A TEXT BOOK OF

STRUCTURAL DESIGN - III

For
SEMESTER – I

FINAL YEAR (BE) DEGREE COURSE IN CIVIL ENGINEERING

**As Per New Revised Syllabus of
Savitribai Phule Pune University, Pune.**

(2012 Pattern)

Dr. M. N. BAJAD

M.E. (Struct.), Research Scholar (NIT), (Gold Medalist) Ph.D
Assistant Professor,
Department of Civil Engineering,
Sinhgad College of Engineering
Vadgaon (BK), Pune.

N 3687

Structural Design – III (BE Civil SEM. I PU)   ISBN 978-93-5164-689-1

First Edition   :   July 2015

©   :   Author

Published By :
NIRALI PRAKASHAN
Abhyudaya Pragati, 1312, Shivaji Nagar,
Off J.M. Road, Pune – 411005
Tel - (020) 25512336/37/39, Fax - (020) 25511379
Email : niralipune@pragationline.com

☞ **DISTRIBUTION CENTRES**

PUNE

Nirali Prakashan   :   119, Budhwar Peth, Jogeshwari Mandir Lane, Pune 411002, Maharashtra
Tel : (020) 2445 2044, 66022708, Fax : (020) 2445 1538
Email : bookorder@pragationline.com, niralilocal@pragationline.com

Nirali Prakashan   :   S. No. 28/27, Dhyari, Near Pari Company, Pune 411041
Tel : (020) 24690204 Fax : (020) 24690316
Email : dhyari@pragationline.com, bookorder@pragationline.com

MUMBAI

Nirali Prakashan   :   385, S.V.P. Road, Rasdhara Co-op. Hsg. Society Ltd.,
Girgaum, Mumbai 400004, Maharashtra
Tel : (022) 2385 6339 / 2386 9976, Fax : (022) 2386 9976
Email : niralimumbai@pragationline.com

☞ **DISTRIBUTION BRANCHES**

JALGAON

Nirali Prakashan   :   34, V. V. Golani Market, Navi Peth, Jalgaon 425001,
Maharashtra, Tel : (0257) 222 0395, Mob : 94234 91860

KOLHAPUR

Nirali Prakashan   :   New Mahadvar Road, Kedar Plaza, 1st Floor Opp. IDBI Bank
Kolhapur 416 012, Maharashtra. Mob : 9850046155

NAGPUR

Pratibha Book Distributors   :   Above Maratha Mandir, Shop No. 3, First Floor,
Rani Jhanshi Square, Sitabuldi, Nagpur 440012, Maharashtra
Tel : (0712) 254 7129

DELHI

Nirali Prakashan   :   4593/21, Basement, Aggarwal Lane 15, Ansari Road, Daryaganj
Near Times of India Building, New Delhi 110002
Mob : 08505972553

BENGALURU

Pragati Book House   :   House No. 1, Sanjeevappa Lane, Avenue Road Cross,
Opp. Rice Church, Bengaluru – 560002.
Tel : (080) 64513344, 64513355,Mob : 9880582331, 9845021552
Email:bharatsavla@yahoo.com

CHENNAI

Pragati Books   :   9/1, Montieth Road, Behind Taas Mahal, Egmore,
Chennai 600008 Tamil Nadu, Tel : (044) 6518 3535,
Mob : 94440 01782 / 98450 21552 / 98805 82331,
Email : bharatsavla@yahoo.com

niralipune@pragationline.com | www.pragationline.com

Also find us on   www.facebook.com/niralibooks

PREFACE

This book titled **"Structural Design - III"** is strictly written according to the New Revised Syllabus of Savitribai Phule Pune University. This book will serve as a text book for the students of final year (B.E.) of degree Course in Civil Engineering.

The present text is presented in 15 chapters. The theory of each chapter is written in simplified language and number of solved problems which cover the practical aspect of theory are included at the end of each chapter. Since, the student usually has his greatest difficulty in applying the theory principles that he has learned to specific situations. To develop this ability among students, special attention has been given to the selection and treatment of illustrative examples. Every solved problem is presented in pictorial form which will help the students to imagine and grasp the practical problems from the field.

It is hoped by the author that solved examples will help the students to bridge the gap between mere cognizance of the general principles and ability to apply them to concrete problems. **I am included Sample Question Papers for In-Semester Assement Exams. (30 Marks) and End Semester Theory Exams. (70 Marks) for practice of the both the Exams. I am also included University Question Papers (May 2008 to May 2015) at the end of each chapter for the benefit of students community.**

Shri Dineshbhai Furia, Mr. Jignesh Furia and Shri M. P. Munde of Nirali Prakashan have a lion's share in publishing this book. I express my sincere thanks to all the team of Nirali Prakashan. Namely Mrs. Depali Lachake (Co-ordinator), Mrs. Roshan Khan and Miss. Rani and Miss Rajashri. I am also sincerely thank to faculty colleagues and staff of SCOE Vadgaon. I am also thankful to renovation family for their support.

Although every care has been taken to check mistakes and misprints, yet it is difficult to claim perfection. Any error, omission and suggestions for the improvement of this volume, brought to my notice, will be thankfully acknowledged and incorporated in the next edition.

Pune   **Author**

SYLLABUS

Unit 1 : Prestressed Concrete - Analysis

Introduction, Basic concepts, materials-various Pre-tensioning and post-tensioning systems, Concept of losses, Stress calculations, and concept of cable profile.

Unit 2 : Prestressed Concrete - Design

Design of post tensioned prestressed concrete simply supported rectangular and flanged sections for flexure and shear including end block.

Design of one way and two way post-tensioned slabs (Single panel only)

Unit 3 : Earthquake Force Calculation And Analysis And Design Of Frames

Review of methods of analysis for frames subjected to gravity and lateral loads. Earthquake loads by seismic coefficient method. Estimation of combined effect of lateral forces and vertical loading on multi storeyed frames. Design any intermediate continuous beam of the frames for combined effect of loadings

Unit 4 : Earth Retaining Structures

Introduction, Functions and types of retaining walls. Analysis and design of RCC cantilever, Type of retaining wall for various types of backfill conditions.

Unit 5 : Combined Footings

Introduction, Necessity and Types of combined footings, Design of slab type and Slab-beam type of combined footing.

Unit 6 : Liquid Retaining Structures

Introduction, Types, Function, Codal provisions, Methods of analysis and design of circular, square, and rectangular water tanks resting on ground.

CONTENTS

Unit II

Unit III

Unit IV

Unit V

Chapter 14 : Combined Footing	14.1-14.46

Unit VI

Chapter 15 : Water Tanks	15.1-15.38

Chapter 1
FUNDAMENTAL PRINCIPLES OF PRESTRESSED CONCRETE

1.1 INTRODUCTION

The prestressing of concrete is a recent development, although the idea of prestressing is not a new one. Even in ancient days, this was practised, for example, in the case of a cart-wheel, upon which the iron tyre is shrunk-on, producing a radial precompression in it.

Several engineers and scientists in different countries have worked since the later part of the last century to develop suitable methods for pre-compressing the concrete. The first practical applications were, however, made in 1928 by an eminent French engineer, M. Eugene Freyssinet, who is regarded as the "Father of prestressing".

In the initial stages of the development of the prestressed concrete, the materials such as mild steel and concrete, as used in ordinary reinforced concrete work, were used to achieve the required degree of prestressing. But soon it was realised that these materials with the then available properties, were not suitable for prestressed concrete work. It was also found that the failures occurred due to loss of prestress on account of "creep" and "shrinkage" of concrete and the "plastic flow" of the steel itself under load.

M. Freyssinet found from his research work that high tensile steel was necessary instead of mild steel, so that after the losses of prestresses, which occurred there still remains sufficient stresses to produce the desired permanent precompression in the concrete. He also developed a concrete of high strength which is another basic requirement for attaining prestressed concrete.

Today, along with these materials and several systems of achieving precompression in the concrete, the prestressed concrete is one of the major structural materials available and has proved more economic than the ordinary reinforced concrete.

1.2 NEED OF PRESTRESSING

Tests on concrete have shown that it is weak in resisting tensile forces and that its tensile strength is about one-tenth of its compressive strength. Even this available tensile strength cannot be used for resisting any loads, as it is used up partly or wholly in resisting internal tensile stresses. These stresses are caused by heat evolved by the cement in setting or by atmospheric influences, difference in rate of drying and therefore shrinkage, etc.

The plain concrete structures may develop cracks in course of time, even if external loads are not applied. Therefore, mild steel bars are provided so that these can take up the tensile stresses and also keep the width of the cracks in the concrete within harmless limits. The reinforced concrete structures are, therefore, designed on the theory, which assumes that the tensile zone of the concrete is cracked and the tensile forces are resisted by the reinforcing bars only. (Refer Fig. 1.1).

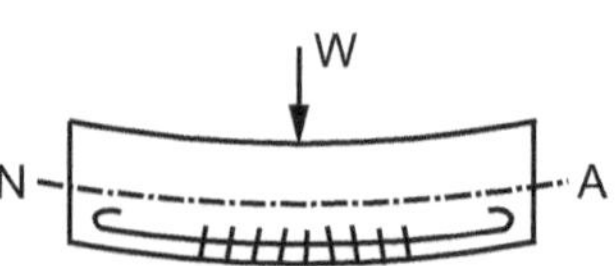

Fig. 1.1 : A simply supported R.C.C. beam, in which tensile zone is assumed to be cracked

By suitably distributing the mild steel bars, the width of these cracks can be kept small and also a good bond of concrete is achieved. It can be assumed that a crack width of 0.2 mm in case of structures in the open air and 0.3 mm in case of structures which are not exposed to the causes of serious corrosion, can be regarded as harmless. These cracks can be a cause of serious damage to the structures, especially in cases where cover to the bars is insufficient.

It was, therefore, already realised in the early days of reinforced concrete construction that these cracks were objectionable and that these should be prevented. This then given rise to an idea of placing the concrete under precompression, so that the cracks could be prevented from occurring. The prestressed concrete in its present form is the fulfillment to that idea.

1.3 BASIC PRINCIPLE OF PRESTRESSING

The basic principle of prestressing is to produce, by any suitable means, sufficient compressive stresses in all those parts of the concrete where tensile stresses would occur when the external loads (i.e. dead and live loads) are applied. These compressive stresses need to be produced in the concrete before the external loads are allowed to act, so that these have to be first neutralised by the tensile stresses developed due to external loading. Any tension can, in that case, actually occur in the concrete only when the tensile stresses exceed the already induced compressive stresses.

Consider an example, a concrete section of size 100 mm × 100 mm which is to be designed to carry an axial tensile force of 50 kN, therefore, tensile stress $= \dfrac{50 \times 10^3 \text{ N}}{100 \times 100 \text{ mm}^2}$

$= 5 \text{ N/mm}^2$ will occur due to this axial tensile force.

Now, if by some any means, we introduce a compressive stress in concrete which is slightly greater than 5 N/mm^2 say 6 N/mm^2, finally the section is subjected to $(6 - 5) = 1$ N/mm^2 compressive prestress. In this way, concrete section is made able to carry tensile force.

Thus, if the induced compressive stresses are greater in magnitude than the tensile stresses developed due to external loading, no tension would occur in the beam and the beam would be capable of carrying the external loads.

The prestressed concrete beams are, therefore, so designed that the induced compressive stresses or precompressive stresses (i.e. prestresses), are greater than the anticipated tensile stresses which would occur due to the external loads.

1.4 COMMON TERMS USED IN PRESTRESSING

The idea along with different terms commonly used is explained by following tests.

Let a concrete beam of rectangular cross-section be cast with a continuous hole by providing a **sheath**, supported at suitable intervals at neutral axis level. After the concrete has hardened, let a high tensile steel rod be placed inside the hole so that it can slide there without any friction and let, it be provided with bearing plates, screw threads and nuts, etc. (Refer Fig. 1.2).

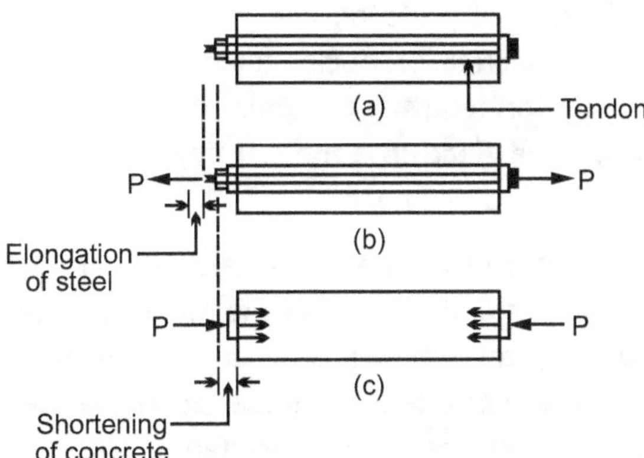

Fig. 1.2 : (a) Concrete beam before stressing; (b) after tensioning force P acting on steel; (c) force P acting on concrete

Let this bar be tensioned, as a result of the tensioning operation, a tensile force, say P is produced in the bar, which is resisted by the nuts and through the medium of the bearing plates it is thrust against the concrete, thereby producing an uniform compressive stress in the concrete.

The concrete in which the compressive stresses are induced in the manner described above is known as **"prestressed concrete"**. The tensile force in the bar is known as **"prestressing force"**, which acts upon the concrete member as an external force producing the compressive stresses in the concrete.

The rod is known as **"tendon"**. Any stretched element used in a concrete member to impart prestress to the concrete is known as tendon. It is generally of steel and may consist of one or more individual wires, cables, stands or a thick bar.

"Cable" is formed from wires by grouping these in a parallel arrangement so as to form bundles. These are known as **"prestressing cables"**.

"Strand" may consist of form two to seven wires twisted together. A number of strands grouped together in a parallel arrangement is known as a "strand cable".

These different types of tendons are used in individual cases as per requirement of prestress to be applied. Thus, for producing small prestressing force, individual tendons are employed and for producing large prestressing forces, concentrated tendons or cables are found more economical and efficient.

The nuts, bearing plates, or other special arrangements at the ends of the beam which keep the tendons in stretched position are known as **"anchorage"**.

It can be seen from the above tests that the prestressing force 'P' acts at the centroid of the bar and that this force is transmitted to the beam through a relatively small area of the bearing plate, involving high local pressure, and hence require a certain length through which it is transmitted to the concrete, producing uniform stresses on the entire section. This length is known as **"transmission length"**. The zone of the beam upto this length is known as the **"transmission zone"** or **"lead-in zone"** or **"end-block"**. This length is generally considered as equal to the depth of the beam.

Because of the bond, the compressive stresses radiate from the tendon into the concrete and cause warping of the concrete at the end of the member. Considerable tensile stresses are, therefore, developed in the transmission zone, acting at right angles to the direction of the prestressing force. The transverse tensile stresses should be determined and adequate mild steel reinforcement provided. These transverse tensile forces are usually referred to as **"splitting forces"** or **"brusting forces"**.

1.5 KINDS OF PRESTRESSING

Prestressed concrete may be classified into a number of ways depending upon construction, method of applying prestressing and purpose of structure. The following are the main kinds of prestressing.

1.5.1 Pre-tensioning

In this method, the tendons are first tensioned on a prestressing bed, and the concreting is done after the required amount of extension is obtained. When the concrete has hardened, the tendons are released, so that the prestressing force is transferred to the concrete. Since tendon force is transferred from steel to concrete through a bond, so it is fully bonded construction. (Refer Fig. 1.3).

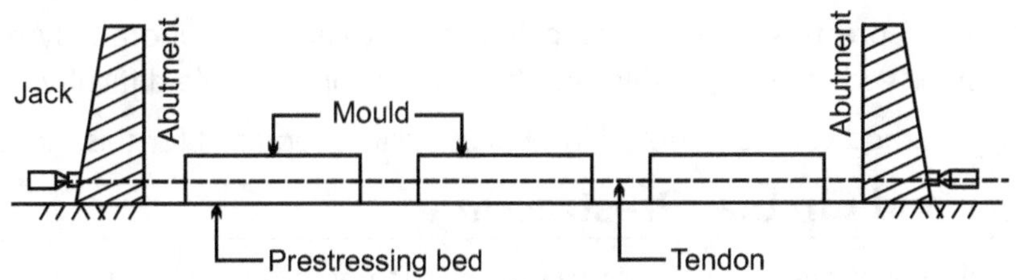

Fig. 1.3 : Prestressing bed

1.5.2 Post-tensioning

In this system, the position of tendons are fixed and hollow ducts are left in the member for placing the tendons and the members are cast. Then the concrete is cured to get its design strength. Now, the tendons are placed at required locations and prestressing force is applied. (Refer Fig. 1.4).

After applying the prestressing force to the tendons through jack and end anchorages, the ducts may be filled completely with cement grout injected under pressure. Such a system is known as **fully bonded system**. The wires in this system are protected against rusting. If the duct is not grouted, an unbonded system is obtained, in which the protection for the tendons from corrosion is provided by galvanising, greasing or some other means. In the latter case, prestressing force is transferred to concrete by end bearing rather than by bond, so it is end anchored construction.

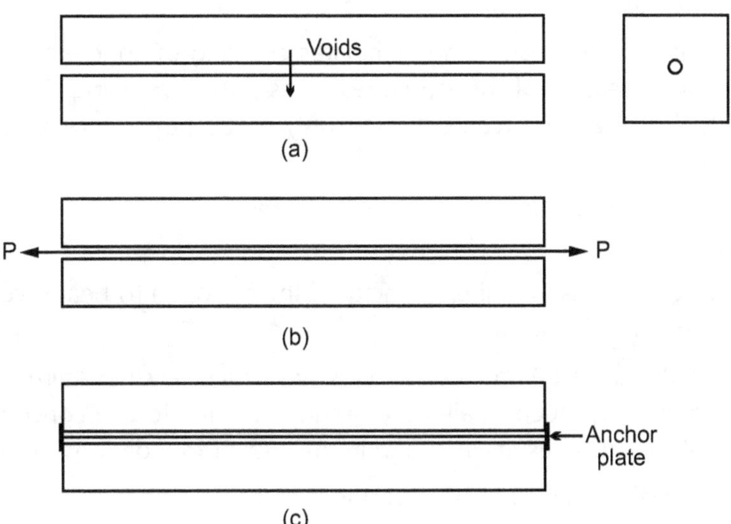

Fig. 1.4

Suitability of the System :

Pre-tensioning method is economically adopted in mass production in factories, which make concrete products of limited size. This is so because, handling as well as transporting large products are highly expensive and may be practically impossible, if the members are too large. The length of prestressed concrete product, that can be economically made by this method may not exceed 20 m. Even this length involves considerable difficulty in transport.

Post-tensioning method can be adopted in sites but skill is required for this method.

1.5.3 Linear and Circular Prestressing

Linear prestressing is applied in straight members such as beams, slab, piles, electric poles, etc.

Circular prestressing is applied for circular structures such as cylindrical tanks, silos where the prestressing tendons are wound around in circle.

However, the prestressing tendons in the linear prestressing need not be necessarily straight. They can be either bent or even curved, but they are not wound in round circles around the structure.

1.5.4 Full and Partial Prestressing

The concrete is said to be fully prestressed if there are no tensile stresses in it under working load. However, if some tensile stresses are produced in the concrete under working load conditions, it is said to be partially prestressed.

1.6 ADVANTAGES OF PRESTRESSED CONCRETE

Prestressed concrete has the following advantages :

- Since, the technique of prestressing eliminates cracking of concrete under all stage of loading the entire section of the structures takes part in resisting the external load. In contrast to this, in the reinforced concrete, only portion of concrete above the natural axis is effective.

- Since concrete does not crack, the possibility of steel to rust and concrete to deteriorate is minimized.

- Absence of cracks results in higher capacity of the structure to bear reversal of stresses, impact, vibration and shock.

- In prestressed concrete beams, dead loads are practically neutralized. The reactions required are therefore, much smaller then required in reinforced concrete. The reduced dead weight of structure results in saving in the cost of foundations.

  The netralisation of dead weight of importance in large bridges.

- The use of curved tendons and the precompression of concrete helps to resists share.

- The quantity of steel required for prestressing about $\frac{1}{3}$ of that required for reinforced concrete, though the steel for the former should have high tensile strength.

- In prestressed concrete, preacast blocks and elements can be assumed and used as one unit. This saves in the cost of shuttering and centring for large structure.

- With the advent of prestressed concrete it has been possible now to construct large size liquid retaining structures not economical to build otherwise. Such structures have low cost and are preferably safe against cracking and consequent leakage.

- Prestressed concrete can be used with advantage in all those structures where tension develops, such as tie and suspender of a bow string girder, railway sleepers, electric poles, upstream face of gravity dam etc.

- Prestressed concrete beams have usually low deflection.

1.7 DISADVANTAGES OF PRESTRESSED CONCRETE

- It requires high quality dense concrete of high strength prefect quality control in production, placement and compaction is required.

- It requires high tensile steel, which is 2.5 to 3.5 times costlier than mild steel.

- It requires complicated tensioning equipment and anchoring devices which are usually covered under patented rights.

- Construction requires prefect supervision at all stages of construction.

1.8 PRESTRESS AT "TRANSFER" AND "WORKING" STAGES

It is known that in the prestressed concrete, the initial prestressing force undergoes some reduction due to various causes, such as, shrinkage and creep of concrete and creep of steel, etc. Therefore, the initially produced prestress is not fully available with the lapse of time, when full live load is operative. It is, therefore, necessary to evaluate the losses of prestress and to find the prestress finally available.

It is thus necessary to investigate stresses in prestressed concrete at two different stages, namely :

- Immediately after the initial prestress is operative, i.e., after the bar is tensioned and is kept in that position, transferring its force permanently on to the concrete, and before any losses have yet occurred. This stage or condition is known as "**transfer**". At this stage, the prestressing force is transferred from steel to concrete and it is assumed that only dead load is operative.

- When the losses of prestress have occurred and the initial prestress is reduced by the subsequent influences. This is the prestress finally available for offsetting any tensile stresses produced by the external loads. This stage or condition is known as "working". At this stage, full working load is operative.

The permissible stresses at "transfer" are naturally higher than those at "working" as the prestress at transfer is reduced by all subsequent influences and is of a temporary nature.

1.9 CABLE PROFILE

The following are the important cable profiles, as shown in Fig. 1.5.

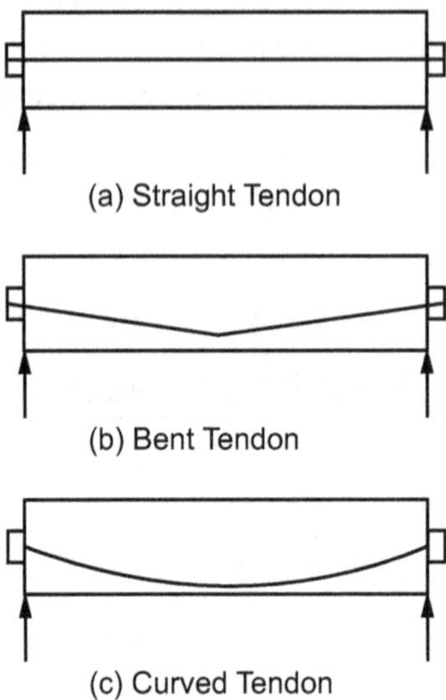

Fig. 1.5 : Profiles of cable

The profile of the cable takes place in a prestressed member corresponding to the shape of the bending moment diagram resulting from the external loads.

1.10 MATERIALS

To design prestress concrete structures, it is necessary to have a knowledge of the physical properties of the materials i.e. steel and concrete. Only a brief description of these materials will be given here. The prestressed concrete structure requires both high tensile steel and high strength concrete.

1.10.1 Steel : Reason of using High Tensile Steel

The mild steel used in ordinary reinforced concrete has a yield point of 200 N/mm^2 to 300 N/mm^2. If such steel is used and if even it is subjected to a stress say 160 N/mm^2 at the stage of tensioning, we find that due to creep and shrinkage of concrete, the net tensile stress left over will be extremely low. In the design of a prestressed concrete member, the estimated loss of prestress due to shrinkage and creep of concrete and steel is of the order of nearly 200 N/mm^2. But high tension steel has an ultimate strength of 2100 N/mm^2 and if initially stressed to say 1200 N/mm^2, there will still be large stress in the reinforcement after making deduction for the loss of prestress.

Example :

We know, creep and shrinkage strain occurring in concrete is roughly 0.0008.

Suppose, if a low tensile strength mild steel is used and stressed to 160 N/mm^2, the resulting strain $= \dfrac{160}{2 \times 10^5}$ = 0.0008 then the net prestrain = (0.0008 – 0.0008) = 0.

Therefore, the resulting prestress $= 0 \times 2 \times 10^5$ = zero.

This will make the prestress as zero.

On the other hand, if a high tensile bar is used and stressed to 1200 N/mm^2, the resulting strain $= \dfrac{1200}{2 \times 10^5}$ = 0.006.

Then the net prestrain = (0.006 – 0.0008) = 0.0052.

Therefore, the resulting prestress = $0.0052 \times 2 \times 10^5$ = 1040 N/mm^2.

    i.e.   This will make the prestress of 1040 N/mm^2

    and   loss of prestress $= \dfrac{1200 - 1040}{1200} \times 100$

        = 13.33% only.

1.10.2 Concrete

The concrete must attain the minimum cube strength at 28 days where ordinary portland cement is used as given below :

    For pre-tensioned system, 45 N/mm^2,

    For post-tensioned system, 35 N/mm^2.

Reasons of using high strength concrete :

- High strengths can be utilized to achieve smaller cross-sections. The weight is consequently reduced and so the longer spans become technically and economically practicable.

- The high strength concrete creeps and shrinks less and so causes less loss of prestressing force.

- Since large prestressing forces are applied to the members by the tendons, high bearing stresses are developed at the ends by the anchoring devices. The anchorages are generally designed for high strength concrete work.

- Brusting stresses liable to at the ends of the beam cannot be satisfactorily resisted by the low strength concrete.

- The stresses transfer to concrete take place by bond action and hence concrete should have a high bond stress which can be offered only by high strength concrete.

1.10.3 Cement Grout

In the case of bonded post-tensioning, cement grouting is done which also serves to protect steel against corrosion. Entry of the grout into the cable, way is provided by means of holes in the anchorage heads. Where the space between the wires is large, such as in Magnel system, a 1 : 1 cement-sand mix is used with a water-cement ratio of 0.5 by volume. In other systems, such as in Freyssinet, neat cement paste with 0.5 water-cement ratio is injected. On a big job, saving of cement is important. In that case, fine sand of about 0.4 mm grain size may be used, with water : cement : sand proportion of about 1 : 1.3 : 0.7 by volume. The grout pressure may be between 0.5 to 0.7 N/mm^2. The injection can be applied at one end of the member until it is forced out at the other end; the end is then plugged and pressure is again applied at the injecting end to compact the grout.

1.11 PRESTRESSING SYSTEM [DEC. 11, MAY 13]

A prestressing system comprises essentially a method of stressing the steel combined with a method of anchoring it to the concrete. The desired precompression in the concrete can be achieved by two different methods, namely, (i) pre-tensioning, and (ii) post-tensioning. In both methods, it is essential to tension the prestressing tendons and these can be tensioned by means of different tensioning devices.

1.11.1 Pre-tensioning System

In this method of obtaining precompression, the tendons are tensioned by suitable tensioning devices, before the concrete is placed in the moulds to form the required element. The concrete is then cast, which hardens around the tendons, so that when they are released, the anchorage action is obtained by bond. The pretensioning can be done by two methods, namely, (i) Hoyer method, and (ii) Individual moulds capable of withstanding the wire reaction.

(i) Hoyer Method :

This method provides an ideal arrangement where the production of many units of the same section such as floor beams, railway sleepers etc. is required.

The bed itself is of concrete with steel abutments, one at each end, sunk deeply enough into the ground to resist the maximum tensioning force without yielding. (Refer Fig. 1.3)

The tendons are anchored to these steel abutments by means of wedges at one end before tensioning and at the other end after tensioning. The bed length may vary from 60 m to 120 m. After the wires are tensioned, the spacing and the vertical positions of the wires should be accurately secured, so as to obviate any displacement during the placing and compaction of concrete. The tensioning force and the extension are accurately measured and recorded. The concreting is then done and the wires are embedded in it. Steam curing can be employed to quicken the hardening of the concrete. The required strength of concrete is then attained in a matter of 8 to 20 hours.

After the unit has attained the necessary strength, to effect the transferring of the prestressing force to concrete, the wires are served by cutting at the abutments and between the unit cast on the same bed. The severing should be done gradually, so that the prestressing force is transferred uniformly to the concrete.

When the units have been separated, they should be handled with great care and kept the "right way up" at all times and lifted at the correct points, so as to avoid tensile stresses in the top fibres.

In order to grip the pre-tensioned wires properly to the bulk heads, the devices shown in Fig. 1.6 are followed.

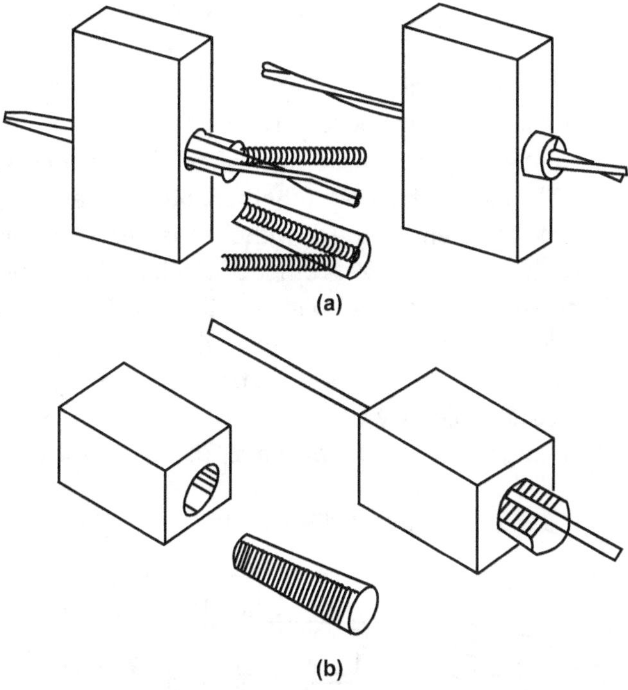

Fig. 1.6

(ii) Individual Mould :

In this method, the prestressing bed is usually formed by the rigid mould itself that is able to withstand the prestressing force, which is subsequently to be transferred to the concrete structural member. The wires are held by wedges in a solid steel plate at one end of the mould and these are tensioned at the other end. The wires are retained in their extended position. The mould is then filled with concrete of high compressive strength, vibrated, compressed and finally steam cured in an oven. After about two hours, concrete attains enough strength to permit the release of wires. The joint is then demoulded and stacked properly.

1.11.2 Post-tensioning System [May 15]

In this method, the concrete is first cast as per designed section and allowed to harden till it attains the required strength as assumed in the design calculations, at which the prestressing force is to be applied. In post-tensioned members, there are several commercially developed systems by which precompression can be imparted to the concrete. Each system usually makes use of a particular type of cables, anchorages and tensioning equipment developed by the investigators of the system. These systems are

(i)	Freyssinet system.	(ii)	Magnel-Blaton system.
(iii)	Gifford-Udall system.	(iv)	Lee-McCall system.
(v)	C.C.L. spiral system.	(vi)	P.S.C. monowire system.

(i) Freyssinet System :

This system was developed by an eminent French engineer, M. Eugene Freyssinet in 1928, and is considered to be the first practical post-tensioning system.

The cable consists of a number of high tensile steel wires of circular cross-section. These are grouped around a central helix and taped together. Because all the wires are stressed simultaneously, it is possible for them to touch without the need for any form of spacers or separators. The final cable is, therefore, both compact and flexible. Despite the compactness, the central helix provides an uninterrupted path for the injection of the cement grout to envelope all the wires for sound bonding and protection from corrosion.

To form these cables, two diameters of wires can be used, namely 5 mm and 7 mm. The number of wires in a particular cable may be 8, 10 or 12.

The Freyssinet Cone anchorage consists of two parts, namely, female cone and male cone. (Refer Fig. 1.7)

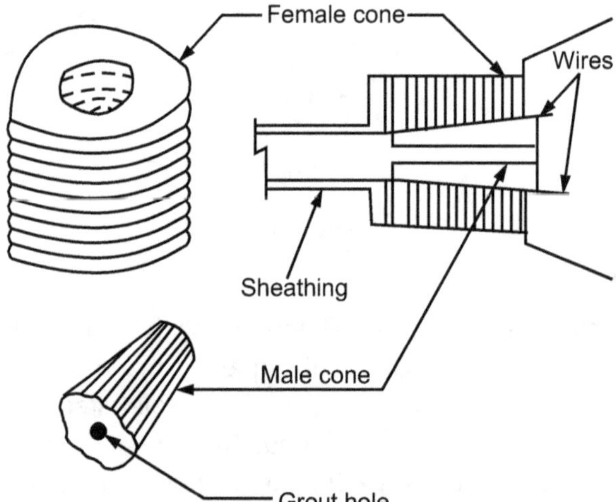

Fig. 1.7 : Freyssinet anchorage

The female cone is a conical steel wound lining, heavily reinforced with high tensile steel spirals to resist bursting forces. The grooves are made so as to accommodate the wires. The male cone is a strong steel tube around which wire mesh reinforced concrete is built to form a similar conical shape, with grooves made in such a way as to space evenly the requisite number of wires. When stressing is to be carried out, the wires are placed around the male cone, which is tapped into the female cone to hold them in position.

The central tube permits grout to be injected through it and no other provision for cable grouting is required except in special cases. Identical anchorages are used at both the jacking and dead ends.

The Freyssinet jack, is used to tension and anchor the wires. The wires coming from the duct pass between the two concentric cones (i.e., female and male cones). The outer or the female cone together with the duct connecting them, are cast in the concrete. The wires are attached to the jack, and its main cylinder is used to tension them. A bearing ring, which is placed between the jack head and the concrete, acts as a seating for the jack. When the necessary extension of the wires is obtained, the secondary cylinder of the jack presses the male cone home and the wires are thus anchored. Finally, grout is injected through the central hole of the male cone.

Advantages of the System :

- The desired stretching force is obtained quickly.
- The plugs may be left in the concrete and they do not project beyond the ends of the member.
- Securing the wires is not expensive.

Disadvantages of the System :

- All the wires of a cable are stretched together. Hence, the stresses in the wires may not be exactly the same.
- The greatest stretching force applied to a cable is from 250 kN to 500 kN. This may not be sufficient.
- The jacks used are heavy and expensive.

(ii) Magnel-Blaton System :

This system was developed in Belgium by the late Prof. G. Magnel in conjunction with the contracting firm of Blaton-Aubert.

In this system, the cable consists of wires which are arranged in a rectangular pattern. The cable is composed of layers of wires and there are four wires per layer. In a single duct upto ninety-six wires can be used. Each wire is separated from the neighbouring wires in the same layer and from those in the adjacent layer by a space of 5 mm. The geometric pattern of the wires is maintained in the same form throughout the length of the cable by means of grills or spacers at regular intervals. These grills offer little frictional resistance to the wires which are free to move relative to each other during tensioning.

The anchorage unit used is known as **sandwich plate** (Refer Fig. 1.8). It consists of a steel plate containing two tapered slots on both the top and the bottom surfaces. A pair of wires can be anchored in each slot by driving home a steel wedge, so that each sandwich plate provides an anchorage for eight wires.

When more than eight wires are used, a stack of sandwich plates is built-up in layers with thin metal shims separating the plates.

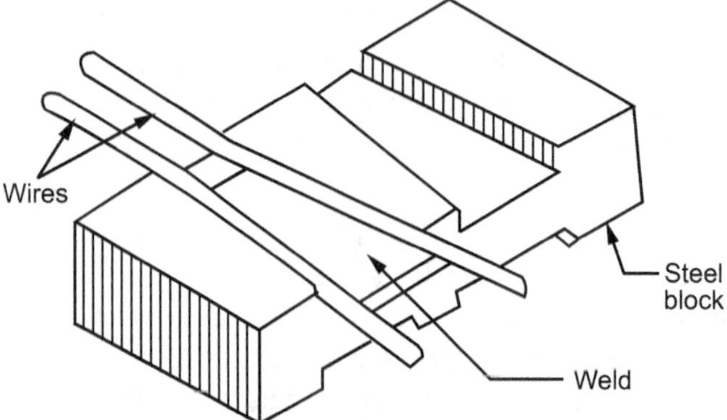

Fig. 1.8 : Magnel-Blaton sandwich plate

Parts and equipment for this system are available in two series. One for use with 5 mm diameter wires and the other for use with 7 mm diameter wires. Each series provides components for fabricating, tensioning, and anchoring cables composed of upto ninety-six wires in one duct.

The duct is cast in the concrete with a steel bearing plate embedded at each end, covered by a thin layer of mortar. The wires are then passed through the grooves of a sandwich plate and are tensioned by a Magnel-Blaton jack. Tensioning of the wires is done at only one end, the other being anchored by driving home a steel wedge between the pair of wires in each groove. Two wires are tensioned at a time and when the required extension is obtained, the wedges are driven home between the wires at the tensioning end. Grout is injected through a hole in the top of the beam, which leads to the cable duct.

(iii) Gifford - Udall System :

This system was developed in the United Kingdom by E. W. Gifford, in conjunction with the concreting firm of Udalls Ltd. It is a universal post-tensioning system, not tied to any particular arrangement of wires and capable of being operated with a light-weight easily handed jack. The cable consists of high tensile steel wires of a diameter varying from 2.5 mm to 8 mm. For the cables containing upto twelve wires, standard spacers are available. The function of these is to keep the wires free from contact with the duct surface, thereby reducing friction losses during stressing and to ensure that the wires are not bunched together in such a way as to prevent the grout from fully bonding them. In the tube anchorage (Refer Fig. 1.9) used in this system, the wires pass from the cable duct into a steel tube which has a square thrust ring at its outer end.

A reinforcing helix is welded to this tube unit to prevent brusting of the concrete. A circular steel bearing plate seats on the thrust ring, and the stressing jack bears onto the plate, tensioning the wires one at a time. The wires pass through the bearing plate through conical holes and when stresses are anchored by means of split cone wedges which are pressed into the holes in the plate. Grout is injected through an additional hole.

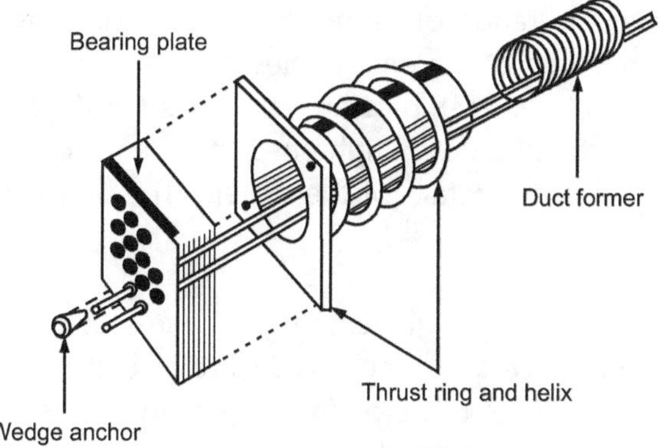

Fig. 1.9 : Gifford-Udall system

(iv) Lee-McCall System :

Lee-McCall system uses high-tensile alloy steel bars (Silico-Manganese steel) as the prestressing tendons, in the place of high-tensile steel wires used in other systems.

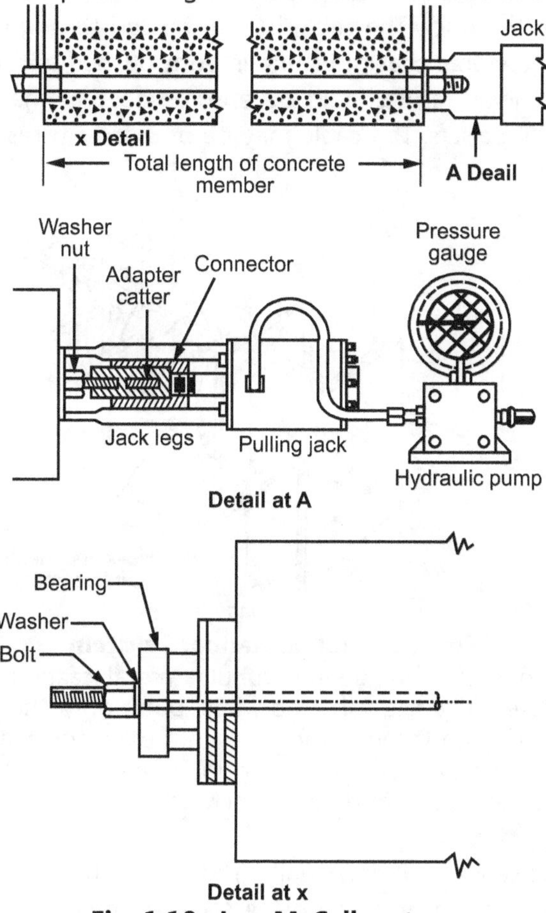

Fig. 1.10 : Lee-McCall system

These bars are provided in the range of 12 mm to 28 mm diameter and in lengths upto 20 meters. The rods are threaded at the ends. Holes are made in the member by means of rubber core. When the concrete has set, bars are introduced in the hole, after removing the core. After the desired stretching, a nut is tightened at its end to prevent its return to the original length. Fig. 1.10 shows the details of the system. The bars can be either bonded or unbonded to the concrete.

(v) C.C.L. Spiral System :

In this system, the cable consists of high tensile steel wires of circular cross-section. The wires are passed through the spacers and the spacers are placed at their correct centres. The end spacer should be such that its distance from the end of the cable is 0.6 m plus an allowance for the jack etc. The intermediate spacers should be at intervals from 0.3 m to 1.3 m depending upon the curvature of the duct. The spacers are then fixed in their final position with soft iron building wire. The tie is placed 7.6 cm behind the spacers on the side remote from the end of the cable fed into the duct. The purpose of the binding wire is to reduce the external diameter of the cable so that the spacers do not slip back when the cable is introduced into the duct. The cable is then passed through the ducts immediately after making up. It is preferable that the cable is both pushed and pulled, especially if the duct has considerable curvature. It should be ensured so that the cables are not twisted when they are fed into the ducts. The cable may be of 8 or 12 wires of 7 mm diameter or a single large strand cable.

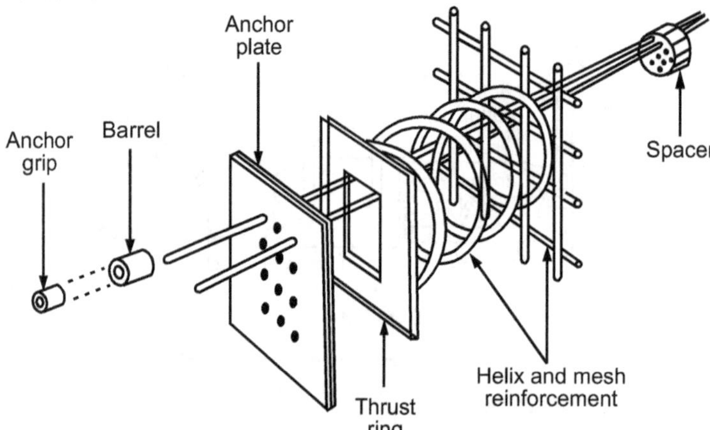

Fig. 1.11 : C.C.L. standard system

The spiral anchorage consists of a tapered tubular metal casting which is cast into the concrete. An anchor plate, drilled to take the wires, butts onto the face of the anchorage. The wires pass from the casting through the holes in the anchor plate. Each wire is stressed individually, and is locked off by a C.C.L. anchor grip. (Refer Fig. 1.11). The sheathing fits into the rear of the anchorage as a push fit during concreting.

(vi) P.S.C. Monowire System :

In this system, wires are tensioned individually. The system uses collect sleeves wedging in conical holes. These sleeves are of single piece serrated internally to give positive grip to wire passing through them. A steel trunked guide leads each wire from its cable position to its point of anchorage through a gentle curvature (Refer Fig. 1.12). The monowire anchorages are available for 1-, 2-, 4-, 8- and 12- wire cables of size upto 7 mm. For 8- and 12-wire cable, a high strength plastic spacer is used to make up the cable and separate the wires for stressing.

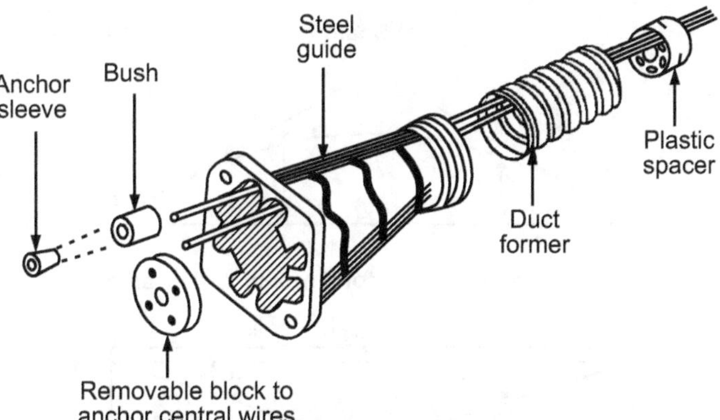

Fig. 1.12 : P.S.C. Monowire system

1.12 DISTINCTION BETWEEN RCC AND PSC
(SUMMER, WINTER 2012, 4 MARKS)

- In RCC beam, the concrete in the compression side of the N.A. alone is effective. The concrete in the tension side of the N.A. is ineffective. But in a prestressed concrete, the entire section is effective.
- RC beams are generally heavy. They always need shear reinforcements besides the longitudinal reinforcements for flexure. Prestressed concrete beams are lighter. By providing, the curved tendons and precompression, a considerable part of the shear is resisted.
- In RC beams, high strength concrete is not needed. But in prestressed concrete beam, high strength concrete and high strength steel are necessary. High strength concrete is needed to resist high stresses at the anchorages. High strength steel is needed to transfer large prestressing force.
- In RC beams, there is no way of testing steel and concrete. In PSC beams, testing of steel and concrete can be made while prestressing.

1.13 FACTORS AFFECTING CABLE PROFILE   (SUMMER 2012, 4 MARKS)

The layout of simple beams is controlled by the maximum moment at midspan and end span so that after these sections are designed, other sections can often be designed by inspection.

A limiting zone for the location of C.G. of steel is first obtained, then the cables are arranged so that their centroid will lie within the zone. The centre of pressure i.e. C-line will not fall above the top kern line, C.G. of steel must be located below top kern at least at a distance $a_1 = M_1/F$

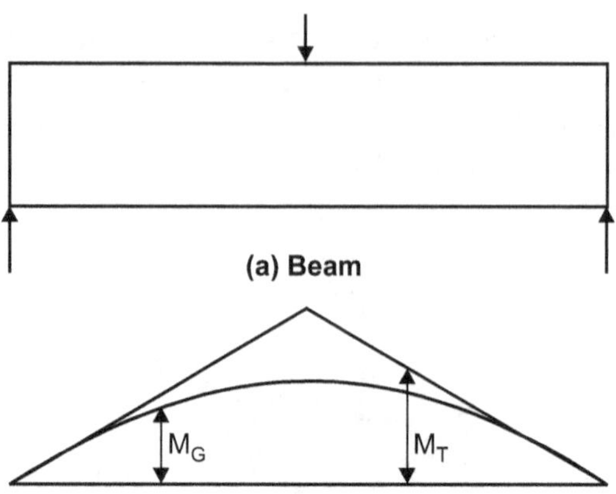

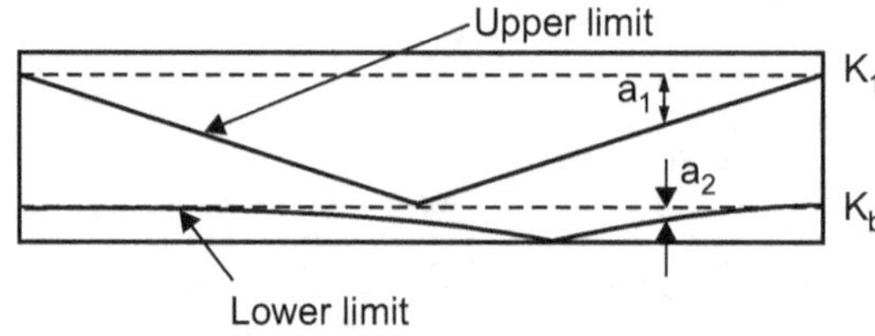

Fig. 1.13

If the C.G. of steel falls above that upper limit at any point, then C-line corresponding to moment M_T and prestress F will fall above top kern resulting in tension in bottom fibre.

1.14 WHY HIGH GRADE MATERIALS ARE USED FOR PRESTRESSED-CONCRETE OR ELEMENTS ? (DEC.11, 12, MAY 13 – 4 M)

Higher strength is necessary in prestressed concrete in order to minimize the cost, to use commercial anchorages, to have high resistance in tension, shear, bond and bearing. High strength concrete is less liable to shrinkage cracks.

Higher modulus of elasticity and smaller creep strain results in small loss of prestressed steel. Generally, 28 to 34 MPa strengths work out to be economical designs.

High strength steel is mostly used as prestressing material. High strength steels are often obtained by alloying, which permits the manufacturer of such steels under normal operation.

High strength steel for prestressing takes one of the three forms : Wires (5-12 mm dia.), strands (2-4 mm dia.) or bars. For post-tensioning, wires are widely employed; they are grouped in parallel into cables. Strands are fabricated in the factory by twisting wires together.

1.15 ASSUMPTIONS IN THE DESING OF PRESTRESSED CONCERETE MEMBERS

Prestressed concrete members are analysed and designed on the basis of the assumptions given below

- A transverse plane section of the member will remain a plan after bending also.

- Within the limits of the deformations taking place, Hooke's law is applicable to concrete and steel components.

- The stress in the reinforcement dose not change along the length of the reinforcement stress changes take place for the concrete component only. Variation the stress in components only. Variation of stress in the reinforcement due to changes in the external loading is ignorable.

1.16 CONCENTRIC PRESTRESSING   [MAY 2015]

Consider a concrete beam with a concentric tendon as shown in Fig. 1.14.

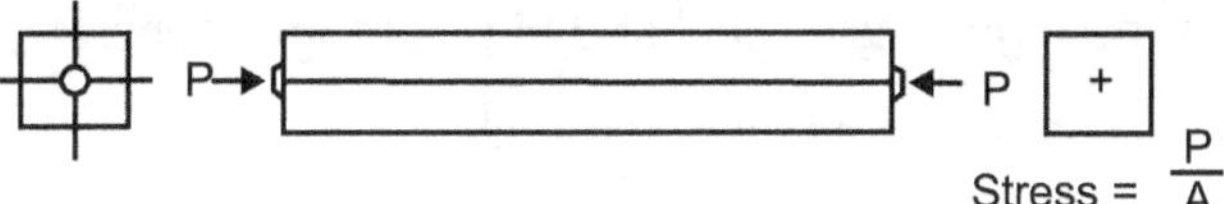

Fig. 1.14 : Concentric prestressing

Uniform prestress in concrete = P/A, which is compressive across the depth of the beam. Generally the applied loads and the dead load of the beam induce tensile stress towards the soffit and are counter balanced more effectively by eccentric tendons.

1.17 ECCENTRIC PRESTRESSING   [MAY 2015]

Fig. 1.15 shows a concrete beam subjected to an eccentric prestressing force of magnitude P located at an eccentricity e. The streses developed at the top and bottom fibres of the beam are obtained by the relations.

$$f_{inf} = \left(-\frac{P}{A} + \frac{P_e}{Z_b}\right)$$

$$= \frac{P}{A}\left(1 + \frac{e_{yb}}{i^2}\right)$$

$$f_{sup} = \left(\frac{P}{A} + \frac{P_e}{Z_t}\right)$$

$$= \frac{P}{A}\left(1 + \frac{e_{yb}}{i^2}\right)$$

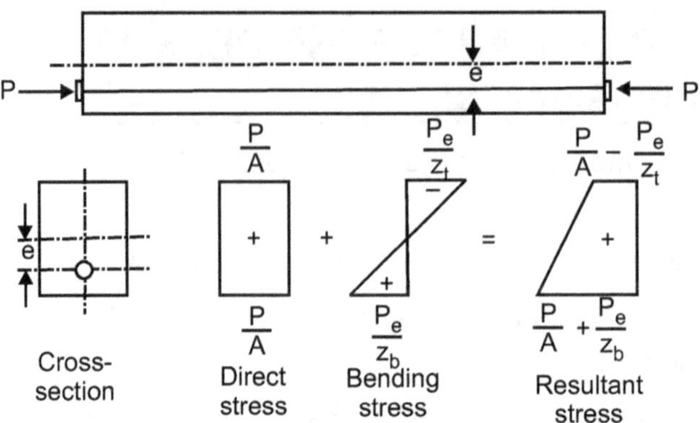

Fig. 1.15 : Eccentric prestressing

IMPORTANT POINTS

- Need of prestressing.
- Kinds of prestressing.
- Reasons for using high tensile steel and high strength concrete.
- Pre-tensioning system and its two methods.
- Post-tensioning system, along with its systems.
- Advantages and disadvantages of pre-stressed concrete.

QUESTIONS

1. (a) Explain why high tensile steel and high grade concrete are used for prestressed concrete construction.

   (b) Differentiate between pre-tensioning and post-tensioning. Enumerate the situations where above methods are preferred.

2. (a) State high-strength materials used for prestressed concrete construction, including grades, compared to the materials used for reinforced concrete construction. Give the specific reasons for using high strength materials for prestressed concrete.

   (b) Explain long line or Hoyer system of pretensioning.

3. (a) Compare reinforced concrete and prestressed concrete from the view point of (i) Safety, (ii) Serviceability, (iii) Economy.

   (b) State and explain various stages of loading.

   (c) Write a short note on partial prestressing.

4. (a) Define the terms full prestressing and partial prestressing.

   (b) What are the short comings of prestressed concrete structure ?

   (c) What are the various possible cable profiles in prestressed concrete ?

5. Write notes on :

   (a) Freyssinet system on prestressing.

   (b) Lee-McCall system.   (c) Magnel-Blaton system.

UNIVERSITY QUESTIONS

Dec. 2011

Q. 1 (a) Explain in brief why high grade materials are used for prestressed concrete elements. **(Section 1.14)**   **(4 Marks)**

   (b) Explain in the system of prestressing. **(Section 1.11)**   **(4 Marks)**

May 2012

Q. 2 (a) Distinguish between RCC and PSC. **(Section 1.12)**   **(4 Marks)**

   (b) Explain the factors affecting the cable profile. **(Section 1.13)**   **(4 Marks)**

Dec. 2012

Q. 3 (a) Compare PSC with RCC. **(Section 1.12)**   **(4 marks)**

   (b) Explain in brief why high grade materials are used for pre-stressed concrete elements. **(Section 1.14)**   **(4 marks)**

May 2013

Q. 4 (a) Explain with neat sketches various systems of Pre-stressing. **(Section 1.11)**

                                                                        (5 Marks)

Q. 5 (a) Explain need of high strength steel and high strength concrete in prestress concrete construction. **(Section 1.14)**   **(7 Marks)**

Q. 6 (a) Explain with sketch, why eccentric prestressing is preferable to concentric prestressing. **(Section 1.16 and 1.17)**   **(8 Marks)**

May 2015

Q. 7 (a) Explain any one method of post tensioning with neat sketches.

(Section 1.11.2) (5 Marks)

◈ ◈ ◈

LOSSES OF PRESTRESS

2.1 INTRODUCTION

The initial prestress undergoes some reduction due to the loss of prestress which occurs due to the shrinkage of concrete and creep of concrete and steel, shortening of concrete at transfer, friction and anchorage slip, etc. These losses need to be estimated and consideration of these taken while preparing designs, in such a way that the remaining working prestress is sufficient to produce the designed compressive stress in the concrete.

Losses of prestress may be classified into the following :

- Loss of prestress during the tensioning process.

- Loss of prestress at the anchorage stage.

- Losses occurring subsequently.

2.2 LOSS OF PRESTRESS DURING THE TENSIONING PROCESS DUE TO FRICTION

[DEC. 11, 12]

There always exists a certain amount of friction in the jacking and anchoring system and on the walls of the duct where the wires fan out at the anchorages with the result, the actual stress in the tendon is less than what is indicated by pressure gauge. The loss due to friction may be classified into

(a) loss due to length effect.

(b) loss due to curvature effect.

(a) **Loss due to length effect :** The length effect means the extent of friction met within a straight tendon due to slight imperfections of the duct. In practice, the duct meant for the straight tendon is not absolutely straight. Hence, the cable will touch the duct or concrete. This loss is also called the loss due to **wobbling effect** or **wave effect**.

The prestressing force P_x in the tendon at any distance 'x' from the jack is given by

$$P_x = P_o \cdot e^{-kx} \qquad \qquad \text{... (2.1)}$$

(b) **Loss due to curvature effect :** In the case of curved ducts, the loss of prestress depends upon the radius of curvature R of the duct and the co-efficient of friction between the duct surface and the tendon.

The tension at any point of the cable is given by

$$P_X = P_o \cdot e^{\frac{-\mu k}{R}} \qquad \ldots (2.2)$$

It is used to combine the length effect and the curvature effect and the tension in the tendon at any point is given by

$$P_X = P_o \cdot e^{-\left(kx + \frac{\mu k}{R}\right)} \qquad \ldots (2.3)$$

I.S. Recommendations :

As per I.S. code (clause 18.5.2.6), for straight or moderately curved structure with curve or straight cables, the value of the prestressing force, P_X at a distance x from the tensioning end shall be calculated by the formula,

$$P_X = P_o \cdot e^{-(\mu\alpha + kx)} \qquad \ldots (2.4)$$

where, P_o – Prestressing force in the prestress steel at the tensioning end in the direction of the tangent to the curve of cable.

α – Cumulative angle in radians through which the tangent to the cable profile has turned between any two points under consideration.

μ – Coefficient of friction in curve, unless otherwise proved by tests, μ may be taken as

0.55 for steel moving on smooth concrete,

0.30 for steel moving on steel fixed to duct, and

0.25 for steel moving on lead.

k – coefficient for wave effect varying from 15×10^{-4} to 50×10^{-4} per metre.

For small values of $(\mu\alpha + kx)$, the formula given above can be expressed as

$$P_X = P_o [1 - \mu\alpha - kx] \qquad \ldots (2.5)$$

The previous expression may be expressed as

$$\frac{P_o - P_X}{P_o} = (\mu\alpha + kx)$$

$$\therefore \qquad \frac{\left[\dfrac{P_o - P_X}{A}\right]}{\left[\dfrac{P_o}{A}\right]} = (\mu\alpha + kx)$$

$$\therefore \qquad \text{Loss of stress} = (\mu\alpha + kx) \times \text{Initial stress} \qquad \ldots (2.6)$$

In circular constructions, where circumferential tendons are tensioned by jacks, values of μ for calculating friction may be taken as :

> 0.45 for steel moving on smooth concrete.

> 0.25 for steel moving on steel bearers fixed to the concrete, and

> 0.10 for steel moving on steel rollers.

This loss is applicable in post-tensioning system only.

2.3 LOSS OF PRESTRESS AT THE ANCHORING STAGE

This loss is due to the fact that anchorage fixtures themselves are subjected to a stretch. It is also possible that the friction wedges holding the wires may slip a little. The amount of this slip may be taken on the average as 2.5 mm. But in the case of direct-bearing anchorages, the slip may be on the average only 0.75 mm.

The loss of prestress due to deformation, slip etc. is given by

$$\Delta f_s \;=\; \frac{\Delta_a \cdot E_s}{L} \qquad\qquad \text{... (2.7)}$$

where, Δ_a – Effective slip.

E_s – Young's modulus for tendon, and

L – Length of the tendon

Any loss of prestress which may occur due to slip of wires during anchoring or due to the strain of anchorage shall be allowed for in the design. Loss due to slip in anchorage is of special importance with short members and necessary additional elongation may be provided at the time of tensioning to compensate for this loss.

It is necessary to note that this loss of prestress depends upon the length of tendons, being high when a tendon is short and low when a tendon is long.

This loss is applicable in post-tensioning system.

2.4 LOSS OF PRESTRESS OCCURRING SUBSEQUENTLY   [MAY 13, 15]

The losses which occur subsequent to prestress are the following :

- Loss of stress due to shrinkage of concrete.

- Loss of stress due to creep of concrete.

- Loss of stress due to elastic shortening of concrete.

- Loss of stress due to relaxation of steel.

The first three types of losses mentioned above take place due to the reduction in the length of concrete resulting in the reduction of the initial extension of the steel.

2.4.1 Loss due to Shrinkage of Concrete

Shrinkage means a contraction of concrete due to chemical changes and drying. It depends upon the quantity of water, type of aggregate used in the mix, surrounding atmospheric conditions and interval of time but is independent of the stresses in the member due to loads.

The loss of stress due to shrinkage of concrete

$$= \text{Shrinkage strain} \times E_s \qquad \qquad \text{... (2.8)}$$

$$\text{where} \quad E_s \; - \; \text{Young's modulus for steel.}$$

For all purposes of design, the shrinkage strain may be taken as 0.0002 to 0.0004.

I.S. Recommendations :

As per I.S. : 1343-1980 (clause 5.2.4.1), the approximate value of shrinkage strain for design is assumed as follows :

$$\text{For pre-tensioning} \; = \; 0.0003 \qquad \qquad \text{... 2.8 (a)}$$

$$\text{For post-tensioning} \; = \; \frac{0.0002}{\log_{10}(t + 2)} \qquad \qquad \text{... 2.8 (b)}$$

$$\text{where } t - \text{ age of concrete at transfer in days.}$$

The value of shrinkage strain for design of post-tensioned concrete may be increased by 50 percent in dry atmospheric conditions, subject to a maximum value of 0.0003.

2.4.2 Loss of Stress due to Creep of Concrete

Creep of concrete is defined as its time-dependent deformation resulting from the presence of stress. The loss of prestress due to creep of concrete under load shall be determined for all the permanently applied loads including the prestress. The creep loss due to live load stresses, erection stresses and other stresses of short duration may be ignored. The loss of prestress due to creep of concrete is obtained as the product of the **modulus of elasticity of the prestressing steel (E_s) and the ultimate creep strain** of the concrete fibre integrated along the line of centre of gravity of the prestressing steel over its entire length.

The total creep strain during any specific period shall be assumed for all practical purposes, to be the creep strain due to sustained stress equal to the average of the stresses at the beginning and end of the period.

As per **IS : 1343-1980 (clause 5.2.5.1)**, the ultimate creep strain may be estimated from the following values of creep coefficient. (i.e. ultimate creep strain/elastic strain at the age of loading).

Age at loading	Creep coefficient
7 days	2.2
28 days	1.6
1 year	1.1

The above ultimate creep strain does not include the elastic strain. For the calculation of deformation at some stage before the total creep is reached, it may be assumed that about half the total creep takes place in first month after loading and that about three-quarters of the total creep takes place in the first six months after loading.

2.4.3 Loss of Stress due to Elastic Shortening of Concrete   [May 12]

(a) **For pretensioned members**, the IS : 1343-1980 (clause 18.5.2.4) recommends that the loss due to shortening of concrete at transfer is proportional to the modular ratio and the initial stress in the concrete.

i.e.   loss of prestress $= f \times m$ ... (2.9)

where $m = \dfrac{E_s}{E_c} =$ modular ratio

f – initial stress in the concrete adjacent to the wire.

(b) **For post-tensioned members**, the IS : code of practice suggests that where there is more than one tendon and which may not be stressed simultaneously, there is a progressive loss of stress during the transfer of the prestress.

In the case of post-tensioned beam with a single concentric tendon, as the tendon is stretched and anchored against concrete, all the elastic strain has occurred in concrete when the jacking force is reached in tendon. Since the force in the cable is measured, after the elastic shortening of the concrete has taken place, no loss of prestress due to this need be accounted for. However, in practice there are more than one tendon. If the tendons are stressed in succession, the prestress is applied gradually. Due to this, the tendon that is stressed first will suffer the maximum loss while one that is tensioned last will not suffer any loss. Accurate calculation for losses is complicated, but for all practical purposes, it may be assumed that average loss of each cable is equal to half the loss in the first cable.

2.4.4 Loss of Stress due to Relaxation of Steel

The loss due to relaxation may be from 2% to 8% of the average initial stress. The correct values may be supplied by the manufacturers of the steel.

As per IS : 1343-1980 (clause 18.5.2.3), the relaxation losses in prestressing steels vary with type of steel, initial prestress, age and temperature, and therefore, shall be determined from experiments. When experimental values are not available, the relaxation losses may be assumed as given in Table 2.1.

Table 2.1 : Relaxation losses for prestressing steel at 1000 H at 27°C

Initial stress	Relaxation loss (N/mm^2)
$0.5\,f_p$	0
$0.6\,f_p$	35
$0.7\,f_p$	70
$0.8\,f_p$	90

Note : t_p is the characteristic strength of prestressing steel.

2.5 REMEDIAL MEASURES TO REDUCE LOSSES IN PSC BEAMS
(WINTER 2011; 2012, MAY 13, 5 MARKS)

1. **Loss due to Friction :** It is found that by using lubricants, coefficient of friction can be reduced. Oils, grease, paraffin etc. are some of the lubricants that may be used.

2. **Loss due to Anchorage Slip :** This loss is of special importance with short members and necessary additional elongation may be provided at the time of tensioning to compensate for this loss.

3. **Loss of Stress Due to Shrinkage :** By minimizing the water/cement ratio and the proportion of cement, shrinkage can be reduced. This may be achieved by using well graded, larger sized aggregates.

2.6 COMMENT ON LOSSES IN SIMPLY SUPPORTED AND BALANCED CANTILEVER POST TENSIONED PRESTRESSED CONCRETE
(SUMMER 2012, 5 MARKS)

1. **Elastic Shortening of Concrete in Post-Tensioned Members :** In post-tensioned construction, wires are stretched with reaction against member itself so the elastic deformation takes place simultaneously and the jacking or initial stresses are independent of elastic shortening. If the tensioning of wires is done in stages, the wires that were anchored will undergo elastic shortening while the jacking is done for the next stage of prestressing. The wires tightened in the very beginning will be subjected to maximum loss of stress and those tightened in the last will not suffer any loss due to elastic shortening of concrete. If the prestressing is done at equal intervals, an average prestressing force could be taken for computing the elastic shortening.

2. **Shrinkage in Concrete :** The loss of stress due to shrinkage is higher in pretensioned members than in the post-tensioned members.

   Loss of stress due to shrinkage is given by

   $$E_s \times \text{Shrinkage strain}$$

   where $\qquad E_s$ = Young's modulus of steel

For post-tensioned member,

$$\text{Shrinkage strain} = \frac{0.0002}{\log_{10}(t+2)}$$

where, t = age of concrete at transfer in days

3. **Anchorage Slip :** In post-tensioned system, an allowance should be made for slipping of steel at the time of transferring the tendon force from the jacks to the member.

Solved Examples

Example 2.1 :

A prestressed concrete beam 250 mm wide and 360 mm deep has a span of 12 m. The beam is prestressed by steel wires of area 350 mm^2 provided at a uniform eccentricity of 60 mm with an initial prestress of 1250 N/mm^2. Determine the percentage loss of stress in the wires

(a)   if the beam is a pre-tensioned beam.

(b)   if the beam is a post-tensioned beam.

Use E_s = 210 kN/mm^2, E_c = 35 kN/mm^2

Ultimate creep strain = 45 $\times 10^{-6}$ mm/mm per N/mm^2 for pre-tensioned beam

= 22 $\times 10^{-6}$ mm/mm per N/mm^2 for post-tensioned beam

Shrinkage of concrete = 300 $\times 10^{-6}$ for pre-tensioned beam

= 215 $\times 10^{-6}$ for post-tensioned beam

Relaxation of steel stress = 5% of initial stress

Anchorage slip = 1.25 mm

Friction coefficient for wave effect, k = 0.00015 m.

Solution :

$$\text{Area of beam section } (A) = 250 \times 360$$
$$= 9 \times 10^4 \text{ mm}^2$$

$$\text{M.I. of beam section } (I) = \frac{1}{12} \times 250 \times 360^3$$
$$= 9.72 \times 10^8 \text{ mm}^4$$

$$\text{Initial prestressing force } (P_i) = 350 \times 1250$$
$$= 437.5 \text{ kN}$$

$$\text{Modular ratio, } m = \frac{E_s}{E_c} = \frac{210}{35} = 6$$

Stress in concrete at the level of steel

$$= \frac{P_i}{A} + \frac{P_i \times e}{I/e}$$

$$= \frac{P_i}{A} + \frac{P_i \times e^2}{I}$$

$$= \frac{437.5 \times 10^3}{9 \times 10^4} \; + \; \frac{437.5 \times 10^3 \times 60^2}{9.72 \times 10^8}$$

$$= 4.86 + 1.62$$

$$= 6.48 \text{ N/mm}^2$$

(A) Losses of Prestress for Pre-Tensioned Beam :

(a) Loss of stress due to elastic shortening of concrete $= m \times \dfrac{P}{A_c}$

$$= 6 \times 6.48 \; = \; 38.88 \text{ N/mm}^2$$

(b) Loss of stress due to creep of concrete $= (45 \times 10^{-6}) \times (210 \times 10^3) \times (6.48)$

$$= 61.24 \text{ N/mm}^2$$

(c) Loss of stress due to shrinkage of concrete $=$ Shrinkage strain $\times E_s$

$$= 300 \times 10^{-6} \times 210 \times 10^3$$

$$= 63.00 \text{ N/mm}^2$$

(d) Relaxation loss $= \dfrac{5}{100} \times 1250 = 62.50 \text{ N/mm}^2$

(e) Loss due to anchorage slip $= 0$

(f) Loss due to friction effect $= 0$

$$\text{Total loss} = 225.62 \text{ N/mm}^2$$

% age loss of stress $= \dfrac{225.62}{1250} \times 100 = 18.05 \%$ **... Ans.**

(B) Losses of Prestress for Post-Tensioned Beam :

(a) Loss due to elastic shortening of concrete $= 0$.

(b) Loss of stress due to creep of concrete

$$= (22 \times 10^{-6} \times 210 \times 10^3) \times 6.48 = 29.94 \text{ N/mm}^2$$

(c) Loss of stress due to shrinkage of concrete

$$= (215 \times 10^{-6} \times 210 \times 10^3) = 45.15 \text{ N/mm}^2$$

(d) Relaxation loss $= \dfrac{5}{100} \times 1250 = 62.50 \text{ N/mm}^2$.

(e) Loss due to anchorage of slip $= \dfrac{\Delta_a}{l} \, E_s = \dfrac{1.25}{12 \times 1000} \times 210 \times 10^3 = 21.88 \text{ N/mm}^2$.

(f) Loss due to friction effect $= (\mu\alpha + kx) \times$ initial stress

$$= (kx) \times \text{initial stress} \qquad \text{(since } \mu = 0)$$

$$= (0.00015 \times 12 \times 1250) \; = \; 22.50 \text{ N/mm}^2$$

$$\text{Total stress} = 181.97 \text{ N/mm}^2$$

$$\% \text{ age loss of stress} = \frac{181.97}{1250} \times 100$$

$$= 14.56\% \qquad\qquad \textbf{... Ans.}$$

Example 2.2 :

A straight post-tensioned concrete member 15 m long with a X-section of 400 mm × 400 mm is prestressed with 900 mm² of steel wires. This steel is made of 4-tendons with 225 mm² per tendon. The tendons are tensioned to a stress of 1050 N/mm². Determine the loss of prestress in each tendon due to elastic shortening of concrete. Find also average percentage loss of prestress.

If it is desired that after the last tendon is tightened, a stress of 1050 N/mm² be maintained in each tendon, compute the actual stress to which the individual tendons should be tightened. Take m = 16.

Solution :

There are four tendons.

$$\text{Loss of prestress in 1}^{st}\text{ tendon} = \frac{m \times P}{A_c}$$

$$\text{where} \quad P - \text{force transmitted by 3 tendons}$$

$$= \frac{6 \times 3 \times 225 \times 1050}{400 \times 400} \text{ N/mm}^2$$

$$= 26.6 \text{ N/mm}^2$$

$$\text{Loss of prestress in 2}^{nd}\text{ tendon} = \frac{m \times \text{force transmitted by 2 tendons}}{A_c}$$

$$= \frac{6 \times 2 \times 225 \times 1050}{400 \times 400} \text{ N/mm}^2$$

$$= 17.7 \text{ N/mm}^2$$

$$\text{Loss of prestress in 3}^{rd}\text{ tendon} = \frac{m \times \text{force transmitted by 1 tendon}}{A_c}$$

$$= \frac{6 \times 1 \times 225 \times 1050}{400 \times 400} \text{ N/mm}^2$$

$$= 8.9 \text{ N/mm}^2$$

$$\text{Loss of prestress in 4}^{th}\text{ tendon} = 0$$

$$\therefore \quad \text{Average loss of prestress} = \frac{26.6 + 17.7 + 8.9 + 0}{4} \text{ N/mm}^2 = 13.3 \text{ N/mm}^2$$

This is also equal to half the maximum loss of prestress

$$\text{i.e.} = \frac{26.6}{2} = 13.3 \text{ N/mm}^2$$

$$\text{Average \% age loss of prestress} = \frac{13.3}{1050} \times 100 = 1.27 \%$$

Adjustment of initial tendons to maintain a final stress of 1050 N/mm².

Initial stress required in first tendon = (1050 + 26.6) = 1076.6 N/mm²

Initial stress required in second tendon = (1050 + 17.7) = 1067.7 N/mm².

Initial stress required in third tendon = (1050 + 8.9) = 1058.9 N/mm².

and Initial stress required in fourth tendon = 1050 N/mm².   **... Ans.**

Example 2.3 :

A post-tensioned cable of a beam 10 m long is initially tensioned to a stress of 1000 N/mm² at one end. If the tendons are curved so that the slope is 1 in 24 at each end, with a cross-sectional area of 600 mm², calculate the loss of prestress due to friction, given the following data :

Coefficient of friction between duct and cable = 0.3.

Friction coefficient for wave effect = 0.0015 per metre.

Solution :

Let θ be the inclination of the cable with the horizontal at each end.

$$\tan \theta = \frac{1}{24}$$

$$\theta = \frac{1}{24} \text{ radian (since } \theta \text{ is small)}$$

$\therefore$ Total angle of turn of cable $= \alpha = 2\theta = 2 \times \frac{1}{24} = \frac{1}{12}$ radian

$\therefore$ Loss of prestress $= (\mu\alpha + kx) \times$ stress in steel at tensioning ends

$$= \left(0.3 \times \frac{1}{12} + 0.0015 \times 10\right) \times 1000 \text{ N/mm}^2$$

$$= 40 \text{ N/mm}^2 \qquad \textbf{... Ans.}$$

Example 2.4 :

A simply supported post-tensioned concrete beam of span 15 m has a rectangular cross-section 300 mm $\times$ 800 mm. The prestress at ends is 1300 kN with zero eccentricity at the supports and an eccentricity of 250 mm at the centre, the cable profile being parabolic.

Assuming $k = 0.15$ per 100 metre

and $\mu = 0.35$

determine the loss of prestress due to friction at the centre of beam.

Solution :

The equation of cable with one end as origin is,

$$y = \frac{4h}{l^2} \, x \, (l - x)$$

Slope at any point $= \dfrac{dy}{dx} = \dfrac{4h}{l^2} (l - 2x)$

Slope of cable at end $= \dfrac{4h}{l^2} (l - 0) = \dfrac{4h}{l} = \dfrac{4 \times 0.25}{15} = \dfrac{1}{15}$

$$\text{Slope of cable at centre} = 0$$

$$\text{Change of slope} = \frac{1}{15}$$

$\therefore$ Angle of deviation of cable from the end to the centre

$$\alpha = \frac{1}{15} \text{ radian } (\alpha \text{ is small})$$

$$k = \frac{0.15}{100} = 0.0015 \text{ per m}$$

$$\mu = 0.35$$

$$\text{at centre, } x = \frac{15}{2}$$

$\therefore$ Loss of prestress $= (\mu\alpha + kx) \times$ stress in steel at tensioning ends

$$= \left(0.35 \times \frac{1}{15} + 0.0015 \times 7.5\right) \times 1300 \times 10^3$$

$$= 44954 \text{ N}$$

$$\text{\% age loss of prestress} = \frac{44954}{1300 \times 1000} \times 100$$

$$= 3.46 \% \qquad \qquad \textbf{... Ans.}$$

Example 2.5 :

Fig. 2.1 shows a tendon profile ACEDB provided for a prestressed concrete beam. The tendon being tensioned from the end A. Calculate the percentage loss of prestress due to friction, from end A to end B.

Take $\mu = 0.30$, $k = 0.0015$ per metre.

Stress in tendon at A = 1050 N/mm².

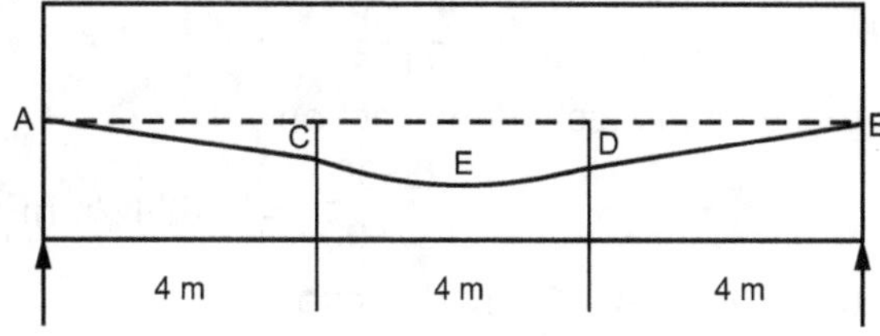

Fig. 2.1

Solution :

The tendon may be analysed in the following three portions :

(i)   straight AC, (ii) curved CED, (iii) straight DB.

Part AC :

$$\text{Loss due to length effect} = (k \times 4) \times \text{stress at A}$$

$$= (0.0015 \times 4) \times 1050 = 6.30 \text{ N/mm}^2$$

$$\text{Stress at C} = (1050 - 6.30) = 1043.7 \text{ N/mm}^2$$

Part CD : Loss due to length and curvature effect

$$= (\mu \times 0.12 + k \times 4) \times 1043.7$$
$$= (0.3 \times 0.12 + 0.0015 \times 4) \times 1043.7$$
$$= 43.8 \text{ N/mm}^2$$
$$\text{Stress at D} = (1043.7 - 43.8) = 999.9 \text{ N/m}^2$$

Part DB :

$$\text{Loss due to length effect} = (k \times 4) \times \text{stress at D}$$
$$= (0.0015 \times 4) \times 999.9 = 6 \text{ N/mm}^2$$
$$\therefore \qquad \text{Stress at B} = (999.9 - 6) = 993.9 \text{ N/mm}^2$$
$$\text{\% age loss of stress from A to B} = \frac{1050 - 993.9}{1050} \times 100$$
$$= 5.34 \% \qquad \qquad \text{... Ans.}$$

Example 2.6 :

A pre-tensioned beam (125 × 300) mm is prestressed by a parabolic tendon. The eccentricity of the tendon is zero at each support and 55 mm at centre of the span. The area of the tendon is 215 mm² and the tendons are initially stressed to 1200 N/mm².

Creep coefficient, ϕ = 1.6,   M40 grade of concrete.

Use E_s = 2 × 10⁵ N/mm²

Find the loss of prestress due to creep of concrete.

Solution :

$$\text{Area of beam section (A)} = 125 \times 300$$
$$= 37500 \text{ mm}^2$$
$$\text{M.I. of beam section} = I = \frac{1}{12}\, bd^3 = \frac{1}{12} \times 125 \times 300^3 = 2.8125 \times 10^8 \text{ mm}^4$$
$$\therefore \qquad \text{Initial prestressing force} = 215 \times 1200$$
$$= 258000 \text{ N}$$

Stress in concrete at the level of steel at end section

$$= \frac{P}{A} = \frac{258000}{37500} = 6.88 \text{ N/mm}^2$$

Stress in concrete at the level of steel at mid-section

$$= \frac{P}{A} + \frac{Pe^2}{I} = 6.88 + \frac{258000 \times 55^2}{2.8125 \times 10^8}$$
$$= 9.65 \text{ N/mm}^2$$

$$\text{Average stress in concrete at the level of steel} = f_c = \frac{6.88 + 9.65}{2}$$

$$f_c = 8.265 \text{ N/mm}^2$$

$\therefore$ Loss of stress in steel due to creep of concrete

$$= \phi m f_c$$

$$= 1.6 \times \frac{E_s}{E_c} \times 8.265$$

$$= 1.6 \times 6.32 \times 8.265$$

$$= 83.63 \text{ N/mm}^2$$

$$\left[\because \; E_c = 5000 \sqrt{f_{ck}} \right.$$
$$= 5000 \sqrt{40}$$
$$\left. = 31622.7 \text{ N/mm}^2 \right] \quad \text{... \textbf{Ans.}}$$

Example 2.7 :

A post-tensioned prestressed concrete beam of simply supported span 16 m having the cross-sectional details as top flange 450 × 150, web 120 × 600 and bottom flange 360 × 200 mm. The beam is prestressed with 3 number of 12/5 Freyssinet parabolic cables with their c.g. at 120 mm from extreme bottom fiber, stressed one at a time from only one end to 900 MPa. Calculate total loss of prestress and jacking force at the age of 120 days, if coefficient of friction = 0.3, coefficient for curvature and wave effect = 0.0026/m length of cable, slip of anchorage at jacking end = 2 mm, creep coefficient = 2.4, $E_s = 2 \times 10^5$ MPa, creep and relaxation of steel = 1% of initial prestress concrete grade = M40.

(Winter 2011, 17 Marks)

Solution :

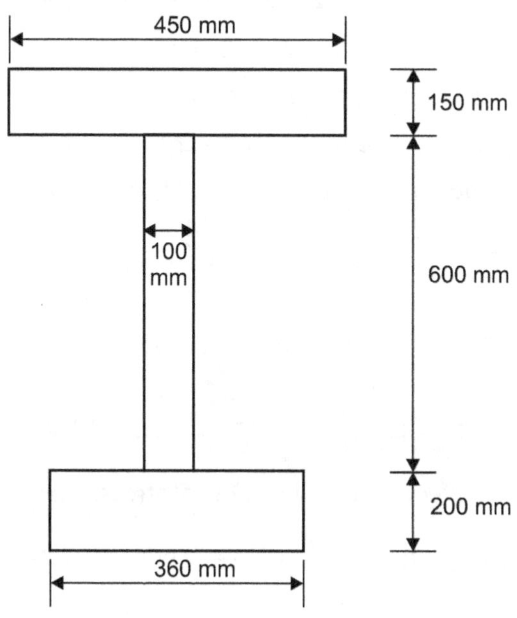

Fig. 2.2

$$A = 450 \times 150 + 120 \times 600 + 360 \times 200 = 2.115 \times 10^3 \text{ mm}^2$$

$$\bar{y}_{bottom} = \frac{450 \times 150 \times 875 + 120 \times 600 \times 500 + 360 \times 200 \times 100}{2.115 \times 10^3}$$

$$= 483.51 \text{ mm},$$

$$y_{top} = 466.49 \text{ mm}$$

$$I = \frac{450 \times 150^3}{12} + 450 \times 150 \,(466.49 - 75)^2 + \frac{120 \times 600^3}{12} + 120 \times 600$$

$$(466.49 - 480)^2 + \frac{360 \times 200^3}{12} + 360 \times 200 \times (483.51 - 100)^2$$

$$= 2.348 \times 10^{10} \text{ mm}^4$$

$$e = 483.51 - 120 = 363.51 \text{ mm}$$

$$\text{Initial prestressing force} = P_i = \frac{900 \times 3 \times 5 \times \frac{\pi}{4} \times 12^2}{1000} = 1526.81 \text{ kN}$$

$$\text{Modular ratio} = m = \frac{E_s}{E_c} = \frac{2 \times 10^5}{5000 \sqrt{40}} = 6.32$$

Stresses in concrete at the level of steel

$$= \frac{P_i}{A} + \frac{P_i \times e}{I/e} = \frac{P_i}{A} + \frac{P_i \cdot e^2}{I} = \frac{1526.81 \times 10^3}{2.115 \times 10^3} + \frac{1526.81 \times 10^3 \times 363.51^2}{2.348 \times 10^{10}}$$

$$= 721.89 + 8.59 = 730.48 \text{ N/mm}^2$$

(a)　Loss due to elastic shortening of concrete = 0

(b)　Loss due to creep of concrete = $24 \times 10^{-6} \times 2.1 \times 10^5 \times 730.48$

(c)　Loss due to shrinkage of concrete

$$= \frac{0.0002}{\log_{10} (t + 2)} = \frac{0.0002}{\log_{10} (120 + 2)} = 1.48 \times 10^{-4} \text{ N/mm}^2$$

(d)　Relaxation loss $= \frac{1}{100} \times 900 = 9 \text{ N/mm}^2$

(e)　Loss due to anchorage slip $= \frac{\Delta_a}{l} \, E_s = \frac{2}{16000} \times 2.1 \times 10^5 = 26.25 \text{ N/mm}^2$

(f)　Loss due to friction effect = $(\mu\alpha + kx) \times$ Initial stress.

$$= (0.3 \times 0.03 + 0.026 \times 16) \times 900 \qquad \left[\because \alpha = \frac{4h}{l} = \frac{4 \times 0.12}{16} = 0.03\right]$$

$$= 382.5 \text{ N/mm}^2$$

$$\text{Total stress} = 417.75 \text{ N/mm}^2$$

$$\therefore \quad \text{\% loss of stress} = \frac{417.75}{900} \times 100 = 46.41\%$$

Example 2.8 :

A post-tensioned prestressed concrete beam of simply supported span 16 m having the cross-sectional details as top flange 500 × 150, web 125 × 400 and bottom flange 300 × 280 mm. The beam is prestressed with 3 number of 12/7 Freyssinet parabolic cables with their c.g. at 100 mm from extreme bottom fiber, stressed one at a time from only one end to 1100 MPa. Calculate total loss of prestress and jacking force at the age of 100 days, if coefficient of friction = 0.3, coefficient for curvature and wave effect = 0.0026/m length of cable, slip of anchorage at jacking end = 1.5 mm, creep coefficient = 2.2, E_s = 2 × 10⁵ MPa, creep and relaxation of steel = 1.1% of initial prestress concrete grade = M40.

(Summer 2012, 17 Marks, May 13, 15, Dec. 11, 12, 14)

Solution :

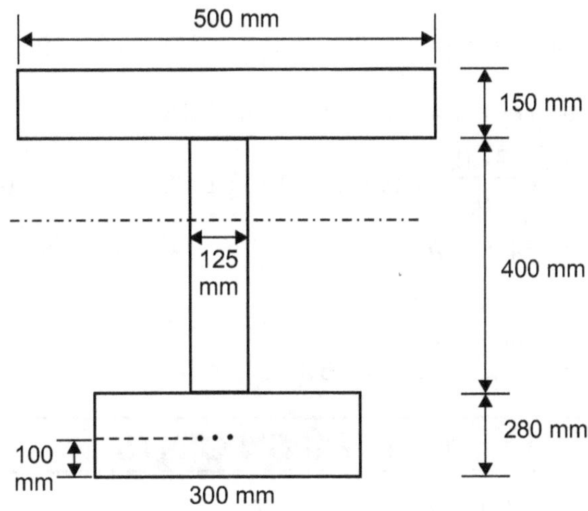

Fig. 2.3

$$A = 500 \times 150 + 125 \times 400 + 300 \times 280$$

$$= 2.09 \times 10^5 \text{ mm}^4$$

$$\bar{y} = 529.84 \text{ mm}$$

$$I = 1.524 \times 10^{10} \text{ mm}^4$$

$$e = 529.84 - 100 = 429.84 \text{ mm}$$

Initial prestressing force, $P_i = \dfrac{1100 \times 3}{1000} \times \dfrac{\pi}{4} \times 12^2 \times 7 = 2612.55$ kN

Modular ratio, $m = \dfrac{E_s}{E_c} = \dfrac{2.1 \times 10^5}{5000 \sqrt{40}} = 6.64$

Stresses in concrete at the level of steel

$$= \frac{P_i}{A} + \frac{P_i \times e}{I/e} = \frac{P_i}{A} + \frac{P_i \cdot e^2}{I}$$

$$= \frac{2612.55 \times 10^3}{2.09 \times 10^5} + \frac{261255 \times 10^3 \times 429.84^2}{1.524 \times 10^{10}}$$

$$= 44.17 \ \text{N/mm}^2$$

(a)   Loss due to elastic shortening of concrete = 0.

(b)   Loss due to creep of concrete = $22 \times 10^{-6} \times 2.1 \times 10^5 \times 44.17 = 204.06 \ \text{N/mm}^2.$

(c)   Loss of stress due to shrinkage of concrete = 0.

(d)   Relaxation loss = $\dfrac{1.1}{100} \times 1100 = 12.1 \ \text{N/mm}^2$

(e)   Loss due to anchorage slip = $\dfrac{\Delta_a}{l} E_s = \dfrac{1.5}{16000} \times 2.1 \times 10^5 = 19.69 \ \text{N/mm}^2.$

(f)   Loss due to friction effect = $(\mu\alpha + kx) \times$ Initial stress

$$= (\frac{0.3 \times 0.1}{4} + 0.0026 \times 16) \times 1100 \qquad [\because \ \alpha = \frac{4h}{l} = \frac{4 \times 0.1}{16} = \frac{0.1}{4}]$$

$$= 54.01 \ \text{N/mm}^2$$

$$\text{Total loss} = 289.86 \ \text{N/mm}^2$$

$$\% \ \text{loss of stress} = \frac{289.86}{1100} \times 100 = 26.35\%$$

IMPORTANT POINTS

- Losses of prestress occurring subsequently.
- Losses of prestress during tensioning and anchoring stage.

QUESTIONS

1.   A simply supported beam (prestressed) has the following data :

Span = 10 m

Section = 200 mm × 300 mm deep

Area of prestressing steel = 160 mm²

Constant eccentricity of prestressing steel = 50 mm.

Initial prestress = 1000 N/mm².

E_s = 210 kN/mm², E_c = 35 kN/mm².

Slip at anchorage = 1 mm.

Relaxation of steel = 5 % of initial stress.

Friction coefficient for wave effect $= 0.00015$ per m.

$$\text{Shrinkage of concrete} = 300 \times 10^{-6} \text{ for pre-tensioning}$$
$$= 200 \times 10^{-6} \text{ for post-tensioning}$$
$$\text{Creep strain} = 40 \times 10^{-6} \text{ mm/mm per N/mm}^2 \text{ for pre-tensioning}$$
$$= 20 \times 10^{-6} \text{ mm/mm per N/mm}^2 \text{ for post-tensioning}$$

Estimate and compare the percentage loss of prestress if

(i)   the beam is pre-tensioned

(ii)   the beam is post-tensioned.

2.   A pre-tensioned beam (200×400) mm is prestressed by 7 mm diameter H.T. wires 12 numbers. The centroid of wires is 100 mm from soffit at centre of span and at support they are concentric.

Estimate TPL (Total Prestress Loss).

$$\text{Use : creep coefficient} = 1.6$$
$$\text{Shrinkage strain} = 300 \times 10^{-6}$$
$$\text{Initial stress in steel} = 1200 \text{ N/mm}^2$$

M40 concrete and assume E_c and E_s.

3.   A post-tensioned prestressed concrete beam 250 mm wide and 400 mm deep is prestressed with wires (area $= 400$ mm^2), located at uniform eccentricity of 100 mm. The wires are initially stressed to 1000 MPa. The beam spans 12 m. Calculate the loss of stress in wires, given that

(i) $E_{steel} = 210$ kN/mm^2

(ii) $E_{concrete} = 35$ kN/mm^2

(iii)   Relaxation of steel $= 5$ % of initial stress.

(iv)   Age of concrete at transfer $= 21$ days.

(v)   Creep coefficient $= 1.6$.

(vi)   Anchorage slip $= 1$ mm.   **(P.U. Dec. 2005)**

4.   A post-tensioned prestressed concrete beam has a parabolic cable profile with zero eccentricity at the end and an eccentricity of 400 mm at the centre, with respect to gross centroid of the section. It covers a span of 25 m and a prestressing force of 400 kN is applied from one end A. Determine the loss in prestressing due to friction at the farther end B and hence, evaluate the force at B. Coefficient of friction is 0.30 and the wobble effect is 0.25% per unit length of span.   **(P.U. Dec. 2005)**

5.   (a)   Enlist the different types of losses in prestress. Explain the time-dependent losses with their usual magnitude.

(b)   Explain the concept of loss of prestress due to slip of anchorages and relaxation of steel in prestressed concrete beams.

(c)   Comment on – "A precise determination of losses in prestressed concrete is a complicated problem".

(d)   Describe the creep action in concrete and explain how the creep loss is estimated in prestressed concrete member.

6.   A post-tensioned prestressed concrete beam section has top flange 450×150, web 120×600 and bottom flange 300×200 mm, is simply supported over a effective span of 16 m. The beam is prestressed with 5 No. of 12/5 Freyssinet parabolic cables with their c.g. at 120 mm from extreme bottom fibre, stressed one at a time from only one end. Calculate total loss of prestress at the age of 150 days, if k = 0.0026 m per length of cable, slip of anchorage = 2 mm, C_c = 2.0, E_s = 2×10^5 MPa, concrete grade = M40, creep and relaxation of steel = 2% of initial prestress.

UNIVERSITY QUESTIONS

Dec. 2011

Q. 1 (a)   Explain in detail the loss of prestress due to friction. **(Section 2.2)**   **(8 Marks)**

(b)   A post tensioned prestressed concrete beam of simply supported span 16 m having the cross-sectional details as top flange 450×150, web 120×600 and bottom flange 360×200 mm, the beam is prestressed with 3 No. of 12/5 Freyssinet parabolic cables with their c.g. at 120 mm from extreme bottom fiber, stressed one at a time from only one end to 900 Mpa. Calculate total loss of prestress and jacking force at the age of 120 days, if coefficient of friction = 0.3, coefficient for curvature and wave effect = 0.0026 / m length of cable, slip of anchorage at jacking end = 2 mm, creep coefficient = 2.4, Es = 2×10^5 Mpa, creep and relaxation of steel = 1% of initial prestress concrete grade = M40.

(Example 2.8)   **(17 Marks)**

May 2012

Q. 2 (a)   Explain in detail the loss of stress due to Elastic shortening in pre and post tensioned prestressed concrete. **(Section 2.4.3)**   **(8 Marks)**

(b)   A post tensioned prestressed concrete beam of simply supported span 16 m having the cross sectional details as top flange 500×150, web 125×400 and bottom flange 300×280 mm. The beam is prestressed with 3 No. of 12/7 Freyssinet parabolic cables with their c.g. at 100 mm from extreme bottom fiber, stressed one at a time from only one end to 1100 Mpa. Calculate total loss of presstress and jacking force at the age of 100 days, if coefficient of friction = 0.3, coefficient for curvature and wave effect = 0.0026/m length of cable, slip of anchorage at jacking end = 1.5 mm, creep coefficient = 2.2, Es = 2×10^5 Mpa, Creep and relaxation of steel = 1.1 % of initial prestress concrete grade = M 40.

(Example 2.8)   **(17 Marks)**

Q. 3 (a) Comment on the losses in simply supported and balanced cantilever post tensioned prestressed concrete. **(Section 2.6)**   **(5 Marks)**

Dec. 2012

Q. 4 (a) Explain in detail loss of pre-stress due to friction. **(Section 2.2)**   **(8 Marks)**

   (b) A pre-stressed concrete beam 200 mm wide and 300 mm deep is pre-stressed with wires having area 320 mm^2 located at constant eccentricity of 50 mm and carrying an initial stress of 1000 N/mm^2. The span of beam is 10 m. Calculate the percentage loss of stress in wires if (a) the beam is pre-tensioned, and (b) the beam is post-tensioned if coefficient of friction for wave effect = 0.0015/m, slip of anchorage = 1 mm, creep coefficient = 1.6, shrinkage of concrete = 300×10^{-6} for pre-tensioning and 200×10^{-6} for post tensioning, relaxation of steel stress = 5% of initial stress, E_s = 210 kN/mm^2 and E_c = 35 kN/mm^2. **(Example 2.8)**   **(17 Marks)**

Q. 5 (a) State remedial measures to be taken to reduce losses in PSC beams.

   (Section 2.5)   **(5 Marks)**

May 2013

Q. 6 (a) Explain with neat sketches various systems of Pre-stressing. **(Section 1.11)** **(5 Marks)**

   (b) Explain in detail various types of losses in post-tensioned members.

   (Section 2.4)   **(5 Marks)**

Q. 7 (a) State what are the remedial measures to be taken to reduce losses in prestress.

   (Section 2.5)   **(8 Marks)**

   (b) A post tensioned prestressed concrete beam is simply supported over a span of 20 m having cross sectional dimensions of top flange as 500 × 200 mm, web 150 × 800 mm, and bottom flange 400 × 250 mm. The beam is prestressed with 5 numbers of 12/5 Freyssinet parabolic cables with their C.G. at 120 mm from extreme bottom fire cables are stressed one at a time from one end only with prestressing force 1000 kN. Calculate total loss of prestress and jacking force at the age of 100 days, if coefficient of friction is 0.3, coefficient of curvature and wave effect = 0.0026/m length of cable, slip of anchorage at jacking end = 2 mm, creep coefficient = 2.4, Es = 200 Gpa, creep and relaxation of steel = 1% of initial prestress, concrete grade = M40.

   (Example 2.8)   **(17 Marks)**

Dec. 2014

Q. 8   A post tensioned prestressed concrete beam of 16 m span is subjected to prestressing force by 5 Nos. of 12/5 Freyssinet parabolic cables with their C.G. at 130 mm from extreme bottom fiber, stressed one at a time from only one end at 800 MPa. Calculated total loss of prestress at the age of 90 days for the following data: Top flange 525 mm × 200 mm. bottom flange 350 mm × 250 mm and web 150 mm × 650 mm, Es = 210 GPa, Ec = 0.382 GPa, coefficient of friction = 0.25, Wobble correction factor = 0.0015 per meter, anchorage slip = 2.5, creep coefficient = 2.4.

(Example 2.8)   **(17 Marks)**

May 2015

Q. 9 (a) Explain the various losses in prestressed concret.   **(Section 2.4) (8 Marks)**

   (b) A post tensioned prestressed concrete beam section has top flange 500 × 150 mm, web 200 × 800 mm and bottom flange 400 × 300 mm is simply supported over an effective span of 16 meter. The beam is prestressed with 6 number of 12/5 Freyssinet parabolic cabls (F_y = 1650 MPa) with their C.G. 100 mm from extreme bottom fiber, stressed one at a time from only one end. Calculate total loss of prestress at the age of 100 days if K = 0.0026/m length of cable, slip of anchorage = 2 mm, C_c = 1.8, E_s = 2 × 10^5 MPa, concrete grade M40, Creep and relaxation = 2% on initial prestress.   **(Example 2.8) (17 Marks)**

Chapter 3

STRESS CALCULATIONS

3.1 INTRODUCTION

According to Lin, three different concepts may be applied to explain and calculate the stress of prestressed concrete. These concepts are as follows :

- Stress concept.
- Load balancing concept.
- Strength concept/pressure line concept/thrust line concept.

3.2 STRESS CONCEPT [May 15]

Stress concept is credited to Eugene Freyssinet, who visualised prestressed concrete as essentially concrete which is transformed from a brittle material into an elastic one by precompression given to it. If an ordinary concrete, whether plain or reinforced, is subjected to only compressive stresses, it behaves as a perfect elastic material because no tension cracks are there. But if it is subjected to flexural stresses, some portion of it will be in tension resulting in tension cracks; the material under such circumstance no longer remains elastic. In prestressed concrete, on the other hand, concrete is visualised as being subjected to two system of forces : internal prestress, which is compressive and external load causing tensile stresses. The tensile stresses caused due to external load are counterbalanced by the compressive stress due to prestress, with the result that final stress in the extreme fibre is either compressive or zero. Due to absence of final tensile stress, no tension cracks would be there in concrete, and it will thus be transformed from brittle to elastic material. To elaborate this point, let us consider two cases :

   (a)   The prestressing force acting at the neutral axis of the beam.

   (b)   The prestressing force acting at an eccentricity to the neutral axis of the beam.

(a) The Prestressing Force Acting at the Neutral Axis of the Beam (Concentric Tendon):

Let a concrete beam, in which prestressing force (P) is applied and placed simply on two supports and let the external load (i.e. dead load and live load) W, act upon it. [Refer Fig. 3.1 (a)]. Then there will be two kinds of stresses in the beam, namely (i) the already existing prestresses (i.e. precompressive stresses) induced by the prestressing force and (ii) the stresses developed due to the bending moments caused by the external loads. The latter will be superimposed upon the former.

Let p_t and p_b be the prestresses at top and bottom fibres respectively which in this case will be the same when the uniform prestressing force act at the neutral axis of the beam. Let f_t

and f_b be the stresses developed at top and bottom fibres respectively by the external load W. At the top fibre, the stress f_t will be compressive and at the bottom fibre the stress f_b will be tensile.

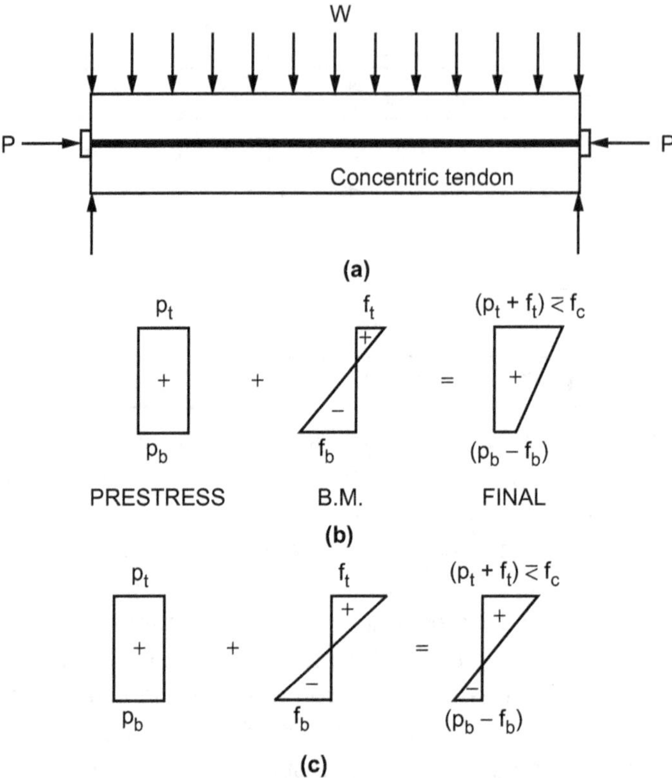

(a) Superimposing bending stresses upon prestress,

(b) Causing no tensile stresses, (c) Causing tensile stresses

Fig. 3.1 : Concentrically prestressed section

Then at the top fibre, the total compressive stress will increase and be equal to the sum of the prestress and the compressive stress due to the external loads (i.e. $p_t + f_t$) and at the bottom fibre the tensile stress will be reduced by an amount of the uniform prestress p_b, and if f_b is less than p_b, then the total stress will be equal to $(p_b - f_b)$, which will be compressive. Thus no tension will occur in the beam [Refer Fig. 3.1 (b)]. If, however, the stress f_b is greater than the prestress p_b, the tensile stress will occur at the bottom fibre as shown in Fig. 3.1 (c). It is assumed that the stress at the top fibre is equal to or less than f_c, the permissible stress.

(b) The Prestressing Force Acting at an Eccentricity to the Neutral Axis of the Beam :

From the above discussion it can be seen that in a simply supported beam, the external loads develop compressive stresses at the top fibre and if the additional compressive stresses due to prestressing are also present there, the beam is placed under greater compression, reducing the compressive strength of the beam to that extent. Consequently, the stresses due to prestressing would not be required there. But, it would be better to have large prestresses available in the bottom fibre as the tensile stresses are developed thereby the external loads and the prestresses will be utilised in neutralising the tensile stresses.

Such a useful stress distribution can be attained if the prestressing force is allowed to act at an eccentricity to the neutral axis of the beam. [Refer Fig. 3.3 (a)]. Then, as in case of an eccentrically loaded column, the direct and the bending stresses will be induced in the beam, due to the prestressing force. This eccentricity can be made such that the bending stress is equal to the direct stress. The prestress will then consist of a triangular compression as shown in Fig. 3.2 (a). Such eccentricity will be the lower limit of the core of the section. The core in case of a rectangular section will be the middle third of the section, being equal to $\frac{1}{3}$ D, where D is the overall depth of the section.

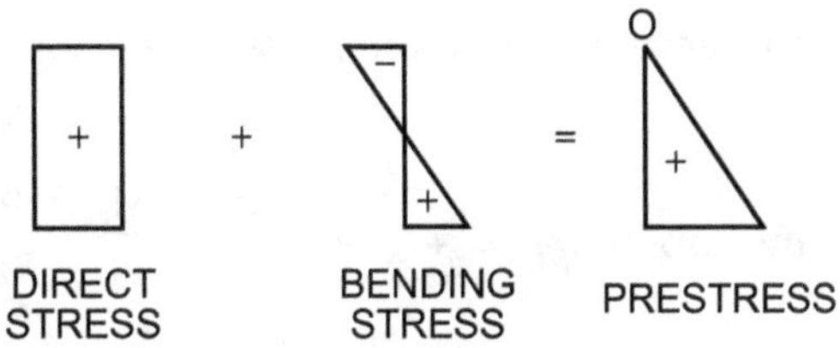

DIRECT STRESS   +   BENDING STRESS   =   PRESTRESS

(a) Stresses due to prestressing force acting at lower limit of core

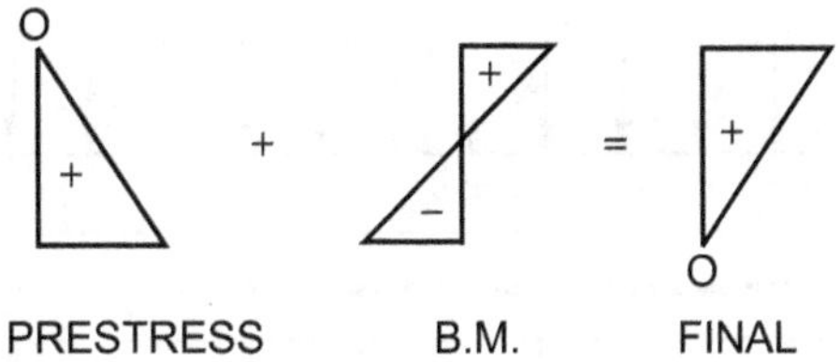

PRESTRESS   +   B.M.   =   FINAL

(b) Stresses due to prestressing force and bending moment

Fig. 3.2

The stresses due to the bending moments produced by the external loads will then be superimposed upon the prestress obtained as above [Refer Fig. 3.2 (b)]. If now the stress at the bottom fibre due to the external loads be equal to the prestress at the bottom fibre as shown in Fig. 3.2 (b), then there will be zero tensile stress at the bottom fibre and the compressive stress equal to that produced by the external loads at the top fibre as shown in Fig. 3.2 (b). If the stresses are within the permissible limits, then the stress in the concrete is fully utilised both at the bottom of the section (i.e. in respect of prestressing force) and at the top (i.e. in respect of the bending).

Thus, it is seen that if the artificially induced compressive stresses are large enough and are present in those parts of the beam where tensile stresses due to the external loads will ordinarily occur, cracking of the concrete can indeed be prevented and the subsequent destruction of concrete due to cracking can be avoided.

Mathematically :

Let, P be the prestressing force supplied by the tendon.

Let, due to dead load, the bending moment at a section be M_d and due to live load, the bending moment at a section be M_L.

The stresses on the section consist of the following :

(i)   Direct stress due to prestressing force $= +\dfrac{P}{A}$.

(ii)   Extreme stress due to bending moment (D.L.) $= \pm\dfrac{M_d}{z}$.

(iii)   Extreme stress due to bending moment (L.L.) $= \pm\dfrac{M_L}{z}$.

(iv)   Extreme stress due to eccentricity of the prestressing force $= \mp\dfrac{P \cdot e}{z}$.

Final stresses are :

$$\text{Stress at the extreme top } (f_{top}) = +\frac{P}{A} + \frac{M_d}{z_t} + \frac{M_L}{z_t} - \frac{P \cdot e}{z_t} \qquad \text{... (3.1)}$$

$$\text{Stress at the extreme bottom } (f_{bottom}) = +\frac{P}{A} - \frac{M_d}{z_b} - \frac{M_L}{z_b} + \frac{P \cdot e}{z_b} \qquad \text{... (3.2)}$$

These are shown in Fig. 3.3.

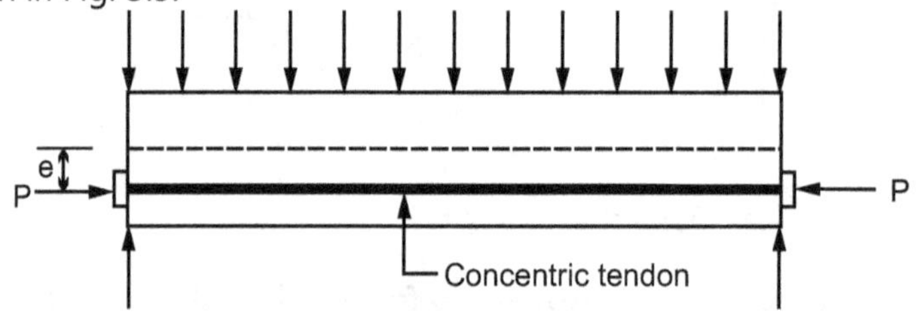

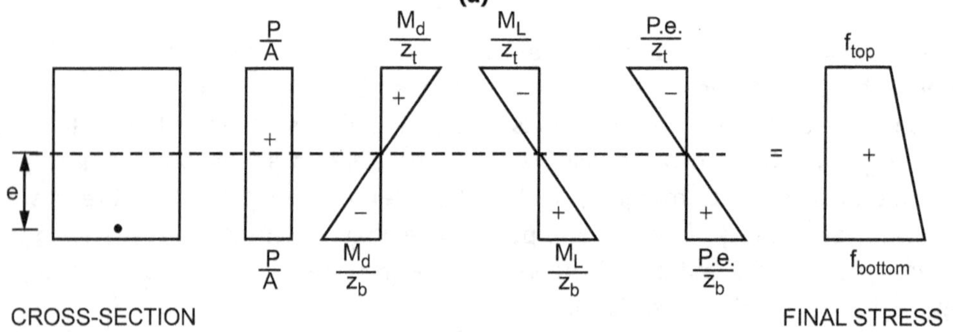

Fig. 3.3 : Eccentrically prestressed section

3.3 LOAD BALANCING CONCEPT   [Dec. 14, May 15]

Load balancing concept was developed by Lin, in which a flexural member is transformed into a member under direct stress. In this method, the cable profile can be adjusted so that the cable may exert upward forces counteracting to some extent the downward external loading. If a beam is so designed that the upward forces transmitted by the cable exactly neutralise the externally applied loading, such method of designing is called load balancing method. In this method, either an inclined tendon or a curved (parabolic) tendon is used.

(a) **Prestressed Beam with Bent Tendon :** Consider a prestressed beam carrying an external load W (Refer Fig. 3.4). The tendon is provided with an inclined profile. By providing bent tendons, the tendons will exert an upward pressure on the concrete beam and will counteract a part of the extended downward loading. For sake of discussion, let us assume that the tendon forms a sharp bend and that there is no frictional loss along the tendon.

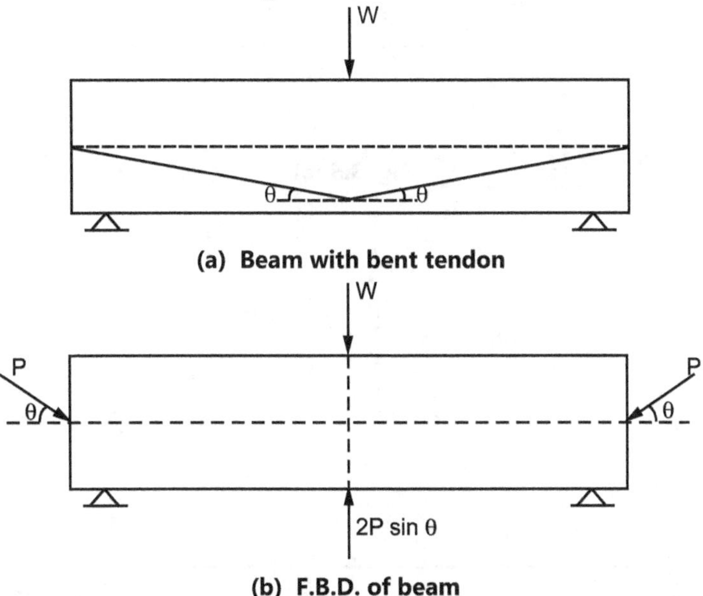

(a) Beam with bent tendon

(b) F.B.D. of beam

Fig. 3.4 : Prestressed beam with bent tendon

For the above beam,

Net downward load at centre $= (W - 2P \sin \theta)$

The axial longitudinal force provided by the tendon

$$= P \cos \theta \approx P \text{ (since } \theta \text{ is small)}$$

$\therefore$ Direct stress on the section $= \dfrac{P \cos \theta}{A}$

and   Net B.M. $= M = \dfrac{(W - 2P \sin \theta) \times l}{4} + \dfrac{wl^2}{8}$

where w = D.L. per unit length of beam

Therefore,   Extreme fibre stress $= \dfrac{P}{A} \pm \dfrac{M}{Z}$ ... (3.3)

From above it is clear that, the profile of the tendon should follow the shape of the B.M. diagram for the given external loads in order it may offer effective upward forces.

For instance, if the loading on the beam is a uniformly distributed load, the tendon may be provided along a parabolic profile.

Important Notes :

   (A)

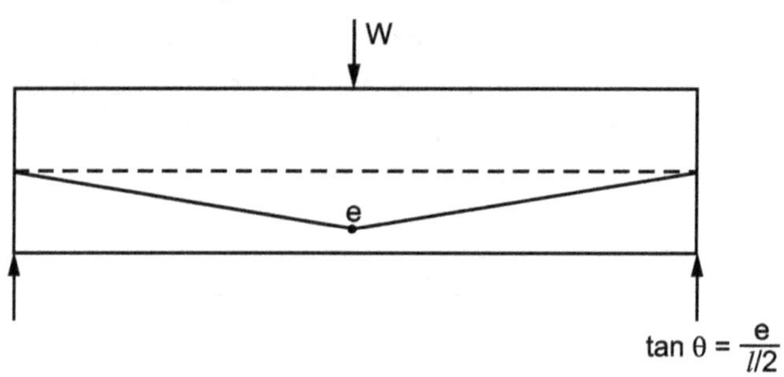

Fig. 3.5 (a)

At mid-section : $f_{top} = +\dfrac{P}{A} + \dfrac{M_d}{Z} + \dfrac{M_L}{Z}$

$f_{bottom} = +\dfrac{P}{A} - \dfrac{M_d}{Z} - \dfrac{M_L}{Z}$

At ends : $f_{top} = +\dfrac{P}{A}$, $f_{bottom} = +\dfrac{P}{A}$

   (B)

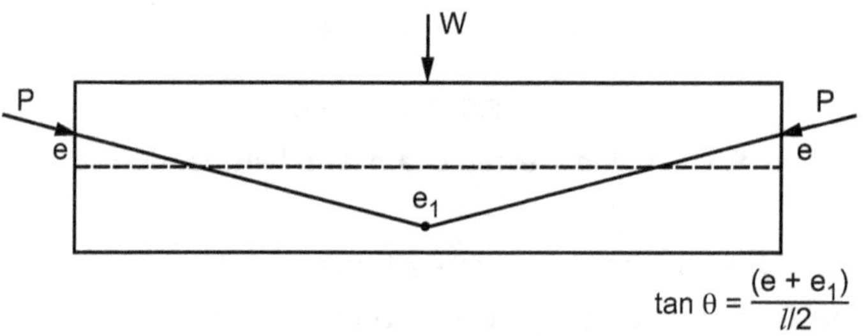

Fig. 3.5 (b)

At mid-section : $f_{top} = +\dfrac{P}{A} + \dfrac{P \cdot e}{Z} + \dfrac{M_d}{Z} + \dfrac{M_L}{Z}$

$f_{bottom} = +\dfrac{P}{A} - \dfrac{P \cdot e}{Z} - \dfrac{M_d}{Z} - \dfrac{M_L}{Z}$

At ends :

$$f_{top} = +\frac{P}{A} + \frac{P \cdot e}{z}$$

$$f_{bottom} = +\frac{P}{A} - \frac{P \cdot e}{z}$$

(C)

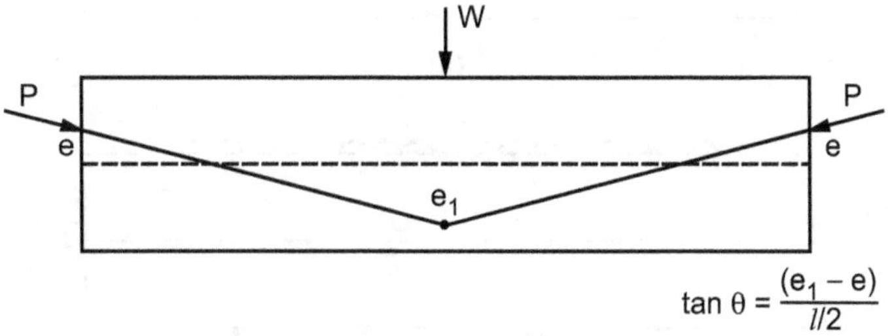

$$\tan \theta = \frac{(e_1 - e)}{l/2}$$

Fig. 3.5 (c)

At mid-section :

$$f_{top} = +\frac{P}{A} - \frac{P \cdot e}{z} + \frac{M_d}{z} + \frac{M_L}{z}$$

$$f_{bottom} = +\frac{P}{A} + \frac{P \cdot e}{z} - \frac{M_d}{z} - \frac{M_L}{z}$$

At ends :

$$f_{top} = +\frac{P}{A} - \frac{P \cdot e}{z}$$

$$f_{bottom} = +\frac{P}{A} + \frac{P \cdot e}{z}$$

(b) Prestressed Beam with Parabolic Tendon :

Consider a prestressed beam carrying an external u.d.l. w/m. The tendon is provided with a parabolic profile. When the cable is provided with a parabolic profile, it will exert a uniform upward pressure w_c/m on the beam and will therefore receive a downward u.d.l. w_c/m.

We have studied in the theory of cables, carrying u.d.l. on the whole span.

Horizontal reaction at each end of the cable $= P_x = \dfrac{w_c l^2}{8 h}$.

where, $\quad$ h – dip of the cable centre below the ends of the cable.

Making approximation $\quad P_x = P$, we get

$$P = \frac{w_c \cdot l^2}{8 h}$$

$\therefore \qquad w_c = \dfrac{8 Ph}{l^2}$ $\hspace{4cm}$ ... (3.4)

Hence, a parabolic tendon carrying a tension P will provide an upward u.d.l.

$$w_c = \frac{8 Ph}{l^2} \text{ per unit length of the beam}$$

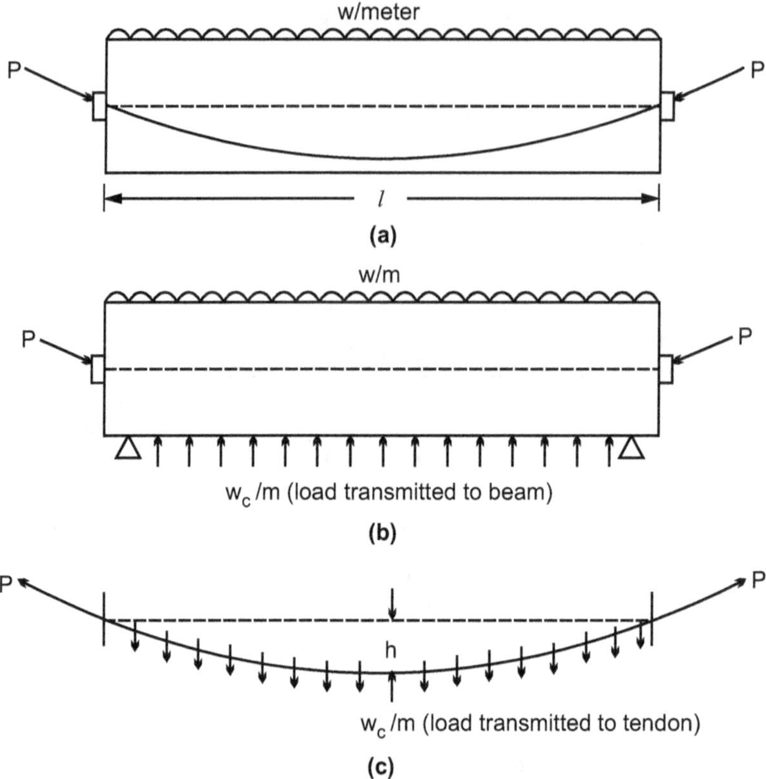

Fig. 3.6 : Prestressed beam with parabolic tendon

Hence, the upward uniform pressure supplied by the parabolic tendon will counteract a part of the external downward uniformly applied load.

The net downward loading on beam $= (w - w_c)$ per unit run.

Therefore,   Extreme fibre stress $= \dfrac{P}{A} \pm \dfrac{M}{z}$ ... (3.5)

where $M = \dfrac{(w - w_c)\, l^2}{8}$

3.4 STRENGTH CONCEPT

Consider a beam of length l provided with a tendon at an eccentricity e. (Refer Fig. 3.7)

Suppose the beam is lying on the ground i.e. the beam is not subjected to any external load. Hence, there is no external B.M. on the beam. But there are two forces acting on the beam, which are equal :

(1)   P-force; which is the tension in the tendon.

(2)   C-force; which is the compressive force acting on concrete. Stresses in concrete are produced entirely due to C-force.

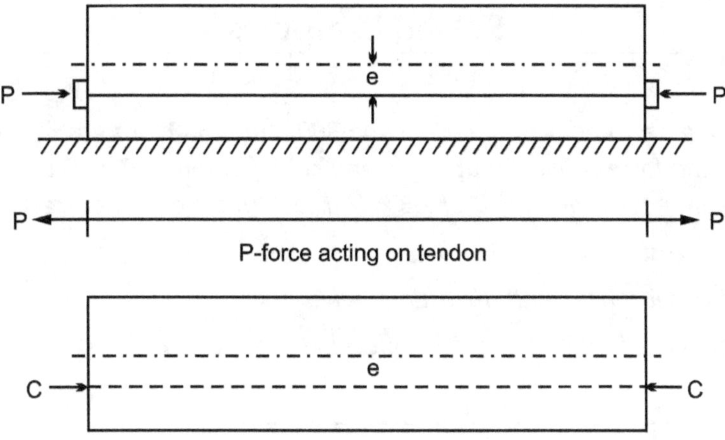

Fig. 3.7

In the absence of any external B.M., the C-force and P-force act at the same level. The line of action of P-force is called P-line. The P-line is tendon line itself. The line of action of C-force is called the C-line (or pressure line). Hence, in the absence of any external B.M., the P-line and the C-line coincide.

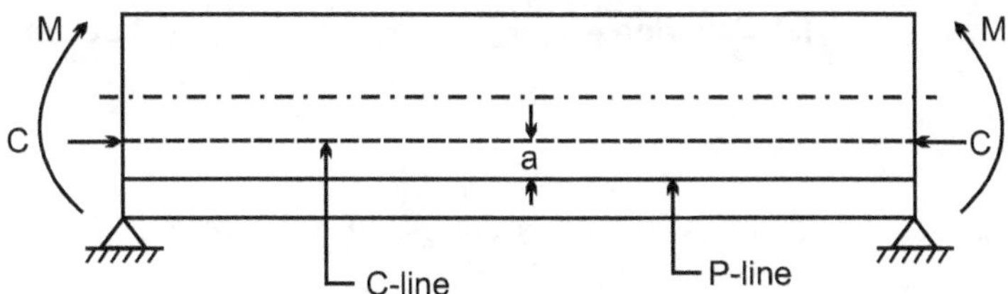

Fig. 3.8

Suppose the beam is subjected to a moment M (Refer Fig. 3.8), then the C-line will be shifted from the P-line by a distance (a) called the lever arm.

$$a = \text{Shift of C-line from P-line}$$

$$= \frac{\text{External moment}}{P}$$

$$= \frac{M}{P}$$

Now, corresponding to the new position of the C-line and its eccentricity, the stress distribution for concrete can be determined as

$$\text{Extreme stress in concrete} = \frac{C}{A} \pm \frac{C \times \text{eccentricity of C}}{z} \qquad \text{... (3.6)}$$

The concept in this analysis is called strength concept.

Solved Examples

Example 3.1 :

A prestress concrete beam of rectangular section 300 mm × 600 mm has a span of 12 m. The effective prestressing force is 980 kN at an eccentricity of 120 mm. The D.L. of the beam is 4.5 kN/m and the beam has to carry a L.L. of 7.5 kN/m. Determine extreme stress

   (a) At the end section,

   (b) At the mid-section without the action of live load,

   (c) At the mid-section with the action of live load.

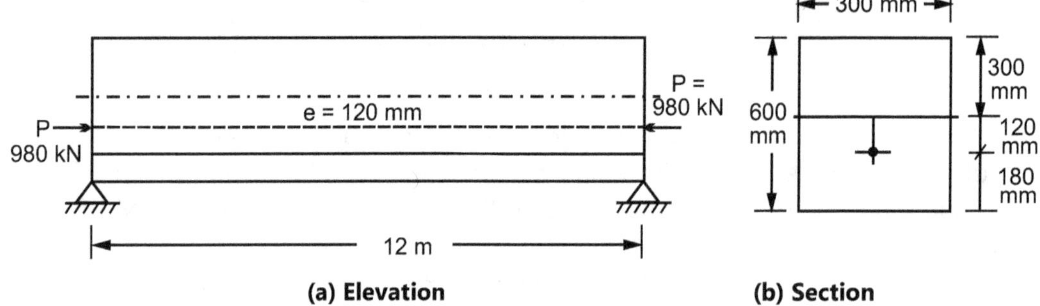

Fig. 3.9

Solution :

$$\text{Area of beam section (A)} = 300 \times 600 = 1.8 \times 10^5 \text{ mm}^2$$

$$\text{Section modulus of section (z)} = \frac{bd^2}{6} = 300 \times \frac{600^2}{6} = 1.8 \times 10^7 \text{ mm}^3$$

$$\text{B.M. due to D.L. (}M_d\text{)} = \frac{4.5 \times 12^2}{8} = 81 \text{ kN-m (at centre) and zero at ends.}$$

$$\text{B.M. due to L.L. (}M_L\text{)} = \frac{7.5 \times 12^2}{8} = 135 \text{ kN-m (at centre) and zero at ends.}$$

$$\text{Direct stress due to prestressing force} = +\frac{P}{A} = +\frac{980 \times 10^3}{1.8 \times 10^5} = +5.44 \text{ N/mm}^2$$

$$\text{Extreme stress due to eccentricity of prestressing force} = \mp\frac{P \cdot e}{z} = \mp\frac{980 \times 10^3 \times 120}{1.8 \times 10^7} = \mp 6.53 \text{ N/mm}^2$$

(A) Analysis of the end section :

$$f_{top} = \frac{P}{A} - \frac{P \cdot e}{z} = 5.44 - 6.53 = -1.09 \text{ N/mm}^2 \text{ (tensile)}$$

$$f_{bottom} = \frac{P}{A} + \frac{P \cdot e}{z} = 5.44 + 6.53 = +11.97 \text{ N/mm}^2 \text{ (compressive)}$$

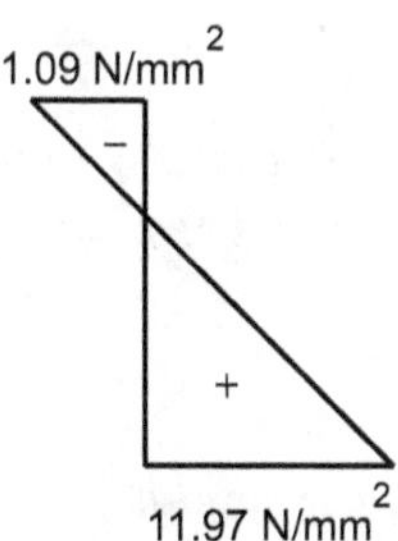

Fig. 3.10

(B) Analysis of mid-section without the action of L.L. :

Extreme stress due to D.L. moment $= \pm \dfrac{M_d}{z} = \pm \dfrac{81 \times 10^6}{1.8 \times 10^7} = \pm 4.50$ N/mm²

$$\therefore \quad f_{top} = +\frac{P}{A} - \frac{P{\cdot}e}{z} + \frac{M_d}{z} = 5.44 - 6.53 + 4.50 = +3.41 \text{ N/mm}^2 \text{ (compressive)}$$

$$f_{bottom} = +\frac{P}{A} + \frac{P{\cdot}e}{z} - \frac{M_d}{z} = 5.44 + 6.53 - 4.50 = +7.47 \text{ N/mm}^2 \text{ (compressive)}$$

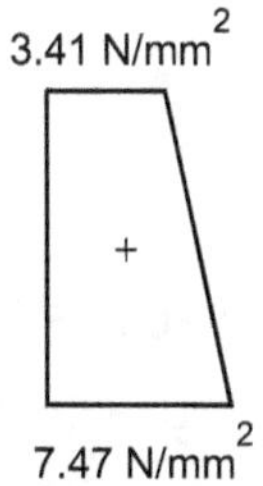

Fig. 3.11

(C) Analysis of mid-section with the action of L.L. :

Extreme stress due to L.L. moment $= \pm \dfrac{M_L}{z} = \pm \dfrac{135 \times 10^6}{1.8 \times 10^7} = \pm 7.50$ N/mm²

$$\therefore \quad f_{top} = +\frac{P}{A} - \frac{P{\cdot}e}{z} + \frac{M_d}{z} + \frac{M_L}{z}$$

$$= +5.44 - 6.53 + 4.50 + 7.50 = 10.91 \text{ N/mm}^2 \text{ (compressive)}$$

$$f_{bottom} = +\frac{P}{A} + \frac{P{\cdot}e}{z} - \frac{M_d}{z} - \frac{M_L}{z}$$

$$= 5.44 + 6.53 - 4.50 - 7.50 = -0.03 \text{ N/mm}^2 \text{ (tensile)}$$

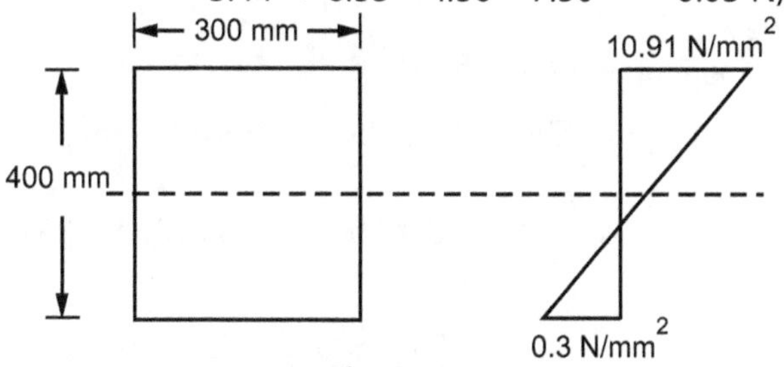

Fig. 3.12

Example 3.2 :

An unsymmetrical I-section beam is prestressed with a force of 400 kN at 300 mm from bottom as shown in Fig. 3.13. If imposed load is 15 kN/m, determine the stresses at the central and the end sections due to

(1)   Prestress and self weight.

(2)   Prestress, self weight and imposed loads.   **[Dec. 14]**

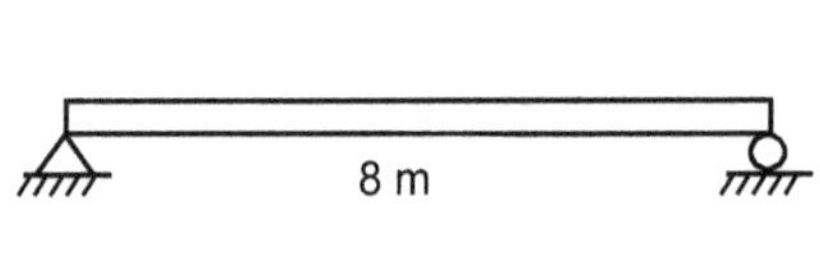

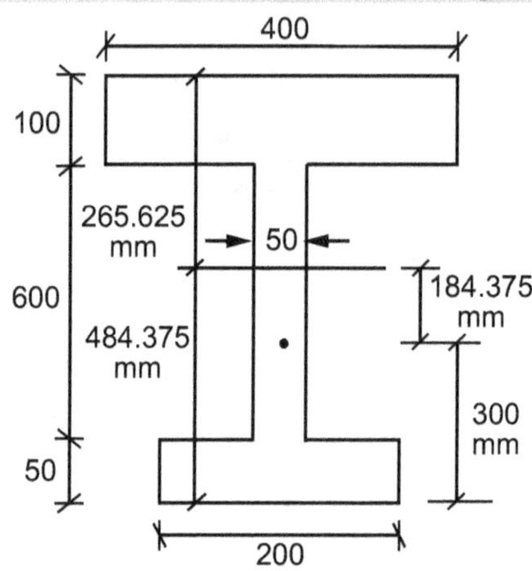

Fig. 3.13

Solution :   Area of section (A) = $(400 \times 100) + (600 \times 50) + (50 \times 200)$

$$= 80{,}000 \text{ mm}^2$$

$$\bar{Y} = \frac{(400 \times 100) \times 700 + (600 \times 50)(350) + (200 \times 50) \times 25}{80{,}000}$$

$$= 484.375 \text{ mm from bottom}$$

$\therefore$ Eccentricity (e) = $(484.375 - 300) = 184.375$ mm

Self weight of beam = $80{,}000 \times 10^{-6} \times 25$

$$= 2 \text{ kN/m}$$

B.M. due to D.L. = $\dfrac{wl^2}{8}$ = $\dfrac{2 \times 8^2}{8}$ = 16 kN-m (at centre) and 0 at ends

Y_{bottom} = 484.375 mm

Y_{top} = $(750 - 484.375)$ = 265.625 mm

$$I = \left(\frac{1}{12} \times 400 \times 100^3\right) + (40{,}000 \times 215.625^2)$$

$$+ \left(\frac{1}{12} \times 50 \times 600^3\right) + (30{,}000 \times 134.375^2)$$

$$+ \left(\frac{1}{12} \times 210 \times 50^3\right) + (10{,}000 \times 459.375^2)$$

$$= 5.295 \times 10^9 \text{ mm}^4$$

$$z_{top} = \frac{I}{Y_{top}} = 20.63 \times 10^6 \text{ mm}^3$$

$$z_{bottom} = \frac{I}{Y_{bottom}} = 10.93 \times 10^6 \text{ mm}^3$$

Case 1 : Prestress + Self weight :

At centre-line :

$$f_{top} = +\frac{P}{A} - \frac{P \cdot e}{z_{top}} + \frac{M_d}{z_{top}}$$

$$= +\frac{400 \times 10^3}{80{,}000} - \frac{400 \times 10^3 \times 184.375}{20.63 \times 10^6} + \frac{16 \times 10^6}{20.63 \times 10^6}$$

$$= +5 - 3.57 + 0.78$$

$$= +2.21 \text{ N/mm}^2 \text{ (compressive)}$$

$$f_{bottom} = +\frac{P}{A} + \frac{P \cdot e}{z_{bottom}} - \frac{M_d}{z_{bottom}}$$

$$= +5 + 6.75 - 1.46$$

$$= 10.29 \text{ N/mm}^2 \text{ (compressive)}$$

At ends : $\quad f_{top} = +\dfrac{P}{A} - \dfrac{P \cdot e}{z_{top}} = +5 - 3.57 = +1.43 \text{ N/mm}^2 \text{ (compressive)}$

$$f_{bottom} = +\frac{P}{A} + \frac{P \cdot e}{z_{bottom}}$$

$$= +5 + 6.75 = 11.75 \text{ N/mm}^2 \text{ (compressive)}$$

Case 2 : Prestress + Self weight + Imposed loads :

At centre-line : $\quad f_{top} = +\dfrac{P}{A} - \dfrac{P \cdot e}{z_{top}} + \dfrac{M_d}{z_{top}} + \dfrac{M_L}{z_{top}}$

$$= +5 - 3.57 + 0.78 + \frac{120 \times 10^6}{20.63 \times 10^6} \quad \left(\text{Since } M_L = \frac{15 \times 8^2}{8}\right.$$

$$= +8.03 \text{ N/mm}^2 \text{ (compressive)} \qquad\qquad = 120 \text{ kNm})$$

$$f_{bottom} = +\frac{P}{A} + \frac{P \cdot e}{z_{bottom}} - \frac{M_d}{z_{bottom}} - \frac{M_L}{z_{bottom}}$$

$$= +5 + 6.75 - 1.46 - 10.98$$

$$= -0.69 \text{ N/mm}^2 \text{ (tensile)}$$

At ends : $\quad f_{top} = +\dfrac{P}{A} - \dfrac{P \cdot e}{z_{top}}$

$$= 5 - 3.57 = +1.43 \text{ N/mm}^2 \text{ (compressive)}$$

$$f_{bottom} = +\frac{P}{A} + \frac{P \cdot e}{z_{bottom}}$$

$$= 5 + 6.75 = +11.75 \text{ N/mm}^2 \text{ (compressive)} \qquad \textbf{... Ans.}$$

Example 3.3 :

(a) An I-shaped prestressed concrete beam spanning 25 m has an effective prestress (just after transfer) of 2500 kN at an eccentricity of 175 mm at the mid-span X-section. Calculate the stresses at mid-span and at the ends in the extreme fibres.

Given that : $A = 0.4 \text{ m}^2$, $I = 0.12 \text{ m}^4$, $z_{top} = 0.2 \text{ m}^3$, $z_{bottom} = 0.16 \text{ m}^3$.

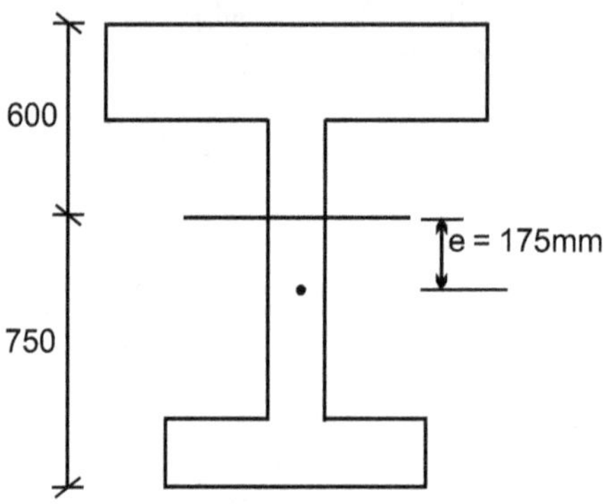

Fig. 3.14

(b) What uniform imposed load can be applied to the above beam, if the maximum permissible stresses anywhere in the beam are 2 N/mm^2, tensile and 14 N/mm^2, compressive.

Solution :

(A) Self-weight of beam $= 0.4 \times 25$

$$= 10 \text{ kN/m}$$

B.M. due to D.L. (M_d) $= \dfrac{10 \times 25^2}{8} = 781.25$ kN-m (at centre) and 0 at ends

B.M. due to prestress (M_p) $= P \times e$

$$= 2500 \times 0.175$$

$$= 437.5 \text{ kN-m}$$

At mid-span : $f_{top} = +\dfrac{P}{A} - \dfrac{P \cdot e}{z_{top}} + \dfrac{M_d}{z_{top}}$

$$= \frac{2500 \times 10^3}{0.4 \times 10^6} - \frac{437.5 \times 10^6}{0.2 \times 10^9} + \frac{781.25 \times 10^6}{0.2 \times 10^9}$$

$$= +6.25 - 2.19 + 3.91$$

$$= +7.97 \text{ N/mm}^2 \text{ (compressive)}$$

$$f_{bottom} = +\frac{P}{A} + \frac{P \cdot e}{z_{bottom}} - \frac{M_d}{z_{bottom}}$$

$$= +\ 6.25 + 2.73 - 4.88$$

$$= +\ 4.10 \ \text{N/mm}^2 \ (\text{compressive})$$

At ends :　　　$f_{top} = +\dfrac{P}{A} - \dfrac{P \cdot e}{z_{top}} = +\ 6.25 - 2.19 = +\ 4.06 \ \text{N/mm}^2 \ (\text{compressive})$

$$f_{bottom} = +\frac{P}{A} + \frac{P \cdot e}{z_{bottom}} = +\ 6.25 + 2.73$$

$$= +\ 8.98 \ \text{N/mm}^2 \ (\text{compressive})$$

(B)　Let M be the applied moment due to applied uniform load at centre.

The moment at the ends is zero.

Therefore, only central section should be examined.

Stresses due to external moment,

$$f_{top} = +\frac{M_L}{z_{top}} = +\frac{M \times 10^6}{0.2 \times 10^9} = +\ 0.005 \ M$$

$$f_{bottom} = -\frac{M_L}{z_{bottom}} = -\frac{M \times 10^6}{0.16 \times 10^9} = -\ 0.00625 \ M$$

∴　Total stresses

$$f_{top} = +\frac{P}{A} - \frac{P \cdot e}{z_{top}} + \frac{M_d}{z_{top}} + \frac{M_L}{z_{top}}$$

$$= 7.97 + 0.005 \ M \ (\text{compressive})$$

$$f_{bottom} = +\frac{P}{A} + \frac{P \cdot e}{z_{bottom}} - \frac{M_d}{z_{bottom}} - \frac{M_L}{z_{bottom}}$$

$$= 4.1 - 0.00625 \ M \ (\text{tensile})$$

f_{bottom} is assumed tensile so as to determine the maximum applied moment.

Now, $7.97 + 0.005 \ M \ngtr 14$

∴　　　　　　　　$M \ngtr 1206 \ \text{kN-m}$　　　　　　　　　　　　　... (1)

and　$4.1 - 0.00625 \ M \ngtr -2$

　　　　　　$-\ 0.00625 \ M \ngtr -\ 2 - 4.10$

　　　　　　　　$M \ngtr 976 \ \text{kN-m}$　　　　　　　　　　　　　... (2)

From (1) and (2),　$M \ngtr 976 \ \text{kN-m}$

∴　　　$\dfrac{w \times l^2}{8} = 976 \Rightarrow w \times 25^2 = 976 \times 8$

∴　　　　$\boxed{w = 12.49 \ \text{kN/m}}$　　　　　　　　　　　　　**... Ans.**

Example 3.4 :

Fig. 3.15 shows a prestressed concrete beam provided with bent tendon. The beam carries a point load of 160 kN at the centre. Determine the stress distribution for the end section and the mid-section of the beam. The D.L. of the beam is 6 kN/m.

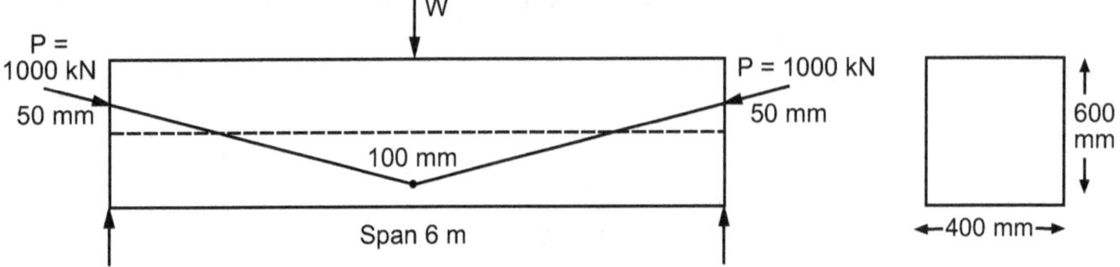

Fig. 3.15

Solution :

$$\text{Area of beam section (A)} = 600 \times 400 = 2.4 \times 10^5 \text{ mm}^2$$

$$\text{Section modulus (z)} = \frac{400 \times 600^2}{6} = 2.4 \times 10^7 \text{ mm}^2$$

Let θ be the inclination of the tendon with the horizontal.

$$\therefore \qquad \sin\theta = \tan\theta = \frac{150}{3000} = \frac{1}{20}$$

Analysis of end section :

$$f_{top} = +\frac{P\cos\theta}{A} + \frac{P\cos\theta \times e}{z} \qquad \left[\because \text{ at end, eccentricity is located at top of centre-line}\right]$$

$$= +\frac{P}{A} + \frac{P \cdot e}{z}$$

$$= +\frac{1000 \times 10^3}{2.4 \times 10^5} + \frac{1000 \times 10^3 \times 50}{2.4 \times 10^7}$$

$$= 4.17 + 2.08 = +6.25 \text{ N/mm}^2 \text{ (compressive)}$$

$$f_{bottom} = +\frac{P}{A} - \frac{P \cdot e}{z} = 4.17 - 2.08 = +2.09 \text{ N/mm}^2 \text{ (compressive)}$$

Analysis of mid-section :

External downward load at centre $= 160$ kN ($\downarrow$).

Upward point load provided by tendon $= 2P\sin\theta = 2 \times 1000 \times \dfrac{1}{20} = 100$ kN ($\uparrow$)

$\therefore$ Net downward point load $= (160 - 100) = 60$ kN ($\downarrow$).

B.M. due to net downward point load $(M_L) = \dfrac{wl}{4} = \dfrac{60 \times 6}{4} = 90$ kN-m.

$$\text{B.M. due to D.L.} = \frac{wl^2}{8} = \frac{6 \times 6^2}{8} = 27 \text{ kN-m.}$$

B.M. due to eccentricity of prestressing force at the end

$$= P \times e$$

$$= \frac{1000 \times 50}{1000} = 50 \text{ kN-m}$$

$$\therefore \quad f_{top} = +\frac{P}{A} + \frac{P \cdot e}{z} + \frac{M_d}{z} + \frac{M_L}{z}$$

$$= 4.17 + 2.08 + \frac{27 \times 10^6}{2.4 \times 10^7} + \frac{90 \times 10^6}{2.4 \times 10^7}$$

$$= 11.13 \text{ N/mm}^2 \text{ (compressive)}$$

$$f_{bottom} = +\frac{P}{A} - \frac{P \cdot e}{z} - \frac{M_d}{z} - \frac{M_L}{z}$$

$$= 4.17 - 2.08 - \frac{27 \times 10^6}{2.4 \times 10^7} - \frac{90 \times 10^6}{2.4 \times 10^7}$$

$$= 4.17 - 2.08 - 1.125 - 3.75$$

$$= -2.785 \text{ N/mm}^2 \text{ (tensile)} \quad \text{... Ans.}$$

Example 3.5 :

Fig. 3.16 shows a prestressed concrete beam provided with a tendon having a parabolic profile. If the total external load on the beam is 35 kN/m on the whole span, calculate the extreme stresses for the mid-span section. The tendon carries a prestressing force of 1000 kN.

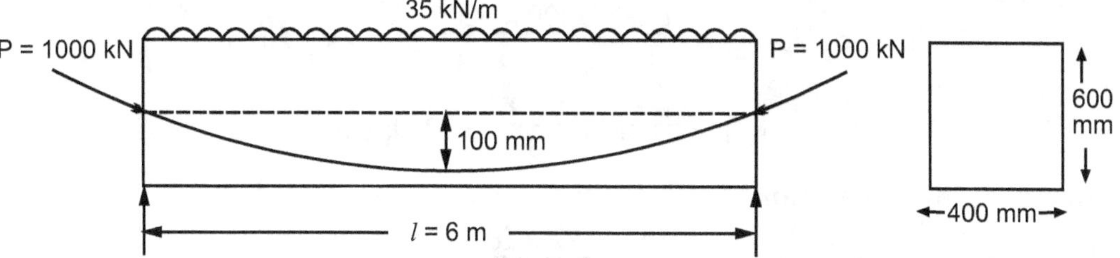

Fig. 3.16

Solution :

$$\text{Area of beam section (A)} = 400 \times 600 = 2.4 \times 10^5 \text{ mm}^2$$

$$\text{Section modulus (z)} = \frac{bd^2}{6} = 2.4 \times 10^7 \text{ mm}^3$$

$$\text{Span of beam } (l) = 6 \text{ m}$$

$$\text{Dip of tendon (h)} = 0.10 \text{ m}$$

Upward u.d. pressure provided by the cable

$$w_c = \frac{8\,Ph}{l^2} = \frac{8 \times 1000 \times 0.10}{6 \times 6}$$

$$= 22.22 \text{ kN/m}$$

$$\therefore \quad \text{Net downward load on beam} = (35 - 22.22)$$

$$= 12.78 \text{ kN/m}$$

$$\text{B.M. due to L.L. } (M_L) = \frac{w_c l^2}{8} = \frac{12.78 \times 6^2}{8} = 57.51 \text{ kN-m}$$

Extreme stress at mid-section :

$$f_{top} = +\frac{P}{A} + \frac{M_L}{z} = +\frac{1000 \times 10^3}{2.4 \times 10^5} + \frac{57.51 \times 10^6}{2.4 \times 10^5}$$

$$= 4.17 + 2.40 = +6.57 \text{ N/mm}^2 \text{ (compressive)}$$

$$f_{bottom} = +\frac{P}{A} - \frac{M_L}{z} = +4.17 - 2.40 = +1.77 \text{ N/mm}^2 \text{ (compressive)} \qquad \textbf{... Ans.}$$

Example 3.6 :

A prestressed concrete beam 400 mm × 600 mm in section has a span of 6 m and is subjected to a u.d.l. of 16 kN/m including the self-weight of beam. The prestressing tendons which are located along the longitudinal axis provide an effective prestressing force of 960 kN. Determine the extreme stresses in concrete for mid-span section using strength concept method.

Solution :

$$\text{Area of section } (A) = 400 \times 600 = 2.4 \times 10^5 \text{ mm}^2$$

$$\text{Section modulus } (z) = \frac{bd^2}{6} = \frac{400 \times 600^2}{6} = 2.4 \times 10^7 \text{ mm}^3$$

$$\text{B.M. due to L.L. } (M_L) = \frac{wl^2}{8} = \frac{16 \times 6^2}{8} = 72 \text{ kN-m}$$

Extreme stress at mid-section :

$$\text{Shift of C-line from P-line} = \frac{M}{P} = \frac{72 \times 10^6}{960 \times 10^3} = 75 \text{ mm.}$$

$$\text{Eccentricity of C-line} = 75 \text{ mm } (= e) \text{ (above centroidal axis)}$$

$$f_{top} = +\frac{C}{A} + \frac{C \cdot e}{z}$$

$$= +\frac{960 \times 10^3}{2.4 \times 10^5} + \frac{960 \times 10^3 \times 75}{2.4 \times 10^7}$$

$$= 4 + 3 = 7 \text{ N/mm}^2 \text{ (compressive)}$$

$$f_{bottom} = +\frac{C}{A} - \frac{C \cdot e}{z}$$

$$= +4 - 3$$

$$= +1 \text{ N/mm}^2 \text{ (compressive)}$$

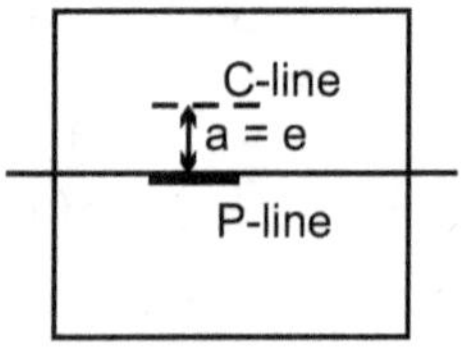

C-line

a = e

P-line

Fig. 3.17

Example 3.7 :

In the above problem, if prestressing tendons are located at the lower third point and provide an effective prestressing force of 960 kN, determine stress at mid-span.

Solution :

From above, a = 75 mm.

Eccentricity of C-line = e = (100 – 75) = 25 mm below centroidal axis.

$$f_{top} \;=\; +\frac{C}{A} - \frac{C \cdot e}{z} \;=\; +\frac{960 \times 10^3}{2.4 \times 10^5} - \frac{960 \times 10^3 \times 25}{2.4 \times 10^7}$$

$$=\; +4 - 1 \;=\; +3 \text{ N/mm}^2 \text{ (compressive)}$$

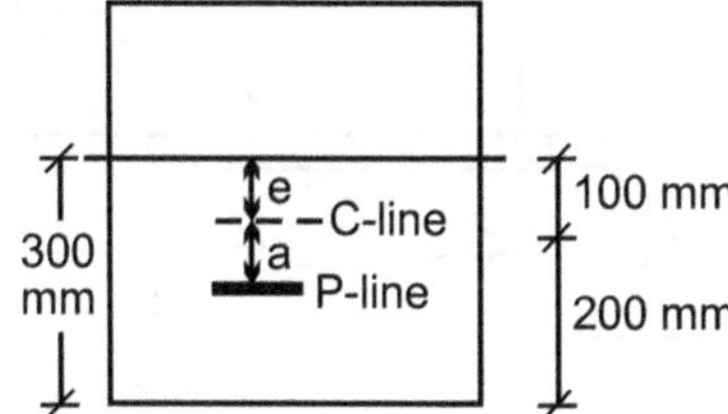

Fig. 3.18

$$f_{bottom} \;=\; +\frac{C}{A} + \frac{C \cdot e}{z} \;=\; +\frac{960 \times 10^3}{2.4 \times 10^5} + \frac{960 \times 10^3 \times 25}{2.4 \times 10^7}$$

$$=\; +4 + 1 \;=\; +5 \text{ N/mm}^2 \text{ (compressive)} \qquad \textbf{...Ans.}$$

Example 3.8 :

A prestressed concrete beam of rectangular section is 125 mm wide and 300 mm deep. The beam is prestressed with a cable provided along the longitudinal centroidal axis. The effective prestressing force is 180 kN. The beam carries a u.d.l. of 2.25 kN/m including the weight of the beam. The beam has a span of 8 m.

Locate the pressure line for the beam.

Solution :

From example, it is clear that

P-line is the longitudinal centroidal axis.

$$\therefore \quad \text{Reaction at each support} \;=\; \frac{2.25 \times 8}{2} \;=\; 9 \text{ kN.}$$

B.M. at any section distance 'x' m from the support,

$$M \;=\; 9x - 2.25 \times x \times \frac{x}{2}$$

$$=\; 9x - 1.125 \, x^2$$

Shift of C-line from P-line at any section distance x m from the support $= \dfrac{M}{P}$.

$$= (9x - 1.125\ x^2) \times \frac{1}{180}$$

Distance from support (x) m	Shift of C-line from P-line $(9x - 1.125\ x^2) \times \dfrac{1}{180}$
0	0
1	0.043475 m = 43.75 mm
2	75 mm
3	93.75 mm
4	100 mm

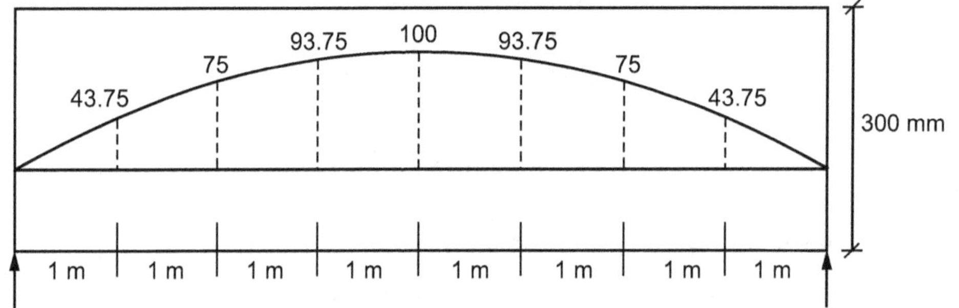

Fig. 3.19

Example 3.9 :

A prestressed concrete beam is prestressed with a tendon bent as shown in Fig. 3.20. The external load on the beam consists of a concentrated load of 180 kN at mid span. If the prestressing force is 1200 kN, calculate the extreme stress in concrete for the mid-span section.

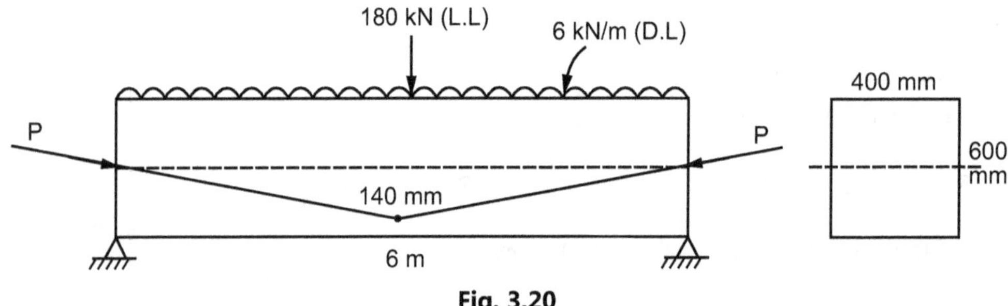

Fig. 3.20

Solution :

$$\text{Area of section (A)} = 400 \times 600 = 2.4 \times 10^5\ \text{mm}^2$$

$$\text{Section modulus (z)} = \frac{bd^2}{6} = 2.4 \times 10^7\ \text{mm}^2$$

$$P = 1200 \text{ kN}$$

$$\text{D.L. of beam} = 0.4 \times 0.6 \times 25 = 6 \text{ kN/m}$$

Stress concept method :

$$\text{B.M. due to L.L. } (M_L) = \frac{wl}{4} = \frac{180 \times 6}{4} = 270 \text{ kN-m}$$

$$\text{B.M. due to D.L.} = \frac{wl^2}{8} = \frac{6 \times 6^2}{8} = 27 \text{ kN-m}$$

$$f_{top} = +\frac{P}{A} - \frac{P \cdot e}{z} + \frac{M_d}{z} + \frac{M_L}{z}$$

$$= \frac{1200 \times 10^3}{2.4 \times 10^5} - \frac{1200 \times 10^3 \times 140}{2.4 \times 10^7} + \frac{270 \times 10^6}{2.4 \times 10^7} + \frac{27 \times 10^6}{2.4 \times 10^7}$$

$$= 5 - 7 + 11.25 + 1.125 = +10.4 \text{ N/mm}^2 \text{ (compressive)}$$

$$f_{bottom} = +\frac{P}{A} + \frac{Pe}{z} - \frac{M_d}{z} - \frac{M_L}{z}$$

$$= +5 + 7 - 1.125 - 11.25 = -0.4 \text{ N/mm}^2 \text{ (tensile)} \qquad \textbf{... Ans.}$$

Strength concrete method :

$$\text{Shift of C-line from P-line} = \frac{M}{P} = \frac{(270 + 27) \times 10^6}{1200 \times 10^3} = 247.5 \text{ mm } (= a)$$

$\therefore \qquad$ Eccentricity of C-line $= (247.5 - 140) = 107.5$ mm (above centroidal axis)

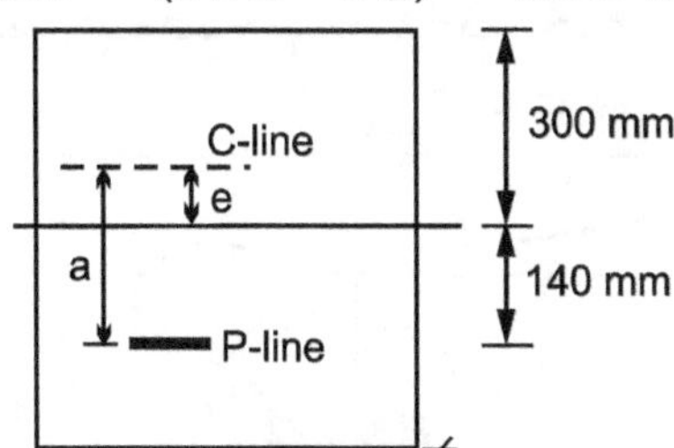

Fig. 3.21

$$f_{top} = +\frac{C}{A} + \frac{C \cdot e}{z} = +\frac{1200 \times 10^3}{2.4 \times 10^5} + \frac{1200 \times 10^3 \times 107.5}{2.4 \times 10^7}$$

$$= +5 + 5.4 = +10.4 \text{ N/mm}^2 \text{ (compressive)}$$

$$f_{bottom} = +\frac{C}{A} - \frac{C \cdot e}{z} = +5.0 - 5.4 = -0.4 \text{ N/mm}^2 \text{ (tensile)}$$

Load balancing concept :

$$\sin \theta = \tan \theta = \frac{140}{3000} = \frac{7}{150}$$

Upward point load transmitted by the tendon at the centre

$$= 2P\ \sin \theta = 2 \times 1200 \times \frac{7}{150} = 112 \text{ kN}$$

Net downward point load at the centre $= (180 - 112) = 68 \text{ kN}$

B.M. at centre due to L.L. (M_L) $= \dfrac{68 \times l}{4} = 102 \text{ kN}$

B.M. at centre due to D.L. (M_d) $= \dfrac{6 \times 6^2}{8} = 27 \text{ kN}$

$$f_{top} = +\frac{P}{A} + \frac{M_d}{z} + \frac{M_L}{z}$$

$$= +5 + 1.125 + \frac{102 \times 10^3 \times 10^3}{2.4 \times 10^7}$$

$$= +5 + 1.125 + 4.25 = +10.4 \text{ N/mm}^2 \text{ (compressive)}$$

$$f_{bottom} = +\frac{P}{A} - \frac{M_d}{z} - \frac{M_L}{z} = +5 - 1.125 - 4.25 = -0.4 \text{ N/mm}^2$$

(tensile) ... **Ans.**

Example 3.10 :
Determine the profile of a load balancing cable for a beam of span 6 m carrying on all inclusive load of 40 kN/m. The prestressing force in the tendon is 1200 kN. The beam section is 400 mm × 600 mm.

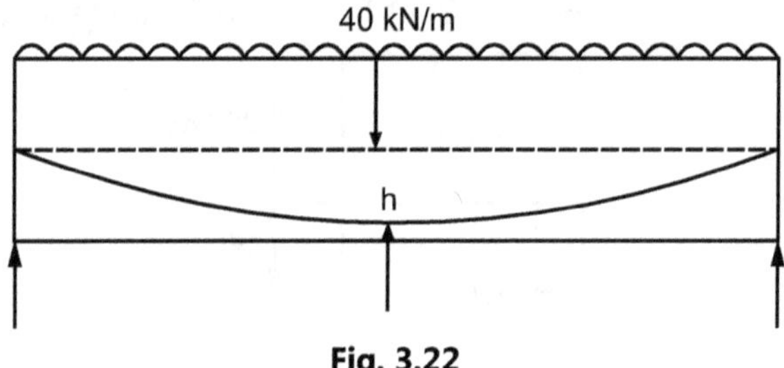

Fig. 3.22

Solution :

Let the dip of the cable be h meters.

Upward pressure provided by the parabolic cable

$$= \frac{8\ Ph}{l^2}$$

$$= \frac{8 \times 1200 \times h}{6^2} = \frac{800\ h}{3} \text{ kN/m}$$

This upward pressure may fully balance the external loading,

$$\frac{800\ h}{3} = 40$$

$$\therefore \qquad h = \frac{40 \times 3}{800} = 0.15 \text{ m} \qquad \qquad \textbf{... Ans.}$$

Example 3.11 :

Find the cable dip 'h' for the beam shown in Fig. 3.23 so that the applied external loads may be balanced. The tension in the cable is P.

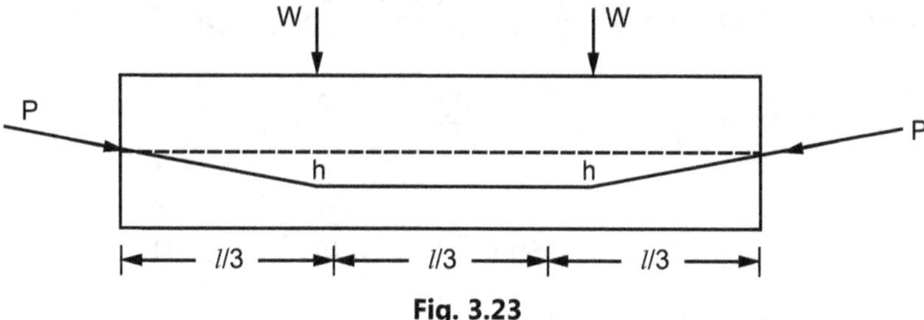

Fig. 3.23

Solution :

Let θ be the inclination of the end parts of the cable with the horizontal.

$$\therefore \qquad \tan \theta = \frac{h}{l/3} = \frac{3h}{l} = \sin \theta \text{ (approximately)}$$

Upward force provided at each one-third span point by the cable $= P \sin \theta$.

In order to balance the external load,

$$P \sin \theta = W$$

$$P \times \frac{3h}{l} = W$$

$$\therefore \qquad h = \frac{Wl}{3P} \qquad \qquad \textbf{... Ans.}$$

Example 3.12 :

A pretensioned beam of rectangular section, 80 mm wide by 120 mm deep is to be designed to support concentrated loads of 4 kN each at one-third of span points over an effective span of 3 m. The permissible stresses in concrete are limited to zero and 1.4 N/mm² in tension at transfer and working load respectively. If 3 mm ϕ wires initially stressed to 1400 N/mm² are used, find the number of wires required and the eccentricity of the prestressing force.

Assuming 20% loss in prestress.

Weight of concrete $= 25$ kN/m³.

Solution :

$$\text{Area of section (A)} = 80 \times 120 = 9600 \text{ mm}^2$$

$$\text{Section modulus (z)} = \frac{bd^2}{6} = 1.92 \times 10^5 \text{ mm}^3$$

$$\text{Dead load of beam} = (0.08) \times (0.12) \times 25 = 0.24 \text{ kN/m}$$

Analysis at transfer :

Let P_i be the prestressing force at transfer.

Let 'e' mm be the eccentricity.

$$\text{B.M. due to D.L } (M_d) = \frac{wl^2}{8} = \frac{0.24 \times 3^2}{8} = 0.27 \text{ kN-m}$$

$$f_{top} = +\frac{P_i}{A} + \frac{M_d}{z} - \frac{P_i \times e}{z}$$

$$f_{top} = +\frac{P_i}{9600} + \frac{0.27 \times 10^6}{1.92 \times 10^5} - \frac{P_i \times e}{1.92 \times 10^5}$$

For the condition of zero stress at top edge, i.e. $f_{top} = 0$.

$$\therefore \quad \frac{P_i}{9600} + 1.41 - \frac{P_i \times e}{1.92 \times 10^5} = 0$$

$$\therefore \quad \frac{P_i}{9600} - \frac{P_i \times e}{1.92 \times 10^5} = -1.41 \qquad \text{... (i)}$$

Analysis at working load :

Final prestressing force $(P_f) = 0.80 \, P_i$

$$\text{Live load B.M.} = \frac{Wl}{3} = \frac{4 \times 3}{3} = 4 \times 1 = 4 \text{ kN-m}$$

From the condition, final stress at bottom edge i.e. $f_{bottom} = -1.40 \text{ N/mm}^2$.

$$f_{bottom} = +\frac{P_f}{A} - \frac{M_d}{z} - \frac{M_L}{z} + \frac{P_f \times e}{z}$$

$$-1.40 = \frac{0.80 \, P_i}{9600} - \frac{0.27 \times 10^6}{1.92 \times 10^5} - \frac{4 \times 10^6}{1.92 \times 10^5} + \frac{0.8 \, P_i \times e}{1.92 \times 10^5}$$

$$\frac{0.8 \, P_i}{9600} + \frac{0.8 \, P_i \times e}{1.92 \times 10^5} = 20.84$$

$$\therefore \quad \frac{P_i}{9600} + \frac{P_i \times e}{1.92 \times 10^5} = 26.05 \qquad \text{... (ii)}$$

Adding equations (i) and (ii), we get

$$\frac{2 \times P_i}{9600} = 24.64$$

$$\therefore \qquad P_i = 118272 \text{ N} \qquad \qquad \text{... Ans.}$$

Substituting in equation (i), we get

$$\frac{1182.72}{9600} - \frac{118272 \times e}{1.92 \times 10^5} = -1.41$$

$$\therefore \qquad\qquad e = 22.3 \text{ mm} \qquad\qquad \text{... Ans.}$$

Number of wires :

$$\text{Area of tendons} = \frac{P_i}{1400} = \frac{118272}{1400} = 84.50 \text{ mm}^2$$

Now, area of 3 mm diameter $\left(A_\phi = \dfrac{\pi}{4} \times 3^2 = 7.07 \text{ mm}^2\right)$.

$$\therefore \qquad \text{Number of wires} = \frac{84.50}{7.07} = 12$$

$$\therefore \qquad\qquad N = 12 \text{ wires} \qquad\qquad \text{... Ans.}$$

Example 3.13 :

A pretensioned concrete beam is 300 mm wide and 600 mm deep. The tendons are provided at a height of 200 mm above the soffit. The initially applied prestressing force is 1500 kN which eventually reduces to 1350 kN after losses. The live load on the beam consists of two point loads of 35 kN each placed at a distance of 4.5 m and 10.5 m from one end. Determine the extreme stresses in concrete for the mid-span section

(i)   Under the initial full prestress and no live load,

(ii) Under the final condition after all losses and full live load.

Solution :

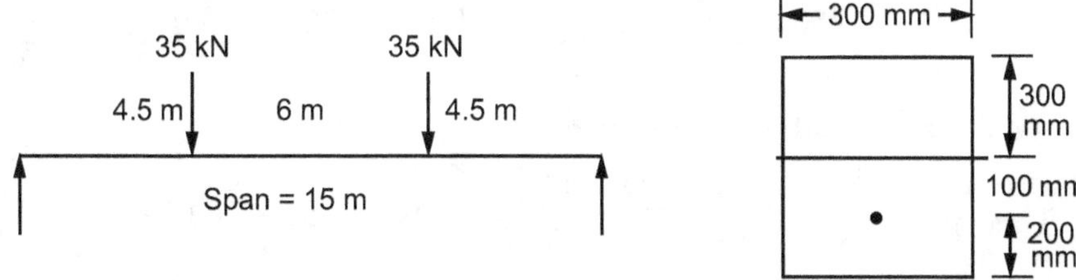

Fig. 3.24

$$\text{Area of beam section (A)} = 300 \times 600 = 1.80 \times 10^5 \text{ mm}^2$$

$$\text{Section modulus (z)} = \frac{bd^2}{6} = \frac{300 \times 600^2}{6} = 1.8 \times 10^7 \text{ mm}^3$$

$$\text{D.L. of beam} = (0.3 \times 6 \times 25) = 4.50 \text{ kN/m}$$

$$\text{B.M. due to D.L. (M}_d) = \frac{4.50 \times 15^2}{8} = 126.5625 \text{ kN-m}$$

$$\text{B.M. due to L.L. (M}_L) = 35 \times 4.5 = 157.50 \text{ kN-m}$$

Case-I : Beam subjected to initial prestressing force and dead load :

$$f_{top} = +\frac{P_i}{A} - \frac{P_i \times e}{z} + \frac{M_d}{z}$$

$$= +\frac{1500 \times 10^3}{1.8 \times 10^5} - \frac{1500 \times 10^3 \times 100}{1.8 \times 10^7} + \frac{126.5625 \times 10^6}{1.8 \times 10^7}$$

$$= + 8.33 - 8.33 + 7.03$$

$$f_{top} = + 7.03 \text{ N/mm}^2$$

$$f_{bottom} = +\frac{P_i}{A} + \frac{P_i \times e}{z} - \frac{M_d}{z} = + 8.33 + 8.33 - 7.03$$

$$= + 9.63 \text{ N/mm}^2 \qquad \text{... Ans.}$$

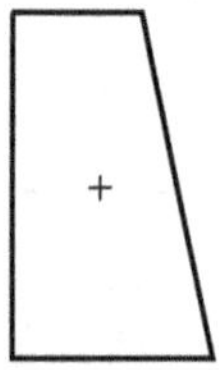

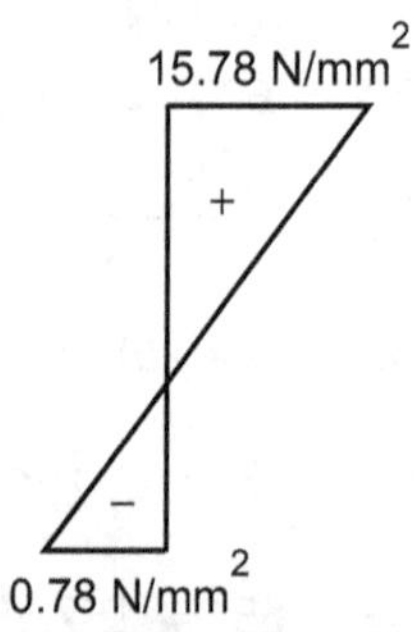

Fig. 3.25

Case-II : Beam subjected to final prestressing force, dead load and live load :

$$f_{top} = +\frac{P_f}{A} - \frac{P_f \cdot e}{z} + \frac{M_d}{z} + \frac{M_L}{z}$$

$$= +\frac{1350 \times 10^3}{1.8 \times 10^5} - \frac{1350 \times 10^3 \times 100}{1.8 \times 10^7} + \frac{126.5625 \times 10^6}{1.8 \times 10^7} + \frac{157.50 \times 10^6}{1.8 \times 10^7}$$

$$= + 7.50 - 7.50 + 7.03 + 8.75 = + 15.78 \text{ N/mm}^2$$

$$f_{bottom} = +\frac{P_f}{A} + \frac{P_f \cdot e}{z} - \frac{M_d}{z} - \frac{M_L}{z} = + 7.50 + 7.50 - 7.03 - 8.75$$

$$= - 0.78 \text{ N/mm}^2 \qquad \text{... Ans.}$$

Fig. 3.26

Example 3.14 :

A prestressed concrete rectangular beam 250 mm wide and 600 mm deep is simply supported on a span of 8 m. At the mid section of the beam, the cable is provided at a height of 200 mm above the soffit. The initial prestressing force is 1000 kN which after losses decrease to 830 kN. Determine the u.d.l. the beam will carry at the final stage for the following cases :

   (i)   The stress at the bottom edge reaches zero.

   (ii) The stress reaches at the bottom edges, a cracking tensile stress of 4 N/mm².

Solution :

$$\text{Area of beam section (A)} = 250 \times 600 = 1.50 \times 10^5 \text{ mm}^2$$

$$\text{Section modulus (z)} = \frac{bd^2}{6} = 1.5 \times 10^7 \text{ mm}^3$$

Case-I : Stress at the bottom edge reaches zero :

$$f_{bottom} = +\frac{P_f}{A} + \frac{P_f \times e}{z} - \frac{M}{z}$$

i.e.
$$+\frac{830 \times 10^3}{1.5 \times 10^5} + \frac{830 \times 10^3 \times 100}{1.5 \times 10^7} - \frac{M}{1.5 \times 10^7} = 0$$

$$\therefore \quad \frac{M}{1.5 \times 10^7} = +11.06$$

$$\therefore \quad M = +11.06 \times 1.5 \times 10^7 = 165.9 \text{ kN-m}$$

Let the u.d.l. on the beam be w kN/m.

$$M = \frac{wl^2}{8} = \frac{w \times 8^2}{8} = 165.9$$

$$\therefore \quad w = 20.74 \text{ kN/m}$$

$$\text{Dead load of beam} = (250 \times 600) \times 10^{-6} \times 25000$$

$$= 3750 \text{ N/m}$$

$$= 3.750 \text{ kN/m}$$

$$\text{Additional safe superimposed load} = (20.74 - 3.750)$$

$$= 16.99 \text{ kN/m} \quad \quad \text{... Ans.}$$

Case -II : When the stress at the bottom edge reaches the cracking tensile stress of 4 N/mm² :

$$f_{bottom} = +\frac{P_f}{A} + \frac{P_f \cdot e}{z} - \frac{M}{z}$$

i.e.
$$-4 = \frac{830 \times 10^3}{1.5 \times 10^5} + \frac{830 \times 10^3 \times 100}{1.5 \times 10^7} - \frac{M}{1.5 \times 10^7}$$

or,
$$-4 = 11.06 - \frac{M}{1.5 \times 10^7}$$

$\therefore \qquad M = (15.06) \times 1.5 \times 10^7 = 225.9 \text{ kN-m}$

Let the u.d.l. for this condition be w kN/m.

$$\frac{wl^2}{8} = 225.9$$

$$w = \frac{225.9 \times 8}{8^2}$$

$$w = 28.24 \text{ kN/m} \qquad\qquad \text{... } \textbf{Ans.}$$

Example 3.15 :

Fig. 3.27 shows the section of a precast slab unit. Each slab unit is supported on a span of 8 m. The section is pretensioned by 6 wires of 5 mm ϕ, with three wires for each rib. The wires are provided at a distance of 50 mm from bottom of ribs. The wires are subjected to an initial stress of 1250 N/mm², the total loss of prestress is 15% of initial stress. Determine the safe u.d.l. on the slab unit.

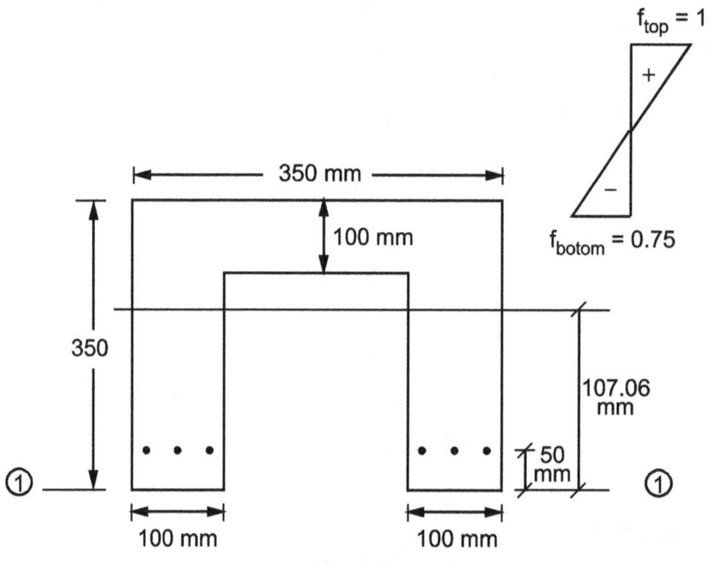

Fig. 3.27

Solution :

Total area of section (A) $= (350 \times 350) - (150 \times 250)$

$\qquad\qquad\qquad\qquad\quad = 85000 \text{ mm}^2$

Distance of centroidal axis from bottom edge (1) - (1)

$$= \frac{(350 \times 350) \times 175 - (150 \times 250) \times 125}{85000}$$

$$= 197.06 \text{ mm}$$

M.I. about the bottom edge (1) - (1)

$$I_{1-1} = \frac{350 \times 350^3}{3} - \frac{150 \times 250^3}{3}$$

$$= 4.22083 \times 10^9 \text{ mm}^4$$

M.I. about the centroidal axis,

$$I = I_{1-1} - A\,\bar{y}^2$$

$$= 4.22083 \times 10^9 - (85000 \times 197.06^2)$$

$$= 9.21001 \times 10^8 \text{ mm}^4$$

Now,

$$z_{top} = \frac{9.21001 \times 10^8}{152.94} = 6015496.3 \text{ mm}^3$$

$$z_{bottom} = \frac{9.21001 \times 10^8}{197.06} = 4668679.6 \text{ mm}^3$$

$$\text{Initial prestress} = 1250 \text{ N/mm}^2$$

$$\text{Final prestress} = 0.85 \times 1250 = 1062.5 \text{ N/mm}^2$$

$$\text{Area of steel wires} = 6 \times \left(\frac{\pi}{4} \times 5^2\right) = 117.81 \text{ mm}^2$$

$$\text{Final prestressing force } (P_f) = 1062.5 \times 117.81 = 125173.12 \text{ N}$$

and

$$\text{eccentricity } (e) = (197.06 - 50) = 147.06 \text{ mm}$$

Now,

$$f_{top} = +\frac{P_f}{A} - \frac{P_f \times e}{z_t} + \frac{M}{z_t}$$

or,

$$\frac{125173.12}{85000} - \frac{125173.12 \times 147.06}{6015496.3} + \frac{M}{6015496.3} = 14 \text{ (given)}$$

or,

$$M = 93781587 \text{ N-mm}$$

$$f_{bottom} = +\frac{P_f}{A} + \frac{P_f \cdot e}{z_b} - \frac{M}{z_b}$$

or,

$$\frac{125173.13}{85000} + \frac{125173.13 \times 147.06}{4668679.6} - \frac{M}{4668679.6} = -0.75$$

$$1.47 + 3.94 - \frac{M}{4668679.6} = -0.75$$

$$\therefore \quad M = 28759066 \text{ N-mm}$$

From above condition,

$$\text{min B.M.} = 28759066 \text{ N-mm}$$

If $\qquad$ w = Safe uniformly distributed load (N/m)

$\therefore \qquad \dfrac{w \times 8^2}{8} \times 1000 = 28759066$

$\therefore \qquad$ w = 3594.88 N/m $\qquad$ **... Ans.**

Example 3.16 :

A rectangular prestressed concrete beam 300 mm × 800 mm is simply supported over a span of 9 m. The beam supports two concentrated loads of 20 kN each at the third points of span. Using the concept of load balancing.

(i) Suggest a suitable cable profile and calculate the prestressing force if the eccentricity is 100 mm.

Neglect self weight.

(ii) For the same cable profile with e = 100 mm, considering the self weight of beam, calculate the prestressing force so that the resultant stress is zero at the bottom fibre of mid-span section. (Using stress concept method).

Solution :

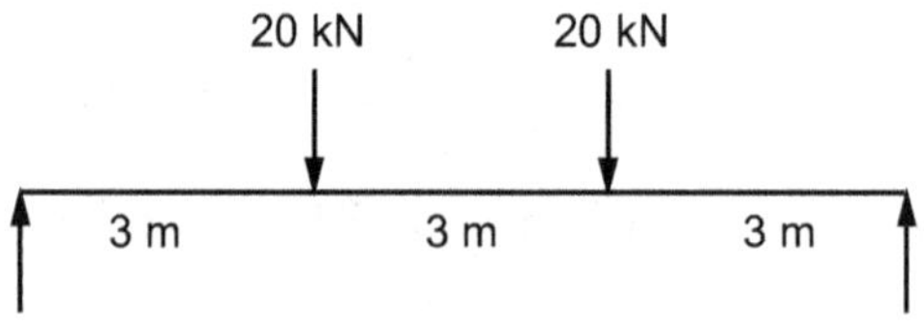

Fig. 3.28

(i) B.M. due to external loads $= 20 \times 3 = 60$ kN-m $\left(\text{i.e. } \dfrac{Wl}{3}\right)$

$\qquad$ B.M. due to eccentricity $= P \times e = P \times 100$

In load balancing method,

$\qquad 60 \times 10^6$ N-mm $= P \times 100$

$\therefore \qquad P = \dfrac{60 \times 10^6}{10^2} = 600$ kN

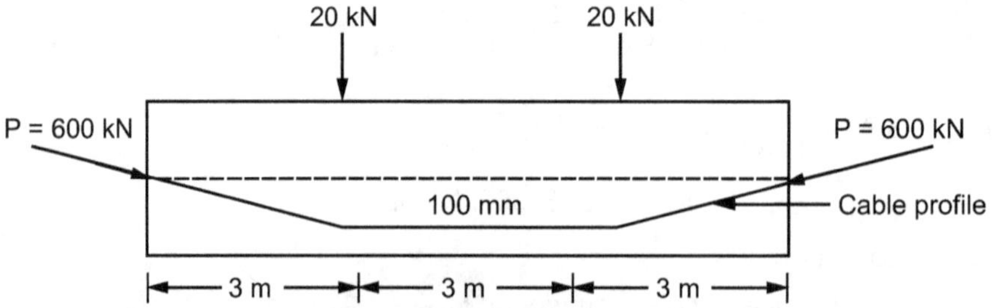

Fig. 3.29

(ii)   Self-weight of beam $= (0.3 \times 0.8 \times 25) = 6$ kN/m

B.M. due to D.L. $(M_d) = \dfrac{wl^2}{8} = \dfrac{6 \times 9^2}{8} = 60.75$ kN-m

$$f_{bottom} = +\frac{P}{A} + \frac{P \cdot e}{z_b} - \frac{M_d}{z_b} - \frac{M_L}{z_b}$$

$$0 = \frac{P}{(800 \times 300)} + \frac{P \times 100}{3.2 \times 10^7} - \frac{60.75 \times 10^6}{3.2 \times 10^7} - \frac{60 \times 10^6}{3.2 \times 10^7}$$

$$0 = \frac{P}{2.4 \times 10^5} + \frac{P}{3.2 \times 10^5} - 1.89 - 1.875$$

$\therefore$

$$3.765 = \frac{P}{10^5}\left(\frac{1}{2.4} + \frac{1}{3.2}\right)$$

$\therefore$

$$P = \frac{3.765 \times 10^5}{0.729166}$$

$$P = 5.164 \times 10^5 \text{ N}$$

$$P = 516.4 \text{ kN} \qquad \text{... \textbf{Ans.}}$$

Example 3.17 :

An unsymmetrical I section is used to support an imposed load of 11 kN/m over a span of 17 m. The sectional details are top flange 650 ×150, web 150 ×650 and bottom flange   350 ×250 mm. The effective prestressing force is 1125 kN is located from 70 mm from soffit of the section at midspan. Cable profile is parabolic concentric at support. Calculate extreme fiber stresses in concrete at midspan, at initial and final stages. Take loss ratio as 0.85 and unit weight of concrete as 25 kN/m³.   **(Winter 2011, May 12, 13, 15, 17 Marks)**

Solution :

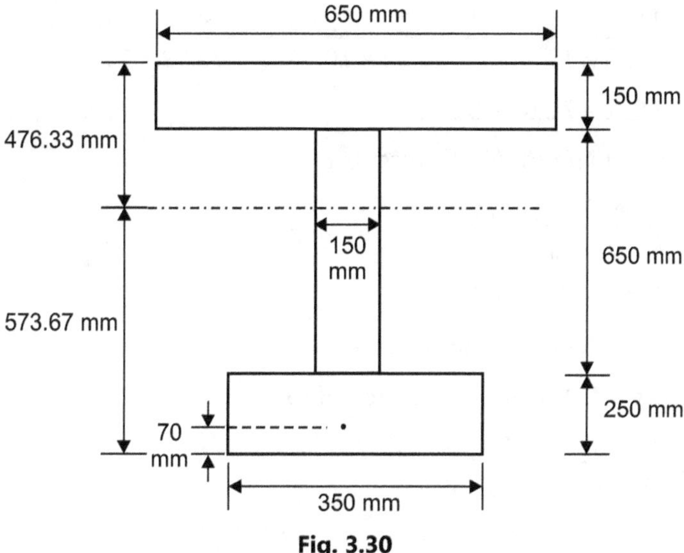

Fig. 3.30

$$A = 650 \times 150 + 150 \times 650 + 250 \times 350 = 2.825 \times 10^5 \text{ mm}^2$$

$$\bar{y}_b = \frac{650 \times 150 \times 975 + 150 \times 650 \times 575 + 250 \times 350 \times 125}{650 \times 150 + 150 \times 650 + 250 \times 350} = 573.67 \text{ mm}$$

$$y_t = 1050 - 573.67 = 476.33 \text{ mm}$$

$$e = 573.67 - 70 = 503.67 \text{ mm}$$

Self weight of beam $= 282500 \times 10^{-6} \times 25 = 7.06 \text{ kN/m}$

$$M_d = \frac{7.06 \times 17^2}{8} = 255.04 \text{ kN-m}$$

$$I = \frac{650 \times 150^3}{12} + 650 \times 150 \; (476.33 - 75)^2 + \frac{150 \times 650^3}{12} + 150 \times 650$$

$$(575 - 573.67)^2 + \frac{350 \times 250^3}{12} + 350 \times 250 \, (573.67 - 125)^2$$

$$= 3.74 \times 10^{10} \text{ mm}^4$$

$$Z_t = \frac{I}{y_t} = \frac{3.74 \times 10^{10}}{476.33} = 78.52 \times 10^6 \text{ mm}^3$$

$$Z_b = \frac{I}{y_b} = \frac{3.74 \times 10^{10}}{573.67} = 65.19 \times 10^6 \text{ mm}^3$$

Case 1 : Prestress + Self weight :

$$f_{top} = \frac{P}{A} = \frac{P \cdot e}{Z_{top}} + \frac{M_d}{Z_{top}}$$

$$= \frac{1125 \times 10^3}{2.825 \times 10^6} - \frac{1125 \times 10^3 \times 503.67}{78.52 \times 10^6} + \frac{255.04 \times 10^6}{78.52 \times 10^6}$$

$$= 3.982 - 7.216 + 3.248$$

$$= 0.014 \text{ N/mm}^2 \text{ (Compressive)}$$

$$f_{bottom} = \frac{P}{A} + \frac{P \cdot e}{Z_{bottom}} - \frac{M_d}{Z_{bottom}}$$

$$= 3.982 + 8.692 - 3.912$$

$$= 8.762 \text{ N/mm}^2 \text{ (Compressive)}$$

Case 2 : Prestress + Self weight + Imposed loads :

$$f_{top} = \frac{\eta P}{A} - \frac{\eta P e}{Z_{top}} + \frac{M_d}{Z_{top}} + \frac{M_L}{Z_{top}}$$

$$= \frac{0.85 \times 1125 \times 10^3}{2.825 \times 10^5} - \frac{0.85 \times 1125 \times 10^3 \times 503.67}{78.52 \times 10^6}$$

$$+ \frac{255.04 \times 10^6}{78.52 \times 10^6} + \frac{11 \times 17^2/8 \times 10^6}{78.52 \times 10^6}$$

$$= 3.385 - 6.134 + 3.248 + 5.061$$

$$= 5.56 \text{ N/mm}^2 \text{ (Compressive)}$$

$$f_{bottom} = \frac{0.85 \times 1125 \times 10^3}{2.825 \times 10^5} + \frac{0.85 \times 1125 \times 10^3 \times 503.67}{65.19 \times 10^6}$$

$$- \frac{255.04 \times 10^6}{65.19 \times 10^6} + \frac{11 \times 17^2/8 \times 10^6}{65.19 \times 10^6}$$

$$= 3.385 + 6.134 - 3.912 - 6.096$$

$$= -0.489 \text{ N/mm}^2 \text{ (Tensile)}$$

Example 3.18 :

An unsymmetrical I section is used to support an imposed load of 10 kN/m over a span of 15 m. The sectional details are top flange 400 × 150, web 150 × 400 and bottom flange 250 × 250 mm. The applied prestressing force is 852 kN is located at from 65 mm from soffit of the section at midspan. Cable profile is parabolic concentric at support. Calculate extreme fiber stresses in concrete at midspan at initial and final stages. Take loss ratio as 0.82 and unit weight of concrete as 25 kN/m³. **(Summer 12, 17 Marks)**

Solution :

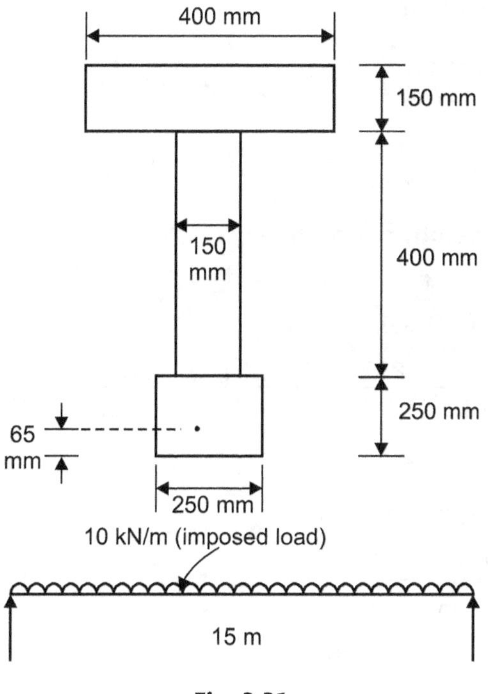

Fig. 3.31

$$M_L = \frac{10 \times 15^2}{8} = 281.25 \text{ kN-m}$$

$$A = 400 \times 150 + 150 \times 400 + 250 \times 250 = 182.5 \times 10^3 \text{ mm}^2$$

$$\bar{y} = \frac{400 \times 150 \times 725 + 150 \times 400 \times 450 + 250 \times 250 \times 125}{(400 \times 150 + 150 \times 400 + 250 \times 250)}$$

$$= 429.11 \text{ mm from bottom}$$

$$e = 429.11 - 65 = 364.11 \text{ mm}$$

Self weight of beam $= 182.5 \times 10^3 \times 10^{-6} \times 25 = 4.5625 \text{ kN/m}$

$$\text{B.M. due to D.L. } (M_d) = \frac{wl^2}{8} = \frac{4.5625 \times 15^2}{8} = 128.32 \text{ kN-m}$$

$$y_{bottom} = 429.11 \text{ mm}$$

$$y_{top} = 370.89 \text{ mm}$$

$$I = \frac{400 \times 150^3}{12} + 400 \times 150 \, (370.89 - 75)^2 + \frac{150 \times 400^3}{12}$$

$$+ \, 150 \times 400 \times (370.89 - 350)^2 + \frac{250^4}{12} + 250^2 \, (429.11 - 125)^2$$

$$= 1.229 \times 10^{10} \text{ mm}^4$$

$$\therefore \quad Z_{top} = \frac{I}{y_{top}} = \frac{1.229 \times 10^{10}}{370.89} = 33.137 \times 10^6 \text{ mm}^3$$

$$Z_{bottom} = \frac{I}{y_{bottom}} = \frac{1.229 \times 10^{10}}{429.11} = 28.641 \times 10^6 \text{ mm}^3$$

1.   Prestress + Self weight : At centre line

$$f_{top} = \frac{P}{A} - \frac{P \cdot e}{Z_{top}} + \frac{M_d}{Z_{top}}$$

$$= \frac{852 \times 10^3}{182.5 \times 10^3} - \frac{852 \times 10^3 \times 364.18}{33.137 \times 10^6} + \frac{128.32 \times 10^6}{33.137 \times 10^6}$$

$$= 4.668 - 9.36 + 3.872$$

$$= -0.82 \text{ N/mm}^2 \text{ (Tensile)}$$

$$f_{bottom} = \frac{P}{A} + \frac{P \cdot e}{Z_{bottom}} - \frac{M_d}{Z_{bottom}}$$

$$= 4.668 + 10.83 - 4.48$$

$$= 11.018 \text{ N/mm}^2 \text{ (Compressive)}$$

2.   **Prestress + Self weight + Imposed load :** At centre line

$$f_{top} = \frac{P}{A} - \frac{Pe}{Z_{top}} + \frac{M_d}{Z_{top}} + \frac{M_L}{Z_{top}}$$

$$= 4.668 - 9.36 + 3.872 + \frac{281.25 \times 10^6}{33.137 \times 10^6}$$

$$= 7.667 \text{ N/mm}^2 \text{ (Compressive)}$$

$$f_{bottom} = \frac{P}{A} + \frac{Pe}{Z_{bottom}} - \frac{M_d}{Z_{bottom}} - \frac{M_L}{Z_{bottom}}$$

$$= 4.668 + 9.36 - 3.872 - 8.487$$

$$= 1.668 \text{ N/mm}^2 \text{ (Compressive)}$$

Example 3.19 :

A pre-stressed concrete beam of simply supported span of 9 m having cross-sectional details as Top flange 250 × 100 mm, web 100 × 500 mm and bottom flange 200 × 200 mm. The beam has a carry superimposed load of 20 kN/m. The pre-stressing force is transmitted by tendons in two cables which are placed in a ducts of 50 × 50 mm. The C.G. of the cable of 12 mm from the soffit of the beam. In each cable, the tendons consist of 14 wires of 5 mm diameter subjected to an initial stress of 1000 N/mm². Calculate extreme fiber stresses in concrete at mid span at initial and final stages. Take loss ratio as 0.85 and unit weight of concrete as 25 kN/m³.

(Winter 2012, 17 Marks)

Solution :

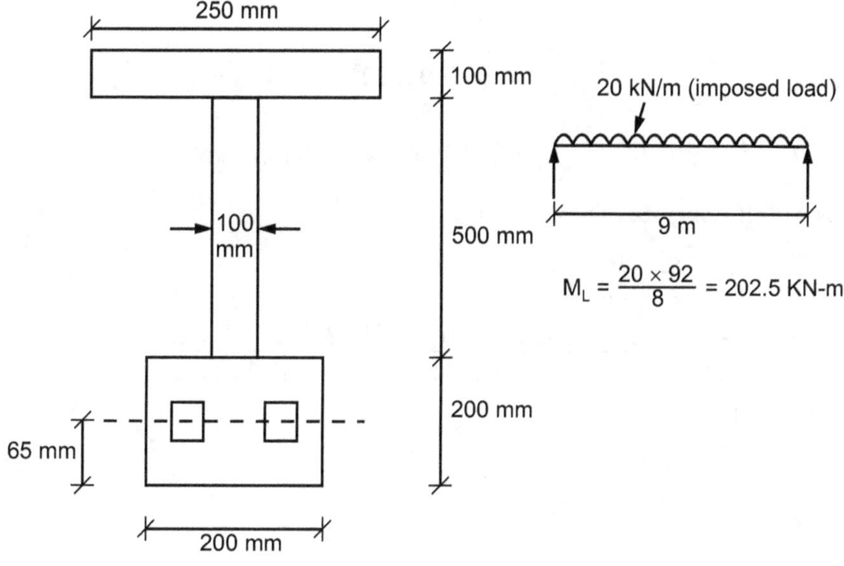

Fig. 3.32

$$M_L = \frac{20 \times 9^2}{8} = 202.5 \text{ kN-m}$$

$$A = 250 \times 100 + 500 \times 100 + 200 \times 200 - 2 \times 50 \times 50 = 110 \times 10^3 \text{ mm}^3$$

$$\bar{y} = \frac{250 \times 100 \times 750 + 100 \times 500 \times 450 + 200 \times 200 \times 100 - 2 \times 50 \times 50 \times 100}{250 \times 100 + 500 \times 100 + 200 \times 200 - 2 \times 50 \times 50}$$

$$= 406.82 \text{ mm from bottom}$$

$$\therefore \quad e = 406.82 - 65 = 341.82 \text{ m}$$

Self weight of beam $= 110 \times 10^3 \times 10^{-6} \times 25 = 2.75 \text{ kN/m}$

$$\text{B.M. due to D.L. } (M_d) = \frac{wl^2}{8} = \frac{2.75 \times 9^2}{8} = 27.84 \text{ kN/m}$$

$$y_{bottom} = 406.82 \text{ mm}$$

$$y_{top} = 393.18 \text{ mm}$$

$$I = 250 \times \frac{100^3}{12} + 250 \times 100 \times (393.18 - 50)^2 + 100 \times \frac{500^3}{12}$$

$$+ 100 \times 500 \times (393.18 - 350)^2$$

$$+ 200 \times \frac{200^3}{12} + 200 \times 200 \times (406.82 - 100)^2$$

$$- 2 \times 50 \times \frac{50^3}{12} - 2 \times 50 \times 50 \times (406.82 - 100)^2$$

$$= 2.965 \times 10^9 + 1.135 \times 10^9 + 3.899 \times 10^9 - 0.469 \times 10^9$$

$$= 7.53 \times 10^9 \text{ mm}^4$$

$$\therefore \quad Z_{top} = \frac{I}{y_{top}} = \frac{7.53 \times 10^9}{393.18} = 19.152 \times 10^6 \text{ mm}^3$$

$$Z_{bottom} = \frac{I}{y_{bottom}} = \frac{7.53 \times 10^9}{406.82} = 18.509 \times 10^6$$

$$P = \frac{\pi}{4} \times 5^2 \times 14 \times \frac{1000}{1000} = 274.89 \text{ kN} \times 2 = 549.78 \text{ kN}$$

1. **Prestress + Self weight :** At mid-span :

$$f_{top} = \frac{P}{A} - \frac{Pe}{Z_{top}} + \frac{M_d}{Z_{top}}$$

$$= \frac{549.78 \times 10^3}{110 \times 10^3} - \frac{549.78 \times 10^3 \times 341.82}{19.152 \times 10^6} + \frac{27.84 \times 10^6}{19.152 \times 10^6}$$

$$= 4.998 - 9.812 + 1.45$$

$$= -3.364 \text{ N/mm}^2 \text{ (Tensile)}$$

$$f_{bottom} = \frac{P}{A} + \frac{Pe}{Z_{bottom}} - \frac{M_d}{Z_{bottom}}$$

$$= 4.998 + 10.157 - 1.504 = 13.651 \text{ N/mm}^2 \text{ (Compressive)}$$

2. Prestress + Self weight + Imposed load : At mid-span

$$f_{top} = \frac{P}{A} - \frac{Pe}{Z_{top}} + \frac{M_d}{Z_{top}} + \frac{M_L}{Z_{top}}$$

$$= 4.998 - 9.812 + 1.45 + \frac{202.5 \times 10^6}{19.152 \times 10^6}$$

$$= 7.209 \ \text{N/mm}^2 \ \text{(Compressive)}$$

$$f_{bottom} = \frac{P}{A} + \frac{Pe}{Z_{bottom}} - \frac{M_d}{Z_{bottom}} - \frac{M_L}{Z_{bottom}}$$

$$= 4.998 + 9.812 - 1.145 - 10.573$$

$$= 3.092 \ \text{N/mm}^2 \ \text{(Compressive)}$$

IMPORTANT POINTS

- Stress concept
  - (i)   Prestressing force acting at neutral axis of the beam.
  - (ii) Prestressing force acting at an eccentricity to neutral axis of the beam.
- Load balancing concept
  - (i)   Prestressed beam with beam tendon.
  - (ii) Prestressed beam with parabolic tendon.

QUESTIONS

1. Fig. 3.33 shows a prestressed concrete beam provided with inclined tendon. The beam carries a point load of 160 kN at the centre. Determine the stress distribution for mid-section of the beam. The dead load of the beam is 6 kN/m.

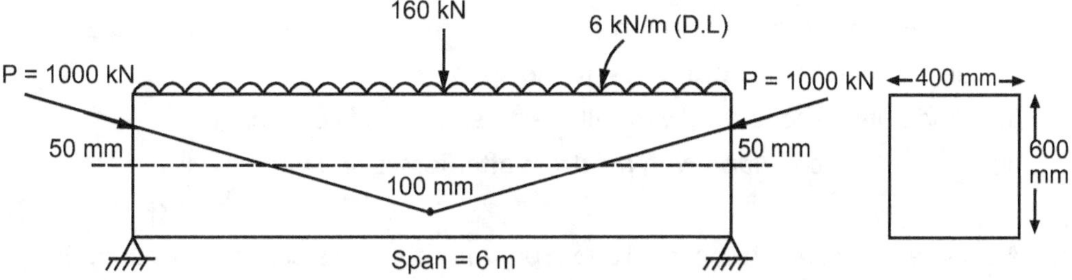

Fig. 3.33

Using
   - (i)   Stress concept method.
   - (ii) Strength concept method.
   - (iii) Load balancing method.

2. A prestressed concrete beam 200 mm × 400 mm is prestressed by a cable which has an eccentricity of 100 mm at centre of span section. The span of beam is 8 m and it is supported by two concentrated loads of 12 kN, each at one third span points. Determine the magnitude of prestressing from load balancing concept when

(a)   self-weight is ignored and live load is considered,

(b)   when live load plus self-weight is considered.   **(P.U. Dec. 2003)**

3. A prestress concrete I-beam supports a live load of 4000 N/m over a simply supported span of 8 m. The beam has an overall depth of 400 mm. The thickness of each flange and web are 60 mm and 80 mm respectively. The width of each flange is 200 mm. The beam is to be prestressed by an effective prestressing force of 235 kN applied at suitable eccentricity such that the resultant stress at the bottom of beam at centre of span is zero.

(i)   Find the eccentricity required for the prestressing force.   **Ans.** e = 84.35 mm

(ii) If the tendon is concentric, what should be the magnitude of the prestressing force for the resultant stress to be zero at the bottom fibre of the central section ?   **Ans.** P = 451936 N

4. A prestressed concrete T-beam is to be designed to support a superimposed load of 4400 kN/m over a span of 5 m. The T-beam is made up of a flange 400 mm wide and 40 mm thick. The rib is 100 mm wide by 200 mm deep. The stress in concrete must not exceed 15 N/mm^2 in compression and zero in tension at any stage.

Calculate the minimum prestressing force necessary and the corresponding eccentricity. Assume 20% loss of prestress after transfer.

5. A post-tensioned concrete beam is 300 mm wide and 600 mm deep. The tendons are provided at a height of 175 mm above the soffit. The initially prestressing force is 1575 kN which reduces to 1350 kN due to losses. The beam carries two live loads of 45 kN each at a distance of 4 m and 8 m from one end. The span of beam is 12 m. Calculate the extreme fibre stress at mid span

(i)   under initial condition with full prestress and no live load,

(ii) under final condition with prestress after losses and with full live load.

                                                          (P.U. Dec. 2000)

6. A prestressed concrete beam (120 × 300) mm is prestressed by a force of 200 kN at an eccentricity of 75 mm throughout. Calculate uniformly distributed superimposed load at the time of cracking, if density of concrete is 25 kN/m^3.

     Maximum tensile stress = 4 N/mm^2.

     A span of beam is 10 m, and beam is simply supported.

7. Analyse the stresses at the centre of beam section as shown in Fig. 3.34. Two cables, each of 10 numbers of wires of 7 mm diameter are tensioned initially upto 1200 N/mm^2. The span of beam is 15 m and it has to carry superimposed loads of 12 kN/m. Assume total loss of prestress 15%.   **(P.U. Dec. 2003)**

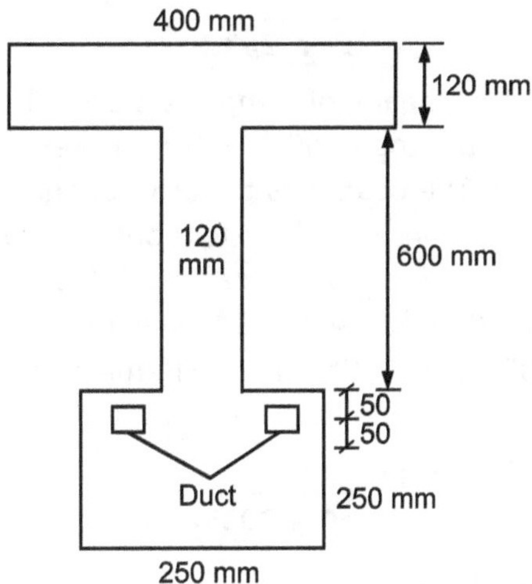

Fig. 3.34

8. (a) Explain load balancing concept for a prestressed concrete section.

   (b) Explain the concept of P-line and C-line as applied to a prestressed concrete beam.

   (c) Write note on 'eccentric prestressing is perferable to concentric prestressing'.

   (d) State, why cables are provided with eccentricity in prestressed concrete. Explain how parabolic cable profile helps to reduce shear force at support.

9. A post-tensioned prestressed concrete beam section has top flange 550 × 150, web 150 × 620 and bottom flange 350 × 400 mm, is simply supported over a effective span of 18 m and carries a superimposed load of 14.5 kN/m over the entire span. Calculate extreme fibre stresses in concrete at midspan at initial and final stage. The 5 No. of 12/5 Freyssinet cables having zero eccentricity at supports and c.g. area of steel at 100 mm from soffit of the section and are stressed to initial prestress of 1050 MPa. Take loss ratio as 0.85 and unit weight concrete as 25 kN/m^3.

UNIVERSITY QUESTIONS

May 2012

Q. 1 An unsymmetrical I section is used to support an imposed load of 10 kN/m over a span of 15 m. the sectional details are top flange 400 × 150, web 150 × 400 and bottom flange 250 × 250 mm. the applied prestressing force is 852 kN is located at from 65 mm from soffit of the section at midspan. Cable profile is parabolic concentric at support. Calculate extreme fiber stresses in concrete at midspan at initial and final stages. Take loss ratio as 0.82 and unit weight concrete as 25 kN/m^3. **(Example 3.17)**   **(17 Marks)**

Dec. 2012

Q. 2   A prestressed concrete beam of simply supported span of 9 m having cross sectional details as top flange 250 × 100 mm, web 100 × 500 mm and bottom flange 200 × 200 mm. The beam has to carry superimposed load of 20 kN/m. The pre-stressing forces is transmitted by tendons in two cable which are placed in ducts of 50 × 50 mm. The C.G. of the cable is 120 mm from the soffit of the beam. In each cable the tendons consist of 14 wires of 5 mm diameter subjected to an initial stress of 1000 N/mm^2. Calculate extreme fiber stresses in concrete at mid span at initial and final stages. Take loss ratio as 0.85 and unit weight of concrete as 25 kN/m^3. **(Example 3.19)**   **(17 Marks)**

May 2013

Q. 3 (a)   An unsymmetrical I-section of size top flange 500 × 200 mm, bottom flange 350 × 250 mm and web 150 × 600 mm is used to support an imposed load of 15 kN/m over a span of 16 m. The effective pre-stressing force of 1250 kN is located at 90 mm from soffit of the section at mid span. Cable profile is parabolic and concentric at support. Calculate the extreme fiber stress in concrete at mid span at initial and final stages. Take loss ratio as 0.82. **(Example 3.17)**   **(15 Marks)**

Dec. 2014

Q. 4 (a)   What is load balancing concept? Explain with sketch. **(Section 3.3)**   **(8 Marks)**

(b)   A beam of unsymmetrical I-section is to support a live load of 10 kN/m over a span of 15 m. The beam is prestressed by a panabolic cable with an eccentricity of 150 mm at the center and zero at the supports with an effective force of 1100 km. The I-section has top flange 750 mm wide and 200 mm deep, bottom flange 400 mm wide and 300 mm deep and web 500 mm and 150 mm wide. Calculate extreme fiber stress in concrete at mid span for the following condition :
(i) Prestress + Self weight
(ii) Prestress + Self weight + Live load. Take mass of concrete as 25 kN/m^3. Assume 15% loss of prestressing. **(Example 3.2)**   **(17 Marks)**

May 2015

Q. 5 (a)   Explain stress concept and load balancing concept.
(Sections 3.2 and 3.3)   **(8 Marks)**

(b)   An unsymmetrical prestressed concrete section has top flange 500 × 200 mm, bottom flange 400 mm × 300 mm, and web 200 mm × 800 mm, it is supported over a span of 15 m carries super imposed load of 13 kN/m, the effective prestressing force is 1000 kN located at 100 mm from soffit of the section at mid span, cable profile is parabolic and concentric at support. Calculate extreme fiber stresses in concrete at mid span at initial and final stage. Take loss ratio as 0.85 and unit weight of concrete as 25 kN/m^3.   **(Example 3.17) (17 Marks)**

Chapter 4

FLEXURAL STRENGTH OF PRESTRESSED CONCRETE SECTION

4.1 MOMENT OF RESISTANCE

The IS : (1343-1980) method for computing the **moment of resistance of rectangular sections or T-sections in which neutral axis lies within the flange**, is based on the rectangular and parabolic stress block as shown in Fig. 4.1.

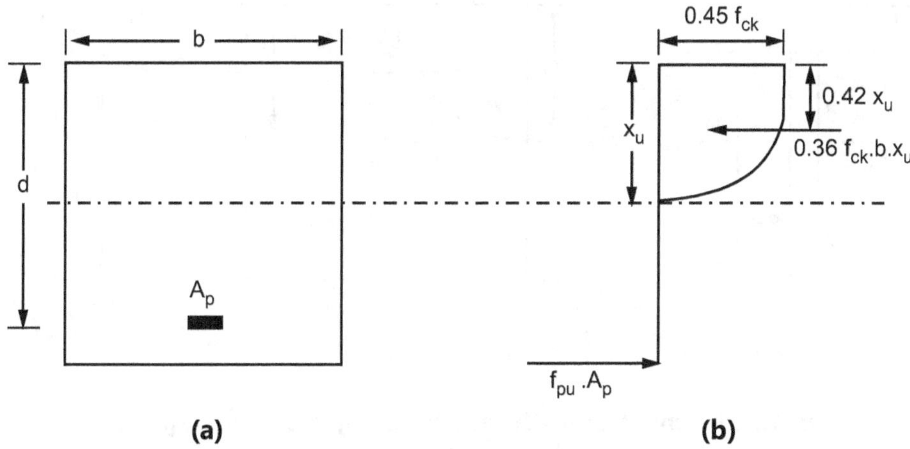

Fig. 4.1 : Moment of resistance of rectangular section

The moment of resistance is obtained as

$$M_u = f_{pu} \cdot A_p (d - 0.42\, x_u)$$

where

    M_u – Ultimate moment of resistance of the section

    f_{pu} – Tensile stress developed in tendons at the failure stage

    A_p – Area of prestressing tendon

    d – Effective depth

    x_u – Neutral axis depth

    f_p – Characteristic tensile strength of the prestressing steel

The value of f_{pu} depends on the effective reinforcement ratio $\left(\dfrac{A_p \cdot f_p}{b \cdot d \cdot f_{ck}}\right)$; given in Table 4.1.

For pre-tensioned and post-tensioned members with effective bond between the concrete and tendons, values of f_{pu} and x_u are given in Table 4.1. The effective prestress after all losses should not be less than 0.45 f_p; for post-tensioned members with unbonded tendons, the values of f_{pu} and x_u are given in Table 4.2.

Now, **the ultimate moment of resistance of flanged sections in which neutral axis falls outside the flange ($x_u > D_f$), is computed by combining the moment of resistance of the web and flange portions and considering the stress blocks as shown in Fig. 4.2.

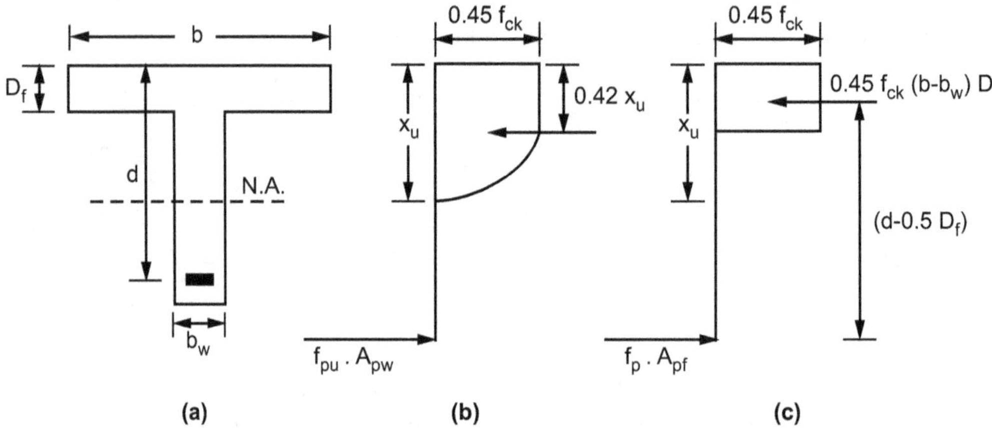

Fig. 4.2 : Moment of resistance for flanged section ($x_u > D_f$)

For this condition, the ultimate moment of resistance is

$$M_u = f_{pu} \cdot A_{pw} (d - 0.42\, x_u) + 0.45\, f_{ck} (b - b_w) D_f (d - 0.5\, D_f)$$

where A_{pw} – Area of prestressing steel for web

                     A_{pf} – Area of prestressing steel for flange

                     D_f – Thickness of flange

Then, $A_p = A_{pw} + A_{pf}$

where, $A_{pf} = 0.45\, f_{ck} (b - b_w) \left(\dfrac{D_f}{f_p}\right)$

For effective reinforcement ratio of $\left(\dfrac{A_{pw} \cdot f_p}{b_w \cdot d \cdot f_{ck}}\right)$, use Table 4.1.

Table 4.1 : Conditions at the ultimate limit state for rectangular beams with pre-tensioned tendons or with post-tensioned tendons having effective bond

$\dfrac{A_p\, f_p}{bd\, f_{ck}}$	Stress in tendon as a proportion of the design strength $\dfrac{f_{pu}}{0.87\, f_p}$		Ratio of the depth of neutral axis to that of the centroid of the tendon in the tension zone x_u/d	
	Pre-tensioning	Post-tensioning with effective bond	Pre-tensioning	Post-tensioning with effective bond
(1)	(2)	(3)	(4)	(5)
0.025	1.0	1.0	0.054	0.054
0.05	1.0	1.0	0.109	0.109
0.10	1.0	1.0	0.217	0.217
0.15	1.0	1.0	0.326	0.316
0.20	1.0	0.95	0.435	0.414
0.25	1.0	0.90	0.542	0.488
0.30	1.0	0.85	0.655	0.558
0.40	0.9	0.75	0.783	0.653

Table 4.2 : Conditions at the ultimate limit state for post-tensioned rectangular beams having unbonded tendons

$\dfrac{A_p\, f_p}{bd\, f_{ck}}$	Stress in tendons as a proportion of the effective prestress f_{pu}/f_p for values of l/d $\left(\dfrac{\text{Effective span}}{\text{Effective depth}}\right)$			Ratio of depth of neutral axis to that of the centroid of the tendons in the tension zone x_u/d for values of l/d $\left(\dfrac{\text{Effective span}}{\text{Effective depth}}\right)$		
	30	20	10	30	20	10
(1)	(2)	(3)	(4)	(5)	(6)	(7)
0.025	1.23	1.34	1.45	0.10	0.10	0.10
0.05	1.21	1.32	1.45	0.16	0.16	0.18
0.10	1.18	1.26	1.45	0.30	0.32	0.36
0.15	1.14	1.20	1.36	0.44	0.46	0.52
0.20	1.11	1.16	1.27	0.56	0.58	0.64

Solved Examples

Example 4.1 :

A pre-tensioned prestressed concrete beam having a rectangular section 150 mm wide × 350 mm deep has an effective cover 50 mm. If f_{ck} = 40 N/mm², f_p = 1600 N/mm² and A_p = 461 mm², calculate ultimate flexural tensile strength of section.

Solution :

The effective reinforcement ratio

$$\frac{f_p \, A_p}{f_{ck} \cdot b \cdot d} = \frac{1600 \times 461}{40 \times 150 \times 300} = 0.40$$

From Table 4.1,

$$\frac{f_{pu}}{0.87 \, f_p} = 0.9 \quad \text{and} \quad \frac{x_u}{d} = 0.783$$

$$\therefore \quad f_{pu} = 0.9 \times 0.87 \times 1600 = 1253 \text{ N/mm}^2$$

$$x_u = 0.783 \times 300 = 234.9 \text{ mm}$$

$$M_u = f_{pu} \, A_p \, (d - 0.42 \, x_u)$$

$$= 1253 \times 461 \times (300 - 0.42 \times 234.9)$$

$$= 116 \text{ kN-m} \qquad \qquad \text{... } \textbf{Ans.}$$

Example 4.2 :

A pre-tensioned T-section has a flange which is 300 mm wide and 200 mm thick. The rib is 150 mm wide by 350 mm deep. The effective depth of cross-section is 500 mm. Given : A_p = 200 mm², f_{ck} = 50 N/mm² and f_p = 1600 N/mm². Calculate the ultimate moment capacity of T-section using I.S. code.

Solution :

Given : f_{ck} = 50 N/mm², b = 300 mm, d = 500 mm, f_p = 1600 N/mm², A_p = 200 mm².

Assuming that neutral axis falls within the flange.

Now, we have
$$\frac{f_p \, A_p}{f_{ck} \cdot b \cdot d} = \frac{1600 \times 200}{50 \times 300 \times 500} = 0.04$$

From Table 4.1,

$$\left(\frac{f_{pu}}{0.87 \, f_p}\right) = 1.0 \quad \text{and} \quad \left(\frac{x_u}{d}\right) = 0.09$$

$$\therefore \quad f_{pu} = (1.0 \times 0.87 \times 1600) = 1392 \text{ N/mm}^2$$

$$x_u = (0.09 \times 500) = 45 \text{ mm}$$

Therefore, the assumption that the neutral axis falls within the flange is correct.

Hence, the ultimate flexural strength of the section is

$$M_u = f_{pu}\, A_p\, (d - 0.42\, x_u)$$

$$= 1392 \times 200 \times (500 - 0.42 \times 45)$$

$$M_u = 134 \text{ kN-m} \hspace{3cm} \textbf{... Ans.}$$

Example 4.3 :

A post-tensioned beam with unbonded tendons is of rectangular section 400 mm wide with an effective depth of 800 mm. The cross-sectional area of the prestressing steel is 2840 mm². The effective prestress in the steel after all losses is 900 N/mm². The effective span of the beam is 16 m. If f_{ck} = 40 N/mm², calculate the ultimate moment of resistance of the section.

Solution :

Given :
$$f_{ck} = 40 \text{ N/mm}^2, \quad b = 400 \text{ mm}, \quad d = 800 \text{ mm},$$

$$f_{pe} = 900 \text{ N/mm}^2, \quad A_p = 2840 \text{ mm}^2, \quad \left(\frac{L}{d}\right) = \frac{16000}{800} = 20$$

The effective reinforcement ratio,

$$\frac{f_{pe}\, A_p}{b \cdot d \cdot f_{ck}} = \left(\frac{900 \times 2840}{400 \times 800 \times 40}\right) = 0.2$$

From Table 4.2,
$$\frac{f_{pu}}{f_{pe}} = 1.16 \quad \text{and} \quad \left(\frac{x_u}{d}\right) = 0.58$$

$$\therefore \quad f_{pu} = 1.16 \times 900 = 1044 \text{ N/mm}^2$$

$$\therefore \quad x_u = (0.58 \times 800) = 464 \text{ mm}$$

$$M_p = f_{pu} \cdot A_p \cdot (d - 0.42\, x_u)$$

$$= 1044 \times 2840 \times (800 - 0.42 \times 464)$$

$$M_p = 1794 \text{ kN-m} \hspace{3cm} \textbf{... Ans.}$$

Example 4.4 :

A pre-tensioned T-section has a flange 1200 mm wide and 150 mm thick. The width and depth of the rib are 300 mm and 1500 mm respectively. The high-tensile steel has an area of 4700 mm² and is located at an effective depth of 1600 mm. If f_{ck} = 40 N/mm² and strength of steel is 1600 N/mm², calculate the flexural strength of T-section.

Solution :

Given :
$$A_p = 4700 \text{ mm}^2, \quad f_{ck} = 40 \text{ N/mm}^2, \quad b = 1200 \text{ mm}$$

$$b_w = 300 \text{ mm}, \quad D_f = 150 \text{ mm}$$

Now,

$$A_{pf} = 0.45 \, f_{ck} \, (b - b_w) \left(\frac{D_f}{f_p}\right)$$

$$= 0.45 \times 40 \times (1200 - 300) \left(\frac{150}{1600}\right)$$

$$= 1518 \text{ mm}^2$$

Therefore,

$$A_{pw} = A_p - A_{pf}$$

$$= (4700 - 1518) = 3182 \text{ mm}^2$$

Also,

$$\frac{A_{pw} \cdot f_p}{b_w \cdot d \cdot f_{ck}} = \left(\frac{3182 \times 1600}{300 \times 1600 \times 40}\right) = 0.265$$

From Table 4.1,

$$\frac{f_{pu}}{0.87 \, f_p} = 1.0 \qquad\qquad \therefore \; f_{pu} = 0.87 \times 1 \times 1600 = 1392 \text{ mm}^2$$

$$\left(\frac{x_u}{d}\right) = 0.56 \qquad\qquad \therefore \quad x_u = 0.56 \times 1600 = 896 \text{ mm}$$

It is clear that, neutral axis lies outside the flange.

Therefore, moment of resistance,

$$M_u = f_{pu} \, A_{pw} \, (d - 0.42 \, x_u) + 0.45 \, f_{ck} \, (b - b_w) \, D_f \, (d - 0.5 \, D_f)$$

$$= 1392 \times 3182 \times (1600 - 0.42 \times 896)$$

$$+ \; 0.45 \times 40 \times (1200 - 300) \times 150 \times (1600 - 0.5 \times 150)$$

$$= (5420 \times 10^6) + (3705 \times 10^6)$$

$$M_u = 9125 \text{ kN-m} \qquad\qquad\qquad\qquad \textbf{... Ans.}$$

Example 4.5 :

A pre-tensioned beam of rectangular section 400 mm wide by 1000 mm overall depth is prestressed by 800 mm² of high tensile steel at an eccentricity of 300 mm. If f_{ck} = 40 N/mm², f_p = 1600 N/mm², estimate the ultimate flexural strength of the section.

Solution :

Given :

$$A_p = 800 \text{ mm}^2, \quad b = 400 \text{ mm}, \quad d = 800 \text{ mm},$$

$$f_{ck} = 40 \text{ N/mm}^2, \quad f_p = 1600 \text{ N/mm}^2$$

The effective reinforcement ratio,

$$\left(\frac{A_p \, f_p}{f_{ck} \cdot b \cdot d}\right) = \left(\frac{800 \times 1600}{40 \times 400 \times 800}\right) = 0.1$$

Refer Table 4.1,

$$\left(\frac{f_{pu}}{0.87 \, f_p}\right) = 1.0 \qquad \therefore \ f_{pu} = (0.87 \times 1600 \times 1) = 1392 \text{ N/mm}^2$$

and

$$\left(\frac{x_u}{d}\right) = 0.217 \quad \therefore \ x_u = (0.217 \times 800) = 173.6 \text{ mm}$$

Hence, the ultimate moment of resistance,

$$M_u = A_p \, f_{pu} \, [d - 0.42 \, x_u]$$

$$= 800 \times 1392 \ [800 - 0.42 \times 173.6]$$

$$M_u = 809 \text{ kN-m} \hspace{4cm} \textbf{... Ans.}$$

Example 4.6 :

Design a post tensioned prestressed concrete 'I' or 'T' section beam for flexure to carry a live load of 8 kN/m over entire simply supported span of 20 m with M40 of concrete and Freyssinet cables of 12/5 (F_y = 1750 MPa) or 12/7 (F_y = 1600 MPa) including design of end block. Draw sketches showing cable profiles and end block reinforcement details. Check fiber stresses in concrete and deflection. **(May 12, 13, 15, Dec. 11, 12, 14)**

Solution : 1. Preliminary Design :

$$\text{Depth of girder} = 40 \text{ to } 50 \text{ mm/m of span}$$

$$= 40 \times 20 \text{ to } 50 \times 20$$

$$= 800 \text{ mm to } 1000 \text{ mm}$$

$$\text{Adopt overall depth} = 900 \text{ mm}$$

$$\text{Top width of flange} = 0.4 \text{ to } 0.5 \text{ h}$$

$$= 0.4 \times 900 \text{ to } 0.5 \times 900$$

$$= 360 \text{ to } 450 \text{ mm}$$

∴   Assume b = 400 mm.

Thickness of top flange = t = 0.2 h = 0.2 × 400 = 800 mm

Thickness of web = b_w = 100 mm.

Assume bottom flange as 350 × 300 mm.

2. Sectional Properties :

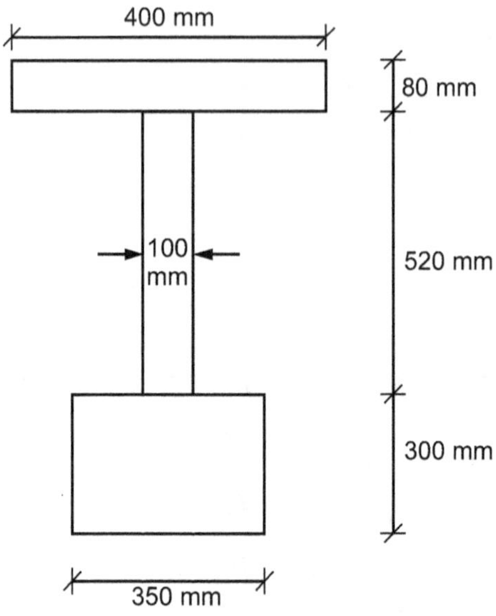

Fig. 4.3

$$A = 400 \times 80 + 100 \times 520 + 350 \times 300 = 189 \times 10^3 \text{ mm}^2$$

$$y_b = \frac{(400 \times 80 \times 860 + 100 \times 520 \times 560 + 350 \times 300 \times 150)}{189 \times 10^3}$$

$$= 383.02 \text{ mm from bottom}$$

∴

$$y_t = 900 - 383.02 = 516.98 \text{ mm}$$

$$I = 400 \times \frac{80^3}{12} + 400 \times 80 \times (516.98 - 40)$$

$$+ 100 \times \frac{520^3}{12} + 100 \times 520 \times (516.98 - 340)^2$$

$$+ 350 \times \frac{300^3}{12} + 350 \times 300 \times (383.02 - 150)^2$$

$$= 7.297 \times 10^9 + 2.8 \times 10^9 + 6.489 \times 10^9$$

$$= 16.586 \times 10^9 \text{ mm}^4$$

$$Z_t = \frac{I}{y_t} = \frac{16.586 \times 10^9}{516.98} = 32.082 \times 10^6 \text{ mm}^3$$

$$Z_b = \frac{I}{y_b} = \frac{16.586 \times 10^9}{383.02} = 43.303 \times 10^6 \text{ mm}^3$$

3. Design Moments and Shear Forces :

$$\text{Self weight} = 25 \times 0.189 = 4.725 \text{ kN/m}$$

$$\text{D.L. moment} = M_d = \frac{W_d\, l^2}{8} = \frac{4.725 \times 20^2}{8} = 236.25 \text{ kN-m}$$

$$\text{L.L.} = W_L = 8 \text{ kN/m}$$

$$\therefore \quad \text{L.L. moment} = M_L = \frac{W_L\, l^2}{8} = \frac{8 \times 20^2}{8} = 400 \text{ kN-m}$$

$$\text{Total shear force} = V = (W_d + W_L)\frac{l}{2}$$

$$= (4.725 + 8) \times \frac{20}{2} = 127.25 \text{ kN}$$

4. Permissible Stresses (As per IS : 1343-1980) : Referring to Fig. 8B of IS : 1343-1980.

$$f_{ck} = 45 \text{ N/mm}^2, \quad f_{ci} = 37 \text{ N/mm}^2$$

$$f_{ct} = 0.427, \quad f_{ci} = 0.427 \times 37 = 15.8 \text{ N/mm}^2$$

For class z type, $\quad f_{tt} = f_{tw} = 0$, since no tension is permitted at transfer and working loads.

From Fig. 7 of IS : 1343-1980,

$$f_{cw} = 0.37\, f_{ck} = 0.37 \times 45 = 16.65 \text{ N/mm}^2$$

5. Check for Section Moduls :

$$Z_b \geq \left[\frac{M_l + (l - n)\, M_d}{(nf_{ct} - f_{tw})} \right]$$

$$\geq \left[\frac{400 \times 10^6 + (1 - 0.85) \times 236.25 \times 10^6}{(0.85 \times 15.8 - 0)} \right]$$

$$\geq 32.42 \times 10^6 \text{ mm}^3 < Z_{b\ provided}$$

Hence O.K.

6. Prestressing Force and Eccentricity :

$$f_{sup} = \left[f_{tt} - \frac{M_d}{Z_t} \right] = 0 - \frac{236.25 \times 10^6}{32.082 \times 10^6} = -7.364 \text{ N/mm}^2$$

$$f_{inf} = \left[\frac{f_{tw}}{\eta} + \frac{M_d\, M_L}{\eta\, Z_b} \right]$$

$$= \left[0 + \frac{(236.25 + 400) \times 10^6}{0.85 \times 43.303 \times 10^6} \right] = 17.286 \text{ N/mm}^2$$

$$e = \frac{Z_t \cdot Z_b \,(f_{inf} - f_{sup})}{A \,(f_{inf} \cdot Z_b + f_{sup} \cdot Z_t)}$$

$$= \frac{1389.25 \times 10^{12} \,(17.286 + 7.364)}{189000 \times 10^6 \,(17.286 \times 43.303 - 7.364 \times 32.082)}$$

$$= 353.69 \text{ mm} \approx 354 \text{ (not possible).}$$

$\therefore$ Maximum possible eccentricity = 50 mm

$$P = \frac{A \cdot f_{inf} \cdot Z_b}{Z_b + A \cdot e} = \frac{189000 \times 17.286 \times 43.303 \times 10^6}{43.303 \times 10^6 + 189000 \times 50}$$

$$= 2.6818 \times 10^6 = 2691.80 \text{ kN/m}$$

Using Freyssinet cables 12 numbers of 5 mm ϕ initially stressed to 1750 N/mm^2.

$\therefore$ Number of cables $= \dfrac{2681.80 \times 10^3}{12 \times \dfrac{\pi}{4} \times 5^2 \times 1750} = 6.5 \approx 7$

7. Permissible Tendon Zone :

(a) At centre of span :

$$e \le \left[\frac{Z_b \cdot f_{ct}}{P} - \frac{Z_b}{A} + \frac{M_d}{P} \right]$$

$$\le \left[\frac{43.303 \times 10^6 \times 15.8}{2681.8 \times 10^3} - \frac{43.303 \times 10^6}{189000} + \frac{236.25 \times 10^6}{2681.8 \times 10^6} \right]$$

$$\le 26.08 \text{ mm}$$

$$e \ge \left[\frac{Z_b \cdot f_{tw}}{P} - \frac{Z_b}{A} + \frac{(M_d + M_l)}{\eta P} \right]$$

$$\ge \left[\frac{43.303 \times 10^6 \times 0}{P} - \frac{43.303 \times 10^6}{189000} + \frac{(236.25 + 400) \times 10^6}{0.85 \times 2681.8 \times 10^6} \right]$$

$$\ge (- 229.12 + 0.279) \ge - 228.84 \text{ mm}$$

(b) At support : $e \le \left[\dfrac{Z_b \cdot f_{ct}}{P} - \dfrac{Z_b}{A} + 0 \right] \le (255.12 - 229.12) \le 26 \text{ mm}$

$$e \ge \left[0 - \frac{Z_b}{A} + 0 \right] \ge - 229.12 \text{ mm}$$

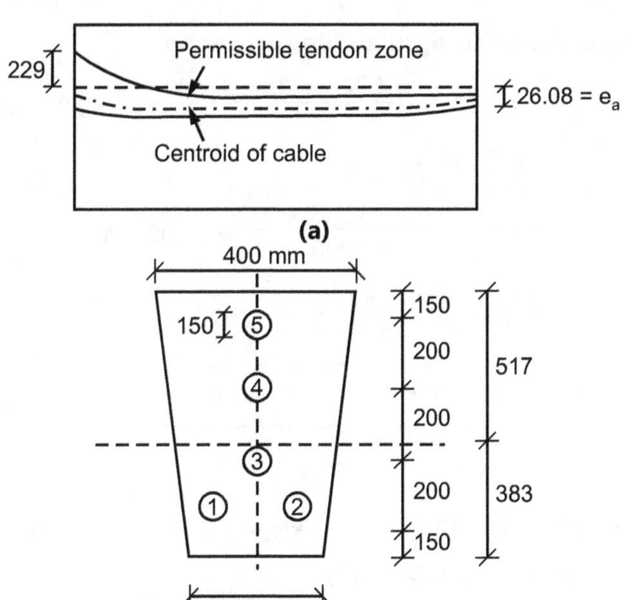

(b) Arrangement of cables at supports

Fig. 4.4

8. Check for Ultimate Flexural Strength :

$$A_p = 12 \times \frac{\pi}{4} \times 5^2 \times 7 = 1649.34 \text{ mm}^2, d = 850 \text{ mm}$$

$f_{ck} = 45 \text{ N/mm}^2, b_N = 100 \text{ mm}, f_{pu} = 1750 \text{ N/mm}^2, b = 400 \text{ mm}, D_f = 80 \text{ mm}$

$$M_u = 1.5 (M_d + M_l) = 1.5 (236.25 + 400) = 954.375 \text{ kN-m}$$

$$A_p = A_{Pw} + A_{Pf}$$

$$A_{Pf} = 0.45 f_{ck} (b - b_w) (D_f/f_p)$$

$$= 0.45 \times 45 (400 - 100) \times \frac{80}{1750} = 277.71 \text{ mm}^2$$

$$A_{Pw} = 1649.34 - 277.71 = 1371.63 \text{ mm}^2$$

$$\therefore \quad \frac{A_{Pw} \cdot f_p}{b_w \, d \, f_{ck}} = \frac{1371.63 \times 1750}{100 \times 850 \times 45} = 0.63$$

Table 11 of IS : 1343.

$$\frac{f_{Pu}}{0.87 f_p} = 0.75, \quad \frac{x_u}{d} = 0.653$$

$$\therefore \quad f_{Pu} = 0.87 \times 0.75 \times 1750 = 1141.88 \text{ N/mm}^2$$

$$x_u = 0.653 \times 850 = 555.05 \text{ mm}$$

$$M_u = f_{Pu} A_{Pw} (d - 0.42 x_u) + 0.45 f_{ck} (b - b_w) D_f (d - 0.5 D_f)$$

$$= 1750 \times 1371.63 (850 - 0.42 \times 555.05)$$

$$+ 0.45 \times 45 (400 - 100) \times (850 - 0.5 \times 80)$$

$$= 1874.38 \times 10^6 \text{ N-mm} = 1874.38 \text{ kN-m} > 954.375 \text{ kN-mm}$$

Hence O.K.

9. Check for Ultimate Shear Strength at Support Section :

$$V_u = 1.5\,(V_d + V_l) = 1.5 \times \left(\frac{4.725 \times 20}{2} + \frac{8 \times 20}{2}\right) = 190.875 \text{ kN/mm}$$

$$f_t = 1.7 \text{ N/mm}^2$$

$$f_{cp} = \frac{\eta P}{A} = \frac{0.85 \times 2681.8 \times 10^3}{189000} = 12.06 \text{ N/mm}^2$$

$$\theta = \frac{\Delta e}{l} = \Delta\left(\frac{583 - 170}{20000}\right) = 0.0826$$

$$V_{co} = 0.67\, b_w\, D\,\sqrt{f_r^2 + 0.8\, f_{cp} \cdot f_t} + \eta P \sin\theta$$

$$= 0.67 \times 100 \times 900\,\frac{\sqrt{1.7^2 + 0.8 \times 12.06 \times 1.7}}{1000} + 0.85 \times 2681.8 \times \sin(0.0826)$$

$$= 284.766 + 188.29 = 473.055 \text{ kN} > 190.875 \text{ kN} \Rightarrow \text{O.K.}$$

Using 10 mm ϕ, 2 legged stirrups (Fe-415)

$$S_v = \frac{A_{sv} \times 0.87\, f_y}{0.4\, b_w} = \frac{2 \times 78.5 \times 0.787 \times 415}{0.4 \times 100} = 1417.12 \text{ mm}$$

Allowing 50 mm cover, $d_t = 850$ mm

$S > 0.75 \times 850 = 637.5$ or $4 \times 100 = 400$ mm

Adopt 10 mm ϕ, 2 legged stirrups @ 400 mm c/c

10. Check for Deflection at Serviceability Limit State : $e_1 = 583$ mm, $e_2 = 170$ mm.

Deflection at centre of span due to prestressing force

$$= \frac{PL^2}{48\, E_c I}\,(- 5e_1 + e_2) = \frac{2681.8 \times 10^3 \times 20^2 \times 10^6\,(- 5 \times 583 - 170)}{48 \times 35.36 \times 10^3 \times 72208 \times 10^6} = 71 \text{ mm } (\uparrow)$$

Deflection due to D.L. and L.L.

$$= \frac{5\,(W_d + W_l)\, l^4}{384\, E_c I} = \frac{5 \times (9.2 + 11)\,(30 \times 10^3)^4}{384 \times 35.36 \times 10^3 \times 72208 \times 10^6} = 83 \text{ mm}$$

If $\phi = 1.6,$

Long term deflection $= [0.87\,(- 71) + 83]\,[1 + 1.6]$

$$= 59 \text{ mm } (\downarrow)$$

Maximum permissible deflection $> \dfrac{\text{Span}}{250} = \dfrac{20 \times 10^3}{250} = 80$ mm   O.K.

IMPORTANT POINTS

- Moment of resistance of rectangular section.
- Effective reinforcement ratio.

QUESTIONS

1. A double tee section having a flange of 1200 mm wide and 150 mm thick is prestressed by 4700 mm^2 of high-tensile steel located at an effective depth of 1600 mm. The ribs have a thickness of 150 mm each. If the cable strength of the concrete is 40 N/mm^2 and tensile strength of the steel is 1600 N/mm^2, determine the flexural strength of the double tee girder using IS : code provisions.

2. A post-tensioned prestressed concrete tee beam with unbonded tendons is made up of a flange 300 mm wide by 150 mm thick and the thickness of the rib is 150 mm. The beam is prestressed by 24 H.T. wires of 5 mm diameter with an effective stress of 65 percent of the ultimate tensile strength of wires. The wires are located at an effective depth of 320 mm. Loss ratio is 0.8. If f_{ck} = 56 N/mm^2 and f_p = 1650 N/mm^2, estimate the flexural strength of the section assuming the span/depth ratio of the beam as 20.

3. A pre-tensioned concrete girder of box section 1 m × 1 m overall dimensions has a uniform wall thickness of 200 mm. The girder is post-tensioned by high-tensile wires of area 2250 mm^2 located at an effective depth of 900 mm. If f_{ck} = 40 N/mm^2 and f_p = 1600 N/mm^2, calculate the ultimate flexural strength of box girder section.

4. A pre-tensioned prestressed concrete tee section having a flange width of 1200 mm and thickness of flange 150 mm, thickness of web being 300 mm is prestressed by 4700 mm^2 of high-tensile steel located at an effective depth of 1600 mm. If f_{ck} = 40 N/mm^2 and f_p = 1600 N/mm^2, estimate the ultimate moment capacity of the pre-tensioned tee section.

5. A simply supported post-tensioned prestressed concrete deck slab of a road bridge is 500 mm thick spanning over 10 m. The slab is prestressed by Freyssinet cables each containing 12 high tensile wires of 8 mm diameter. The cables are spaced at 500 mm centres at an effective depth of 450 mm. If f_{ck} = 40 N/mm^2, f_p = 1600 N/mm^2, estimate the

    (a) ultimate flexural strength of the slab for 1 m width;

    (b) maximum permissible uniformly distributed ultimate live load on slab assuming a load factor of 1.5 for dead load.

UNIVERSITY QUESTIONS

Dec. 2011

Q. 1   Design a post tensioned prestressed concrete 'I' section beam for flexure to carry a live load of 10 kN/m over entire simply supported span of 15 m with M 40 grade of concrete and Freyssinet cables of 12/5 (f_y = 1750 Mpa) or 12/7 (f_y = 1500 Mpa), including the design of end block. Draw sketches showing cable profiles and end block reinforcement details. Check fiber stresses in concrete and deflection.
(Example 4.6)   **(25 Marks)**

May 2012

Q. 2 Design a post tensioned prestressed concrete 'I' or 'T' section beam for flexure to carry a live load 13 kN/m over entire simply supported span of 17 m with M45 grade of concrete and Freyssinet cables of 12/5 (f_y = 1750 Mpa) or 12/7 (f_y = 1500 Mpa), including the design of end block. Draw sketches showing cable profiles and end block reinforcement details. Check fibre stresses in concrete and deflection.
(Example 4.6) **(25 Marks)**

Dec. 2012

Q. 3 Design a post tensioned pre-stressed concrete 'I' or 'T' section beam for flexure to carry a live laod of 8 kN/m over entire simply supported span of 20 m with M_{40} of concrete and Freyssinet cables of 12/5 (F_y = 1750 MPa) or 12/7 (F_y = 1600 MPa) including design of end block. Draw sketches showing cable profiles and end block reinforcement details. Check fiber stresses in concrete and deflection.
(Example 4.6) **(25 Marks)**

May 2013

Q. 4 Design a post-tension prestressed concrete beam using I section for flexure to carry a live load of 15 kN/m over simply supported span of 18 m with M40 grade of concrete and freyssinet cables of 12/5 (f_y = 1750 Mpa) or 12/7 (f_y = 1500 Mpa), design the end block also. Draw sketches showing details of cable profile, end block reinforcement, check fiber stress in concrete and deflection.
(Example 4.6) **(25 Marks)**

Dec. 2014

Q. 5 Design a post tensioned prestressed concreted beam to carry a live load of 15 kN/m over simply supported span of 18 m only for flexure. The characteristic strength of concrete is 35 MPa. Use Freyssinet cables of 12/5 with f_y = 1750 MPa. Also design end block. Draw cable profiles at various sections. Check fiber stresses in concrete and deflection at mid-span. **(Example 4.6)** **(25 Marks)**

May 2015

Q. 6. Design a post tensioned presstressed concrete beam using I-section for flexure to carry a live load of 15 kN/m over simply supported span of 17 m with M 45 grade of concrete and Freyssinet cable of 12/5 (f_y = 1750 MPa) or 12/7 (f_y = 1500 MPa). Design the End block also. Draw sketches showing details of cable profile, end block reinforcement check for fiber stresses in concrete and deflection is must.
(Example 4.6) (25 Marks)

Chapter 5
SHEAR RESISTANCE OF PRESTRESSED CONCRETE MEMBERS

5.1 SHEAR RESISTANCE

There are two major modes of shear cracking in structural concrete beam. These are referred as web-shear cracks and flexure-shear cracks, as shown in Fig. 5.1.

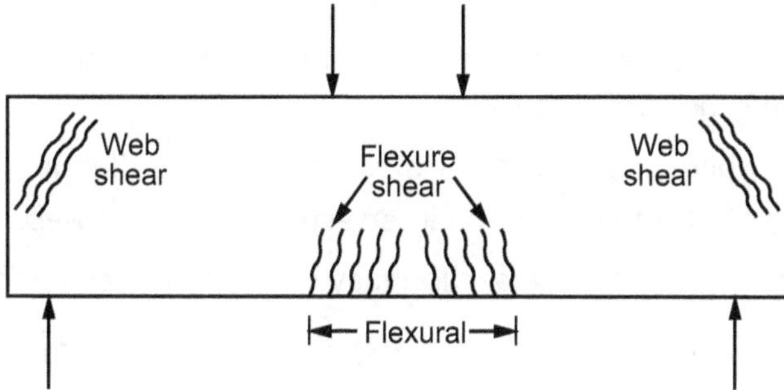

Fig. 5.1

Web-shear cracks generally start from an interior part, when the local principal tensile stress exceeds the tensile strength of concrete. This is likely to develop in highly prestressed beams with thin webs, particularly when the beam is subjected to large concentrated loads near a simple support (section uncracked in flexure).

Flexure-shear cracks are first initiated by flexural cracks in the inclined direction. Flexure-shear cracks develop when the combined shear and flexural tensile stresses produce a principal tensile stress exceeding the tensile strength of concrete (section cracked in flexure).

As per Clause 22.4 (IS : 1343-1980) :

The ultimate shear resistance of the concrete alone V_c, should be considered at both sections uncracked and cracked in flexure, the lesser value taken.

i.e. $V_c \left\langle \begin{matrix} V_{co} \\ V_{cr} \end{matrix} \right.$, lesser of V_{co} and V_{cr} taken.

5.1.1 Section Uncracked in Flexure (V_{co}) [Clause 22.4.1]

The ultimate shear resistance of a section uncracked in flexure $V_c = V_{co}$ is given by

$$V_{co} = 0.67\ bD\ \sqrt{f_t^2 + 0.8\ f_{cp}\ f_t} \qquad\qquad \text{... (5.1)}$$

where, b – Width of member, but for T, I and L beams, it should be b_w (width of rib)

D – Overall depth of member

f_t – Maximum principal tensile stress i.e. $0.24\sqrt{f_{ck}}$

f_{ck} – Characteristic compressive strength of concrete

f_{cp} – Compressive stress at the centroid of section due to prestress $\left(\dfrac{P_i}{A}\right)$

For inclined and curved tendons, vertical component of prestress normal to the longitudinal axis of the member may be added to V_{co}.

In flanged members, where the centroidal axis occurs in the flange, the principal tensile stress should be limited to $0.24\sqrt{f_{ck}}$ at the intersection of flanged web.

In this calculation, $0.8 \times f_{cp}$ at this intersection may be used in calculating V_{co}.

5.1.2 Sections Cracked in Flexure (V_{cr}) [Clause 22.4.2]

The ultimate shear resistance of a section cracked in flexure $V_c = V_{cr}$ is given by

$$V_{cr} = \left(1 - 0.55\ \frac{f_{pe}}{f_p}\right)\ \tau_c \cdot bd + M_o\ \frac{V}{M}\ \ngtr\ 0.1\ bd\ \sqrt{f_{ck}} \qquad \text{... (5.2)}$$

where, f_{pe} – Effective prestress after all losses have occurred

$\ngtr\ 0.6\ f_p.$

f_p – Characteristic strength of prestressing steel

τ_c – Ultimate shear stress capacity of concrete

b – Breadth of member (for flanged section, $b = b_w$)

d – Effective depth of section (y_t + eccentricity)

M_o – Moment required to produce zero stress in concrete

$$= 0.8\ f_{pt} \times \frac{I}{y}$$

f_{pt} – Stress due to prestress only at depth (d)

y – Distance of extreme tension fibre from centroid of section

I – M.I. about centroid of section

V, M – S.F. and B.M. at a section under consideration

For inclined tendons, vertical component of prestress is to be neglected.

Table 5.1 : Design shear strength of concrete, ξ_c, N/mm² (Clause 22.4.2)

$100\,\dfrac{A_p}{bd}$	Concrete grade		
	M 30	M 35	M 40 and above
(1)	(2)	(3)	(4)
0.25	0.37	0.37	0.38
0.50	0.50	0.50	0.51
0.75	0.59	0.59	0.60
1.00	0.66	0.67	0.68
1.25	0.71	0.73	0.74
1.50	0.76	0.78	0.79
1.75	0.80	0.82	0.84
2.00	0.84	0.86	0.88
2.25	0.88	0.90	0.92
2.50	0.91	0.93	0.95
2.75	0.94	0.96	0.98
3.00	0.96	0.99	1.01

Note : A_p is the area of prestressing tendon.

5.2 DESIGN OF SHEAR REINFORCEMENT [CLAUSE 22.4.3]

1. If design shear force (V_{uD}) < 0.5 V_c and in a member of minor importance,

    – No shear reinforcement is required.

2. If 0.5 V_c < V_{uD} < V_c, then provide nominal shear reinforcement

$$\frac{A_{sv}}{b_{sv}} = \frac{0.4}{0.87\,f_y}$$

3. V_{uD} > V_c – provide design shear reinforcement

$$\frac{A_{sv}}{S_v} = \frac{V_{uD} - V_c}{0.87\,f_y \cdot d_t}$$

where d_t – Depth from the extreme compression fibre either to the long bars or to the centroid of tendons, whichever is greater.

5.3 SPACING OF SHEAR REINFORCEMENT

1. The maximum spacing of stirrups should not exceed 0.75 d_t nor $4 \times$ web thickness.

2. If $V_{UD} > 1.8\,V_c$, then maximum spacing should be reduced to 0.5 d_t. The lateral spacing of the individual legs of the stirrups provided at a cross-section should not exceed 0.75 d_t.

3. If $V_{UD} \geq V_{c\,max}$ – then redesign the section.

$V_{c\,max}$ is taken from Table 5.2.

V_{UD} is calculated at a distance 'd' from the effective support. This will give us critical shear failure.

Table 5.2 : Maximum shear stress ($V_{c\,max}$)

Concrete grade	M 30	M 35	M 40	M 45	M 50	M 55 and over
Maximum shear stress, (N/mm²)	3.5	3.7	4.0	4.3	4.6	4.8

Solved Examples

Example 5.1 :

A simply supported beam of 25 m span subjected to a load of 20 kN/m inclusive of self weight and effective prestress force 1300 kN, as shown in Fig. 5.2.

Use M 40 grade of concrete and tensile strength of steel 1600 MPa.

The cable is parabolic with maximum eccentricity at mid-span and zero at ends.

Design beam for shear.

Area of steel provided 1810 mm².

Assume any suitable data, if required.

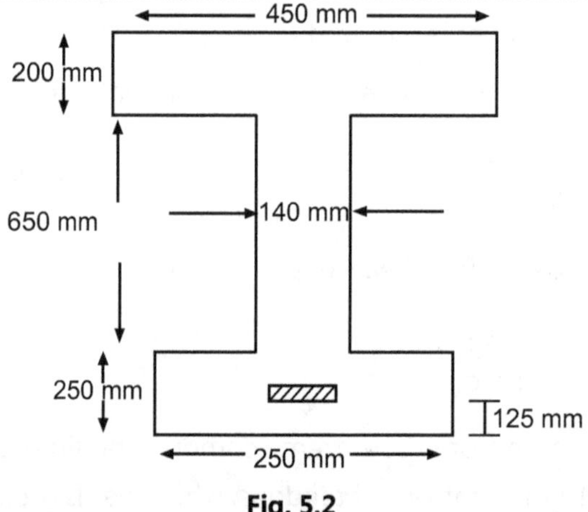

Fig. 5.2

Solution :

First calculate the neutral axis, let neutral axis lies from bottom of beam.

$$y_b = \frac{(450 \times 200) \times (1000) + (650 \times 140) \times (250 + 325) + (250 \times 250) \times 125}{(450 \times 200 + 650 \times 140 + 250 \times 250)}$$

$$y_b = 616.6 \text{ mm}$$

$$\therefore \quad y_t = (1100 - 616.6) = 483.4 \text{ mm}$$

Now, **the ultimate shear resistance for uncracked section is as**

$$V_{co} = 0.67 \, bD \sqrt{f_t^2 + 0.8 \, f_{cp} \times f_t} + P_v$$

where
$$f_t = 0.24 \sqrt{f_{ck}} = 0.24 \sqrt{40} = 1.52 \text{ N/mm}^2$$

$$f_{cp} = \frac{P}{A} = \frac{1300 \times 10^3}{243500} = 5.33 \text{ N/mm}^2$$

and
$$P_v = \text{Vertical component of prestressing force}$$

$$= P \sin \theta$$

where θ is the slope of parabolic tendon profile at support.

Since, the cable is provided in parabolic shape,

i.e.
$$y = \frac{4e}{l^2} (lx - x^2)$$

$$\frac{dy}{dx} = \tan \theta = \frac{4e}{l^2} (l - 2x)$$

At support, $x = 0$, $\dfrac{dy}{dx} = \tan \theta = \dfrac{4e}{l^2}$

$$\theta = \frac{4e}{l^2} \quad [\because \tan \theta \cong \theta, \text{ if } \theta \text{ is small}]$$

$$\theta = \frac{4 \times 491.6}{25000} = 0.0786 \text{ radians}$$

Effective depth, $d = e + y_t$

$$975 = e + 483.4$$

$$e = 491.6 \text{ mm}$$

$$\therefore \quad P_v = P \sin \theta = 1300 \times \sin \left\{ 0.0786 \times \frac{180}{\pi} \right\} = 102 \text{ kN}$$

$$\therefore \quad V_{co} = 0.67 \times 140 \times 1100 \sqrt{1.52^2 + 0.8 \times 5.33 \times 1.52} + 10.2$$

$$V_{co} = 408 \text{ kN}$$

The ultimate shear resistance for cracked flexure is as

$$V_{cr} = \left(1 - 0.55\,\frac{f_{pe}}{f_p}\right) \tau_c \cdot b \cdot d \; + \; M_o \cdot \frac{V}{M} \; \nleqslant \; 0.1\, bd\,\sqrt{f_{ck}}$$

where τ_c is calculated as

$$\frac{100\,A_p}{bd} \;=\; \frac{100 \times 1810}{140 \times 975} \;=\; 1.326$$

Referring Table 5.1, we get,

$$\tau_c \;=\; 0.75 \text{ N/mm}^2$$

$$f_{pe} \;\ngtr\; 0.6\, f_p \;=\; 0.6 \times 1600 \;=\; 960 \text{ N/mm}^2$$

and

$$M_o \;=\; 0.8\, f_{pt}\,\frac{I}{y}$$

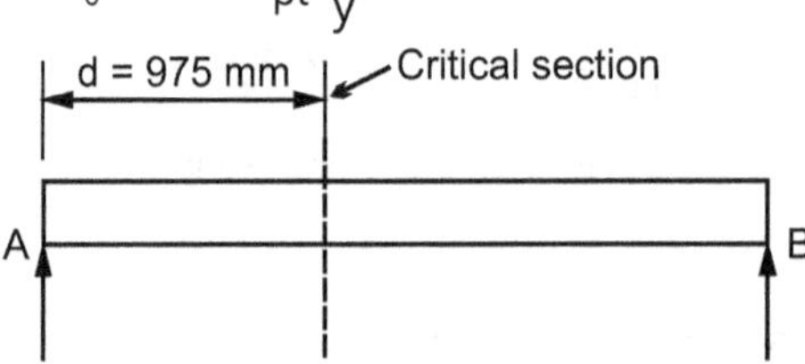

Fig. 5.3

Now, y at a distance 'd' from support, is calculated as

$$y \;=\; \frac{4e\,(ld - d^2)}{l^2} \;=\; \frac{4 \times 491.6 \times (25000 \times 975 - 975^2)}{(25000)^2}$$

$$y \;=\; 73.7 \text{ mm}$$

and

$$I \;=\; 3.23 \times 10^{10} \text{ mm}^4$$

$$f_{pt} \;=\; \frac{P}{A} + \frac{P \cdot e \cdot y}{I} \;=\; \frac{1300 \times 10^3}{243500} + \frac{1300 \times 10^3 \times (73.7)^2}{3.23 \times 10^{10}}$$

$$=\; 5.34 \text{ N/mm}^2 \; [\because \text{ at critical section, } e = y]$$

$$\therefore \quad M_o \;=\; 0.8 \times 5.34 \times \frac{3.23 \times 10^4}{(73.7)} \;=\; 1872.88 \times 10^6 \text{ N-mm}$$

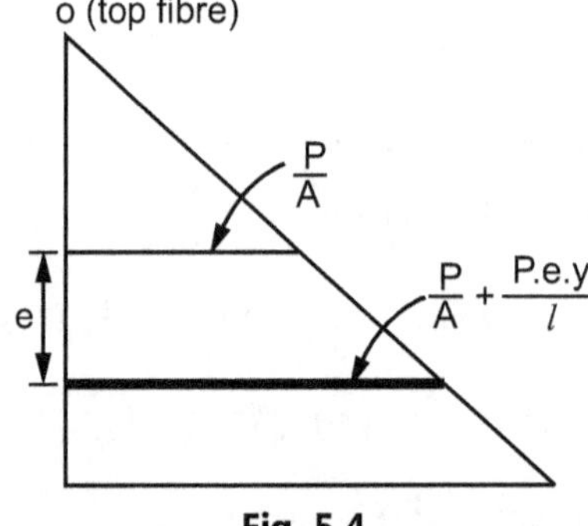

Fig. 5.4

Now,

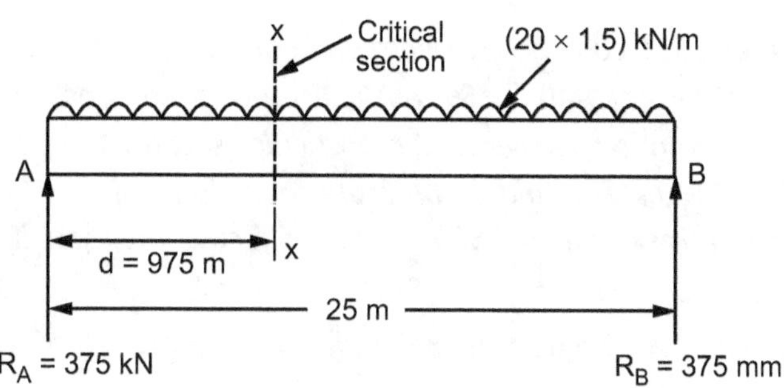

Fig. 5.5

Shear force (V) at critical section X-X;

$$V = 375 - (20 \times 1.5) \times 0.975 = 345.75 \text{ kN} \approx 346 \times 10^6 \text{ N-mm}$$

Also, bending moment (M) about critical section X-X

$$= 375 \times 0.975 - 20 \times 1.5 \times \frac{0.975^2}{2}$$

$$= 351.375 \times 10^6 \text{ N-mm}$$

$$\therefore \quad V_{cr} = \left(1 - 0.55 \times \frac{960}{1600}\right) \times 0.75 \times 140 \times 975 + \frac{1872.88 \times 10^6 \times 346 \times 10^6}{351.375 \times 10^6}$$

$$V_{cr} = 1913 \text{ kN}$$

$$\therefore \quad V_c \text{ is lesser of} \begin{cases} V_{co} = 408 \text{ kN} \\ V_{cr} = 1913 \text{ kN} \end{cases}$$

$$\text{Adopt value } V_c = 408 \text{ kN.}$$

Since V_{uD} = 346 kN is more than 0.5 V_c (= 0.5 × 408 kN)

therefore, we provide nominal shear reinforcement.

Using 2 legged 8 ϕ $\left(A_\phi = 2 \times \frac{\pi}{4} \times 8^2 \approx 100 \text{ mm}^2\right)$.

$$\text{Spacing,} \quad S_v = \frac{0.87 \, f_y \, A_{sv}}{0.4 \times b} = \frac{0.87 \times 415 \times (100)}{0.4 \times 140}$$

$$= 644.73 \text{ mm c/c}$$

But maximum permissible spacing,

$$S_v \leq 0.75 \times d_t = 0.75 \times 975 = 731 \text{ mm}$$

$$\leq 4 \times b_w = 4 \times 140 = 560 \text{ mm}$$

Adopt 500 mm c/c.

Provided 2 legged 8 ϕ @ 500 mm c/c.

Example 5.2 :

The cross-section of a prestressed concrete beam is an unsymmetrical I-section with an overall depth of 1300 mm. Thickness of web is 150 mm. Distance of top and bottom fibres from the centroid are 545 and 755 mm respectively. At a particular section, the beam is subjected to an ultimate moment M = 2130 kN-m and an ultimate shear force of 237 kN. Effective depth d = 1100 mm, f_{ck} = 45 N/mm² and f_p = 1500 N/mm². Effective prestress in tendons after losses f_{pe} = 890 N/mm², f_{pt} = 19.3 N/mm², I = 665 × 10⁸ mm⁴, A_p = 2310 mm². Estimate the ultimate shear resistance of the section cracked in flexure using IS : 1343 code specifications.

Solution :

$$M_o = \frac{0.8\, f_{pt} \cdot I}{y_b} = \frac{0.8 \times 19.3 \times 665 \times 10^8}{755}$$

$$= 138 \times 10^7 \text{ N-mm}$$

$$\frac{100\, A_p}{b_w d} = \frac{100 \times 2310}{150 \times 1100} = 1.40$$

From Table 5.1 for f_{ck} = 45 N/mm².

$$\tau_c = 0.77$$

The ultimate shear resistance of section cracked in flexure is

$$V_{cr} = \left[1 - 0.55\, \frac{f_{pe}}{f_p}\right] \tau_c \cdot b \cdot d + M_o\, \frac{V}{M}$$

$$= \left[1 - 0.55 \times \frac{890}{1500}\right] (0.77 \times 150 \times 1100) + (138 \times 10^7) \left[\frac{237 \times 10^3}{2130 \times 10^6}\right]$$

$$= 240 \times 10^3 \text{ N} = 240 \text{ kN}$$

But　　　　$V_{cr} \ngtr 0.1 \times bd \times \sqrt{f_{ck}}$

$$\ngtr 0.1 \times 150 \times 1100 \sqrt{45}$$

$$\ngtr 110.685 \text{ kN}$$

∴　　　　$V_{cr} = 240$ kN　　　　　　　　　　**... Ans.**

Example 5.3 :

The support section of a prestressed concrete beam 100 mm × 250 mm is required to support an ultimate shear force of 60 kN. The compressive prestress at centroid is 5 N/mm², f_{ck} = 40 N/mm², effective cover to R/F = 50 mm. If f_y = 415 N/mm², design suitable R/F in the section using IS : 1343 code recommendations.

Solution :

Given :　　　　$b = 100$ mm,　　　　　$f_y = 415$ N/mm²

$D = 250$ mm,　　　　　$f_{cp} = 5$ N/mm²

$d = 200$ mm,　　　　　$f_t = 0.24 \sqrt{f_{ck}} = 0.24 \sqrt{40} = 1.517$ N/mm²

$V = 60$ kN,　　　　　$f_{ck} = 40$ N/mm²

For the support section uncracked in flexure,

$$V_{co} = 0.67\, bD \sqrt{f_t^2 + 0.8\, f_{cp}\, f_t}$$

$$= (0.67 \times 100 \times 250) \sqrt{1.517^2 + 0.8 \times 5 \times 1.517}$$

$$= 48407 \text{ N} = 48.407 \text{ kN}$$

$$\text{Balance shear force} = (V_{UD} - V_{co})$$

$$= (60 - 48.4) = 11.6 \text{ kN}$$

Using 6 mm ϕ two legged stirrups,

Spacing is given by,

$$S_V = \left[\frac{A_{sv} \times 0.87\, f_y \times d}{(V_{UD} - V_{co})} \right]$$

$$= \left[\frac{2 \times \left(\dfrac{\pi}{4} \times 6^2 \right) \times 0.87 \times 250 \times 200}{11.6 \times 10^3} \right]$$

$$= 212 \text{ mm}$$

$$\text{Maximum possible spacing} = S_V \ngtr 0.75\, d$$

$$\ngtr 0.75 \times 200$$

$$\ngtr 150 \text{ mm}$$

Provided 6 mm ϕ two legged stirrups at 150 mm centres.　　　　**... Ans.**

IMPORTANT POINTS

- Ultimate shear resistance for section uncracked in flexure and cracked in flexure.
- Formulae for ultimate shear resistance uncracked in flexure V_c.
- Formulae for ultimate shear resistance cracked in flexure V_{cr}.

QUESTIONS

1. Design for shear of a post-tensioned beam with the following data :

   Ultimate bending moment (M) = 250 kN-m.

   Ultimate shear force (V) = 100 kN.

   Area of prestressing strands = 506 mm².

   Ultimate tensile strength of strands (f_p) = 1820 N/mm².

   Cube strength of concrete (f_{ck}) = 40 N/mm².

   Prestressing force (P) = 500 kN, Eccentricity (e) = 150 mm.

   Width of section (b) = 400 mm, Overall depth (D) = 550 mm.

   Effective depth (d) = 425 mm.

   Effective stress in steel $= \dfrac{500 \times 10^3}{506}$ = 988 N/mm², and assume any suitable data, if required.

2. The support section of a prestressed concrete beam, 120 mm wide and 250 mm deep, is required to support an ultimate shear force of 60 kN. The compressive prestress at the centroidal axis is 5 N/mm². The characteristic cube strength of concrete is 40 N/mm². The cover to the tension reinforcement is 50 mm. If the characteristic tensile strength of steel in stirrups is 250 N/mm², design the suitable reinforcements at the section using IS : 1343 code specifications.

3. An unsymmetrical I-section bridge girder has the following sectional properties :

   Area of cross-section = 777 × 10³ mm², second moment of area = 22 × 10¹⁰ mm⁴, width and thickness of top flange = 1200 mm and 360 mm respectively and thickness of web = 240 mm. The centroid of the section is located at 580 mm from the top. The girder is used over a span of 40 m. The tendons with a cross-section of 700 mm² are parabolic with an eccentricity of 1220 mm at the centre of span and zero at the supports. The effective prestress in the wires is 800 N/mm². If the tensile strength of concrete is 4.5 N/mm², estimate the ultimate shear resistance of the section uncracked in flexure. Overall depth is 2000 mm.

Chapter 6

DEFLECTION OF PRESTRESSED
CONCRETE MEMBERS

6.1 INTRODUCTION

The deflection of prestressed concrete member is also an important consideration in designing the size of the member and the amount of prestressing force. It is necessary that the member must be designed to remain sufficiently stiff against deflection so that the member remains not only strong but serviceable at working loads. Large deflections of members will make the member appear unsightly from architectural considerations. Such large deflections may adversely damage finishes and partitions. In the case of beams of large spans, deflection limitation may become the criteria for the design. The various factors influencing the deflections of members are :

(1)   Dead load and live load.

(2)   Magnitude of the prestressing force.

(3)   The profile of the cable.

(4)   The geometry of the section of the member.

(5)   Shrinkage and creep of the concrete.

(6)   Stress relaxation of the tendons.

(7)   End conditions of the member, etc.

The methods of deflection calculations are different in the "pre-crack" condition and "post-crack" condition.

In the "pre-cracking" stage, the whole cross-section is effective and the deflections in this stage are computed by using the second moment of area of the gross concrete section.

In the "post-cracking" stage, a prestressed concrete beam behaves in a manner similar to that of a reinforced concrete beam and the computation of deflections in this stage is made by considering moment curvature relationships which involve the section properties of the cracked beam.

In both cases, the effect of creep and shrinkage of concrete is to increase the long-term deflections under constantly prevailing loads. Such deflections are determined by either using long-term modulus of elasticity or by magnifying short-term deflection by a suitable correcting factor.

6.2 SHORT-TERM DEFLECTIONS OF UNCRACKED MEMBERS

Short-term deflections of prestressed members are governed by the bending moment distribution along the span and the flexural rigidity of the members.

Generally, the variation of the tension in the tendons has negligible effect on the short-term deflection caused by the loads provided the beam remains uncracked and the strain increases with stress in concrete and steel. In uncracked condition of the beam, the short-term deflections are determined by elastic theory.

In this case, we consider the moment due to eccentricity of the tendons. The moment diagram due to eccentricities of the tendons can be drawn and the deflections at mid-point are directly calculated from the second moment area theorem.

6.3 EFFECT OF TENDON PROFILE ON DEFLECTIONS

In most of the cases of prestressed beams, tendons are provided with eccentricity towards the soffit of beams so that the sagging moment produced by the external loads are counteracted to some extent.

The forces transmitted by the tendon on the beam deflect the beam upwards. The upward deflections produced due to some symmetrical cable profiles are summarized below in Table 6.1.

Table 6.1 : Value of central deflection (δ) for different cable profiles

Sr. No.	Cable - profile	Bending moment diagram due to cable	Deflection due to cable	Central deflection (δ)
01.	Straight Tendons 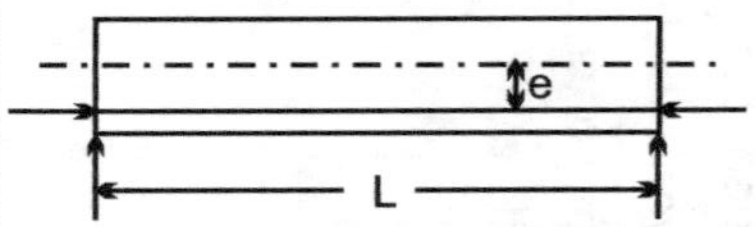	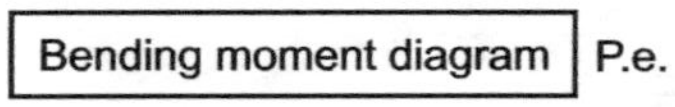 Bending moment diagram — $P.e.$	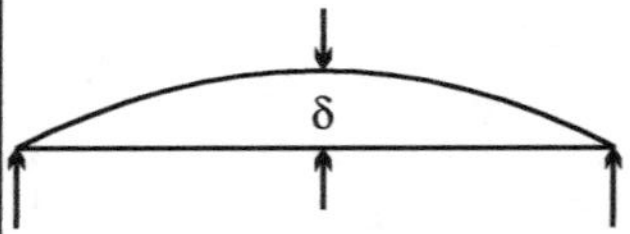 δ	$\dfrac{P.e.L^2}{8\,EI}$
02.	Trapezoidal Tendons 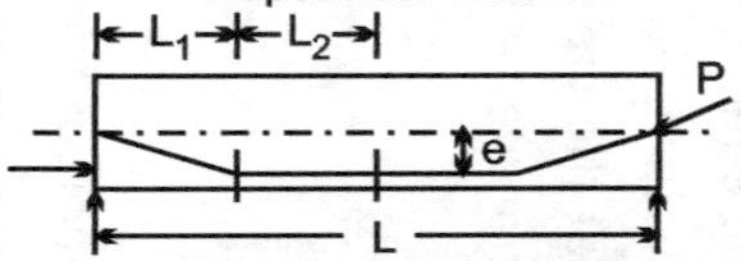 (L_1, L_2)	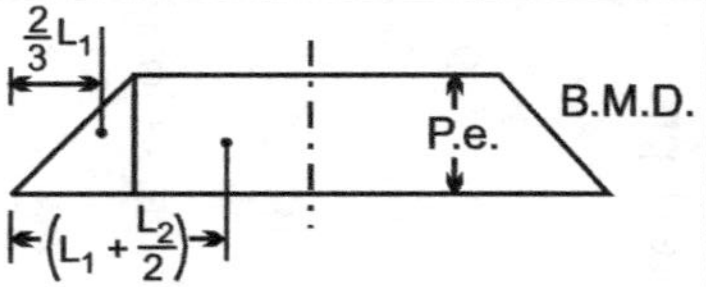 B.M.D. — $P.e.$; $\dfrac{2}{3}L_1$, $\left(L_1 + \dfrac{L_2}{2}\right)$	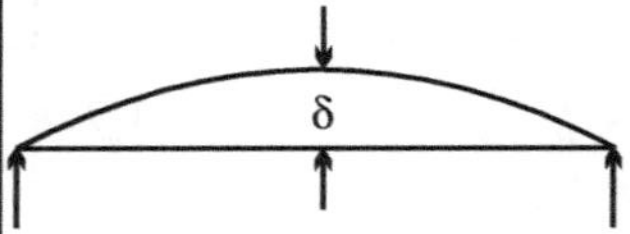 δ	$\dfrac{Pe}{6\,EI}\left[2l^2 + 6l_1 l_2 + 3l_2^2\right]$
03.	Parabolic Tendons (Central Anchors) 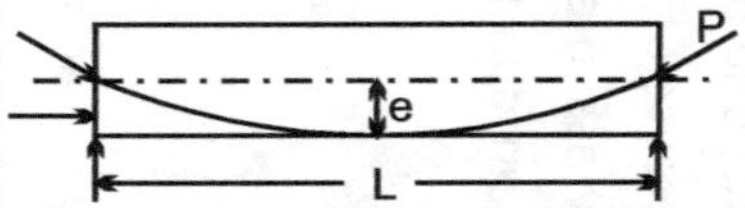	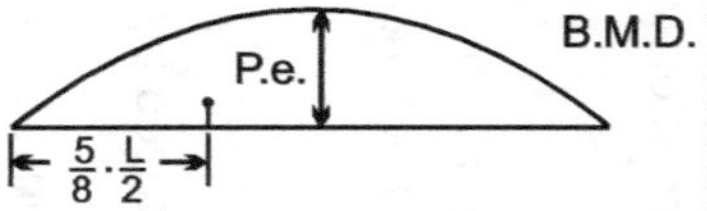 B.M.D. — $P.e.$; $\dfrac{5}{8}\cdot\dfrac{L}{2}$	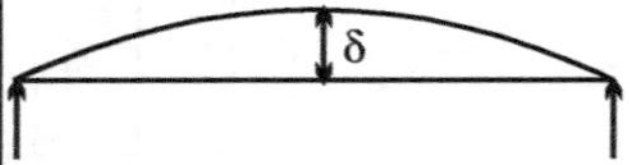 δ	$\dfrac{5\,PeL^2}{48\,EI}$
04.	Parabolic Tendons (Eccentric Anchors) 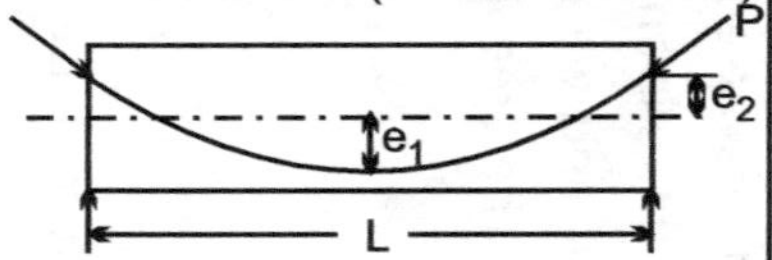	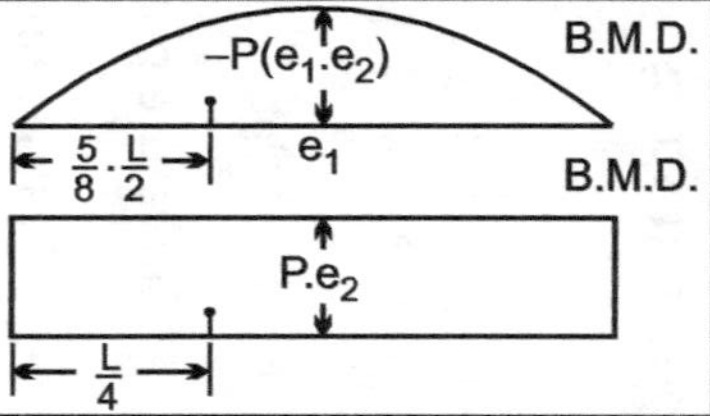 B.M.D. — $-P(e_1.e_2)$, e_1, $\dfrac{5}{8}\dfrac{L}{2}$; B.M.D. — $P.e_2$, $\dfrac{L}{4}$	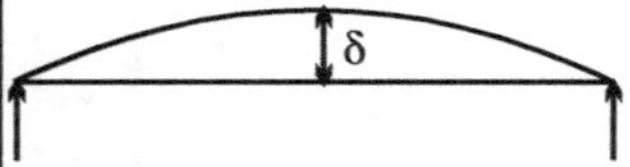 δ	$\dfrac{PL^2}{48\,EI}\left[-5e_1 + e_2\right]$
05.	Sloping Tendons (Eccentric Anchors) 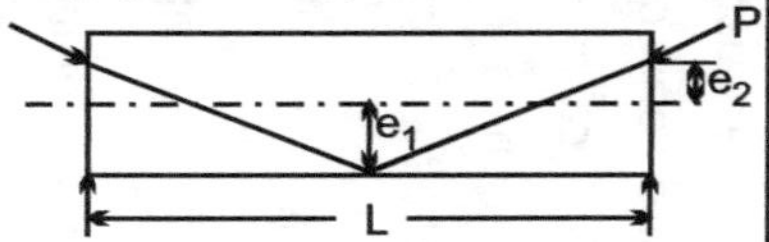	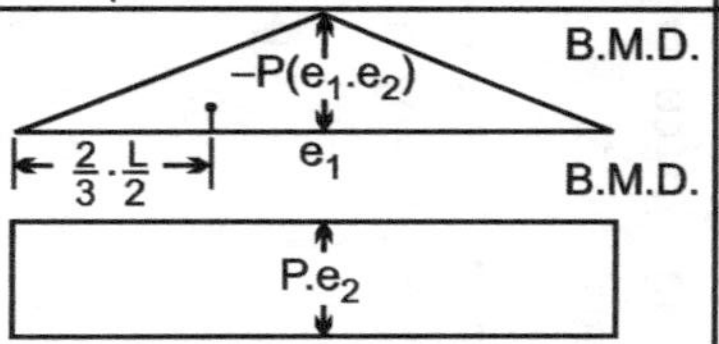 B.M.D. — $-P(e_1.e_2)$, e_1, $\dfrac{2}{3}\dfrac{L}{2}$; B.M.D. — $P.e_2$	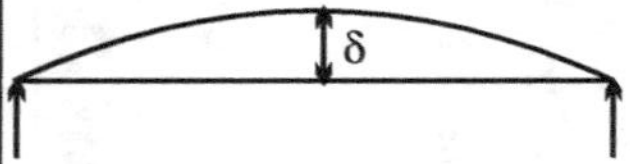 δ	$\dfrac{PL^2}{24\,EI}\left[-2e_1 + e_2\right]$
06.	Parabolic and Straight Tendons 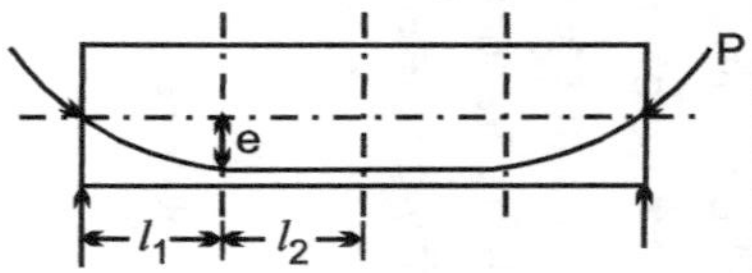 (l_1, l_2)	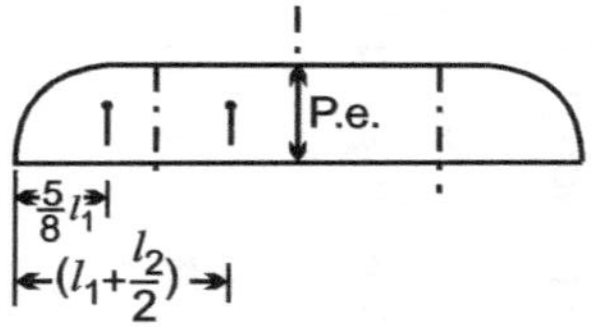 $P.e.$; $\dfrac{5}{8}l_1$, $\left(l_1 + \dfrac{l_2}{2}\right)$		$\dfrac{-Pe}{12\,EI}\left[5l_1^2 + 12l_1 l_2 + 6l_2^2\right]$

Notes :

(1) Upward deflections are considered as negative ($\uparrow$, –).

(2) Deflections due to self weight and imposed loads $= \dfrac{5}{384} \dfrac{(w_d + w_L)\, L^4}{EI}$ and it is taken as downward deflection ($\downarrow$, +).

(3) P = effective prestressing force.

(4) e = eccentricity.

(5) L = length of the beam.

(6) w_d = self weight of the beam/m.

(7) w_L = imposed load/m.

(8) Deflection due to concentrated loads (w) $= \dfrac{WL^3}{48\,EI}$.

6.4 LONG-TIME DEFLECTION

Creep and shrinkage of concrete, and stress relaxation of steel produce changes in the deflection of beams.

There are two opposing effects producing deformations, namely prestress effect and transverse load effect. At any stage, the resultant curvature ϕ_t, at any section is given by

$$\phi_t = \phi_{mt} + \phi_{pt} \qquad \qquad \text{... (6.1)}$$

where ϕ_{mt} – Curvature produced by transverse loads

ϕ_{pt} – Curvature produced by prestress

When maintained under sustained transverse loads, due to the effect of creep, there will be increase of strain and consequently there is an increase of curvature. However, the change in stress in the practical cases is small and we may assume that the creep of concrete takes place practically at constant stress. The creep strain due to transverse loads at any time 't' may be determined as

$$\phi_{mt} = (1 + \phi)\, \phi_i \qquad \qquad \text{... (6.2)}$$

where ϕ – Creep coefficient

ϕ_i – Initial curvature caused by the application of transverse load.

Curvature produced by prestress (ϕ_{pt}) depends on the combined effect of creep and shrinkage of concrete and stress relaxation of the steel.

According to A.M. Neville :

The curvature produced due to prestress at time 't' is given by

$$\phi_{pt} = -\frac{P_i e}{E}\left[1 - \frac{\Delta P_i}{P_i} + \left(1 - \frac{\Delta P_i}{2P_i}\right)\phi\right] \qquad \ldots (6.3)$$

where, P_i – Initial prestress

P_t – Prestress after a time 't'

$\Delta P_i = (P_i - P_t)$ = loss of prestress due to creep, shrinkage and stress relaxation.

Let, δ_{it} = Initial deflection due to transverse loads

δ_{ip} = Initial deflection due to prestress.

Then the total long-time deflection after time 't' is given by

$$\delta_t = \delta_{it}(1 + \phi) - \delta_{ip}\left\{1 - \frac{\Delta P_i}{P_i} + \left(1 - \frac{\Delta P_i}{2P_i}\right)\phi\right\} \qquad \ldots (6.4)$$

Note : In the expression above, –ve sign indicates upward deflection.

According to Lin, the long-time deflection after time 't' is given by

$$\delta_t = \left[\delta_{it} - \delta_{ip} \cdot \frac{P_t}{P_i}\right](1 + \phi) \qquad \ldots (6.5)$$

Solved Examples

Example 6.1 :

A prestressed concrete beam with a cross-section 120 mm wide and 300 mm deep is used to support a uniformly distributed live load of 3 kN/m over an effective span of 6 m. The beam is prestressed by a straight cable carrying an effective prestressing force of 180 kN at a constant eccentricity of 50 mm.

Given : E_c = 38 kN/mm², modulus of rupture = 5 N/mm², area of the cable = 200 mm² and modular ratio = 6.

Estimate the deflection of the beam at the following stages :

(a) Working load.

(b) Cracking load.

Solution :

The loaded prestressed concrete beam with its rectangular section is shown in Fig. 6.1.

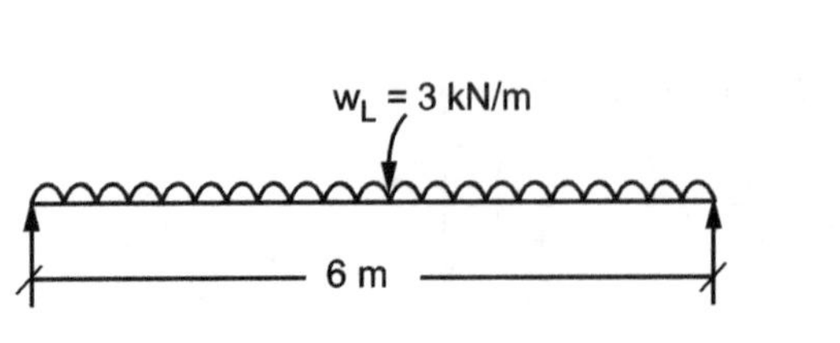

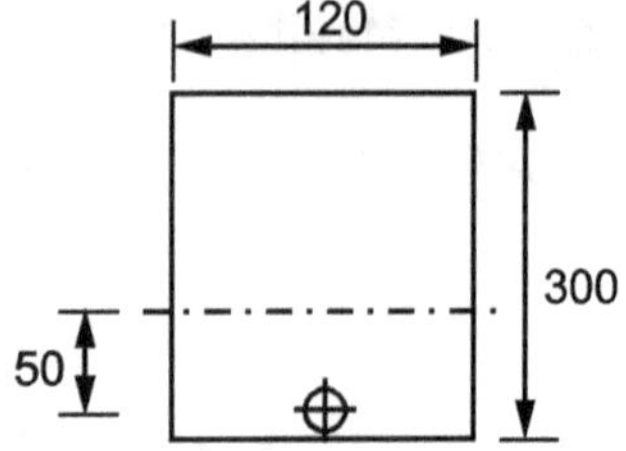

Fig. 6.1

P = 180 kN	Modular ratio = 6
e = 50 mm	Modulus of rupture = 5 N/mm²
E_c = 38 kN/mm²	

$$I = \frac{1}{12} \times 120 \times 300^3 = 27 \times 10^7 \text{ mm}^4$$

$$z = \frac{I}{150} = 18 \times 10^5 \text{ mm}^3$$

Now, Self weight of the beam (w_d) = $(0.120 \times 0.300 \times 25)$ = 0.90 kN/m

Imposed load (w_L) = 3.00 kN/m

Total load ($w_d + w_L$) = 3.90 kN/m

$$\text{Deflection due to total load} = \frac{5\,(w_d + w_L)\,L^4}{384 \times EI} \ (\downarrow)$$

$$= \frac{5 \times 3.90 \times 10^{-3} \times (6 \times 10^3)^4}{384 \times 38 \times 27 \times 10^7} = 6.41 \text{ mm} \ (\downarrow)$$

$$\text{Deflection due to prestressing force} = \frac{PeL^2}{8\,EI} \ (\uparrow)$$

$$= \frac{180 \times 50 \times (6 \times 10^3)^2}{8 \times 38 \times 27 \times 10^7} = 3.94 \text{ mm} \ (\uparrow)$$

(a) At working load :

Resultant deflection = $(6.41 - 3.94)$ = 2.47 mm ($\downarrow$)   ... **Ans.**

(b) At cracking load :

$$\text{Working moment} = \frac{(w_d + w_L)\,l^2}{8} = \frac{3.90 \times 6^2}{8} = 17.55 \text{ kN-m}$$

$$\text{Resultant stress at bottom fibre} = \frac{P}{A} + \frac{P \cdot e}{z} - \frac{M}{z}$$

$$= \frac{180 \times 10^3}{120 \times 300} + \frac{180 \times 10^3 \times 50}{18 \times 10^5} - \frac{17.55 \times 10^6}{18 \times 10^5}$$

$$= (5 + 5 - 9.75) = 0.25 \text{ N/mm}^2$$

Now, extra moment required to cause cracking $= fz$

$$= \frac{(5 + 0.25) \times 18 \times 10^5}{10^6} = 9.45 \text{ kN-m}$$

$\therefore$ Total cracking moment $= (17.55 + 9.45) = 27 \text{ kN-m}$

$\therefore$ Cracking load $= \dfrac{M \times 8}{l^2} = \dfrac{27 \times 8}{6^2} = 6 \text{ kN-m}$

$\therefore$ Deflection due to cracking load $= \dfrac{5 \times (6 \times 10^{-3}) \times (6 \times 10^3)^4}{384 \times 38 \times 27 \times 10^7} \; (\downarrow)$

$$= 9.86 \text{ mm} \; (\downarrow)$$

$\therefore$ Resultant deflection $= (9.86 - 3.94) = 5.92 \text{ mm} \; (\downarrow)$ **... Ans.**

Example 6.2 :

A concrete beam with a cross-sectional area of 36×10^3 mm² and radius of gyration of 75 mm is prestressed by a parabolic cable carrying an effective stress of 1200 N/mm². The span of the beam is 8 m. The cable composed of 6 wires of 7 mm diameter, has an eccentricity of 50 mm at the centre and zero at the supports. Neglecting all losses, find the central deflection of the beam as follows :

(a) Self weight + prestress, and

(b) Self weight + prestress + live load of 3 kN/m.

Assume $E_c = 36$ kN/mm² and density of concrete $= 25$ kN/m³.

Solution :

Given : $A = 36 \times 10^3$ mm², $w_d = \dfrac{36 \times 10^3 \times 25}{10^6} = 0.9$ kN/m

          $L = 8000$ mm, $P = 6 \times 38.5 \times 1200 = 276.9$ kN

          $e = 50$ mm, $I = A \times 75^2 = (36 \times 10^3 \times 75^2) = 202.5 \times 10^6$ mm⁴

Now, Deflection due to self weight $= \dfrac{5 \, w_d \, L^4}{384 \, EI} \; (\downarrow)$

$$= \left(\frac{5 \times 0.9 \times 10^{-3} \times 8000^4}{384 \times 36 \times 202.5 \times 10^6} \right) = 6.58 \text{ mm} \; (\downarrow)$$

Deflection due to live load $= \left(\dfrac{6.58}{0.9} \times 3 \right) = 21.93 \text{ mm} \; (\downarrow)$

Deflection due to prestressing force $= \dfrac{5 \, PeL^2}{48 \, EI} \; (\uparrow)$

$$= \left(\frac{5 \times 276.9 \times 50 \times 8000^2}{48 \times 36 \times 202.5 \times 10^6} \right) = 12.66 \text{ mm } (\uparrow)$$

(a)   Deflection due to (self weight + prestress) :

$$= (12.66 - 6.58) = 6.08 \text{ mm } (\uparrow)$$

(b)   Deflection due to (self weight + prestress + live load)

$$= (6.58 - 12.66 + 21.93) = 15.85 \text{ mm } (\downarrow) \quad \text{... \textbf{Ans.}}$$

Example 6.3 :

A rectangular concrete beam of cross-section 120 mm wide and 250 mm deep is simply supported over a span of 6 m and is prestressed by means of a symmetric parabolic cable, at a distance of 50 mm from the bottom of the beam at mid-span and 75 mm from the top of the beam at support sections. If the force in the cable is 300 kN and modulus of elasticity of concrete is 36 kN/mm², calculate :

(a)   The deflection at mid-span when the beam is supporting its own weight.

(b)   The concentrated load which must be applied at mid-span to restore it to the level of supports.

Solution :

Given : $P = 300$ kN, $E_c = 36$ kN/mm², $e_1 = 75$ mm, $e_2 = 50$ mm,

$$I = 1562.5 \times 10^5 \text{ mm}^4, \quad L = 6000 \text{ mm}$$

Now, Self weight of the beam $(w_d) = (0.120 \times 0.250 \times 25) = 0.75$ kN/m

$$\text{Deflection due to self weight} = \left(\frac{5 \times 0.00075 \times 6000^4}{384 \times 36 \times 1562.5 \times 10^5} \right) = 2.25 \text{ mm } (\downarrow)$$

$$\text{Deflection due to prestressing force} = \frac{PL^2}{48 \text{ EI}} \, (- 5e_1 + e_2) \, (\uparrow)$$

$$= \frac{300 \times 6000^2}{48 \times 36 \times 1562.5 \times 10^5} \, (-5 \times 75 + 50)$$

$$= 13 \text{ mm } (\uparrow)$$

(a)   Deflection due to (prestress + self weight)

$$= (13 - 2.25) = 10.75 \text{ mm } (\uparrow)$$

(b)   If $Q = $ concentrated load required at the centre of span, then

$$\frac{QL^3}{48 \text{ EI}} = 10.75$$

$$\therefore \qquad Q = \left(\frac{10.75 \times 48 \times 36 \times 1562.5 \times 10^5}{6000^3} \right) = 13.44 \text{ kN} \qquad \text{... \textbf{Ans.}}$$

Example 6.4 :

A concrete beam with a section 90 mm wide and 180 mm deep is prestressed by two wires of 7 mm diameter initially stressed to 920 N/mm². The wires are located in a parabolic profile with an eccentricity of 36.8 mm at the centre span (3m) and concentric at the supports. The beam supports two concentrated live loads of 7 kN each spaced 1 m apart. The modulus of elasticity of concrete is 30.9 kN/mm². Compute the initial deflection of the beam at the centre of span under (prestress + self weight) and the final deflection, including live loads, assuming 15% loss in prestress due to various causes. Compare these deflections with the limits prescribed in the IS : 1343-1980.

Assume, creep coefficient (ϕ) = 1.6.

Solution :

The concrete beam prestressed by a parabolic cable and supporting concentrated loads at one third points is shown in Fig. 6.2.

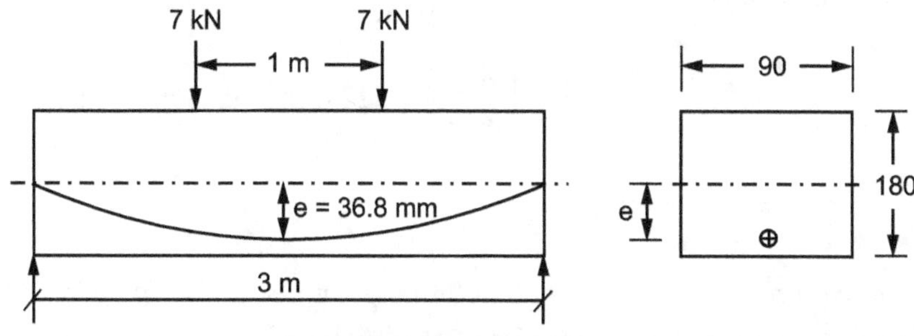

Fig. 6.2

$E_c = 30.9 \text{ kN/mm}^2$, $I = \dfrac{1}{12} \times 90 \times 180^3 = 43.74 \times 10^6 \text{ mm}^4$, $P = (2 \times 38.4 \times 920) = 70.8 \text{ kN.}$

Self weight of the beam (w_d) = $(0.09 \times 0.18 \times 25)$ = 0.405 kN/m

$$\text{Deflection due to self weight} = \frac{5 w_d L^4}{384 \, EI} \, (\downarrow) = \left(\frac{5 \times 0.000405 \times 3000^4}{384 \times 30.9 \times 43.74 \times 10^6} \right)$$

$$= 0.32 \text{ mm}$$

$$\text{Deflection due to live load} = \frac{Wa}{24 \, EI} \, (3L^2 - 4a^2) \, (\downarrow)$$

$$= \frac{7 \times 1000}{24 \times 30.9 \times 43.74 \times 10^6} \, (3 \times 3000^2 - 4 \times 1000^2)$$

$$= 4.96 \text{ mm}$$

Deflection due to prestressing force $= \dfrac{5\ PeL^2}{48\ EI}\ (\uparrow)$

$$= \left(\dfrac{5 \times 70.8 \times 36.8 \times 3000^2}{48 \times 30.9 \times 43.74 \times 10^6}\right) = 1.80 \text{ mm}$$

(a) Deflection due to (prestress + self weight)

$$= (1.8 - 0.32)\ = 1.48 \text{ mm } (\uparrow)$$

(b) Deflection due to (prestress + self weight + live load) including effect of creep

$$= [(-\ 0.85 \times 1.8) + 0.32 + 4.96]\ (1 + 1.6)$$

$$= 9.75 \text{ mm } (\downarrow)$$

But according to IS : 1343-1980,

Maximum permissible limiting deflection $= \left(\dfrac{\text{span}}{250}\right)$

$$= \left(\dfrac{3000}{250}\right)\ = 12 \text{ mm} > 9.75 \text{ mm (Hence safe)}$$

... Ans.

Example 6.5 :

A concrete beam with a rectangular section 100 mm wide and 300 mm deep, is stressed by 3 cables, each carrying an effective force of 240 kN. The span of the beam is 10 m. The first cable is parabolic with an eccentricity of 50 mm below the centroidal axis at the centre of span and 50 mm above the centroidal axis at the supports. The second cable is parabolic with zero eccentricity at the supports and an eccentricity of 50 mm at the centre of span. The third cable is straight with a uniform eccentricity of 50 mm below the centroidal axis. Estimate the instantaneous deflection due to

(a) Prestress + self weight; and

(b) Prestress + self weight + live load of 5 kN/m.

Assume, modulus of elasticity of concrete of 38 kN/mm².

Solution :

The concrete beam of rectangular section prestressed by three cables is shown in Fig. 6.3.

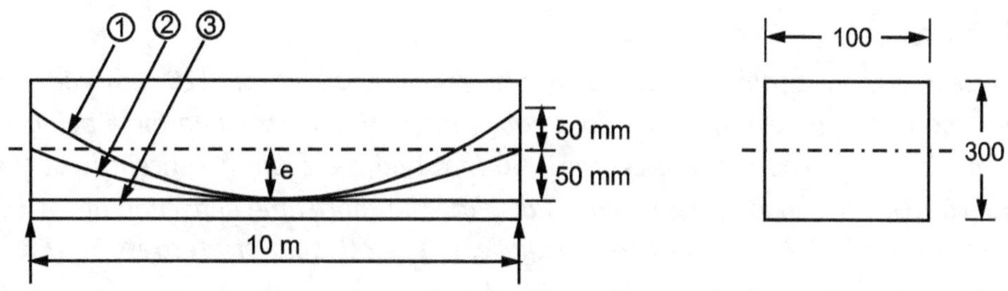

Fig. 6.3

$$P = 240 \text{ kN (3 cables 1, 2 and 3)}, \quad e_1 = e_2 = 50 \text{ mm}$$

$$I = \left(\frac{1}{12} \times 100 \times 300^3\right) = 225 \times 10^6 \text{ mm}^4$$

$$\text{Self weight of the beam} = (0.1 \times 0.3 \times 25) = 0.75 \text{ kN/m}$$

$$\therefore \quad \text{Deflection due to self weight} = \left(\frac{5 \times 0.00075 \times 10000^4}{384 \times 38 \times 225 \times 10^6}\right) = 11.42 \text{ mm } (\downarrow)$$

$$\text{Deflection due to live load} = \left(\frac{11.42}{0.00075} \times 0.005\right) = 76.1 \text{ mm } (\downarrow)$$

Deflection due to cables 1, 2 and 3,

$$\delta_1 = \frac{PL^2}{48 \, EI} \, (-5e_1 + e_2) = \frac{240 \times (10 \times 1000)^2}{48 \times 38 \times 225 \times 10^6} \, [-5 \times 50 + 50]$$

$$= -15.8 \text{ mm } (\uparrow)$$

$$\delta_2 = -\frac{5 \, PeL^2}{48 \, EI} = -\left(\frac{5 \times 240 \times 50 \times (10 \times 1000)^2}{48 \times 38 \times 225 \times 10^6}\right)$$

$$= -14.6 \text{ mm } (\uparrow)$$

$$\delta_3 = -\frac{PeL^2}{8 \, EI} = -\left(\frac{240 \times 50 \times 10000^2}{8 \times 38 \times 225 \times 10^6}\right) = -17.5 \text{ mm } (\uparrow)$$

$$\therefore \quad \text{Total deflection } (\delta_1 + \delta_2 + \delta_3) = (15.8 + 14.6 + 17.5) = 47.9 \text{ mm } (\uparrow)$$

(a) Deflection due to (self weight + prestress)

$$= (47.9 - 11.42) = 36.48 \text{ mm } (\uparrow)$$

(b) Deflection due to (self weight + prestress + live load)

$$= (-47.9 + 11.42 + 76.1) = 39.62 \text{ mm } (\downarrow) \qquad \textbf{... Ans.}$$

Example 6.6 :

A prestressed concrete beam of span 10 m is of rectangular section 120 mm wide and 300 mm deep and is prestressed by a parabolic cable, the initial prestressing force being 280 kN. The eccentricity of the cable at the centre is 50 mm and the cable is concentric at the ends. The beam carries a live load of 2.20 kN/m. Calculate the short-time deflection at the centre of span. Take E_c = 40 kN/mm^2 and creep coefficient ϕ = 2.0. Loss of prestress = 18% of the initial stress after a duration of 6 months. Find the long-time deflection at the centre. Assume that the beam is subjected to dead load and live load simultaneously when the prestress is applied.

Solution :

Given : P_i = 280 kN,   Live load = 2.20 kN/m

e = 50 mm,   Dead load = 0.90 kN/m

E_c = 40 kN/mm^2,   Loss of prestress = 18 percent

ϕ = 2.0,   = 0.18 P_i

L = 10 m, I = 2.7 × 10^8 mm^4

(a) Short-time deflection :

$$\text{Deflection due to prestress} = \frac{5\, P_i e L^2}{48\ EI}\ (\uparrow)$$

$$= \left(\frac{5}{48} \times \frac{280 \times 50 \times 10000^2}{40 \times 2.7 \times 10^8}\right) = 13.50 \text{ mm } (\uparrow)$$

Deflection due to self weight and live load

$$= \left(\frac{5}{384} \times \frac{(2.20 + 0.90)\ 10^{-3} \times 10000^4}{40 \times 2.7 \times 10^8}\right) (\downarrow)$$

$$= 37.3 \text{ mm } (\downarrow)$$

∴   Net deflection = (37.3 – 13.50) = 23.8 mm (↓)   ... **Ans.**

(b) Long-time deflection :

Initial deflection due to transverse loads = 37.3 mm.

Initial deflection due to prestress only = 13.50 mm.

According to Neville's formula,

$$\delta_t = \delta_{it}\, (1 + \phi) - \delta_{ip} \left\{\left(1 - \frac{\Delta P_i}{P_i}\right) + \left(1 - \frac{\Delta P_i}{2P_i}\right)\phi\right\}$$

$$= 37.3\, (1 + 2) - 13.5 \left\{\left(1 - \frac{0.18\ P_i}{P_i}\right) + \left(1 - \frac{0.18\ P_i}{2P_i}\right)2\right\}$$

$$= (111.9 - 35.64) = 76.26 \text{ mm } (\downarrow)$$

Or, By Lin's formula,

$$\delta_t = \left[\delta_{it} - \delta_{ip} \cdot \frac{P_t}{P_i} \right] (1 + \phi) = [37.3 - 13.5 \times 0.82] (1 + 2)$$

$$= 78.69 \text{ mm } (\downarrow) \hspace{4cm} \text{... Ans.}$$

IMPORTANT POINTS

- Factors influencing deflections.
- Deflections due to self weight and imposed load formulae.
- Deflection due to concentrated load formulae.

QUESTIONS

1. A prestressed concrete beam 120 mm wide and 250 mm deep is used to support an imposed load of 12.5 kN/m over a span of 3 m. The beam is prestressed by a straight cable, containing 7 wires of 5 mm dia., stressed to 1200 MPa at an eccentricity of 50 mm.

   Given :   (i) E_c = 36 kN/mm²

   (ii)   Modulus of rupture of concrete = 4 N/mm².

   (iii)   Modular ratio = 6.

   Estimate the deflection of the beam at :

   (i)   Working load, (ii) Cracking load.   **(P.U. Dec. 2005)**

2. A rectangular concrete beam of cross-section 150 mm wide and 300 mm deep is simply supported over a span of 8 m and is prestressed by means of a symmetric parabolic cable, at a distance of 75 mm from the bottom of the beam at mid-span and 125 mm from the top of the beam at support sections. If the force in the cable is 350 kN and E_c = 38 kN/mm², calculate :

   (a)   The deflection at mid-span when the beam is supporting its own weight and

   (b)   The concentrated load which must be applied at mid-span to restore it to the level of supports.

3. A concrete beam with a cross-sectional area of 32×10^3 mm² and radius of gyration of 72 mm is prestressed by a parabolic cable carrying an effective stress of 1000 N/mm². The span of beam is 8 m. The cable, composed of 6 wires of 7 mm diameter, has an eccentricity of 50 mm at the centre and zero at the supports. Neglecting all losses, find the central deflection of the beam as follows :

   (a)   Self weight + prestress, and

   (b) Self weight + prestress + live load of 2 kN/m.

4. A concrete beam having a rectangular section 150 mm wide by 300 mm deep is prestressed by a parabolic cable having an eccentricity of 75 mm at centre of span towards the soffit and an eccentricity of 25 mm towards the top at support reactions. The effective force in the cable is 350 kN. The beam supports a concentrated load of 20 kN at the centre of span in addition to the self weight. If modulus of elasticity of the concrete is 38 kN/mm² and span is 8 m, calculate :

   (a) Short-term deflection at centre of span under prestress, self-weight and live load.

   (b) Long-term deflection assuming the loss ratio is 0.8 and creep coefficient is 1.6.

Chapter 7

STRESS DISTRIBUTION IN END BLOCKS

7.1 ANCHORAGE STRESS

In the anchorage zone or the end block of a post-tensioned prestressed concrete element, the state of stress distribution is complex. In most post-tensioned members, the pre-stressing wires are introduced in ducts (pre-formed in the members) and then stressed and anchored at the end faces. As a result of this, large forces, concentrated over relatively small areas, are applied on the end blocks. These highly discontinuous forces which are applied at the end, while changing progressively to continuous linear distribution, develop transverse and shear stresses. According to St. Venant's principle, the stress distribution can be computed from the simple bending theory. **The zone between the end of the beam and the section where only longitudinal stress exists is generally referred to as the lead-in-zone or anchorage-zone or end block. It is believed that the length of the zone is equal to or greater than the depth of the beam**. The transverse stresses developed in the anchorage zone are tensile in nature and since concrete is weak in tension, adequate reinforcement should be provided to resist this tension. Hence, from the point of view of the designer, it is essential to have a good knowledge of the distribution of the stresses in the anchorage zone so that he can provide an adequate amount of steel, properly distributed to sustain the transverse tensile stresses.

Fig. 7.1 (a) shows a prestressing force 'P' applied to the section 'AB', through a small area. The stress trajectories transfer the force from bearing face AB across the lead-in-zone to face CD, where the stress $p = \dfrac{P}{BD}$. These lines of forces (or stress trajectories) can be considered to be acting as individual struts. The curvature of this struts, being convex towards the centre line of the block, induces compressive stresses in zone I. In zone II, the curvature is reversed in direction (i.e. concave towards the centroidal axis) and the struts tend to deflect outwards, separating from each other and consequently developing transverse tensile stresses. In zone III, the struts are straight and parallel so that no transverse stresses are induced, only longitudinal stresses develop in this zone. The transverse tensile stresses, as high as 0.3 to 0.5 p may occur deep inside the concrete, this zone is known as bursting zone, which is clear from Isobar of transverse stress Refer Fig. 7.1 (b). Also, the corners of the end section are found to be subjected to high spalling tensile stress may be as high as 0.68 p. It is therefore, necessary to provide one layer of reinforcement very near to the end (just behind the anchorage), to take care of **spalling zone**.

Fig. 7.1 (c) shows the idealised stress distribution in an end block with the compressive and tensile stress paths. The effect of transverse tensile stress is to develop a zone of bursting tension in a direction perpendicular to the anchorage force, resulting in horizontal cracking. Since concrete is weak in tension, suitable reinforcements are provided in the transverse direction to resist the bursting tension.

Fig. 7.1 (d) shows the advantage of distributing the total prestressing force (P) over a large number of points of application of the prestressing force on the end block. When the force on each bearing surface is $\frac{P}{2}$, the tensile stresses act only on half the length $\left(\frac{D}{2}\right)$ and the resultant forces are halved and more uniform in the stress distribution.

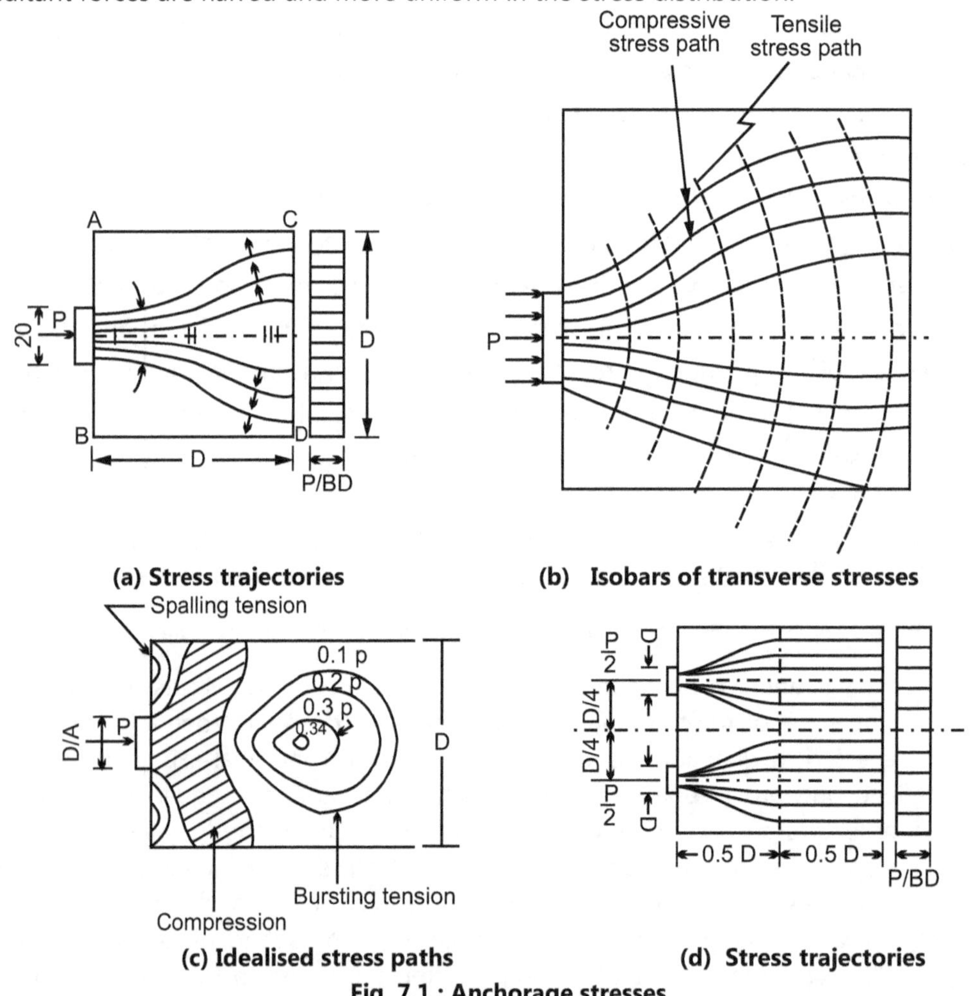

(a) Stress trajectories　　　　**(b) Isobars of transverse stresses**

(c) Idealised stress paths　　　　**(d) Stress trajectories**

Fig. 7.1 : Anchorage stresses

7.1.1 Computation of Bursting Force

A number of investigators have studied the stress distribution in the anchorage zone using empirical equations or theoretical solutions based on two or three-dimensional elasticity or experimental techniques. The main aim of stress analysis in the anchorage zone is to obtain the transverse tensile stress distribution in the end block from which the total transverse bursting tension could be computed.

The provision of the Indian standard code IS : 1343-1980, for computation of the bursting tensile force is based on the ratio of punching to bearing area.

As per clause 18.6.2.2 of IS : 1343-1980, the bursting tensile force (F_{bst}) is obtained from the expression

$$F_{bst} \ = \ P_k \left[0.32 - 0.3 \left(\frac{y_{po}}{y_o} \right) \right] \qquad \text{... (7.1)}$$

where, P_k – tendon jacking force

y_{po} – side of the loaded area

y_o – side of the end block

The reinforcement is designed to sustain this bursting tension and it is assumed to act at its design strength of 0.87 f_y, except that the stress should be limited to a value corresponding to a strain of 0.1 percent, when the concrete cover to the reinforcement is less than 50 mm. The bursting force will be distributed in a region extending from 0.1 y_o to y_o from the loaded face of the end block.

If groups of anchorages are encountered, the end block is divided into a series of symmetrically loaded prisms and each prism is analysed for bursting tensile forces using the recommended expression.

7.1.2 Bearing Stress (Clause 18.6.2.1 of IS : 1343-1980)

On the areas immediately behind external anchorages, the permissible unit bearing stress on the concrete, after accounting for all losses due to relaxation of steel, elastic shortening, creep of concrete, slip and/or seating of anchorages, etc. shall not exceed

$$0.48 \, f_{ci} \sqrt{\frac{A_{br}}{A_{pun}}} \quad \text{or} \quad 0.8 \, f_{ci}, \ \text{whichever is smaller.} \qquad \text{... (7.2)}$$

where f_{ci} – the cube strength at transfer

                             A_{br} – the bearing area and

                             A_{pun} – the punching area.

During tensioning, the allowable bearing stress specified in above may be increased by 25 percent, provided that this temporary value does not exceed f_{ci}.

Solved Examples

Example 7.1 :

The end block of a post-tensioned beam is 90 mm wide and 180 mm deep. A prestressing wire 7 mm in diameter, stressed to 1200 N/mm² has to be anchored against the end block at the centre. The anchorage plate is 50 mm by 50 mm. The wire bears on the plate through a female cone of 20 mm diameter. Given, the permissible stress in concrete at transfer (f_{ci}) = 20 N/mm² and the permissible shear in steel is 94.5 N/mm². Determine the thickness of the anchorage plate.

Solution :

$$\text{Force in wire} = \left(\frac{\frac{\pi}{4} \times 7^2 \times 1200}{1000}\right) = 46.2 \text{ kN}$$

$$\text{Average stress, } f_c = \left(\frac{46.2 \times 10^3}{90 \times 90}\right) = 5.70 \text{ N/mm}^2$$

$$\text{Permissible bearing pressure} = 0.48 \times 20 \times \sqrt{\frac{90 \times 90}{50 \times 50}} = 17.28 \text{ N/mm}^2$$

or, $(0.8 \times 20) = 16$ N/mm², whichever is smaller.

Now, the actual bearing stress is only 5.70 N/mm².

$$\text{Female cone diameter} = 20 \text{ mm}$$

$$\text{Punching circumference} = \pi \times 20 = 62.86 \text{ mm}$$

If t = thickness of anchorage plate, then

$$(62.86 \times 94.5 \times t) = 46.2 \times 10^3$$

$$\therefore \qquad t = 7.8 \text{ mm}$$

Use an anchorage plate of 8 mm thickness.   **... Ans.**

Example 7.2 :

The end block of a post-tensioned bridge girder is 600 mm wide by 1200 mm deep. Two cables each comprising 97 high-tensile wires of 7 mm diameter, are anchored using square anchor-plates of side length 410 mm with their centres located at 600 mm from the top and bottom edges of the beam. The jacking force in each cable is 4500 kN. Design a suitable anchorage zone reinforcement using Fe-415 grade HYSD bars conforming to IS : 1343 code provisions.

Solution :

Depth of anchor plate (y_{po}) = 410 mm

Depth of equivalent prism (y_o) = 600 mm

Jacking force in each cable (P_k) = 4500 kN

$$\text{Bursting tension, } f_{bst} = P_k \left[0.32 - 0.3 \left(\frac{y_{po}}{y_o} \right) \right]$$

$$= 4500 \left[0.32 - 0.3 \times \frac{410}{600} \right] = 517.5 \text{ kN}$$

$$\text{Area of steel, } A_{st} = \frac{F_{bst}}{0.87 \, f_y} = \left(\frac{517.5 \times 10^3}{0.87 \times 415} \right) = 1434 \text{ mm}^2$$

Using 10 mm diameter bars,

$$\text{Number of bars required} = \frac{1434}{\frac{\pi}{4} \times 10^2 \approx 79} = 19$$

Adopt 10 mm diameter bars at 150 mm c/c in the horizontal and vertical directions over a length of 600 mm from the end face of the beam.   **... Ans.**

Example 7.3 :

The solid end-block of a post-tensioned prestressed beam of 25 m span, with three cables, each of 7-15 mm strands, tensioned to 1200 kN is shown in Fig. 7.2. The anchorage plates are square with a solid length of 180 mm. Design the end-block for bursting forces and sketch the details of reinforcement according to provision of IS : 1343-1980.

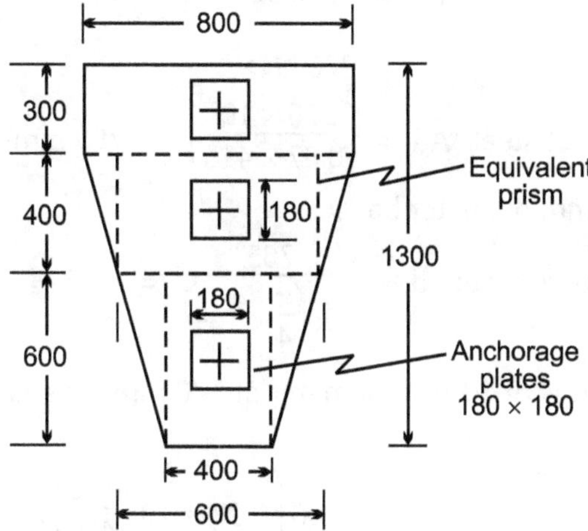

Fig. 7.2 : End block with anchorages

Solution :

The end block has been divided into three equal areas, with one anchorage located approximately at the centroid of each area. The sections of the equivalent prisms corresponding to each anchorage force are shown in Fig. 7.2.

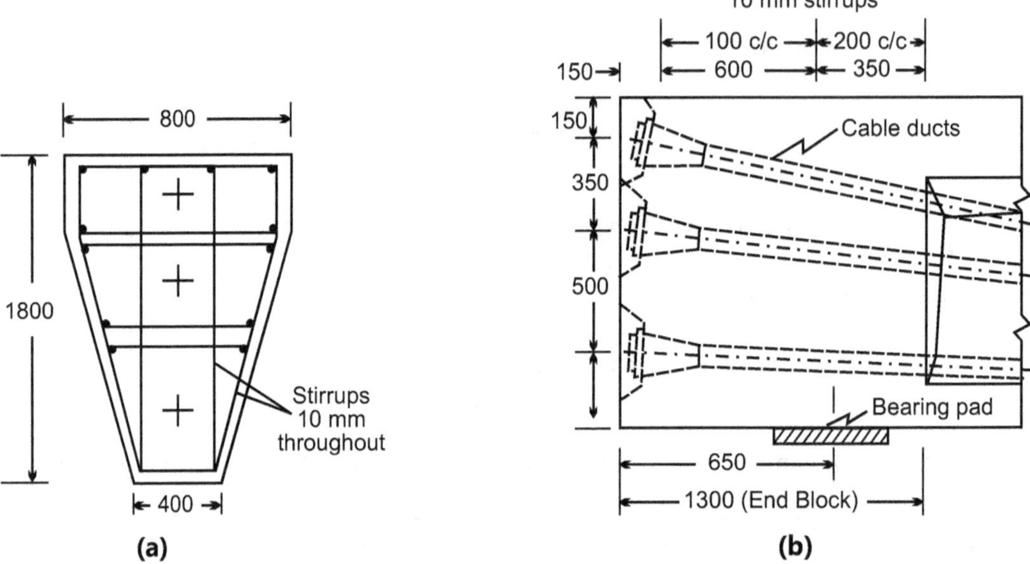

Fig. 7.3 : Details of end block reinforcement

The bursting tension may be calculated for each prism as

For vertical bursting force,

$$F_{bst} = P_k\left[0.32 - 0.3\left(\frac{y_{po}}{y_o}\right)\right] = 1200\left[0.32 - 0.3 \times \frac{180}{600}\right]$$

$$= 276 \text{ kN}$$

$$\text{Area of steel, } A_{st} = \left(\frac{276 \times 10^3}{0.87 \times 415}\right) = 765 \text{ mm}^2$$

Using 2 legged of 10 mm diameter bars,

$$\text{Number of bars required} = \frac{765}{2 \times \left(\frac{\pi}{4} \times 10^2\right)} = 4.87 \approx 5$$

Provide 2-legged stirrups of 10 mm diameter at 100 mm c/c spacing.

For horizontal bursting force,

$$F_{bst} = 1200\left[0.32 - 0.3\left(\frac{180}{400}\right)\right]$$

$$= 222 \text{ kN}$$

Resistance of 4-10 mm stirrups (100 mm c/c)

$$= (4 \times 2 \times 78.5 \times 0.87 \times 415)$$

$$= 226.7 \text{ kN} \qquad\qquad \text{... O.K.}$$

In the same way, the bursting forces are evaluated for the centre and top anchorage and it is found that the required resistance can be provided by 10 mm stirrups at 100 mm centres. A possible arrangement of the stirrups in the end block is shown in Fig. 7.3. Since the bursting forces do not extend over the whole length of the end block, the spacing of the stirrups is increased from 100 mm to 200 mm at the end remote from the anchorages.

7.1.3 Anchorage Zone Reinforcement

The main reinforcement in the anchorage zone should be designed to withstand the bursting tension, which is determined by the transverse stress distribution on the critical axis, usually coinciding with the line of action of the largest individual force. For plate and embedded (Freyssinet) type of anchorages, the typical arrangement of reinforcement in end blocks is shown in Fig. 7.4. Mats, helics, loops or links are generally provided in perpendicular directions. Tests have shown that helical reinforcement is more efficient than mat reinforcement. In view of the short available bond lengths, loops, hooks or right-angle bends are necessary, even with deformed bars.

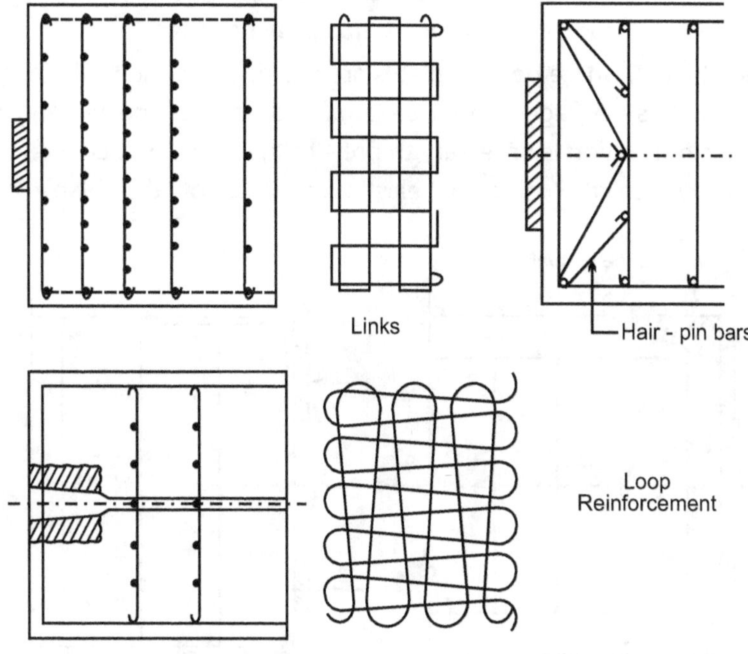

Fig. 7.4 : Arrangement of reinforcement in end blocks

In cases, where spalling or secondary tension develops at the corners, suitable steel in the form of hair-pin bars should be provided to prevent the failure of corner zones. Suitable pockets are generally provided behind the anchorages so that the secondary reinforcements can be bent as shown in Fig. 7.5 and the pocket filled with mortar after prestressing operations.

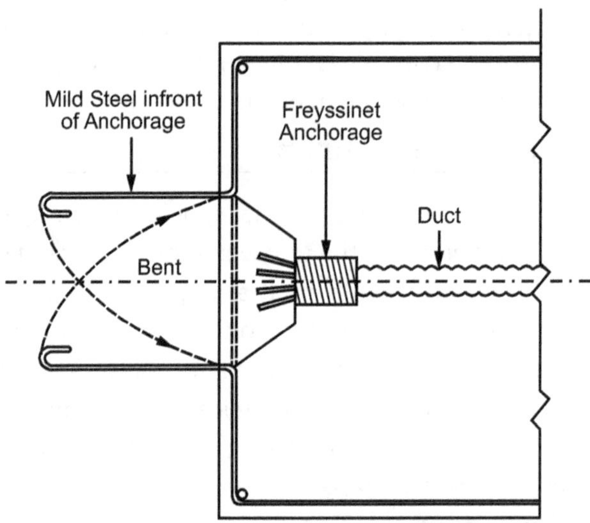

Fig. 7.5 : Pockets behind anchorages

In the case of end blocks, where bearing plates are positioned close to the edges of block as shown in Fig. 7.6, the steel cage should be arranged so that the bearing plates do not overlap with it. This precaution is necessary to prevent the spalling of concrete at the corners during stressing due to the different elastic modulus of the plane containing the reinforcement.

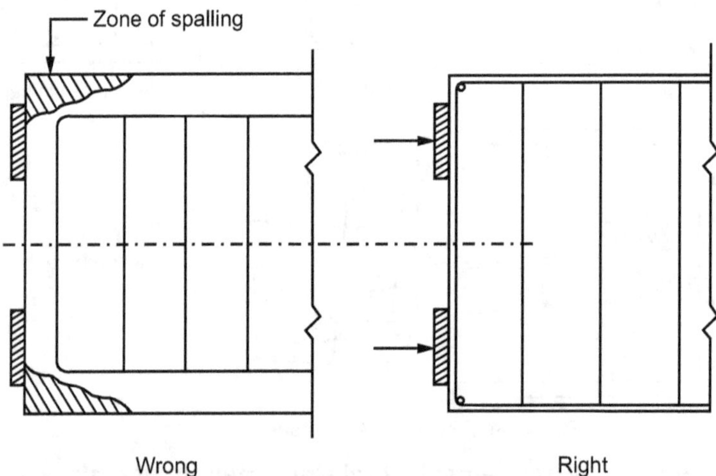

Fig. 7.6 : Arrangement of steel cage in anchorage zone

7.2 TRANSFER OF PRESTRESS IN PRETENSIONED MEMBERS

Length of Transfer/Transmission Length :

In a pre-tensioned system, when a wire is released from its temporary anchorage on the prestressing bed, the end of the wire swells as a result of the recovery of the lateral contraction and develops a wedge effect. This is to enable the prestressing force to become zero at the end of the wire. This is generally referred to as the **Hoyer effect**. The swelling of the wire is only a few thousandths of a millimetre, but inspite of that it produces considerable radial pressures on the concrete, giving rise to large frictional forces. (Refer Fig. 7.7).

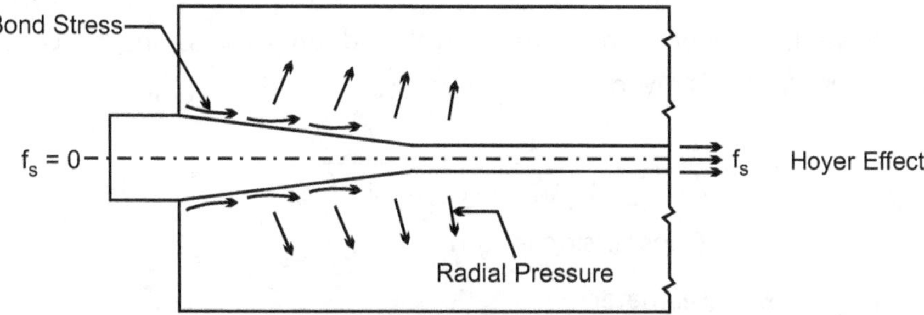

Fig. 7.7

The transmission of prestressing force from steel to concrete is generally through a bond comprising of (i) adhesion, (ii) friction, and (iii) shearing resistance. At intermediate points along the length of a beam, the bond stress is resisted by adhesion, while in the transfer zone, the tendons invariably slip and sink into the concrete, destroying most of the adhesion. Consequently, the bond stresses are due to the friction and shearing resistance. The distribution of bond stress, stress in steel and concrete in transmission zone are shown in Fig. 7.8.

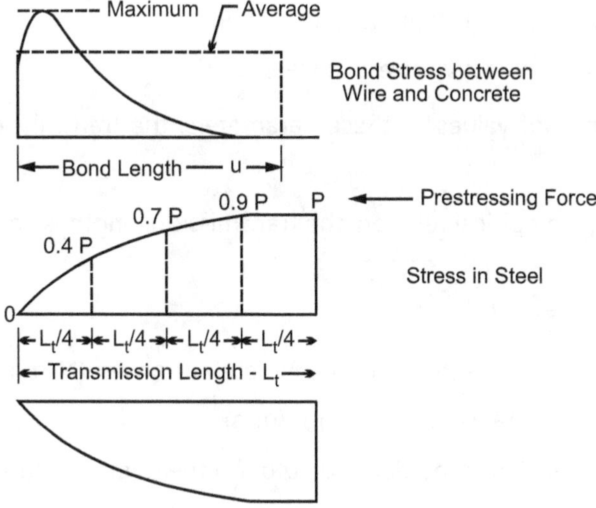

Fig. 7.8 : Distribution of bond stresses

The maximum bond stress is reached in the zone of transverse compression. When the bond stress is zero, the stress in steel and concrete reach their maximum values and uniform stress distribution is effective from this section. The length needed for achieving the uniform stress distribution is termed as **transmission length**.

7.2.1 Computation of Transmission Length

The transmission length depends mainly on the diameter, surface characteristics of the wire, the elastic properties of steel and concrete, and the coefficient of friction between steel and concrete.

Based on the wedge action, Hoyer has developed an expression for computing the transmission length, which is given by

$$L_t = \frac{\phi}{2\mu} (1 + \gamma_c) \left(\frac{\alpha_e}{\gamma_s} - \frac{f_{pi}}{E_c} \right) \left(\frac{f_{pe}}{2f_{pi} - f_{pe}} \right) \qquad ... (7.3)$$

where, L_t – Transmission length

ϕ – Diameter

μ – Coefficient of friction between steel and concrete

γ_c – Poisson's ratio for concrete

γ_s – Poisson's ratio for steel

α_e – Modular ratio $\left(\dfrac{E_s}{E_c} \right)$

E_c – Modulus of elasticity of concrete

f_{pi} – Initial stress in steel

f_{pe} – Effective stress in steel

Under the normal range of values of these parameters, the transmission length is likely to vary from 80 to 160 ϕ.

As per Krishna Murthy's empirical relation, the transmission length is computed as :

$$L_t = \sqrt{\frac{\sqrt{f_{cu}} \times 10^3}{\beta}} \qquad ... (7.4)$$

where f_{cu} – Cube strength of concrete at transfer (N/mm²)

L_t – Transmission length (mm)

β – Constant, depending upon the details of strand and wire

The values of constant β for some of the typical wires and strands are given in Table 7.1.

Table 7.1 : Values of constant β

Sr. No.	Details of wire or strand	β
1.	2 mm dia. wire.	0.144
2.	5 mm dia. wire	0.0235
3.	7 mm dia. wire	0.0174
4.	10 mm dia., 7 wire strand	0.144
5.	12.5 mm dia., 7 wire strand	0.058
6.	18 mm dia., 19 wire strand	0.0235
7.	19 mm dia., 7 wire strand	0.0235
8.	Twin twisted wires or 6.25 mm dia., 7 wire strand	0.077

This empirical formula is applicable for both plain smooth wires and strands.

Example 7.4 :

Calculate the transmission length at the end of a pre-tensioned beam as per Hoyer's method using the following data :

Span of beam = 50 m.

Diameter of wires used = 5 mm.

Coefficient of friction between steel and concrete = 0.1.

Poisson's ratio for steel = 0.30.

Poisson's ratio for concrete = 0.15.

E_s = 210 kN/mm^2, E_c = 30 kN/mm^2.

Ultimate tensile strength of steel wire, f_{pu} = 1500 N/mm^2.

Initial stress in steel, f_{pi} = 0.7 f_{pu}.

Effective stress in steel, f_{pe} = 0.6 f_{pu}.

Solution :

Using Hoyer's expression,

$$L_t = \frac{\phi}{2\mu}\,(1 + \gamma_c)\left(\frac{\alpha_e}{\gamma_s} - \frac{f_{pi}}{E_c}\right)\left(\frac{f_{pe}}{2f_{pi} - f_{pe}}\right)$$

$$= \frac{\phi}{(2 \times 0.1)}\,(1 + 0.15)\left(\frac{7}{0.30} - \frac{0.7 \times 1500}{30 \times 10^3}\right)\left(\frac{0.6 \times 1500}{2 \times 0.7 \times 1500 - 0.6 \times 1500}\right)$$

$$= 100\,(\phi) = 100 \times 5 = 500 \text{ mm}$$

If the beam is simply supported over a span of 50 m, there should be atleast 700 mm of beam projection beyond the centre of supports at each end. Therefore, the total length of the beam required to be cast at site is given by

$$\text{Overall length} = (50 + 2 \times 0.5) \text{ m} = 51 \text{ m} \qquad \text{... Ans.}$$

Example 7.5 :

Estimate the transmission length at the ends of a pre-tensioned beam prestressed by 7 mm diameter wires. Assume the cube strength of concrete at transfer as 40 N/mm². (Adopt Krishna Murthy's empirical relation).

Solution :

For 7 mm diameter smooth wires, $\beta = 0.0174$ (from Table 7.1) and $f_{cu} = 40$ N/mm².

$$\text{Thus,} \qquad L_t = \sqrt{\frac{\sqrt{40} \times 10^3}{0.0174}} = 603 \text{ mm} = 86 \, \phi \qquad \text{... Ans.}$$

7.3 BOND STRESSES IN PRETENSIONED BEAMS

Bond stress : The magnitude of bond stresses developed between concrete and steel and its variation in the transfer zone of pre-tensioned beams is shown in Fig. 7.9.

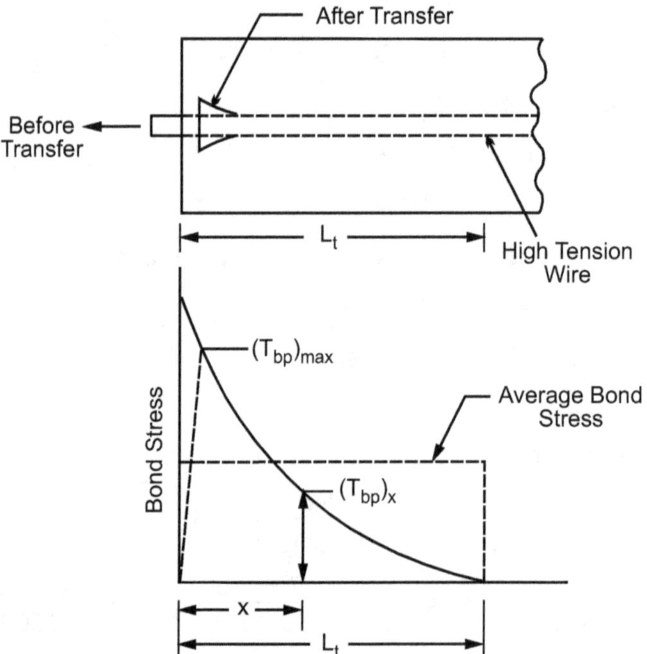

Fig. 7.9 : Bond stress in pre-tensioned beams

The bond stress is zero at the ends but builds up rapidly to a maximum over a very short length. This value decreases as the stress in the wire builds up. At a distance equal to the transmission length, the bond stress is almost zero while the stress in steel and concrete reach their maximum values.

If $(\tau_{bp})_{max}$ = Maximum value of bond stress

$(\tau_{bp})_x$ = Bond stress at a distance x from the free end

ϕ = Diameter of the wire

f_s = Stress in steel at a distance 'x' from the free end

f_{se} = Effective stress in steel at the end of transfer zone

Based on several tests, Marshall proposed the following relations :

$$(\tau_{pb})_x = (\tau_{bp})_{max}\, e^{-4\psi x/\phi} \qquad \text{... (7.5)}$$

$$f_s = f_{se}\,(1 - e^{-4\psi x/\phi}) \qquad \text{... (7.6)}$$

where, $\quad \psi\ -\ $ Constant, expressed as the ratio of change in bond stress to steel stress

$x\ -\ $ Distance measured from the free end, expressed in mm

Based on tests using wires of 2 mm to 5 mm diameter stressed to 1575 and 1000 N/mm^2 respectively in conjunction with a concrete having a cube crushing strength of 80 N/mm^2, the values of maximum bond stress $(\tau_{bp})_{max}$ and constant ψ were found to be 7.42 N/mm^2 and 0.00725 respectively. However, the magnitude of the average bond stress is considerably less than the maximum local bond stress. The stress in a steel wire gradually increases from zero at the end of the beam to 100 percent of the effective stress at the end of transmission length.

Example 7.6 :

A pre-tensioned beam is prestressed using 5 mm diameter wires with an initial stress of 85 percent of the ultimate tensile strength of steel (f_{pu} = 1600 N/mm^2). The cube strength of concrete at transfer is 40 N/mm^2.

(a) Calculate the transmission length.

(b) Compute the bond stress at $\dfrac{1}{4}$ and $\dfrac{1}{2}$ the transmission length from the end, and

(c) Calculate the overall average bond stress.

Solution :

(a)   The transmission length is calculated by

$$L_t = \sqrt{\dfrac{\sqrt{f_{cu}} \times 10^3}{\beta}}$$

For 5 mm wire, $\qquad \beta = 0.0235$

$$L_t = \sqrt{\frac{\sqrt{40 \times 10^3}}{0.0235}} = 519 \text{ mm}$$

(b) The bond stress is given by

$$(\tau_{bp})_x = (\tau_{bp})_{max} \cdot e^{-4\psi x/\phi}$$

$$= 7.42\, e^{-(4 \times 0.00725\, x)/\phi}$$

If $\phi = 5$ mm, then $\quad (\tau_{bp})_x = 7.42 \cdot e^{-(4 \times 0.00725\, x)/5}$

$$= 7.42\, e^{-0.0058\, x}$$

Now, bond stress at $\dfrac{L_t}{4}\left(= \dfrac{519}{4} = 129.75 \text{ mm}\right)$ is given by

$$(\tau_{bp}) = (7.42\, e^{-0.0058 \times 129.75}) = 3.5 \text{ N/mm}^2$$

Bond stress at $\dfrac{L_t}{2}$ (= 259.50 mm) from the end is given by

$$\tau_{bp} = (7.42\, e^{-0.0058 \times 259.50}) = 1.65 \text{ N/mm}^2$$

(c) Overall average bond stress is given by

$$(\tau_{bp})_{avg} = \left(\frac{19.6 \times 0.85 \times 1600}{\pi \times 5 \times 519}\right) = 3.27 \text{ N/mm}^2 \qquad \textbf{... Ans.}$$

IMPORTANT POINTS

- Formulae of bursting force.
- Anchorage stress with stress trajectories.
- Computation of transmission length by Krishna Murthy relation.
- Hoyer's effect in transfer of prestress in pretensioned members.

QUESTIONS

1. Explain anchorage zone reinforcement.
2. Describe transfer in predestined members.
3. Write in short bond stresses in pretension Beams.

Chapter 8

DESIGN OF PRESTRESSED CONCRETE SECTION

8.1 DESIGN OF RECTANGULAR AND FLANGED SECTIONS

Prestressed sections under the action of flexure should satisfy the limits specified for permissible stresses at the stage of transfer of prestress and at service loads. Expression for the minimum section modulus, prestressing force and the corresponding eccentricity are developed. For this, a rectangular beam (b × d) is considered in which the tendon is placed as shown in Fig. 8.1.

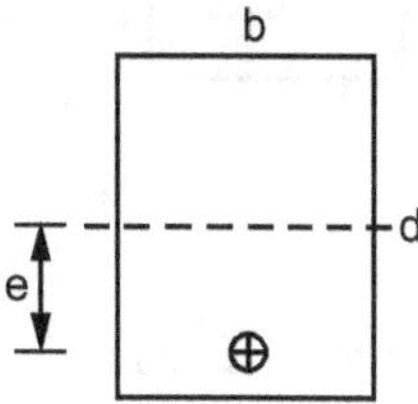

Fig. 8.1

Now, consider the fundamental conditions for stresses at transfer and service loads for the two extreme fibres of the sections.

Initial Stress Condition (At transfer) :

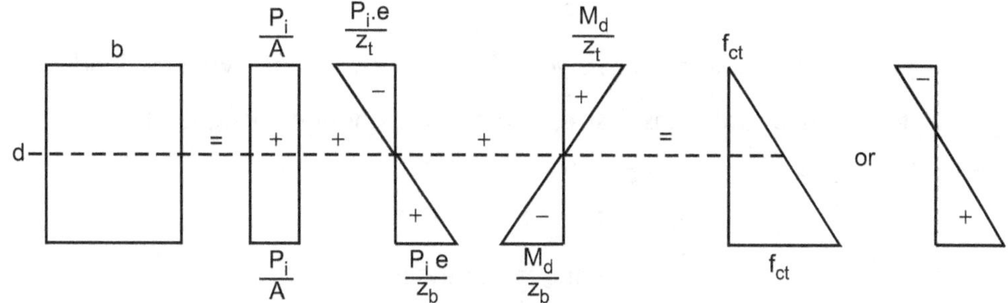

Fig. 8.2

For top fibres : $\dfrac{P_i}{A} - \dfrac{P_i e}{z_t} + \dfrac{M_d}{z_t} \geq f_{tt}$ ... (8.1)

For bottom fibres :

$$\frac{P_i}{A} + \frac{P_i e}{z_b} - \frac{M_d}{z_b} \leq f_{ct} \qquad ...(8.2)$$

where, f_{tt} – Allowable tensile stress in concrete at initial transfer of prestress

          f_{ct} – Allowable compressive stress in concrete at initial transfer of prestress

Final prestress (at working/service condition) :

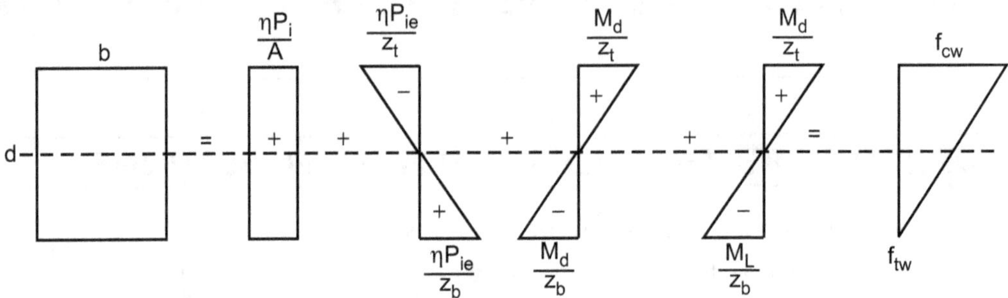

Fig. 8.3

For top fibres :

$$\eta\frac{P_i}{A} - \eta\frac{P_ie}{z_t} + \frac{M_d}{z_t} + \frac{M_l}{z_t} \le f_{cw} \qquad \text{... (8.3)}$$

For bottom fibres :

$$\eta\frac{P_i}{A} + \eta\frac{P_ie}{z_b} - \frac{M_d}{z_b} - \frac{M_l}{z_b} \ge f_{tw} \qquad \text{... (8.4)}$$

where, η – Loss ratio or loss factor $= \dfrac{P_f}{P_i}$

f_{cw} – Allowable compressive stress in concrete under working load

f_{tw} – Allowable tensile stress in concrete under working load

For top fibres, from equations (8.1) and (8.3),

$$(f_{cw} - \eta\, f_{tt}) = f_{tr} \qquad \text{... (8.5)}$$

$$= \text{Range of stress for top fibre}$$

i.e. $\dfrac{M_l}{z_t} - \eta\dfrac{M_d}{z_t} + \dfrac{M_d}{z_t} \le f_{tr}$

or, $\dfrac{M_l + (1 - \eta)\, M_d}{z_t} \le f_{tr} \qquad \text{... (8.6)}$

Similarly, for bottom fibres, from equations (8.2) and (8.4),

$$(\eta\, f_{ct} - f_{tw}) = f_{br} \qquad \text{... (8.7)}$$

$$= \text{range of stress for bottom fibre}$$

i.e. $\dfrac{M_l + (1 - \eta)\, M_d}{z_b} \le f_{br} \qquad \text{... (8.8)}$

Hence, we get the required section moduli as

$$z_t \geq \frac{M_l + (1 - \eta)\, M_d}{f_{tr}} \qquad \ldots (8.9)$$

$$z_b \geq \frac{M_l + (1 - \eta)\, M_d}{f_{br}} \qquad \ldots (8.10)$$

To find prestressing force : From equation (8.1),

$$\left(\frac{P_i}{A} - \frac{P_i e}{z_t}\right) \geq \left(f_{tt} - \frac{M_d}{z_t}\right) \qquad \ldots (8.11)$$

From equation (8.4),

$$\left(\frac{P_i}{A} + \frac{P_i e}{z_b}\right) \geq \left(f_{tw} + \frac{M_d + M_l}{z_b}\right) \frac{1}{\eta} \qquad \ldots (8.12)$$

Solving equations (8.5) and (8.6), we get following after eliminating 'e',

where,
$$\boxed{P_i = \frac{A(f_{inf} \cdot z_b + f_{sup} \cdot z_t)}{(z_t + z_b)}} \qquad \ldots (8.13)$$

Prestress in concrete at bottom of section (inferior) $= f_{inf} = \left(\frac{P_i}{A} + \frac{P_i e}{z_b}\right)$.

Prestress in concrete at top of section (superior) $= f_{sup} = \left(\frac{P_i}{A} - \frac{P_i e}{z_t}\right)$.

Similarly, after eliminating 'P_i' from equations (8.5) and (8.6), we get

$$\boxed{e = \frac{z_t\, z_b\, (f_{inf} - f_{sup})}{A\, (f_{sup} \cdot z_t + f_{inf} \cdot z_b)}} \qquad \ldots (8.14)$$

After calculation, if 'e' goes beyond the cross-section of beam, then adjust value of 'e' and fix up the value of eccentricity and find out the prestressing force required.

$$\boxed{P_{i\,(revised)} = \frac{A\, f_{inf}\, z_b}{z_b + A \cdot e}} \qquad \ldots (8.15)$$

Important Notes :

(1) At transfer stage, for top fibres, $f_{tt} = 0$.

So equation (8.1) can be written as

$$\frac{P_i}{A} - \frac{P_i e}{z_t} + \frac{M_d}{z_t} = 0$$

i.e.
$$\frac{P_i}{A} + \frac{M_d}{z_t} = \frac{P_i\,e}{z_t} \qquad \text{... (8.16)}$$

and at working stage, for bottom fibres, $f_{tw} = 0$.

So equation (8.4) can be written as

$$\eta\frac{P_i}{A} - \frac{M_d}{z_b} - \frac{M_l}{z_b} = -\eta\,\frac{P_i\,e}{z_b}$$

or,
$$\eta\,\frac{P_i\,e}{z_b} = \frac{M_d + M_l}{z_b} - \eta\frac{P_i}{A} \qquad \text{... (8.17)}$$

If $z_t = z_b$ and loss ratio is not considered, then from equations (8.9) and (8.10), we get after adding,

$$2\frac{P_i e}{z} = \frac{M_d + M_l}{z} + \frac{M_d}{z}$$

$$\boxed{e = \frac{2\,M_d + M_l}{2\,P_i}} \qquad \text{... (8.18)}$$

Also, in designing the beam, it should be noted down

$$z = \frac{M_l}{f_c} \qquad \text{... (8.19)}$$

and
$$P = \frac{f_c \cdot A}{2} \qquad \text{... (8.20)}$$

Since the stress varies from 0 at one extreme fibre to f_c at the other extreme fibre.

(2) Limiting zone for prestressing force :

The prestressing force along the length of beam is generally adjusted by varying the eccentricity of the prestressing force. After having once determined the magnitude of the prestressing force for the critical section, it is possible to fix up the limiting zone for the force bounded by the upper and lower limits expressed as a function of the minimum and maximum moments, sectional properties, prestressing force and permissible stresses in concrete at transfer and working loads.

From the following expressions, we find the permissible tendon zone.

    (i)   At centre of span :

$$e \leq \left[\left(\frac{z_b \cdot f_{ct}}{P}\right) - \left(\frac{z_b}{A}\right) + \left(\frac{M_d}{P}\right)\right] \qquad \text{... (8.21)}$$

$$e \geq \left[\left(\frac{z_b \cdot f_{tw}}{P}\right) - \left(\frac{z_b}{A}\right) + \left(\frac{M_d + M_l}{\eta P}\right)\right] \qquad \text{... (8.22)}$$

(ii)   At support :

$$e \leq \left[\left(\frac{z_b \cdot f_{ct}}{P} \right) - \left(\frac{z_b}{A} \right) \right] \qquad \text{... (8.23)}$$

$$e \geq \left[\left(\frac{z_b \cdot f_{tw}}{P} \right) - \left(\frac{z_b}{A} \right) \right] \qquad \text{... (8.24)}$$

8.2 DESIGN OF SECTIONS FOR THE LIMIT STATE OF COLLAPSE IN FLEXURE

The maximum design value of the moment of resistance of rectangular and flanged sections vary from $0.08\ f_{ck}\ bd^2$ to $0.2\ f_{ck}\ bd^2$, depending upon the recommendations of the stress block parameter.

The maximum ultimate moment of resistance of a rectangular section, according to IS : 1343-1980 is given by

$$M_{ud} = 0.21\ f_{ck}\ bd^2$$

The dimensions based on this expression are the minimum values. It is often preferable to use a larger section.

In case of flanged section,

$$\frac{h_f}{d} = 0.2 \text{ to } 0.25, \quad \frac{b_w}{b} = 0.2 \text{ to } 0.3$$

may be taken so that the ultimate moment varies from $0.08\ f_{ck}\ bd^2$ to $0.12\ f_{ck}\ bd^2$.

Assuming a suitable value for the breadth of the compression face b, generally of the order of 0.5 h for T-sections and 0.6 to 0.8 h for I-sections, the effective and overall depth of the section is designed by providing suitable cover requirements.

8.3 STEP BY STEP PROCEDURE USED IN DESIGN OF PRESTRESSED CONCRETE FLANGED BEAM [Dec. 2014]

Preliminary design of prestressed concrete sections for flexure can be performed by a very simple procedure based on a knowledge of the internal C-T couple acting in the section. In practice the depth h of the section is either given, know or assumed as is the total moment, M_T on the section. Under the working load, the lever arm for the internal couple could very between 30 to 80% of the overall height h and averages about 0.65 h. Hence, the required effective prestress F can be computed from the equation.

$$F = T = \frac{M_T}{0.65\ h}$$

If we assume the lever arm to be 0.65 h, Fig. 8.4. If the effective unit prestress is f_s for the steel, then the area of steel required is,

$$A_{Ps} = \frac{F}{f_{se}} = \frac{M_T}{0.65\ h\ f_{se}}$$

The total prestress $A_{Ps}\ f_{se}$ is also the force C on the section. This force will produce an average unit stress on the concrete of

$$\frac{C}{A_c} = \frac{T}{A_c} = \frac{A_{Ps}\, f_{se}}{A_c}$$

For preliminary design, the average stress can be assumed to be about 50% of the maximum allowable stress f_c, under the working load hence,

$$\frac{A_{Ps}\, f_{se}}{A_c} = 0.50\, f_c$$

$$A_c = \frac{A_{Ps}\, f_{se}}{0.50\, f_c}$$

Note that in the above, procedure the only approximations made are the coefficients of 0.65 and 0.50. These coefficients vary widely, depending on the shape of the section. However, with experience and knowledge, they can be closely approximated for each particular section and the preliminary design can be made rather accurately.

The above procedure is based on the design for working load, with little or no tension in the concrete. Preliminar designs can also be made on the basis of ultimate strength theories with proper load factors.

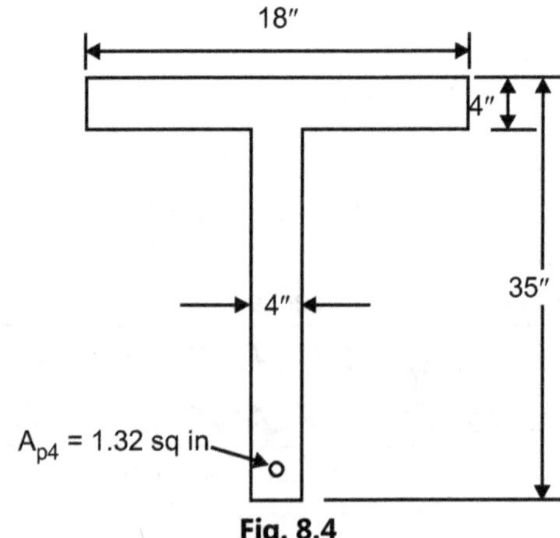

Fig. 8.4

Solved Examples

Example 8.1 :

A pre-tensioned concrete beam of rectangular section is required to support a design ultimate moment of 150 kN-m. Desing the section if f_{ck} = 50 N/mm² and f_p = 1800 N/mm².

Solution :

$$\text{If } b = \text{Breadth of the section and}$$
$$d = \text{Effective depth of the section}$$

$$\text{and assuming } b = \frac{d}{2}$$

Using an average value of constant 0.15, we have,

$$M_u = 0.15\, f_{ck} \cdot b \cdot d^2$$

$$150 \times 10^6 = 0.15 \times 50 \times \frac{d}{2} \times d^2$$

$$\therefore \qquad d = 340 \text{ mm}, \quad b = 170 \text{ mm}$$

Now, using Table 7 of IS : 1343 code and IS : 456,

$$f_{pu} = 0.87\, f_p, \quad \frac{x_u}{d} = 0.48 \quad \text{or} \quad x_u = 0.48 \times 340 = 167 \text{ mm}$$

We know,
$$M_u = f_{pu} \cdot A_p\, (d - 0.42\, x_u)$$

$$A_p = \left[\frac{M_u}{0.87\, f_p\, (d - 0.42\, x_u)}\right]$$

$$= \left[\frac{150 \times 10^6}{0.87 \times 1800\,(340 - 0.42 \times 167)}\right] = 355 \text{ mm}^2$$

Adopt a section, 170 mm wide by 400 mm deep, with 355 mm² of high-tensile steel located at an effective depth of 340 mm.

Example 8.2 :

A post-tensioned bonded beam of unsymmetrical I-section is required to support a design ultimate moment of 1200 kN-m. Determine the overall depth and thickness of the compression flange required if f_{ck} is 35 N/mm² and f_p = 1500 N/mm².

Solution :

For flanged section,

$$M_{ud} = 0.08\, f_{ck}\, bd^2$$

$$\text{assuming } b = \frac{d}{2} \text{ and } b_w = 0.25\, b$$

$$\therefore \qquad 1200 \times 10^6 = 0.08 \times 35 \times \frac{d}{2} \times d^2$$

$$\therefore \qquad d \approx 950 \text{ mm}, \quad b = 475 \text{ mm}$$

Thickness of top flange (D_f) = $0.2 \times d$ = 0.2×950 = 190 mm

Thickness of the web = b_w = $0.25 \times b$ = 0.25×475 = 120 mm.

Assuming the neutral-axis depth, $x_u = D_f = 190$ mm.

$$M_u = 0.87\, f_p \cdot A_p\, (d - 0.42\, x_u)$$

$$\therefore \qquad A_p = \left[\frac{M_u}{0.87\, f_p\, (d - 0.42\, x_u)}\right]$$

$$= \left[\frac{1200 \times 10^6}{0.87 \times 1500\,(950 - 0.42 \times 190)}\right] = 1060 \text{ mm}^2 \qquad \textbf{... Ans.}$$

Example 8.3 :

A post-tensioned prestressed beam of rectangular section 250 mm wide is to be designed for an imposed load of 12 kN/m, u.d.l. on span of 12 m. The stress in concrete must not exceed 17 N/mm² in compression or 1.4 N/mm² in tension at any time and the loss of prestress may be assumed to be 15%. Calculate :

(a) The minimum possible depth of beam.

(b) For the section provided, the minimum prestressing force and the corresponding eccentricity.

Solution :

Given :

$$\text{Imposed load} = 12 \text{ kN/m}, \quad \eta = 0.85$$

$$\text{Breadth of section (b)} = 250 \text{ mm}$$

$$f_{ct} = f_{cw} = 17 \text{ N/mm}^2$$

$$f_{tt} = f_{tw} = -1.4 \text{ N/mm}^2$$

$$\text{Overall depth of section} = h$$

$$\text{Live load moment (M}_l) = \frac{12 \times 12^2}{8} = 216 \text{ kN-m} = 216 \times 10^6 \text{ N-mm}$$

$$\text{D.L. moment (M}_d) = \left[\frac{\text{b.h. } 1 \times 24 \times 12^2}{8}\right] = 432 \text{ bh N-mm}$$

Range of stress at bottom fibre

$$f_{br} = (\eta \, f_{ct} - f_{tw}) = [0.85 \times 17 - (-1.4)]$$

$$= 15.85 \text{ N/mm}^2$$

(a) Minimum section modulus is given by

$$z_b = \left[\frac{M_l + (1 - \eta) \, M_d}{f_{br}}\right]$$

$$\therefore \quad \frac{bh^2}{6} = \left[\frac{(216 \times 10^6) + (1 - 0.85) \, 432 \, bh}{15.85}\right]$$

$$\text{or,} \quad \frac{250 \times h^2}{6} = \left[\frac{216 \times 10^6 + 0.15 \times 432 \times 250 \times h}{15.85}\right]$$

on simplifying, $h^2 - 24.5 \, h - 325000 = 0$

$$\therefore \quad \boxed{h = 580 \text{ mm}} \quad \text{required depth of beam.}$$

(b) For section, $b = 250 \text{ mm}, \ h = 580 \text{ mm}$

$$\text{Area of section = (A)} = 145 \times 10^3 \text{ mm}^2$$

$$z_b = z_t = \frac{bh^2}{6} = 14 \times 10^6 \text{ mm}^3$$

Dead load moment, $M_d = 432 \times b \times h = 626.4 \times 10^5 \text{ N-mm}$

$$f_{sup} = \left(f_{tt} - \frac{M_d}{z_t}\right) = \left[-1.4 - \frac{626.4 \times 10^5}{14 \times 10^6}\right] = -5.9 \text{ N/mm}^2$$

$$f_{inf} = \left(f_{tw} + \frac{M_l}{z_b} + \frac{M_d}{z_b}\right) \times \frac{1}{\eta}$$

$$= \left[-1.4 + \frac{626.4 \times 10^5}{14 \times 10^6} + \frac{2160 \times 10^5}{14 \times 10^6}\right] \times \frac{1}{0.85}$$

$$= 22 \text{ N/mm}^2$$

Minimum prestressing force is given by

$$P_i = \frac{A\,(f_{inf} \cdot z_b + f_{sup} \cdot z_t)}{z_b + z_t}$$

$$= \frac{145 \times 10^3\,[(22 - 5.9) \times 14 \times 10^6]}{14 \times 10^6 + 14 \times 10^6}$$

$$= 1170000 \text{ N}$$

$$\approx 1170 \text{ kN}$$

Corresponding eccentricity 'e' is given by

$$e = \frac{z_t\, z_b\,(f_{inf} - f_{sup})}{A\,(f_{sup} \cdot z_t + f_{inf} \cdot z_b)}$$

$$= \frac{(14 \times 10^6)^2 \times (22 + 5.9)}{145 \times 10^3\,(22 - 5.9) \times 14 \times 10^6}$$

$$e = 167.5 \text{ mm}$$

$\therefore$ Minimum prestressing force $P_i = 1170$ kN

eccentricity, $e = 167.5$ mm   ... **Ans.**

Example 8.4 :

An unsymmetrical I-section having the following properties is used for a bridge girder :

The thickness of top and bottom flanges are 200 mm and 250 mm respectively.

The width of top and bottom flanges are 750 mm and 450 mm respectively.

The thickness of web is 150 mm, overall depth of beam = 1000 mm

and area of X-section = 345000 mm2.

$z_t = 95 \times 10^6$ mm³, $z_b = 75 \times 10^6$ mm³ *and the position of the centroid of section is 440 mm from the top. If permissible tensile and compressive stresses at transfer and working loads are not to exceed 0 in tension and 15 N/mm² in compression.*

Determine the prestressing force required and the corresponding eccentricity to resist self weight and applied moments of 1012 kN-m and 450 kN-m respectively.

The loss ratio is 0.85.

Solution :

Given :

$$f_{tt} = f_{tw} = 0$$

$$f_{ct} = f_{cw} = 15 \text{ N/mm}^2$$

$$f_{sup} = \left(f_{tt} - \frac{M_d}{z_t}\right) = \left[0 - \frac{1012 \times 10^6}{95 \times 10^6}\right] = -10.6 \text{ N/mm}^2$$

$$f_{inf} = \left[f_{tw} + \frac{M_d}{z_b} + \frac{M_l}{z_b}\right]\frac{1}{\eta}$$

$$= \left[0 + \frac{1012 \times 10^6}{75 \times 10^6} + \frac{450 \times 10^6}{75 \times 10^6}\right] \times \frac{1}{0.85} = +23 \text{ N/mm}^2$$

$\therefore$ Prestressing force, P_i

$$P_i = \frac{A (f_{inf} \cdot z_b + f_{sup} \cdot z_t)}{(z_t + z_b)}$$

$$= \frac{345 \times 10^3 (23 \times 75 - 10.6 \times 95) \times 10^6}{(75 + 95) \times 10^6}$$

$$= 146 \times 10^4 \text{ N}$$

Eccentricity, e

$$e = \left[\frac{z_t \cdot z_b (f_{inf} - f_{sup})}{A (f_{sup} \cdot z_t + f_{inf} \cdot z_b)}\right]$$

$$= \frac{95 \times 75 \times 10^6 \times (23 + 10.6)}{345 \times 10^3 (23 \times 75 - 10.6 \times 95) \times 10^6}$$

$$= 967 \text{ mm}$$

But maximum possible eccentricity (if c.g. of cables of 100 mm from bottom)

$$= (1000 - 440 - 100) = 460 \text{ mm}$$

Providing the maximum possible eccentricity $e = 460$ mm.

Then the prestressing force P_i required to develop the prestress f_{inf}, is obtained as,

$$P_i = \frac{A \, f_{inf} \, z_b}{z_b + A \cdot e}$$

$$= \frac{345 \times 10^3 \times 23 \times 75 \times 10^6}{75 \times 10^6 + (345 \times 10^3) \times 460}$$

$$= 2547 \times 10^3 \text{ N}$$

$$P_i = 2547 \text{ kN} \qquad \text{... \textbf{Ans.}}$$

Example 8.5 :

A rectangular prestressed concrete beam has a span of 12 m and has to carry a live   load of 15 kN/m excluding the self weight of the beam. Given : safe stress in concrete = 16 N/mm² and safe stress in steel = 1050 N/mm². Design the beam using 6 mm tendons. Weight of concrete = 24 kN/m³.

Solution :

$$\text{Live load moment } (M_L) = \frac{wl^2}{8} = \frac{15 \times 12^2}{8} = 270 \text{ kN-m}$$

$$\text{Section modulus required } (z) = \frac{M_L}{f_c} = \frac{270 \times 10^6}{16} = 1.69 \times 10^7 \text{ mm}^3$$

Let the width of the beam (b) = 300 mm, then

$$z = \frac{bd^2}{6} = \frac{300 \, d^2}{6} = 1.69 \times 10^7$$

$$\therefore \qquad d = 580 \text{ mm}$$

Hence, the section of the beam is 300 mm × 580 mm.

Now,   D.L. of the beam $= 0.30 \times 0.580 \times 24 = 4.176$ kN/m

$$\text{Dead load moment } (M_d) = \frac{4.176 \times 12^2}{8} = 75.168 \text{ kN-m}$$

$$\therefore \qquad \text{Prestressing force } (P) = \frac{f_c \cdot A}{2} = \frac{16}{2} \times (300 \times 580) = 1392 \text{ kN}$$

$$\therefore \qquad \text{Area of tendons} = \frac{1392 \times 10^3}{1050} = 1326 \text{ mm}^2$$

$$\text{Number of 6 mm diameter wires required} = \frac{1326}{28} = 48 \text{ wires.}$$

These can be arranged in 6 cables with 8 wires per cable.

$$\text{Eccentricity, } e = \frac{2\,M_d + M_l}{2P} = \frac{2 \times 75.168 + 270}{2 \times 1392000} \times 10^6 = 151 \text{ mm ... \textbf{Ans.}}$$

Example 8.6 :

Design a pretensioned roof purlin of effective span 6 m to support a service uniformly distributed load of 5 kN/m.

Assume the following data :

$$f_{ck} = 50 \text{ N/mm}^2, \quad E_c = 5000 \sqrt{f_{ck}} = 35.36 \text{ kN/mm}^2$$

$$f_{ci} = 30 \text{ N/mm}^2, \quad \eta = 0.8.$$

7 mm high tensile wires with $f_p = 1600$ N/mm² are available for use. Design a suitable symmetrical I-section as class-I type member and determine number of wires required and the eccentricity. Sketch the cross-section showing details of reinforcement.

Solution :

Preliminary dimensions of I-section :

Generally, we take * approximate overall depth

$$= 50 \text{ to } 60 \text{ mm per metre span}$$

For 6 m span,

$$\text{overall depth (h)} = 50 \times 6 \text{ to } 60 \times 6 \text{ mm}$$

$$= 300 \text{ mm to } 360 \text{ mm}$$

$$\approx 320 \text{ mm}$$

$$\text{* Width of top flange (b)} = 0.4 \text{ to } 0.5 \text{ h}$$

$$= 0.4 \times 320 = 128 \text{ mm}$$

$$= 0.5 \times 320 = 160 \text{ mm}$$

$$\text{Adopt width of top flange (b)} = 160 \text{ mm}$$

$$\text{* Thickness of top flange (t)} = 0.2 \text{ h}$$

$$= 0.2 \times 320 = 64 \text{ mm}$$

Since, sloping flanges are employed, increase flange thickness by 20%.

$$\therefore \text{ Average thickness of flange} = (64 \pm 0.2 \times 64) = 76.8 \text{ mm}$$

Adopt thickness of top flange with sloping = 80 mm.

$$\text{*Thickness of web (b}_w\text{)} = 50 \text{ mm}$$

Fig. 8.5 shows the cross-sectional dimensions of I-section selected based on empirical and practical considerations.

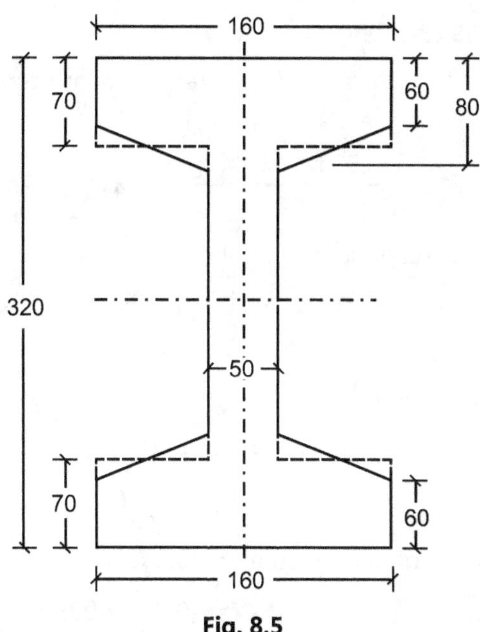

Fig. 8.5

Properties of section :

$$A = 2 \times (160 \times 70) + 180 \times 50 = 31400 \text{ mm}^2$$

$$I = \frac{1}{12} \times 50 \times 180^3 + 2 \times \left[\frac{1}{12} \times 160 \times 70^3 + 160 \times 70 \times 125^2 \right] = 3835 \times 10^5 \text{ mm}^4$$

$$z \, (= z_t = z_b) = \frac{I}{y} = \frac{3835 \times 10^5}{160} = 240 \times 10^4 \text{ mm}^3$$

Design moments and shear forces :

$$\text{Self weight of I-section} = 25 \frac{\text{kN}}{\text{m}^3} \times 31400 \times 10^{-6} \text{ m}^2 = 0.785 \text{ kN/m}$$

$$\therefore \quad \text{B.M. due to dead load } (M_d) = \left(\frac{0.785 \times 6^2}{8} \right) = 3.53 \text{ kN-m}$$

$$\text{B.M. due to live load } (M_l) = \frac{5 \times 6^2}{8} = 22.50 \text{ kN-m}$$

and $\qquad$ Shear force $(V) = V_d + V_l$ (at support)

$$= \frac{w_d \cdot l}{2} + \frac{w_l \cdot l}{2}$$

$$= \frac{0.785 \times 6}{2} + \frac{5 \times 6}{2} = 17.35 \text{ kN}$$

Permissible stresses (IS : 1343-1980) :

Permissible stresses for M 50 grade of concrete, and pre-tensioned work (referring to Fig. 8 B of IS : 1343)

$$f_{ct} = \frac{0.51\, f_{ci} + 0.44\, f_{ci}}{2} = 0.475\, f_{ci} = 0.475 \times 30 = 14.25 \text{ N/mm}^2$$

From Fig. 7 of IS : 1343 corresponding to zone-I,

$$f_{cw} = 0.37\, f_{ck} = (0.37 \times 50) = 18.5 \text{ N/mm}^2$$

and for class-I type member,

$$f_{tt} = f_{tw} = 0$$

$$\text{Tensile strength of concrete} = f_t = 0.24 \sqrt{f_{ck}}$$

$$= 0.24 \sqrt{50} = 1.697 \text{ N/mm}^2$$

$$\text{Initial stress in high tensile steel} = (0.8 \times f_p)$$

$$= (0.8 \times 1600) = 1280 \text{ N/mm}^2$$

Check for minimum section modulus :

$$z_b \geq \left[\frac{M_l + (1 - \eta)\, M_d}{(\eta\, f_{ct} - f_{tw})} \right]$$

$$\geq \left[\frac{(22.50 \times 10^6) + (1 - 0.8)\, 3.53 \times 10^6}{(0.8 \times 14.25) - 0} \right]$$

$$\geq 203.5 \times 10^4 \text{ mm}^3 \leq 240 \times 10^4 \text{ mm}^3 \text{ (provided). Hence, safe.}$$

Prestressing force :

$$f_t = \left[f_{tt} - \left(\frac{M_d}{z_t} \right) \right] = \left[0 - \frac{3.53 \times 10^6}{240 \times 10^4} \right] = -1.47 \text{ N/mm}^2 \ (f_{sup})$$

$$f_b = \left[\left(\frac{f_{tw}}{\eta} \right) + \left(\frac{M_d + M_l}{\eta} \right) \right] = \left[0 + \frac{(3.53 + 22.50) \times 10^6}{240 \times 10^4} \right] = 13.55 \text{ N/mm}^2 \ (f_{inf})$$

$$P = \left[\frac{A\, (f_t\, z_t + f_b\, z_b)}{z_t + z_b} \right] = \left[\frac{A\, (f_t + f_b)}{2} \right]; \text{ since } z_t = z_b.$$

$$= \left[\frac{31400\, (-1.47 + 13.55)}{2} \right] = 189.66 \text{ kN}$$

Using high tensile wires of 7 mm diameter initially stressed to 1280 N/mm²,

$$\text{Number of wires} = \left(\frac{189.66 \times 10^3}{\frac{\pi}{4} \times 7^2 \times 1280}\right) \approx 4$$

Eccentricity of the prestressing force is computed as :

$$e = \left[\frac{z_b \cdot z_t \cdot (f_b - f_t)}{A(f_t \cdot z_t + f_b \cdot z_b)}\right] = \left[\frac{z(f_b - f_t)}{A(f_t + f_b)}\right] \qquad \text{(since } z_t = z_b)$$

$$= \left[\frac{240 \times 10^4 \times (13.55 + 1.47)}{31400 \times (13.55 - 1.47)}\right] = 95 \text{ mm}$$

Check for ultimate flexural strength :

$$M_u \text{ (required)} = 1.5 (M_d + M_l) = 1.5 (3.53 + 22.50) = 39.05 \text{ kN-m}$$

$$A_p = 4 \times 38.5 = 154 \text{ mm}^2, \qquad\qquad b = 160 \text{ mm}$$

$$f_p = 1600 \text{ N/mm}^2, \qquad\qquad d = (160 + 95) = 255 \text{ mm}$$

$$f_{ck} = 50 \text{ N/mm}^2$$

$$\text{Ratio}\left[\frac{A_p f_p}{bd f_{ck}}\right] = \left[\frac{154 \times 1600}{160 \times 255 \times 50}\right] = 0.120$$

From Table-11 of IS : 1343,

$$\left(\frac{f_{pu}}{0.87 f_p}\right) = 1.00 \quad \text{and} \quad \left(\frac{x_u}{d}\right) = 0.26$$

$$\therefore \qquad\qquad f_{pu} = 1 \times 0.87 \times 1600 = 1392 \text{ N/mm}^2$$

and

$$x_u = 0.26 \times 255 = 66.3 \text{ mm} < 70 \text{ mm. Hence, safe.}$$

So,

$$M_u = A_p \cdot f_{pu} (d - 0.42 x_u)$$

$$= 1392 \times 154 (255 - 0.42 \times 66.3)$$

$$= 48.69 \times 10^6 \text{ N-mm} > 39.05 \times 10^6 \text{ N-mm. Hence, safe.}$$

So separate untensioned reinforcement is not required.

But according to IS : 1343 code, minimum longitudinal reinforcement should not be less than 0.15 percent of cross-sectional area of concrete section.

$$\therefore \qquad \text{Longitudinal steel} = \frac{0.15}{100} \times 31400 = 47 \text{ mm}^2.$$

$\therefore$ Provide 4 bars of 6 mm diameter mild steel bars.

Check for ultimate shear strength at support (uncracked in flexure) :

$$V_{uD} \text{ (required)} = 1.5 (V_d + V_l)$$

$$= 1.5 \times 17.35 = 26.0 \text{ kN}$$

$$V_{co} = 0.67 \, bD \sqrt{f_t^2 + 0.8 \, f_{cp} \cdot f_t}$$

Here,

$$f_{cp} = \left(\frac{\eta \times P}{A}\right) = \left(\frac{0.8 \times 189.66 \times 10^3}{31400}\right) = 4.83 \text{ N/mm}^2$$

$$b = b_w \quad \text{and} \quad D = h$$

$\therefore$

$$V_{co} = 0.67 \times 50 \times 320 \sqrt{1.697^2 + 0.8 \times 4.83 \times 1.697}$$

$$= 32.9 \text{ kN} \, > \, 26.0 \text{ kN. Hence, safe.}$$

Here, $V_{uD} > \dfrac{1}{2} V_{co}$, no need to provide shear reinforcement. But we provide the minimum shear reinforcement. Thus,

$$\frac{A_{sv}}{S_v} = \left(\frac{0.4 \, b_w}{0.87 \, f_y}\right) = \frac{0.4 \times 50}{0.87 \times 230} = 0.09 \text{ mm}^2/\text{mm}$$

Provide 6 mm ϕ mild steel single legged stirrups at 150 mm c/c.

Check for deflection :

The deflection due to the prestressing force $= \left(\dfrac{Pe \cdot L^2}{8 \, EI}\right) (\uparrow)$

$$= \left(\frac{189.66 \times 95 \times 6000^2}{8 \times 35.36 \times 3835 \times 10^5}\right) = 5.97 \text{ mm} \, (\uparrow)$$

The deflection due to self weight and live load $= \left[\dfrac{5 \, (w_d + w_l) \, L^4}{384 \, EI}\right] (\downarrow)$

$$= \frac{5 \times (0.785 + 5) \times 10^{-3} \times 6000^4}{384 \times 35.36 \times 3835 \times 10^5} = 7.19 \text{ mm} \, (\downarrow)$$

Assuming, creep coefficient $\phi = 1.6$,

Long-term deflection is computed as

$$= [-0.8 \times 5.97 + 7.19] \, (1 + 1.6)$$

$$= 6.27 \text{ mm} \, (\downarrow)$$

But maximum permissible deflection as per IS : 1343,

$$\left(\frac{\text{span}}{250}\right) = \left(\frac{6000}{250}\right) = 24 \text{ mm.}$$

Hence, limit state of deflection is safisfied.

Now, the details of reinforcement provided in the section are shown in Fig. 8.5.

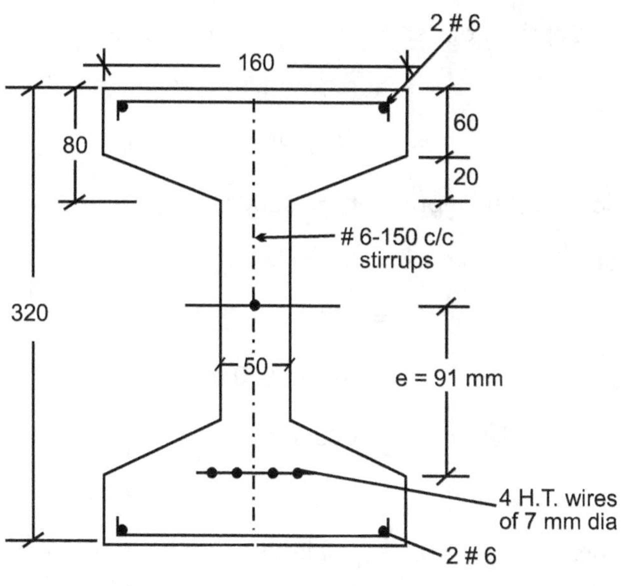

Fig. 8.6

Example 8.7 :

Design a post-tensioned prestressed concrete beam to suit the following data :

Effective span = 30 m,   M 50 grade concrete (f_{ck} = 50 N/mm²)

Live load = 11 kN/m, f_{ci} = 41 N/mm².

$$f_t = 0.24\sqrt{f_{ck}} = 0.24\sqrt{50} = 1.7 \ N/mm^2$$

$$E_c = 5000\sqrt{f_{ck}} = 35.36 \ N/mm^2$$

Loss ratio (η) = 0.85.

High tensile wires of 8 mm diameter – 12 numbers in each cable with Freyssinet anchorages are available in use.

Initial stress in wires = 1100 N/mm².

Ultimate tensile strength of wires = f_p = 1500 N/mm².

Design the beam as class-I type structure to confirm to I.S. code specifications.

Solution :

1.   Preliminary cross-sectional dimensions :

An unsymmetrical I-section (Tee-section) is selected.

$$\text{Depth of girder} = 40 \text{ to } 50 \text{ mm/m of span}$$

$$= (40 \times 30) = 1200 \text{ mm}$$

$$= (50 \times 30) = 1500 \text{ mm}$$

$$\text{Adopt overall depth} = h = 1300 \text{ mm}$$

$$\text{Top width of flange} = 0.4 \text{ to } 0.5 \text{ h}$$

$$= (0.4 \times 1300) \text{ to } (0.5 \times 1300)$$

$$= 520 \text{ to } 650 \text{ mm}$$

$$\text{Adopt top width of flange} = b = 600 \text{ mm}$$

$$\text{Thickness of top flange, } t = 0.20 \text{ h} = (0.20 \times 1300) \approx 250 \text{ mm (adopt)}$$

Thickness of web = b_w = Minimum of 150 mm to house cable ducts of 50 mm diameter with a cover of 50 mm on either side.

The dimensions of bottom flange are based on number of cables and number of each cable in a row. The dimensions should be such that a clear cover of 50 mm between the cables and their rows is available. Assuming that three cables are provided in a horizontal row and the diameter of the cable is 50 mm, the minimum width required to house three cables in a row with a clear cover of 50 mm between them is 350 mm. So, 350 mm wide by 300 mm deep bottom flange is adopted. The cross-sectional dimensions of the girder are shown in Fig. 8.7.

2. Sectional properties :

$$A = (600 \times 250) + (750 \times 150) + (300 \times 350) = 367500 \text{ mm}^2$$

$$y_b = \frac{(600 \times 250 \times 1175) + (750 \times 150 \times 675) + (300 \times 350 \times 150)}{367500}$$

$$= 730 \text{ mm (from bottom)}$$

$$y_t = (1300 - 730) = 570 \text{ mm}$$

$$I = 72208 \times 10^6 \text{ mm}^4$$

$$z_t = 127 \times 10^6 \text{ mm}^3$$

$$z_b = 99 \times 10^6 \text{ mm}^3$$

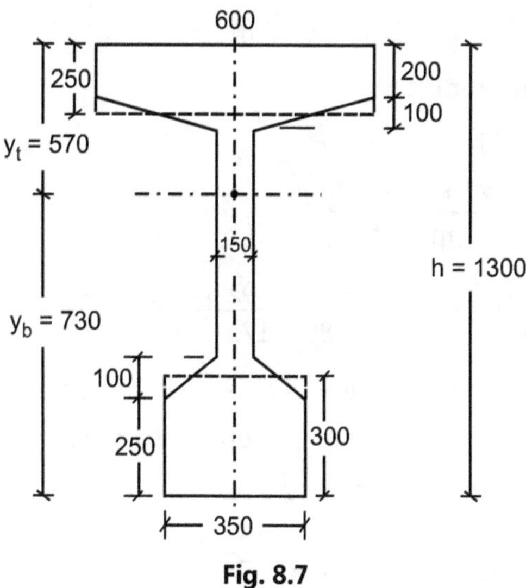

Fig. 8.7

3. Design moments and shear forces :

$$\text{Self weight } (w_d) = (25 \times 0.3675) = 9.2 \text{ kN/m}$$

$$\text{Dead load moment } (M_d) = \left(\frac{w_d \cdot l^2}{8}\right) = \left(\frac{9.2 \times 30^2}{8}\right) = 1035 \text{ kN-m}$$

$$\text{Live load } (w_l) = 11 \text{ kN/m}$$

$$\text{Live load moment } (M_l) = \left(\frac{11 \times 30^2}{8}\right) = 1237.5 \text{ kN-m}$$

$$\text{Total shear force } (V) = (w_d + w_l) \cdot \frac{l}{2}$$

$$= \frac{1}{2} \times 30 \times (9.2 + 11) = 303 \text{ kN}$$

4. Permissible stresses (As per IS : 1343-1980) :

$$f_{ck} = 50 \text{ N/mm}^2, \ f_{ci} = 41 \text{ N/mm}^2$$

Since the beam is post-tensioned, referring to Fig. 8 of IS : 1343 code, the permissible compressive stress in concrete is

$$f_{ct} = 0.427 \, f_{ci} = (0.427 \times 41) = 17.5 \text{ N/mm}^2$$

For class-I type member, $f_{tt} = f_{tw} = 0$; since no tension is permitted at transfer and working loads.

The permissible compressive stress in concrete under working loads is interpolated from Fig. 7 of IS : 1343 code.

$$f_{cw} = 0.37\, f_{ck} = (0.37 \times 50) = 18.5 \text{ N/mm}^2$$

5. Check for section modulus :

Minimum section modulus :

$$z_b \geq \left[\frac{M_l + (1 - \eta)\, M_d}{(\eta f_{ct} - f_{tw})}\right]$$

$$\geq \left[\frac{1237.5 \times 10^6 + (1 - 0.85) \times 1035 \times 10^6}{0.85 \times 17.5 - 0}\right]$$

$$\geq 93.63 \times 10^6 \text{ mm}^3 < 99 \times 10^6 \text{ mm}^3 \text{ (provided)} \qquad \text{Hence safe.}$$

The I-section selected satisfies the requirements regarding the section modulus.

6. Prestressing force and eccentricity :

$$f_{sup} = \left[f_{tt} - \frac{M_d}{z_t}\right] = \left[0 - \frac{1035 \times 10^6}{127 \times 10^6}\right]$$

$$= -8.14 \text{ N/mm}^2$$

$$f_{inf} = \left[\frac{f_{tw}}{\eta} + \frac{M_d + M_l}{\eta\, z_b}\right] = \left[0 + \frac{(1237.5 + 1035) \times 10^6}{0.85 \times 99 \times 10^6}\right]$$

$$= 27.0 \text{ N/mm}^2$$

$$\text{Eccentricity} = e = \left[\frac{z_t \cdot z_b\, (f_{inf} - f_{sup})}{A\, (f_{inf} \cdot z_b + f_{sup} \cdot z_t)}\right]$$

$$e = \left[\frac{127 \times 99 \times 10^{12}\, (27.0 + 8.14)}{367500 \times 10^6\, (27 \times 99 - 8.14 \times 127)}\right]$$

$$= 733.0 \text{ mm, which is impracticable.}$$

Hence,   Maximum possible eccentricity $= [733.0 - 150]$

$$= 583 \text{ mm}$$

Then, the prestressing force corresponding to this eccentricity,

$$P = \left[\frac{A \cdot f_{inf} \cdot z_b}{z_b + A \cdot e}\right] = \left[\frac{(367500 \times 27 \times 99 \times 10^6)}{(99 \times 10^6) + (367500 \times 583)}\right]$$

$$= 3136 \times 10^3 \text{ N} = 3136 \text{ kN}$$

Using Freyssinet cables, 12 numbers of 8 mm diameter initially stressed to 1100 N/mm².

$$\text{Number of cables} = \left[\frac{3136 \times 10^3}{12 \times 50 \times 1100}\right] \approx 5$$

7. Permissible tendon zone :

The permissible tendon zone at the centre of span and the support section is computed as,

(a) At centre of span :

$$e \leq \left[\left(\frac{z_b \cdot f_{ct}}{P}\right) - \left(\frac{z_b}{A}\right) + \frac{M_d}{P}\right]$$

$$\leq \left[\left(\frac{99 \times 10^6 \times 17.5}{3136 \times 10^3}\right) - \left(\frac{99 \times 10^6}{367500}\right) + \left(\frac{1035 \times 10^6}{3136 \times 10^3}\right)\right]$$

$$\leq 613 \text{ mm}$$

$$e \geq \left[\left(\frac{z_b \cdot f_{tw}}{P}\right) - \left(\frac{z_b}{A}\right) + \left(\frac{M_d + M_l}{\eta P}\right)\right]$$

$$\geq \left[0 - \left(\frac{99 \times 10^6}{367500}\right) + \frac{(1035 + 1237.5) \times 10^6}{0.85 \times 3136 \times 10^3}\right]$$

$$\geq 583 \text{ mm}$$

(b) At support section :

$$e \leq \left[\left(\frac{z_b \cdot f_{ct}}{P}\right) - \left(\frac{z_b}{A}\right) + 0\right]$$

$$\leq 283 \text{ mm}$$

$$e \geq \left[0 - \frac{z_b}{A} + 0\right]$$

$$e \geq -269 \text{ mm}$$

The permissible tendon zone is shown in Fig. 8.8.

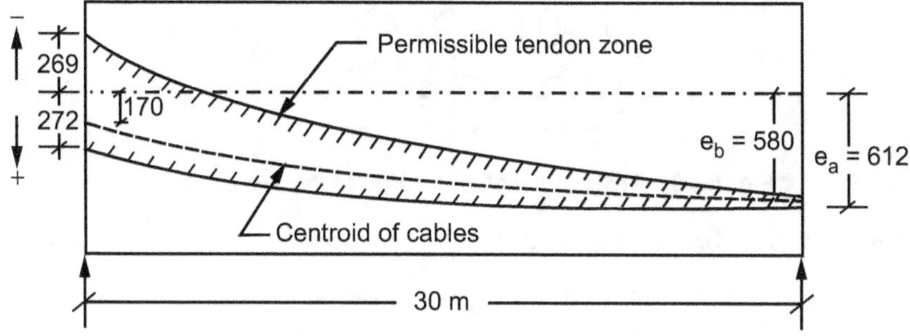

Fig. 8.8 : Permissible tendon zone

The arrangement of cables at support sections and at centre of span are shown in Figs. 8.9 and 8.10.

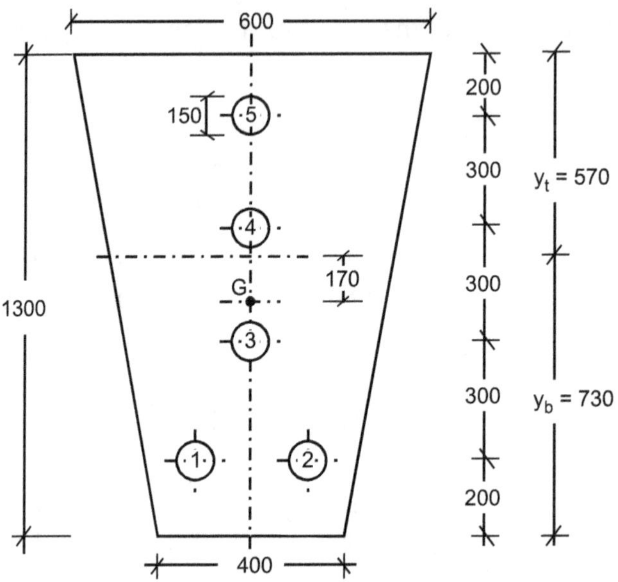

Fig. 8.9 : Arrangement of cables at supports

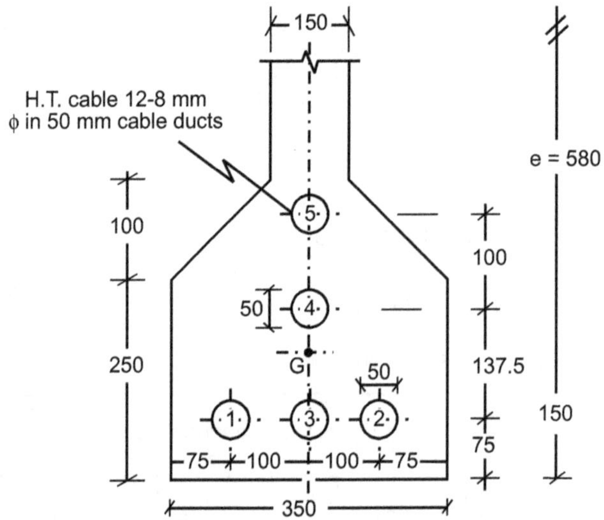

Fig. 8.10 : Arrangement of cables at centre of span

8. Check for ultimate flexural strength :

At centre of span-section, the section properties are as :

$$A_p = (12 \times 50 \times 5) = 3000 \text{ mm}^2, \qquad d = 1150 \text{ mm}$$

$$f_{ck} = 50 \text{ N/mm}^2, \qquad\qquad b_w = 150 \text{ mm}$$

$$f_{pu} = 1500 \text{ N/mm}^2, \qquad\qquad b = 600 \text{ mm}$$

$$D_f = 250 \text{ mm}$$

$$\text{Design ultimate moment, } M_{ud} = 1.5 \, (M_d + M_l)$$

$$= 1.5 \, (1035 + 1237.5)$$

$$= 3408 \text{ kN-m}$$

$$A_p = A_{pw} + A_{pf}$$

Now,

$$A_{pf} = 0.45 \, f_{ck} \, (b - b_w) \left(\frac{D_f}{f_p}\right)$$

$$= 0.45 \times 50 \times (600 - 150) \left(\frac{250}{1500}\right)$$

$$= 1680 \text{ mm}^2$$

$$\therefore \quad A_{pw} = [3000 - 1680] = 1320 \text{ mm}^2$$

$$\left(\frac{A_{pw} \, f_p}{b_w \cdot d \cdot f_{ck}}\right) = \left(\frac{1320 \times 1500}{150 \times 1150 \times 50}\right) = 0.23$$

Referring to Table - 11 of IS : 1343;

$$\frac{f_{pu}}{0.87 \, f_p} = 0.92 \quad \text{and} \quad \left(\frac{x_u}{d}\right) = 0.45$$

$$\therefore \quad f_{pu} = (0.92 \times 0.87 \times 1500) = 1200.6 \text{ N/mm}^2$$

$$x_u = (0.45 \times 1150) = 517.5 \text{ mm}$$

It is clear that, neutral axis lies outside the flange. Therefore, moment of resistance,

$$M_u = f_{pu} \cdot A_{pw} \, (d - 0.42 \, x_u) + 0.45 \, f_{ck} \, (b - b_w) \, D_f \, (d - 0.5 \, D_f)$$

$$= (1320 \times 1200.6) \, (1150 - 0.42 \times 517.5) + (0.45 \times 50) \, (600 - 150)$$

$$\times 250 \times (1150 - 0.5 \times 250)$$

$$= 4072 \times 10^6 \text{ N-mm}$$

$$= 4072 \text{ kN-m} > 3408 \text{ kN-m}$$

Hence, the section satisfies the limit state of ultimate flexural strength and supplementary reinforcement is not necessary. However, it is to be provided to safeguard against shrinkage cracking.

9.   Check for ultimate shear strength at support section :

Required ultimate shear, $V_u = 1.5 \, (V_d + V_l)$

$$= (1.5 \times 303) = 454.5 \text{ kN}$$

$$f_t = 1.7 \text{ N/mm}^2 \text{ (given)}$$

$$f_{cp} = \left(\frac{\eta P}{A}\right) = \left(\frac{0.85 \times 3136 \times 10^3}{367500}\right) = 7.25 \text{ N/mm}^2$$

$$\text{Slope of cable} = \theta = \left(\frac{4e}{L}\right) = \left[\frac{4 \times (583 - 170)}{30 \times 1000}\right] = 0.055$$

$$V_{co} = 0.67 \, b_w \, D \sqrt{f_t^2 + 0.8 \, f_{cp} \cdot f_t} + \eta \, P \sin\theta$$

$$= 0.67 \times 150 \times 1300 \, \frac{\sqrt{1.7^2 + 0.8 \times 7.25 \times 1.7}}{(1000)} + 0.85 \times 3136 \times 0.055$$

$$= 613 \text{ kN} > 454.5 \text{ kN}. \quad \text{Hence safe.}$$

Minimum shear reinforcement :

Using 10 mm diameter two legged stirrups (Fe-415 HYSD bars),

$$\text{Spacing} = S_v = \left(\frac{A_{sv} \times 0.87 \, f_y}{0.4 \, b_w}\right)$$

$$= \left(\frac{2 \times 78.5 \times 0.87 \times 415}{0.4 \times 150}\right) = 950 \text{ mm}$$

But the maximum spacing of stirrups is limited to 0.75 d_t or 4 b_w, whichever is smaller.

Allowing for 50 mm cover; d_t = 1250 mm

$$\text{Spacing} > (0.75 \times 1250) = 937.5 \text{ or } (4 \times 150) = 600 \text{ mm}$$

Adopt 10 mm diameter two legged stirrups at 600 mm c/c throughout the span.

10. Check for deflection at serviceability limit state :

Eccentricity of cable at centre of span = e_1 = 583 mm.

Eccentricity of cable at support section = e_2 = 170 mm.

Deflection at centre of span due to prestressing force

$$= \left[\frac{PL^2}{48 \, E_c \, I} \, (-5e_1 + e_2)\right]$$

$$= \left[\frac{3136 \times 10^3 \times 30^2 \times 10^6}{48 \times 35.36 \times 10^3 \times 72208 \times 10^6} \, (-5 \times 583 - 170)\right] \quad \text{(Here } e_2 = -e_2\text{)}$$

$$= 71 \text{ mm} \, (\uparrow)$$

Deflection due to dead and live loads

$$= \left[\frac{5\,(w_d + w_l)\,L^4}{384\,E_c \cdot I}\right]$$

$$= \left[\frac{5 \times (9.2 + 11) \times (30 \times 10^3)^4}{384 \times 35.36 \times 10^3 \times 72208 \times 10^6}\right]$$

$$= 83 \text{ mm } (\downarrow)$$

If creep coefficient $= \phi = 1.6$,

Long-term deflection is evaluated as

$$= [0.85 \times (-71) + 83]\,(1 + 1.6)$$

$$= 59 \text{ mm } (\downarrow)$$

But Maximum permissible deflection $\ngtr \left(\dfrac{\text{span}}{250}\right) = \left(\dfrac{30 \times 10^3}{250}\right) = 120 \text{ mm}.$

Hence, deflection is within permissible limit.

11. End block design :

Equivalent prisms on which the anchorage forces are considered to be effective are shown in Fig. 8.11.

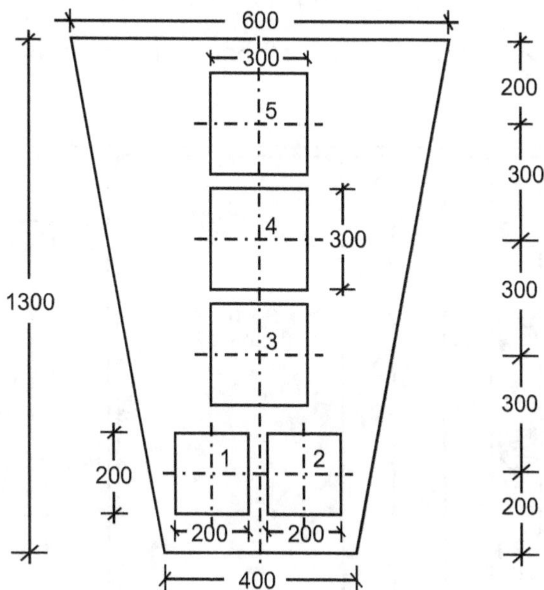

Fig. 8.11 : Equivalent prisms for anchorage forces

For cables 1 and 2,

$$P_k = \left(\frac{3136}{5}\right) = 627 \text{ kN}$$

$$y_{po} = 150 \text{ mm}, \quad y_o = 200 \text{ mm}$$

$$\therefore \quad \text{Bursting tension} = P_k \left[0.32 - 0.3 \left(\frac{y_{po}}{y_o} \right) \right]$$

$$= 627 \, [0.32 - 0.3 \times 0.75]$$

$$= 59.6 \text{ kN}$$

For cables 3, 4, and 5,

$$P_k = 627 \text{ kN}, \quad y_{po} = 150 \text{ mm}, \quad y_o = 300 \text{ mm}$$

$$\text{Bursting tension} = 627 \, [0.32 - 0.3 \times 0.5]$$

$$= 106.6 \text{ kN}$$

Using mild steel links and considering the larger bursting tension,

$$A_{st} = \left(\frac{106.6 \times 10^3}{0.87 \times 250} \right) = 490 \text{ mm}^2$$

$$\text{Number of 8 mm diameter bars} = \left(\frac{490}{50} \right) \approx 10.$$

Provide 8 mm diameter bars at 100 mm c/c both in the horizontal and vertical directions as shown in Fig. 8.12.

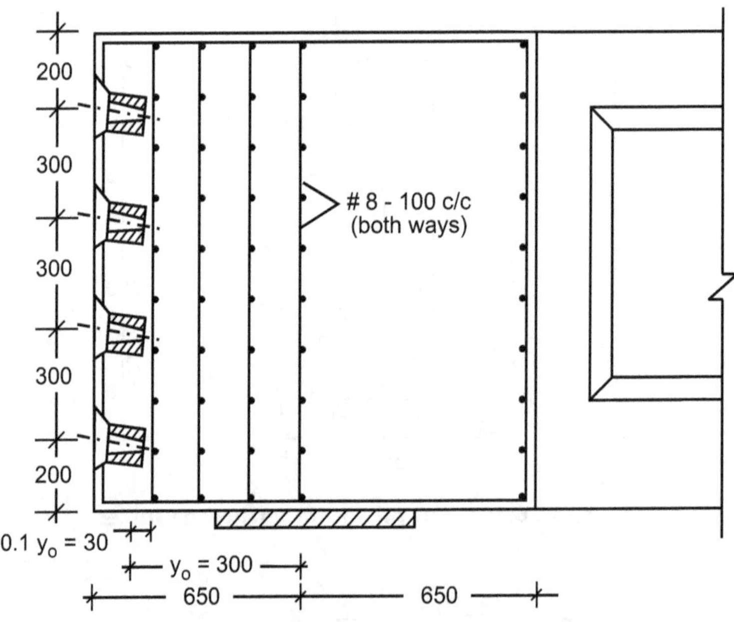

Fig. 8.12 : End block reinforcements

12. Supplementary reinforcement :

As per IS : 1343-1980, the minimum longitudinal reinforcement should not be less than 0.15 percent of the cross-sectional area.

$$A_{st} = \left(\frac{0.15 \times 367500}{100}\right) = 551.25 \text{ mm}^2$$

Provide 16 mm diameter HYSD bar.

Minimum web reinforcement = 0.15 percent of web area in plan

$$= \left(\frac{0.15}{100} \times 750 \times 150\right) \approx 169 \text{ mm}^2$$

Provide 10 mm diameter HYSD bar.

The reinforcement details in girder are as shown in Fig. 8.13.

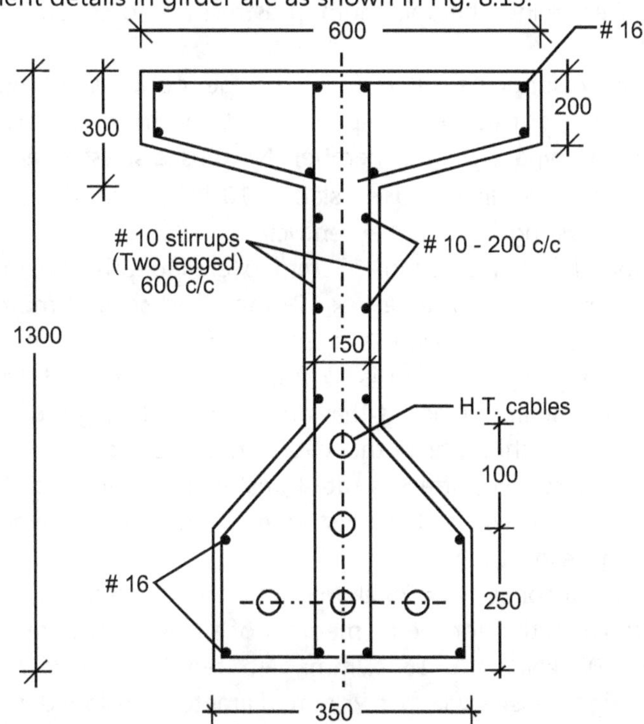

Fig. 8.13 : Reinforcements in P.S. girder

IMPORTANT POINTS

- Formula : $M_{ud} = 0.08\, P_c h\, bd^2$

  P_i, Minimum prestress $= \dfrac{A\,(f_{in}\,f \cdot z_b + f_{sup} \cdot z_t)}{(z_t + z_b)}$

  $P_{i\ (revised)} = \dfrac{A f_{in}\,f\,z_b}{z_b + A_e}$

Minimum section modulus,

$$z_b = \left[\frac{M_l + (1 - n)\, M_d}{P_b}\right]$$

$$\text{Eccentricity, } e = \frac{z_t\, z_b\, (P_{inf} - f_{sup})}{A\, (f_{sup} \cdot z_t + f_{inf} \cdot z_b)}$$

QUESTIONS

1. A post-tensioned prestressed concrete beam of rectangular section 250 mm wide by 580 mm deep is to be designed to support an imposed load of 12 kN/m uniformly distributed over a span of 12 m. The stress in concrete must not exceed 17 N/mm² in compression or 1.4 N/mm² in tension at any stage and the loss of prestress is 15 percent. Determine the minimum prestressing force and the corresponding eccentricity.

2. Design a simply supported slab for a bridge deck using the following data : span = 10 m, permissible compressive strength in concrete at transfer = f_{ct} = 16.5 N/mm², type-1/class-1 member (No tensile stress at any stage), safe stress in steel = 950 N/mm², live load on slab = 10 kN/m², loss of stress = 18 percent. Design the prestressing force and eccentricity.

3. A post-tensioned beam of span, 15 mm overall depth 900 mm, has a uniform symmetrical cross-section of area 2×10^5 mm² and second moment of area being 212×10^8 mm⁴ units. The prestress is provided by a cable tensioned to a force of 1450 kN at transfer. If the beam is to support a uniformly distributed live load of 21 kN/m and the minimum load is that due to the self weight of the beam, calculate the vertical limits within which the cable must lie along the beam length. The permissible compressive stresses at transfer and working load are 14 and 16.8 N/mm² respectively. The tensile stresses at transfer and working load are zero and 1.75 N/mm² respectively.
   Assume density of concrete = 25 kN/m³ and loss of prestress = 20 percent.

4. Design a suitable section for the tie member of a truss to support a maximum design tensile force 200 kN. f_{ct} = 16 N/mm². No tensile stresses are permitted. Loss ratio = 0.8. High tensile wire of 7 mm diameter tensioned to 100 N/mm², are available for use, f_p = 1600 N/mm². Tensile strength of concrete = 3 N/mm². Load factor against collapse = 1.5 and load factor against cracking = 1.25.

UNIVERSITY QUESTIONS

Dec. 2014

Q. 1 (a) State the step by step procedure used in design of prestressed concrete flanged beam. **(Section 8.3)**   **(7 Marks)**

Chapter 9
PRESTRESSED CONCRETE SLABS

9.1 INTRODUCTION

Design of prestressed concrete one-way slabs : The design of prestressed concrete one-way slabs spanning between parallel supports is based on the principles of designing members for flexure as outlined in section. One-way slabs may be supported across the entire width of the slab by beams, piers or abutments or bearing walls, which are positioned perpendicular to the longitudinal axis of the span or the supports may be at an angle to the span directions. One-way slabs may be continuous over one or several supports.

Simple or continuous slabs are analysed for design moments by considering a unit width of the slab. The prestressing force and the eccentricity of the cable required at prominent sections to resist the dead and live load moments are determined and the spacing of the cables or wires fixed based on the availability of the type of tendons. In the case of slabs subjected to heavy concentrated loads, transverse reinforcements in the form of mild steel or deformed bars or prestressed cables will be required to resist transverse moments.

An approximate estimate of these moments may be made by using the data of Westergaard[9] or Kawal[10] or Kist and Bouma[11]. Concentric tendons are generally preferred for transverse prestressing of one-way slabs to prevent objectionable deflections in the transverse direction. The slabs designed should conform to the requirements of serviceability and strength. The serviceability requirement includes limiting deflections and cracking under working loads as prescribed in the codes.

Solved Examples

Example 9.1 :

The deck slab of a road bridge of span 10 m is to be designed as a one-way prestressed concrete slab, with parallel post-tensioned cables in each of which the force at transfer is 500 kN. If the deck slab is required to support a uniformly distributed live load of 25 kN/m^2, with the compressive and tensile stress in concrete at any stage not exceeding 15 and zero N/mm^2 respectively, calculate the maximum horizontal spacing of the cables and their positions at the mid-span section. Assume the loss ratio as 0.80.

Solution :

The live and dead load moments are computed considering one metre width of slab.

$$M_q = 25 \times \frac{10^2}{8}$$

$$= 312.5 \text{ kN/m}$$

Let, h – Overall depth of slab

b – Width of slab

$\therefore$ $M_g = \dfrac{bh}{10^6} \times 24 \times \dfrac{10^2}{8}$

$$= \dfrac{300\, bh}{10^6} \text{ kN/m}$$

$$= 300\, bh \ \text{N/mm}$$

$$f_{ct} = f_{cw} = 15 \text{ N/mm}^2$$

$$f_{tt} = f_{tw} = 0$$

Range of stress, $f_{br} = 0.8 \times 15 + 0 = 12 \text{ N/mm}^2$

Hence, the minimum section modulus required is

$$Z_b = \dfrac{bh^2}{6} = \left[\dfrac{M_q + (1-\eta)\, M_q}{f_{br}}\right]$$

or $\dfrac{1000 \times h^2}{6} = \dfrac{(312.5 \times 10^6) + (1-0.8)\,300 \times 1000 \times h}{12}$

or $h^2 - 30h + 156250 = 0$

Solving $h = 410 \text{ mm}$

$$A = 1000 \times 410 = 41 \times 10^4 \text{ mm}^2$$

$$Z_b = zt = 1000 \times \dfrac{410^2}{6} = 28 \times 10^6 \text{ mm}^3$$

and $M_g = 123 \times 10^6 \text{ N/mm}$

$$f_{sup} = 0 - \dfrac{123 \times 10^6}{28 \times 10^6}$$

$$= 4.4 \text{ N/mm}^2$$

$$f_{inf} = 0 + \dfrac{(312.5 + 123)\, 10^6}{0.8 \times 28 \times 10^6}$$

$$= 19.4 \text{ N/mm}^2$$

The minimum prestressing force required is

$$P = \dfrac{A}{2}\,(f_{inf} + f_{sup})$$

$$= \dfrac{41 \times 10^4}{2}\,(19.4 - 4.4)$$

$$= 3075 \times 10^3 \text{ N} = 3075 \text{ kN}$$

$$e = \frac{Z \left(f_{inf} - f_{sup}\right)}{A \left(f_{inf} + f_{sup}\right)}$$

$$= \left[\frac{28 \times 10^6 \ (19.4 + 4.4)}{41 \times 10^4 \ (19.4 - 4.4)}\right]$$

$$= 109 \text{ mm}$$

$$\text{Spacing of cables} = \frac{1000 \times 500}{3075}$$

$$= 162 \text{ mm}$$

The slab is to be checked for the limit state of collapse and deflection. If the high-tensile steel designed is insufficient to provide the ultimate moment with desired load factors, supplementary (un-tensioned) reinforcement consisting of deformed bars is designed to cater for the balance moment.

9.2 DESIGN OF PRESTRESSED CONCRETE TWO-WAY SLABS

The design of a two-way slab supported on all four sides involves the computation of bending moments in the principal directions of the slab. The slabs may be supported on masonry walls or beams and may or may not be continuous over the supports. Transverse loads are resisted by the development of two-way slab action, resulting in moments in the longer and shorter span directions. The magnitude and nature of moments developed in two-way slabs depend mainly upon the type of load, ratio of the sides of slab and the degree of restraint at the supports.

The moments developed in a two-way slab may be determined by the elastic analysis, such as those of Westergaard and Pigeaud or alternatively by the ultimate load methods, such as Johansen's yield line method[12] or Hillerborg's strip method[13]. The bending moment coefficients shown in Table 9.1 are provided for by the British Standard BS : 8110 for the design of two-way slabs, simply supported on all four sides without any adequate provision to resist torsion and the lifting of corners.

Table 9.1 : Bending moment coefficients for slabs spanning in two directions at right angles, simply supported on four sides (British Standard BS:8110)

L_y/L_x	1.0	1.1	1.2	1.3	1.4	1.5	1.75	2.0
α_x	0.062	0.074	0.084	0.093	0.099	0.104	0.113	0.118
α_y	0.062	0.061	0.059	0.055	0.051	0.046	0.037	0.029

Bending moment coefficients compiled in Table 9.1 are useful for the design of restrained slabs supported on four sides with provision for torsion at corners as provided in the British as well as Indian standard codes[14]. These coefficients are based on the modified distributions of elastic bending moments proposed by Westergaard. Moment coefficients based on the yield line theory and compiled in Table 9.1 and on strip methods suggested by the author[15, 16, 17] are strictly applicable for the limit state of collapse only. It is also significant to note that coefficients predicted by the simple yield line theory using on orthotropic layout of reinforcement are found to be identical with those derived by the strip method. The moment coefficients derived from the ultimate load methods are generally lower in magnitude than those evaluated from elastic theories thus naturally resulting in savings in reinforcement. However, slabs designed by the ultimate load method should be checked for excessive deflections and/or crack widths under service loads according to the principles of limit state design[18].

In the case of two-way slabs which are fully prestressed (class 1), the serviceability criterion to be satisfied is generally the constraint imposed on upward deflections under prestress and self-weight, so that tensile stresses are completely eliminated under service loads. The question of limiting cracks within permissible limits arises only in slabs which are designed as partially prestressed systems.

Deflections of slabs which are not cracked under service loads can be estimated by using the deflection coefficients of Timoshenko[19]. The shear coefficients are useful for computing the shear forces developed at the supports.

In prestressed slabs, due to the load balancing effect, the shear forces and stresses developed being negligibly small, shear reinforcements are generally not required.

Table 9.2 : Bending Moment Coefficients for Rectangular Panels Supported on Four Sides with Provision for Torsion at Corners (IS: 456)

No.	Type of panel and moments considered		B.M. coefficient α_x for short span								B.M. coefficient α_y for long span (for all values of L_y/L_x)
			1.0	1.1	1.2	1.3	1.4	1.5	1.75	2.0 (or more)	
1.	Interior panels	X	0.032	0.037	0.043	0.047	0.051	0.053	0.060	0.065	0.032
		Y	0.024	0.028	0.032	0.036	0.039	0.041	0.045	0.049	0.024
2.	One short edge discontinuous	X	0.037	0.043	0.048	0.051	0.055	0.057	0.064	0.068	0.037
		Y	0.028	0.032	0.036	0.039	0.041	0.044	0.048	0.052	0.028
3.	One long edge discontinuous	X	0.037	0.044	0.052	0.057	0.063	0.067	0.077	0.085	0.037
		Y	0.028	0.033	0.039	0.044	0.047	0.051	0.059	0.065	0.028
4.	Two adjacent edges discontinuous	X	0.047	0.053	0.060	0.065	0.071	0.075	0.084	0.091	0.042
		Y	0.035	0.040	0.045	0.049	0.053	0.056	0.069	0.069	0.035
5.	Two short edges discontinuous	X	0.045	0.049	0.052	0.056	0.059	0.060	0.069	0.069	-
		Y	0.035	0.037	0.040	0.043	0.044	0.045	0.052	0.052	0.035
6.	Two long edges discontinuous	X	-	-	-	-	-	-	-	-	0.045
		Y	0.035	0.043	0.051	0.057	0.063	0.068	0.088	0.088	0.035
7.	Three edges discontinuous	X	0.057	0.064	0.071	0.076	0.080	0.084	0.097	0.097	-
		Y	0.043	0.048	0.053	0.057	0.060	0.064	0.073	0.073	0.043
8.	Three edges discontinuous	X	-	-	-	-	-	-	-	-	0.057
		Y	0.043	0.051	0.059	0.065	0.071	0.076	0.096	0.096	0.043
9.	Four edges	X	0.056	0.056	0.072	0.079	0.085	0.089	0.107	0.107	0.056

Table 9.2 : Bending Moment Coefficients for the Design of Rectangular Slabs by Yield Line Theory

B.M. coefficient α_x for short span

Values of L_y/L_x

No.	Type of panel and moments considered		1.0	1.1	1.2	1.3	1.4	1.5	1.75	2.0 (or more)	B.M. coefficient α_y for long span (for all values of L_y/L_x)
1.	Interior panels	X	0.025	0.028	0.031	0.035	0.039	0.043	0.045	0.050	0.025
		Y	0.017	0.019	0.021	0.024	0.026	0.028	0.030	0.033	0.017
2.	One edge discontinuous	X	0.030	0.033	0.037	0.040	0.043	0.047	0.051	0.054	0.030
		Y	0.020	0.022	0.025	0.027	0.029	0.031	0.034	0.036	0.020
3.	Two adjacent edges discontinuous	X	0.032	0.036	0.040	0.045	0.048	0.051	0.057	0.063	0.032
		Y	0.021	0.024	0.027	0.030	0.032	0.034	0.038	0.042	0.021
4.	Two short edges discontinuous	X	0.036	0.040	0.043	0.047	0.050	0.053	0.055	0.058	-
		Y	0.024	0.026	0.029	0.031	0.033	0.035	0.037	0.039	0.024
5.	Two long edges discontinuous	X	-	-	-	-	-	-	-	-	0.048
		Y	0.032	0.034	0.037	0.040	0.045	0.050	0.057	0.065	0.032
6(a).	Three edges discontinuous (one long edge	X	0.039	0.044	0.048	0.053	0.056	0.060	0.063	0.068	-
		Y	0.026	0.029	0.032	0.035	0.037	0.039	0.042	0.045	0.026
6(b).	Three edges discontinuous (one short edge continuous)	X	-	-	-	-	-	-	-	-	0.55
		Y	0.037	0.041	0.045	0.049	0.051	0.054	0.064	0.074	0.037
7.	Four edges discontinuous	X	0.042	0.048	0.054	0.060	0.064	0.068	0.076	0.083	0.042
		Y									

X – Negative moment at continuous edge, Y – Positive moment at midspan

Limited experimental investigations[20, 21] on slabs designed by the strip method indicate that the designs are safe with respect to the limit states of serviceability and strength, with actual load factors against collapse exceeding the theoretical values.

Example 9.2 :

Design a post-tensioned prestressed concrete two-way slab, 6 m by 9 m, with discontinuous edges, to support an imposed load of 3 kN/m². Cables of four wires of 5 mm diameter carrying an effective force of 100 kN are available for use. Design the spacings of cables in the two directions and check for the safety of the slab against collapse and excessive deflection at service loads. Assume f_{ck} = 40 N/mm², f_p = 1600 N/mm² and E_c = 38 kN/mm², L_x = 6 m and L_y = 9 m.

Solution :

$$\text{Ratio of } L_y/L_x \ = \ 1.5$$

$$\text{Thickness of slab} \ = \ \frac{\text{Span}}{50} \ = \ \frac{6000}{50} \ = \ 120 \text{ mm}$$

$$\text{Self-weight of slab} \ = \ 0.12 \times 24 \times 1$$

$$= \ 2.88 \text{ kN/m}^2$$

$$\text{Live load on slab} \ = \ 3.00 \text{ kN/m}^2$$

$$\text{Finishes, etc.} \ = \ 0.12 \text{ kN/m}^2$$

$$\text{Total service load} \ = \ 6.00 \text{ kN/m}^2$$

Total ultimate design load,

$$W_{ud} \ = \ (1.4 \times 3.00) + (1.6 \times 3.00) \ = \ 9.00 \text{ kN/m}^2$$

Referring to Table 9.2 working moments in the middle strips are given by

$$M_{sx} \ = \ 0.089 \times 6.0 \times 6^2$$

$$= \ 19.3 \text{ kN/m}$$

$$M_y \ = \ 0.056 \times 6.0 \times 6^2$$

$$= \ 12.1 \text{ kN/m}$$

Total moment in the middle strip (x direction)

$$= \ 19.3 \times 0.75 \times 9$$

$$= \ 130 \text{ kN/m}$$

Using a minimum cover of 30 mm for the tendons at the centre of slab, the distance between the top kern and the centroid of cable

$$= \ 120 - 20 - 40 \ = \ 50 \text{ mm}$$

If $\quad\quad\quad\quad$ P = Total prestressing force required in the x direction

$$P \times 50 = 130 \times 10^6$$

$$P = 26 \times 10^5 \text{ N}$$

$$= 2600 \text{ N}$$

Force in each cable = 100 kN

∴ $\quad$ Number of cables in x direction (middle strip) = 26

$$\text{Spacing of cables} = \frac{0.75 \times 9 \times 1000}{26} = 260 \text{ mm}$$

Adopt a spacing of 250 mm (four cables per metre).

Total moment in the middle strip (y direction)

$$= 12.1 \times 0.75 \times 6 = 55 \text{ kN/m}$$

Providing a cover of 40 mm to cables in y direction.

Distance between cable and top kern = 120 – 40 – 40 = 40 mm

∴ $\quad$ Prestressing force required $= \dfrac{(55 \times 10^6)}{40 \times 10^3} = 1380 \text{ kN}$

∴ $\quad$ Number of cables in y direction (middle strip)

$$= \frac{1380}{100} = 14$$

$$\text{Spacing of cables} = \frac{0.75 \times 6 \times 1000}{14} = 320 \text{ mm}$$

The cable profile is parabolic with maximum eccentricity at the centre and concentric at the supports.

Check for limit state of collapse :

Ultimate moment (x direction) $= 0.089 \times 9.00 \times 6^2$

$$= 29 \text{ kN/m}$$

$$A_p = (4 \times 4 \times 20)$$

$$= 320 \text{ mm}^2$$

$$\left(\frac{A_p\, f_p}{bd\, f_{ck}}\right) = \left(\frac{320 \times 1600}{1000 \times 90 \times 40}\right) = 0.142$$

Referring to conditions at the ultimate limit state (IS : 1343-1980)

$$\left(\frac{f_{pu}}{0.87 f_p}\right) = 1.0$$

∴ $\quad\quad\quad\quad$ $f_{pu} = (0.87 \times 1600) = 1392 \text{ N/mm}^2$

and
$$\left(\frac{x_u}{d}\right) = 0.29$$

$$x_u = (0.29 \times 90) = 26.1 \text{ mm}$$

$$M_u = f_p \, A_p \, (d - 0.42 \, x_u)$$

$$= 1392 \times 320 \left(\frac{90 - 0.42 \times 26.1}{10^6}\right)$$

$$= 35.2 \text{ kN/m}$$

The ultimate moment capacity of the slab is higher than the minimum value required. A similar check may be made in the y direction also.

Check for deflection under service loads :

The tendons following a parabolic profile in x and y directions induce uniformly distributed loads acting upwards, which are given by

$$\text{Equivalent load (x direction)} = \frac{8Pe}{L_x^2} = \frac{8 \times 400 \times 0.03}{36}$$

$$= 2.66 \text{ kN/m}$$

$$\text{Equivalent load (y direction)} = \frac{8Pe}{L_y^2} = \frac{8 \times 320 \times 0.02}{81}$$

$$= 0.64 \text{ kN/m}$$

$$\therefore \quad \text{Unbalanced service load} = 6.00 - 2.66 - 0.64$$

$$= 2.70 \text{ kN/m}^2$$

$$= 0.0027 \text{ N/mm}^2$$

Using deflection coefficients recommended by Timoshenko, for an aspect ratio of $\frac{L_y}{L_x} = 1.5$, the deflection is given by

$$a_{max} = \alpha \left(\frac{qL_x^4}{D}\right)$$

where,
$$\alpha = \text{Coefficient} = 0.00772$$

$$q = \text{u.d.l.} = 0.0027 \text{ N/mm}^2$$

$$D = \text{flexural rigidity} = \frac{Eh^3}{12\,(1 - v_c^2)}$$

$$= \frac{38000 \times 120^3}{12\,(1 - 0.15^2)} = 5.62 \times 10^9$$

$$\therefore \qquad a_{max} = 0.00772 \left(\frac{0.0027 \times 600^4}{5.62 \times 10^9} \right) = 4.85 \text{ mm}$$

$$\text{Maximum permissible long term deflection} = \frac{6000}{250} = 24 \text{ mm}$$

Check for stresses :

$$\text{Unbalanced load} = 2.7 \text{ kN/m}^2$$

Moment due to this load (x direction)

$$= 0.089 \times 2.7 \times 6^2 = 8.7 \text{ kN/m}$$

$$\text{Stresses developed} = \frac{8.7 \times 10^6}{(1000 \times 120^2)/6} = 3.33 \text{ N/mm}^2$$

(Compression at top and tension at soffit of slab.)

Direct stress due to prestressing force

$$= \frac{400 \times 1000}{1000 \times 120} = 3.66 \text{ N/mm}^2 \text{ (compression)}$$

$\therefore$ Maximum compressive stress in concrete at the top of slab

$$= 3.66 + 3.33 = 7.00 \text{ N/mm}^2$$

which is less than the permissible stress of 13 N/mm^2.

The maximum shear-stress under ultimate load is

$$= \frac{0.424 \times 9.00 \times 6000}{(1000 \times 90)} = 0.26 \text{ N/mm}^2$$

which is negligibly small and hence no shear reinforcements are necessary.

Example 9.3 :

A post-tensioned prestressed concrete two way slab 7 × 8.5 m with discontinuous edges to support imposed load of 5 kN/m². Use S3 (three strands, each having cross-sectional area 100 mm²) having f_y = 1900 MPa. Check the safety of the slab against collapse and deflection at service load, take the grade of concrete = M45.

(May 12, 13, 15, Dec. 11, 12, 14, 20 Marks)

Solution :

$$\text{Ratio } \frac{L_y}{L_x} = \frac{8.5}{7} = 1.21$$

$$\text{Thickness of slab} = \frac{\text{Span}}{50} = \frac{7000}{50} = 140 \text{ mm}$$

$$\text{Self weight of slab} = 0.14 \times 24 \times 1 = 3.36 \text{ kN/m}^2$$

$$\text{Live load on slab} = 5 \text{ kN/m}^2$$

$$\text{Finishes, etc.} = 0.12 \text{ kN/m}^2$$

$$\text{Total service load} = 8.48 \text{ kN/m}^2$$

$$\text{Total ultimate design load} = (14 \times 5) + (1.6 \times 5) = 15 \text{ kN/m}^2$$

$$M_x = 0.072 \times 8.48 \times 7^2 = 29.92 \text{ kN-m}$$

$$M_y = 0.056 \times 8.48 \times 7^2 = 23.27 \text{ kN-m}$$

Total moment in the middle strip (x direction)

$$= 29.92 \times 0.6 \times 8.5 = 152.59 \text{ kN-m}$$

Using a minimum cover of 20 mm for the tendons at the centre of slab, the distance between the top kern and the centroid of cable = 140 – 20 – 40 = 80 mm.

If $\quad\quad\quad\quad\quad\quad P$ = Total prestressing force required in x direction

$$P \times 80 = 152.59 \times 10^6$$

$$\therefore \quad\quad\quad P = 1907.37 \times 10^6 \text{ N} = 1907.37 \text{ kN}$$

Assume force in each strand = 100 kN

Number of cables in x direction (middle strip) = 19 (approximate) $\approx$ 20.

$$\text{Spacing of cables} = \frac{0.6 \times 8.5 \times 1000}{20} = 255 \text{ m}$$

Adopt a spacing of 250 mm (four cables per metre)

Total moment in the middle strip (y direction)

$$= 23.27 \times 0.6 \times 7 = 97.734 \text{ kN-m}$$

Providing a cover of 40 mm to cables in y direction,

Distance between cable and top kern = 140 – 40 – 40 = 60 mm

$$\therefore \quad \text{Prestressing force required} = \frac{97.734 \times 10^6}{45 \times 10^3} = 2172 \text{ N}$$

$\therefore \quad$ Number of cables in y direction (middle strip)

$$= \frac{2172}{100} = 21.72 \approx 22$$

$$\text{Spacing of cables} = \frac{0.6 \times 7 \times 1000}{22} = 190.91 \text{ mm}$$

The cable profile is parabolic with maximum eccentricity at the centre and concentric at the supports.

Check for limit state of collapse :

Ultimate moment (x direction) $= 0.072 \times 15 \times 7^2 = 52.92 \text{ kN-m}$

$$A_p = 3 \times 100 = 300 \text{ mm}^2$$

$$\frac{A_p \, f_p}{bd \, f_{ck}} = \frac{300 \times 1900}{1000 \times 110 \times 45} = 0.115$$

From IS : 1343 – 1980

$$\frac{f_{pu}}{0.87 \, f_p} = 1$$

$$\therefore \qquad f_{pu} = 0.87 \times 1900 = 1653 \text{ N/mm}^2$$

$$\frac{x_u}{d} = 0.29$$

$$x_u = 0.29 \times 110 = 31.9 \text{ mm}$$

$$\therefore \qquad M_u = f_p \, A_p \, (d - 0.42 \, x_u)$$

$$= \frac{1653 \times 300 \, (110 - 0.42 \times 31.9)}{10^6}$$

$$= 47.90 \text{ kN-m}$$

The ultimate moment capacity of the slab is higher than the minimum required value.

Check for deflection :

$$\text{Equivalent load (x direction)} = \frac{8Pe}{l_x^2} = \frac{8 \times 300 \times 0.03}{49} = 1.47 \text{ kN/m}$$

$$\text{Equivalent load (y direction)} = \frac{8Pe}{l_y^2} = \frac{8 \times 300 \times 0.02}{8.5^2} = 1 \text{ kN/m}$$

$$\therefore \quad \text{Unbalanced service load} = 8.48 - 1.47 - 1 = 6 \text{ kN/m}^2 = 0.006 \text{ N/mm}^2$$

$$q_{max} = \alpha \left(\frac{qL_x^4}{D} \right)$$

$\alpha = 0.00772$, $q = \text{UDL} = 0.006 \text{ N/mm}^2$.

$$D = \text{Flexural rigidity} = \frac{Eh^3}{12 \, (1 - V_c^2)}$$

$$= \frac{500 \sqrt{45} \times 110^3}{12 \, (1 - 0.5^2)} = 3.81 \times 10^9$$

$$\therefore \qquad q_{max} = 0.00772 \left(\frac{0.006 \times 7000^4}{3.81 \times 10^9} \right) = 29.26 \text{ mm}$$

$$\text{Maximum permissible long term deflection} = \frac{7000}{250} = 28 \text{ mm}$$

IMPORTANT POINTS

- Principles of designing members for flexure.
- Some important conceptions.
- Requirements of serviceability and strength.

QUESTIONS

1. What are the salient design features of prestressed concrete one-way and two-way slab panels ?

2. Design a post-tensoined prestressed concrete two-way slab, 6 m by 8 m in size, to support a live load of 3 kN/m^2. If cables of four wires of 5 mm diameter stressed to 1000 N/mm^2 are available for use, determine the number of cables in the two principal directions. The stresses in concrete not to exceed 15 N/mm^2 in compression and tensile stresses are not permitted under service loads. The loss ratio is 0.8. Check for the limit states of serviceability and collapse.

UNIVERSITY QUESTIONS

Dec. 2011

Q. 1   A post tensioned prestressed concrete two way slab, 6.5 × 9 m with discontinuous edges to support imposed load of 4 kN/m^2. Use S3 (three strands, each having cross sectional area 100 mm^2) having f_y = 1900 Mpa. Check the safety of the slab against collaps and deflection at services load, take the grade of concrete = M40.

(Example 9.3)   **(20 Marks)**

May 2012

Q. 2   A post tensioned prestressed concrete two way slab, 7 × 8.5 m with discontinuous edges to support imposed load of 5 kN/m^2. Use S3 (three strands, each having cross sectional area 100 mm^2) having f_y = 1900 MPa. Check the safety of the slab against collapse and deflection at service load take the grade concrete = M45.

(Example 9.3)   **(20 Marks)**

Dec. 2012

Q. 3   A post tensioned prestressed concrete two way slab, 6.5 × 9 m with discontinuous edges to support imposed load of 4 kN/m^2. Use S3 (three strands, each having cross sectional area 100 mm^2) having f_y = 1900 Mpa. Check the safety of the slab against collapse and deflection at service load. Take the grade of concrete = M40.

(Example 9.3)   **(20 Marks)**.

May 2013

Q. 4   A post-tension prestress concrete two way slab of 7 m × 9 m with discontinuous edges to support imposed load of 5 kN/m^2 use S3 cable having area of each 100 mm^2 and f_y = 1800 Mpa. Check the safety of slab against collapse and deflection at service load. Use M40 concrete. **(Example 9.3)**   **(18 marks)**

Dec. 2014

Q. 5   A post tensioned prestressed concrete slab of size 7 m × 10 m with discontinuous edges is subjected to live load of 3.5 kN/m^2.Use three strands, each having cross sectional area 100 mm^2 having f_y = 1900 MPa. Use M35 grade of concrete. Check the safety of slab against collapse and deflection at working load.
(Example 9.3)   **(18 Marks)**

May 2015

Q. 6   A post tensioned prestressed concrete two-way slab of 7 m × 8 m with discontinuous edge to support imposed load of 4 kN/m^2 using S3 strands each having cross sectional area 100 mm^2 and f_y = 1900 MPa check the safety of the slab at collapse and deflection at service load. Use M45 grade of concrete.
(Example 9.3)   **(20 Marks)**

Chapter 10
EARTHQUAKE LOADS

DETERMINATION OF EARTHQUAKE LOADS BASED ON IS : 1893

10.1 INTRODUCTION

The chapter highlights the analysis and calculation required for the determination of design lateral forces of multi-storeyed earthquakes resistant structures as per **IS : 1893 (PART-I) 2002**. The study of occurrence of earthquake and its vibrational effects on structures have been studied by structural engineers since past many years. The various approaches to seismic analysis have been developed to design the structures subjected to earthquake.

The IS : 1893 has been updated in 2002 and it can be effectively used for the analysis and design of the structures which must be safe against earthquake. The analysis of (G + 5) storey building frame for lateral forces considering earthquake has been illustrated with an example in this chapter.

10.2 DETERMINATION OF LATERAL DESIGN FORCES

The procedure recommended for the determination of lateral forces in the code are based on the approximation that effects of yielding can be accounted for by linear analysis of building using the design spectrum. This analysis is carried by dynamic analysis procedure **(clause 7.8 of IS - 1893 (Part - I) : 2002)**. A simplified method may also be adopted that will be referred as equivalent lateral force procedure **(clause 7.5 of IS : 1893 (Part - I) : 2002)**, also recognized as equivalent lateral force procedure or equivalent static procedure. The main difference between the equivalent lateral force procedure and dynamic analysis procedure lies in the magnitude and distribution of natural vibration modes of the building, which are determined by distribution of mass and stiffness over height. In the equivalent lateral force procedures, the magnitude of forces is based on an estimation of the fundamental period and on the distribution of forces as given by simple formulas for regular buildings. The present chapter deals in detail the equivalent lateral method of seismic analysis.

10.3 EQUIVALENT LATERAL FORCE PROCEDURE

As discussed above, the equivalent lateral force procedure is the simplest method of analysis because the force depends on the code-based fundamental period of structures with same empirical modifier. The design lateral force shall first be computed for the building as a whole. The design lateral forces are distributed along the height of the building at various floor levels. The design lateral forces obtained at each floor level are then distributed to individual lateral load resisting elements depending on the floor diaphragm action. In case of rigid diaphragm (Reinforced concrete monolithic slab-beam floors or those consisting of prefabricated/precast elements with topping reinforcement screed can be taken a right diaphragm) action, the total shear in any horizontal plane is distributed to the various elements of lateral force resisting system on the basis of relative rigidity **(clause 7.2.2 IS 1893 (Part - I) : 2002)**.

The following are the major steps to determine the forces by equivalent static procedures.

10.4 DETERMINATION OF DESIGN SEISMIC BASE SHEAR

The total design lateral force or design seismic base shear (V_B) along principal direction shall be determined by the following expression **(clause 7.5.3 : IS 1893 (Part - I) : 2002)**.

$$V_B = A_h W$$

where, A_h – Design horizontal seismic coefficient for a structure.

                          W – Seismic weight of the building as per clause 7.4.2.

A_h shall be determined by the following expression (clause 6.4.2) :

$$A_h = \left(\frac{z}{2}\right)\left(\frac{I}{R}\right)\left(\frac{Sa}{g}\right)$$

provided that for any structure with T ≤ 0.1 sec, the value of A_h will not be taken less than $\frac{z}{2}$ irrespective of the value of $\frac{I}{R}$.

In factor $\left(\frac{z}{2}\right)$; z is the zone factor given in Table 10.1 of IS - 1893 (Part - I) 2002 for the maximum considered earthquake (MCE) and service life of structure in a zone. The value 2 in the denominator of z is used so as to reduce the maximum considered earthquake (MCE) zone factor to the factor for design basis earthquake (DBE). z can also be determined from the seismic zone map of India, as shown in Fig. 10.1. The object of this map is to divide the area of the country into a number of zones in which one may reasonably expect earthquake shaking of more or less of same maximum intensity in future. The whole country has been divided into four zones, starting from zone II to V. The intensity as per comprehensive Intensity scale (MSK64) broadly associated with the various zones is VI (or less), VII, VIII and IX (and above) for zones II, III, IV and V respectively. The values of z range from 0.10 to 0.36 corresponding to zone II to zone V as given in Table 10.1.

1993-1984

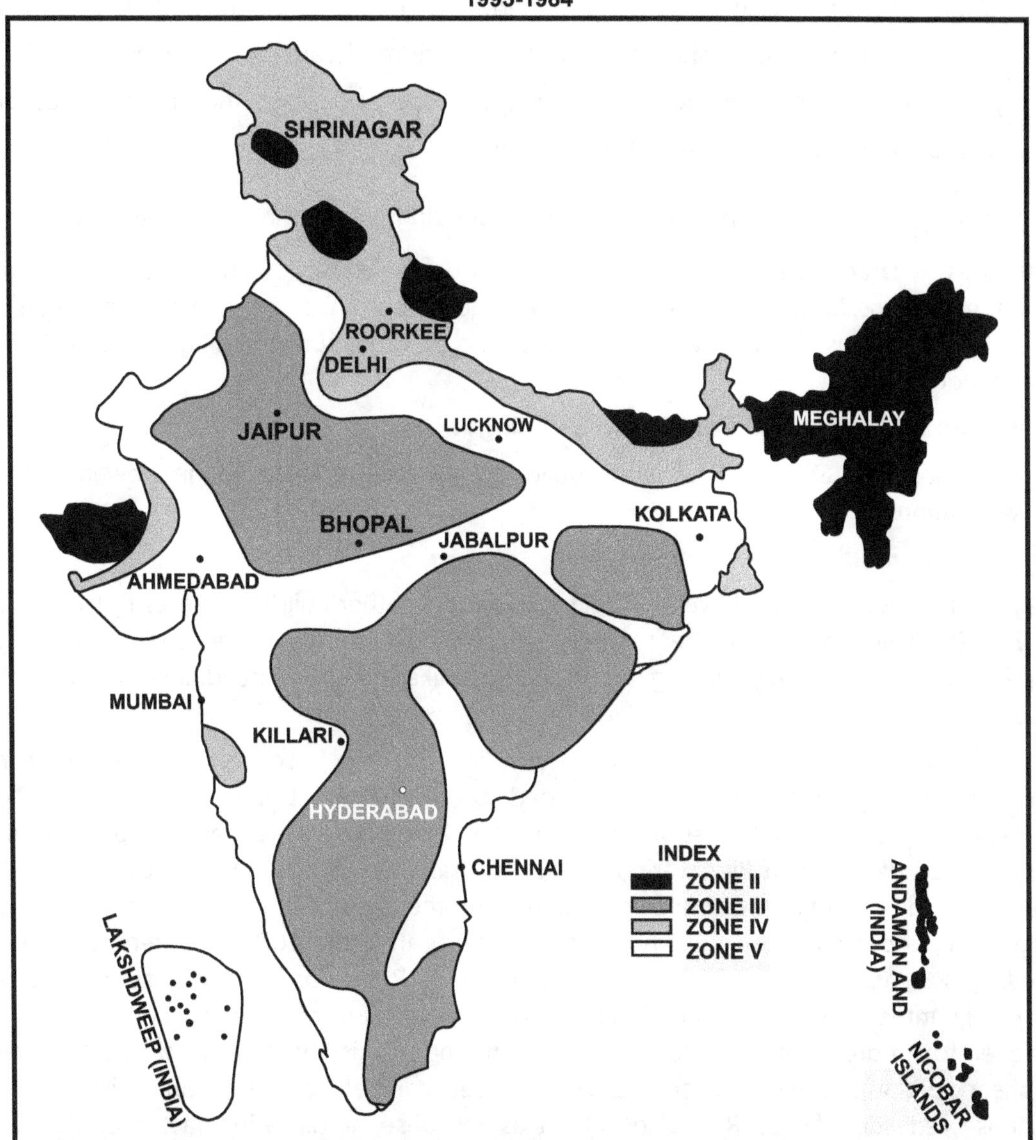

Fig. 10.1 : Revised seismic zoning map of India IS : 1893-2002

Table 10.1 : Zone factor

Seismic zone	II	III	IV	V
Seismic intensity	Low	Moderate	Severe	Very severe
z	0.10	0.16	0.24	0.36

From Table 10.1, it is clear that, zone II having low seismic intensity zone and minor damage will occur. Zone III is in moderate intensity zone where moderate damage may occur. Zone IV represents severe intensity zone where major property damage may be expected and zone V falls in very severe intensity of earthquake.

In factor $\left(\dfrac{I}{R}\right)$; I is the importance factor, depending upon the functional use of the structures, characterized by hazardous consequence of its failure, post-earthquake functional needs, historical value, or economic importance. The minimum value of importance factor is given in Table 10.2. According to Table 10.2, buildings are classified in two categories.

(i) Important Service and Community Buildings :

(Such as Hospitals, Schools, Emergency buildings like telephone exchange, power stations, railway stations, etc.)

(ii) All Other Buildings :

Important service buildings have an 'I' factor 1.5, and all other buildings are assigned a value of 1.0. The value of 'I' may be more than assigned value as proposed in Table 10.2, depending upon economy, strategy considerations like multistory buildings having several residential units.

R is the response reduction factor, depending on the perceived seismic damage performance of the structure, characterized by ductile or brittle deformations. This characteristic represents the structure's ductility, damping as well as the past seismic performance of structure with various structural framing systems. The factor 'R' is to be assigned to different types of building structures on the basis of empirical or semi-empirical judgement, experienced by building performance as in Table 10.3 for different types of building systems. Table 10.3 shows a low value of R approaching I.5 assigned to an extremely brittle building i.e. unreinforced masonry wall buildings and a high value of R (5) is assigned to a more ductile structure like special moment resistant frame reinforced concrete or shear special moment resistant frame reinforced concrete or shear wall buildings. The response reduction factor R is also known as response modification factor or behavior factor.

$\dfrac{Sa}{g}$ = Average response acceleration coefficient for rocks or soil sites as given by Fig. 10.2 and by the equations described in clause 6.4.5 for different soil conditions based on approximate natural periods of the structures. These values are given for 5% of damping of the structures, for other values of damping, it is modified according to Table 10.4.

The fundamental natural period for building is given in clause 7.6 of IS - 1893 (Part-I) : 2002 and is summarized.

$$T_a = 0.075 \, h^{0.75}$$

moment resisting RC frame building without brick infill panels.

$$= 0.085 \, h^{0.85}$$

moment resisting steel frame building without brick infill panels.

$$= \frac{0.09 \, h}{\sqrt{d}}$$

all other buildings including moment-resisting frame buildings with brick infill panels.

where,

h – height of building in m and

d – base dimension of the building at the plinth level in m, along the considered direction of the lateral force.

W – seismic weight of building which is the sum of the seismic weight of floors. The seismic weight at any floor level would be equal to dead weight of the floor system plus weight of column and walls in inverse proportion to its distance from the floors plus appropriate amount of imposed load as specified in clause 7.3 of IS-1893 (Part-I) : 2002. Imposed load on roof level need not be considered. The percentage of imposed load will be considered from Table 10.5.

10.5 DISTRIBUTION OF DESIGN BASE SHEAR

The computed base shear is distributed along the height of building. The shear force, at any level, depends on the mass at that level and deformed shape of the structure. The design base shear is distributed along the height of the building (clause 7.7 of I.S. 1893 (Part-I) : 2002 as per the following expression :

$$Q_i = V_B \, \frac{W_i \, h_i^2}{\sum\limits_{i=1}^{n} W_i \, h_i^2}$$

where,

Q_i – Design lateral force at floor i

W_i – Seismic weight of floor i

h_i – Height of ith floor measured from base, and

n – Number of storeys in the building is the number of levels at which the masses are located.

Table 10.2 : Importance Factors, I (Clause 6.4.2)

Sr. No.	Structure	Importance factor
(1)	(2)	(3)
(i)	Important service and community buildings, such as hospitals, schools, monumental structures, emergency buildings, like telephone exchange, television stations, radio stations, railway stations, fire station buildings, large community halls like cinemas, assembly halls and subway stations, power stations.	1.5
(ii)	All other buildings.	1.0

Notes :

(1) The design engineer may choose values of importance factor I greater than those mentioned above.

(2) Buildings not covered in SI No. (i) and (ii) above may be designed for higher value of I, depending on economy, strategy considerations like multi-storey buildings having several residential units.

(3) This does not apply to temporary structures like excavations, scaffolding etc. of short duration.

Table 10.3 : Response Reduction Factor (1), R, for Building Systems (Clause 6.4.2)

Sr. No.	Lateral Load Resisting System	R
(1)	(2)	(3)
(i) (ii) (iii)	Building Frame Systems Ordinary RC moment-resisting frame (OMRF)[2] Special RC moment-resisting frame (SMRF)[3] Steel frame with (a) Concentric braces (b) Eccentric braces	3.0 5.0 4.0 5.0
(iv) (v)	Steel moment resisting frame designed as per SP 6 (6) Load bearing masonary will buildings[5] (a) Unreinforced (b) Reinforced with horizontal RC bands (c) Reinforced with horizontal RC bands and vertical bars at corners of rooms and jumps of openings.	5.0 1.5 2.5 3.0

...Conti.

(vi)	Ordinary reinforced concrete shear walls[6]	3.0
(vii)	Ductile shear walls[7]	4.0
	Buildings with Dual System[8]	
(viii)	Ordinary shear wall with OMRF	3.0
(ix)	Ordinary shear wall with SMRF	4.0
(x)	Ductile shear wall with OMRF	4.5
(xi)	Ductile shear wall with SMRF	5.0

(1) The values of response reduction factors are to be used for buildings with lateral load resisting elements, and not just for the lateral load resisting elements built in isolation.

(2) OMRF are those designed and detailed as per 456 or IS 800 but not meeting ductile detailing requirements as per IS 13920 or SP 6 (6) respectively.

(3) SMRF defined in 4.15.2 in 1893 (part 1) : 2002.

(4) Buildings with shear walls and include buildings having shear walls and frames, but where

   (a) frames are not designed to carry lateral loads, or

   (b) frames are designed to carry lateral loads but do not fulfil the requirements of 'dual systems'.

(5) Reinforcement should be as per IS 4326.

(6) Prohibited in zones IV and V.

(7) Ductile shear walls are those designed and detailed as per IS 13920.

(8) Building with dual systems consists of shear walls (or braced frames) and moment resisting frames such that :

   (a) the two systems are designed to resist the total design force in proportion to their lateral stiffness considering the interaction of the dual system at all floor levels; and

   (b) the moment resisting frames are designed to independently resist atleast 25 percent of the design seismic base shear.

Table 10.4 : Multiplying Factors for Obtaining Values for Other Damping
(Clause 6.4.2)

Damping percent	0	2	5	7	10	15	20	25	30
Factors	3.20	1.40	1.00	0.90	0.80	0.70	0.60	0.55	0.50

Table 10.5 : Percentage of Imposed load to be considered in Seismic Weight Calculation (Clause 7.3.1)

Imposed uniformly distributed floor loads (kN/m²)	Percentage of imposed load
(1)	(2)
Upto and include 3.0	25
Above 3.0	50

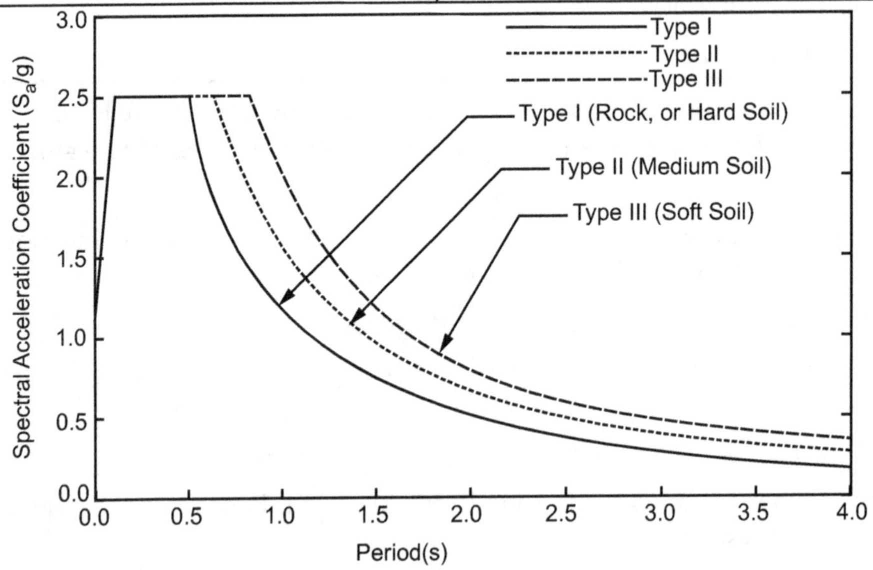

Fig. 10.2 : Response spectra for rock and soil sites for 5% damping

Portal Method :   (Summer 12, 8 Marks)

Lateral shear in each storey is distributed equally in each panel. Portal method is based on this concept. Since the interior columns connects two panels, it will carry twice the shear compared to exterior column. The distribution can also be visualised by dividing a frame into a number of portals and assuming that each leg carries equal shear.

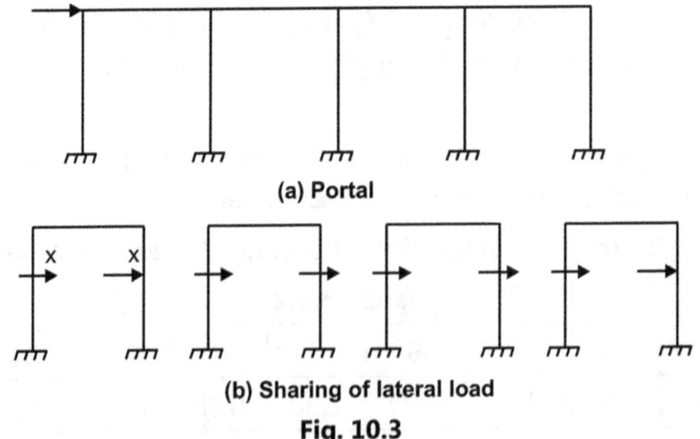

Fig. 10.3

Portal method is based on following assumptions :

1.   There is a point of inflection at the centre of each girder.

2.   There is a point of inflection at the centre of each rigidly connected column. This does not apply to columns with pinned bases where the moment is zero.

3.   The shear resisted by an exterior column of any storey is equal to 1/2n of the total storey shear and the shear resisted by each of the (n – 2) adjacent interior columns is 1/n, where n is the number of bays in any storey. In Fig. 10.3 (b), n = 4. Hence, shear resisted by exterior column = P/2 × 4 = P/8 and interior column = 2 × P/8 = P/4.

In portal method, the shear in column is determined first and then other forces and moments.

10.6 PRELIMINARY DATA FOR EXAMPLE FRAME

A floor plan of a typical office building is shown in Fig. 10.4. The plan is regular in nature in the sense that it's all columns are equally spaced. Thus, entire building space frame can be divided into a number of vertical frames. An interior frame B-B as shown in Fig. 10.5 is considered for analysis. Following are some of the salient features of the frame.

1.   Type of structure   :   Multi-storeyed rigid jointed frame
2.   Zone   :   IV
3.   Layout   :   As shown in Fig. 10.4
4.   Number of storeys   :   Six (G + 5) as shown in Fig. 10.5
5.   Ground storey height   :   5.0 m
6.   Floor to floor height   :   3.5 m
7.   External wall thickness   :   250 mm
8.   Internal wall thickness   :   125 mm
9.   Live load   :   3 kN/m^2
10.   Ceiling plaster thickness   :   6 mm
11.   Floor finishes   :   0.6 kN/m^2
12.   Materials   :   M 20 and Fe 415
13.   Size of beam   :   250 mm × 350 mm
14.   Size of column   :   300 mm × 400 mm
15.   Thickness of slab   :   150 mm

The soil below the foundation is assumed to be hard strata and damping of structures is 5%. The total base shear has been determined and its distribution along the height of building as per IS 1893 (Part-I) 2002 is shown in the present example.

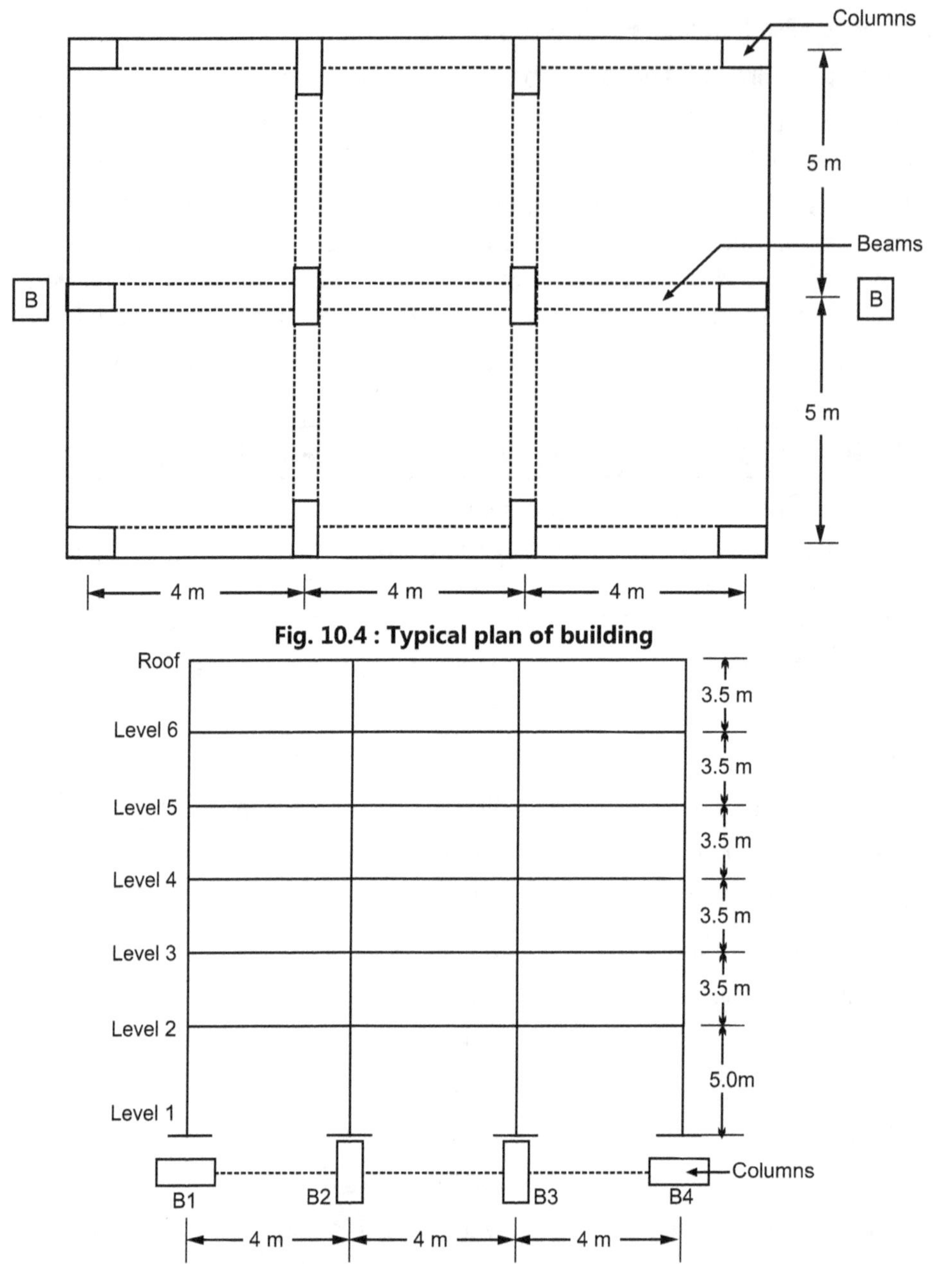

Fig. 10.4 : Typical plan of building

Fig. 10.5 : Details of frame along grid B.B.

Seismic Weight of Building :

The seismic weight of the whole building is the sum of the seismic weights of all the floors.

(a) Seismic weight of building at roof level :

(i) Weight of lime terracing $= (12 \text{ m} \times 5 \text{ m}) \times 0.15 \times 19 \text{ kN/m}^3 = 171 \text{ kN}$

(ii) Self-weight of slab $= (12 \text{ m} \times 5 \text{ m}) \times 0.15 \times 25 \text{ kN/m}^3 = 225 \text{ kN}$

(iii)   Weight of ceiling plaster $= (12 \text{ m} \times 5 \text{ m}) \times 0.006 \text{ m} \times 20 \text{ kN/m}^3 = 7.20 \text{ kN}$

(iv)   Self-weight of beam $= \{(12 \text{ m} \times 5 \text{ m}) \times 0.15 \times 19 \text{ kN/m}^3\} +$

$$\left\{4 \times \left(\frac{5}{2} + \frac{5}{2}\right) \times (0.35 - 0.15) \times 0.25 \times 25 \text{ kN/m}^3\right\}$$

$$= 40.0 \text{ kN}$$

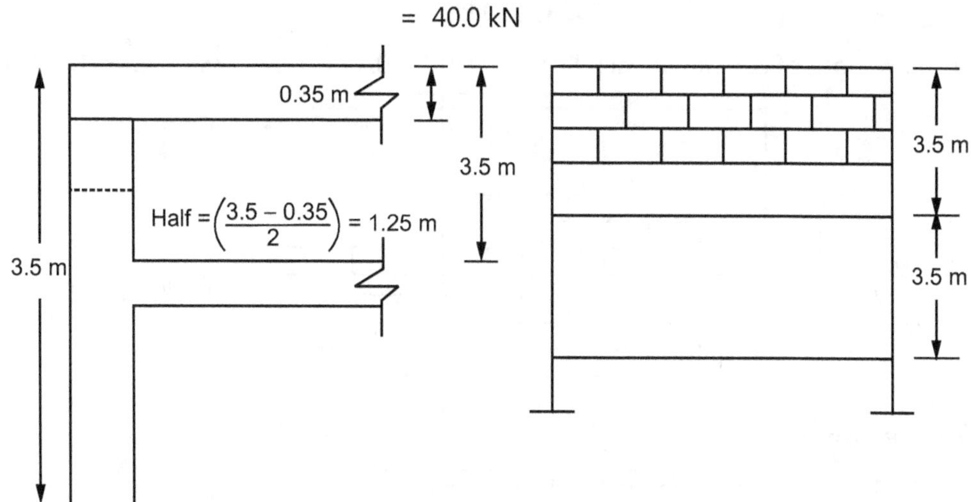

Fig. 10.6

(v)   Weight of brick work :

$$= \left\{12 \times 0.125 \times \left(\frac{3.5 - 0.35}{2}\right) \times 19\right\} + \left\{2 \times 5 \times 0.250 \times \left\{\frac{3.5 - 0.35}{2}\right\} \times 19\right\}$$

$$+ \left\{2 \times 5 \times 0.125 \times \left(\frac{3.5 - 0.35}{2}\right) \times 19\right\}$$

$$= 157.10 \text{ kN}$$

(vi) Self-weight of column acting half on roof level :

$$= 4 \times 0.300 \times 0.400 \times \left\{\frac{3.5 - 0.35}{2}\right\} \times 25 = 18.90 \text{ kN}$$

(vii) Live load on roof level (as per clause 7.3.2) = 0 kN

Total load at roof level = **619.20 kN**

(b) Seismic Weight of Building at 5th, 4th, 3rd and 2nd floor :

(i)   Self-weight of slab = 225 kN

(ii)   Weight of ceiling plaster = 7.20 kN

(iii)   Weight of floor finishes $= 12 \times 5 \times 0.60 = 3.6$ kN

(iv)   Self-weight of beam $= 40$ kN $\{12 \times 0.125 \times (3.5 - 0.35) \times 19\}$

(v)   Weight of brick work $= \begin{array}{l} + \{2 \times 5 \times 0.25 \times (3.5 - 0.35) \times 19\} \\ + \{2 \times 5 \times 0.125 \times (3.5 - 0.35) \times 19\} \end{array}$

$= 314.20$ kN

(vi) Self-weight of column at each floor : $4 \times (0.3 \times 0.4) \times (3.5 - 0.35) \times 25 = 37.8$ kN

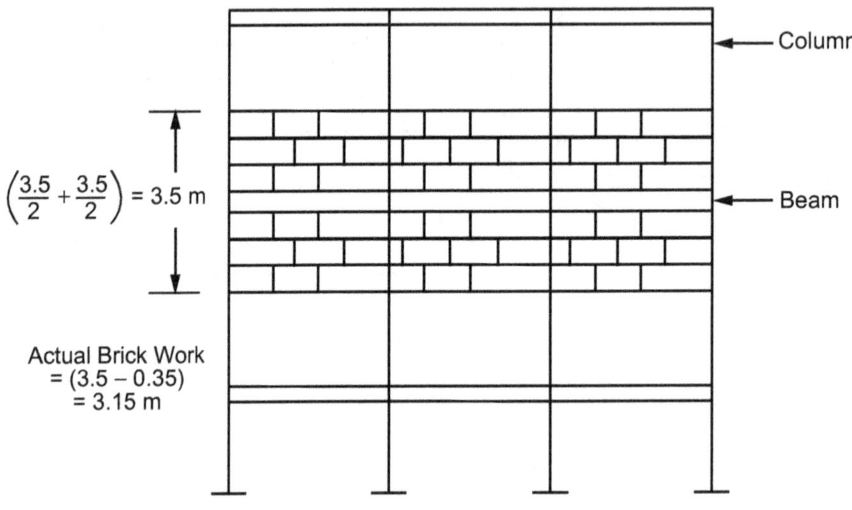

Fig. 10.7

(vii)   Live load on floor $= 25\%$ of live load

(as per clause 7.3.1) $= \dfrac{25}{100} \times 3 = 0.75$ kN/m^2 $= 12 \times 5 \times 0.75$

$= 45$ kN

Total weight $=$ **705.20 kN**

(c) Seismic weight of building at first floor level :

(i)   Self-weight of slab $= 225$ kN

(ii)   Weight of ceiling plaster $= 7.20$ kN

(iii)   Weight of floor finishes $= 12 \times 5 \times 0.60 = 3.6$ kN

(iv)   Self-weight of beam $= 40$ kN

(v)   Weight of brick work $= \{12 \times 0.125 \times (4.25 - 0.35) \times 19\}$

$+ \{2 \times 5 \times 0.125 \times (4.25 - 0.35) \times 19\}$

$$+ \{2 \times 5 \times 0.250 \times (4.25 - 0.35) \times 19\}$$

$$= 389.025 \text{ kN}$$

(vi) Self-weight of column on each floor $= 4 \times 0.3 \times 4 \times (4.25 - 0.35) \times 25$

$$= 46.80 \text{ kN}$$

(vii)   Live load on floor $= 45 \text{ kN}$

Total weight $= \textbf{789.025 kN}$

Therefore, total seismic weight of building

$$W = \frac{(619.20 \text{ kN})}{(\text{roof level})} + \frac{(4 \times 705.20)}{(2^{nd},\ 3^{rd},\ 4^{th} \text{ and } 5^{th} \text{ floor})} + \frac{(789.025 \text{ kN})}{(1^{st} \text{ floor})}$$

$$= 4229.025 \text{ kN}$$

Determination of base shear as per IS-1893 (Part-I) : 2002 :

The total seismic base shear is given by

$$V_A = A_h \cdot W$$

where, A_h – Design horizontal acceleration spectrum values.

It is determined by the following expression :

$$A_h = \left(\frac{z}{2}\right)\left(\frac{I}{R}\right)\left(\frac{Sa}{g}\right) = \frac{0.24}{2} \times \frac{1.5}{5.0} \times 1.71 = 0.062$$

z (Zone factor) $= 0.24$ (Building is in zone IV)

I (Importance) $= 1.5,$ Building is used as telephone exchange.

R (Response reduction factor) $= 5.0$ (Assume special RC moment resisting frame)

$\dfrac{Sa}{g}$ (Spectral acceleration) $= 1.71$

$$\left(T = \frac{0.09\,h}{\sqrt{d}} = \frac{0.09 \times 22.5}{\sqrt{12}} = 0.584, \ \frac{Sa}{g} = \frac{1}{T}, \text{ for hard strata}\right)$$

$\therefore$ Total base shear $(V_B) = 0.062 \times 4229.025$

$$= 262.20 \text{ kN}$$

Vertical Distribution of Base Shear to Different Floors :

The design base shear (V_B) computed shall be distributed along the height of the building as per the following expression :

$$Q_i = V_B \frac{W_i h_i^2}{\sum\limits_{i=1}^{n} W_i h_i^2}$$

Using the above equation, base shear is distributed as follows :

Level	W_i (kN)	h_i (metre)	$W_i h_i^2$	$\dfrac{W_i h_i^2}{\sum W_i h_i^2}$	Q_i (kN)
1	2	3	4	5	6
Roof (level 7)	619.20	22.5	313470.0	0.344	90.35
Fifth floor (level 6)	705.20	19.0	254577.2	0.279	73.38
Fourth floor (level 5)	705.20	15.5	169424.3	0.186	48.83
Third floor (level 4)	705.20	12.0	101548.8	0.112	29.27
Second floor (level 3)	705.20	8.5	50950.7	0.056	14.68
First floor (level 2)	789.025	5.0	19725.63	0.022	5.68
Ground floor (level 1)	–	0.00	–		
			$\sum$ 909696.63	$\sum$ 1.0	$\sum$ 262.20

10.7 SEISMIC COEFFICIENT METHOD

The seismic force to be resisted shall be computed as follows :

(a) $\qquad F_h = \propto h \, W_m$

Where,

$\qquad F_h$ = Horizontal seismic force to be resisted.

$\qquad \propto_h$ = Design horizontal seismic coefficient

$\qquad W_m$ = Weight of the mass under consideration ignoring reduction due to buoyancy or uplift

(b) $\qquad F_v = \propto v \, W_m$

Where,

$\qquad F_v$ = Vertical seismic force to be resisted and

$\qquad \propto_v$ = Design vertical seismic coefficient.

IMPORTANT POINTS

- Equivalent lateral force procedure.
- Steps to determine forces by equivalent static procedures.
- Design base shear $\displaystyle P_i = \frac{V_B\, W_i\, h_1^2}{\sum\limits_{i\,=\,1} W_i\, h_i^2}$

QUESTIONS

1. A multistorey building has the following data :

   Plan dimension (overall) = 16 m × 8 m

   Number of bays in X-direction = 4 @ 4 m each.

   Number of bays in Z-direction = 2 @ 4 m each.

   Floor to floor height in Y-direction = 5.0 m.

   Number of storeys   = 4 nos.

   Total height of building = 20 m.

   Size of columns and beams (all) = 300 mm × 600 mm.

   Slab thickness = 150 mm

   Live load = 3 kN/sq.m.

   Floor finish = 1 kN/sq.m.

   Brick masonry wall on all beams (excluding top floor) = 230 mm.

   Seismic zone = IV.

   Hard strata and 5% damping.

   Assume required data.

   Estimate the seismic forces at each floor level as per IS : 1893-2002.

2. A multistorey building has the following data :

   Plan dimension (overall) = 15 m × 8 m

   Number of bays in X-direction = 3 @ 5 m each.

   Number of bays in Z-direction = 2 @ 4 m each.

   Floor to floor height in Y-direction = 4.0 m.

   Number of storeys = 5 nos.

   Live load intensity = 3 kN/sq.m.

   Floor finish = 0.75 kN/sq.m.

   Thickness of slab = 150 mm.

   Size of beams = 300 mm × 500 mm.

   Size of columns = 300 mm × 600 mm.

Brick wall thickness = 230 mm.

Seismic zone = IV.

Hard strata and 5% damping.

 Assume required data.

Evaluate the seismic forces at each floor level as per IS : 1893-2002.

UNIVERSITY QUESTIONS

Dec. 2012

(b)　A multistory building has the following data

Plan dimension (overall) = 20 m × 15 m

Number of boys in X - direction = 4 @ 5 m each

Number of boys in Z - direction = 3 @ 5 m each

Floor to floor height in Y direction = 3.2 m

No. of storeys = 4 Nos.

Total height of building = 12.8 m

Size of column and beam = 300 mm × 600 mm

Slab thickness = 150 mm

Live load floor = 3 kN/sq.m

RCC frame infield with brick masonry.

Seismic zone = IV

Hard strata and 5% damping

Estimate the seismic forces at each floor level as per IS : 1893-2002 by seismic coefficient. Assume suitable data if necessary. **(Example 10.6)**　　　　**(18 Marks)**

Dec. 2014

Q. 6 (a)　Explain Seismic coefficient method. **(Section 10.7)**　　　　　　　　**(8 Marks)**

11.1 INTRODUCTION

Steel or timber structures are fabricated separately and joined together by rivets, bolts, welds or nails. Unless the joints are specially designed for rigidity, they are too flexible to transfer moments of significant magnitude from one member to another. In contrast, for most reinforced concrete members, concrete is usually poured in one single operation. Reinforcement provided is not terminated at ends of a member, but is extended through the joints into adjacent members, thus providing continuity. During construction adequate care is taken to bound new concrete to the old by carefully cleaning the latter, by extending reinforcement through the joints and by other means.

11.2 INTERACTION BETWEEN PARTS OF THE STRUCTURE

In the various types of construction in reinforced concrete, the designer is faced with a highly indeterminate type of structure in three dimensions, which cannot be exactly analysed as a planer structure, for example the intermediate beams of Fig. 11.1 cannot be analysed precisely without considering the vertical deflection and torsional stiffness of the girders and the stiffness of the columns. Similarly, the beams framing into the columns have moments which are influenced by the column joint rotations and hence by any torsion present in the girders. In practice design of structures, however, such aspects are normally ignored as a result of which actually an approximate design of the structure is accomplished.

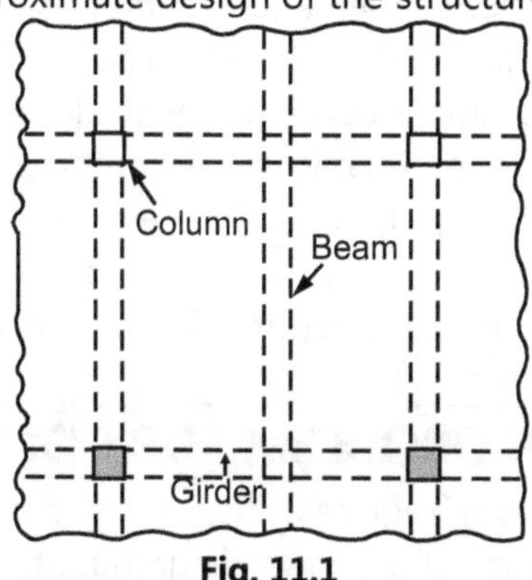

Fig. 11.1

A designer usually adopts approximate method of analysis for the structures. All such analyses are based on some assumptions which may not even be quite in accordance with facts. The conclusions from such analysis, however, can be considered close to facts. A good designer understands not only the nature of the approximations involved in the assumptions made, but also the resulting approximation in the conclusions.

One important and simplifying assumption in designing structures is that analysis in two dimensions is adequate for most of the structures. The closeness of this assumption depends on the nature of the loading the floors will be subjected to. For uniform floor load, the assumption fits in better than in case of concentrated loads.

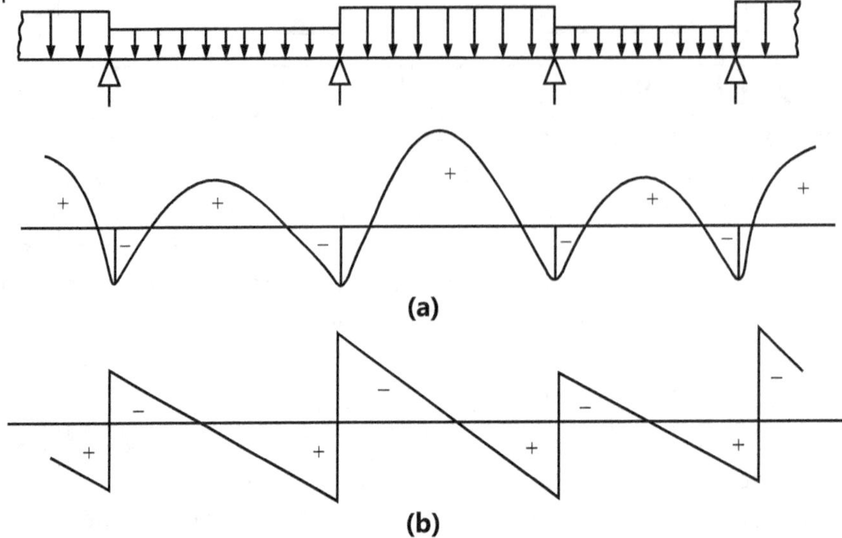

Fig. 11.2 : Typical B.M. and S.F. diagrams for continuous beam

Bending moment diagrams for continuous beams normally show negative moment over supports and positive moments near mid-span. The presence of columns changes the magnitude of such negative moments slightly. Loading pattern of adjacent slab has some effect on the magnitudes of the negative moments slightly. Loading pattern of adjacent slab has some effect on the magnitudes of the negative and positive bending moments on spans and therefore, have to be considered. The moment diagram in any span may be considered as the sum of two parts, on the simple beam moment diagram for that span and the other the moments across the span due to negative support moments.

Shear force diagram differs only slightly from that of a series of simple spans. In any span, the shear force diagram for a given loading consists of the sample beam shear force plus the shear force on account of the effect of continuity. The continuity shear force is usually relatively small except in end spans.

11.3 GENERAL DESIGN PROBLEM FOR CONTINUOUS BEAMS

Each span of a continuous beam requires a separate design for negative and positive bending moment conditions. Fig. 11.3 shows diagrammatically the design conditions for continuous slabs, rectangular beams and T-beams. Depending on the nature of the moments the faces have been marked as T and C, T designating tension face and C the compression face.

Rectangular beams as in Fig. 11.3 (a) are usually designed as a doubly reinforced section at location of maximum negative bending moment. At zone of maximum positive bending moments, the sections are relatively under reinforced or nearly balanced.

For zones having negative bending moment less than the maximum, the section may be considered as doubly reinforced or under reinforced depending on the actual conditions.

T-beams are actually inverted rectangular beams at the supports with only the width of stem i.e. b_w effective in compression as shown in Fig. 11.3 (b) for maximum negative moments. Such beams are designed as doubly reinforced rectangular section and for positive bending moment as T-beam section which is usually under reinforced. Shear force rarely governs in case of one-way slab. Width of web or rib of continuous beams will normally be controlled from the point of view of accommodation of the bars, even though sometimes such widths will be governed by shear or moment requirements.

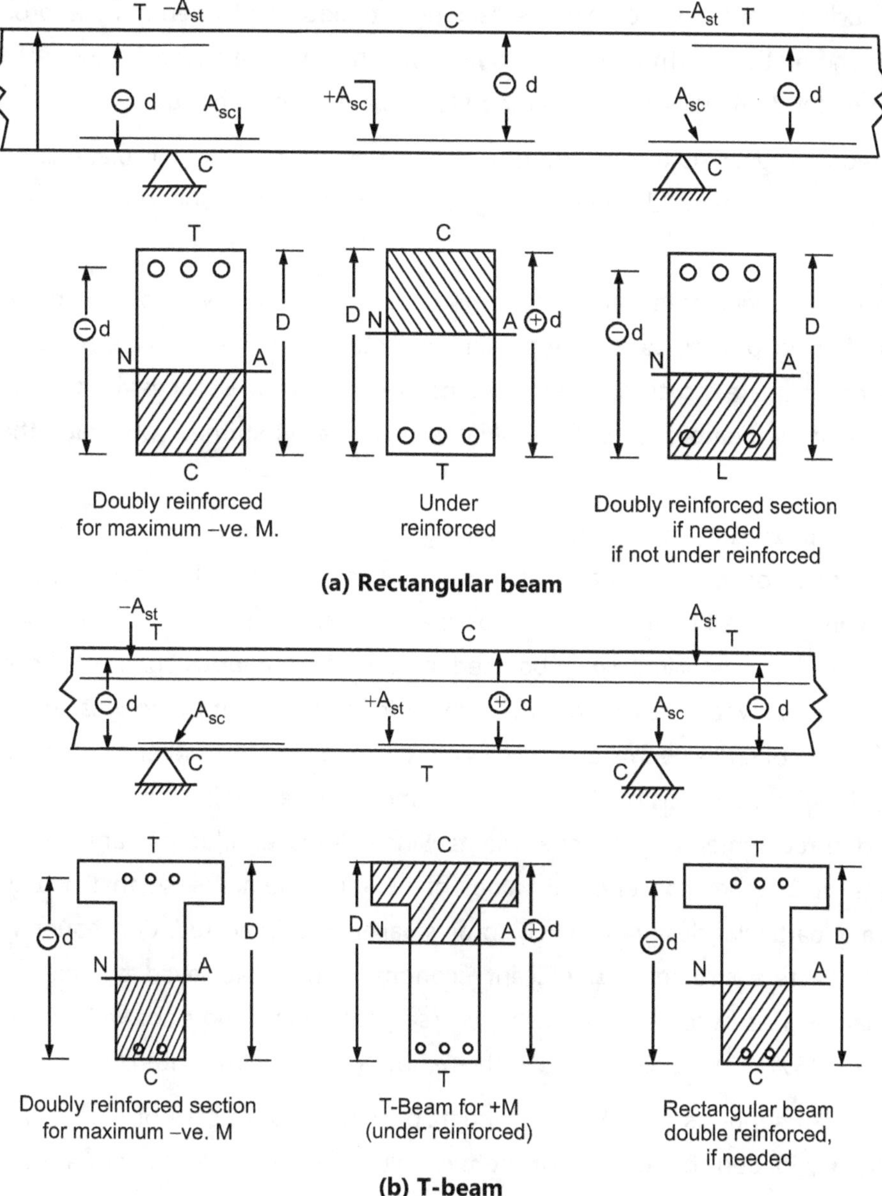

Fig. 11.3 : Design procedures for continuous beams

11.4 METHOD OF ANALYSIS

A number of methods have been developed over the years for the analysis of continuous beams. The so called classical methods, such as applications of the theorem of three moments, Castigliano's theorem and method of consistent deformation are useful mainly in the analysis of continuous beams with few spans. For more complicated cases, usually met in practice, such methods prove to be exceedingly tedious and alternative approaches are preferred. The method of moment distribution which is an interactive solution of the slope deflection method provides a useful method for analysis of continuous beams.

Such methods of analysis are however, used in cases where exact calculations of bending moments are required and where there exist considerable variations in the spans of continuous beams.

Inspite of the development of refined methods for the analysis of beams, increasing attention is being paid to various approximate methods of analysis. The reason is that in case of indeterminate structures, before complete analysis, it is necessary to estimate the proportions of its members in order to know their relative stiffness on which the analysis depends.

Sometimes approximate calculation of bending moments and shear force can be made by the coefficient of bending moments at various critical sections. Coefficients recommended by IS as given in Table 11.1 may be used for analysis of usual types of construction span and storey heights. The coefficients may be used in case of continuous spans of three or more approximate equal when they do not differ by more than 15% of the longest span. The fact that reinforced concrete beams are never simply supported, but either rest on supports of considerable width, such as walls or are built monolithically with columns has also been considered in recommending the coefficients. Since all these influences are considered, the coefficients yield rather conservative values of bending moments, so that actual accurate values in any particular design are likely to be smaller than indicated. Consequently in many reinforced concrete structures significant economy can be achieved by making a more precise analysis. This becomes absolutely necessary for beams and slabs with spans differing by more than 15% or sustaining load which are not uniformly distributed.

For moments at supports where two unequal spans meet or in case of two adjacent spans are not equally loaded the average of the two values for negative moment at support may be taken for design.

Table 11.1 : Bending moments and shear force values as per IS 456

Type of load	Span moments		Support moments	
	Near middle of end span	At middle of interior span	At support next to end	At other interior supports
Dead load and imposed load (fixed)	$+\dfrac{W_dL}{12}$	$+\dfrac{W_dL}{24}$	$-\dfrac{W_dL}{10}$	$-\dfrac{W_dL}{12}$
Imposed load (not fixed)	$+\dfrac{W_sL}{10}$	$+\dfrac{W_sL}{12}$	$-\dfrac{W_sL}{9}$	$-\dfrac{W_sL}{9}$

For a member built into masonry wall developing partial restraint negative moment at the face of support can be taken as WL/24.

Load	S.F. at end supports	S.F. at exterior face of support next to end support		S.F. at all other interior supports
		Outer side	Inner side	
Dead load and imposed load (fixed)	$0.4\,W_4$	$0.6\,W_d$	$0.55\,W_d$	$0.5\,W_d$
Imposed load (not fixed)	$0.45\,W_s$	$0.6\,W_s$	$0.6\,W_s$	$0.6\,W_s$

$$W_d = \text{Total dead load per span}$$

$$W_s = \text{Total uniformly distributed live load per span}$$

$$L = \text{Effective span}$$

In case of a two span continuous structures for no end restraint the negative and positive bending moments can be taken as,

$$\left[-\frac{W_dL}{9}-\frac{W_sL}{9}\right] \text{ or } -\frac{WL}{9} \text{ and } \left[+\frac{W_dL}{16}+\frac{W_sL}{10}\right]$$

or $+\dfrac{WL}{12}$ respectively, where $W = W_d + W_s$. For end restraint, in the form of spandrel and column, the positive moment at centre of span may be taken as $+\dfrac{WL}{14}$.

For beams of prismatic sections and having two or more approximately equal spans not greater than the shorter by more than 20% and loads considered uniformly distributed with live load not exceeding 3 (dead load), A.C.I. suggest use of the following coefficients in terms of the clear span L_n. Such coefficients are usually to be used for monolithic construction.

End span :

For positive BM with discontinuous end unrestrained $= +\dfrac{WL_n^2}{11}$

For positive BM with discontinuous end integral with support $= +\dfrac{WL_n^2}{14}$.

For negative BM at exterior face of first interior support

$$= -\dfrac{WL_n^2}{8} \text{ for two spans and } -\dfrac{WL_n^2}{10} \text{ for more than two spans}$$

For negative BM at interior face of end support for members built integrally with support

$-\dfrac{WL_n^2}{24}$.

If support is a spandrel beam and $-\dfrac{WL_n^2}{16}$, if support is a column for interior span positive

B.M. $= +\dfrac{WL_n^2}{16}$.

Negative B.M. at supports other than the penultimate support $= -\dfrac{WL_n^2}{11}$.

Negative B.M. at face of all supports.
   (i)   For slabs with spans not exceeding 3.05 m and

   (ii) Beams if ratio of $\sum \dfrac{\text{column stiffness}}{\text{beam stiffness}} > 8$, at each end of the span $= -\dfrac{WL_n^2}{12}$.

   Shear in end members at face of first interior support $= \dfrac{1.15\, WL_n}{2}$.

Shear at face of other supports $= \dfrac{WL_n}{2}$.

Use of such coefficients are very convenient for preliminary designing, as they do not require knowledge of the member sizes. When moments are calculated by other methods, it is a good practice to always compute the equivalent within the above limitations.

Solved Examples

Example 11.1 :

Design an interior span of a continuous T-beam of effective span 6 m. The beams are placed 4 m centres and carry slab of thickness 100 mm. Loading on the slab may be taken as W_d = 3000 N/m^2 inclusive of self-weight of slab and W_s = 6000 N/m^2.

Assume σ_{cbc} = 7 N/mm^2, σ_{st} = 140 N/mm^2

                 σ_{sc} = 130 N/mm^2, m = 13.0

                 K = 0.394, j = 0.868

                 Q = 1.20 N/mm^{-2}, τ_{bd} = 0.80 N/mm^2

$$\tau_{max} = 1.80 \ N/mm^2$$

Value of Q' for doubly reinforced beam may be taken as 1.50. Design also if Fe 415 steel be used.

Solution :

Assume total depth as $\dfrac{6000}{12}$ = 500 mm and width of rib b_w = 250 mm.

Loading on beam :

$$\text{Dead load from slab} = (3000)\ (4) = 12000 \ N/m$$

$$\text{Self-weight of beam} = \frac{250}{1000}\left(\frac{500-100}{100}\right)(24000) = 2400 \ N/m$$

$$\text{Total } W_d = 14400 \ N/m$$

$$\text{Live load } W_s = (4)\ (6000)$$

$$= 24000 \ N/m$$

For intermediate span :

$$\text{Negative B.M.} = \frac{W_d\, l_{ef}^2}{12} + \frac{W_s\, l_{ef}^2}{9}$$

$$= \frac{14400\ (6)^2}{12} + \frac{24000\ (6)^2}{9}$$

$$= 139200 \ Nm$$

Effective depth d required for doubly reinforced section for carrying the moment, assuming Q' = 1.50 is given by

$$d = \sqrt{\frac{139200\ (1000)}{250\ (150)}} = 609.26$$

$$\text{Make total depth} = 650 \ mm$$

$$\text{with } b_w = 250 \ min$$

Take $\qquad\qquad\qquad d = 610 \ mm$

$$\text{Revised self-weight of beam} = \frac{250}{1000}\left(\frac{550}{1000}\right)(24000)$$

$$= 3300 \ N/m$$

Revised bending moments,

$$\text{Negative B.M.} = \frac{15300\ (6)^2}{12} + \frac{24000\ (6)^2}{9}$$

$$= 141900 \ N/m$$

$$\text{Positive B.M.} = \frac{W_d \, l_{eff}}{24} + \frac{W_s \, l_{eff}}{12} = 94950 \text{ N/m}$$

$$\text{Maximum shear force} = 0.5 \, W_d + 0.6 \, W_s$$

$$= 0.5 \, (6) \, (15300) + 0.6 \, (24000) \, (6)$$

$$= 132300 \text{ N}$$

$$\text{Maximum shear stress} = \frac{132300}{(250) \, (610)}$$

$$= 0.8675 \text{ N/mm}^2$$

$$< \tau_{i \, max}$$

Economical depth for T-beam is given by

$$d = \frac{D_f}{2} + \sqrt{\frac{M_c}{b_w \cdot \sigma_{st}}} = 50 + \sqrt{\frac{94950 \, (1000) \, (50)}{(250) \, (140)}}$$

$$= 418.20 \text{ mm}$$

Check section for positive bending moment :

Flange width b_f will be smaller of the following :

(i)
$$\frac{l_o}{6} + b_w + 6D_f = \frac{0.7 \, (6000)}{6} + 250 + 6 \, (100)$$

$$= 1550 \text{ mm}$$

(ii)　b_w + clear distance between beams = 4000 mm

$$\text{Adopt } b_f = 1550 \text{ mm}$$

Approximate lever arm

(i)
$$d - \frac{D_f}{2} = 610 - \frac{100}{2} = 560 \text{ mm}$$

or　(ii)
$$0.90d = 549 \text{ mm}$$

With $j_d = 560$ mm,
$$A_{st} = \frac{94950 \, (100)}{140 \, (560)}$$

$$= 1211.10 \text{ mm}^2$$

$$\text{Minimum } A_{st} = 518.5 \text{ mm}^2$$

Use 6 numbers 16 mm diameter bars,

$$A_{st} \text{ provided} = 1206 \text{ mm}^2$$

The six bars cannot be accommodated in one layer. Arrange them in two layers with 4 numbers at bottom and 2 numbers above with a 16 mm diameter spacer in between. Effective cover of positive moment steel then

$$= 25 + \frac{16}{2} + \frac{32}{6} \quad (2)$$

$$= 44 \text{ mm}$$

$$\text{Total depth} = 610 + 44 = 654 \text{ mm}$$

$$\text{Adopt 660 mm with d} = 660 - 45 = 615 \text{ mm}$$

With revised self-weight of 3360 N/m

$$\text{Revised negative B.M.} = 142080 \text{ Nm}$$

$$\text{Positive B.M.} = 95040 \text{ Nm}$$

Check for positive B.M. of 95040 Nm

Neglecting compression in rib,

$$1550(100) \, (n - 50) = 13 \, (1206) \, (615 - n),$$

where,

$$n = 101.90 \text{ mm}$$

Hence neutral axis falls below the flange depth.

Centre of compressive force below top

$$= \frac{101.90 + 2 \, (1.90)}{101.90 + 1.90} \left(\frac{100}{3} \right)$$

$$= 33.94 \text{ mm}$$

$$\text{Lever arm} = 615 - 33.94$$

$$= 581.06 \text{ mm}$$

Hence steel area provided is adequate.

Maximum compressive stress in concrete is given by

$$\frac{1}{2} \sigma'_{cbc} \left(1 + \frac{1.90}{101.90} \right) (1550) \, (100) \, (581.06) = 95040 \, (1000)$$

where,

$$\sigma'_{cbc} = 2.072 \text{ N/mm}^2 < 7 \text{ N/mm}^2$$

Reinforcement for negative bending moments

$$\text{Effective depth of beam} = 610 \text{ mm with 50 mm effective cover}$$

$$M_c = Qbd^2 = 1.2 \, (250) \, (610)^2 = 11630000 \text{ N/mm}$$

$$M_s = M - M_c = 142080000 - 11163000 = 30450000 \text{ N/mm}$$

$$A_{st_1} = \frac{111630000}{140 \, (0.868) \, (610)} = 1505.93 \text{ mm}^2$$

$$A_{st_2} = \frac{30450000}{140 \, (610 - 45)} = 384.96 \text{ mm}^2$$

$$\text{Total } A_{st} = A_{st_1} + A_{st_2} = 1890.89 \text{ mm}^2$$

For compressive steel,

$$\sigma_{st} = 7\frac{0.394\,(610) - 45}{0.394\,(610)} = 5.689 \text{ N/mm}^2$$

$$A_{sc} = \frac{30450000}{[1.5\,(13) - 1]\,(5.689)\,(610 - 45)}$$

$$= 512.10 \text{ mm}^2$$

4 Nos. 16 mm diameter bars will be quite adequate for steel in compression when A_{sc} provided = 804.25 mm^2

IMPORTANT POINTS

- Advantages of continuous beams.

- Some important conceptions.

- Analysis and assumptions in continuous beams.

QUESTIONS

1. Design the interior span of a rectangular beam supported on 500 m square column and beam continuous over 8 m span. The beams support slab 120 mm thick and are placed 4 m centres and are cast monolithic with the slab. The loading on the slab is due to self-weight, floor finish and plastering and live load of magnitude 5000 N/m^2. Use M20 grade concrete and σ_{st} = 140 N/mm^2, for bars upto 20 mm diameter, for bars above 20 mm diameter σ_{st} = 130 N/mm^2 (or 230 N/mm^2 for Fe 415 steel).

2. Design an interior span of a continuous one-way slab supported on beams at 5 m centres. Moment coefficient as per IS 456 for maximum positive and maximum negative bending moments can be used. Assume dead load as 1200 N/m^2 + self weight of slab and live load as 5000 N/m^2. Assume allowable stresses for M20 grade concrete and σ_{st} = 140 N/mm^2, for bars upto 20 mm diameter (or 190 N/mm^2 for deformed medium tensile steel bars conforming to IS 1139-1966).

Chapter 12
APPROXIMATE ANALYSIS OF MULTISTORYED FRAMES

12.1 INTRODUCTION

Analysis of multistoreyed structures involves large number of unknowns, also geometric properties of cross-section of members and material properties are per-requisites of exact analysis. Therefore, it becomes necessary to perform some approximate analysis to arrive at an estimate of member sizes. This type of analysis is also useful in checking the results obtained by computer program which uses more elaborate computations.

In approximate methods of analysis, statically indeterminate structure is converted to statically determinate structure by making appropriate assumptions and then analysed for member forces using laws of statics. This chapter deals with commonly used approximate methods of analysis for rigid jointed multistoreyed, multibay two-dimensional frames.

Following are approximate methods of analysis :

1. Substitute frame method for vertical loads.

2. Any one of the following methods for vertical loads :

    (a) Portal method

    (b) Cantilever method.

12.2 SUBSTITUTE FRAME METHOD

This method is used for the analysis of multistorey frames subjected to vertical (gravity) loads only. In this method, only a part of the frame is considered for the analysis. The part considered is called a substitute frames. Here, it is assumed the moments transferred from one floor to another floor are negligible and hence analysis can be made floor by floor. So, a substitute frame is consisting of floor beams and columns above and below it. Columns are considered as fixed at far ends.

To find moments and shears in the second floor of multistorey frame shown in Fig. 12.1 the substitute frame shown in Fig. 12.1 is considered.

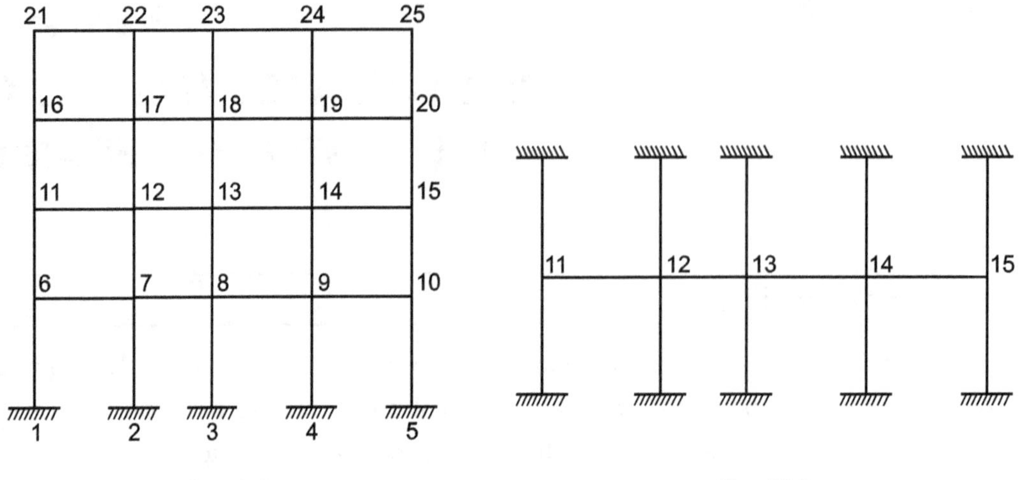

Fig. 12.1   **Fig. 12.2**

In the multistorey frame, both dead load and live load together constitute the vertical load. Dead load acts throughout the frame and at all times. Live load may act throughout the frame or on a part of it at a particular time. Hence, for analysis, various combinations of live loads are to be considered.

Critical live load positions are shown in Fig. 12.3 to get various design moment in beams.

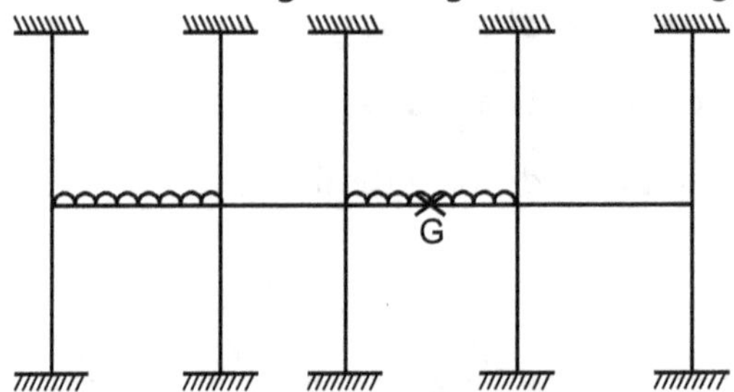

Fig. 12.3 : Live loading for maximum positive moment at G

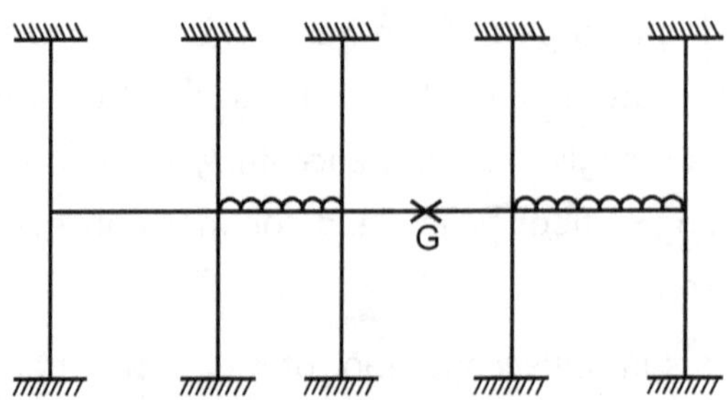

Fig. 12.4 : Live loading for maximum negative moment G

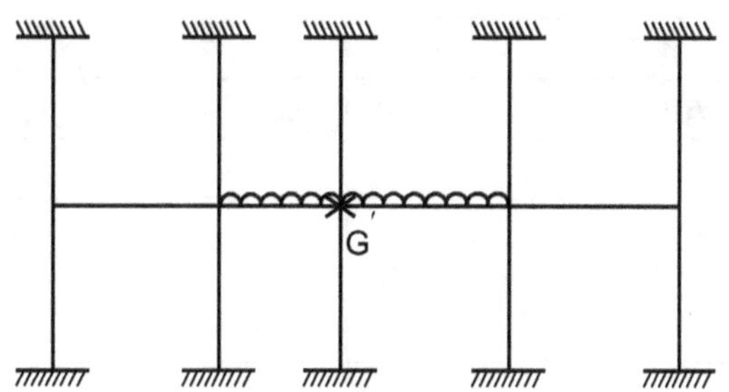

Fig. 12.5 : Live loading for maximum negative moment at G

The design moment in the column is obtained for any on series of alternate loading of spans. Moment distribution is done for only two cycles and hence it is called the **two cycle method**. A joint moment is mainly due to the loading on the two adjacent spans. Hence, to find the moment at a joint. Only two adjacent spans are considered.

12.3 STEP BY STEP ANALYSIS PROCEDURE OF SUBSTITUTE FRAME METHOD

1) Distribution Factor (D.F)

Joint	Member	Relative Stiffness (R.S)	Total Stiffness (T.S)	Distribution Factor D.F. = R.S./ T.S.
		4EI / L - Fixed at one end and S.S. at other, 3EI/ L - S.S. at both ends and O - Overhanging member		
?	?	?	?	?

2) Load Calculations :

Live load (Per meter run) of floor = L.L. intensity × Spacing

Dead load (Per meter run) of floor = D.L. intensity × Spacing

D.L. on beam = D.L. of floor + self weight of beam

L.L. on beam = Live load (per meter run) of floor

3) Fixed End Moment (F.E.M. due to D.L. and L.L) :

Member	D.L. on beam	L.L. on beam	D.L. + L.L.	F.E.M. due to DL = $DL \times (\text{span of beam})^2 / 12 = WL^2/12$	F.E.M. due to D.L. + L.L. = $(\text{D.L.} + \text{L.L.}) \times (\text{span of beam})^2 / 12 = WL^2/12$

4) Design Moments in Beams :

(a) To Determine the Maximum Moments and mid-span in AB and CD

(D.L. + L.L. on AB and CD, D.L. on BC)

Note : Use F.E.M. due to W = D.L. + L.L. for member AB and C.D. and F.E.M. due to W = D.L. for member BC.

Joint	A		B		C		D
Member	AB		BA	BC		CB	CD	DC
DF	–		–	–		–	–	–
F.E.M. balance carryover moment Balance	–		–	–		–	–	–
Total Moment							
Free moment at center of span $= WL^2/8$	–			–			–	
Mid-span moment = Free moment at center – Average of total moment	–			–			–	

(b) to determine the maximum moments at mid span in B.C.

(D.L. on AB and CD, DL + LL on BC)

Procedure same as above step 4 (a)

(5) Design Moments in Columns

(a) Loading Conditions : Case-I

D.L. + L.L. on AB and CD, DL on BC

Joint	A	B	C	D
F.E.M. case I [step 4 (a)] Carryover moment (COM) case I [Step 4 (a)]				
F.E.M. + COM				
Column Moment = D.F. of column $\times (-1)$ [F.E.M. + COM]				

(b) Loading Condition : Case II

D.L. + L.L. on AB and CD, D.L. + L.L. on BC

Procedure same as above step 5(a).

6. Design Moments at Joints :

(a) For Maximum Moment at Joint A

The condition of loading to obtain maximum movement at joint A is as D.L. + L.L. on AB, D.L. on AB and BC the effect of D.L. on other span is neglected.

Joint	A		B		C		D
Member D.F	AB	BA	BC	CB	CD		DC
FEM Balance Carryover moment Balance							
Final							

(b) For Maximum movement at Joint B

Loading conditions are

D.L. + L.L on AB and BC, D.L. + on AB, BC and CD

Procedure same as above step 6(a)

(c) For Maximum Moment at Joint C

Loading Conditions are D.L. + L.L. on BC and CD, D.L. on AB

Procedure same as above step 6(a)

(d) For Maximum Moment at Joint D

Loading conditions are D.L. + L.L on CD D.L. on BC and CD

Procedure same as above step 6(a).

12.4 PORTAL MOTHOD

The portal method is an approximate analysis used for analyzing building frames subjected to lateral loading such as the one shown in Fig. 12.6. This method is more appropriate for low rise (height is less than width) building frames. In the analysis, the following assumptions are made :

1.	An inflection point is located at mid-height of each column,

2.	An inflection point is located at centre of each beam, and

3.	The horizontal shear divided among all the columns on the basis that each interior column takes twice as much as the exterior columns.

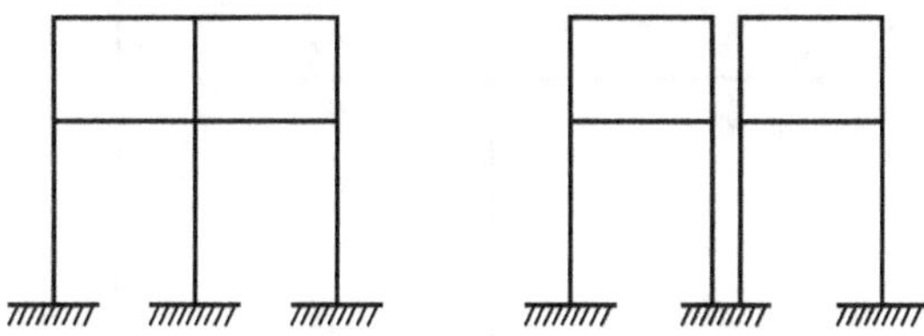

(a) Building frame under lateral loading	(b) Equivalent portals

Fig. 12.6

The basis of third assumption should be clear from Fig. 12.6 which indicates that interior column will resist the shear of two columns of individual portals.

Solved Examples

Example 12.1 :

Analyse the intermediate frame of a multistoried frame shown in Fig. 12.7

Given :

$$\text{Spacing of frame} = 4.0 \text{ m}$$
$$\text{D.L. on floors} = 4 \text{ kN/m}^2$$
$$\text{L.L. on floors} = 3 \text{ kN/m}^2$$
$$\text{Self weight of beams} = 5 \text{ kN/m for beams of span 9 m}$$
$$= 4 \text{ kN/m for beams of span 6 m}$$
$$= 3 \text{ kN/m for beams of span 3 m}$$

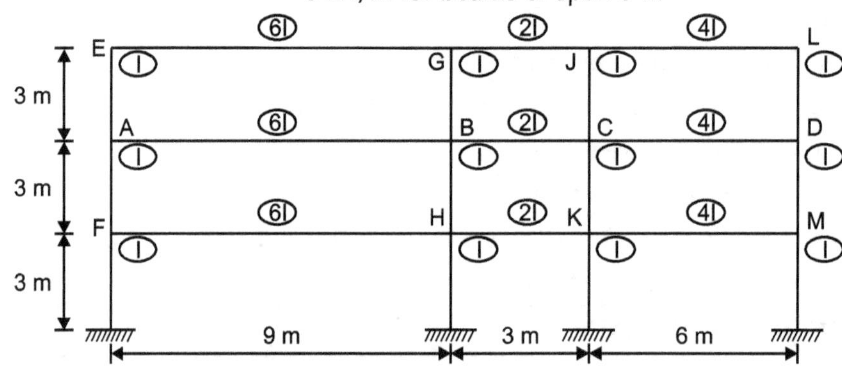

Fig. 12.7

Solution :

The analysis for the second floor is given below. Similar analysis may be carried out to all the other floors to get the complete solution.

The substitute frame is as shown in Fig. 12.8.

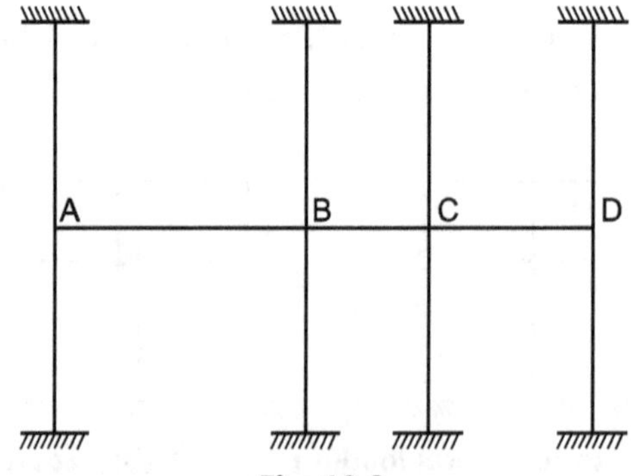

Fig. 12.8

The distribution factors are calculated in Table 12.1

Table 12.1

Joint	Members	Relative stiffness	Sum	D.F
A	AE	$\dfrac{I}{3}$	$\dfrac{4I}{3}$	$\dfrac{1}{4}$
	AB	$\dfrac{6I}{9}$		$\dfrac{1}{2}$
	AF	$\dfrac{I}{3}$		$\dfrac{1}{4}$
B	BG	$\dfrac{I}{3}$	$\dfrac{6I}{3}$	$\dfrac{1}{6}$
	BA	$\dfrac{6I}{9}$		$\dfrac{1}{3}$
	BC	$\dfrac{2I}{3}$		$\dfrac{1}{3}$
	BH	$\dfrac{I}{3}$		$\dfrac{1}{6}$
C	CJ	$\dfrac{I}{3}$	$\dfrac{6I}{3}$	$\dfrac{1}{6}$
	CB	$\dfrac{2I}{3}$		$\dfrac{1}{3}$
	CD	$\dfrac{4I}{6}$		$\dfrac{1}{3}$
	CK	$\dfrac{I}{3}$		$\dfrac{1}{6}$
D	DL	$\dfrac{I}{3}$	$\dfrac{4I}{3}$	$\dfrac{1}{4}$
	DC	$\dfrac{4I}{6}$		$\dfrac{1}{2}$
	DM	$\dfrac{I}{3}$		$\dfrac{1}{4}$

Load calculation :

Live load (Per metre run) of floor = L.L. intensity × Spacing

Dead load (per metre run) of floor = D.L. intensity × Spacing

D.L. on beam = D.L. of floor + self weight of beam

L.L. on beam = Live load (per metre) of floor

Loads :

$$\text{Live load per meter run of girder} = 3 \times 4 = 12 \text{ kN/m}$$

$$\text{Dead load per meter run girder} = 4 \times 4 = 16 \text{ kN/m}$$

$$\text{Dead load on 9 m beam} = 16 + 5 = 21 \text{ kN/m}$$

$$\text{Dead load on 3 m beam} = 16 + 3 = 19 \text{ kN/m}$$

$$\text{Dead load on 6 m beam} = 16 + 4 = 20 \text{ kN/m}$$

Fixed End Moment (FEM due to D.L. and L.L.					
Member	D.L. on beam [kN/m]	L.L. on Beam [kN.m]	D.L. + L.L.	FEM due to D.L. = D.L. $\times$ (Span of beam)^2 / 12 = $WL^2/12$ (kN-m)	FEM due to D.L. + L.L. = (D.L. + L.L.) (span of beam)^2 / 12 = WL^2 / 12 [kN/m]
AB	21	12	33	$21 \times 9 \times 9 / 12 = 141.75$	$33 \times 9 \times 9 / 12 = 222.75$
BC	19	12	31	$19 \times 3 \times 3 / 12 = 14.25$	$31 \times 3 \times 3 / 12 = 23.25$
CD	20	12	32	$20 \times 6 \times 6 / 12 = 60$	$32 \times 6 \times 6 / 12 = 96$

Design Moments in Beams :

(1)   To determine the maximum moment at mid-spans in AB and CD.

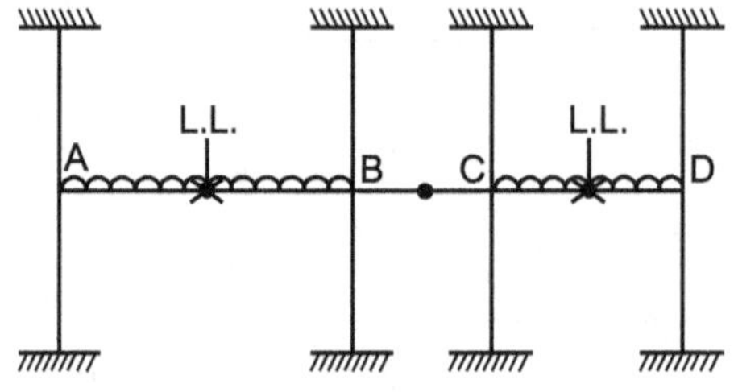

Fig. 12.9

Live load on AB and CD, dead load on ABCD.

D.F	$\frac{1}{2}$		$\frac{1}{3}$	$\frac{1}{3}$		$\frac{1}{3}$	$\frac{1}{3}$		$\frac{1}{2}$
FEM	− 222.75	+ 222.75		− 14.25	+ 14.25		− 96.0		+ 96.0
BAL	+ 111.38	− 69.5		− 69.5	+ 27.25		+ 27.25		− 48.0

...Conti.

COM	– 34.75	+ 55.69	+ 13.88	– 34.75	– 24.0	+ 13.88
BAL	+17.38	– 23.19	– 23.19	+ 19.58	+19.58	– 6.94
	– 128.74	+ 185.75	– 93.06	+ 26.33	– 73.17	+ 54.94
Free moment at center of span = $\dfrac{WL^2}{8}$	334.12		21.38		144	
Mid-span moment	$\dfrac{334.12 - 128.74 + 185.75}{2} =$ 176.88		$\dfrac{21.38 - 93.06 + 26.33}{2} =$ – 38.32		$144 - \dfrac{73.17 + 58.94}{2}$ = 79.95	

(2) To determine the maximum moment at mid span in BC.

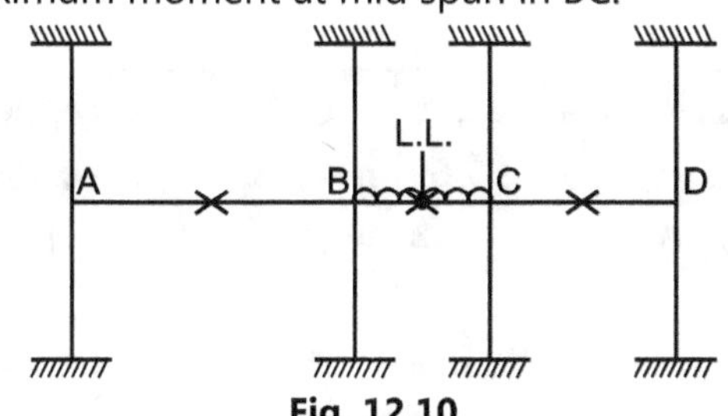

Fig. 12.10

Live load on BC, dead load on ABCD.

D.F.	$\dfrac{1}{2}$	$\dfrac{1}{3}$	$\dfrac{1}{3}$	$\dfrac{1}{3}$	$\dfrac{1}{3}$	$\dfrac{1}{2}$
FEM	– 141.75	+ 141.75	– 23.25	+ 23.25	– 60.0	+ 60.0
BAL	+ 70.88	– 39.5	– 39.5	+ 12.25	+ 12.5	– 30.0
COM	– 19.75	+ 35.44	+ 6.13	– 19.75	– 15.0	+ 6.13
BAL	+ 9.88	– 13.86	– 13.86	+ 11.58	+ 11.58	– 3.06
	– 80.74	+ 123.83	– 70.48	+ 27.33	– 51.17	+ 33.07
Free moment mid-span= $\left(\dfrac{WL^2}{8}\right)$	212.63		34.88		90	
Final moment at mid-span	$212.63 - \dfrac{80.74 + 123.83}{2}$ = 110.35		$34.88 - \dfrac{70.48 + 27.33}{2}$ = – 14.02		$90 - \dfrac{51.17 + 33.07}{2}$ = 47.88	

Digital Moments in Columns :

For maximum moments in columns, alternate spans should be loaded with love load.

In present case, there are two possibilities

(i) Loading conditions are : Live load on AB and CD, while dead load on ABCD.

(ii) Loading conditions are : Live load on BC, while dead load on ABCD.

Therefore, the possible cases for maximum moment in columns are the same as the two cases considered above. In the above moment distribution table, column moments are not noted down. At each cycle, distribution factor times unbalanced moment should have been noted as column moment. Column moments are not considered for distribution in beams. It can be determined after completing the moment distribution for the beam.

Column moment = Distribution factor of column $\times$ (– 1) [FEMs + COMs]

These calculations are shown in tabular form below :

(i) Live load on AB and CD, dead load on ABCD.

	A		B		C		D
FEMs	**– 222.75**	**+ 222.75**	**– 14.25**	**+ 14.25**	**– 96.0**		**+ 96.0**
COMs	**– 34.75**	**+ 55.69**	**+ 13.88**	**– 34.75**	**– 24.0**		**+ 13.88**
FEMs + COMs	– 257.50	278.44	– 0.37	– 20.5	– 120		109.88
Column moment							
at top	64.38	– 46.4			20		27.47
at bottom	64.38	– 46.4			20		– 27.47

(ii) Live load on BC only, dead load on ABCD.

	A		B		C		D
FEMs	**– 141.75**	**+ 141.75**	**– 23.25**	**+ 23.23**	**– 60.0**		**+ 60.0**
COMs	**– 19.75**	**+ 35.44**	**+ 6.13**	**– 19.75**	**– 15.0**		**+ 6.13**
FEMs + COMs	– 161.5	177.19	– 17.22	3.5	– 75		66.13
Column moment							
at top	40.38	29.53			12.5		– 16.53
At bottom	40.38	29.53			12.5		– 16.53

Design Moments in Columns :

	A	B	C	D
Column moment in columns				
at top	64.38	– 46.	20	– 27.47
at bottom	64.38	– 46.	20	– 27.47

Design Moments at Joints :

Moment at joints are negative (tension at top) moments and their maximum values occur only when adjoining panels are loaded with lives loads.

For Maximum Moment at Joint A :

The condition of loading to obtain maximum moment at joint A is as,

Live load on AB only while dead load on AB and BC.

The effect of dead load on other span is neglected.

	A D.L. + L.L.		B D.L.		C D.L.		D
D.F.	$\frac{1}{2}$	$\frac{1}{3}$	$\frac{1}{3}$	$\frac{1}{3}$	$\frac{1}{3}$		$\frac{1}{2}$
FEMs	– 222.75	+ 222.75	– 14.25	...	....		...
BAL	+ 111.38	– 69.5	– 69.5	...	...		...
COM	– 34.75	....	...	...	...		...
BAL	+ 17.38	...	...	...	...		....
Final	– 128.74						

For Maximum Moment at Joint B :

Loading conditions are : Live load on AB and BC, while dead load ABCD.

	A D.L. + L.L.		B D.L. + L.L.		C D.L.		D
D.F.	$\frac{1}{2}$	$\frac{1}{3}$	$\frac{1}{3}$	$\frac{1}{3}$	$\frac{1}{3}$		$\frac{1}{2}$
FEM	– 222.75	+ 222.75	– 23.25	+ 23.25	– 60.0	+ 60.0	
BAL	+ 111.38	– 66.50	– 66.50	+ 12.25	+ 12.25		...
COM	...	+ 55.69	+ 6.13	...	...		...
BAL	...	– 20.60	– 20.60	...	...		....
Final		+ 191.34	– 104.22				

For Maximum Moment at Joint C :

Loading conditions are : Live load on BC and CD, while dead load on AB.

	A D.L.		B D.L. + L.L.		C D.L. + L.L.		D
D.F.	$\frac{1}{2}$	$\frac{1}{3}$	$\frac{1}{3}$	$\frac{1}{3}$	$\frac{1}{3}$		$\frac{1}{2}$
FEMs	– 141.75	+ 141.75	– 23.25	+ 23.25	– 96.0	+ 96.0	
BAL	...	– 39.5	– 39.5	+ 24.25	+ 24.25	– 48.0	
COM	...	....	...	– 19.75	– 24.0		...
BAL	...	...	...	+ 14.58	+ 14.58		....
Final				+ 42.33	– 81.17		

For maximum moment at joint D :

Loading conditions are : Live load on CD only, while dead load on BC and CD. The effect of dead load on other spans is neglected.

D.F.	$\frac{1}{2}$	$\frac{1}{3}$	$\frac{1}{3}$	$\frac{1}{3}$	$\frac{1}{3}$	$\frac{1}{2}$
FEMs	...	...	...	+ 14.25	− 96.0	+ 96.0
BAL	...	...	...	+ 27.25	+ 27.25	− 48.0
COM	...	....	...	...	...	+ 13.63
BAL	...	...	...	...	...	− 6.81
Final						+ 54.82

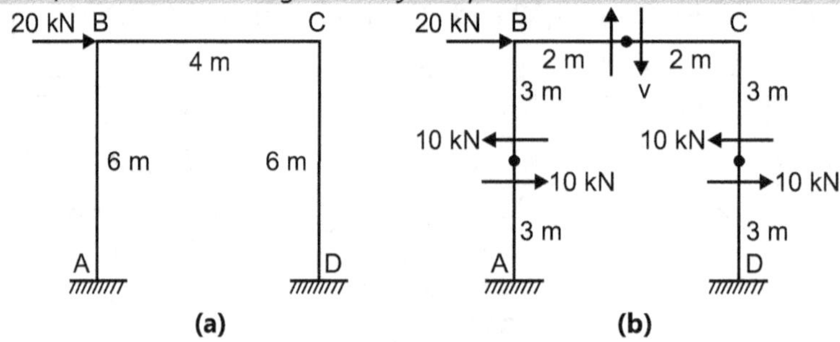

Example 12.2 :

Analyse the portal frame shown in Fig.12.11 by the portal method.

Fig. 12.11

Solution :

Let use assume that points of contraflexure occur at the middle point of the beam and at the middle points of the columns.

Column shear :

Let $\quad$ Q = horizontal shear for each column

$\qquad 2Q = 20$

$\therefore \qquad Q = 10$ kN

Column methods :

B.M. at the upper and lower end of each column = $10 \times 3 = 30$ kNm

Beam moments :

Moment at the end of the beam = Moment at the top of the column = 30 kNm.

Beam shear :

Let V = S.F. for the beam : B.M. at B = $V \times 2 = 30$

$$\therefore \quad V \;=\; 15 \text{ kN}$$

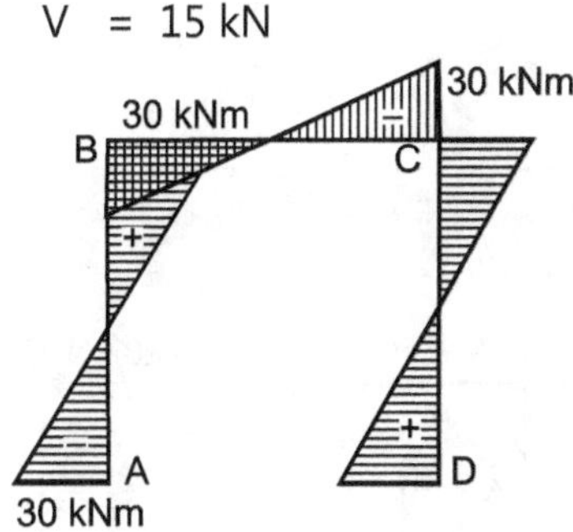

Fig. 12.12 : BMD

Alternative solution

Let,
$$P_1 \;=\; \text{Horizontal force acting at last storey } (n) = 20 \text{ kN}$$
$$Q_1 \;=\; \text{Shear for each end column at first storey}$$
$$2\,Q_1 \;=\; \text{shear for each intermediate column at first storey}$$
$$n \;=\; \text{No. of storey} = 1$$

Storey	Column shear (Q)
(last) n	$P_1 = Q_n$ (No. of end column) $+ Q_n$ (No. of intermediate column) / 2 $20 = Q_1 \times 2 + 2\,Q_1 \times 0$ $Q_1 = 10$ kN

Storey	Column Moments	
	End column	**Intermediate column**
n = 1	Force $\times$ distance $= Q_n \times$ column height (h) / 2 $= 10 \times (6/2) = 30$ kNm	$2\,Q_n \times$ column height (h) / 2 Not applicable

Storey	Beam Moments	
	End beam moments	**Intermediate beam moments**
n = 1	Sum of end column moment (above the floor and below the floor) at joint = 0 + 30 = 30 kNm	([sum of intermediate column moment (above the floor and below the floor) at joint] – [end beam moments]) = 0

Shear in beams :   Beam moment $= V \times$ Beam length / 2

$$M \;=\; V \times \frac{L}{2}$$

$$V \;=\; \frac{2 \times M}{L} \;=\; \frac{2 \times 30}{4} \;=\; 15 \text{ kN}$$

Where,   V = S.F. beam

M = Beam moment

L = Beam length

Example 12.3 :

Analyse the portal frame shown in Fig. 12.13

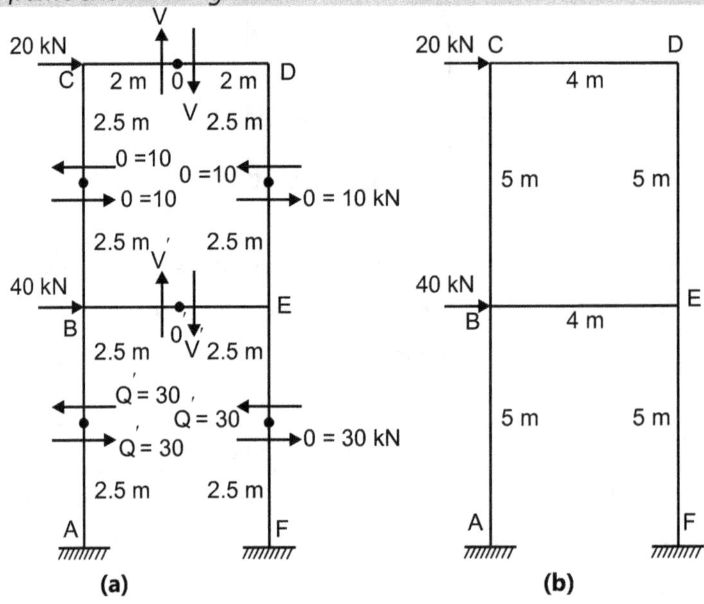

Fig. 12.13

Let, P_1 = Horizontal force acting at last storey (n) = 20 kN]

P_2 = Horizontal force acting at (n – 1) storey = 40 kN

Q_1 = Shear for each end column at first storey

$2 Q_1$ = Shear for each intermediate column at first storey

n = No. of storey = 2

Storey	Column shear (Q)
(last) n = 2	$P_1 = Q_n$ (No. of end column) + $2 Q_n$ (No. of intermediate column) $20 = Q_2 \times 2$ $Q_2 = 10$ kN
n – 1 = 2 – 1 = 1	$P_1 + P_2 = Q_{n-1}$ (No. of end column) + $2 Q_{n-1}$ (No. of intermediate column) $20 + 40 = Q_1 \times 2$ $Q_1 = 30$ kN

Storey	Column moments	
	End column	**Intermediate column**
n = 2	Force × Distance = Q_n × Column height (h) / 2	$2 Q_n$ × Column height (h) / 2 = 0

	$Q_2 \times 5/2 = 10 \times 2.5 = 25$ kNm	
n – 1 = 2 – 1 = 1	$Q_{n-1} \times h/2$ $Q_1 \times 5/2 = 30 \times 2.5 = 75$ kNm	$Q_{n-1} \times h/2 = 0$

Storey	Beam Moments	
	End beam moments	**Intermediate Beam moments**
n	Sum of end column moment (above the floor and below the floor) at joint	{[sum of intermediate column moment (above the floor and below the floor) at joint] – [end beam moments]}
2	0 + 25 = 25 kNm	0
1	25 + 75 = 100 kNm	0

Shear in beams :

$$\text{Beam moment} = V \times \frac{\text{Beam length}}{2}$$

$$M = V \times \frac{L}{2}$$

$$V = 2 \times \frac{M}{L}$$

Where, V = S.F. in beam

  M = Beam moment

  L = Beam length

Story	Beam					
	End beam			**Intermediate beam**		
	Moment (M)	**Length (L)**	**Shear = 2 M/L**	**Moment (M)**	**Length (L)**	**Shear = 2 M/L**
2	25	4	2(25)/4 = 12.5 kN	NA	NA	NA
1	100	4	2(100)/4 = 50 + 12.5 = 62.5 kN	NA	NA	NA

Alternative solution :

Column shear :

Let Q = Horizontal shear for each column of upper storey.

  $2Q = 20$ $\therefore$ $Q = 10$ kN

Let, Q' = Horizontal shear for each column of the lower storey.

$$\therefore \quad 2Q' = 20 + 40 = 60$$
$$\therefore \quad Q' = 30 \text{ kN}$$

Column moments :

B.M. at the top and bottom of each upper storey column
$$= 10 \times 2.5 = 25 \text{ kNm}$$

B.M. at the top and bottom of each lower storey column
$$= 30 \times 2.5 = 75 \text{ kNm}$$

Beam moments :

B.M. at each end of the upper beam = B.M. at the top of each column = 25 kNm

B.M. at each end of the lower beam = sum of the moments in the column just above adjust below the beam = 25 + 75 = 100 kNm.

Beam Shear :

$$V = \text{S.F. for upper beam}$$
$$V' = \text{S.F. for lower beam}$$
$$V \times 2 = 25$$
$$\therefore \quad V = 12 - 5 \text{ kN}$$
$$V' \times 2 = 100$$
$$V' = 50 \text{ kN}$$

Axial force for each upper column $= V = 12.5 \text{ kN}$

Axial force for each lower column $= V + V' = 12.5 + 50 = 62.5 \text{ kN}$

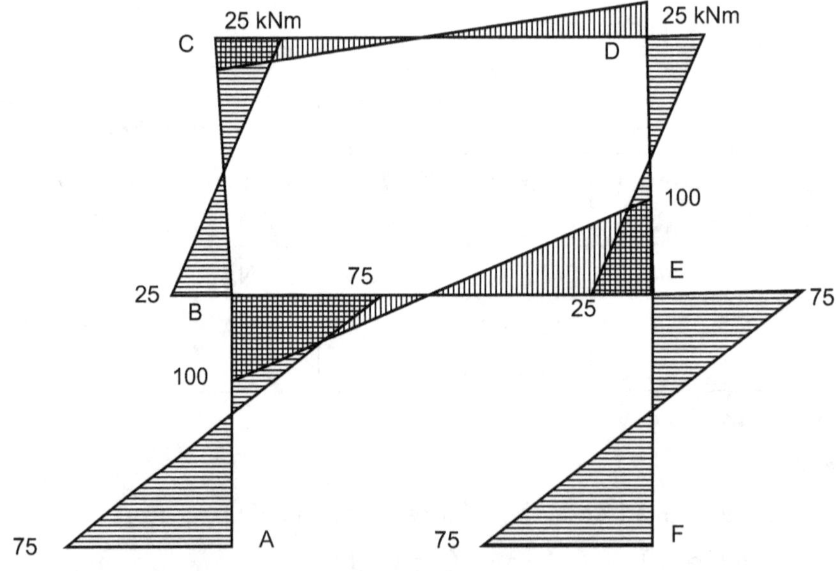

Fig. 12.14 : BMD

Example 12.4 :

Analyse the frame shown in Fig. 12.15

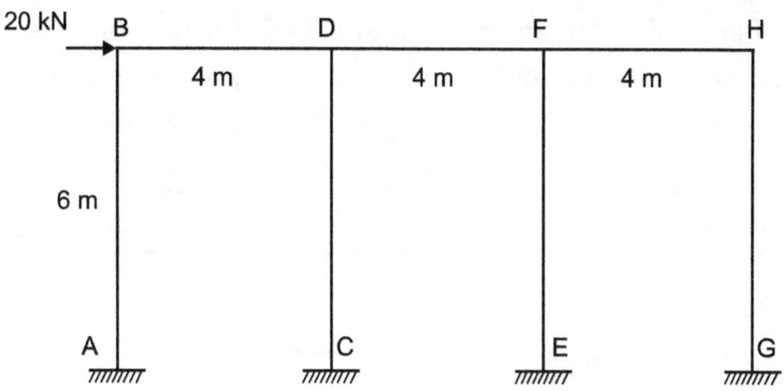

Fig. 12.15

Let, P_1 = Horizontal force acting at last storey (n) = 20 kN

P_2 = Horizontal force acting at (n – 1) storey

P_3 = Horizontal force acting at (n – 2) storey

Q_1 = Shear for each end column at first storey

$2Q_1$ = shear for each intermediate column at first storey.

n = No. of storey = 1

Storey	Column Shear (Q)
(last) n = 1	$P_1 = Q_n$ (No. of end column) + 2 Q_n (No. of intermediate column) 20 = Q_1(2) + 2Q_1 (2) 20 = 6Q_1 Q_1 = 3.33 kN

Storey	Column moments	
	End column	**Intermediate column**
N = 1	Force × Distance = Q_n × Column height (h) / 2 = Q_1 (6/2) Q1 = 3.33 kN	2 Q_n × Column height (h) / 2 2Q_1 (6/2) 2(3.33)(3) = 20 kNm

Storey	Beam Moments	
	End Beam Movements	**Intermediate Beam Movement**
n	Sum of end column moment (above the floor and below the floor) at joint.	{[Sum of intermediate column moment (above the floor and below the floor) at joint] – [End beam moments]}
1	0 + 10 = 10 kNm	(0 + 20) – 10 = 10 kNm

Shear in Beams :

$$\text{Beam Moment} = V \times \frac{\text{Beam length}}{2}$$

$$M = V \times \frac{L}{2}$$

$$V = 2 \times \frac{M}{L}$$

Where, V = S.F. in beam

M = Beam Moment

L = Beam Length

Story	Beam					
	End beam			**Intermediate beam**		
	Moment (M)	Length (L)	Shear = 2 M/L	Moment (M)	Length (L)	Shear = 2 M/L
1	10	4	2(10)/4 = 5 kN	10	4	= 2(10)/4 = 5 kN

Solution : Let us assume points of contraflexure at the middle points of each component.

Column shear :

Let, Q = S.F. for each end column

∴ S.F. for each intermediate column = $2Q$

∴ $Q + 2Q + 2Q + Q = 20$; $6Q = 20$;

∴ $Q = \frac{10}{3}$ kN

Horizontal shear for each intermediate column = $\frac{10}{3}$ kN

Horizontal shear for each intermediate column = $\dfrac{20}{3}$ kN

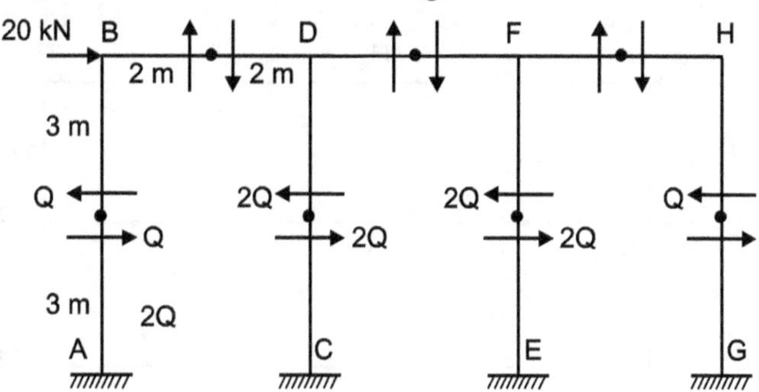

Fig. 12.16

Column moments :

End columns AB and GH

$$\text{B.M. at top of the column} \;=\; \frac{10}{3} \times 3 = 10 \text{ kNm}$$

$$\text{B.M. at bottom of the column} \;=\; \frac{10}{3} \times 3 = 10 \text{ kNm}$$

Intermediate columns CD and EF

$$\text{B.M. at the top of the column} \;=\; \frac{20}{3} \times 3 = 20 \text{ kNm}$$

$$\text{B.M. at the bottom of the column} \;=\; \frac{20}{3} \times 3 = 20 \text{ kNm}$$

Beam moments :

$$\text{B.M. at B or H} \;=\; \text{B.M. at top of end column} = 10 \text{ kNm}$$

$$\text{B.M. at D on either side of D} \;=\; \frac{\text{B.M. at the top of column CD}}{2} = \frac{20}{2} = 10 \text{ kNm}$$

Beam shears :

Let $\qquad V$ = S.F. for end beams BD and FH; $V \times 2 = 10$

$\therefore \qquad V$ = 5 kN

Let $\qquad V'$ = S.F. for the beams DF; $V' \times 2 = 10$

$\therefore \qquad V'$ = 5 kN

Axial force for each end column = SF for beam BD or FH = 5 kN

Axial force for each intermediate column = 0

Example 12.5 :

Analyse the frame shown in Fig. 12.17.

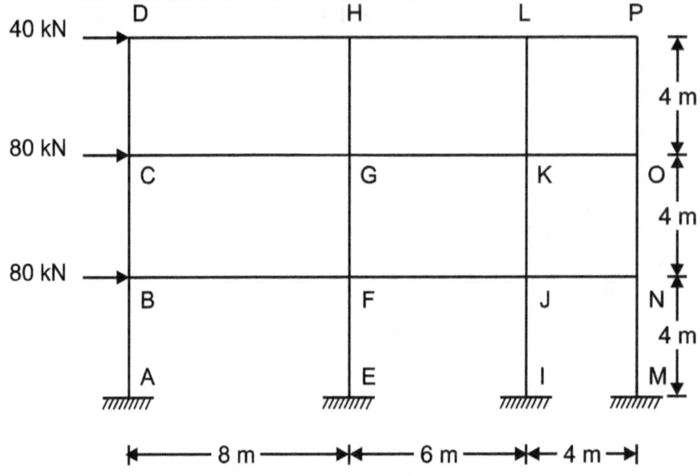

Fig. 12.17

Let, P_1 = Horizontal force acting at last storey (n) = 40 kN

P_2 = Horizontal force acting at (n − 1) storey = 80 kN

P_3 = Horizontal force acting at (n − 2) storey = 80 kN

Q_1 = Shear for each end column at first storey

$2Q_1$ = Shear for each intermediate column at first storey

n = No. of storey = 3

Storey	Column Shear (Q)
(last) n = 3	$P_1 = Q_n$ (No. of end column) + 2 Q_n (No. of intermediate column) $40 = Q_3(2) + 2Q_3(2)$ $40 = 6Q_3$ $Q_3 = 6.66$ kN
n − 1 = 3 − 1 = 2	$P_1 + P_2 = Q_{n-1}$ (No. of end column) + 2 Q_{n-1} (No. of intermediate column) $40 + 80 = Q_2(2) + 2Q_2(2)$ $120 = 6Q_2$ $Q_2 = 20$ kN
n − 2 = 3 − 2 = 1	$P_1 + P_2 + P_3 = Q_{n-2}$ (No. of end column) + 2 Q_{n-2} (No. of intermediate column) $40 + 80 + 80 = Q_1(2) + 2Q_1(2)$ $200 = 6Q_1$ $Q_1 = 33.33$ kN

Storey	Column moments	
	End Column	**Intermediate Column**
$n = 3$	Force $\times$ Distance = $Q_n \times$ Column height (h) / 2 $= Q_3 (4/2)$ $= 6.66(2) = 13.33$ kNm	$2\,Q_n \times$ Column height (h) / 2 $= 2Q_3 (2)$ $= 2(6.66)\,2 = 26.66$ kNm
$n - 1 =$ $3 - 1 = 2$	$Q_{n-1} \times h/2$ $= Q_2(2)$ $= 20(2)$ $= 40$ kNm	$2\,Q_{n-1} \times h / 2$ $= 2Q_2 (2)$ $= 2(20)\,2$ $= 80$ kNm
$n - 2 =$ $3 - 2 = 1$	$Q_{n-2} \times h/2$ $= Q_1(2)$ $= 33.33(2)$ $= 66.66$ kNm	$2\,Q_{n-2} \times h / 2$ $= 2(Q_1)\,2$ $= 2(33.33)\,2$ $= 133.32$ kNm

Storey	Beam Moments	
	End Beam Moments	**Intermediate Beam moments**
n	Sum of end column moment (above the floor and below the floor) at joint	{[sum of intermediate column moment (above the floor and below the floor) at joint] – [end beam moments]}
3	0 + 13.33 = 13.33 kNm	(0 + 26.66) – 13.33 = 13.33 kNm
2	13.33 + 40 = 53.33 kNm	(26.66 + 80) – 53.33 = 53.33 kNm
1	40 + 66.66 = 106.66 kNm	(80 + 133.32) – 106.66 = 106.66 kNm

Shear in Beams :

$$\text{Beam Movement} \quad = \quad \frac{V \times \text{beam length}}{2}$$

$$M \quad = \quad V \times \frac{L}{2}$$

$$V \quad = \quad 2 \times \frac{M}{L}$$

Where, V = S.F. in beam

                M = Beam moment

                L = Beam length

Story	Beam								
	End Beam (DH)			End Beam (LP)			Intermediate beam (HL)		
	Moment (M)	Length (L)	Shear = 2 M/L	Moment (M)	Length (L)	Shear = 2 M/L	Moment (M)	Length (L)	Shear = 2 M/L
3	13.33	8	3.33	13.33	4	6.66	13.33	6	4.44
2	53.33	8	13.33	53.33	4	26.66	53.33	6	17.77
1	106.66	8	26.66	106.66	4	53.33	106.66	6	35.55

Solution :

We will assume that points of countraflexure occur at the middle points of the individual components

Column shear :

Storey 3 :

Let, Q_3 = shear for each end column

$\therefore$ Shear for each intermediate column = $2 Q_3$

$\therefore \quad Q_3 + 2Q_3 + 2Q_3 + Q_3 = 40;$

$$6 Q_3 = 40$$

$$\therefore \quad Q_3 = \frac{20}{3} \text{ kN}$$

$$\therefore \quad \text{Shear for end column} = \frac{20}{3} \text{ kN};$$

$$\text{Shear for intermediate column} = \frac{40}{3} \text{ kN}$$

Storey 2 :

Let Q_2 = Shear for each end column

$\therefore$ Shear for each intermediate column = $2 Q_2$

$\therefore \quad Q_2 + 2 Q_2 + 2Q_2 + Q_2 = 40 + 80$

$$6 Q_2 = 120$$

$$\therefore \quad Q_2 = 20 \text{ kN}$$

$\therefore \quad$ Shear for end column = 20 kN

$\therefore \quad$ Shear for intermediate column = 40 kN

Storey 1 :

Let Q_1 = Shear for each end column

$\therefore$ Shear for each intermediate column = $2 Q_1$

$\therefore \quad Q_1 + 2Q_1 + 2Q_1 + Q_1 = 40 + 80 + 80$

$$\therefore \quad 6Q_1 = 200$$

$$\therefore \quad Q_1 = \frac{100}{3} \text{ kN}$$

$$\therefore \quad \text{Shear for end column} \ = \frac{100}{3} \text{ kN;}$$

$$\text{Shear for intermediate column} \ = \frac{200}{3} \text{ kN}$$

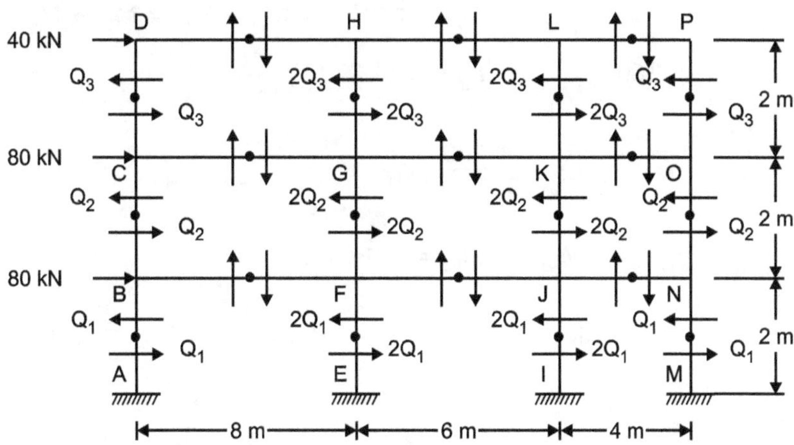

Fig. 12.18

Column moments :
Storey 3 :

End columns : Moment at top or bottom $= \dfrac{20}{3} \times 2 = \dfrac{40}{3}$ kNm

Intermediate column : Moment at top bottom $= \dfrac{40}{3} \times 2 = \dfrac{80}{3}$ kNm

Storey 2 :

End columns : Moment at top or bottom $= 20 \times 2 = 40$ kNm

Intermediate columns : Moment at top or bottom $= 40 \times 2 = 80$ kNm

Storey 1 :

End columns : Moment at top or bottom $= \dfrac{100}{3} \times 2 = \dfrac{200}{3}$ kNm

Intermediate columns : Moment at top or bottom $= \dfrac{200}{3} \times 2 = \dfrac{400}{3}$ kNm

Beam moments :

Storey 3 :

$$M_{dh} = M_{dc} = \frac{40}{3} \text{ kNm;} \qquad M_{hd} = M_{dh} = \frac{40}{3} \text{ kNm;} \qquad M_{hd} = M_{hl} = M_{hg}$$

$$\frac{40}{3} + M_{hl} = \frac{80}{3} \qquad \therefore \ M_{hl} = \frac{40}{3} \text{ kNm;} \qquad M_{lp} = M_{lp} = M_{po} = \frac{40}{3} \text{ kNm}$$

Storey 2 :

$$M_{cg} \;=\; M_{cd} + M_{cb} = \frac{40}{3} + 40 = \frac{160}{3} \text{ kNm}$$

$$M_{gc} \;=\; M_{gk} = \frac{160}{3} \text{ kNm}; \; M_{gc} + M_{gk} = M_{gh} + M_{gf}$$

$$\frac{160}{3} + M_{gk} \;=\; \frac{80}{3} + 80 = \frac{320}{3} \text{ kNm}$$

$$\therefore \qquad M_{gk} \;=\; \frac{160}{3} \text{ kNm}$$

$$M_{kg} \;=\; M_{kg} = \frac{160}{3} \text{ kNm}$$

$$M_{ko} \;=\; M_{gk} = M_{op} + M_{on} = \frac{40}{3} + 40 = \frac{160}{3} \text{ kNm}$$

Storey 1 :

$$M_{bf} \;=\; M_{bc} + M_{ba} = 40 + \frac{200}{3} = \frac{320}{3} \text{ kNm}$$

$$M_{fb} \;=\; M_{bf} = \frac{320}{3} \text{ kNm}; \; M_{fb} + M_{fl} = M_{fg} + M_{fe}$$

$$\frac{320}{3} + M_{fb} \;=\; 80 + \frac{400}{3} = \frac{640}{3} \text{ kNm}; \; M_{fb} = \frac{320}{3} \text{ kNm}$$

$$M_{if} \;=\; M_{fi} = \frac{320}{3} \text{ kNm}$$

$$M_{jn} - M_{nj} \;=\; M_{no} + M_{nm} = 40 + \frac{200}{3} = \frac{320}{3} \text{ kNm}$$

Shear in beams

$$\text{SF in DH} \;=\; \frac{2 \times \left(\frac{40}{3}\right)}{8} = \frac{40}{3} \text{ kN}; \qquad \text{SF in HL} = \frac{2 \times \frac{40}{3}}{6} = \frac{40}{9} \text{ kN}$$

$$\text{SF in LP} \;=\; \frac{2 \times \frac{40}{3}}{4} = \frac{40}{3} \text{ kN}; \qquad \text{SF in CG} = \frac{2 \times \frac{160}{3}}{8} = \frac{40}{3} \text{ kN}$$

$$\text{SF in GK} \;=\; \frac{2 \times \frac{160}{3}}{6} = \frac{160}{9} \text{ kN} \qquad \text{SF in KO} = \frac{2 \times \frac{160}{3}}{4} = \frac{80}{3} \text{ kN}$$

$$\text{SF in BF} \;=\; \frac{2 \times \frac{320}{2}}{8} = \frac{80}{9} \text{ kN} \qquad \text{SF in FJ} = \frac{2 \times \frac{320}{3}}{6} = \frac{320}{9} \text{ kN}$$

$$\text{SF in JN} \;=\; \frac{2 \times \dfrac{320}{3}}{4} = \frac{160}{3}\ \text{kN}$$

12.5 STEP BY STEP ANALYSIS PROCEDURE OF PORTAL FRAME METHOD

(1) Column Shear (Q) :

Let,

P_1 – Horizontal force acting at last storey (n)

P_2 – Horizontal force acting at (n − 1) storey

P_3 – Horizontal force acting at (n − 2) storey

Q_1 – Shear for each end column at first storey

$2Q_1$ – Shear for each intermediate column at first storey

n – No. of storey

Storey	Column Shear (Q)
(last) n	$P_1 = Q_n$ (No. of end column) + 2 Q_n (No. of intermediate column)
n − 1	$P_1 + P_2 = Q_{n-1}$ (No. of end column) + $2Q_{n-1}$ (No. of intermediate column)
n − 2	$P_1 + P_2 + P_3 = Q_{n-2}$ (No. of end column) + 2 Q_{n-2} (No. of intermediate column)

(2) Column Moments :

Storey	Column Moments	
	End Column	**Intermediate column**
n	Force × Distance = Q_n × Column height (h)/2	$2Q_n$ × Column height (h) / 2
n − 1	$Q_{n-1} \times h/2$	$2Q_{n-1} \times h/2$
n − 2	$Q_{n-2} \times h/2$	$2Q_{n-2} \times h/2$

(3) Beam Moments :

Storey	Beam Moments	
	End Beam Moment	**Intermediate Beam Moment**
n	Sum of end column moment (above the floor and below the floor) at joint.	{Sum of intermediate column moment (above the floor and below the floor) at joint − [End beam moments]}
n − 1	Same as above	
n − 2	Same as above	

(4) Shear in Beams

$$\text{Beam moment} = V \times \frac{\text{Beam length}}{2}$$

$$M = V \times \frac{L}{2}$$

$$V = 2 \times \frac{M}{L}$$

Where,   V = S.F. in beam

M = Beam moment

V = Beam length

Storey	Beam					
	End Beam			Intermediate Beam		
	Moment (M)	Length (L)	Shear = 2 M/L	Moment (M)	Length (L)	Shear = 2 M/L

12.6 CANTILEVER METHOD

The cantilever method of analysis is more appropriate for all structures i.e. for a structure that has height grater than its width. This method is based on the assumption that the building frame acts like a cantilever beam with the columns as longitudinal fibres of the beam.

Example 12.6 :

Analyse the frame shown in Fig. 12.19 by cantilever method. Area of each exterior columns is one half of the area of the interior column.

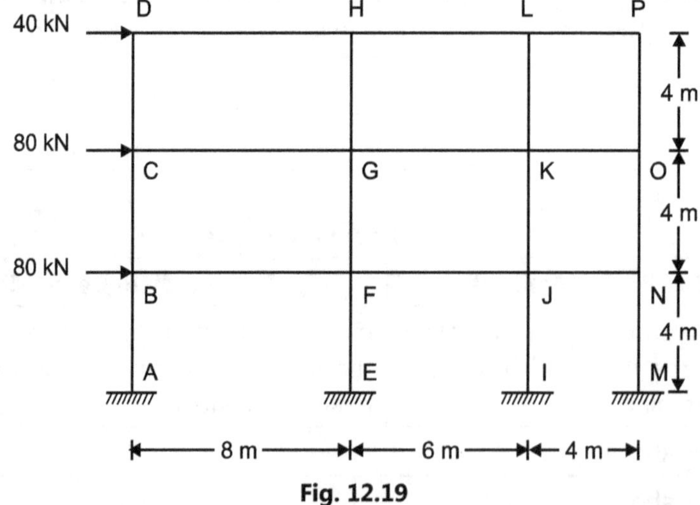

Fig. 12.19

CG of Frame :

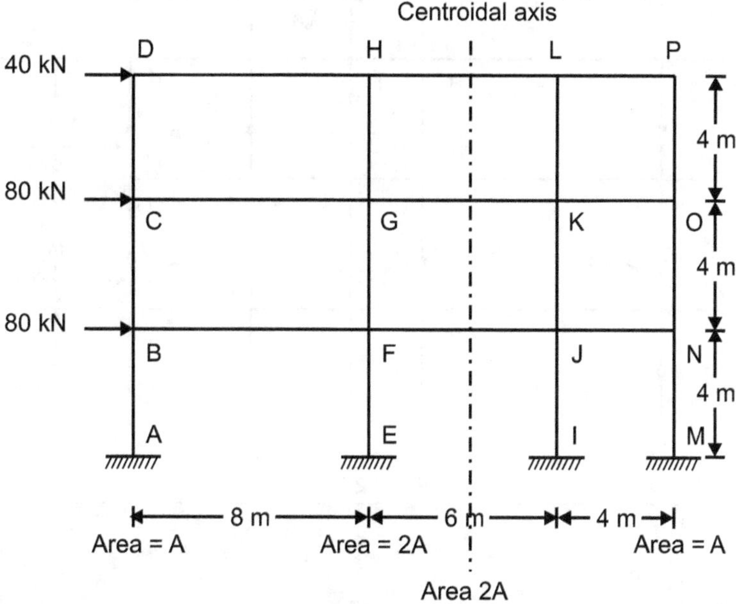

Fig. 12.20

Solution :

We will assume that points of contraflexure occur at the middle of each member.

Let the area of each end column = A

∴   Area of each intermediate column = 2A

Total area of columns = A + 2A + 2A + A = 6A

Let the distance of the centre of gravity of the columns be $\bar{x}$ from the axis of the column ABCD taking moments about the column ABCD.

$$6A\,\bar{x} \;=\; (A \times 0) + (2A)\,8 + (2A)14 + A(18);$$

$$6A\,\bar{x} \;=\; 62\,A$$

$$\therefore \qquad \bar{x} \;=\; 10.33 \text{ m}$$

Consider the structure just above the points of contraflexure of the columns of the first storey. The distances of the various columns from the centre of gravity of the columns are shown in Fig. 12.21. Let, the axial force in the column AB = P_1 (tensile).

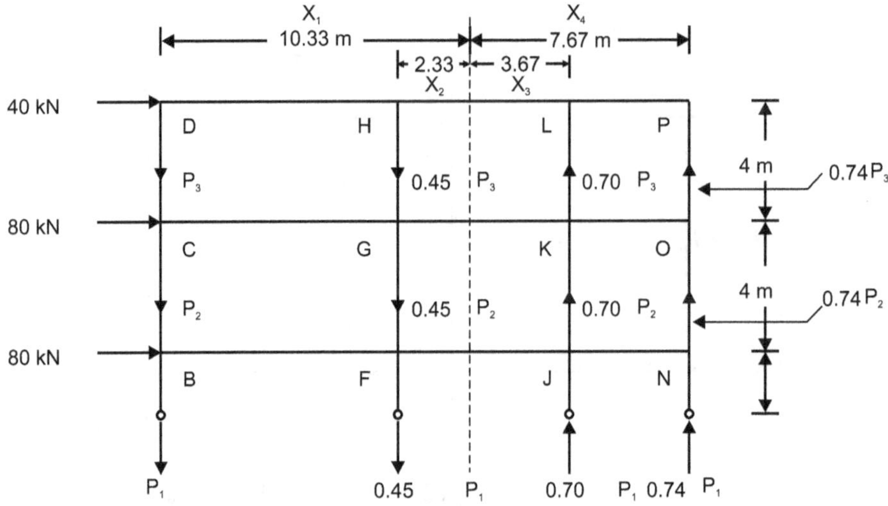

Fig. 12.21

Story	Axial force notation	Stress in column $(\sigma_c) = (P/A)(x/x)$	Axial force in terms of P = stress x area	Axial force (taking moment @ contraflexure of End column)
3	P_3	$\sigma_c CD = \dfrac{P_3}{A}\dfrac{10.33}{10.33} = \dfrac{P_3}{A}$	$P_{CD} = \dfrac{P_3}{A} A = P_3$ (tensile)	
		$\sigma_c GH = \dfrac{P_3}{A}\dfrac{2.33}{10.33} = 0.22\dfrac{P_3}{A}$	$P_{GH} = 0.22\dfrac{P_3}{A} 2A = 0.45\,P_3$ (tensile)	$(40 \times 10) + (80 \times 6) + (80 \times 2) + (0.45P_1 \times 8) = (0.74P_1 \times 18)$ [$P_1 = 53.27$ kN]
		$\sigma_c KL = \dfrac{P_3}{A}\dfrac{3.67}{10.33} = 0.35\dfrac{P_3}{A}$	$P_{KL} = 0.35\dfrac{P_3}{A} 2A = 0.70\,P_3$ (Comp.)	
		$\sigma_c OP = \dfrac{P_3}{A}\dfrac{7.67}{10.33} = 0.74\dfrac{P_3}{A}$	$P_{OP} = 0.74\dfrac{P_3}{A} A = 0.74\,P_3$ (Comp.)	
2	P_2	$\sigma_c BC = \dfrac{P_2}{A}\dfrac{10.33}{10.33} = \dfrac{P_2}{A}$	$P_{BC} = \dfrac{P_2}{A} = A = P_2$ (tensile)	
		$\sigma_c FG = \dfrac{P_2}{A}\dfrac{2.33}{10.33} = 0.22\dfrac{P_2}{A}$	$P_{FG} = 0.22\dfrac{P_2}{A} 2A = 0.45\,P_2$ (tensile)	$(40 \times 6) + (80 \times 2) + (0.45P_2 \times 8) = (0.70P_2 = 14) + (0.74\,P_2 \times 18)$ [$P_2 = 20.49$ kN]
		$\sigma_c JK = \dfrac{P_2}{A}\dfrac{3.67}{10.33} = 0.35\dfrac{P_2}{A}$	$P_{JK} = 0.35\dfrac{P_2}{A} 2A = 0.70\,P_2$ (Comp.)	
		$\sigma_c NO = \dfrac{P_2}{A}\dfrac{7.67}{10.33} = 0.74\dfrac{P_2}{A}$	$P_{NO} = 0.74\dfrac{P_2}{A} A = 0.74\,P_2$ (Comp.)	
3	P_1	$\sigma_c AB = \dfrac{P_1}{A}\dfrac{10.33}{10.33} = \dfrac{P_1}{A}$	$P_{AB} = \dfrac{P_1}{A} = A = P_1$ (tensile)	$40 \times 2 + 0.45\,P_3 \times 8 = 0.70\,P_3 \times 14 +$
		$\sigma_c EF = \dfrac{P_1}{A}\dfrac{2.33}{10.33} = 0.22\dfrac{P_1}{A}$	$P_{EF} = 0.22\dfrac{P_1}{A} 2A = 0.44\,P_1$ (tensile)	

		$\sigma_c \text{IJ} = \dfrac{P_1}{A}\ \dfrac{3.67}{10.33} = 0.35\ \dfrac{P_1}{A}$	$P_{IJ} = 0.35\ \dfrac{P_1}{A}\ 2A = 0.70\ P_1\ (\text{Comp.})$	$0.74\ P_3 \times 18$ $[P_3 = 4.09$ kN]
		$\sigma_c \text{MN} = \dfrac{P_1}{A}\ \dfrac{7.67}{10.33} = 0.74\ \dfrac{P_1}{A}$	$P_{MN} = 0.74\ \dfrac{P_1}{A}\ A = 0.74\ P_1\ (\text{Comp.})$	

Story	Beam	Beam shear (shear force in beam) it is algebraic sum of all the forces acting on column on right or left part of beam (just above the beam and just below the beam)
3	DH	$-P_3 = 4.09$ kN
	HL	$-P_3 - 0.45P_3 = -1.45\ P_3 = -1.45 \times 4.09 = -5.93$ kN
	LP	$-0.74P3 = -0.74 \times 4.09 = -3.02$ kN
2	CG	$-(P_2 - P_3) = -(19.52 - 4.09) = -15.43$ kN
	GK	$-(P_2 - P_3) - 0.45\ (P_2 - P_3) = -1.45\ (P_2 - P_3) = -1.45\ (15.43) = -22.37$ kN
	KO	$-0.74\ (P_2 - P_3) = -0.74\ (15.43) = -11.41$ kN
1	BF	$-(P_1 - P_2) = -(53.27 - 19.5) = -33.77$ kN
	FJ	$-(P_1 - P_2) - 0.45\ (P_1 - P_2) = -1.45\ (P_1 - P_2) = -1.45\ (33.77) = 48.96$ kN
	JN	$-0.74\ (P_1 - P_2) = -0.74\ (33.77) = -24.98$ kN

Story	Beam	Beam span	Beam shear (S.F. in beam) w kN	Beam moment = wl/2 kNm
3	DH	8	4.09	16.36
	HL	6	5.93	17.79
	LP	4	3.02	6.04
2	CG	8	15.43	61.72
	GK	6	22.37	67.11
	KO	4	11.41	22.82
1	BF	8	33.77	135.08
	FJ	6	48.96	146.88
	JN	4	24.98	49.96

Joint	$\sum$ Beam moment = $\sum$ Column Moment	
D	$M_{DC} = M_{DH}$	$M_{DC} = M_{DH} =$
H	$M_{HG} = M_{HD} + M_{HL}$	$M_{HG} =$
L	$M_{LK} = M_{LH} + M_{LP}$	$M_{LK} =$
P	$M_{PO} = M_{PL}$	$M_{PO} = M_{PL} =$
C	$M_{CB} + M_{CD} = M_{CG}$	$M_{CB} =$
G	$M_{GF} + M_{GH} = M_{GC} + M_{GK}$	$M_{GF} =$
K	$M_{KJ} + M_{KL} = M_{KG} + M_{KO}$	$M_{KJ} =$
O	$M_{ON} + M_{OP} = M_{OK}$	$M_{ON} =$
B	$M_{BA} + M_{DC} = M_{BF}$	$M_{BA} =$
F	$M_{FE} + M_{FG} = M_{FB} + M_{FJ}$	$M_{FE} =$
J	$M_{JI} + M_{JK} = M_{JF} + M_{JN}$	$M_{JI} =$
N	$M_{NM} + M_{NO} = M_{NI}$	$M_{NM} =$

$$\text{Stress in the column AB} = \frac{P_1}{A} \text{ (tensile);}$$

$$\text{Stress in the column EF} = \frac{2.33}{10.33} \cdot \frac{P_1}{A} \text{ (tensile)}$$

$$\text{Stress in the column IJ} = \frac{3.6}{10.33} \cdot \frac{P_1}{A} \text{ (compressive);}$$

$$\text{Stress in the column MN} = \frac{7.67}{10.33} = \frac{P_1}{A} \text{ (compressive)}$$

Now we can determine the axial forces in the various columns.

$$\text{Axial force in AB} = \frac{P_1}{A} \cdot A = P_1 \text{ (tensile)}$$

$$\text{Axial force in EF} = \frac{2.33}{10.33} \cdot \frac{P_1}{A} \times 2A = 0.45\, P_1 \text{ (tensile)}$$

$$\text{Axial force in IJ} = \frac{3.6}{10.33} \cdot \frac{P_1}{A} \times 2A = 0.70\, P_1 \text{ (compressive)}$$

$$\text{Axial force in MN} = \frac{7.67}{10.33} \cdot \frac{P_1}{A} \times A = 0.74\, P_1 \text{ (compressive)}$$

Taking moments about the point of contraflexure of the column AB

$$(40 \times 10) + (80 \times 6) + (80 \times 2) + (0.45\, P_1 \times 8) = (0.70\, P_1 \times 14) + (0.74\, P_1 \times 18)$$

$$\therefore \qquad P_1 = \frac{1040}{16.72} = \textbf{62.2 KN}$$

Storey 2

The forces in the columns of this storey will also be in the same proportion as they are in storey 1.

$$\text{Let the force in the column BC} = P_2 \text{ (Tensile)}$$

$$\text{Force in the column FG} = 0.45\,P_2 \text{ (tensile)}$$

$$\text{Force in the column JK} = 0.70\,P_2 \text{ (compressive)}$$

$$\text{Force in the column NO} = 0.74\,P_2 \text{ (compressive)}$$

Taking moments about the point of contraflexure of the column BC.

$$(40 \times 6) + (80 \times 2) + (0.45\,P_2 \times 8) = (0.70\,P_2 \times 14) + (0.74\,P_2 \times 18);$$

$$P_2 = \frac{400}{16.72} = 20.49 \text{ kN}$$

Storey 3 :

Let the force in the column CD = P_3 (tensile)

$$\text{Force in the column GH} = 0.45\,P_3 \text{ (tensile)}$$

$$\text{Force in the column KL} = 0.70\,P_3 \text{ (compressive)}$$

$$\text{Force in the column OP} = 0.74\,P_3 \text{ (compressive)}$$

Taking moments about the point of contraflexure of the column CD.

$$40 \times 2 + 0.45\,P_3 \times 8 = 0.70\,P_3 \times 14 + 0.74\,P_2 \times 18$$

$$\therefore \qquad P_3 = \frac{80}{16.72} = 4.78 \text{ kN}$$

Beam shears :

Since, the axial force in the columns are known we can easily find the shear forces in the beams.

Storey 3 :

$$\text{S.F. in beam DH} = -P_3 = -4.78 \text{ kN}$$

$$\text{S.F. in beam HL} = -P_3 - 0.45\,P_3 = -1.45\,P_3 = -1.45 \times 4.78 = -6.93 \text{ kN}$$

$$\text{S.F. in beam LP} = -0.74\,P_3 = -0.74 \times 4.78 = -3.54 \text{ kN}$$

Storey 2 :

$$\text{S.F. in beam CG} = -(P_2 - P_3) = -(23.92 - 4.78) = -19.14 \text{ kN}$$

$$\text{S.F. in beam GK} = -(P_2 - P_3) = -0.45\,(P_2 - P_3) = -1.45\,(P_2 - P_3) - 1.45\,(19.14)$$

$$= -27.75 \text{ kN}$$

$$\text{S.F. in beam KO} = -0.74\,(P_2 - P_3) = -0.74\,(19.14) = -14.16 \text{ kN}$$

Storey 1 :

$$\text{S.F. in beam BF} = -(P_1 - P_2) = -(62.2 - 23.92) = -38.28 \text{ kN}$$

$$\text{S.F. in Beam FJ} = -(P_1 - P_2) - 0.45 = (P_1 - P_2) = -1.45\,(P_1 - P_2) = -1.45\,(32.28)$$

$$= -55.51 \text{ kN}$$

S.F. in Beam JN $= -0.74 \, (P_1 - P_2) - 0.74 \, (38.28) = -28.33$ kN

Beam Moment :

$$\text{The B.M. for any beam} \; = \; \text{S.F. in the beam} \times \frac{\text{Span}}{2}$$

Storey 3 :

$$\text{B.M. for DH} \; = \; 4.78 \times \frac{8}{2} = 19.12 \text{ kNm;}$$

$$\text{B.M. for HL} \; = \; 6.93 \times \frac{6}{2} = 20.79 \text{ kNm;}$$

$$\text{B.M. for LP} \; = \; 3.54 \times \frac{4}{2} = 7.08 \text{ kNm}$$

Storey 2 :

$$\text{B.M. for CG} \; = \; 19.14 \times \frac{8}{2} = 76.56 \text{ kNm;}$$

$$\text{B.M. for GK} \; = \; 27.75 \times \frac{6}{2} = 83.25 \text{ kNm}$$

$$\text{B.M. for KO} \; = \; 14.16 \times \frac{4}{2} = 28.32 \text{ kNm}$$

Storey 1 :

$$\text{B.M. for BF} \; = \; 38.28 \times \frac{8}{2} = 153.12 \text{ kNm;}$$

$$\text{B.M. for FJ} \; = \; 55.51 \times \frac{6}{2} = 166.53 \text{ kNm}$$

$$\text{B.M. for IN} \; = \; 28.33 \times \frac{4}{2} = 56.66 \text{ kNm}$$

Column Moments :

Joint D	M_{dc}	$= M_{dh} = 19.12$ kNm
Joint H	M_{hg}	$= M_{hd} + M_{hl} = 19.12 + 20.79 = 39.91$ kNm
Joint L	M_{lk}	$= M_{lh} + M_{lp} = 20.79 + 7.08 = 27.87$ kNm
Joint P	M_{po}	$= M_{pl} = 7.08$ kNm;
	M_{cd}	$= M_{dc} = 19.12$ kNm;
	M_{gh}	$= M_{hg} = 39.91$ kNm
	M_{kl}	$= M_{lk} = 27.87$ kNm;
	M_{op}	$= M_{po} = 7.08$ kNm
Joint C	$M_{cb} + M_{cd}$	$= M_{cg} \, ; \; M_{cb} = M_{cg} - M_{cd} = 76.56 - 19.12 = 57.44$ kNm
Joint G	$M_{gf} + M_{gh}$	$= M_{gc} + M_{gk} \, ; \; M_{gf} = M_{gc} + M_{gk} - M_{gh}$

$$= 76.56 + 83.25 - 39.91 = 119.9 \text{ kNm}$$

Joint K $M_{kj} + M_{kl} = M_{kg} + M_{ko};\ M_{kj} = M_{kg} + M_{ko} - M_{kl}$

$$= 83.25 + 28.32 - 27.87 = 83.7 \text{ kNm}$$

Joint O $M_{on} + M_{op} = M_{ok};\ M_{on} = M_{ok} - M_{op} = 28.32 - 7.08 = 21.24 \text{ kNm}$

$M_{bc} = M_{cb} = 57.44 \text{ kNm};\ M_{fg} = 119.9 \text{ kNm}$

$M_{jk} = M_{kj} = 83.7 \text{ kNm};\ M_{no} = M_{on} = 21.24 \text{ kNm}.$

Joint B $M_{ba} + M_{bc} = M_{bf};\ M_{ba} = M_{bf} - M_{bc} = 153.12 - 57.12 = 95.68 \text{ kNm}$

Joint F $M_{fe} + M_{fg} = M_{fb} + M_{fi};$

$M_{fe} = M_{fb} + M_{fi} - M_{fg}$

$$= 153.12 + 166.53 - 119.9$$

$$= 199.75 \text{ kNm}$$

Joint J $M_{ji} + M_{jk} = M_{if} + M_{jn};$

$M_{ji} = M_{if} + M_{jn} - M_{jk}$

$$= 166.53 + 56.66 - 83.7$$

$$= 139.49 \text{ kNm}.$$

Joint N $M_{nm} + M_{no} = M_{nf};\ M_{nm} = M_{nj} - M_{no} = 56.66 - 21.24 = 35.42 \text{ kNm}$

$M_{ab} = 95.68 \text{ kNm};\ M_{ef} = 199.75 \text{ kNm}$

$M_{ij} = 139.49 \text{ kNm};\ M_{nm} = 35.42 \text{ kNm}$

12.7 STEP BY STEP ANALYSIS PROCEDURE OF CANTILEVER METHOD

(1) Find the distance of the **centre of gravity of the columns ($\bar{x}$)** from the axis of end column by taking the moments about the end column, (total area of column)

$\bar{x}$ = Moment of all individual column @ end column.

(2) Axial Forces in the Various Column

(a) Stress in the column = $(P/A) \times (x / \bar{x})$

Where,

P = Axial force in column

A = Area of column

x = Centroidal distance of column from the vertical centroidal axis of the frame

$(\bar{x})$ = C.G. of frame.

(b) Axial force in column (in term of P) = Stress × Area

(c) Find P by taking moments about the point of coutraflexure of the column

(we will assume that point of contraflexure occur at the middle of each member)

Storey	Axial force Notation	Stress in column (σ_c) = $(P/A) \times (X/\bar{x})$	Axial force in term of P = Stress × Area	Axial force (taking moment @ contraflexure of end column)
n	P_n			
n – 1	P_{n-1}			
n – 2	P_{n-2}			

(3) Beam Shear (shear force in Beam)

It is algebraic sum of all forces acting on column on right or left part of beam (just above the beam and just below the beam).

(4) Bending Moment (Beam Moment)

B.M. for any Beam = S.F. in Beam × Span / 2

Storey	Beam	Beam span	Beam shear (S.F. in beam) w	Beam Moment = wl/2

(5) Column Moment :

Find out column moment by considering each joint of frame (example as below)

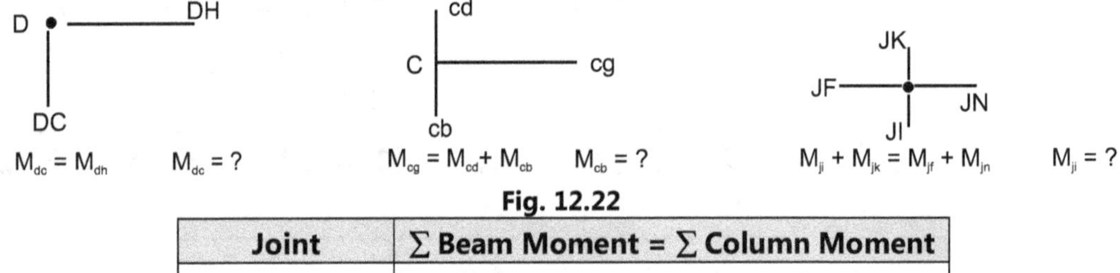

Fig. 12.22

Joint	$\sum$ Beam Moment = $\sum$ Column Moment

QUESTIONS

1. Write detailed note on substitute frame method.
2. Write detailed note on portal method.
3. Write detail note on approximate method or analysis.
4. Explain in detail cantilever method of analysis.

UNIVERSITY QUESTIONS

Dec. 2011

Q. 1 Fig. 12.23 shows an intermediate frame of a multistoried building the frame are spaced 4 m centre to centre. Analyze a rigid jointed frame taking live load of and dead load 2.8 kN/m^2, 3 kN/m^2 for the panels with AB and BC respectively. The self weight of the beam may be taken as follows. Beams of 8m span = 5.5 kN/m and beams of 4.5 m span = 3.5 kN/m.

The relative stiffnesses of the members are marked on the Fig. 12.23 Use portal method for analyzing the frame for horizontal forces and proper substitute frame for vertical loads. Design the section for beam ABC for combined effect of vertical and horizontal loads. Adopt 15% redistribution of moments for vertical load moments Use M20, Fe 415.

(Example 12.1, 12.2 and 12.4) (25 Marks)

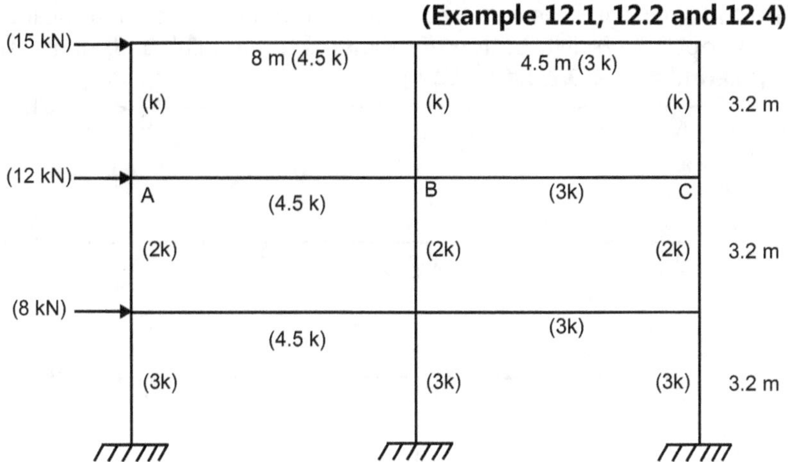

Fig. 12.23

Q. 2 (a) Write detailed note on substitute frame method. **(Section 12.2)**   **(8 Marks)**

(b) Analyze a rigid jointed frame shown in Fig. 12.24 by cantilever method for lateral loads. Flexural rigidity for all members is same. Analyze beam DEF using proper substitute frame, it if is subjected to vertical ultimate live and dead load including of its self weight intensitites 15 kN/m and 16 kN/m on DE and 19 kN/m and 20 kN/m of EF respectively. Calculate maximum span moment for span DE and support moment at E. design section for combined effect of vertical and horizontal loads. Adopt 12% redistribution of moments for vertical load moments. Use M20, Fe 500. **(Example 12.4)**   **(17 Marks)**

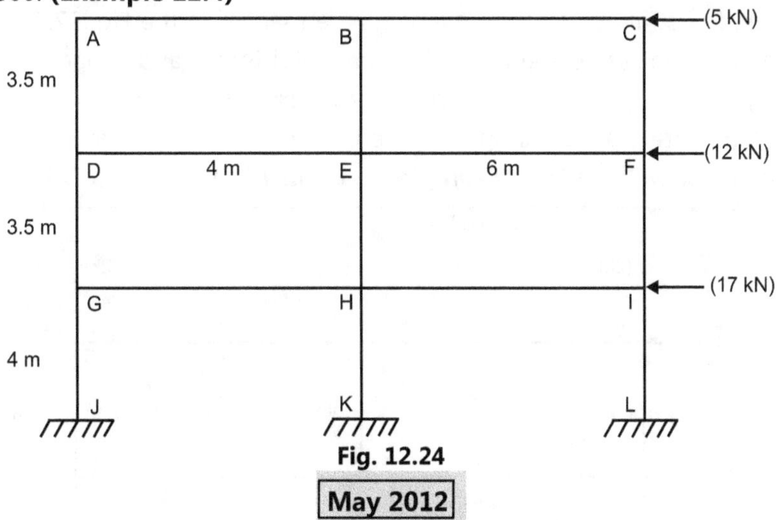

Fig. 12.24

May 2012

Q. 3 (a) Write detailed note on Portal method. **(Section 12.4)**   **(8 Marks)**

(b) Analyze a rigid jointed frame shown in Fig. 12.25 by cantilever method for lateral loads. Flexural rigidity for all members is same. Analyze beam DEF using proper substitute frame, if it is subjected to vertical ultimate live and dead load including of its self weight. Intensities of 12 kN/m and 14 kN/m on DE and 17 kN/m and 18 kN/m on EF respectively. Calculate maximum span moment for span DE and support moment at E. design section for combined effect of vertical and horizontal loads. Adopt 15% redistribution of moments for vertical load moments use M20, Fe 415. **(Example 12.2, 12.3 and 12.4)**   **(17 Marks)**

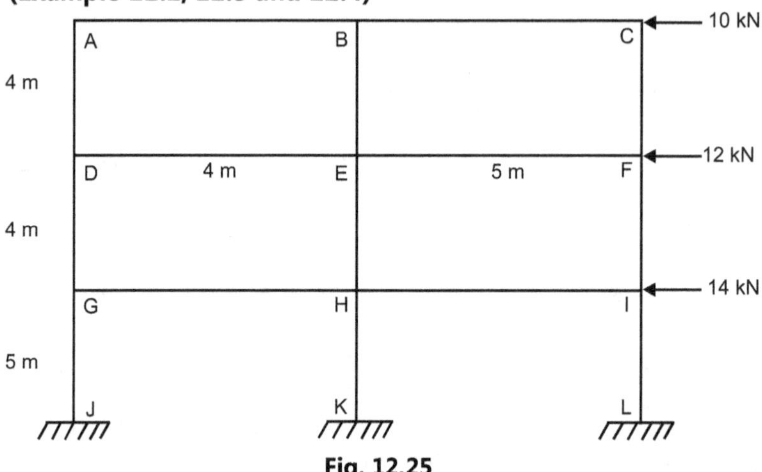

Fig. 12.25

Q. 4   Fig. 12.26 shows an intermediate frame of multistoried building the frame are spaced 4.4 m centre to centre. Analyze a rigid jointed frame taking live load of and dead load of 2.5 kN/m^2 and 4 kN/m^2 respectively for all slab panels. The self weight of the beam may be taken for beams of 6 m and 4 m span as 3.5 kN/m and 2.5 kN/m respectively.

The relative stiffnesses of the members are marked in the Fig. 12.26 Use cantilever method for analyzing the frame for horizontal forces and proper substitute frame for vertical loads, Design the section for beam ABC for combined effect of vertical and horizontal loads. Adop 12% redistribution of moments for vertical load moment Use M20, Fe 500. **(Example 12.1 and 12.4)**   **(25 Marks)**

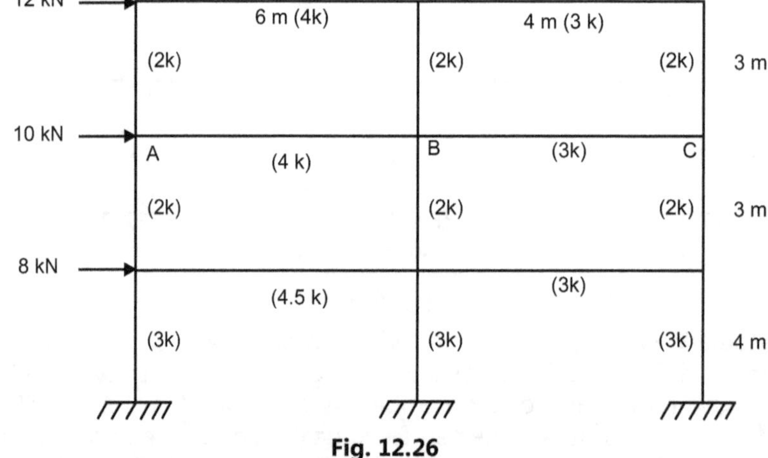

Fig. 12.26

Dec. 2012

Q. 5 (a) Write detail note on approximate method of analysis. **(Section 12.1)**   **(7 Marks)**

Q. 6   Analyse a rigid joint frame shown in Fig. 12.27 by portal method for lateral loads. Flexural rigidity of all members is same. Analyse the beam GHI using proper substitute frame, if it is subjected to vertical ultimate live and dead load including of its self weight intensities of 12 kN/m and 15 kN/m on GH and 13 kN/m and 17 kN/m on HI respectively. Calculate maximum span moment at H. Design section for combined effect of vertical and horizontal load. Adopt 15% redistribution of moments for vertical load moment. Use M20 Fe 500.

(Example 12.2 and 12.3)(25 Marks)

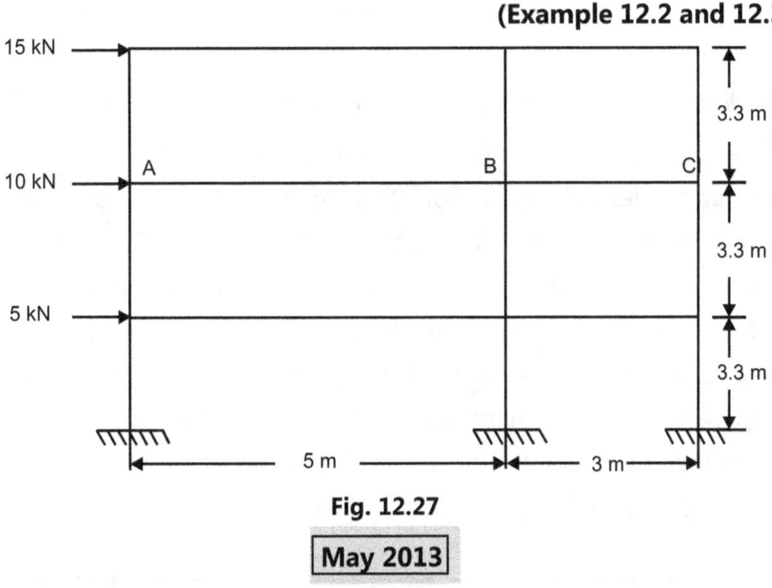

Fig. 12.27

May 2013

Q. 7   Fig. 12.28 shows and intermediate frame of multistoried building frames are spaced at 4.5m centre analyze a rigid jointed frame taking live load 3 kN/m^2 and dead load as 4 kN/m^2 for panels AB and BC respectively. Self weight of beam may be taken as for 7 m span = 5 kN/m and for 5 m span = 4 kN/m. The relative stiffness of the member are shown in the Fig. Use portal method for horizontal loads and proper substitute frame for vertical loads. Design the beam ABC for combined effect of horizontal and vertical loads. Use 20% redistribution of moments for vertical load moments. Use m25 and Fe 500.

(Example 12.1, 12.2 and 12.3)   **(25 Marks)**

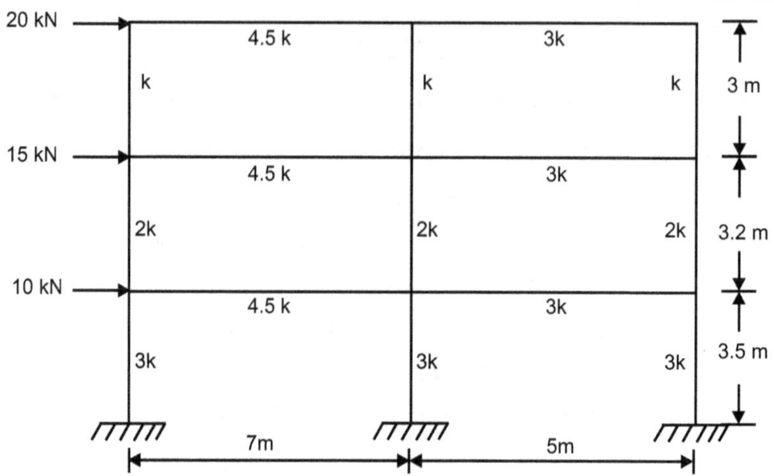

Fig. 12.28

Q. 8 (a) Write detail note on substitute frame method. **(Section 12.2)**   **(8 Marks)**

(b) Analyze the rigid jointed frame as shown in Fig. 12.29 by cantilever method for lateral loads. Flexural rigidity for all members is same. Analyze beam GHI using proper substitute frame, if it is subjected to vertical ultimate live and dead load including its self weight of intensities 15 kN/m and 12 kN/m on span GH and 20 kN/m and 15 kN/m on HI respectively. The horizontal forces are shown in Fig. 12.29. Calculate maximum span moment for HI and support moment at H. Design section for combined effect of vertical and horizontal loads. Adopt 15% redistribution of moments for vertical load moment. Use M20 and Fe 500.

(Example 12.1 and 12.4)   **(17 Marks)**

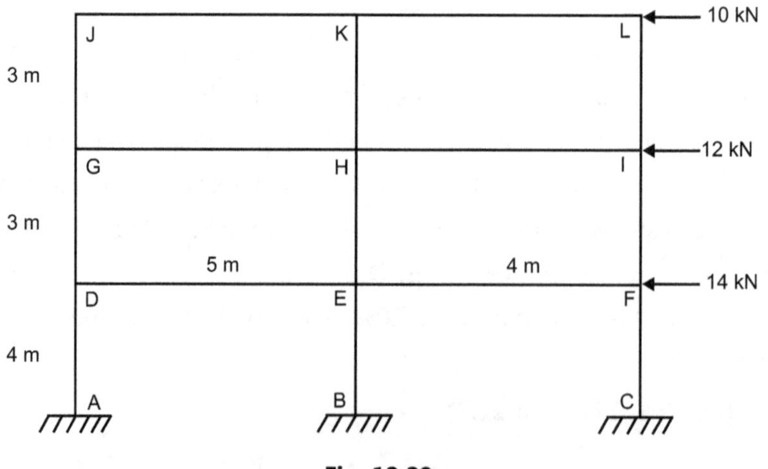

Fig. 12.29

Dec. 2014

Q. 9   Analyse the multistoried building frame of shown in Fig. 12.30 For vertical load by substitute frame and for horizontal load by cantilever method. The frames are spaced 3.5 m c/c. The dead load and live load acting on panels with GH and HI are 3.6 kN/m^2 and 3.5 kN/m^2 respectively. The relatives stiffness of each member is marked on the Fig. 12.30. Also design continuous beam GHI for combined effect of vertical and horizontal loads. 15% redistribution of moments is permitted for vertical load moments. Use M20 and Fe 415 materials.

(Example 12.1 and 12.4)   **(25 Marks)**

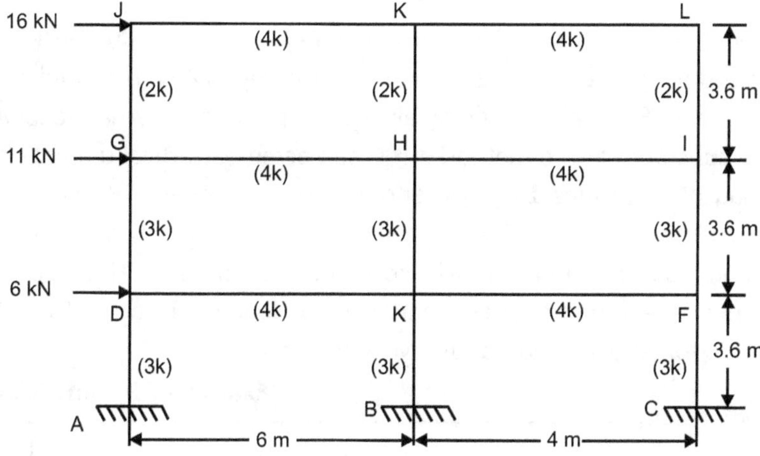

Fig. 12.30

May 2015

Q. 10   Fig. 12.31 shows an intermediate frame of multistoried building the frames are spaced at 4 m centre to centre analyse the rigid jointed frame taking live load as 3.5 kN/m^2 and dead load as 3 kN/m^2 for panel AB and BC respectively. The self weight of beam AB is taken as 4 kN/m and for BC as 3.0 kN/m. The relative stiffness of all members is same. Use Portal method for horizontal load and proper substitute frame for vertical loading. Design the beam ABC for combined effect of horizontal and vertical loading using 15% redistribution of moments for vertical load moments. Use M20 and Fe 415.   **(Examples 12.2, 12.3, and 12.4) (25 Marks)**

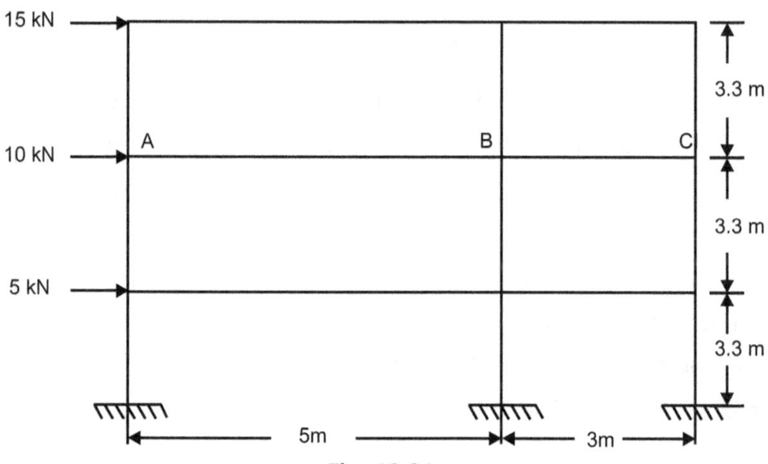

Fig. 12.31

Q. 11 (a)   Explain in detail Cantilever Method of analysis.   **(Section 12.6) (7 Marks)**

(b)   Analyze the rigid jointed frame as shown in Fig. 12.32 by cantilever method for lateral loads. Flexural rigidity of all members is same. Analyze beam GHI using proper substitute frame method if it is subjected to vertical ultimate dead load and live load of intensities 15 kN/m and 18 kN/m on span GH and 18 kN/m and 22 kN/m on HI respectively. The horizontal forces are as shown in Fig. 12.32 Calculate maximum span moment for GH and support moment at H. Design beam GHI for combined effect of horizontal and vertical loading using 10% redistribution of moments for vertical loading. Use M25 and Fe 415.

(Example 12.1 and 12.4) (18 Marks)

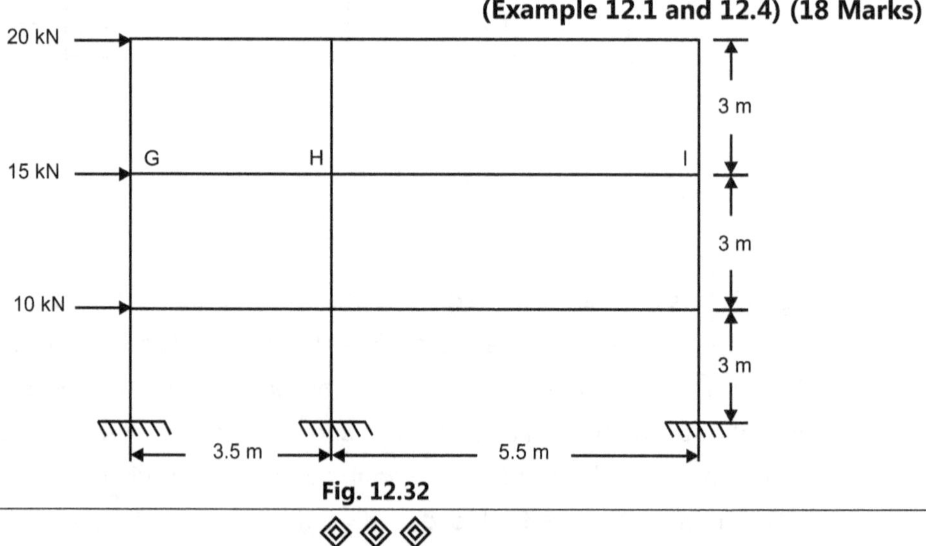

Fig. 12.32

◈ ◈ ◈

Unit IV

Chapter 13
RETAINING WALLS

13.1 INTRODUCTION

Retaining wall is a structure to retain earth, coal, ore or water, etc. Retaining walls are mainly provided in construction of hill roads, embankments, bridge abutments, basement in building, water reservoir, etc. The material retained by wall is known as backfill. The backfill may be horizontal or inclined with top. The inclined backfill is known as surcharge. The surcharge may be due to external loads acting on it. The design of retaining wall should be in such a way that it can resist all forces coming on it.

13.2 TYPES OF RETAINING WALLS

Retaining walls are classified according to the method of achieving stability. Considering the stability factor the retaining walls are classified as follows :

    (i)   Gravity walls,

    (ii)   Cantilever retaining walls,

    (iii)   Counterfort retaining walls,

    (iv)   Buttressed walls.

    (i)   **Gravity Walls :** These walls are constructed in brick masonry, stones or plain cement concrete. When the forces acting on walls are resisted by the dead weight of wall, the walls are known as gravity walls. The dimensions are so proportioned that tensile stresses shall not be developed at any section. The gravity wall with different materials is as shown in Fig. 13.1. The gravity walls are economical for low heights.

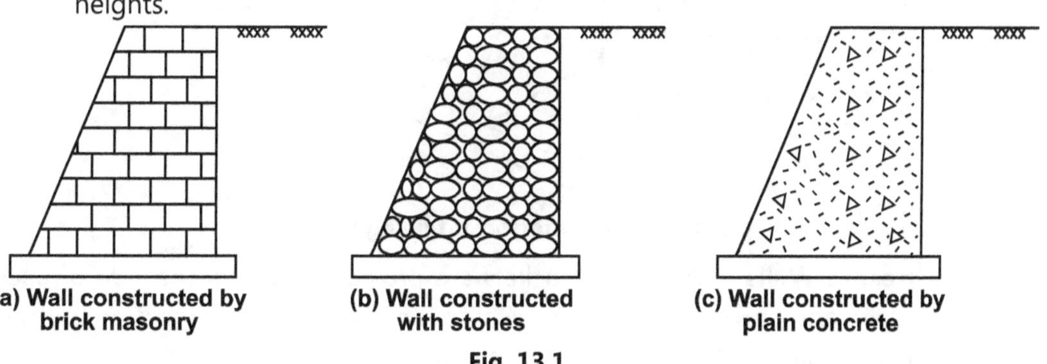

(a) Wall constructed by brick masonry   (b) Wall constructed with stones   (c) Wall constructed by plain concrete

Fig. 13.1

(ii) **Cantilever Retaining Walls :** These walls are constructed as inverted T or L. In case of inverted T, it consists of three parts (i) stem, (ii) heel, (iii) toe. All these parts are acting as cantilever. In case of L type, it consists of two parts : (a) stem and (b) heel. Both the parts are acting as cantilevers. In these types all parts act as cantilevers, so known as cantilever retaining wall. This type of wall proves economical for height 6 m to 7 m. The stability is provided partly by dead weight of wall and partly by the material on the heel portion. Sometimes to increase the resistance in sliding, keys are provided below ground level as shown in Fig. 13.2 (b).

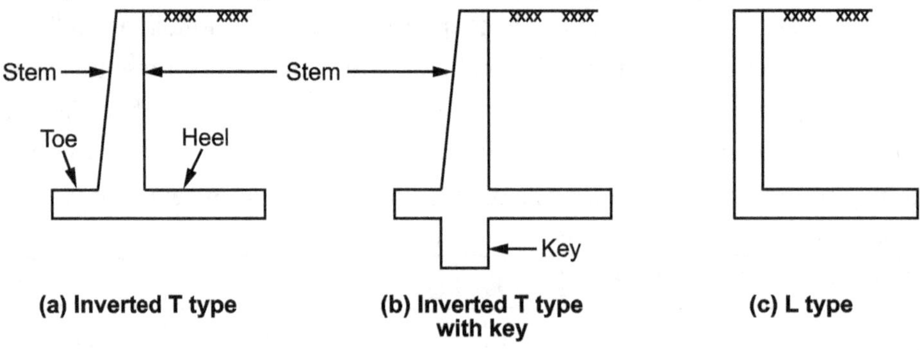

(a) Inverted T type   (b) Inverted T type with key   (c) L type

Fig. 13.2

(iii) **Counterfort Retaining Wall :** This wall proves economical for height greater than 7 m. In this type, the base slab and stem between the brackets span horizontally and designed as continuous slab. The brackets are known as counterforts. The spacing between the counterforts is generally between $\frac{1}{3}$ to $\frac{1}{2}$. Counterforts are provided on backfill side.

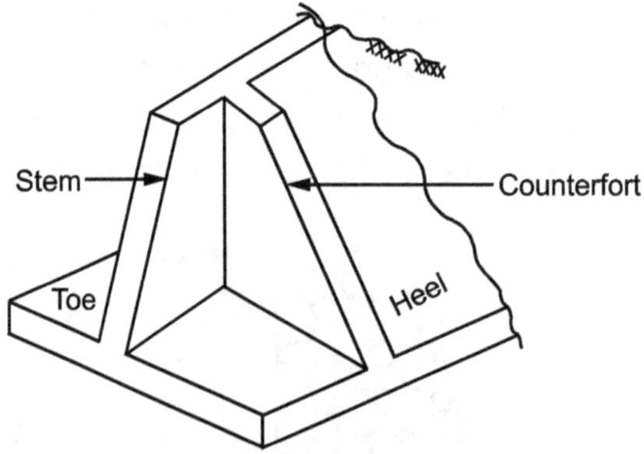

Fig. 13.3 : Counterfort retaining wall

(iv) **Buttressed Walls :** When the brackets are provided on opposite side of backfill, the walls are known as buttressed walls. The brackets are known as buttressed retaining walls.

13.3 EARTH PRESSURE

The lateral pressure exerted on retaining wall depends upon the nature and displacement or deformation of material. Different theories have been developed to define the lateral pressure on the retaining wall such as Terzaghi's theory, E. Culman theory, Prandtt theory, Rankine theory, etc.

Different Types of Pressure :

Depending upon the displacement or deformation of soil, the earth pressure is divided into three types :

- (a)   Active earth pressure,
- (b)   Passive earth pressure,
- (c)   Rest pressure.

- **(a)   Active Pressure :** When a dry cohesionless soil exerts pressure on wall, due to which the wall may slightly deform or move away from the soil fill. If this happens, a wedge of soil gets separated from the rest of fill and will tend to slide down the rupture plane. The shear resistance will act up the plane to oppose the movement of the wedge. In this, the pressure exerted by the soil on the wall is known as active pressure.

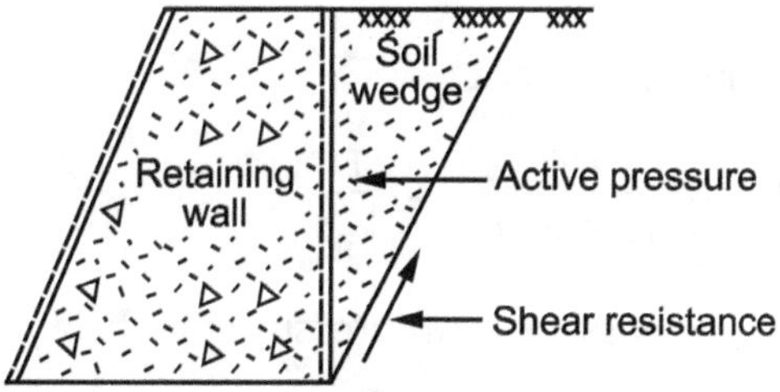

Fig. 13.4

- **(b)   Passive Pressure :** Consider a retaining wall retains the dry cohesionless soil. When some external force is acting on retaining wall, due to which the wall is pushed towards the soil. If this happens, a wedge of soil gets separated from the rest of fill and will tend to move up the plane. The shear resistance will act down the rupture plane to oppose the movement of the wedge. In this, the pressure exerted by the soil on the wall is known as passive pressure.

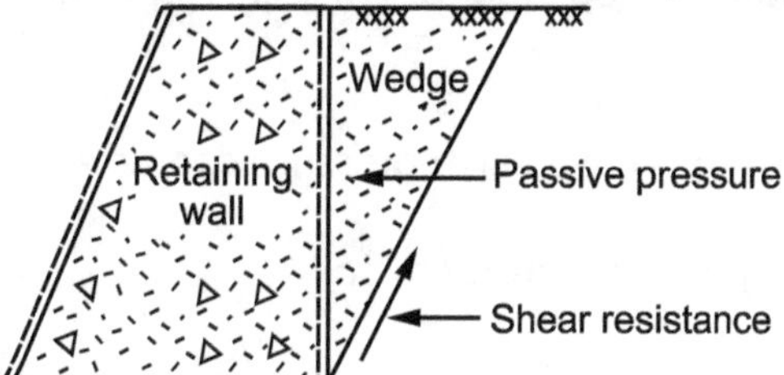

Fig. 13.5

(c) **Rest Pressure :** Consider a retaining wall retains the soil. In this case, the soil wedge does not slide and the wall does not deform. In this, the pressure exerted by the soil on the wall is known as rest pressure.

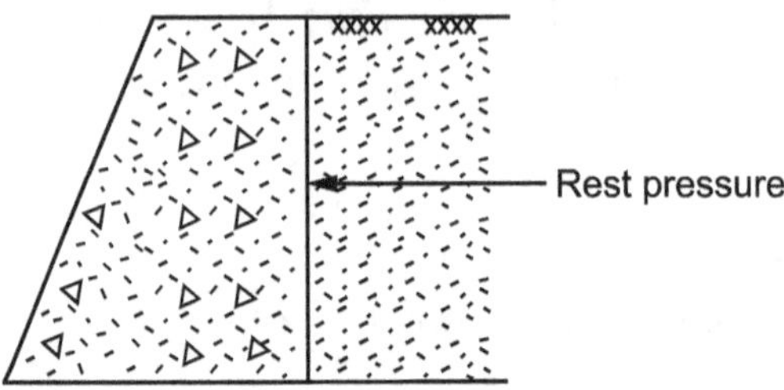

Fig. 13.6

13.4 EARTH PRESSURE COEFFICIENT

(a)   Active earth pressure coefficient :

$$k_a = \left(\frac{1 - \sin\phi}{1 + \sin\phi}\right)$$

where k_a = Active earth pressure coefficient

ϕ = Angle of internal friction of soil

(b)   Passive earth pressure coefficient :

$$k_p = \left(\frac{1 + \sin\phi}{1 - \sin\phi}\right) = \frac{1}{k_a}$$

where k_p = Passive earth pressure coefficient

13.5 ACTIVE EARTH PRESSURE ON RETAINING WALLS FOR VARIOUS CASES

Case I : Retaining wall retaining dry or moist soil without surcharge :

Consider a wall of height H, retaining dry or moist soil. The lateral pressure distribution is triangular with zero pressure at top and $p = k_a\,\gamma_d\,H$ pressure at bottom as shown in Fig. 13.7.

where k_a = Active earth pressure coefficient

γ_d = Dry density of soil

$$k_a = \left(\frac{1 - \sin\phi}{1 + \sin\phi}\right)$$

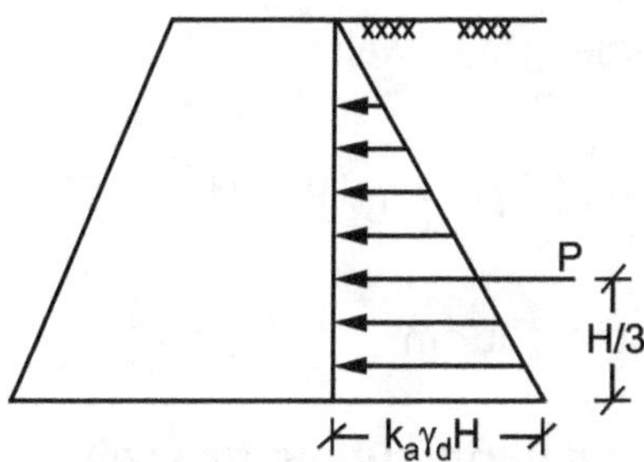

Fig. 13.7

$\therefore$ Total pressure per unit length of the wall :

$$P = \frac{1}{2} k_a \cdot \gamma_d \cdot H \cdot H = \frac{1}{2} k_a \gamma_d H^2$$

When the soil is moist soil, density of soil is γ_d.

$$\therefore \qquad P = \frac{1}{2} k_a \gamma_d H^2$$

Total pressure acts at H/3 from the bottom.

Case II : Retaining wall retaining submerged soil :

Consider a wall of height H, retaining submerged soil. The lateral pressure distribution is as shown in Fig. 13.8.

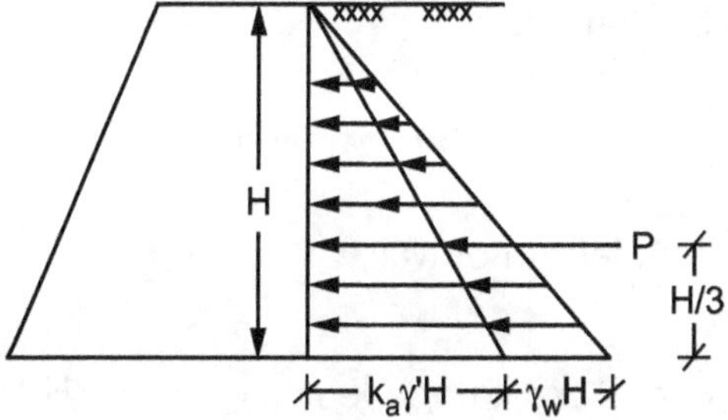

Fig. 13.8

Lateral pressure intensity at bottom,

$$p = k_a \gamma' H + \gamma_w H$$

where γ' = Weight of submerged soil

$$\gamma' = \gamma_{sat} - \gamma_w = \gamma_w \left(\frac{S - 1}{1 + e} \right)$$

where   S = Specific gravity of solids

e = Void ratio

$\therefore$ Total pressure per unit length of wall :

$$P = \frac{1}{2}(k_a\gamma'H + \gamma_w H) \times H$$

Total pressure acts at H/3 from the bottom.

Case III : Retaining wall retaining partly submerged soil :

Consider a wall of height H, retaining partly submerged soil. The lateral pressure distribution is as shown in Fig. 13.9.

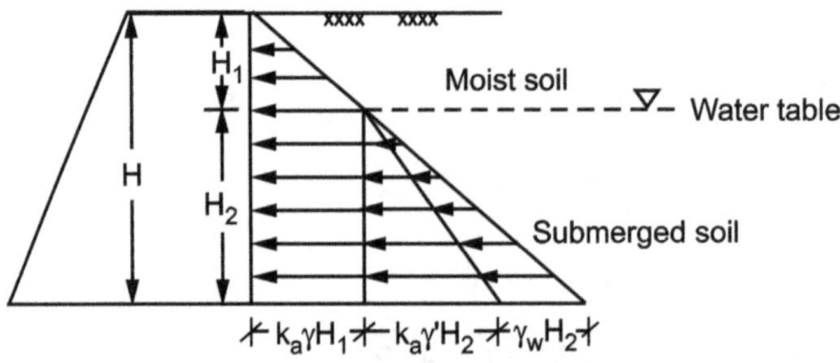

Fig. 13.9

Lateral pressure intensity at bottom,

$$p = k_a\gamma H_1 + k_a\gamma'H_2 + \gamma_w H_2$$

$\therefore$ Total pressure per unit length of wall,

$$P = \left(\frac{1}{2}k_a\gamma H_1 H_1 + k_a\gamma H_1 H_2 + \frac{1}{2}k_a\gamma'H_2 H_2 + \frac{1}{2}k_a\gamma_w H_2 H_2\right)$$

$$= \frac{1}{2}k_a\gamma H_1^2 + k_a\gamma H_1 H_2 + \frac{1}{2}k_a\gamma'H_2^2 + \frac{1}{2}k_a\gamma_w H_2^2$$

Case IV : Retaining wall retaining soil with uniform surcharge :

Consider a wall of height H, retaining wall with uniform surcharge w N/m² on the top of level surface. The surcharge load can be calculated in terms of equivalent height of soil.

i.e. $$h_e = \frac{w}{\gamma}$$

The lateral pressure distribution is as shown in Fig. 13.10.

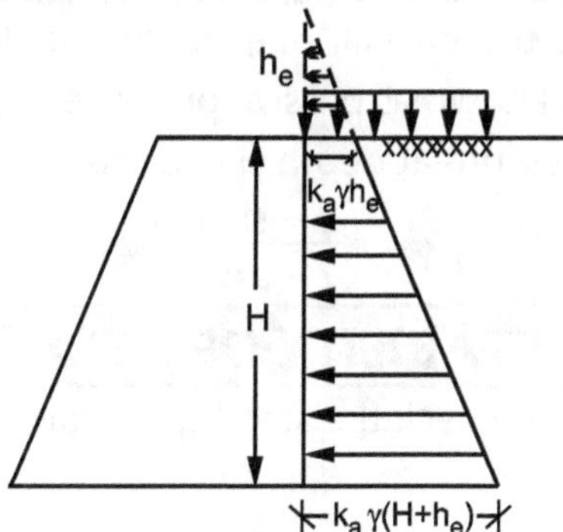

Fig. 13.10

Lateral pressure intensity at bottom,

$$p = k_a\gamma\,(H + h_e)$$

Total pressure per unit length of wall,

$$P = \frac{1}{2}\left[k_a\gamma h_e + k_a\gamma\,(H + h_e)\right] \times H$$

Case V : Retaining wall retaining soil with inclined surcharge :

Consider a retaining wall with height H, retaining soil along with inclined surcharge as shown in Fig. 13.11.

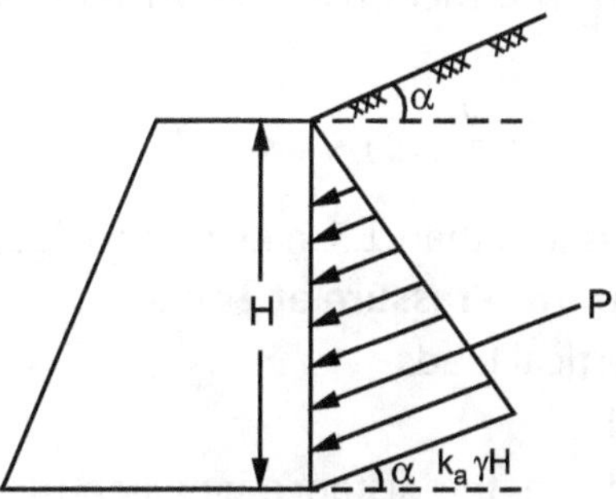

Fig. 13.11

$$k_a = \cos\alpha\,\frac{\cos\alpha - \sqrt{\cos^2\alpha - \cos^2\phi}}{\cos\alpha + \sqrt{\cos^2\alpha - \cos^2\phi}}$$

Pressure intensity at bottom,

$$p = k_a\gamma H$$

Total pressure per unit length of wall,

$$P = \frac{1}{2}\,k_a\cdot\gamma\cdot H\cdot H = \frac{1}{2}\,k_a\gamma H^2$$

13.6 PASSIVE EARTH PRESSURE

If retaining wall moves towards the backfill due to external loads, it will compress the soil and the pressure thus exerted is known as passive pressure.

The intensity of passive earth pressure at depth H in a retaining wall is given by

$$p_p = k_p \cdot \gamma H = \left(\frac{1 + \sin \phi}{1 - \sin \phi}\right) \gamma H$$

13.7 CONDITION FOR STABILITY OF RETAINING WALL

Before designing, it is necessary to check the stability of wall. Following checks are made :

    (a)   Check against overturning,

    (b)   Check against sliding,

    (c)   Check for maximum pressure at toe.

(Maximum pressure should not be greater than the bearing capacity of soil.)

(a)   **Check Against Overturning :** The lateral pressure due to earthfill and surcharge tends to overturn the retaining wall about toe. The overturning moment is stabilized due to soil on the heel and weight of retaining wall. Stabilizing moment is at least equal to or greater than the overturning moment.

$$\text{F.S.} = \frac{\text{Stabilizing moment}}{\text{Overturning moment}} = 2$$

(b)   **Check Against Sliding :** Retaining wall tends to slide due to horizontal pressure. This force is resisted by frictional force developed between the base of wall and the soil underneath. The frictional resistance at least is greater than 50% of the sliding force.

$$\therefore \qquad \text{F.S.} = \frac{\mu \, \Sigma W}{P} = 1.5$$

If the factor of safety is less than 1.5, a key is provided under the base slab.

(c)   **Check Against Maximum Pressure at Toe :**

ΣW = Sum of vertical loads

b = Base width

e = Eccentricity i.e. the distance between the centre of base to the point of intersection of vertical loads

p_1 = Intensity of maximum pressure at toe

p_2 = Intensity of maximum pressure at heel

$$p_1 = \frac{\Sigma W}{b} \left(1 + \frac{6e}{b}\right)$$

$$p_2 = \frac{\Sigma W}{b} \left(1 - \frac{6e}{b}\right)$$

$p_1 \ngtr$ Bearing capacity of soil

$p_2 > 0$ i.e. there is no tension developed in the base

13.8 PRELIMINARY PROPORTIONING OF CANTILEVER RETAINING WALL

The dimensions of a retaining wall should be assumed before starting the design. These assumptions are based on some particle considerations as discussed below.

1. **Height of Wall:**

   The overall height of the wall is equal to the height of the back fill at the face of wall (i.e. difference in elevation of front and back) plus the depth of foundation. The minimum depth of foundation should be such that :

   (i) The foundation is not affected by the upper surface of earth which may be affected by erosion, roots of plants, frost, etc. usually this requires a minimum depth of 900 mm.

   (ii) A good hard soil should be available below the footing to resist the pressures from wall. The allowable bearing pressure on the soil should be found out.

2. **Base Width and Position of Stem on the Base of Footing :**

   A simplified formula can be obtained to find out the base width and position of stem on the base of footing considering that the resultant of forces should pass through the middle third of the base. Assume an average unit weight of concrete and earth be 'r.' As the unit weight of concrete is usually more than the backfill, the assumption is conservative neglect the weight of toe for the derivation of the formula.

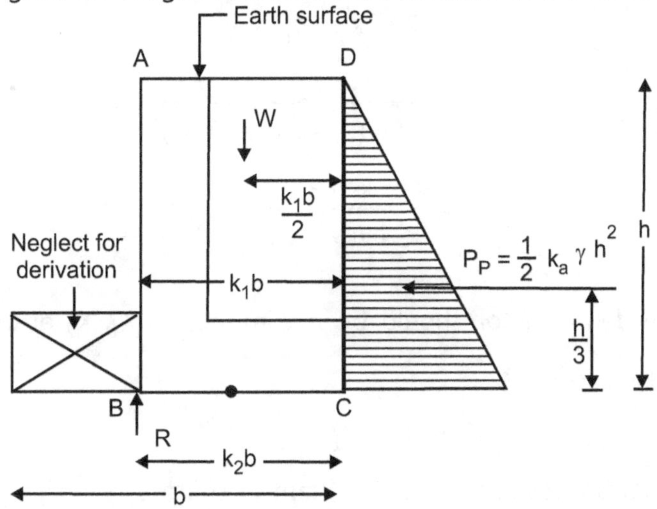

Fig. 13.12 : Preliminary Propertions of a cantilever retaining wall

Refering to Fig. 13.12, the equal total weight of the area ABCD is equal to the reaction R and is given by.

$$R = W = rh (K_1 b)$$

Taking moments about heel (point C)

$$P_a \times \frac{h}{3} + W \times \frac{K_1 \cdot b}{2} = R (K_2 b)$$

$$\therefore \quad K_a \, r \, \frac{h^2}{2} \times \frac{h}{3} + rh \, (K_1 \, b) \left(\frac{K_1 \, b}{2} \right) = r \, h \, K_1 \, b \, (K_2 \, b)$$

Simplifying and readjusting

$$K_a \, \frac{rh^3}{\sigma} = rh \, K_1 \, K_2 \, b^2 - \frac{1}{2} \, K_1^2 \, rhb^2$$

Dividing both sides by $\dfrac{r \, h^3}{\sigma}$

$$K_a = \sigma \, K_1 \, K_2 \, \frac{b^2}{h^2} - 3K_1^2 \, \frac{b^2}{h^2}$$

$$K_a = 3 \, \frac{b^2}{h^2} \, K_1 \, (2 \, K_2 - K_1)$$

$$\therefore \qquad \frac{b^2}{h^2} = \frac{K}{3 \, K_1 \, (2 \, K_2 - K_1)} \qquad \qquad \text{...(1)}$$

To get the economical solution, the term $\dfrac{b}{h}$ should be minimized, i.e. $\dfrac{b^2}{h^2}$ should be minimized.

$$\text{Now,} \qquad \frac{b^2}{h^2} = \frac{K_a / 3}{2 \, K_1 \, K_2 - K_1^2}$$

$$= \frac{K_a / 3}{K_2^2 - (K_1^2 - 2K_1 \, K_2 + K_2^2)}$$

$$= \frac{K_a / 3}{K_2^2 - (K_1 - K_2)^2}$$

To minimize $\dfrac{b^2}{h^2}$ the denominator should be maximized, as K_1, K_2 are both positive, this condition is satisfied when

$$(K_1 - K_2) = 0 \text{ i.e. } K_1 - K_1 = 0 \qquad \qquad \text{...(2)}$$

Thus, we get an important result that the resultant of soil pressure should be in a line with the front face of the wall.

Also, the resultant should lie in middle third of base which follows that the width of toe should be equal to $\dfrac{b}{3}$.

As the resultant of force is expected to lie at face of toe, the moments about that point should be zero.

(i)   For 'L' shaped wall

$$\gamma\,bh \times \frac{b}{6} - \frac{Ph}{3} = 0$$

$$b = \sqrt{\frac{2P}{\gamma}}$$

(ii) For 'T' shaped wall

$$\frac{2}{3}\gamma\,bh \times \frac{b}{3} - \frac{Ph}{3} = 0$$

(a)   h shaped wall   (b) T shaped wall

$$\therefore\ b = \sqrt{\frac{3P}{2\gamma}}$$

The width of base and toe fixed by the above equations, are the minimum required. Also, the pressure under the toe should not exceed the allowable bearing pressure on soil. This condition may necessitate to increase the width of base.

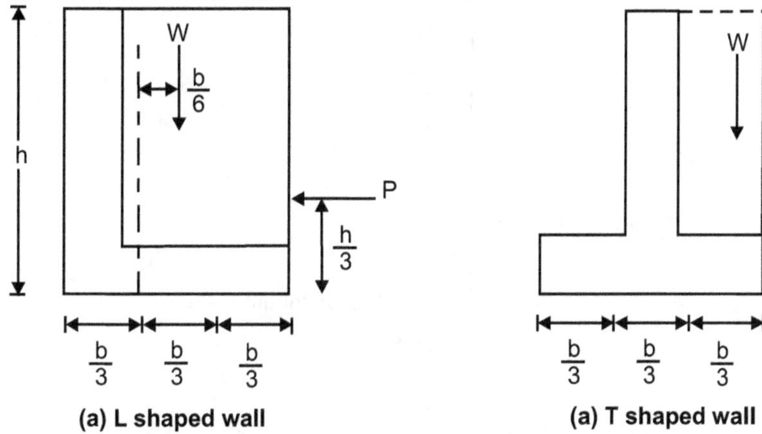

Fig. 13.13

The base width can also be fixed by considerations of sliding, however, the above equations are used in general and if the sliding is not satisfied, a base key is provided. Alternatively, as a thumb rule, the width of base may be takes as 0.5 times to 0.7 times the overall height of the wall.

4.   **Thickness of Base Slab :**

The thickness of base slab may be considered as $\frac{h}{15}$ to $\frac{h}{12}$ where h is the overall height of the wall with a minimum thickness of 300 mm.

5.   **Thickness of Stem :**

The thickness of stem at top may be taken as 150 mm to 200 mm and at the base, for preliminary calculations, it may be assumed as $\frac{h}{12}$ to $\frac{h}{8}$ where h is the overall height of the wall. It is better to calculate the actual required thickness considering moment criterion.

13.9 DESIGN OF CONTILEVER RETAINING WALL

The design of contilever retaining wall consists of design of stem, design of toe design of heel and design of base key, if provided. These are explained below and reinforcements are shown in Fig. 13.14.

The minimum concrete cover to the main reinforcement may be kept as 40 mm as all the components of the wall are in direct contact with the earth. The contilever retaining wall should be treated as a slab while applying the IS limitations like minimum reinforcement, crack control, permissible shear stress etc. for stem, the minimum secondary reinforcement shall not be based on average depth. The stem may be divided into 2 or 3 convenient parts and minimum reinforcement shall be based on larger thickness of the respective part. Deflection need not be checked as it is of minor importance. Where the appearance on the face is important, a better on that face is provided to counteract the effect of deflection. The usual better is about 20 mm to 25 mm per metre height of the wall.

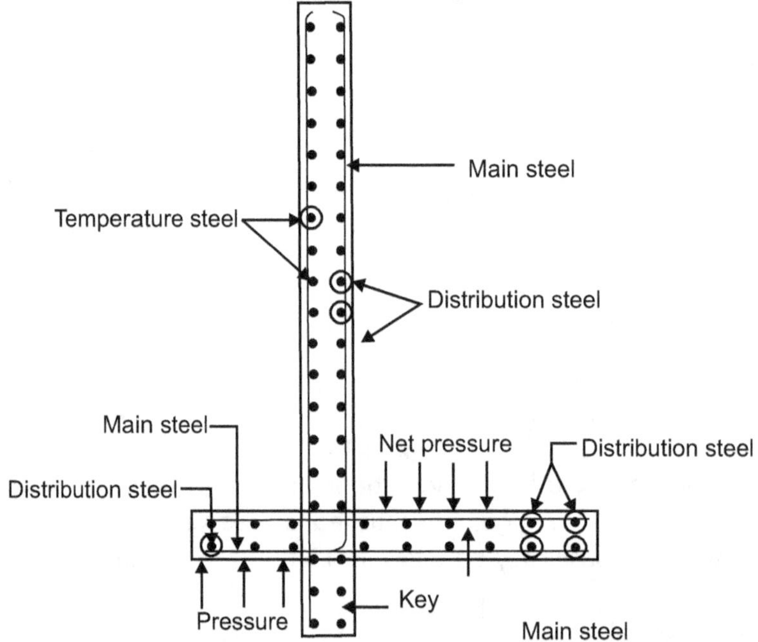

Fig. 13.14 : Reinforcement details-cantilever wall

1. **Design of Stem :**

    Calculate the maximum bending moment and shear force caused by the horizontal earth pressure. Design the wall for moment steel which may be curtailed where not required for flexure if rules for curtailment are satisfied. It would be sufficient to assume that the rules of curtailment are satisfied if the bars in stem are curtailed at a distance equal to the development length of bar from the point of theoretical cut off. The horizontal secondary reinforcement is provided (0.15 per cent for mild steel and 0.12

per cent for HYSD bars) at the inner face of the wall. At the external face the reinforcement should be provided horizontally and vertically. This reinforcement in each direction may be half the minimum reinforcement to serve as a temperature reinforcement.

2. Design of Heel :

The heel is subjected to an upward soil pressure and downward weight of earth above it, the net pressure on heel acts in downward direction causing tension at top face of the heel. The reinforcement is designed for this moment.

3. Design of Toe :

The moment due to earth pressure causes tension at the bottom face of the toe. Here the weight of the frontfill may reduce the moment but this will not taken into account as the frontfill may get scoured or may be excavated. The reinforcement for toe is designed at the bottom face.

It should be noted that all the components of cantilever retaining wall are acting as cantilevers and the reinforcement should be properly anchored.

4. Base Key :

The dimension of base key are calculated considering stability requirements. It is a practice to extend temperature bars of stem into the key.

13.10 BEHAVIOUR OF CANTILEVER RETAINING WALL [DEC. 2011]

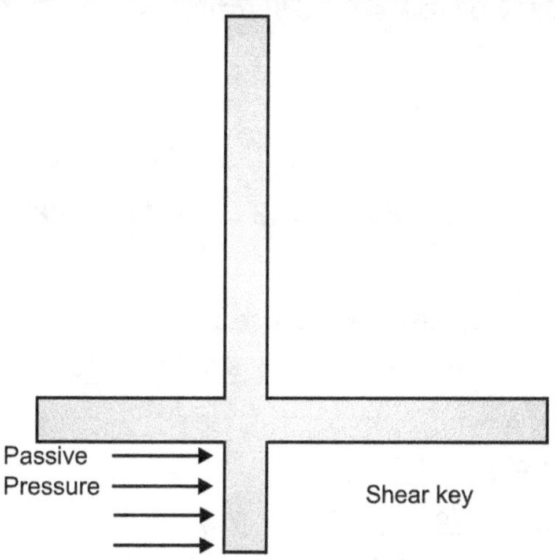

Fig. 13.15 : Stability of cantilever retaining wall

Fig. 13.15 shows a cantilever retaining wall subjected to the following forces :

(i)   Self-weight W_1 of the stem and W_2 of the base slab.

(ii) Weight W_3 of the column of soil supported on heel slab BC and downward load due to surcharge if any, say W_4.

(iii) Lateral pressure due to backfill, P_a and surcharge P_s resulting being P.

The following are various modes of failure of a retaining wall.

(a) Overturning about the toe.

(b) Sliding.

(c) Failure of soil due to excessive pressure at toe or tension at heel.
(d) Bending failure of stem or heel slab or toe steel.

Solved Examples

Example 13.1 :

Design a cantilever retaining wall to retain earth 3.5 m above ground level. The density of earth is 15000 N/m³ and its angle of friction of soil is 30º. The safe bearing capacity of soil is 150 kN/m² and coefficient of friction between soil and wall is 0.6. Use M20 grade of concrete and HYSD 415.

Solution :

Data : Height of wall above ground level $= 3.5$ m

Density of earth $= \gamma = 15000$ N/m³

Angle of internal friction $= 30º$

Coefficient of friction between soil and wall $(\mu) = 0.6$

Safe bearing capacity of soil $= 150$ kN/m²

Step I : Design constants : M 20 and Fe 415

$$k_{u\,max} = 0.48$$

$$R_{u\,max} = 0.36\, f_{ck}\, k_{u\,max}\, (1 - 0.42\, k_{u\,max})$$

$$= 0.36 \times 20 \times 0.48\, (1 - 0.42 \times 0.48)$$

$$= 2.76 \text{ N/mm}^2$$

Step II : Coefficient of active earth pressure :

$$k_a = \frac{1 - \sin\phi}{1 + \sin\phi} = \frac{1 - \sin 30}{1 + \sin 30} = \frac{1}{3} = 0.333$$

Step III : Depth of foundation :

$$D_f = \frac{P_o}{\gamma}\left(\frac{1 - \sin\phi}{1 + \sin\phi}\right)^2$$

$$= \frac{150}{15}\left(\frac{1}{3}\right)^2 = 1.11 \text{ m}$$

Let us assume the depth of foundation $= 1.1$ m

$\therefore$ Total depth of wall including base slab $= 3.5 + 1.1 = 4.6$ m

Step IV : Preliminary dimensions of the wall components :

(a)   Base width :

Base width of wall $= 0.60\,H = 0.60 \times 4.6 = 2.76$ m

$\therefore$ Provide base width $= 2.8$ m

(b)   Toe projection :

Toe projection of wall $= \dfrac{1}{3} \times$ Base width

$$= \dfrac{1}{3} \times 2.8 = 0.93 \text{ m} \approx 0.9 \text{ m}$$

(c)   Thickness of base slab :

Thickness of base slab $= \dfrac{H}{13} = \dfrac{4.6}{13} = 0.35$ m

(d)   Thickness of stem : Thickness of stem can be fixed from B.M. consideration.

Clear height of stem wall $= 4.6 - 0.35$

$$h = 4.25 \text{ m}$$

$\therefore$ Pressure intensity at bottom $= p_a = k_a \cdot \gamma \cdot H$

$\therefore$ Total earth pressure $= P = \dfrac{1}{2} \times p_a \cdot h$

$$= \dfrac{1}{2} \times \dfrac{1}{3} \times 15000 \times (4.25)^2$$

$$= 45156.25 \text{ N}$$

The total pressure acts at (h/3) from top of base.

$\therefore$ Maximum B.M. at base of stem

$$= P \times \text{Distance of pressure from base slab}$$

$$= 45156.25 \times \dfrac{4.25}{3}$$

$$= 63.97 \times 10^3 \text{ N-m}$$

$$= 63.97 \times 10^3 \times 10^3 \text{ N-mm}$$

$$\text{Ultimate moment} = 1.5 \times 63.97 \times 10^6 \text{ N-mm}$$

$\therefore$ Thickness of stem at bottom

$$= \sqrt{\dfrac{M_u}{R_{u\,max}\,b}}$$

$$= \sqrt{\frac{1.5 \times 63.97 \times 10^3 \times 10^3}{2.76 \times 1000}}$$

$$= 186.45 \text{ mm}$$

So provide overall thickness of step $=$ 250 mm throughout.

$$\therefore \quad \text{Effective thickness} = 250 - \text{Clear cover} - \frac{\text{Diameter of bar}}{2}$$

$$= 250 - 40 - \frac{16}{2} = 202 \text{ mm}$$

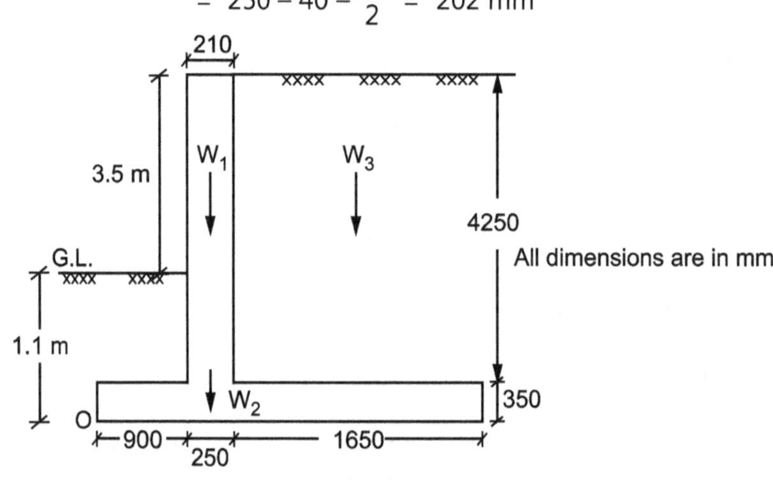

Fig. 13.16

Step V : Check for stability of the wall : Before designing, it is necessary to check the stability of wall. Following checks are made considering one meter length.

(a)   Check against overturning.

(b)   Check against sliding.

(c)   Check against maximum pressure at toe.

(a)   Check against overturning :

Sr. No.	Description of load	Magnitude of load in newton	Distance of C.G. from 'O' in metres	Moment about 'O' in N-m
1.	Weight of stem wall (W₁)	$0.25 \times 4.25 \times 25000$ $= 26562.5$	$0.9 + \frac{0.25}{2} = 1.025$	27226.56
2.	Weight of base slab (W₂)	$2.8 \times 0.35 \times 25000$ $= 24500$	$\frac{2.8}{2} = 1.4$	34300
3.	Weight of earthfill over heel slab (W₃)	$1.65 \times 4.25 \times 15000$ $= 105187.5$	$0.9 + 0.25 + \frac{1.65}{2} = 1.975$	207745.31
		$\Sigma W = 156250$		MR = 269271.87

Total earth pressure on the full height of wall tending to overturn,

$$P = \frac{1}{2}\,\gamma h^2\, k_a$$

$$= \frac{1}{2} \times 15000 \times (4.25)^2 \times \frac{1}{3} = 45156.25 \text{ N}$$

Total pressure acts at $\dfrac{h}{3}$ i.e. $\dfrac{4.25}{3} = 1.42$ m

$\therefore \qquad$ Total overturning moment $= P \times \dfrac{h}{3}$

$$= 45156.25 \times \frac{4.25}{3}$$

$$= 63.97 \times 10^3 \text{ N-m}$$

$\therefore \qquad$ F.S. $= \dfrac{\text{Stabilizing moment}}{\text{Overturning moment}} = \dfrac{269271.87}{63.97 \times 10^3} = 4.2 > 2$

Hence safe.

(b)   Check against sliding :

Total force tending to slide $= P = 45156.25$ N

Total force opposing sliding $= \mu\, \Sigma\, W$

$$= 0.6 \times 156250 = 93750 \text{ N}$$

Factor of safety against sliding $= \dfrac{93750}{45156.25} = 2.08 > 1.55$ Hence safe.

Net moment $=$ Stabilizing moment – Overturning moment

$$= 269271.87 - 63.97 \times 10^3$$

$$= 205301.87 \text{ N-m}$$

Let $\bar{x}$ be the distance from 'A'.

$$\bar{x} = \frac{\text{Net moment}}{\Sigma\, W} = \frac{205301.87}{156250} = 1.31 \text{ m}$$

Eccentricity (e) $= \dfrac{b}{2} - \bar{x} = \dfrac{2.8}{2} - 1.31 = 0.09$ m

Maximum pressure at toe 'A' and minimum pressure at A_3 is given by

$$p = \frac{\Sigma W}{b}\left(1 \pm \frac{6e}{b}\right)$$

$\therefore \qquad p_{max}$ at toe $= \dfrac{\Sigma W}{b}\left(1 + \dfrac{6e}{b}\right)$

$$= \frac{156250}{2.8}\left(1 + \frac{6 \times 0.09}{2.8}\right)$$

$$= 65841.45 \text{ N/m}^2 \; < \; 150000 \text{ N/m}^2 \; \text{Hence safe.}$$

and $\qquad p_{min}$ at heel $= \dfrac{\Sigma W}{b}\left(1 - \dfrac{6e}{b}\right)$

$$= \frac{156250}{2.8}\left(1 - \frac{6 \times 0.09}{2.8}\right)$$

$$= 44551.40 \text{ N/m}^2$$

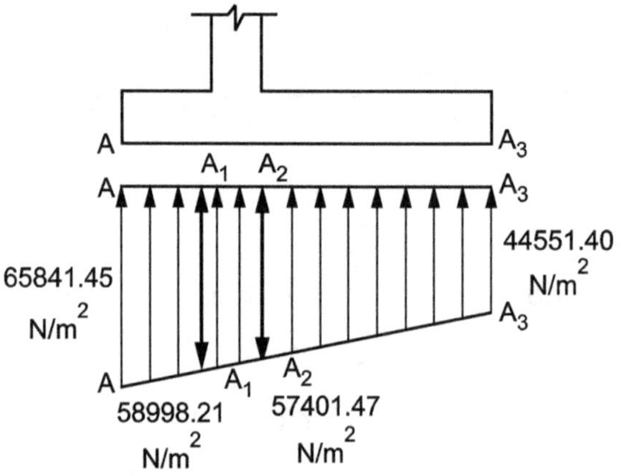

Fig. 13.17

Step VI : Design of toe slab :

Forces acting on slab :

(i)   Upward soil reaction varying from 65841.45 N/m² to 58998.21 N/m².

(ii)   Downward pressure due to self weight of slab

$$= 0.35 \times 25000 = 8750 \text{ N/m}^2$$

Net upward pressure at 'A' $= 65841.45 - 8750$

$$= 57091.45 \text{ N/m}^2$$

Net upward pressure at 'A_1' $= 58998.21 - 8750$

$$= 50248.21 \text{ N/m}^2$$

B.M. of net upward pressure at O

$$= \text{Area of trapezoidal section} \times \text{C.G. of trapezoidal from O.}$$

$$= \frac{1}{2}(57091.45 + 50248.21) \times 0.9 \times \frac{(57091.45 + 2 \times 50248.2)}{(57091.45 + 50248.21)} \times \frac{0.9}{3}$$

$$= 21274.36 \text{ N-m}$$

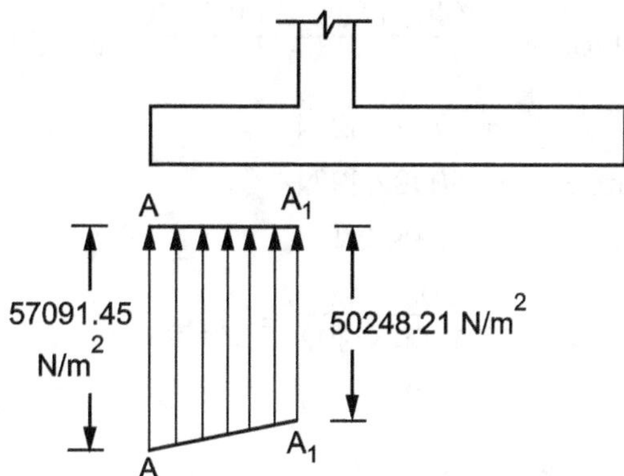

Fig. 13.18

$$\therefore \quad d = \sqrt{\frac{B.M.}{R_u \cdot b}} = \sqrt{\frac{1.5 \times 21274.36 \times 10^3}{2.76 \times 1000}} = 107.52 \text{ mm}$$

So provide thickness at A_1A_1 as 350 mm and reduce to 200 mm at AA.

Provide 40 mm clear cover and 16 mm ϕ bars.

$$\therefore \quad d = 350 - 40 - 8 = 302 \text{ mm}$$

$$A_{st} = \frac{0.5 \, f_{ck}}{f_y}\left[1 - \sqrt{1 - \frac{4.6 \, M_u}{f_{ck} \, bd^2}}\right]$$

$$= \frac{0.5 \times 20}{415}\left[1 - \sqrt{1 - \frac{4.6 \times 1.5 \times 21274.36 \times 10^3}{20 \times 1000 \times (302)^2}}\right] \times 1000 \times 302$$

$$= 298.95 \text{ mm}^2$$

$$A_{st \, min} = 0.12\% \, bD$$

$$= \frac{0.12}{100}(1000 \times 350)$$

$$= 420 \text{ mm}^2$$

$$\therefore \quad \text{Spacing of 16 mm } \phi = \frac{201 \times 1000}{420} = 478.57 \text{ mm say 470 mm}$$

Provide 16 mm ϕ @ 470 mm c/c.

Step VII : Check for shear : Intensity of pressure at a distance d = 302 mm from wall.

$$\therefore \quad \text{Pressure intensity at d} = 44551.40 + \frac{(57091.45 - 50248.21)}{0.9} \times 0.302$$

$$= 46847.69 \text{ N/m}^2$$

$$\text{and} \quad \text{Net vertical force} = \left(\frac{46847.69 + 44551.40}{2}\right) \times 0.598 \times 1$$

$$= 27328.32 \text{ N}$$

$$\therefore \quad \text{Ultimate S.F.} = 40992.49 \text{ N}$$

$$= 40.99 \text{ kN}$$

$$p_t = \frac{100 \times 420}{1000 \times 302} = 0.14$$

$$\tau_c = 0.28$$

$$\therefore \quad V_{uc} = \tau_c \times b \cdot d$$

$$= \frac{0.28 \times 1000 \times 302}{1000}$$

$$= 84.56 \text{ kN} > 40.99 \text{ kN} \quad \text{Hence safe.}$$

Step VIII : Design of heel slab :

(a) Downward weight of soil = 105187.5 N acting at 0.825 m

(b) Downward weight of heel slab = $1.65 \times 0.35 \times 25000 = 14437.5$ N acting at 0.825 m

$\therefore$ Total downward force = 119625 N

Upward force due to soil pressure

$$= \frac{1}{2}(57041.47 + 44551.40) \times 1.65$$

$$= 83814.18 \text{ N}$$

$$\text{C.G. from A}_2 = \frac{(57041.47 + 2 \times 44551.40)}{57041.47 + 44551.40} \times \frac{1.65}{3} = 0.79$$

It acts at 0.79 m from A_2.

$$\therefore \quad \text{Net B.M. at A}_2 = 105187.5 \times 0.825 + 14437.5 \times 0.825 - 83814.18 \times 0.79$$

$$= 32477.43 \text{ N-m}$$

$$d = \sqrt{\frac{M_u}{R_u \cdot b}}$$

$$= \sqrt{\frac{1.5 \times 32477.43 \times 10^3}{2.67 \times 1000}}$$

$$= 135.08 \text{ mm}$$

So provide 350 mm at stem junction and reduce to 200 mm at end.

Provide 40 mm clear cover and 16 mm ϕ.

$$d = 350 - 40 - 8$$
$$= 302 \text{ mm}$$

$$A_{st} = \frac{0.5 \times 20}{415}\left(1 - \sqrt{1 - \frac{4.6 \times 1.5 \times 32477.43 \times 10^3}{20 \times 1000 \times (302)^2}}\right) \times 1000 \times 302$$

$$= 461.65 \text{ mm}^2$$

Spacing of 16 mm $\phi = \dfrac{201 \times 1000}{461.65} = 435.4 \text{ mm}$

$\therefore$ Provide 16 mm ϕ @ 430 mm c/c.

Step IX : Check for shear :

Intensity of pressure at 'd' from face of wall

$$= 44551.4 + \left(\frac{57401.47 - 44551.4}{1.65}\right) \times 1.348$$

$$= 55049.52 \text{ N/m}^2$$

$$\text{Net vertical force} = \left(\frac{55049.52 + 44551.4}{2}\right) \times 1.348$$

$$= 67131.02 \text{ N} \quad \text{(considering unit width)}$$

$\therefore$ Ultimate shear force $= 1.5 \times 67131.02 = 100696.53 \text{ N}$

$$p_t = \frac{100 \times 461.65}{1000 \times 302} = 1.52$$

$$\tau_c \approx 0.72$$

$$V_{uc} = \tau_c \times b \times d$$

$$= 0.72 \times 1000 \times 302 \times 10^{-3}$$

$$= 217.44 \text{ kN} > 100.7 \text{ kN} \quad \text{Hence O.K.}$$

Step X : Design of stem :

$$M_u = 1.5 \times 63.97 \times 10^6$$

$$= 95.955 \times 10^6 \text{ N-mm}$$

$\therefore$ $d = 202 \text{ mm}$

$$A_{st} = \frac{0.5 \times 20}{415}\left[1 - \sqrt{1 - \frac{4.6 \times 95.955 \times 10^6}{20 \times 1000 \times (202)^2}}\right] \times 1000 \times 202$$

$$= 1569.31 \text{ mm}^2$$

$\therefore$ Spacing of 16 mm $\phi = \dfrac{201 \times 1000}{1569.31} = 128.0 \text{ mm}$

$\therefore$ Provide 16 mm ϕ @ 120 mm c/c.

Curtailment of bar : Assuming theoretical point of cut off at $0.8 \times 4.25 = 3.4$ m from top of stem,

$$\text{B.M.} = 1.5\left[\frac{15000 \times (3.4)^3}{6} \times \frac{1}{3}\right] = 49130 \text{ N-m}$$

B.M. at 3.4 m is nearly half of B.M. at bottom.

∴   Provide 16 mm ϕ @ 240 mm c/c.

Step XI : Distribution steel :

(a)   Toe and heel :

$$A_{st} = 0.15 \% \ bD$$

$$= \frac{0.15 \times 1000 \times \left(\frac{350 + 200}{2}\right)}{100} = 412.5 \text{ mm}^2$$

Provide 8 ϕ @ 120 mm c/c.

(b)   Stem :

$$A_{st} = \frac{0.15 \times 1000 \times 250}{100} = 375 \text{ mm}^2$$

Provide 8 ϕ @ 260 mm c/c on both faces.

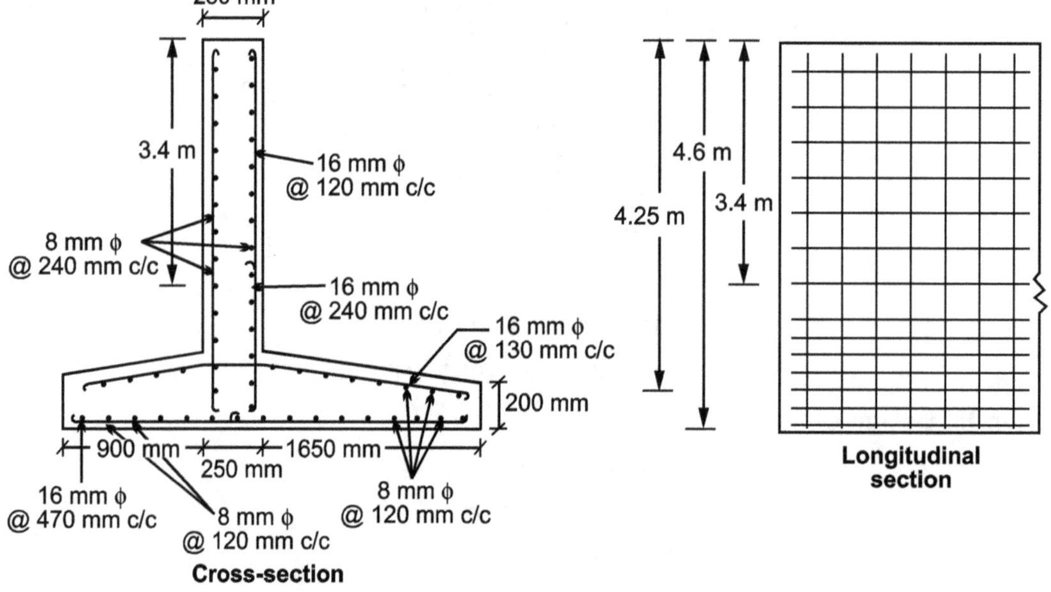

Fig. 13.19

Example 13.2 :

Design a cantilever retaining wall to retain earth for the following data :

(i)   Height above the base = 4.5 m

(ii)   Unit weight of backfill (γ) = 18.5 kN/m²

(iii)   Angle of repose (ϕ) = 30°

(iv)   Coefficient of friction = 0.55

> (v)   Safe bearing capacity of soil = 200 kN/m²
>
> (vi)   Horizontal backfill with surcharge = 10 kN/m²
>
> (vii) M 20 and Fe 500.

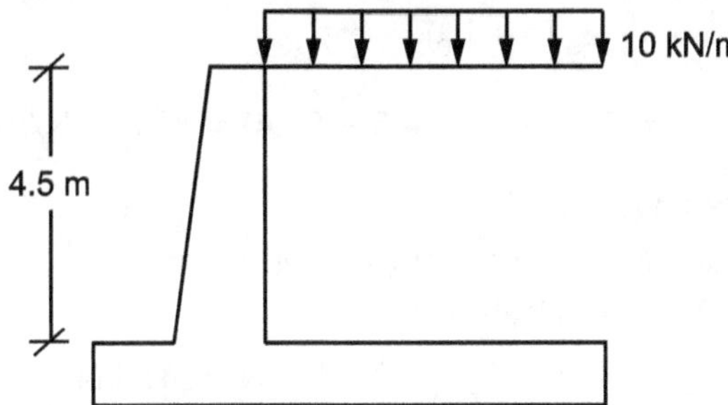

Fig. 13.20

Step I : Design constants :

$$k_{u\ max} = 0.46$$

$$R_{u\ max} = 0.36\, f_{ck}\, k_{u\ max}\, (1 - 0.42\, k_{u\ max})$$

$$= 0.36 \times 20 \times 0.46\, (1 - 0.42 \times 0.46)$$

$$= 2.67\ \text{N/mm}^2$$

Step II : Coefficient of active earth pressure :

$$k_a = \frac{1 - \sin\phi}{1 + \sin\phi} = \frac{1 - \sin 30}{1 + \sin 30} = \frac{1}{3}$$

Step III : Preliminary dimensions of the wall components :

(a)   Base width :

Base width of slab = 0.7 H = 0.7 × 4.5 = 3.15 m

So provide base width = 3.5 m

(b)   Toe projection :

$$\text{Toe projection} = \frac{1}{3} \times \text{Base width} = \frac{1}{3} \times 3.5 = 1.167\ \text{m}$$

So provide 1 m.

(c)   Thickness of base slab :

$$\text{Thickness of base slab} = \frac{H}{10} = \frac{4.5}{10} = 0.45\ \text{m}$$

∴   Provide thickness of base slab = 0.5 m.

(d)   Thickness of stem : Consider unit length.

Equivalent height of surcharge,

$$h_e = \frac{w}{\gamma} = \frac{10}{18.5} = 0.54\ \text{m}$$

Intensity of pressure at top of stem

$$= \gamma k_a h_e = 18.5 \times \frac{1}{3} \times 0.54 = 3.33 \text{ kN/m}^2$$

Intensity of pressure at bottom

$$= \gamma k_a (h + h_e)$$

$$= 18.5 \times \frac{1}{3} \times (4.5 + 0.54) = 31.08 \text{ kN/m}^2$$

The forces acting on stem wall :

Uniform horizontal pressure due to superimposed load,

$$P_1 = \gamma \cdot h_e \cdot k_a \cdot h \times 1$$

$$= 3.33 \times 4.5 = 14.99 \text{ kN} \approx 15 \text{ kN}$$

Force P_1 acts at $\dfrac{4.5}{2}$ from top of heel.

Triangular earth pressure due to backfill,

$$P_2 = \frac{1}{2} \gamma k_a \cdot h \cdot h \times 1$$

$$= \frac{1}{2} \times 18.5 \times \frac{1}{3} \times (4.5)^2 \times 1$$

$$= 62.44 \text{ kN}$$

Force P_2 acts at $\dfrac{4.5}{3}$ from top of heel.

$$\therefore \quad \text{B.M.} = P_1 \times \frac{4.5}{2} + P_2 \times \frac{4.5}{3} = 15 \times \frac{4.5}{2} + 62.44 \times \frac{4.5}{3}$$

$$= 127.41 \text{ kN-m}$$

$$\therefore \quad \text{Ultimate B.M.} = 1.5 \times 127.41 = 191.11 \text{ kN-m}$$

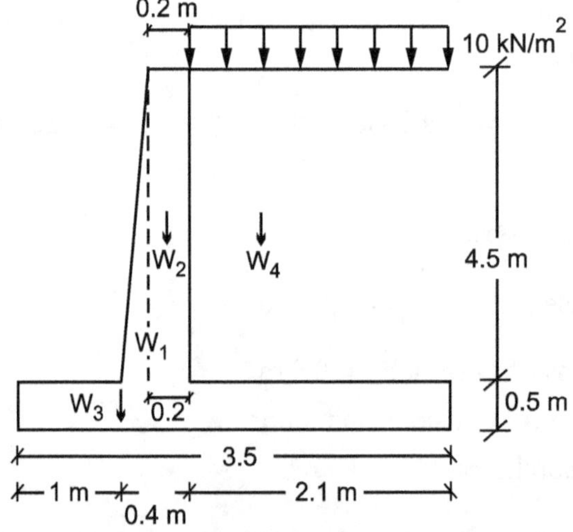

Fig. 13.21

$$d = \sqrt{\frac{M_u}{R_u \cdot b}} = \sqrt{\frac{191.11 \times 10^6}{2.67 \times 1000}} = 267.54 \text{ mm}$$

Provide total width of stem $= 400$ mm

Step IV : Check for stability of the wall : Before designing, it is necessary to check the stability of wall. Following checks are made :

(a)   Check against overturning,

(b)   Check against sliding,

(c)   Check against maximum pressure at toe.

(a)   Check against overturning :

Sr. No.	Description of load	Magnitude of load (kN)	Distance of C.G. from A_1 (m)	Moment about A_1 (kN-m)
1.	Weight of triangular part of stem (W_1)	$\frac{1}{2} \times 0.2 \times 4.5 \times 25 = 11.25$	$1 + \frac{2}{3} \times 0.2 = 1.133$	12.75
2.	Weight of rectangular part of stem (W_2)	$25 \times 4.5 \times 0.2 = 22.5$	$1 + 0.2 + \frac{0.2}{2} = 1.3$	29.25
3.	Weight of base slab (W_3)	$3.5 \times 0.5 \times 25 = 43.75$	$\frac{3.5}{2} = 1.75$	76.56
4.	Weight of earthfill (W_4)	$2.1 \times 4.5 \times 18.5 = 174.83$	$1 + 0.4 + \frac{2.1}{2} = 2.45$	428.34
5.	Surcharge (W_5)	$2.1 \times 10 \times 1 = 21$	2.45	51.45
		$\Sigma W = 273.33$ kN		M.R. $= 598.35$ kN-m

Ultimate stabilizing moment $= 1.5 \times 598.35 = 897.53$ kN-m

Overturning moment $= 191.11$ kN-m

$$\text{F.S. against overturning} = \frac{897.53}{191.11} = 4.7 > 2 \text{ Hence safe.}$$

(b)   Check against sliding :

Total ultimate force tending to slide $= (P_1 + P_2) \times 1.5$

$$= 15 + 62.44$$

$$= 77.44 \times 1.5$$

Total force opposing sliding $= \mu \, \Sigma W$

$$= 0.6 \times 273.33 \times 1.5$$

$$\text{F.S. against sliding} = \frac{\mu \, \Sigma W}{P}$$

$$= \frac{0.6 \times 273.33 \times 1.5}{77.44 \times 1.5}$$

$$= 3.53 \ > \ 2 \ \text{Hence safe}$$

(c) Check against maximum pressure :

$$\text{Net moment} = \text{Stabilizing moment} - \text{Overturning moment}$$

$$= 897.53 - 191.11 = 706.42 \text{ kN-m}$$

Let $\bar{x}$ be the distance from A_1.

$$\bar{x} = \frac{M}{P} = \frac{706.42 \times 10^3}{273.33 \times 1.5 \times 10^3} = 1.72 \text{ m}$$

$$\text{Eccentricity (e)} = \frac{b}{2} - \bar{x}$$

$$= \frac{3.5}{2} - 1.72 = 0.03 \text{ m}$$

$$\text{Maximum pressure at toe} = \frac{\Sigma W}{b}\left(1 + \frac{6e}{b}\right) = \frac{273.33}{3.5}\left(1 + \frac{6 \times 0.03}{3.5}\right)$$

$$= 82.11 \text{ kN/m}^3 \ < \ 200 \text{ kN/m}^2$$

$$\text{Minimum pressure at heel} = \frac{\Sigma W}{b}\left(1 - \frac{6e}{b}\right)$$

$$= \frac{273.33}{3.5}\left(1 - \frac{6 \times 0.03}{3.5}\right)$$

$$= 74.08 \text{ kN/m}^2 \ > \ 0$$

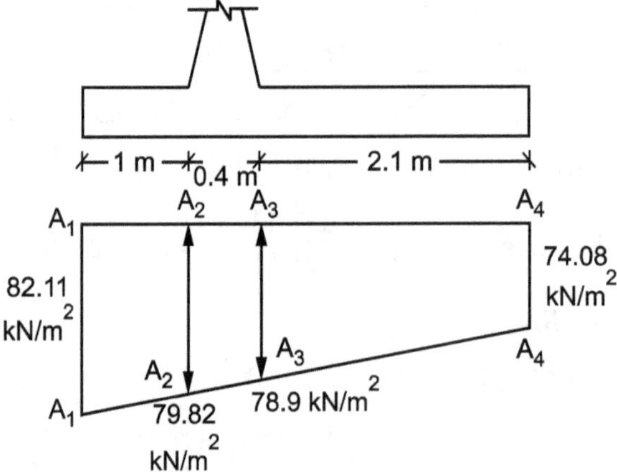

Fig. 13.22

Step V : Design of toe slab :

Forces acting on the slab :

(i)   Upward soil reaction varying from 82.11 kN/m² to 78.9 kN/m².

(ii) Downward pressure due to self weight of slab

$$= 0.5 \times 25000$$

$$= 12500 \ \text{N/m}^2 = 12.5 \ \text{kN/m}^2$$

Net upward pressure at A $= 82.11 - 12.5$

$$= 69.61 \ \text{kN/m}^2$$

Net upward pressure at $= 79.82 - 12.5$

$$= 67.32 \ \text{kN/m}^2$$

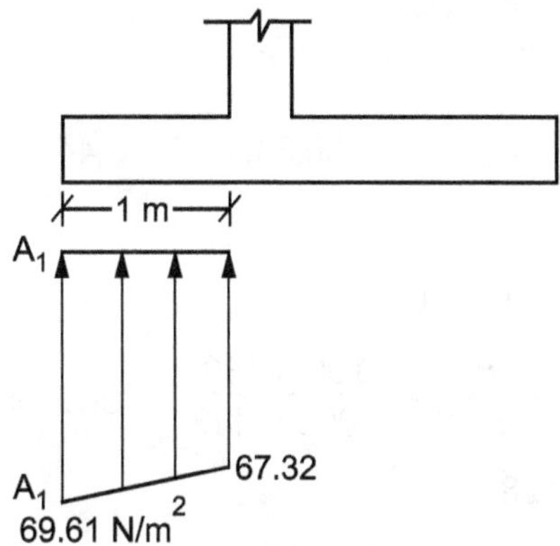

Fig. 13.23

$\therefore$ B.M. due to net upward pressure

$$= \frac{1}{2}(69.61 + 67.32) \times 1 \times \left(\frac{69.61 + 2 \times 67.32}{69.61 + 67.32}\right) \times \frac{1}{3}$$

$$= 34.04 \ \text{kN-m}$$

$\therefore$ Ultimate B.M. $= 1.5 \times 34.04$

$$= 51.06 \ \text{kN-m}$$

$\therefore$

$$d = \sqrt{\frac{M_u}{R_u \times b}} = \sqrt{\frac{51.06 \times 10^6}{2.67 \times 1000}}$$

$$= 138.29 \ \text{mm}$$

$$d_{provided} = 500 - 50 - \frac{16}{2} = 442 \ \text{mm} > 138.29 \ \text{mm}$$

$$A_{st} = \frac{0.5 \ f_{ck}}{f_y}\left[1 - \sqrt{1 - \frac{4.6 \ M_u}{f_{ck} \ bd^2}}\right] bd$$

$$= \frac{0.5 \times 20}{500}\left[1 - \sqrt{1 - \frac{4.6 \times 51.06 \times 10^6}{20 \times 1000 \times (442)^2}}\right] \times 1000 \times 442$$

$$= 269.81 \ \text{mm}^2$$

$$A_{st\,min} = \frac{0.12}{100} \times 1000 \times 442 = 530.4 \text{ mm}^2$$

$$\text{Spacing of 16 mm } \phi = \frac{201 \times 1000}{530.4} = 378.96 \text{ mm}^2$$

Provide 16 mm ϕ @ 370 mm c/c.

Step VI : Check for shear at 'd' from face of stem :

$$\text{Pressure intensity at 'd'} = 79.82 + \left(\frac{82.11 - 79.82}{1}\right) \times 0.442$$

$$= 80.83 \text{ kN/m}^2$$

$\therefore$ S.F. at 'd' from face of wall

$$= \frac{1}{2} \times (82.11 + 80.83) \times (1 - 0.442) = 45.46 \text{ kN}$$

$$\text{Ultimate S.F. at 'd'} = 1.5 \times 45.46$$

$$= 68.19 \text{ kN}$$

$$p_t = \frac{100\,A_{st}}{bd} = \frac{100 \times 530}{1000 \times 442} = 0.12 \; < \; 0.15$$

$\therefore$ $$\tau_c = 0.28$$

$\therefore$ $$V_{uc} = \tau_c\,bd = 0.28 \times 1000 \times 0.442 = 123.76 \text{ kN} \; > \; 68.19 \text{ kN}$$

Step VII : Design of heel slab :

(a)   Downward weight of soil = 174.83 kN/m² acts at 1.05 m from face of wall.

(b)   Downward weight of heel slab = 2.1 × 0.5 × 25 = 26.25 kN/m² acts at 1.05 m from face of wall.

$\therefore$ Maximum B.M. at face of wall

$$= 174.83 \times 1.05 + 26.25 \times 1.05 - \frac{1}{2}(78.9 + 74.08) \times 2.1 \left(\frac{78.9 + 2 \times 74.08}{78.9 + 74.08}\right) \times \frac{2.1}{3}$$

$$= 166.89 \text{ kN-m}$$

$\therefore$ Ultimate B.M. $= 1.5 \times 166.89 = 250.34$ kN-m

$\therefore$ $$d = \sqrt{\frac{M_u}{R_u \cdot b}} = \sqrt{\frac{250.34 \times 10^6}{2.67 \times 1000}}$$

$$= 306.2 \text{ mm} \; < \; 442 \text{ mm}$$

$$\text{Area of reinforcement, } A_{st} = \frac{0.5 \times 20}{500}\left(1 - \sqrt{1 - \frac{4.6 \times 250.34 \times 10^6}{20 \times 1000 \times (442)^2}}\right) \times 1000 \times 442$$

$$= 1416.1 \text{ mm}^2$$

$$\text{Spacing of 16 mm } \phi = \frac{201 \times 1000}{1416.1} = 141.94$$

Provide 16 mm ϕ @ 110 mm c/c.

Step VIII : Check for shear :

Intensity of pressure at 'd' from face of wall

$$= 74.8 + \left(\frac{78.9 - 74.8}{2.1}\right) \times (2.1 - 0.442)$$

$$= 78.04 \text{ kN/m}^2$$

$\therefore$ S.F. at 'd' from face of wall

$$= \frac{1}{2} \times (78.04 + 74.08) \times 1.658 = 126.1 \text{ kN}$$

$\therefore$ Ultimate S.F. at 'd' $= 1.5 \times 126.1$

$$= 189.15 \text{ kN}$$

A_{st} provided $= 1828 \text{ mm}^2$

$$p_t = \frac{1000 \, A_{st}}{1000 \times 442} = \frac{1000 \times 1828}{1000 \times 442} = 0.41$$

$$\tau_c = 0.44$$

p_t	τ_c
0.25	0.36
0.50	0.48

$\therefore$ $V_{uc} = \tau_c \cdot bd = 0.44 \times 1000 \times 442 \times 10^{-3}$

$$= 194.5 \text{ kN} > 189.15 \text{ kN}$$

Step IX : Design of stem :

$$M_u = 191.11 \text{ kN-m}$$

$$A_{st} = \frac{0.5 \, f_{ck}}{f_y}\left[1 - \sqrt{1 - \frac{4.6 \, M_u}{f_{ck} \, bd^2}}\right] bd$$

$$= \frac{0.5 \times 20}{500}\left[1 - \sqrt{1 - \frac{4.6 \times 191.11 \times 10^6}{20 \times 1000 \times (442)^2}}\right] \times 1000 \times 442$$

$$= 1057.75 \text{ mm}^2$$

Spacing of 16 mm $\phi = \dfrac{201 \times 1000}{1057} = 190.16 \text{ mm}$

Provide 16 mm ϕ @ 190 mm c/c.

Curtailment of bars : Assuming theoretical point of cut off at $0.8 \times 4.5 = 3.6$ m,

$\therefore$ $B.M. = 1.5\left[\dfrac{18.5 \times (3.6)^3}{6} \times \dfrac{1}{3}\right] + 1.5 \,(3.33 \times 3.6 \times 1 \times 2.25)$

$$= 71.93 + 26.97$$

$$= 98.9 \text{ kN-m}$$

B.M. at 3.6 m is nearly half of moment at bottom.

∴   Provide 16 mm φ @ 380 mm c/c.

Step X : Distribution steel :

(a)   Toe and heel :

$$A_{st} = 0.15\% \, bD = \frac{0.15 \times 1000 \times 500}{100} = 750 \text{ mm}^2$$

Provide 10 mm φ @ 100 mm c/c.

(b)   Stem :

$$A_{st} = \frac{0.15 \times \left(\dfrac{200 + 400}{2}\right) \times 1000}{100} = 450 \text{ mm}^2$$

Provide 8 mm φ @ 240 mm c/c on both faces.

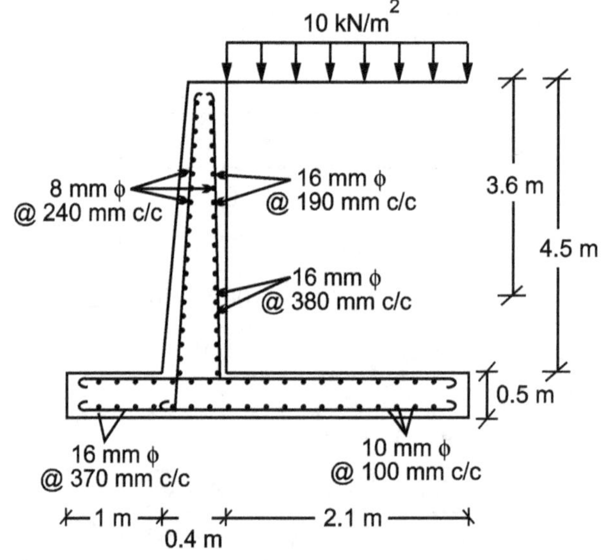

Fig. 13.24

Example 13.3 :

Design L-type retaining wall for the following data :

Height above the base = 4.3 m

Unit weight of backfill = 18 kN/m²

Angle of repose (φ) = 30°

Coefficient of friction = 0.55

Materials :   M 20 Fe 415.

Solution :

Data : Height above the base = 4.3 m

Unit weight of backfill $= 18$ kN/m²

Angle of repose $(\phi) = 30°$

Coefficient of friction $= 0.55$

Step I : Design constants : M 20 and Fe 415

$$k_{u\ max} = 0.48$$

$$R_{u\ max} = 0.36\ f_{ck}\ k_{u\ max}\ (1 - 0.42\ k_{u\ max})$$

$$= 0.36 \times 20 \times 0.48\ (1 - 0.42 \times 0.48)$$

$$= 2.76\ \text{N/mm}^2$$

Step II : Coefficient of active earth pressure :

$$k_a = \frac{1 - \sin\phi}{1 + \sin\phi} = \frac{1 - \sin 30}{1 + \sin 30} = \frac{1}{3}$$

Step III : Preliminary dimensions of wall components :

(a)   Base width :

Base width of slab $= 0.7 \times 4.3 = 3.0$ m

Provide base width 3.0 m.

(b)   Thickness of base slab :

Thickness of base slab $= \dfrac{H}{13} = 0.33$ m

Provide thickness of base slab $= 0.35$ m

(c)   Thickness of stem considering unit length :

Intensity of pressure at bottom of wall,

$$p_a = \gamma k_a \cdot h = 18 \times \frac{1}{3} \times 4.3 = 25.8\ \text{kN/m}^2$$

$$\text{Total earth pressure} = \frac{1}{2}\ p_a \cdot h = \frac{1}{2} \times 25.8 \times 4.3 = 55.47$$

The total pressure acts at $\dfrac{4}{3}$ from bottom of stem.

$\therefore$ Maximum B.M. at base $= 55.47 \times \dfrac{4.3}{3} = 79.51$ kN-m

$\therefore$ Ultimate B.M. at base $= 1.5 \times 79.51 = 119.27$ kN-m

Thickness of stem at bottom $= \sqrt{\dfrac{M_u}{R_u \cdot b}} = \sqrt{\dfrac{119.27 \times 10^6}{2.76 \times 1000}} = 207.88$ mm

Provide width of stem at top $= 250$ mm

Width of stem at bottom = 400 mm

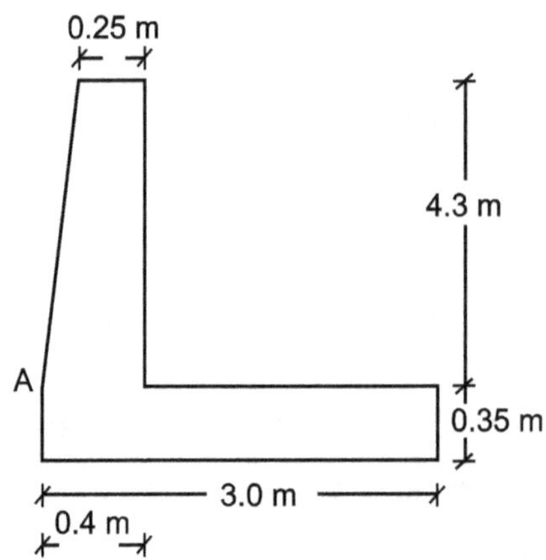

Fig. 13.25

Step IV : Check for stability of wall : Before designing, it is necessary to check the stability of wall.

    (a)   Check against overturning,

    (b)   Check against sliding,

    (c)   Check against maximum pressure.

(a)   Check against overturning :

Sr. No.	Description of load (N)	Magnitude of load (kN)	Distance of C.G. from A (m)	Moment about A (kN-m)
1.	Weight of rectangular portion of stem (W_1)	$0.25 \times 4.3 \times 25 = 26.875$	$0.15 + \dfrac{0.25}{2} = 0.275$	7.39
2.	Weight of triangular portion of stem (W_2)	$\dfrac{1}{2} \times 0.15 \times 4.3 \times 25 = 8.06$	$\dfrac{2}{3} \times 0.15 = 0.1$	0.806
3.	Weight of base slab (W_3)	$0.35 \times 3.0 \times 25 = 26.25$	$\dfrac{3.0}{2} = 1.5$	39.375
4.	Weight of earthfill (W_4)	$2.60 \times 4.3 \times 18 = 201.24$	$0.4 + \dfrac{2.60}{2} = 1.700$	342.11
		$\Sigma W = 262.43$		M.R. = 389.68

    Ultimate stabilizing moment = $1.5 \times 389.68 = 584.52$ kN-m

      Overturning moment = 119.27 kN-m

$$\text{Factor of safety against overturning} = \frac{\text{Stabilizing moment}}{\text{Overturning moment}}$$

$$= \frac{584.52}{119.27} = 4.9 > 2 \text{ Hence safe.}$$

(b)   Check against sliding :

    Total ultimate force tending to slide = 1.5×55.47 = 83.21 kN

$$\text{Total force opposing sliding} = \mu \, \Sigma W = 0.55 \times 262.43$$
$$= 144.34 \text{ kN}$$

$$\text{Factor of safety against sliding} = \frac{\mu \, \Sigma W}{P} = \frac{144.34}{83.21} = 1.73 \; > \; 1.55$$

(c)   Check against maximum pressure at toe :

$$\text{Net moment} = \text{Stabilizing moment} - \text{Overturning moment}$$
$$= 389.45 - 119.27 = 270.18 \text{ kN-m}$$

Let $\bar{x}$ be the distance from 'A'.

$$\bar{x} = \frac{\text{Net moment}}{\Sigma W} = \frac{270.18}{262.43} = 1.03$$

$$\text{Eccentricity (e)} = \frac{b}{2} - \bar{x}$$

$$= \frac{3}{2} - 1.03 = 0.47 \text{ m}$$

$$\text{Maximum pressure at A} = \frac{\Sigma W}{b}\left(1 + \frac{6e}{b}\right)$$

$$= \frac{262.43}{3}\left(1 + \frac{6 \times 0.47}{3}\right)$$

$$= 169.70 \text{ kN/m}^2 \; < \; 200 \text{ kN/m}^2$$

$$\text{Minimum pressure} = \frac{\Sigma W}{b}\left(1 - \frac{6e}{b}\right)$$

$$= \frac{262.43}{3}\left(1 - \frac{6 \times 0.47}{3}\right)$$

$$= 5.25 \text{ kN/m}^2 \; > \; 0$$

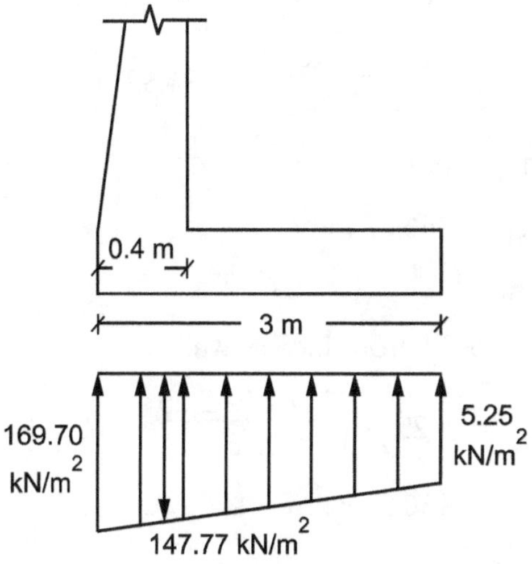

Fig. 13.26

Step V : Design of heel slab :

(a)   Downward weight of soil = 201.24 acts at 1.3 m

(b)   Downward weight of heel slab = $2.60 \times 0.35 \times 25$ = 22.750 kN/m^2 acts at 1.30 m

Maximum B.M. at face of wall

$$= 201.24 \times 1.3 + 22.75 \times 1.3 - \left(\frac{147.77 + 5.25}{2}\right) \times 2.6 \times \left(\frac{147.77 + 2 \times 5.25}{147.77 + 5.25}\right) \times \frac{2.6}{3}$$

$$= 178.32$$

$\therefore$ Maximum ultimate moment = 1.5×178.32 = 267.48 kN-m

$$d = \sqrt{\frac{M_u}{R_u \cdot b}} = \sqrt{\frac{267.48 \times 10^6}{2.76 \times 1000}} = 311.03 \text{ mm}$$

Provide 360 mm at face of wall to 200 mm on opposite side.

$\therefore$ Effective depth = $360 - 40 - \dfrac{16}{2}$ = 312 mm

$$A_{st} = \frac{0.5\, f_{ck}}{f_y}\left[1 - \sqrt{1 - \frac{4.6\, M_u}{f_{ck}\, bd^2}}\right] bd$$

$$= \frac{0.5 \times 20}{415}\left[1 - \sqrt{1 - \frac{4.6 \times 267.48 \times 10^6}{20 \times 1000 \times (312)^2}}\right] \times 1000 \times 252$$

$$= 2388.60 \text{ mm}^2$$

$$A_{st\,min} = \frac{0.12}{100} \times 1000 \times 252 = 302.4 \text{ mm}^2$$

Spacing of 20 mm ϕ = $\dfrac{314.15 \times 1000}{2388.60}$ = 131.52

Provide 20 mm ϕ @ 130 mm c/c.

$A_{st\,provided}$ = 446.67 mm^2

Step VI : Check for shear :

Intensity of pressure at 'd' from face of wall

$$= 5.25 + \left(\frac{147.77 - 5.25}{2.6}\right) \times 2.288$$

$$= 130.67 \text{ kN/m}^2$$

$\therefore$ S.F. at 'd' from face of wall

$$= \left(\frac{130.67 + 5.25}{2}\right) \times 2.6$$

$$= 176.7 \text{ kN}$$

Ultimate S.F. at 'd' from face of wall

$$= 1.5 \times 176.7$$

$$= 265.05 \text{ kN}$$

$$p_t = \frac{100 \, A_{st}}{bd}$$

$$= \frac{100 \times 2388.6}{1000 \times 312}$$

$$= 0.77$$

$$\tau_c = 0.355$$

$$V_{uc} = \tau_c \cdot bd$$

$$= 0.355 \times 1000 \times 252$$

$$= 89.46 \text{ kN} > 233.46 \text{ kN}$$

Step VII : Design of stem :

$$M_u = 119.27 \text{ kN-m}$$

$$A_{st} = \frac{0.5 \times 20}{415}\left[1 - \sqrt{1 - \frac{4.6 \times 119.27 \times 10^6}{20 \times 1000 \times (312)^2}}\right] \times 1000 \times 312$$

$$= 1146.78 \text{ mm}^2$$

$$\text{Spacing of 16 mm } \phi = \frac{201 \times 1000}{1147}$$

$$= 175.24 \text{ mm}$$

Provide 16 mm ϕ @ 170 mm c/c.

Curtailment of bars : Assuming theoretical point of cut-off at $0.8 \times 4.3 = 3.44$ m,

$$\therefore \qquad \text{B.M.} = 1.5\left[\frac{1.8 \times (3.44)^3}{6} \times \frac{1}{3}\right] = 61.06 \text{ kN-m}$$

B.M. at 3.44 m is nearly half of maximum B.M.

$\therefore$ Provide 16 mm ϕ @ 340 mm c/c.

Step VIII : Distribution steel :

(a) Heel slab : $A_{st \, min} = \dfrac{0.15}{100} \times bD = \dfrac{0.15}{100} \times 1000 \times 360 = 540 \text{ mm}^2$

Provide 8 mm ϕ @ 90 mm c/c.

(b)   Stem : $A_{st\ min} = \dfrac{0.15}{100} \times 1000 \times \left(\dfrac{250 + 400}{2}\right) = 487.5\ \text{mm}^2$

Provide 8 mm ϕ @ 200 mm c/c on both sides.

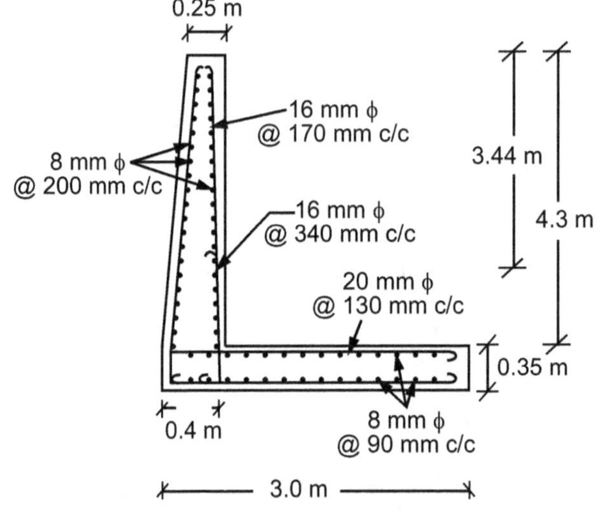

Fig. 13.27

Example 13.4 :

Design a T shaped retaining wall for two layered levelled backfill for the following data :

Upper layer : height = 2.4 m, ϕ = 30°, γ = 17.5 kN/m³.

Lower layer : height = 2.4 m, ϕ = 31°, γ = 18.5 kN/m³.

Safe bearing capacity of the underlying strata = 170 kN/m². The coefficient of friction between the base slab and the underlying strata = 0.55. Draw lateral pressure diagram and details of reinforcement of stem and base showing curtailment if any.

(May 12, 13, 20 Marks)

Solution :

$$k_A = \dfrac{1 - \sin\phi}{1 + \sin\phi} = \dfrac{1 - \sin 30°}{1 + \sin 30°}$$

Depth of foundation below ground level $= \dfrac{P_o}{w}\left(\dfrac{1 - \sin\phi}{1 + \sin\phi}\right)^2 = \dfrac{150}{16}\left(\dfrac{1 - \sin 30°}{1 + \sin 30°}\right)^2 = 1.05\ \text{m}$

Total height of wall above foundation level = 4.5 + 1.05 = 5.55 m

Approximate base width,

$$B = H\sqrt{\dfrac{(1 - \sin\phi)/(1 + \sin\phi)}{(1 - k)(1 + 3k)}}$$

Now, $k = 1 - \dfrac{P_o}{2Hw} = \dfrac{1 - 150}{2 \times 5.55 \times 16} = 0.155$

$\therefore \qquad B = 5.55 \sqrt{\dfrac{(1/3)}{(1 - 0.155)(1 + 3 \times 0.155)}} = 2.9$ m

$\qquad\qquad B = 0.6\,H = 0.6 \times 5.55 = 3.33 \approx 34$ m

Converting surcharge into equivalent depth of earth (h_1)

$\qquad w \cdot h_1 = \text{surcharge} = 15 \Rightarrow h_1 = 15/16 = 0.9375$ m

$\qquad k_A w \cdot h_1 = \dfrac{1}{3} \times 16 \times \dfrac{15}{16} = 5$ kN/m^2

$\qquad k_A w\,(H + h_1) = \dfrac{1}{3} \times 16 \times (5.55 + 0.9375) = 34.6$ kN/m^2

Resultant active earth pressure

$\qquad P = \dfrac{5 + 34.6}{2} \times 5.55 = 109.89$ kN

$\qquad \text{Lever arm} = \dfrac{34.6 + 2 \times 5}{34.6 \times 5} \times \dfrac{5.55}{3} = 2.08$ m

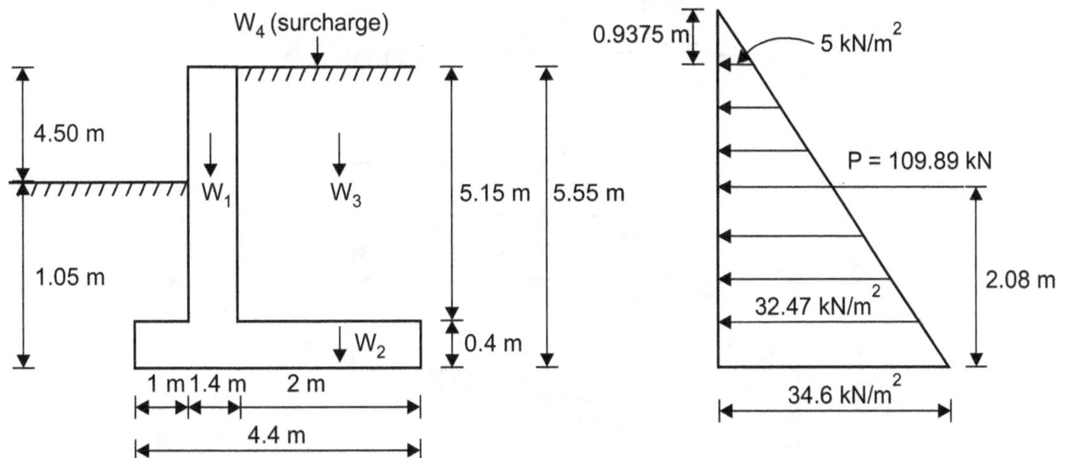

Fig. 13.28

Check for base width : Assume the average thickness of stem, heel and toe as 400 mm.

Description (N)	C.G. from D (m)	Moment @ D (N-m)
$W_1 = 515 \times 0.4 \times 1 \times 25000 = 51500$	2.2	113300
$W_2 = 3.4 \times 0.4 \times 1 \times 25000 = 34000$	1.7	57800
$W_3 = 2 \times 5.15 \times 1 \times 16000 = 164800$	1.0	164800
$W_4 = 0.9375 \times 2 \times 1 \times 16000 = 30000$	1.0	30000

Total = 280300		365900
P = 109890	2.08	228571
		M = 594471

Resultant strikes the base at a distance Z from D $= \dfrac{594471}{280300} = 2.12$ m

$$\frac{2}{3} \times 3.4 = 2.267 \text{ m} > 2.12 \text{ m}$$

$\therefore$ No tension develops at the base

$$e = 2.12 - \frac{1}{2} \times 3.4 = 0.42 \text{ m}$$

Pressure distribution at base :

$$\text{Pressure} = \frac{W}{B}\left(1 \pm \frac{6e}{B}\right)$$

$$P_{max} = \frac{280300}{3.4}\left(1 + \frac{6 \times 0.42}{3.4}\right) = 143550 \text{ N/m}^2 < 150 \text{ kN/m}^2$$

$$P_{min} = \frac{280300}{3.4}\left(1 - \frac{6 \times 0.42}{3.4}\right) = 21340 \text{ N/m}^2$$

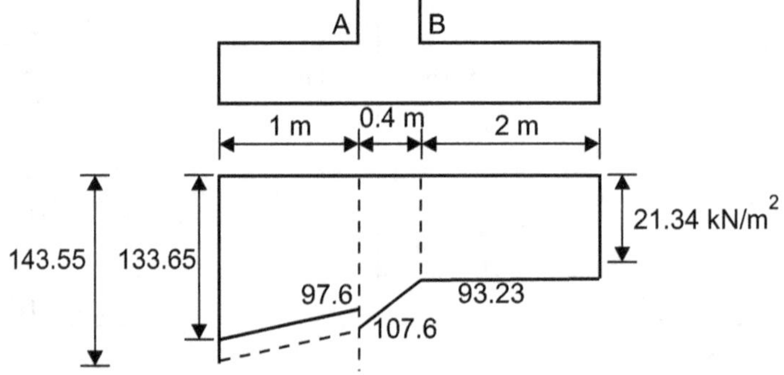

Fig. 13.29

$$\text{Pressure at A} = 21.34 + \frac{143.55 - 21.34}{3.4} \times 2.4 = 107.6 \text{ kN/m}^2$$

$$\text{Pressure at B} = 21.34 + \frac{143.55 - 21.34}{3.4} \times 2 = 93.23 \text{ kN/m}^2$$

Design of stem : Maximum B.M. at AB level

$$= \left(\frac{5 + 32.47}{2} \times 5.15\right)\left[\frac{32.47 + 2 \times 5}{3.247 + 5} \times \frac{5.15}{3}\right] = 187.735 \text{ kN-m}$$

$$\text{Maximum S.F.} = (5 + 34.6) \times \frac{1}{2} \times 5.15 = 102 \text{ kN}$$

$$d = \sqrt{\frac{187.735 \times 1000 \times 1000}{0.812 \times 1000}} = 480.83 \text{ mm}$$

Provide D = 525 mm, d = 475 mm

$$A_{st} = \frac{187.735 \times 10^6}{275 \times 0.9155 \times 475} = 1570 \text{ mm}^2$$

Provide 16 mm ϕ @ 125 mm c/c ($A_{st\ provided}$ = 1608 mm^2)

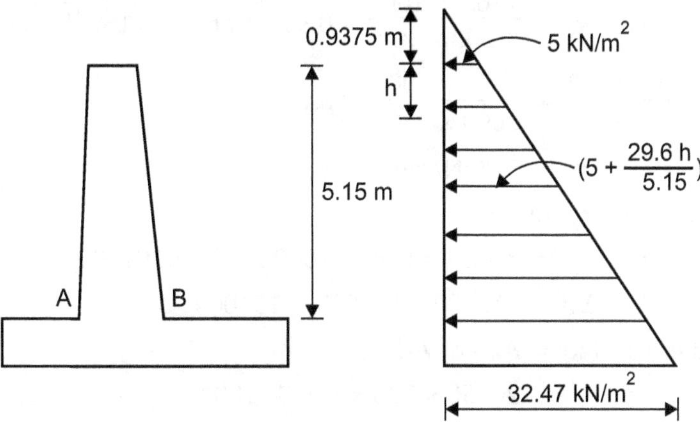

Fig. 13.30

Curtain half bars in top 1/3 portion of the wall.

Check for shear :

$$\text{Nominal shear stress} = \frac{102000}{475 \times 1000} = 0.215 \text{ N/mm}^2$$

$$\frac{A_{st} \times 100}{bd} = \frac{1608 \times 100}{1000 \times 475} = 0.3385 \approx 0.34$$

Taper the stem from 525 mm to 200 mm at top keeping the average thickness as 400 mm approximately.

Design of toe :

$$\text{Weight of toe slab} = 0.4 \times 1 \times 1 \times 25 = 10 \text{ kN/m}^2$$

$$\text{Average upward pressure} = \frac{133.55 + 97.6}{2} = 11.66 \text{ kN/m}^2$$

$$\text{B.M.}_A = 116.6 \times 1 \times \frac{107.6 + 2 \times 143.55}{107.6 + 143.55} \times \frac{1}{3} = 61.08 \text{ kN-m}$$

$$d = \sqrt{\frac{61.08 \times 1000 \times 1000}{0.812 \times 1000}} = 274.3 \text{ mm}$$

$$\text{Provide } D = 400 \text{ mm}, \quad d = 350 \text{ mm}$$

$$A_{st \text{ required}} = \frac{61.08 \times 1000 \times 1000}{275 \times 0.9155 \times 350} = 693.2 \text{ mm}^2$$

Extend tension steel of stem in toe ($A_{st \text{ provided}} = 1608 \text{ mm}^2$).

Check for shear :

$$\text{Shear force} = 116.6 \text{ kN}$$

$$\text{Nominal shear stress,} \quad \tau_v = \frac{116.6 \times 1000}{1000 \times 350} = 0.33 \text{ N/mm}^2 < 0.16 \sqrt{f_{ck}} = 0.7155 \text{ N/mm}^2$$

$$\frac{A_{st} \times 100}{bd} = \frac{1608 \times 100}{1000 \times 350} = 0.46$$

$$\tau_c = 0.29 \text{ N/mm}^2$$

$\tau_v > \tau_c$, shear R/F is required.

$$\text{Shear concrete can carry} = \tau_c \cdot bd = 0.29 \times 1000 \times 350 = 101500 \text{ N}$$

$$V_s = 116600 - 101500 = 15100 \text{ N}$$

$$8 \text{ mm } \phi, 2 \text{ legged at spacing} = A_{sv} \cdot \sigma_{sv}/(d/V_s)$$

$$= 2 \times 50 \times 230 \times 350/15100$$

$$= 533 \text{ mm c/c}$$

$$\text{Maximum spacing} = 0.75d = 0.75 \times 350 = 262.5 \text{ mm}$$

Use 8 mm ϕ, 2 legged shear stirrups @ 250 mm c/c.

Design of heel :

$$\text{Self weight of heel} = 0.4 \times 2 \times 1 \times 25000 = 20000 \text{ N}$$

$$\text{Upward pressure of soil} = \frac{93.23 + 21.34}{2} \times 2 = 114.57 \text{ kN}$$

$$\text{Acting at } \frac{93.23 + 2 \times 21.34}{93.23 + 21.34} \times \frac{2}{3} = 0.79 \text{ m from B.}$$

$$\text{B.M. at B} = 164800 \times 1 + 20000 \times 1 - 114570 \times 0.79 = 124290 \text{ N-m}$$

$$d = \sqrt{\frac{124290 \times 1000}{0.812 \times 1000}} = 391.24 \text{ mm}$$

Provide D = 400 mm, d = 350 mm.

$$A_{st \text{ required}} = \frac{124290 \times 1000}{275 \times 0.9155 \times 350} = 1410.5 \text{ mm}^2$$

Provide 16 mm ϕ @ 125 mm c/c. $A_{st \text{ provided}} = 1608 \text{ mm}^2$

Check for shear :

$$\text{Shear force} = 164800 + 30000 + 20000 - 114570 = 100230 \text{ N}$$

$$\text{Nominal shear stress} = \frac{100230}{1000 \times 350} = 0.286 \text{ N/mm}^2 \text{ O.K.}$$

$$\text{Bars shall be extended} = 58 \times 20 = 1160 \text{ mm from B.}$$

Check against sliding :

$$\text{Sliding force} = \text{Earth pressure} = 109890 \text{ N}$$

$$\text{Frictional force} = \text{H.W.} = 0.6 \times 280300 = 168180 \text{ N}$$

$$\text{F.S.} = \frac{168180}{109890} = 1.53 > 1.5$$

$\therefore$ No key is required.

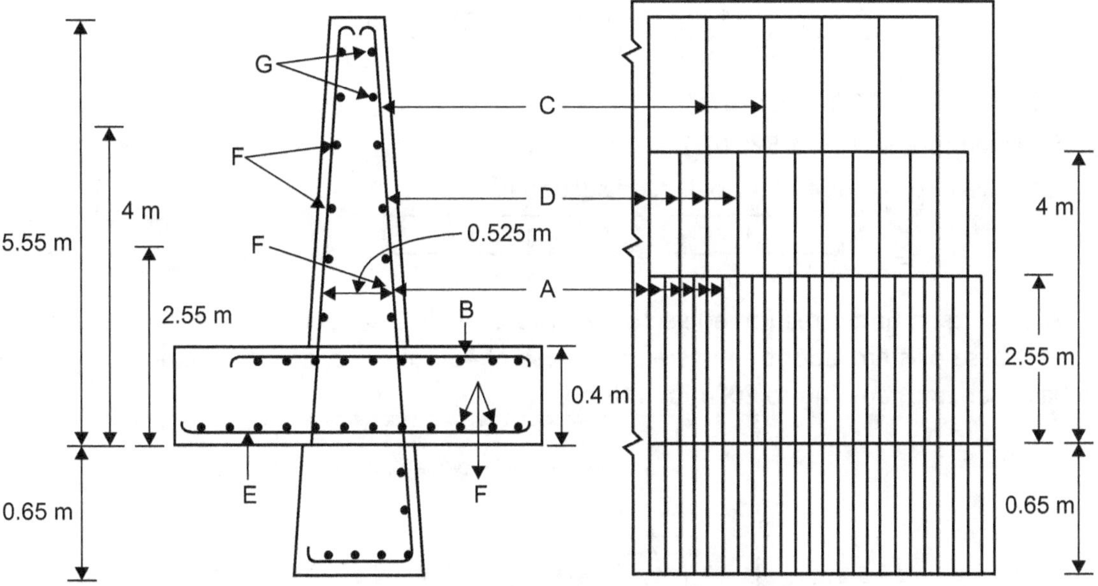

Fig. 13.31

Example 13.5 : *Design a RCC retaining wall to retain earthen embankment 4.2 m high above G.L. The embankment is surcharge at an angle of 20° to horizontal. The unit weight of earth is 18 kN/m³. Angle of repose 30° good foundation for wall is available at a depth of 1.1 m below ground level. SBC of soil 160 kN/m². Coefficient of friction between concrete and soil may be taken as 0.62. Use M20 grade concrete and Fe 415 steel. Sketch the reinforcement details.*

(Dec. 2012, 25 Marks)

Solution : 1. Dimensions of retaining wall :

$$\text{Minimum depth of foundation} = \frac{P}{w}\left(\frac{1 - \sin\phi}{1 + \sin\phi}\right)^2$$

$$= \frac{160}{18}\left(\frac{1}{3}\right)^{2} = 0.98 \text{ m} \approx 1 \qquad \text{(1.1 m is given in data)}$$

$$\text{Overall depth of wall, H} = 4.2 + 1.1 = 5.3 \text{ m}$$

$$\text{Thickness of slab base} = \frac{H}{12} = \frac{5300}{12} = 441.67 \text{ mm}$$

$$\text{Adopt thickness of base slab} = 450 \text{ mm}$$

$$\text{Height of stem, h} = (5.3 - 0.45) = 4.85 \text{ m}$$

$$\text{Width of base slab, b} = 0.5 \text{ H to } 0.6 \text{ H}$$

$$0.5 \text{ H} = 2.65 \text{ m}$$

$$0.6 \text{ H} = 3.18 \text{ m}$$

$$\therefore \qquad \text{Adopt b} = 3 \text{ m}$$

2. Design of stem : Maximum B.M. at base

$$M = k_a \left(\frac{wh^3}{6}\right) = \left(\frac{1 - \sin\phi}{1 + \sin\phi}\right)\frac{wh^3}{6} = \frac{1}{3} \times \left(\frac{18 \times 4.85^3}{6}\right)$$

$$\therefore \qquad M = 107.17 \text{ kN-m}$$

Factored moment $= 1.5 \times 107.17 = 161 \text{ kN-m}$

Effective depth required for balanced section is

$$d = \sqrt{\frac{M_u}{0.138 \times f_{ck} \times b}} = \sqrt{\frac{161 \times 10^6}{0.138 \times 20 \times 10^3}} = 242 \text{ mm}$$

Assuming an under reinforced section and to provide a suitable thickness to resist shear force at base of stem, adopt an overall thickness of 450 mm, which is the same as thickness of base slab and tapering to 200 mm at top.

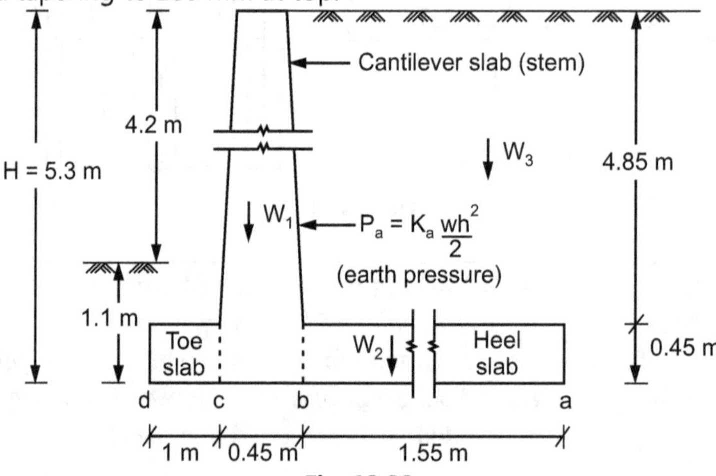

Fig. 13.32

Adopt effective depth of base of stem = 400 mm.

$$M_u = 0.87 \, f_y \, A_{st} \, d \left[1 - \frac{A_{st} \, f_y}{bd \, f_{ck}}\right]$$

$$161 \times 10^6 = 0.87 \times 415 \times A_{st} \times 400 \left[1 - \frac{415 \times A_{st}}{(10^3 \times 400 \times 20)} \right]$$

$$\therefore \qquad A_{st} = 1180 \text{ mm}^2$$

Provide 16 mm ϕ bars @ 150 mm c/c (A_{st} = 1340 mm^2)

$$\text{Distribution steel} = 0.12\% \text{ of c/s} = 0.0012 \times 1000 \times 450$$

$$= 540 \text{ mm}^2/\text{m}$$

Provide 10 mm ϕ bars @ 250 mm c/c on both faces (A_{st} = 630 mm^2)

3. Suitability calculations :

Loads	Magnitude of load (kN)	Distance from a (m)	Moment @ a (kN-m)
$W_1 = (0.2 \times 4.85 \times 24)$	23.28	1.65	38.412
$\quad + (0.5 \times 0.25 \times 4.85 \times 24)$	14.55	1.83	26.63
$W_2 = (3 \times 0.45 \times 24)$	32.40	1.50	48.60
$W_3 = (1.55 \times 18 \times 4.85)$	135.32	0.78	105.55
Moment of earth pressure $= k_a \dfrac{wh^3}{\sigma} = \dfrac{1}{3} \times 18 \times \dfrac{4.85}{6}$	–	–	114.08
Total	205.55		333

Distance of point of application of resultant from end a

$$= z = \left(\frac{\sum M}{\sum W} \right) = \frac{333}{205.55} = 1.62 \text{ m}$$

$$\text{Eccentricity, } e = \left(z - \frac{b}{2} \right) = \left(1.62 - \frac{3}{2} \right) = 0.1 \text{ m}$$

$$\frac{b}{6} = \frac{3}{6} = 0.5 \Rightarrow e < \frac{b}{6}$$

Maximum and minimum pressures at the base are given by

$$\sigma_{max/min} = \frac{\sum W}{b} \left(1 + \frac{6e}{b} \right) = \frac{205.55}{3} \left(1 + \frac{6 \times 0.1}{3} \right)$$

$$\sigma_{max} = 82.22 \text{ kN/m}^2$$

$$\sigma_{min} = 54.81 \text{ kN/m}^2$$

The maximum stress is within permissible limits of SBC of soil = 160 kN/m². The pressure distribution at the bar is trapezoidal and maximum and minimum pressures are shown in figure below :

$$\frac{(82.22 - 54.81)}{3} = 9.14$$

$$82.22 - 9.14 = 73.08$$

$$\frac{(73.08 - 54.81)}{1.55} = 11.78$$

$$73.08 - 11.78 = 61.3$$

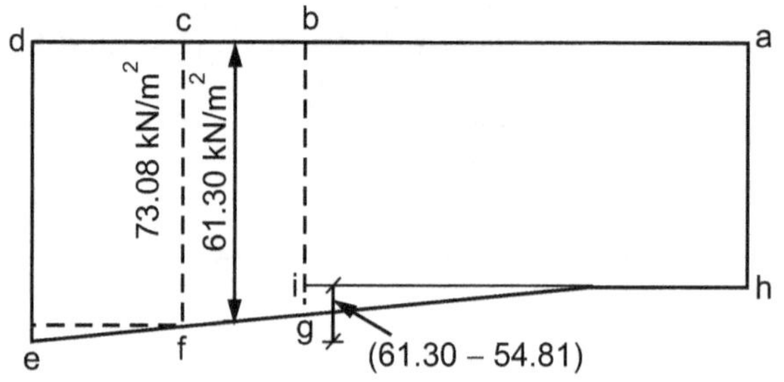

Fig. 13.33

4. Design of heel slab :

Maximum B.M. on heel slab is calculated by taking moments of all forces @ b.

Loads	Magnitude of load (kN)	Distance from b (m)	Moment @ b (kN-m)
$W_3 = (1.55 \times 4.85 \times 18)$	135.32	0.775	104.87
Self weight of heel slab ($1.55 \times 0.45 \times 24$)	16.7	0.775	12.94
Total			117.81
Induct for upward pressure 'abih' (54.81×1.55)	84.96	0.775	65.84
Upward pressure 'ghi' $\frac{1}{2} \times 1.55 \times 6.41$	4.97	0.516	2.56
Total deduction			68.4

Maximum service BM in heel slab at b = M = (117.81 − 68.4) = 49.41 kN-m

Factored moment $M_u = 1.5 \times 49.41 = 74.115$ kN-m

$$M_u = (0.87\, f_y\, A_{st}\, d)\left[1 - \frac{A_{st}\, f_y}{bd\, f_{ck}}\right]$$

$$74.115 \times 10^6 = (0.87 \times 415 \times A_{st} \times 400)\left[1 - \frac{415 \times A_{st}}{10^3 \times 400 \times 20}\right]$$

$$A_{st} = 527.9 \text{ mm}^2$$

Provide 12 mm ϕ bars @ 200 mm c/c (A_{st} = 565 mm^2)

Distribution steel = $(0.0012 \times 1000 \times 450)$ = 540 mm^2

Provide 12 mm ϕ bars @ 200 mm c/c (A_{st} = 565 mm^2)

5. **Design of the slab :**

The maximum B.M. in toe slab is determined by taking moments of forces @ point C.

Loads	Magnitude of load (kN)	Distance from c (m)	Moment @ C (kN-m)
Upward pressure cdif (73.08×1)	73.08	0.5	36.54
Upwards pressure ife $\left(\frac{1}{2} \times 1 \times 9.14\right)$	4.57	0.67	3.06
Total			**39.60**
Deduct self weight of toe slab $(1 \times e \times 0.45 \times 24)$	10.8	0.5	5.40
Dead weight of soil over toe slab $(0.75 \times 1 \times 18)$	13.5	0.5	6.75
Total deduction			**12.15**

Maximum service load BM in toe slab = 39.60 – 12.15 = 27.45 kN-m

Factored BM = M_u = 1.5 × 27.45 = 41.175 kN-m

$$41.175 \times 10^6 = 0.87 \times 415\, A_{st} \times 400\left[1 - \frac{415\, A_{st}}{10^3 \times 400 \times 20}\right]$$

$$A_{st} = 289.6 \text{ mm}^2 < A_{st\,(min)}$$

Hence provide minimum R/F of 0.12%.

$$A_{st\,(min)} = 0.012 \times 1000 \times 450 = 540 \text{ mm}^2$$

Provide 12 mm ϕ bars @ 200 mm c/c (A_{st} = 565 mm^2)

Distribution R/F is same as in heal slab comprising 12 mm ϕ bars @ 200 mm c/c.

6. **Check for safety against sliding :**

Total horizontal earth pressure,

$$P = k_a \cdot \frac{wH^2}{2} = \frac{1}{3} \times 18 \times \frac{5.3^2}{2} = 84.27 \text{ kN}$$

$\mu = 0.62$, $\mu w = 0.62 \times 215.64 = 133.70$

Factor of safety against sliding $= \dfrac{133.70}{84.27} = 1.58 > 1.5$. Hence O.K.

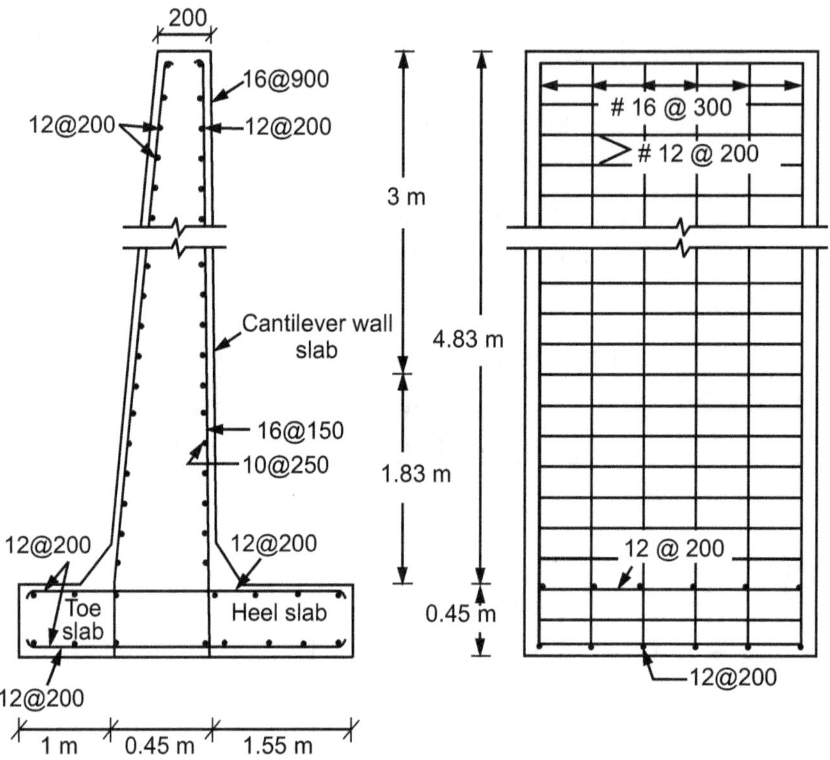

Fig. 13.34

Example 13.6 :

Design a retaining wall to retain the earth 4 m high. The top surface is horizontal behind the wall. The soil behind the wall is a well drained medium dense sand with following properties:

Unit weight = 17 kN/m³

Angle of internal friction, $\phi = 30°$

The material under wall base is the same as above with a safe bearing capacity of 150 kN/m². The coefficient of friction between base and soil is 0.55. Design the wall using M20 grade concrete and HYSD reinforcement of grade Fe 415.

Solution :

(1) Coefficients of earth pressure

$$\phi = 30°$$

$$K_a = \frac{1 - \sin \phi}{1 + \sin \phi} = \frac{1 - 0.5}{1 + 0.5} = \frac{1}{3}$$

$$K_P = \frac{1 + \sin \phi}{1 - \sin \phi} = 3$$

(2) Preliminary proportions of wall dimensions

(i) Height - Assuming 1 m depth foundation

The overall height of wall = 4 + 1 = 5 m

(ii) Width of base :

For cantilever 'T' shaped wall, the minimum base width may be taken as

$$b = \sqrt{\frac{3\,P}{2\gamma}}$$

$$p = \frac{1}{2}\,K_a\,\gamma\,h^2 = \frac{1}{2} \times \frac{1}{3} \times 17 \times 5^2 = 70.83 \text{ kN}$$

$$b = \sqrt{\frac{3 \times 70.83}{2 \times 17}} = 2.5 \text{ m}$$

Toe width $= 0.33 \times 2.5 = 0.83$ m

Consider total width of foundation = 2.7 m and width of toe = 0.8 m.

(iii) Thickness of base slab :

$$\text{Thickness} = \frac{h}{15} \text{ to } \frac{h}{12}$$

H = 5000 mm, i.e. 333 mm to 416 mm consider uniform thickness of 350 mm.

(iv) Thickness of stem

This many be assumed considering the moment criterion.

Maximum moment at the base of stem $= \dfrac{1}{6}\,K_a\,\gamma\,h^3 = \dfrac{1}{6} \times \dfrac{1}{3} \times 17 \times 4.65^3$

$$= 94.96 \text{ kN m}$$

$$M_u = 1.5 \times 94.96$$

$$= 142.44 \text{ kN m}$$

$$d_{required} = \sqrt{\frac{142.44 \times 10^6}{2.76 \times 1000}}$$

$$= 227.2 \text{ mm}$$

$$D = 227.2 + 40 \text{ (cover)} + 10 \text{ (assume 20 \# bar)}$$

$$= 277.2 \text{ mm}$$

Provide an overall thickness of 350 mm at the base and 200 mm at the top.

The proposed arrangement is shown in Fig. 13.35 A base key of size 0.35 × 0.55 m is provided to resist sliding.

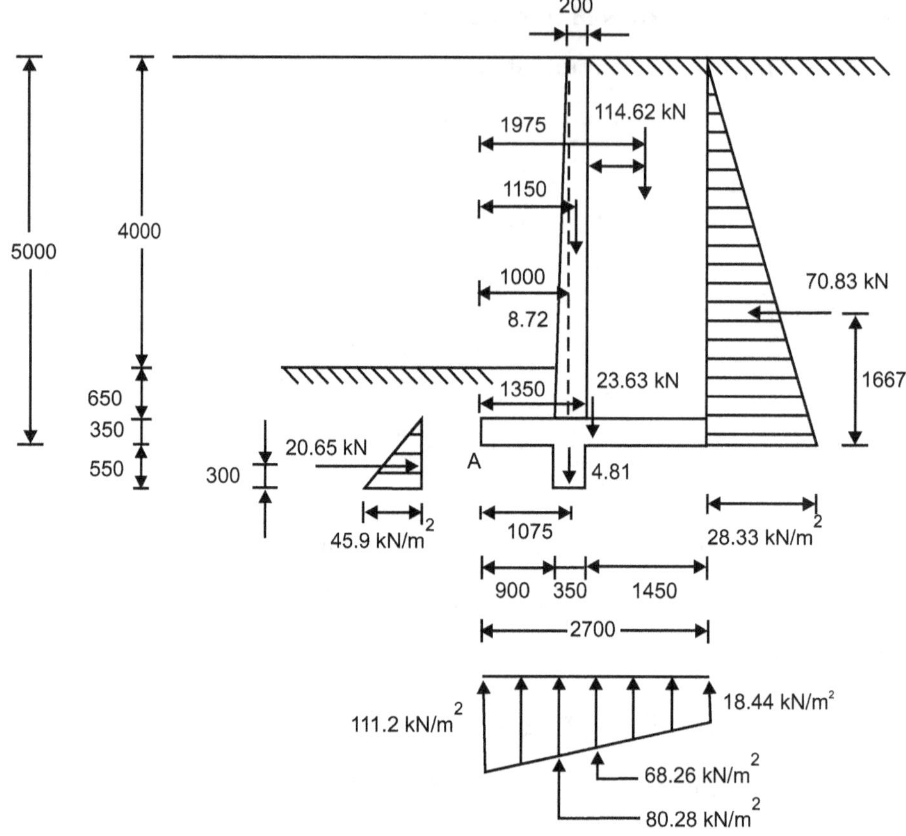

Fig. 13.35 : Soil pressure diagram

(3) Wall stability

Consider 1 m length of wall. Horizontal pressure at depth y from top

$$= K_a\, \gamma\, y = \frac{1}{3} \times 17 \times Y = 5.67\, Y \text{ kN / m}^2$$

Horizontal pressure at base $= 5.67 \times 5$

$$= 28.33 \text{ kN/m}^2$$

Stability calculations			
Load type	**Horizontal load (kN)**	**Distance from A (m)**	**Moment about A (kNm)**
Active pressure	$0.5 \times 28.33 \times 5 = 70.83$	1.667	− 118.07
	Total 70.83		− 118.07
	Vertical load (kN)		

...Conti.

Wall	$0.50 \times 0.15 \times 4.65 \times 25$	= 8.72	1.00	8.72
	$0.20 \times 4.65 \times 25$	= 23.25	1.15	26.74
Key	$0.35 \times 0.55 \times 25$	= 4.81	1.075	4.88
Base	$2.70 \times 0.35 \times 25$	= 23.63	1.35	31.90
Backfill	$1.45 \times 4.65 \times 17$	= 114.62	1.975	226.37
	Total	175 kN		298.61

Distance of c.g. of vertical force from the face of the toe i.e. from point A

$$= \frac{298.61 - 118.07}{175} = 1.028 \text{ m}$$

Eccentricity, $e = \dfrac{2.7}{2} - 1.028 = 0.322$ m

(i) Base properties are :

$$\text{Area A} = 1 \times 2.7 = 2.7 \text{ m}^3$$

$$\text{Modulus Z} = \frac{1}{6} \times 1 \times 2.7^2 = 1.215 \text{ m}^3$$

Maximum pressure at A

$$= \frac{175}{2.7} + \frac{175 \times 0.322}{1.215}$$

$$= 64.82 + 46.38$$

$$= 111.2 \text{ kN / m}^2 < 150 \text{ kN / m}^2 \qquad \text{...(safe)}$$

Minimum pressure at B

$$= 64.82 - 46.38$$

$$= 18.44 \text{ kN/m}^2 > 0 \qquad \text{...(safe)}$$

(ii) Factor of safety against overturning

Overturning moment $= 118.07$ kNm

Stabilizing moment $= 298.61$ kNm

Factor of safety $= \dfrac{298.61}{118.07} = 2.53 > 1.55 \qquad$ ...(safe)

(iii) Factor of safety against sliding :

Sliding force $=$ Active pressure $= 70.83$ kN

Passive pressure under the base of key

$$= 3 \times 17 \times 0.9 = 45.9 \text{ kN/m}^2$$

Friction under the base

Resistance to sliding $= +$ Passive resistance takes on a depth of
900 mm key i.e. to the top of the base

$$= MW + \frac{1}{2} K_p \gamma h^2$$

$$= 0.55 \times 175 + \frac{1}{2} \times 3 \times 17 \times 0.9^2$$

$$= 96.25 + 20.65$$

$$= 116.9 \text{ kN}$$

$$\text{Factor of safety} = \frac{116.9}{70.83} = 1.65 > 1.55 \qquad \text{...(safe)}$$

Note that if the key is not provided, this check would be critical and the base width has to be increased.

(4) Structural design

The structural design consists of design of stem, design of heel, design of toe and design of Key. These are designed below

(i) Stem :

$$\text{Pressure at the base} = 5.67 \times 4.65 = 26.37 \text{ kN/m}$$

$$\text{shear} = \frac{1}{2} \times 26.37 \times 4.65 = 61.31 \text{ kN}$$

$$\text{moment} = 61.31 \times \frac{4.65}{3} = 95.06 \text{ kNm}$$

$$V_u = 1.5 \times 61.31 = 91.96 \text{ kN}$$

$$M_u = 1.5 \times 95.03 = 142.55 \text{ kNm}$$

Assuming 20 mm diameter bars and 40 mm clear cover

$$d = 350 - 40 - 10 = 300 \text{ mm}$$

$$\frac{M_u}{bd^2} = \frac{142.55 \times 10^6}{1000 \times 300 \times 300} = 1.58$$

$$P_t = 0.487$$

$$A_{st} = 1461 \text{ mm}^2$$

Proxide 16 mm # (a) 130 mm c/c $= 1546$ mm

Let us now find the depth Y_1 from the top of the wall where half the bars can be curtailed

$$\text{At depth } Y_1 \qquad M_1 = \frac{1}{6} K_a \gamma y_1^3$$

$$= \frac{1}{6} \times \frac{1}{3} \times 17 \, Y_1^3$$

$$= 0.994 \, Y_1^3 \text{ kNm}$$

$$M_{u1} = 1.5 \, M_1$$

$$= 1.416 \, Y_1^3 \text{ kNm}$$

$$\text{Effective depth } d_1 = (200 - 50) + \frac{150}{4.65} Y_1$$

$$= (150 + 32.26\ Y_1)\text{ mm}$$

$$\text{Assume lever arm} = 0.9\ d_1$$

$$A_{st1} = \frac{1.416\ Y_1^3 \times 10^6}{0.87 \times 415 \times 0.9 \times (150 + 32.26\ Y_1)}$$

$$= \frac{A_{st}}{2} = \frac{1530}{2} = 765$$

$$\text{Which gives } \frac{4358\ Y_1^3}{150 + 32.26\ Y_1} = 765$$

$$\text{i.e. } 4358\ Y_1^3 = 114750 + 24679\ Y_1$$

$$\text{Simplifying } Y_1^3 - 5.66\ Y_1 - 26.33 = 0$$

Solving by successive trial $Y_1 = 3.6$ m

The bars should extend a development length from the theoretical point of cut off, i.e. at $3600 - 47 \times 16 = 2848$ mm from top curtail half the bars at 2.8 m from top.

$$\text{Shear at base} = 91.96\text{ kN}$$

$$\tau_v = \frac{91.96 \times 10^3}{1000 \times 300} = 0.307\text{ N/mm}^2$$

$$\frac{100\ As}{bd} = \frac{100 \times 1546}{1000 \times 300} = 0.052$$

$$\tau_c = 0.486\text{ N/mm}^2 \qquad\qquad …(safe)$$

Shear at theoretical cut off point,

$$\text{i.e. at} \qquad Y = 3.6\text{ m}$$

$$V = \frac{1}{2} \times \frac{1}{3} \times 17 \times 3.6^2 = 36.72\text{ kN}$$

$$V_u = 55.08\text{ kN}$$

$$d = 150 + 32.26 \times 3.6 = 266.1\text{ mm}$$

$$\tau_v = \frac{55.08 \times 10^3}{1000 \times 266.1} = 0.207\text{ N/mm}^2$$

$$\frac{100\ As}{bd} = \frac{100 \times 773}{1000 \times 266.1} = 0.29$$

$$\tau_c = 0.379\text{ N/mm}^2 \qquad\qquad …(safe)$$

$$\text{Development length} = 47 \times 16$$

$$= 752\text{ mm}$$

The bars should be anchored for 752 mm inside the support. The bars are anchored in toe and key and used as toe and key reinforcement.

Deflection need not be checked.

Maximum spacing for crack control for minimum secondary reinforcement provide 0.12% of gross area for HYSD bar.

At base

$$A_s = \frac{0.12}{100} \times 350 \times 1000$$

$$= 420 \text{ mm}^2$$

Use 10 mm # @ 180 mm c/c = 436 mm^2

At 2.7 m from top

$$D = 200 + \frac{150}{4.65} \times 2.7 = 287 \text{ mm}$$

$$A_s = \frac{0.12}{100} \times 287 \times 1000 = 344 \text{ mm}^2$$

Use 10 mm #@ 220 mm c/c = 357 mm^2

Maximum spacing at base = 3×300

$$= 900 \text{ mm or } 450 \text{ m}$$

i.e.   450 mm

Maximum spacing at top = 3×150

$$= 450 \text{ mm}$$

For crack control on outer face use 0.06% both ways on other face

At base, use 10 mm #@ 360 mm c/c

At 2.7 m from top, use 10 mm # @ 440 mm c/c.

(ii) Heel : Total downward pressure

= Weight of earth + Self weight of heel

= $4.65 \times 17 + 0.35 \times 25$

= $79.05 + 8.75$

= 87.8 kN/m^2

The net pressures are calculated in Fig. 13.36

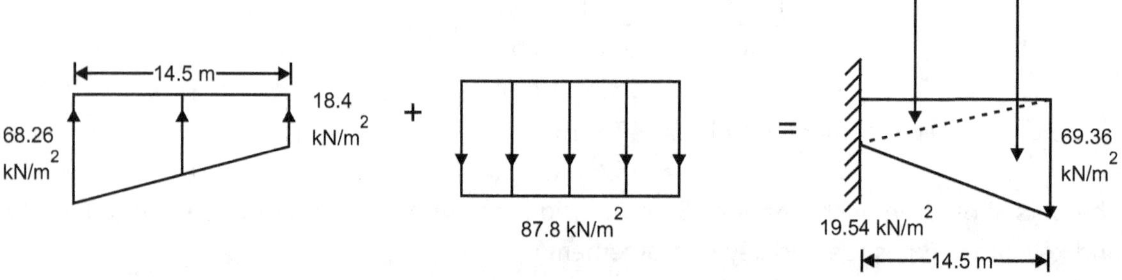

Fig. 13.36 : Net pressure on heel

$$\text{Shear} \;=\; \frac{1}{2} \times 19.54 \times 1.45 + \frac{1}{2} \times 69.36 \times 1.45$$

$$=\; 14.16 + 50.29 = 64.45 \text{ kN}$$

$$V_u \;=\; 96.67 \text{ kN}$$

$$\text{Moment} \;=\; 14.16 \times \frac{1.45}{3} + 50.29 \times \frac{2}{3} \times 1.45$$

$$=\; 6.84 + 48.61$$

$$=\; 55.45 \text{ kNm}$$

$$M_u \;=\; 83.18 \text{ kNm}$$

$$d \;=\; 350 - 40 - 10 = 300 \text{ mm}$$

$$\frac{M_u}{bd^2} \;=\; \frac{83.18 \times 10^6}{1000 \times 300 \times 300} = 0.924$$

$$pt \;=\; 0.272$$

$$A_{st} \;=\; 816 \text{ mm}^2$$

Provide 12 mm #@ 130 mm c/c = 869 mm^2

$$\tau_y \;=\; \frac{96.67 \times 10^3}{1000 \times 300} = 0.322 \text{ N/mm}^2$$

$$\frac{100\, A_s}{bd} \;=\; \frac{100 \times 869}{1000 \times 300} = 0.29$$

$$\tau_c \;=\; 0.379 \text{ N/mm}^2$$

$$\tau_y \;<\; \tau_c \qquad\qquad\qquad \text{...OK}$$

$$\text{Anchorage } 47 \times 12 \;=\; 564 \text{ mm}$$

There is 1200 mm available for anchorage

Distribution steel :

$$A_s \;=\; \frac{0.12}{100} \times 350 \times 1000$$

$$=\; 420 \text{ mm}^2$$

Provide 10 mm # @ 180 mm c/c = 436 mm^2

Provide 10 mm # @ 360 mm c/c both ways at bottom face for crack control.

(iii) Toe :

Total downward pressure

$$=\; \text{self weight of toe} = 0.35 \times 25$$

$$=\; 8.75 \text{ kN/m}^2$$

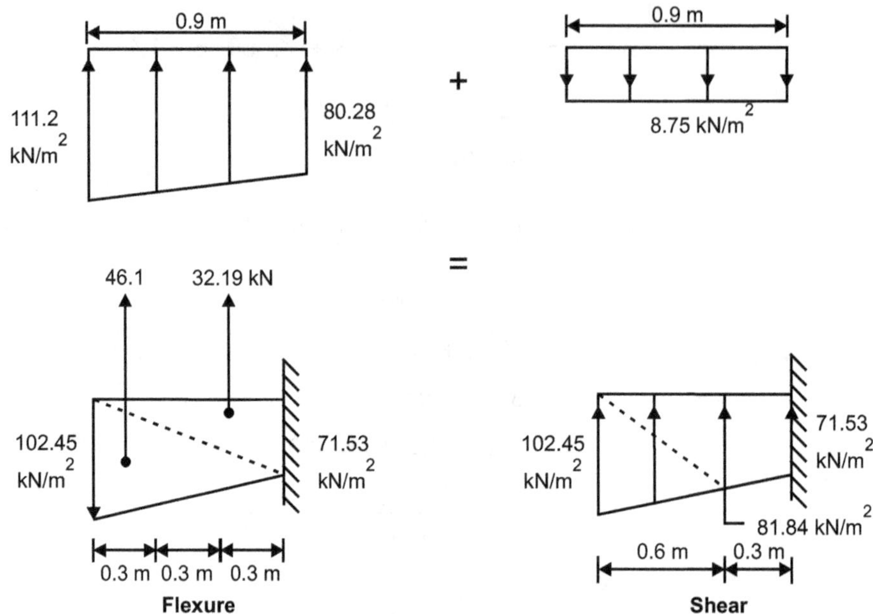

Fig. 13.37 : Net pressure on toe

Shear at distance (reinforcement confined by compressive reaction)

$$= \frac{102.45 + 81.84}{2} \times 0.6 = 55.29 \text{ kN}$$

$$V_u = 1.5 \times 55.29 = 82.93 \text{ kN}$$

$$\text{Moment} = 46.1 \times 0.6 + 32.19 \times 0.3$$
$$= 37.32 \text{ kNm}$$

$$M_u = 1.5 \times 37.32 = 56 \text{ kNm}$$

$$d = 350 - 40 - 10 = 300 \text{ mm}$$

$$\frac{M_u}{bd^2} = \frac{56 \times 10^6}{1000 \times 300 \times 300} = 0.62$$

$$p_t = 0.178$$

$$A_{st} = 534 \text{ mm}^2$$

Half the reinforcement of stem i.e. 16 mm # @ 260 mm c/c = 773 mm^2 anchored in toe will serve as toe reinforcement. The anchorage is provided by bend and a straight length of the bars along the toe.

$$\text{Let internal radius of bend } r = 200 \text{ mm}$$

$$a = 260 \text{ mm}$$

$$L_d = 47 \times 16$$
$$= 752 \text{ mm}$$

At centre of bend,

$$\text{Anchorage} = 244 \text{ mm}$$

$$\sigma_s = 0.87 \times 415 \times \frac{752 - 244}{752}$$

$$= 243.9 \text{ N/mm}^2$$

$$F_{bt} = 243.9 \times 201 \times 10^{-3} = 49 \text{ kN}$$

Design bearing strength

$$= \frac{1.5 \, F_{CK}}{1 + \frac{2\phi}{\propto}} = \frac{1.5 \times 20}{1 + \frac{2 \times 16}{260}} = 26.71 \text{ N/mm}^2$$

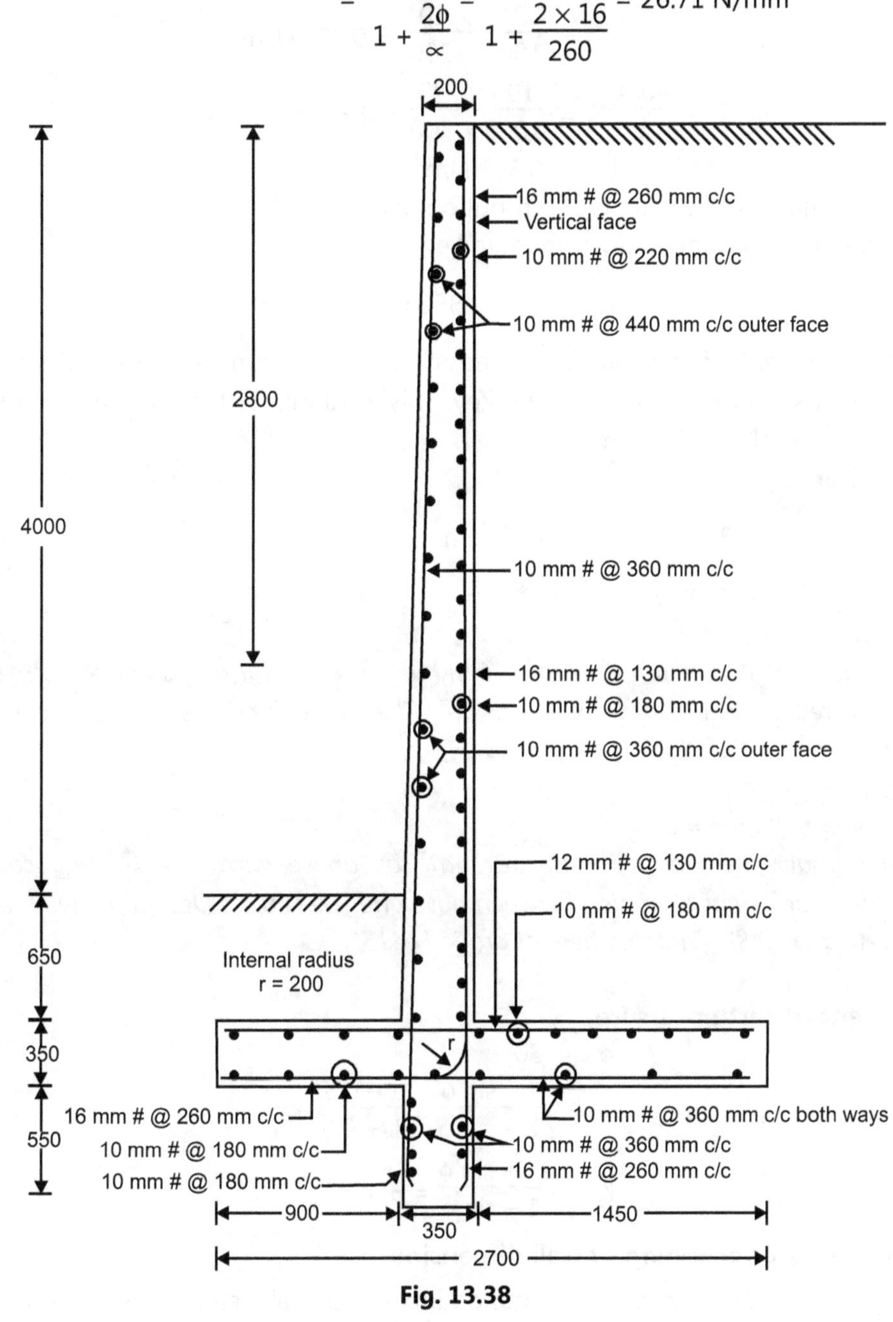

Fig. 13.38

$$\text{Actual bearing stress} \quad = \frac{F_{bt}}{r\phi} = \frac{49 \times 10^3}{200 \times 16}$$

$$= 15.3 \text{ N/mm}^2$$

$$< 26.71 \text{ N/mm}^2$$

Provide 200 mm internal radius of bend

$$\tau_y = \frac{82.93 \times 10^3}{1000 \times 300} = 0.276 \text{ N/mm}^2$$

$$\frac{100 \, A_s}{bd} = \frac{100 \times 773}{1000 \times 300} = 0.26$$

$$\tau_c = 0.351 \text{ N/mm}^2 \qquad\qquad\qquad \text{...(safe)}$$

Provide 10 mm # @ 180 mm c/c distribution bars.

(ii) Key : Provide minimum reinforcement in key

$$A_S = \frac{0.12}{100} \times 350 \times 1000 = 420 \text{ mm}^2$$

Half the reinforcement of stem are anchored in key = 773 mm^2. Also extend temperature reinforcement of stem on outerface in the key. This is 10 #@ 360 mm c/c = 170 mm^2. Total area in key = 773 + 218 = 991 mm^2

Distribution bars :

$$\frac{0.12}{100} \times 350 \times 1000 = 420 \text{ mm}^2$$

Provide 10 mm #@ 360 mm c/c on both faces.

Example 13.7 :

Design a retaining wall to retain the earth 4 m high. The top surface is horizontal behind the wall but subjected to a surcharge of 17 kN/m^2. The soil behind the wall is a well drained medium dense sand with following properties

Unit weight γ = 17 kN/m^3

Angle of internal friction ϕ = 30°

The material under the wall base is the same as above with safe bearing capacity of 150 kN/m^2. The coefficient of friction between base and soil is 0.55. Design the wall using M20 grade concrete and HYSD reinforcement of grade Fe415.

Solution :

(1) Coefficient of earth pressure :

$$\phi = 30°$$

$$k_a = \frac{1 - \sin \phi}{1 + \sin \phi} = \frac{1 - 0.5}{1 + 0.5} = \frac{1}{3}$$

$$K = \frac{1 + \sin \phi}{1 - \sin \phi} = 3$$

(2) Preliminary proportioning of wall dimensions :

(i) Height : Assuming 1 m depth of foundation, the overall height of wall 4 + 1 = 5 m

(ii) Width : For cantilever 'T' shaped wall the minimum width of the base may be taken as

$$b = \sqrt{\frac{3\,P}{2\gamma}}$$

$$P = \frac{1}{2} K_a\,\gamma\,h^2 + K_a\,W_s\,h$$

$$P = \frac{1}{2} \times \frac{1}{3} \times 17 \times 5^2 + \frac{1}{3} \times 17 \times 5$$

$$= 70.83 + 28.33$$

$$= 99.16 \text{ kN}$$

$$b = \sqrt{\frac{3 \times 99.16}{2 \times 17}}$$

$$b = 2.96 \text{ m}$$

$$\text{Toe width} = \frac{b}{3} = 0.99 \text{ m}$$

Consider total width foundation and $= 3.2$ m

$$\text{Width of toe} = 1 \text{ m}$$

(iii) Thickness of base slab : equivalent height of surcharge.

$$= \frac{W_s}{\gamma} = \frac{17}{17} = 1.0 \text{ m}$$

$$h = 5 + 1 = 6 \text{ m}$$

$$\text{Thickness} = \frac{h}{15} \text{ to } \frac{h}{12} = 400 \text{ mm to } 500 \text{ mm}$$

Consider uniform thickness of 450 mm

(iv) Thickness of stem : This may be assumed considering the moment criterion

$$h = 5.0 - 0.45 = 4.55 \text{ m}$$

maximum moment at the base of stem

$$= \frac{1}{6} K_a \cdot \gamma \cdot h^3 + \frac{1}{2} k_a\,W_s\,h^2$$

$$= \frac{1}{6} \times \frac{1}{3} \times 17 \times 4.55^3 + \frac{1}{2} \times \frac{1}{3} \times 17 \times 4.55^2$$

$$= 88.96 + 58.66$$

$$= 147.6 \text{ kNm}$$

$$Mu = 1.5 \times 147.6 = 221.25 \text{ kNm}$$

$$d = \sqrt{\frac{221.25 \times 10^6}{1000 \times 2.76}}$$

$$= 283 \text{ mm}$$

Assuming 16 mm diameter bars

$$D = 283 + 40 \text{ (cover)} + 8 = 331 \text{ mm}$$

Consider D = 400 mm reduce to 200 mm at top.

The proposed arrangement is is shown in Fig. 13.20.

A base key of size 400 mm × 750 mm is provided to resist sliding.

(3) Wall stability :

Consider 1 m length of wall surcharge is equivalent to additional height.

$$= \frac{W_s}{\gamma} = \frac{17}{17} = 1 \text{ m}$$

Total equivalent height = 5 + 1 = 6 m

Horizontal pressure at depth y from top of surcharge

$$= K_a \gamma \cdot y = \frac{1}{3} \times 17 \times y = 5.67 \, y \text{ KN/m}^2$$

Horizontal pressure at top of the wall

$$= 5.67 \times 1 = 5.67 \, y \text{ kN/m}^2$$

Horizontal pressure at the base of the wall

$$= 5.67 \times 6 = 34 \text{ kN/m}^2$$

Stability calculations are tabulated in table.

Stability calculations :

Load type	Horizontal load (kN)		Distance from A (m)	Moment @ A (kNm)
Active	5.67×5	= 28.35	2.500	– 70.88
pressure	$0.5 \times 28.33 \times 5$	= 70.83	1.667	– 118.07
	Total	99.18		– 188.95
	Vertical load (kN)			
Wall	$0.5 \times 0.2 \times 4.55 \times 25$	= 11.38	1.133	12.89
	$0.2 \times 4.55 \times 25$	= 22.75	1.30	29.58
Key	$0.40 \times 0.75 \times 25$	= 7.50	1.20	9.00
Base	$3.2 \times 0.45 \times 25$	= 36.00	1.60	57.60
Backfill	$1.8 \times 4.55 \times 17$	= 139.23	2.30	320.23
Surcharge	1.8×17	= 130.60	2.30	70.38
	Total	247.46 kN		499.68 kNm

Distance of c.g. of vertical forces from the face of the toe (point A)

$$= \frac{499.68 - 188.95}{247.46}$$

$$= 1.26 \text{ m}$$

$$\text{Eccentricity e} = \frac{3.2}{2} - 1.26$$

$$= 0.34 \text{ m}$$

(i)   Base properties are

$$\text{Area } A = 1 \times 3.2 = 3.2 \text{ m}^2$$

$$z = \frac{1}{6} \times 1 \times 3.2^2 = 1.707 \text{ m}^3$$

Maximum soil pressure at A

$$= \frac{247.46}{3.2} + \frac{247.46 \times 0.34}{1.707}$$

$$= 77.33 + 49.29$$

$$= 126.62 \text{ kN/m}^2 < 150 \text{ kN/m}^2 \qquad \qquad ...(OK)$$

Minimum soil pressure at B

$$= 77.33 - 49.29$$

$$= 28.04 \text{ kN/m}^2 > 0 \qquad \qquad ...(OK)$$

The earth pressures and forces are shown in Fig. 13.39.

(ii)   Factor of safety against overturning   with surcharge   without surcharges

	with surcharge	without surcharges	
Overturning moment	188.95 kNm	118.07 kNm	
Stabilizing moment	499.68 kNm	4.930 kNm	
Factor of safety	2.644 71.55	3.63 > 1.55	...(OK)

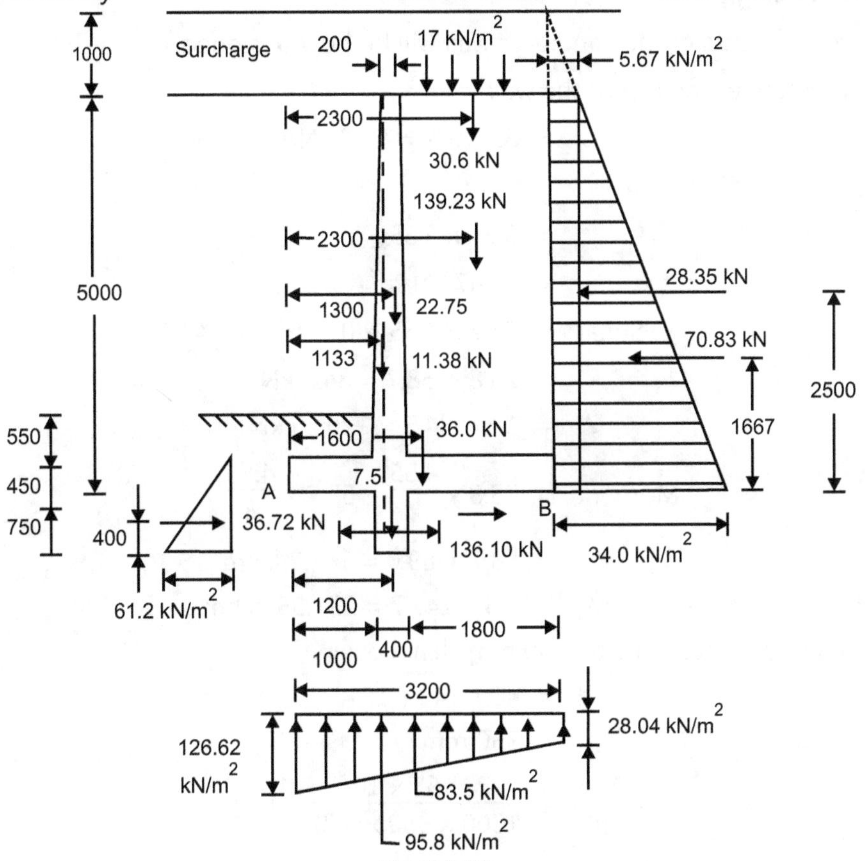

Fig. 13.39

(ii)   Factor of safety against sliding

Sliding force = active pressure = 99.18 kN

Passive pressure under the base of key

$$= 3 \times 17 \times 1.2 = 61.2 \text{ kN/m}^2$$

Resistance to sliding   = Friction under the base + Passive resistance taken on a depth of earth 1200 mm (on key) i.e. to the top of the base

$$= \mu W + \frac{1}{2} \times 61.2 \times 1.2$$

$$= 0.55 \times 247.46 + 36.72 + 136.10 + 36.72$$

$$= 172.82 \text{ kN}$$

$$\text{Factor of safety} \quad = \frac{172.82}{99.18} = 1.74 > 1.55 \qquad \text{...(OK)}$$

The assumed section is thus satisfactory.

(4) Structural design :

All the components of the cantilever wall will be bow designed.

(i)   Stem : Pressure at the top of the wall

$$= 5.67 \times 1 = 5.67 \text{ kN/m}^2$$

Pressure at the base of the wall

$$= 5.67 \times 5.55$$

$$= 31.47 \text{ kN/m}^2$$

$$\text{Shear} \quad = 5.67 \times 4.55 + 0.5 \times 25.8 \times 4.55$$

$$= 25.8 + 58.7 = 84.5 \text{ kN}$$

$$V_u \quad = 1.5 \times 84.5 = 126.75 \text{ kN}$$

$$\text{Moment} \quad = 25.8 \times \frac{4.55}{2} + 58.7 \times \frac{4.55}{3}$$

$$= 58.7 + 89.0 = 147.7 \text{ kNm}$$

$$M_u \quad = 1.5 \times 147.7 = 221.55 \text{ kNm}$$

Assuming 20 mm diameter bars and 40 mm clear cover

$$d \quad = 400 - 40 - 10$$

$$= 350 \text{ mm}$$

$$\frac{M_u}{bd^2} \quad = \frac{221.55 \times 10^6}{1000 \times 350 \times 350} = 1.81$$

$$P_t \quad = 0.569, \ A_{st} = 1992 \text{ mm}^2$$

Provide 20 mm #@ 150 mm c/c = 2093 mm^2 Let us now find out the depth Y_1 from the top of the wall where half the bars can be curtailed.

At depth Y_1

$$M_1 = 5.67 \frac{Y_1^3}{6} + 5.67 \frac{Y_1^2}{2}$$

$$= \left(0.945\, Y_1^3 + 2.835\, Y_1^2\right) \text{ kNm}$$

$$\text{Effective depth } d_1 = (200 - 50) + \frac{200}{4.55} y_1$$

$$= 150 + 43.96\, y_1$$

$$A_{st1} = \frac{2093}{2} = 1047 \text{ mm}^2$$

$$\text{Assuming lever arm} = 0.9\, d_1$$

$$A_{st1} = \frac{1.5 \left(0.945\, Y_1^3 + 2.835\, Y_1^2\right) \times 10^6}{0.87 \times 415 \times 0.9\, (150 + 43.96\, Y_1)}$$

$$= 1047$$

Simplifying, we get

$$Y_1^3 + 3\, Y_1^2 - 10.55\, Y_1 - 36 = 0$$

Solving by trial and error

$$Y_1 = 3.36 \text{ m}$$

The bars should extend a development length from the theoretical point of cut off, i.e. upto $3360 - 47 \times 20 = 2420$ mm from top.

Curtail half the bars at 2.4 m from top

$$\text{Share at base} = 126.75 \text{ kN}$$

$$\tau_v = \frac{126.75 \times 10^3}{1000 \times 350}$$

$$= 0.362 \text{ N/mm}^2$$

$$\frac{100\, A_s}{bd} = \frac{100 \times 2093}{1000 \times 350}$$

$$= 0.598$$

$$= 0.511 \text{ N/mm}^2$$

$$\tau_v < \tau_c \qquad\qquad \text{...(OK)}$$

Shear at theoretical cut off point at 3.36 m from top

$$= 5.67 \times 3.36 + \frac{1}{2} \times \frac{1}{3} \times 17 \times 3.36$$

$$= 51.04 \text{ kN}$$
$$V_u = 76.56 \text{ kN}$$
$$d = 150 + 43.96 \times 3.36$$
$$= 298 \text{ mm}$$
$$\tau_v = \frac{76.56 \times 10^3}{1000 \times 298}$$
$$= 0.257 \text{ N/mm}^2 \qquad \text{...(safe)}$$
$$\text{Development length} = 20 \times 47$$
$$= 940 \text{ mm}$$

The bars should be properly anchored inside the support. Half the bars are anchored in toe and used as toe reinforcement. Remaining half the bars are anchored in key and used as key reinforcements.

Deflection need not be checked.

Maximum spacing for crack control

$$\text{At base spacing} = 3 \times 350 = 1050 \text{ or } 450 \text{ i.e. } 450 \text{ mm}$$

At base spacing $= 3 \times 150 = 450$ mm.

For minimum secondary reinforcement provide 0.12 per cent of the gross area for HYSD bars.

(a) Inner face:

$$\text{At base } A_s = \frac{0.12}{100} \times 400 \times 1000$$
$$= 480 \text{ mm}^2$$

Use 10 mm #@ 160 mm/cc = 491 mm^2

At 2.8 m from top, D = 200 + 43.96 × 2.4 = 305.5 mm

$$A_s = \frac{0.12}{100} \times 305.5 \times 1000$$
$$= 367 \text{ mm}^2$$

Use 10 mm #@ 200 mm cc = 392 mm.

(b) Outer face : Provide 0.06% both ways.

At base, $A_s = 240$ mm^2

Use 10 mm #@ 320 mm c/c = 245 mm^2

At 2.4 m from top $A_s = 184$ mm^2

Use 10 mm # @ 400 mm c/c = 196 mm^2

(ii) Heel :

Total downward pressure

$$= \text{Weight of earth + Self – Weight of heel + Surcharge}$$

$$= 4.55 \times 17 + 0.45 \times 25 + 17$$
$$= 105.6 \text{ kN/m}^2$$

The net pressures on heel are calculated in Fig. 13.40

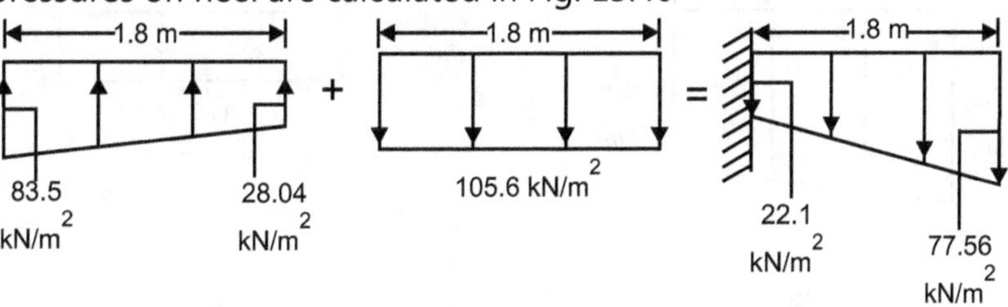

Fig. 13.40 : Net pressure on heel

$$\text{Shear} = \frac{1}{2} \times 22.1 \times 1.80 + \frac{1}{2} \times 77.56 \times 1.80$$
$$= 19.90 + 69.8$$
$$= 89.7 \text{ kN}$$
$$V_u = 134.55 \text{ kN}$$
$$\text{Moment} = 19.9 \times 0.6 + 69.8 \times 1.2 = 95.7 \text{ kNm}$$
$$M_u = 143.55 \text{ kNm (tension top)}$$
$$d = 450 - 40 - 10 = 400 \text{ mm}$$
$$\frac{M_u}{bd^2} = \frac{143.55 \times 10^6}{1000 \times 400 \times 400} = 0.897$$
$$P_t = 0.263, \quad A_{st} = 1052 \text{ mm}^2$$

Provided 16 mm #@ 190 mm C/C = 1058 mm²

$$\tau_v = \frac{134.55 \times 10^3}{1000 \times 400}$$
$$= 0.336 \text{ N/mm}^2$$
$$\frac{100 A_s}{bd} = \frac{100 \times 1058}{1000 \times 400}$$
$$= 0.265$$
$$\tau_c = 0.367 \text{ N/mm}^2 \qquad \qquad ...(OK)$$
$$\text{Anchorage} = 16 \times 47 = 752 \text{ mm}$$

There is 1400 mm available for anchorage distribution steel.

$$\frac{0.12}{100} \times 450 \times 1000 = 540 \text{ mm}^2$$

Provide 10 mm #@ 140 mm c/c = 560 mm²

Provide 10 mm #@ 280 mm c/c both ways on outer face for crack control.

(iii) Toe :

Total downward pressure

$$= \text{self weight of toe} = 0.45 \times 25 = 11.2 \text{ kN}$$

The net pressures are calculated in Fig. 13.41

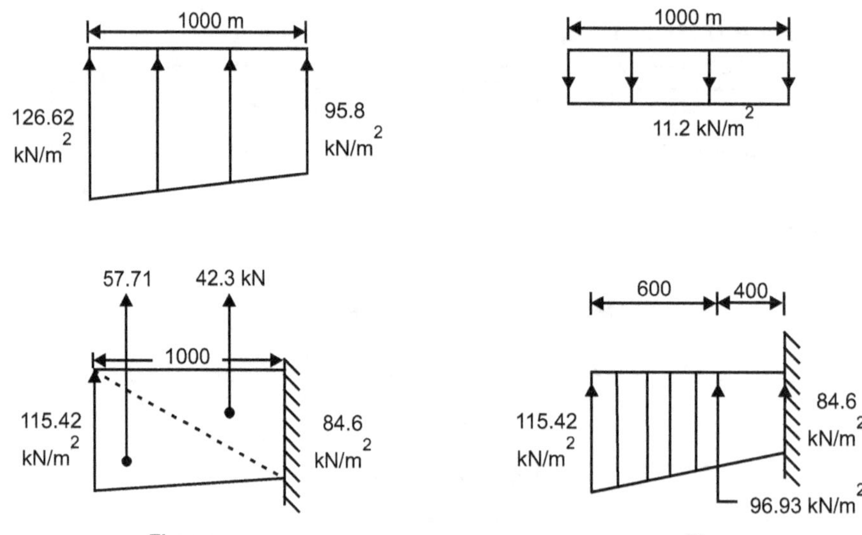

Fig. 13.41 : Net pressure on toe

Share (at d = 400 mm)

$$V = \frac{1}{2} \times 115.42 \times 0.6 + \frac{1}{2} \times 96.93 \times 0.6$$

$$= 34.63 + 29.07 = 63.7 \text{ kN}$$

$$V_u = 1.5 \times 63.7$$

$$= 95.5 \text{ kN}$$

$$\text{Moment } M = \frac{115.42}{2} \times \frac{2}{3} + \frac{84.6}{2} \times \frac{1}{3}$$

$$= 52.57 \text{ kNm}$$

$$M_u = 78.86 \text{ kNm}$$

$$\frac{M_u}{bd^2} = \frac{78.86 \times 10^6}{1000 \times 400 \times 400}$$

$$= 0.493$$

$$P = 0.141$$

$$A_{st} = 564 \text{ mm}^2$$

Half the reinforcement of stem i.e. 20 mm #@ 300 mm c/c = 1046 mm^2 anchored in toe will serve as toe reinforcement. The anchorage is provided by bend. And a straight length of bar along the toe.

$$L_d = 47 \times 20 = 940 \text{ mm}$$

$$\text{Let the radius of bend } r = 250 \text{ mm}, \ a = 360 \text{ mm}$$

$$\text{At centre of bend anchorage} = 347 \text{ mm}$$

$$\sigma_s = 0.87 \times 415 \times \frac{1126 - 347}{1126}$$

$$= 249.8 \text{ N/mm}^2$$

$$F_{bt} = 249.8 \times 314 \times 10^{-3} = 78.4 \text{ kN}$$

$$\text{Design bearing strength} = \frac{1.5 \, f_{CK}}{1 + \dfrac{2\phi}{\propto}}$$

$$= \frac{1.5 \times 20}{1 + \dfrac{2 \times 20}{360}}$$

$$= 27 \text{ N/mm}^2$$

$$\text{Actual bearing stress} = \frac{f_{bt}}{r\phi}$$

$$= \frac{78.4 \times 10^3}{200 \times 20}$$

$$= 19.6 \text{ N/mm}^2 \qquad \qquad ...(OK)$$

Provide 200 mm internal radius,

$$\tau_v = \frac{95.5 \times 10^3}{1000 \times 400}$$

$$= 0.239 \text{ N/mm}^2$$

$$\frac{100 \, As}{bd} = \frac{100 \times 1046}{100 \times 400}$$

$$= 0.262$$

$$\tau_c = 0.365 \text{ N/mm}^2$$

Provide 10 mm#@ 140 mm c/c distribution bars.

(iv) Key :

Provide minimum reinforcement in key

$$A_s = \frac{0.12}{100} \times 400 \times 1000$$

$$= 480 \text{ mm}^2$$

Half the reinforcement of stem are anchored in key = 1046 mm^2

Also extend temperature reinforcement of stem on outer face in the key.

This is 10 mm#@ 360 mm c/c = 218 mm^2

$$\text{Total area in key} \;=\; 1046 + 218 = 1264 \text{ mm}$$

Face as distribution bars,

$$A_S \;=\; 2 \times 261 = 512 \text{ mm}^2$$

(v) Sketch : The cross section of the designed retaining wall with reinforcement detail is shown in Fig. 13.42.

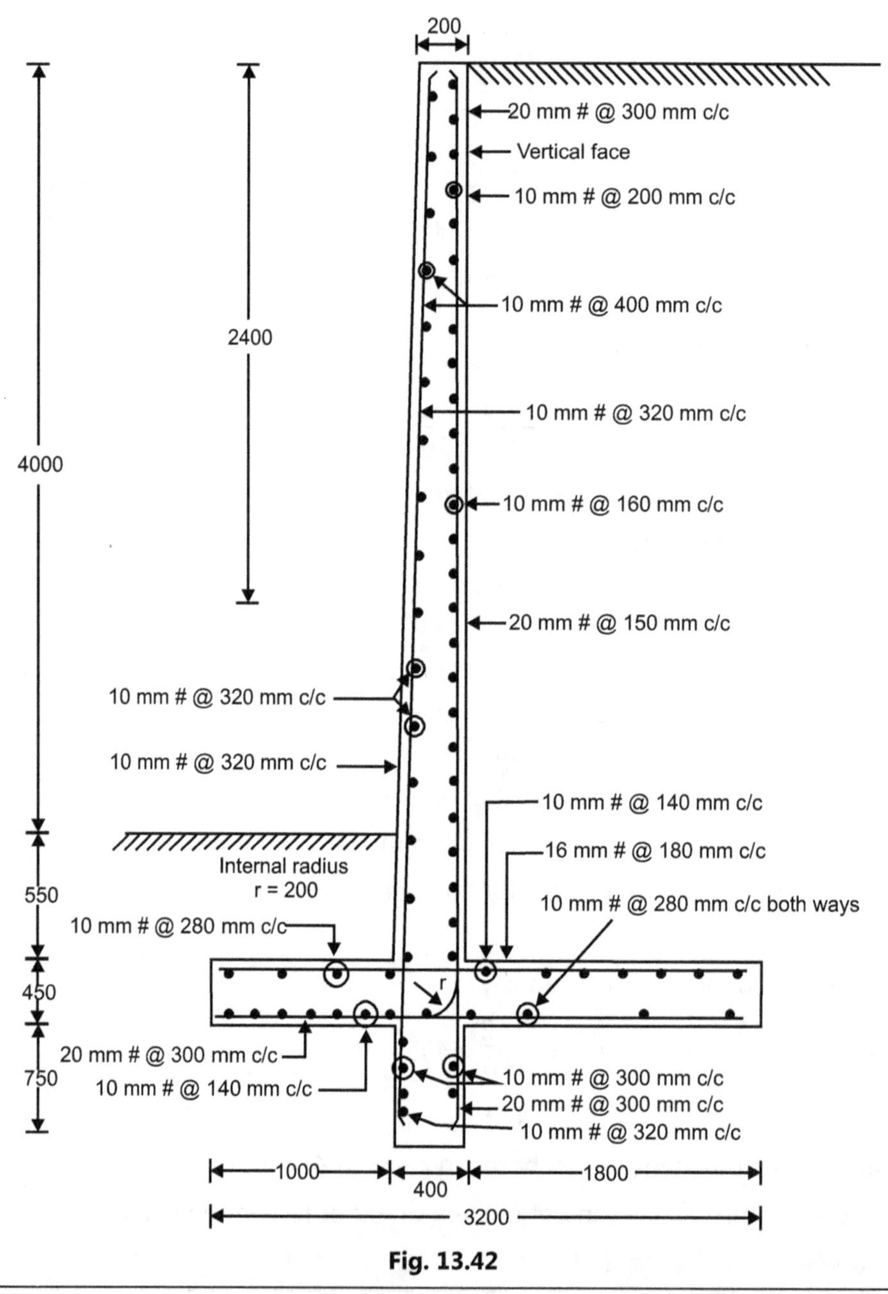

Fig. 13.42

Example 13.8 :

Design a T-shaped cantilever retaining wall to retain earth embankment 3 m high above ground level. The unit weight of earth is 18 kN/m^3 and its angle of repose is 30°. The embankment is horizontal at its top. The safe bearing capacity of soil may be taken as 100 kN/m^2 and the coefficient of friction between soil and concrete as 0.5 use M 15 mix. Take

σ_{st} = *140 N/mm^2*   **[May 2015]**

Solution :

1. Design constants :

For M15 concrete and mild steel reinforcement, we have the following values:

$$C = \sigma_{cbc} = 5\ N/mm^2 \quad t = \sigma_{st} = 140\ N/mm^2$$

$$m = 19,\ K = 0.404;\ j = 0.865 \text{ and}$$

$$R = 0.874$$

2. Depth of foundation

$\gamma = 18\ kN/m^2 = 1800\ N/m^3$

The minimum depth of foundation is

$$y_{min} = \frac{q_o}{\gamma}\left(\frac{1 - \sin\phi}{1 + \sin\phi}\right)^2$$

$$= \frac{100}{18}\left(\frac{1 - \sin 30°}{1 + \sin 30°}\right)^2$$

$$= 0.62\ m$$

However, keep depth = 1 m to accommodate thickness of base wall below the ground surface. Hence, height of wall above its base = H = 3 + 1 = 4 m.

3. Dimensions of base :

The ratio of the length of toe slab (DE) to the base width is given by

$$\propto\ =\ 1 - \frac{q_o}{2.2\ \gamma H} = 1 - \frac{100}{2.2 \times 18 \times 4} = 0.365$$

$$\text{Keep} \propto\ =\ 0.37$$

The width of base is

$$b = 0.95\ H\sqrt{\frac{K_a}{(1 - \propto)(1 + 3\propto)}}$$

$$k_a = \frac{1 - \sin \phi}{1 + \sin \phi}$$

$$= \frac{1 - \sin 30°}{1 + \sin 30°} = \frac{1}{3}$$

$$b = 0.95 \times 4 \sqrt{\frac{1}{3(1 - 0.37)(1 + 3 \times 0.37)}}$$

$$= 1.90 \text{ m}$$

The base width from the consideration of sliding is,

$$b = \frac{0.7 \, HK_a}{(1 - \propto)\mu}$$

$$= \frac{0.7 \times 4}{1 - 0.37} \times \frac{1}{3 \times 0.5}$$

$$= 2.96 \text{ m}$$

This width is excessive normal practice is to provide b between 0.4 to 0.6 H. Taking maximum value of 0.6 H.

$$b = 0.6 \, H = 0.6 \times 4 = 2.4 \text{ m}$$

  Hence, provide to = 2.4 m. The wall be unsafe against sliding. This is well be made safe by providing a shear key at the base.

$$\text{Width of toe slab} = 0.37 \times 2.4 = 0.89 \text{ m}$$

$$\text{Provide toe slab} = 0.9 \text{ m long}$$

Let the thickness of base be $\frac{1}{12}\,H \approx 0.3$ m for preliminary calculations.

4. **Thickness of stem :** height AB = 4 – 0.3 = 3.7 m

  Consider one meter length of retaining wall.

$$\text{Maximum bending moment at B} = k_a \, \gamma \frac{H_1^3}{6}$$

$$= \frac{1}{3}\frac{18}{6}(3.7)^3$$

$$= 50.65 \text{ kN-m}$$

$$= 50.65 \times 10^6 \text{ N-mm}$$

Hence the effective depth is d $= \sqrt{\dfrac{50.65 \times 10^6}{1000 \times 0.874}}$

$= 241$ mm

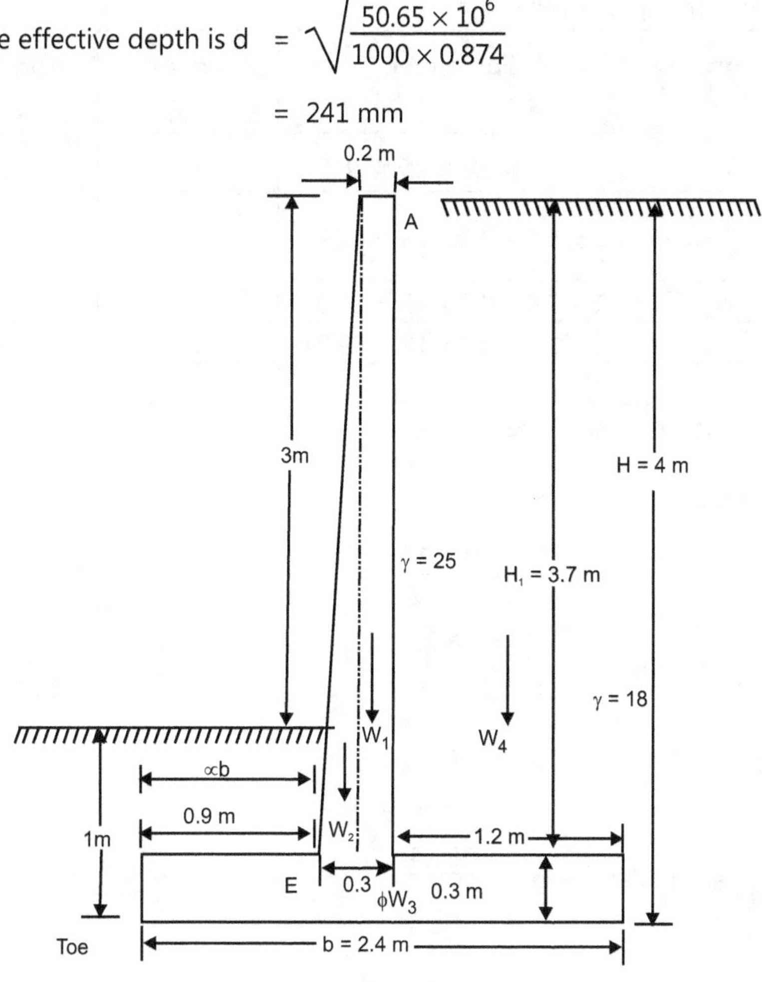

Fig. 13.43

Keep d = 240 mm and total thickness = 300 mm so that an effective cover of 60 mm is available. Reduce the total thickness to 200 mm at the top so that effective depth of 140 mm is available at top.

5. Stability of wall :

Fully dimensioned wall is shown in Fig. 13.14.

Let, W_1 = Weight of rectangular portion of stem

W_2 = Weight of triangular portion of stem

W_3 = Weight of base slab

W_4 = Weight of soil on heel slab

The calculation are arranged in Table

Sr. No	Designation	Force (kN)	Lever arm (m)	Moment about (kN-m)
1.	W_1	$1 \times 0.2 \times 3.7 \times 25 = 18.5$	1.1	20.35
2.	W_2	$\frac{1}{2} \times 0.1 \times 3.7 \times 25 = 4.63$	0.97	4.49
3.	W_3	$1 \times 2.4 \times 0.3 \times 25 = 18.0$	1.2	21.60
4.	W_4	$1 \times 1.2 \times 3.7 \times 18 = 79.97$	1.8	143.86
		$\Sigma W = 121.05$		$M_R = 190.30$

The total resisting moment $M_R = 190.30$ kN-m

$$\text{Earth pressure} \qquad P = K_a \, \gamma \frac{H^2}{2}$$

$$= \frac{1}{3} \times \frac{18}{2} \, (4)^2$$

$$= 48 \text{ kN}$$

Overtuning :

$$\text{overtuning moment,} \quad M_o = 48 \times \frac{4}{3}$$

$$= 64 \text{ kN-m}$$

$$\therefore \quad \text{F.S. against overtuning} = \frac{190.3}{64}$$

$$= 2.97 > 2 \qquad\qquad \text{Hence safe}$$

Sliding :

$$\text{F.S. against sliding} = \frac{\mu \Sigma W}{P}$$

$$= \frac{0.5 \times 121.05}{48}$$

$$= 1.26 < 1.5 \qquad\qquad \text{Hence unsafe.}$$

To make it safe against sliding we will have to provide a share key.

Pressure distribution net moment $\Sigma M = 190.3 - 64 = 126.3$ kN-m

$\therefore$ Distance $\bar{x}$ of the point of application of resultant from toe is

$$\bar{x} = \frac{\Sigma M}{\Sigma W}$$

$$= \frac{126.3}{121.05} = 1.04 \text{ m}$$

$$\text{Eccentricity,} \quad e = \frac{b}{2} - \bar{x} = 1.2 - 1.04 = 0.16 \text{ m}$$

This is less than $\dfrac{b}{6} \left(= \dfrac{2.4}{6} = 0.4 \text{ m} \right)$

$$\begin{aligned}
\text{Pressure } P_1 \text{ at toe} &= \frac{\Sigma W}{b} \left(1 + \frac{6e}{b} \right) \\[2mm]
&= \frac{121.05}{2.4} \left(1 + \frac{6 \times 0.16}{2.4} \right) \\[2mm]
&= 70.61 \text{ kN/m}^2 < 100 \qquad \text{Hence safe} \\[2mm]
\text{Pressure } P_2 \text{ at heel} &= \frac{\Sigma W}{b} \left(1 - \frac{6e}{b} \right) \\[2mm]
&= \frac{121.05}{2.4} \left(1 - \frac{6 \times 0.16}{2.4} \right) \\[2mm]
&= 30.26 \text{ kN/m}^2
\end{aligned}$$

Pressure P at the junction of stem with toe slab is

$$\begin{aligned}
P &= 70.61 - \frac{70.61 - 30.26}{2.4} \times 0.9 \\[2mm]
&= 55.48 \text{ kN/m}^2
\end{aligned}$$

Pressure P′ at the junction of stem with heel slab is

$$\begin{aligned}
P' &= 70.61 - \frac{70.61 - 30.26}{2.4} \times 1.2 \\[2mm]
&= 50.44 \text{ kN/m}^2
\end{aligned}$$

6. Design of toe slab :

The upward pressure distribution on the toe slab is shown in Fig. 13.44. The weight of the soil above the toe slab is neglected. Thus, two forces are acting on

(i)   Upward soil pressure

(ii) Downward weight of slab

Downward weight of slab per unit area

$$= 0.3 \times 1 \times 1 \times 25 = 7.5 \text{ kN/m}^2$$

Hence net pressure intensities will be

$$= 70.61 - 7.5 = 63.11$$

k/m^2 under D and $55.48 - 7.5 = 47.98$ kN/m^2 under E.

Total force = S.F. at E $= \dfrac{1}{2}(63.11 + 47.98)\, 0.9 = 50$ kN

$$\bar{x} \text{ from E} = \left(\frac{47.98 + 2\times 63.11}{47.98 + 63.11}\right)\frac{0.9}{3}$$

$$= 0.47 \text{ m}$$

$\therefore$ B.M. at E $= 50 \times 0.47 = 23.52$ kN-m $= 23.52 \times 10^6$ N-m

Let us keep total depth = 260 mm and effective depth of 200 mm so that 60 mm effective cover is available. Thickness can be reduced to 200 mm at the edge.

$$A_{st} = \frac{23.52 \times 10^6}{140 \times 0.865 \times 200} = 971 \text{ mm}^2$$

This reinforcement has to be provided at the bottom face. If alternate bars of stem reinforcement are bent and continued in the toe slab, area available $= \dfrac{1}{2}\times 201$

$= 1005 \text{ mm}^2$

This reinforcement will consist of 16 ϕ bar @ 200 mm c/c. Let us check this reinforcement for development length.

$$L_d \approx 58.3\,\phi = 58.3 \times 16 = 933 \text{ mm.}$$

Providing 50 mm. Clear side cover, actual length. Available = 900 – 50 + anchorage value of hook

$$= 850 + 13 \times 16 = 850 + 208 = 1058 > L_d. \quad \text{Hence safe.}$$

$$\text{Distribution reinforcement} = \frac{0.15}{100} \times 1000 \left[\frac{260 + 200}{2}\right]$$

$$= 345 \text{ mm}^2$$

$$\text{Using 8 mm } \phi \text{ bars, } A\phi = 50.3 \text{ mm}^2$$

$$\therefore \qquad \text{Spacing} = \frac{1000 \times 50.3}{345} = 146 \text{ mm}$$

Hence, provide these @ 140 mm c/c.

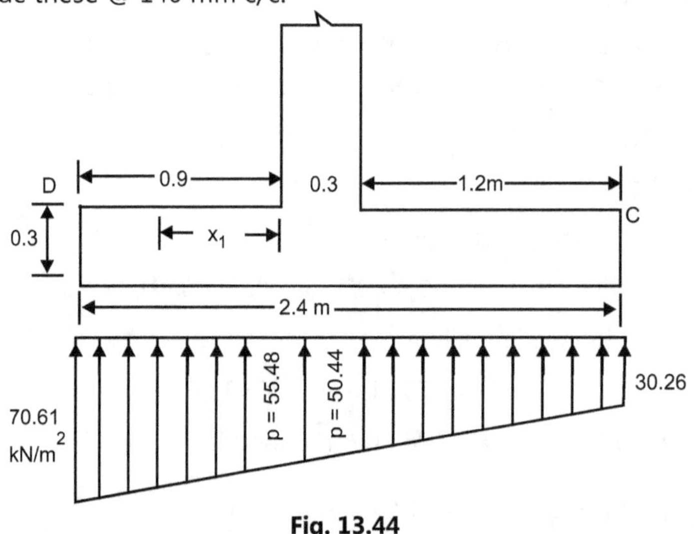

Fig. 13.44

7. Design of heel slab :

Three forces acts on it:

(i) Downward weight of soil 3.7 m high

(ii) Downward weight of heel slab

(iii) Upward soil pressure

$$\text{Total weight of soil} = 1.2 \times 3.7 \times 1 \times 18 = 80 \text{ kN acting at 0.6 m from B.}$$

Total weight of heel slab : $1.2 \times 0.26 \times 1 \times 25 = 7.8$ acting at 0.6 m from B

$$\text{Total upward soil reaction} = \frac{1}{2}(50.44 + 30.26)\,1.2$$

48.42 kN acting at $\left(\dfrac{50.44 + 2 \times 30.26}{50.44 + 30.26}\right)\dfrac{1.2}{3} = 0.55$ m From B.

$\therefore$

$$\text{Total force} = \text{S.F at B} = 80 + 7.8 - 48.42 = 39.38 \text{ kN}$$

$$\text{B.M at B} = (80 \times 0.6) + (7.8 \times 0.6) - (48.42 \times 0.55)$$

$$= 26.05 \text{ kN-m} = 26.05 \times 10^6 \text{ N-mm}$$

$\therefore$

$$d = \sqrt{\frac{26.05 \times 10^6}{1000 \times 0.874}} = 173 \text{ mm}$$

However keep the same total depth (= 260 mm) as that of toe slab, so that available effective depth = 200 mm. The thickness reduced to 200 mm at the edge.

$$A_{st} = \frac{26.05 \times 10^6}{140 \times 0.864 \times 200} = 1077 \text{ mm}^2$$

Using 12 mm ϕ bars $A\phi = 113 \text{ mm}^2$

$\therefore$

$$\text{Spacing} = \frac{1000 \times 113}{1077} \approx 105 \text{ mm}$$

Hence, provide these @ 100 mm c/c. Take the reinforcement into the toe slab from a distance of 58.3 ϕ = 58.3 × 12 = 7 mm to the left of B, and its ends should be hooked.

$$\text{Distribution steel} = \frac{0.15}{100} \times 1000 \left[\frac{260 + 200}{2}\right]$$

$$= 345 \text{ mm}^2$$

$\therefore$

$$\text{Spacing} = \frac{1000 \times 50.3}{345} = 146 \text{ mm.} \qquad \text{Hence proved.}$$

Three @ 140 mm c/c.

$$\text{Shear stress } \tau_v = \frac{39.38 \times 1000}{1000 \times 200} = 0.20 \text{ N/m}$$

This is much less than the permissible shear stress even at the minimum percentage of steel.

8. Reinforcement in the stem :

We had earlier assumed the thickness of heel slab as 0.3 m, while it has now been fixed as 0.26 m only. Hence revised.

$$H_1 = 4 - 0.26 = 3.74 \text{ m}$$

$$M = k_a\,\gamma\,\frac{H_1^3}{6} = \frac{1}{3} \times \frac{18}{3}\,(3.74)^3 = 52.31 \text{ kN/m}$$

$$= 52.31 \times 10^6 \text{ N-mm}$$

$$\therefore\quad d = \sqrt{\frac{52.31 \times 10^6}{1000 \times 0.874}}$$

$$= 245 \text{ mm}$$

Keep d = 250 mm so that D = 310 mm reduce the total thickness at the top.

$$A_{st} = \frac{52.31 \times 10^6}{140 \times 0.865 \times 250}$$

$$= 1728 \text{ mm}^2 \text{ using 16 mm } \phi \text{ bars, } A\phi = 201 \text{ mm}^2$$

$$\therefore\quad S = \frac{1000 \times 201}{1728} = 166 \text{ mm}$$

however provide 16 mm ϕ bars @ 100 mm c/c.

Actual A_{st} provided $= 1000 \times \dfrac{201}{100} = 2010 \text{ mm}^2$

Continue alternate bars in the toe slab to serve as tensile reinforcement there. Discontinue the remaining half bars after a distance of 58.3 ϕ = 58.3 × 16 ≈ 930 mm beyond B, in the toe slab.

Between A and B, some of the bars can be curtailed. Consider a section at depth h below the top of the stem. The effective depth d at that section is

$$d' = 140 + \frac{250 - 140}{3.74}\,h = (140 + 29.4\,h) \text{ mm} \qquad \ldots(1)$$

(where h is in metres)

Now, $A_{st} \propto \dfrac{H^3}{d'}$ or $H = (A_{st}\,d)^{1/3}$

Hence, $\dfrac{h}{H_1} = \left(\dfrac{A_{st}\,'d'}{A_{st}\,d}\right)^{1/3}$ $\ldots(2)$

Where A_{st}' = Reinforcement at depth h

     d' = Effective depth at depth h

     A_{st} = Reinforcement at depth H_1

     d = Effective depth at depth H_1

$$\text{If} \qquad A_{st}' = \frac{1}{2} A_{st}, \quad \frac{A_{st}'}{A_{st}} = \frac{1}{2}$$

$$\therefore \qquad \frac{h}{H_1} = \left(\frac{1}{2} \cdot \frac{d'}{d}\right)^{1/3}$$

Substituting d = 250 mm and d' = (140 + 29.4 h), we get,

$$h = H_1 \left[\frac{140 + 29.4\,h}{2 \times 250}\right]^{1/3}$$

$$= 3.74 \left[\frac{140 + 29.4\,h}{500}\right]^{1/3}$$

$$= 0.471\,[140 + 29.4\,h]^{1/3} \qquad\qquad ...(3)$$

This can be solved by trial and error noting that if the effective thickness of stem were constant, h would have been equal to $\dfrac{H_1}{(2)^{1/3}} \approx 0.79\,H_1 \approx 2.96$ m.

Solving equation (3) by trial we get h = 2.86 m. Thus, half the bars can be curtailed at this point. However, the bars should be extended by a distance of 12 ϕ (= 12 × 16 = 192 mm) or d (= 250 mm) whichever is more beyond the point. H = 2.86 – 0.25 = 2.61 m. Hence, curtail half the bars at a height 2.6 m below the top. If we wish to curtail half of the remaining bars so that remaining reinforcement is one fourth of that provided at B, we have $\dfrac{A_{st}'}{A_{st}} = \dfrac{1}{4}$. Hence, from equation (2), $\dfrac{h}{H_1} = \left(\dfrac{1}{4}\dfrac{d'}{d}\right)^{1/3}$

$$\text{Or} \qquad h = H_1 \left[\frac{140 + 29.4\,h}{4 \times 250}\right]^{1/3}$$

$$= 3.74 \left[\frac{140 + 29.4\,h}{1000}\right]^{1/3}$$

$$= 0.374\,[143 + 29.4\,h]^{1/3} \qquad\qquad ...(4)$$

This can be solved by trial and error noting that if the effective thickness of stem were constant, h would have been equal to $\dfrac{H_1}{(4)^{1/3}} = 0.63\,H_1 \approx 2.36$ m.

Solving (4) by trial and error we get h = 2.2 m. However the bars should be extended by 250 mm beyond this

$$\therefore \qquad h = 2.2 - 0.25 = 1.95 \text{ m}$$

Hence, stop half the remaining bars by 1.95 m below the top of the stem. Continue rest of bars to the top of the step.

Check for shear :

$$\text{Shear force} = P = K_a\,\gamma\,\frac{H^2}{2} = \frac{1}{3} \times \frac{18}{2}\,(3.74)^2$$

$$= 41.96 \text{ kN}$$

$$\tau_v \;=\; \frac{41.96 \times 1000}{1000 \times 250} = 0.17 \text{ N/mm}^2 < \tau_c \qquad\qquad \text{Hence safe}$$

Distribution and temperature reinforcement

$$\text{Average thickness of stem} \;=\; \frac{1}{2}(310 + 200) = 255 \text{ mm}$$

$$\therefore \quad \text{Distribution reinforcement} = \frac{0.15}{100} \times 1000 \times 255$$

$$= 383 \text{ mm}$$

Using 8 mm ϕ bars, $A\phi = 50.3 \text{ mm}^2$

$$\therefore \qquad\qquad \text{Spacing} \;=\; \frac{1000 \times 50.3}{383} = 131 \text{ mm}$$

Hence, provide 8 mm ϕ bars @ 130 mm c/c at the inner face of the wall, along its length. For temperature reinforcement, provide 8 mm ϕ @ 260 mm c/c both ways, in the outer face.

9. Design of shear key :

The wall is unsafe in sliding and hence share key will have to be provided below the stem at shown in Fig. 13.45.

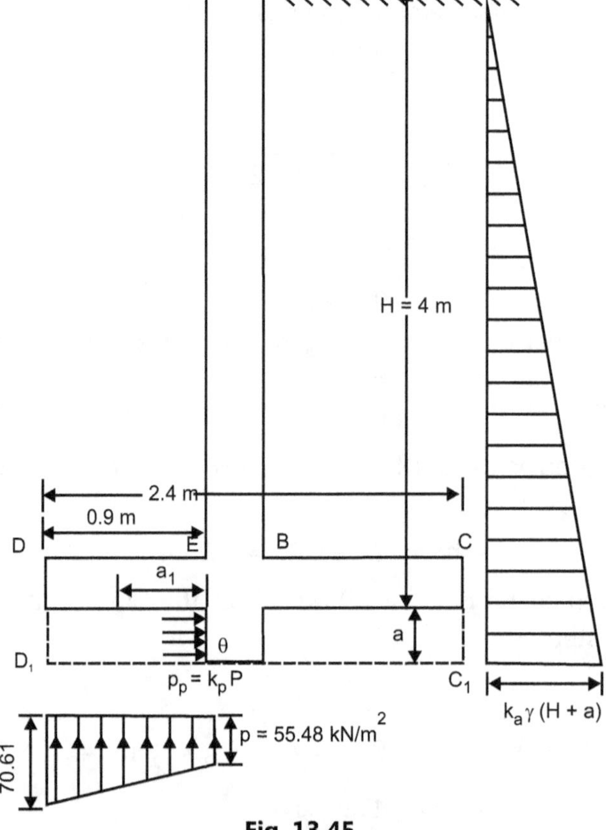

Fig. 13.45

Let the depth of key $= a$. Intensity of passive pressure P_p developed in front of the key depends upon the soil pressure P in front of the key.

$$P_p = K_p P = 3 \times 55.48 = 166.4 \text{ kN/m}^2$$

$\therefore$ Total passive pressure $P_p = P_p\, a = 166.4\, a$ $\qquad\qquad$ ...(1)

$$\text{Sliding force at level } D_1C_1 = \frac{1}{3} \times \frac{18}{2} (4 + a)^2 \text{ or}$$

$$P_H = 3 (4 + a)^2 \qquad\qquad ...(2)$$

Weight of soil between bottom of base and

$$D_1C_1 = 2.4\, a \times 18 = 43.2\, a$$

$\therefore$
$$\Sigma W = 121.05 + 43.2\, a$$

Hence for equilibrium of the wall, permitting

$$\text{F.S.} = 1.5 \text{ against sliding, we have}$$

$$1.5 = \frac{\mu \Sigma W + P_p}{P_H}$$

$$= \frac{0.5(121.05 + 43.2\, a) + 166.4\, a}{3 (4 + a)^2}$$

Or $\quad a^2 - 33.8\, a + 2.54 = 0$

which gives $a \approx 0.09 \text{ m} = 90 \text{ mm}$.

However, provide a minimum value of $a = 0.3 \text{ m} = 300 \text{ mm}$ keep width of key $= 300$ mm. It should be noted that passive pressure taken into account above will be developed only when a length a_1 given below is available in front of the key:

$$a_1 = a \tan \theta = a \tan \left(45° + \frac{\phi}{2}\right) = a \sqrt{K_p},$$

Where $\left(45° + \dfrac{\phi}{2}\right)$ = Shearing angle of passive resistance.

$\therefore$
$$a_1 = 0.3 \sqrt{3} = 0.52 \text{ m}$$

Actual length of the slab available $= DE = 0.9$ m

Hence satisfactory,

$$\text{Now size of key} = 300 \text{ mm} \times 300 \text{ mm}$$

$$P_H = 3 (4 + a)^2 = 3 (4 + 0.3)^2 = 55.47 \text{ kN}$$

$$P_p = 166.4\, a = 166.4 \times 0.3 = 49.92 \text{ kN}$$

Hence,
$$\Sigma W = 121.05 + 43.2\, a = 121.05 + 43.2 \times 0.3$$

$$= 134.01 \text{ kN}$$

Actual force to be resisted by the key, at

$$\text{F.S.} = 1.5 \text{ is} = 1.5\, P_H - \mu \Sigma W$$

$$= 1.5 \times 55.47 - 0.5 \times 134.01 = 16.2 \text{ kN}$$

$\therefore$ $\qquad$ Share stress $= \dfrac{16.2 \times 1000}{300 \times 1000} = 0.054 \text{ N/mm}^2$ $\qquad\qquad$ (safe)

$$\text{Bending stress} \quad = \frac{16.2 \times 150 \times 1000}{\frac{1}{6} \times 1000 \times (300)^2} = 0..16 \text{ N/mm}^2 \qquad \text{(safe)}$$

The details of reinforcement etc. are shown in Fig. 13.46.

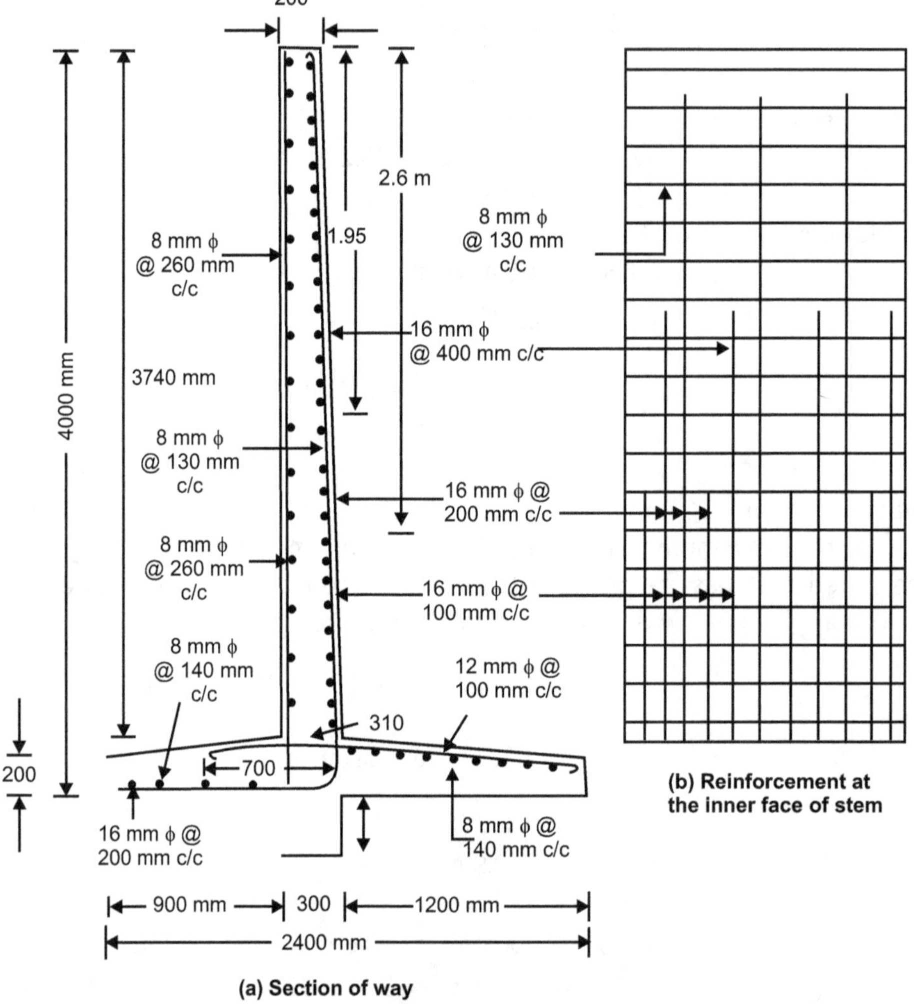

Fig. 13.46

IMPORTANT POINTS

- Types of retaining walls.
- Types of earth pressures.
- Active earth pressure on retaining walls for various cases.
- Conditions for stability of retaining walls.
- Steps to be followed in design of retaining walls.

QUESTIONS

1. A cantilever type retaining wall has 5.5 meter height. The unit weight of soil is 19 kN/m³ and angle of repose is 30°. The bearing capacity of soil is 220 kN/m². Design the 'T' shaped retaining wall. Use M 20 and Fe 415. $\mu = 0.5$.

2. Design a cantilever 'T' shaped retaining wall for the following data :
   (a) Height of wall = 5.5 m   (b) Superimposed load = 9 kN/m²
   (c) Angle of repose = 30   (d) Weight of soil = 18 kN/m³
   (e) Coefficient of friction between the concrete and ground = 0.55
   (f) Safe bearing capacity of soil = 210 kN/m²
   (g) A parapet wall of one meter high shall also be provided.
   (h) M 20 and Fe 250.

3. A reinforced concrete retaining wall has 4.75 meter height. The soil slopes at the rate of 1 vertical to 2 horizontal. The weight of soil is 16.5 kN/m³ and angle of repose is 30°. The safe bearing capacity of soil is 225 kN/m³ at 1.2 m below the ground level. Use M 25 and Fe 415.

4. Design a cantilever 'L' shaped (without toe) retaining wall to the following requirements :
   (a) Height of wall = 5 m   (b) Weight of soil = 16 kN/m²
   (c) Angle of repose = 30°   (d) Coefficient of friction = 0.6
   (e) Safe bearing capacity of soil = 190 kN/m³
   (f) M 20 and Fe 415.

5. Design a cantilever 'J' shaped (without heel) retaining wall for height of 4.7 m. The unit weight of soil is 18 kN/m³ and angle of repose is 30°. The bearing capacity of soil is 150 kN/m². Use M 20 and Fe 500.

6. Design a T-shaped retaining wall for two layered levelled backfill for the following data :
   Upper layer, height = 3 m; ϕ = 32°, γ = 18 kN/m³
   Lower layer, height = 3 m; ϕ = 30°, γ = 19 kN/m³
   Safe bearing capacity of the underlying strata = 160 kN/m². The coefficient of friction between the base slab and the underlying strata = 0.52. Draw lateral pressure diagram and details of reinforcement of stem and base showing curtailment if any. Use M 20, Fe 415.

UNIVERSITY QUESTIONS

Dec. 2011

Q. 1 (a) Explain the behavior of cantilever retaining wall. **(Section 13.10)**   **(5 Marks)**

May 2012

Q. 2   Design a T shaped retaining wall for two layered leveled backfill for the following data.

Upper layer, height = 2.4 m, ϕ = 30 °, γ = 17.5 kN/m³

Lower layer, height = 2.4 m, ϕ = 31°, γ = kN/m^3

Safe bearing capacity of the underlying strata = 170 kN/m^2. The coefficient friction between the base slab and the underlying strata = 0.55. Draw lateral pressure diagram and details of reinforcement of stem and base showing curtailment if any. **(Example 13.4)** **(20 Marks)**

Dec. 2012

Q. 3 Design a RCC retaining wall to retain earthen embankment 4.2m high above G.L. the embankment is surcharge at an angle of 20° to horizontal. The unit weight of earth is 18 kN/m^3. Angle of repose 30° good foundation for wall is available at a depth of 1.1 m below ground level. SBC of soil 160 kN/m^2. coefficient of friction between concrete and soil may be taken as 0.62, Use M20 grade concrete and Fe415 steel. Sketch the reinforcement details. **(Example 13.5)** **(25 Marks)**

May 2013

Q. 4 Design a T-shaped retaining wall for two layered leveled backfill for the following data.
Upper layer, height = 2.5 m, θ = 30°, density of material = 16 kN.m^3
Lower layer, Height = 2.5, θ = 32°, density of material = 18 kN/m^3
Safe bearing capacity of underlying strata is 195 kN/m^2 the coefficient of friction between base and underlying strata is 0.45. Draw lateral pressure diagram and details of reinforcement in stem and base slab including curtailment if any. Use M25 and Fe500. **(Example 13.4)** **(25 Marks)**

Dec. 2014

Q. 5 Design a cantilever T-shaped retaining wall to retain soil, 4 m above the ground. The surcharge angle is 14° at the top of retaining wall. The unit weight of the soil is 17.5 kN/m^3, angle of repose is 35° and S.B.C of soil is 180 kN/m^2 at 1.2 m below ground level. Show the pressure distribution at base of wall and reinforcement details at toe slab, heel slab and vertical wall. Use M20 concrete and Fe415 steel. **(Example 13.8)** **(25 Marks)**

May 2015

Q. 6 Design a T-shape cantilever retaining wall with the following data :
(a) Height of soil to be retained above base = 4.5 m
(b) Unit weight of soil = 17 kN/m^3
(c) Angle of repose = 23°
(d) SBC of soil = 200 kN/m^2
(e) Coefficient of friction between base and soil = 0.45
(f) Material = M25 and Fe – 500
(g) Leveled backfill.
Show all necessary stability checks and details of reinforcement in stem, heel and toe. **(Example 13.8) (25 Marks)**

Chapter 14
COMBINED FOOTING

14.1 INTRODUCTION [MAY 12]

Load from the building is transferred to the soil through footing. If the footing is supporting on a single column only then the footing will be known as **isolated footing**. When the footing supports more than single column, the footing is known as **combined footing**.

14.2 NEED AND SUITABILITY OF COMBINED FOOTING [DEC. 12]

Need :

In combined footing, a common footing is provided for two or more columns. Combined footing is very rigid hence the column settle together and thereby eliminate possibility of settlement.

Suitability :

Combined footings are provid under the following situations.

(1) When loads on adjacent columns are very high.

(2) Bearing capacity of soil is relatively very less.

(3) There is possibility of heavy differential settlement.

14.3 BASIC CONCEPT [DEC. 12]

The shape of footing is designed in such a way that the centre of gravity of column load should match with centre of gravity of the footing provided.

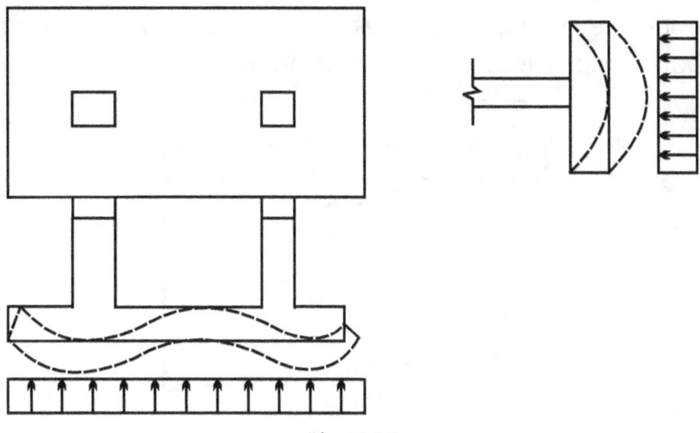

Fig. 14.1

By providing footing in this way, gives distribution of soil pressure nearly uniform. But at the time of fixing dimension, care is taken that the pressure due to external load should not be greater than the bearing capacity of soil and also no part of the footing is under tension.

Footing resists the loads by flexure. Isolated footing acts as cantilever beams. But in case of combined footing, the moment under the column is sagging bending moment and moment between the column is hogging bending moment. In transverse direction, moment diagram is as saucers. The diagram for B.M. is as shown in Fig. 14.1.

14.4 TYPES OF FOOTINGS

Depending upon the shape of the footing, footings are classified as :

   (i)　　Rectangular combined footing,

   (ii)　　Trapezoidal combined footing,

   (iii)　　Strap beam type combined footing,

   (iv)　　Raft footing.

(i) Rectangular Combined Footing :

A combined footing is usually rectangular, if the distance can be extended from face of column, such that C.G. of column load should match with C.G. of footing.

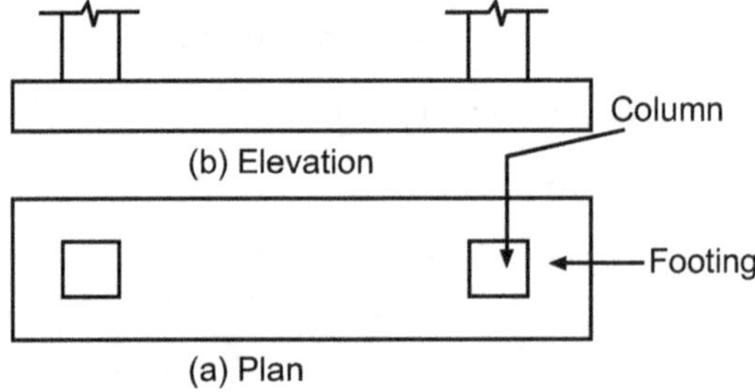

Fig. 14.2

(ii) Trapezoidal combined Footing :

If the distance beyond the column face is restricted i.e. if the length of footing available is limited, then the footing is provided as trapezoidal footing.

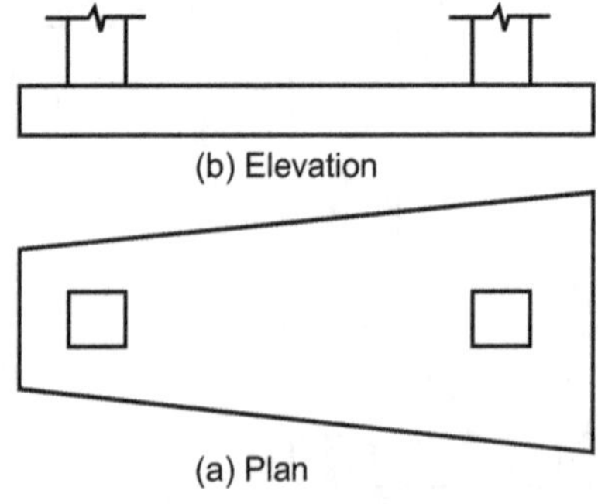

Fig. 14.3

(iii) Strap Beam Type Combined Footing :

When one of the column is on the property line, then isolated footings of two columns are connected by a beam known as strap beam. Due to provision of strap beam, pressure on the soil is evenly distributed.

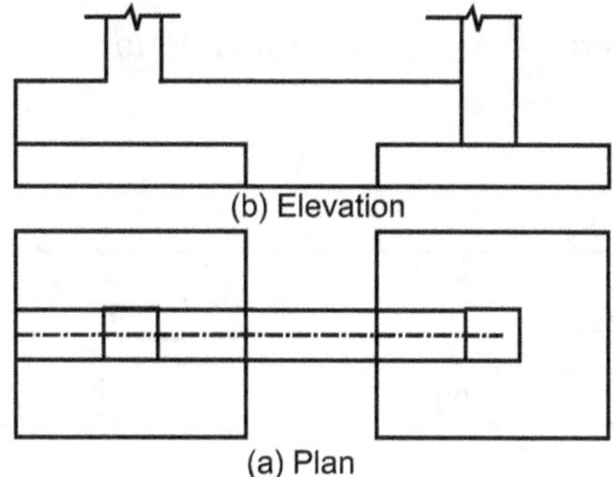

Fig. 14.4

(iv) Raft Foundations :

When the columns are closely spaced, the isolated footing becomes uneconomical. In such cases, a slab of uniform thickness is provided below the structure. This type of foundation is known as raft foundation.

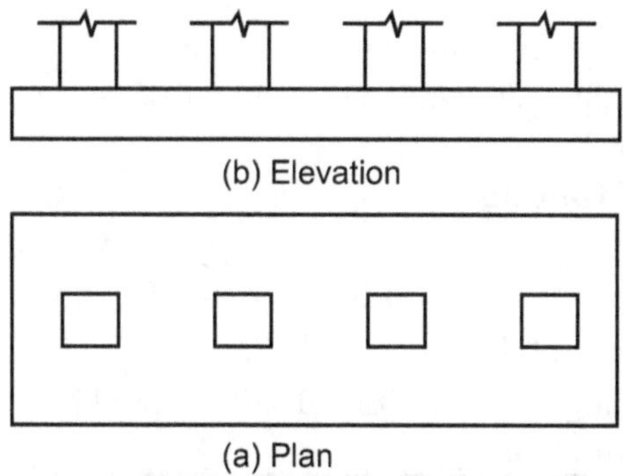

Fig. 14.5

14.5 STEPS TO BE FOLLOWED IN DESIGN OF FOOTINGS

(i)   Design constants (Depending upon grade of concrete and grade of steel).
(ii)   Dimensions of footings.
(iii)   S.F.D. and B.M.D. (Find points of zero S.F. and points of contraflexure).
(iv)   Area of reinforcement.
(v)   Check depth for one way shear.
(vi)   Check depth for two way shear.
(vii)   Reinforcement along width of footing.
(viii) Check for development length.

SOLVED EXAMPLES

Example 14.1 :

Design a combined footing for two R.C.C. columns C_1 and C_2 carrying 400 kN and 500 kN respectively. Column C_1 is 230 mm × 230 mm and column C_2 is 300 mm × 300 mm. Centre to centre distance between columns is 3.0 m. The safe bearing capacity of the soil is 150 kN/m². Use M 20 and Fe 415.

Solution :

The data is as shown in Fig. 14.6.

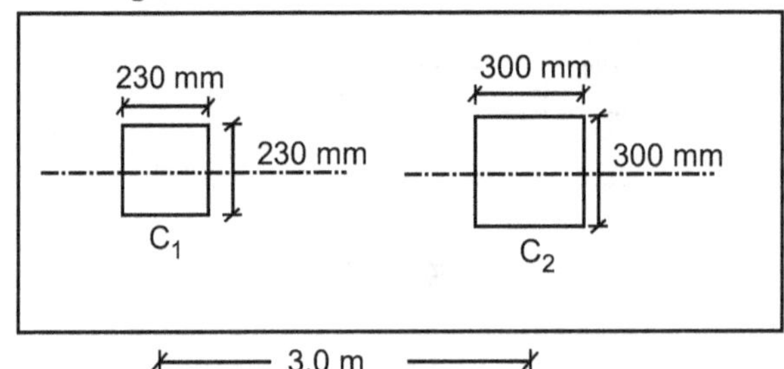

Fig. 14.6

Step I : Design constants : M 20 and Fe 415.

$$k_{u\ max} = 0.48$$

$$R_u = 0.36\ f_{ck}\ k_{u\ max}\ (1 - 0.42\ k_{u\ max})$$
$$= 0.36 \times 20 \times 0.48\ (1 - 0.42 \times 0.48)$$
$$= 2.76\ N/mm^2$$

Step II : Dimensions of footing :

Load on footing :

(i) Ultimate load of column C_1 = 1.5 × 400 = 600 kN

(ii) Ultimate load of column C_2 = 1.5 × 500 = 750 kN

(iii) Self weight of footing = 0.1 × 1350 = 135 kN
(10% of total column load)

Total load on footing = 1485 kN

$\therefore$ Required area of footing $= \dfrac{\text{Total load}}{\text{Ultimate safe bearing capacity of soil}}$

$$= \dfrac{1485}{1.5 \times 150} = 6.6\ m^2$$

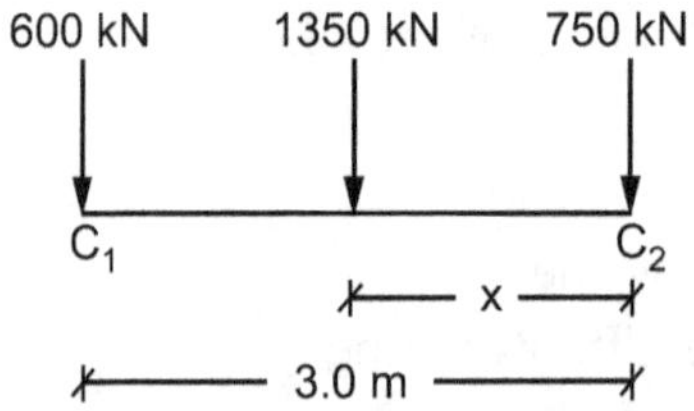

Fig. 14.7

Taking moment @ C_2,

$$600 \times 3 = 1350 \times x$$

$\therefore \qquad x = 1.33 \text{ m from column } C_2$

$\therefore \qquad \dfrac{L}{2} = 0.5 + (3 - 1.33) = 2.17$

$\therefore$ Adopt   Length of footing $= 4.6$ m

$\therefore \qquad$ Width of footing $= \dfrac{A}{L} = \dfrac{6.6}{4.6} = 1.43$ m

$\therefore$ Provide dimensions of footing : $1.5 \text{ m} \times 4.6 \text{ m}$

Let $\bar{x}$ be the distance of C.G. of column loads $(C_1 + C_2)$ from centre line of column C_1.

$\therefore \qquad \bar{x} = \dfrac{750 \times 3}{1350} = 1.67$ m

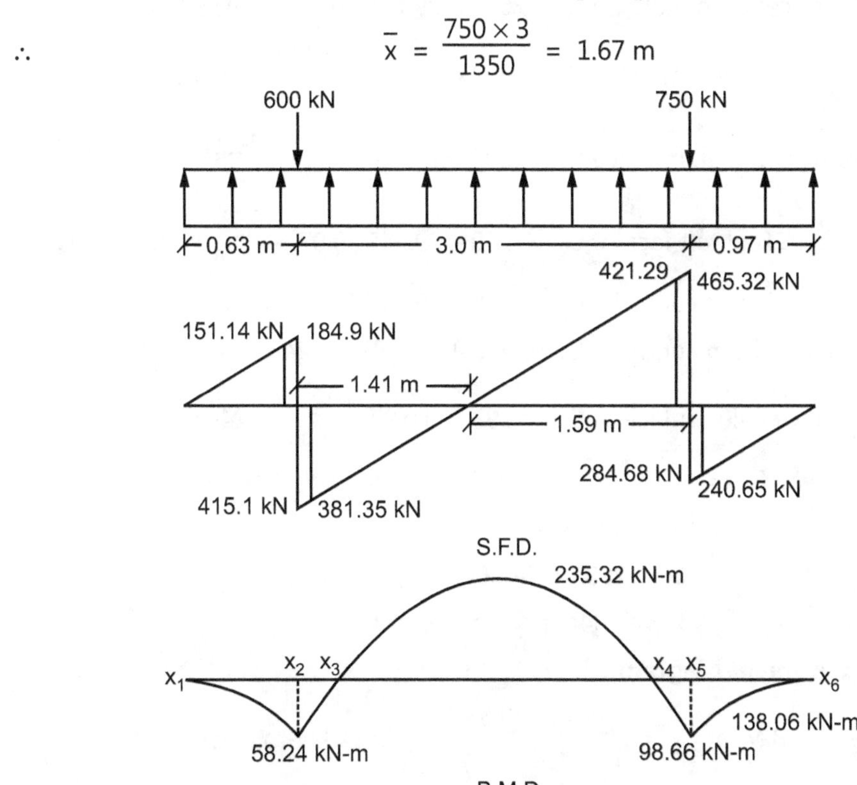

Fig. 14.8

The footing projections should be provided in such a way that C.G. of footing coincides with C.G. of column loads.

$$l_1 + l_2 = 4.6 - 3 = 1.6$$

$$l_1 + \bar{x} = \frac{L}{2} = \frac{4.6}{2} = 2.3$$

$$l_1 + 1.67 = 2.3$$

$$\therefore \qquad l_1 = 0.63 \text{ m}$$

$$\therefore \qquad l_2 = 1.6 - 0.63 = 0.97 \text{ m}$$

$$\therefore \qquad \text{Net upward soil pressure} = \frac{1350}{4.6 \times 1.5} = 195.65 \text{ kN/m}^2 < 1.5 \times 150 = 225 \text{ kN/m}^2$$

Step III : S.F.D. and B.M.D. :

Load/m along the length of footing $= 1.5 \times 195.65 = 293.48$ kN/m

(i) S.F. Diagrams :

S.F. just left of centre of column $C_1 = 293.48 \times 0.63 = 184.9$ kN

S.F. just right of centre of column $C_1 = 600 - 293.48 \times 0.63 = 415.1$ kN

$$\text{S.F. at left of column face } C_1 = 293.48 \left(0.63 - \frac{0.23}{2}\right) = 151.14 \text{ kN}$$

$$\text{S.F. at right of column face } C_1 = 600 - 293.48 \left(0.63 + \frac{0.23}{2}\right) = 381.35 \text{ kN}$$

$$\text{S.F. at left face of } C_2 = 750 - 293.48 \left(0.97 + \frac{0.3}{2}\right) = 421.29 \text{ kN}$$

S.F. just left of centre of $C_2 = 750 - 293.48 \,(0.97) = 465.32$ kN

S.F. just right of centre of $C_2 = 293.48 \times 0.97 = 248.68$ kN

$$\text{S.F. at right of column face of } C_2 = 293.48 \left(0.97 - \frac{0.3}{2}\right) = 240.65 \text{ kN}$$

Point of zero shear force :

$$\text{S.F.}_x = 293.48\, x - 600$$

$$\therefore \qquad 0 = 293.48\, x - 600$$

$$\therefore \qquad x = 2.044 \text{ m from left end}$$

(ii) Bending moment diagram :

$$\text{B.M. at } C_1 = \frac{293.48 \times (0.63)^2}{2} = 58.24 \text{ kN-m (sagging)}$$

$$\text{B.M. at zero S.F.} = \frac{293.48 \times (2.044)^2}{2} - 600\,(2.044 - 0.63) = 235.32 \text{ kN-m}$$

$$\text{(hogging)}$$

$$\text{B.M. at } C_2 = \frac{293.48 \times (0.97)^2}{2}$$

$$= 138.06 \text{ kN-m (sagging)}$$

Points of contraflexure :

$$B.M._{xx} = 293.48 \times \frac{x^2}{2} - 600\,(x - 0.63)$$

$$0 = 293.48 \times \frac{x^2}{2} - 600\,(x - 0.63)$$

$$146.74\,x^2 - 600\,x + 378 = 0$$

$$\therefore \quad x = 0.77 \text{ m} \text{ and } x = 3.31 \text{ m}$$

$$\therefore \quad \text{S.F. at } 0.77 \text{ m} = 600 - 293.48 \times 0.77 = 374.02 \text{ kN}$$

S.F. at 1.29 m from right (i.e. 3.31 m from left)

$$= 750 - 293.48 \times 1.29 = 371.41 \text{ kN}$$

Shear force and bending moment diagrams are as shown in Fig. 14.8.

Step IV : Depth of footing :

Depth of footing from B.M. consideration :

$$d = \sqrt{\frac{M_u}{R_u \cdot b}} = \sqrt{\frac{235.32 \times 10^6}{2.76 \times 1500}}$$

$$= 238.42 \text{ mm}$$

$$D = d + \text{clear cover} + \frac{\phi}{2}$$

$$= 238.42 + 50 + \frac{16}{2}$$

$$= 296.41 \text{ mm}$$

Provide overall depth 350 mm.

$$\therefore \quad d_{provided} = 350 - 50 - \frac{16}{2}$$

$$= 292 \text{ mm}$$

Step V : (a) Area of reinforcement for hogging B.M. between columns C_1 and C_2 :

$$A_{st} = \frac{0.5\,f_{ck}}{f_y}\left[1 - \sqrt{1 - \frac{4.6\,M_u}{f_{ck}\,bd^2}}\right]bd$$

$$= \frac{0.5 \times 20}{415}\left[1 - \sqrt{1 - \frac{4.6 \times 235.32 \times 10^6}{20 \times 1500 \times (292)^2}}\right] \times 1500 \times 292$$

$$= 2538.46 \text{ mm}^2$$

Using 16 mm ϕ,

$$\text{Number of bars} = \frac{2538.46}{201} = 12.62$$

Provide 13 bars of 16 mm diameter.

$\therefore$ Provide 20 mm ϕ bars at 110 mm c/c.

(b)   Area of reinforcement for sagging B.M. under column C_1 :

$$A_{st} = \frac{0.5\, f_{ck}}{f_y}\left[1-\sqrt{1-\frac{4.6\, M_u}{f_{ck}\, bd^2}}\right] bd$$

$$= \frac{0.5 \times 20}{415}\left[1-\sqrt{1-\frac{4.6 \times 58.24 \times 10^6}{20 \times 1500 \times (292)^2}}\right] \times 1500 \times 292$$

$$= 567.98 \text{ mm}^2$$

Minimum area of reinforcement :

$$A_{st\, min} = 0.12\%\ bD = \frac{0.12}{100} \times 1500 \times 350 = 630 \text{ mm}^2$$

Using 16 mm ϕ bars,

$$\text{Number of bars} = \frac{630}{201} = 3.13$$

Provide 4 bars of 16 mm diameter.

(c)   Area of reinforcement for B.M. under column C_2 :

$$A_{st} = \frac{0.5\, f_{ck}}{f_y}\left[1-\sqrt{1-\frac{4.6\, M_u}{f_{ck}\, bd^2}}\right] bd$$

$$= \frac{0.5 \times 20}{415}\left[1-\sqrt{1-\frac{4.6 \times 138.06 \times 10^6}{20 \times 1500 \times (292)^2}}\right] \times 1500 \times 292$$

$$= 1403.51 \text{ mm}^2$$

Using 16 mm ϕ bars,

$$\text{Number of bars} = \frac{1403.51}{201}$$

$$= 6.98$$

Provide 7 bars of 16 mm diameter.

Provide 16 mm ϕ bars at 110 mm c/c.

Step VI : Check depth for one way shear consideration between columns :

(a)   Between X_2 - X_5 :

$$p_t = \frac{100\, A_{st}}{bd}$$

$$= \frac{100 \times 13 \times \frac{\pi}{4} \times (16)^2}{1500 \times 292} = 0.90$$

p_t	τ_c
0.75	0.56
1.0	0.62
0.9	0.6

$\therefore \qquad \tau_c = 0.6 \text{ N/mm}^2$

$\therefore \qquad$ Shear resisted by concrete $= \tau_c \, bd$

$$= 0.6 \times 1500 \times 292 \times 10^{-3}$$

$$= 262.80 \text{ kN}$$

Shear force at critical section 'd' from face of column on right side

$$= 465.32 - 293.48 \,(0.292 + 0.15)$$

$$= 335.60 \text{ kN} > 262.8 \text{ kN}$$

Design of shear reinforcement :

Design shear force $= 335.6$ kN

Shear strength of concrete $(V_{uc}) = 181$ kN

Shear reinforcement is provided for

$$V_s = V_{uD} - V_{uc} = 335.6 - 162.06 = 173.54 \text{ kN}$$

Provide 2-legged stirrups of 10 mm ϕ HYSD steel bars.

$\therefore \qquad A_{sv} = 2 \times \dfrac{\pi}{4} \times (10)^2 = 157.1 \text{ mm}^2$

$\therefore \qquad$ Spacing of stirrups $= \dfrac{A_{sv} \times 0.87 \, f_y \, d}{V}$

$$= \dfrac{157.1 \times 0.87 \times 415 \times 292}{173.54 \times 10^3} = 95.43 \text{ mm}$$

Provide 2-legged stirrups of 10 mm ϕ HYSD steel bars of grade Fe415 at 90 mm spacing.

(b) Between X_1 - X_2 :

$$p_t = \dfrac{100 \, A_{st}}{bd} = \dfrac{100 \times 4 \times 201}{1500 \times 292} = 0.18$$

p_t	τ_c
0.15	0.28
0.25	0.36
0.18	0.304

Shear resisted by concrete $= \tau_c\, bd = 0.304 \times 1500 \times 292 \times 10^{-3}$

$$= 133.15 \text{ kN}$$

Shear force at critical section 'd' on left of face of column A

$$= 184.91 - 293.48 \times 0.407$$

$$= 65.46 \text{ kN} \ < \ 133.15 \text{ kN}$$

(c)   Between $X_5 - X_6$:

$$p_t \ = \ \frac{100\, A_{st}}{bd} \ = \ \frac{100 \times 7 \times 201}{1500 \times 292} \ = \ 0.32$$

p_t	τ_c
0.25	0.36
0.50	0.48
0.32	0.394

Shear resisted by concrete $= 0.394 \times 1500 \times 292 \times 10^{-3} \ = \ 172.57 \text{ kN}$

Shear force at critical section 'd' on right of column c_2

$$= 284.68 - 293.48 \left(\frac{0.3}{2} + 0.292 \right)$$

$$= 154.96 \text{ kN} < 172.57 \text{ kN}$$

Step VII : Check depth for two way shear :

(a)   The critical section for two way shear shall be periphery at a distance d/2 from the face of the column C_1.

$$\therefore \qquad b_o \ = \ 4 \left(230 + \frac{600}{2} + \frac{600}{2} \right) \ = \ 3320 \text{ mm}$$

Effective soil pressure acting upward $= 195.65 \text{ kN/m}^2$

Shear force $=$ Column load $-$ Upward pressure on the area within the periphery

$$= 600 - (195.65 \times 0.83 \times 0.83)$$

$$= 465.22 \text{ kN}$$

Nominal shear stress $= \tau_v \ = \ \dfrac{V}{bd} \ = \ \dfrac{465.22 \times 10^3}{3320 \times 600} \ = \ 0.23 \text{ N/mm}^2$

Permissible shear stress $= k_s \times 0.25 \sqrt{f_{ck}}$

$$k_s \ = \ 1.0$$

$$\therefore \qquad \tau_{uc} \ = \ 1 \times 0.25 \sqrt{20} \ = \ 1.12 \text{ N/mm}^2 \ > \ 0.23 \text{ N/mm}^2$$

(b) The critical section for two way shear shall be periphery at a distance d/2 from the periphery of the column C_2.

$$b_o = 4\left(300 + \frac{600}{2} + \frac{600}{2}\right) = 3600 \text{ mm}$$

Effective soil pressure acting upward $= 195.65 \text{ kN/m}^2$

$$\text{Shear force} = \text{Column load} - \begin{bmatrix} \text{Upward soil pressure on} \\ \text{the area within periphery} \end{bmatrix}$$

$$= 750 - 195.65 \,(0.9 \times 0.9) = 591.52 \text{ kN}$$

$$\text{Nominal shear stress} = \tau_v = \frac{V}{bd} = \frac{591.52 \times 10^3}{1000 \times 600} = 0.99 \text{ N/mm}^2$$

$$\text{Permissible shear stress} = k_s \times 0.25 \sqrt{f_{ck}} = 1 \times 0.25 \sqrt{20}$$

$$= 1.11 \text{ N/mm}^2 > 0.99 \text{ N/mm}^2$$

Step VIII : Reinforcement along width of footing :

(a) **Under column C_1 :** The projection of footing along the width

$$= \frac{1}{2}(1500 - 230) = 635 \text{ mm}$$

$$\text{Width of footing} = (230 + 2 \times 292) = 814 \text{ mm}$$

$$\text{Soil pressure on the footing} = \frac{600 \times 10^3}{0.814 \times 1.5} = 491.4 \text{ kN/m}^2$$

Consider unit width of footing.

$\therefore$ Maximum bending at face of column

$$= \frac{491.40 \times (0.635)^2}{2} = 99.07 \text{ kN-m}$$

$\therefore$

$$d = \sqrt{\frac{M_u}{R_u \cdot b}} = \sqrt{\frac{99.07 \times 10^6}{2.76 \times 1000}} = 189.45 \text{ mm} < 292 \text{ mm}$$

$\therefore$

$$A_{st} = \frac{0.5\,f_{ck}}{f_y}\left[1 - \sqrt{1 - \frac{4.6\,M_u}{f_{ck}\,bd^2}}\right] bd$$

$$= \frac{0.5 \times 20}{415}\left[1 - \sqrt{1 - \frac{4.6 \times 99.07 \times 10^6}{20 \times 1000 \times (292)^2}}\right] \times 1000 \times 292$$

$$= 1013.11 \text{ mm}^2 > A_{st\,min}$$

Using 16 mm ϕ bars,

$$\text{Spacing} = \frac{201 \times 1000}{1013.11} = 198.39 \text{ mm}$$

Provide 16 mm ϕ @ 190 mm c/c.

(b)   Under column C_2 :

The projection of footing along the width

$$= \frac{1}{2}(1500 - 300) = 600 \text{ mm}$$

$$\text{Width of footing} = (300 + 2 \times 292) = 884 \text{ mm}$$

$$\text{Soil pressure on the footing} = \frac{\text{Load}}{\text{Area}} = \frac{750 \times 10^3}{0.884 \times 1.5} = 565.61 \text{ kN/m}^2$$

$\therefore$ Maximum bending at face of column

$$= \frac{565.61 \times (0.6)^2}{2} = 101.81 \text{ kN-m}$$

$\therefore$

$$d = \sqrt{\frac{M_u}{R_u \cdot b}} = \sqrt{\frac{101.81 \times 10^6}{2.76 \times 1000}}$$

$$= 192.01 \text{ mm} < 292 \text{ mm}$$

$$A_{st} = \frac{0.5 \times 20}{415}\left[1 - \sqrt{1 - \frac{4.6 \times 101.81 \times 10^6}{20 \times 1000 \times (292)^2}}\right] \times 1000 \times 292$$

$$= 1932.36 \text{ mm}^2$$

Using 16 mm ϕ bars,

$$\text{Spacing} = \frac{201 \times 1000}{1932.36} = 104 \text{ mm}$$

Provide 16 mm ϕ @ 100 mm c/c.

Step IX : Distribution reinforcement : The distribution reinforcement is provided at locations where transverse reinforcement is not provided. This reinforcement is along the direction of transverse reinforcement.

$\therefore$ Provide 8 mm ϕ @ 100 mm c/c.

Step X : Check for development length :

At point of zero bending moment : The point of zero B.M. is at 0.77 m from left. In IS456 - 1978 following condition is given for development length.

$$\frac{1.3 \, M_1}{V} + L_o > L_d$$

$$M_1 = \text{Moment of resistance of steel bars available at zero B.M.}$$

$$= 0.87 \, f_y \, A_{st} \, (d - 0.42 \, x_{u \, max})$$

$$= 0.87 \times 415 \times 2783.94 \, (292 - 0.42 \times 0.48 \times 292)$$

$$= 234.32 \times 10^6 \text{ N-mm}$$

$$\text{S.F.} = 374.02 \times 10^3 \text{ N}$$

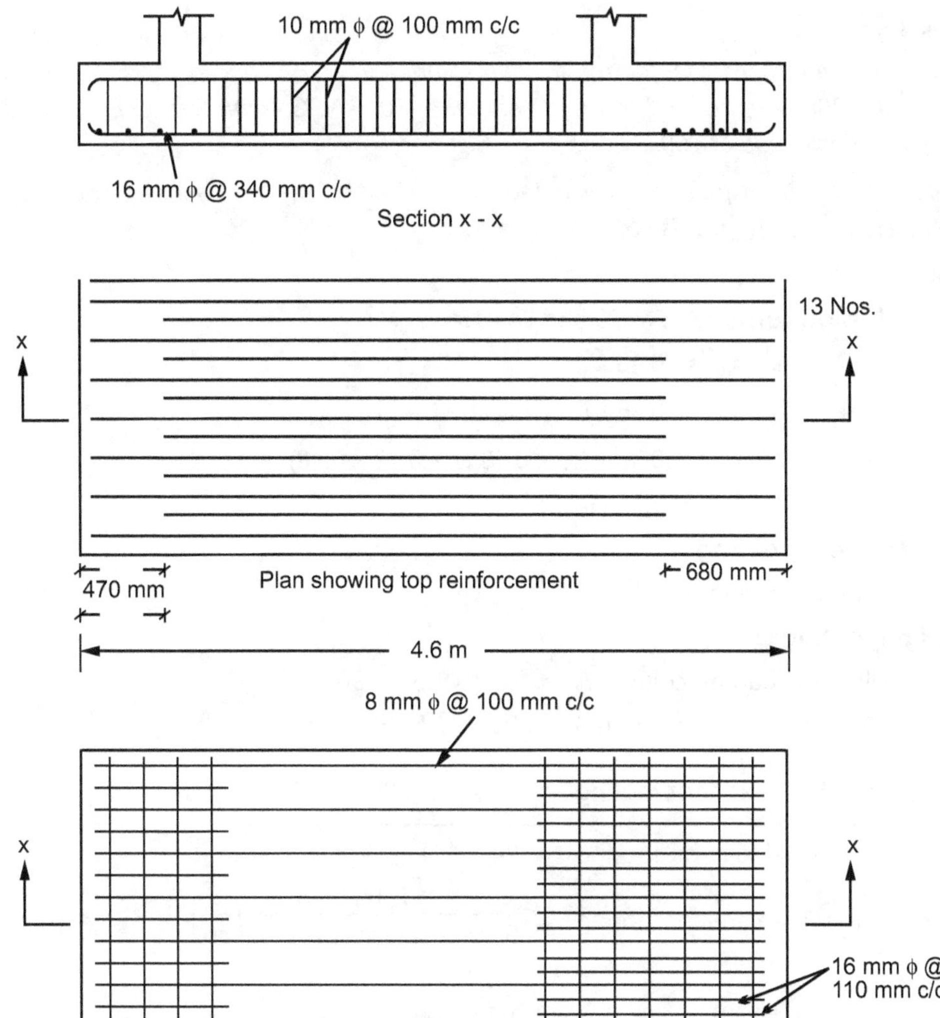

Fig. 14.9

$$L_o = d \text{ or } 12\,\phi \text{ whichever is greater}$$
$$= 292 \text{ or } 12 \times 20 = 292 \text{ mm}$$

$$\therefore \quad L_d = \frac{0.87\,f_y\,\phi}{4\tau_{bd}}$$

$$\therefore \quad L_d = \frac{0.87 \times 415 \times 20}{4 \times 1.6 \times 1.2} = 940.23 \text{ mm}$$

$$\therefore \quad \frac{1.3 \times 234.32 \times 10^6}{374.02 \times 10^3} + 292 = 1106.44 > 940.23 \text{ mm}$$

Example 14.2 :

Design a combined trapezoidal footing for two columns A and B spaced at 5.5 m c/c. Column A is 300 mm × 300 mm size and transmits a load of 500 kN. Column B is 400 mm × 400 mm in size and carries a load of 900 kN.

The maximum length of footing is restricted to 7.5 m only. The safe bearing capacity of soil may be taken as 100 kN/m². Use M 20 and Fe 415.

Solution :

Step I : Design constants : M 20 and Fe 415.

$$k_{u\,max} = 0.48$$

$$R_u = 0.36\, f_{ck}\, k_{u\,max}\, (1 - 0.42\, k_{u\,max})$$

$$= 0.36 \times 20 \times 0.48\, (1 - 0.42 \times 0.48)$$

$$= 2.76 \text{ N/mm}^2$$

Step II : Size of footing :

Length of footing = 7.5 m

Load on footing :

(a)   Ultimate load on column A = 600×1.5 = 900 kN

(b)   Ultimate load on column B = 900×1.5 = 1350 kN

(c)   Self weight of footing = $\dfrac{10}{100} \times 2250$ = 225 kN

Total load on footing = 2475 kN

$$\text{Required area of footing} = \frac{\text{Total load}}{\text{Safe bearing capacity of soil}}$$

$$= \frac{2475}{1.5 \times 100} = 16.5 \text{ m}^2$$

Providing trapezoidal footing.

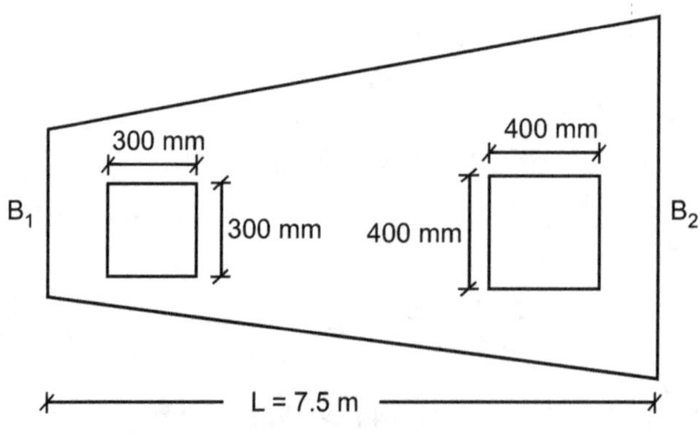

Fig. 14.10

$$\text{Area of footing} = \left(\frac{B_1 + B_2}{2}\right) L$$

$$= \left(\frac{B_1 + B_2}{2}\right) \times 7.5 = 16.5$$

$$\therefore \qquad B_1 + B_2 = 4.4 \text{ m} \qquad\qquad \dots (1)$$

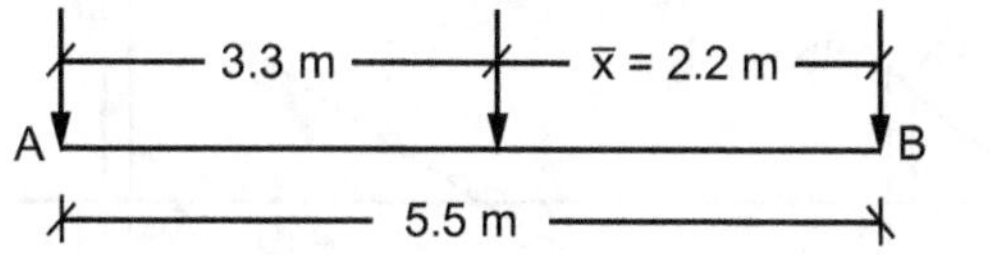

Fig. 14.11

Distance of C.G. of load from column B :

$$900 \times 5.5 = 2250 \times \bar{x}$$

$$\therefore \qquad \bar{x} = 2.2 \text{ m}$$

C.G. of footing :

$$\left(\frac{B_2 + 2B_1}{B_1 + B_2}\right) \frac{l}{3} = \left(\frac{B_1 + 2B_2}{4.4}\right) \times \frac{7.5}{3}$$

$$= \frac{1.705}{3} (B_2 + 2B_1)$$

Equating C.G. of column to C.G. of footing,

C.G. of column from $B_2 = 2.2 + 1 = 3.2$ m

$$3.2 = \frac{1.705}{3} (2B_1 + B_2)$$

$$\therefore \qquad 2B_1 + B_2 = 5.63 \qquad\qquad \dots (2)$$

From equations (1) and (2), we get,

$$B_1 = 1.23 \text{ m} \quad \text{and} \quad B_2 = 3.17 \text{ m}$$

$$\text{Net upward soil pressure} = \frac{2250}{7.5 \left(\dfrac{1.23 + 3.17}{2}\right)}$$

$$= 136.36 \text{ kN/m}^2 < 1.5 \times 100$$

$$= 150 \text{ kN/m}^2$$

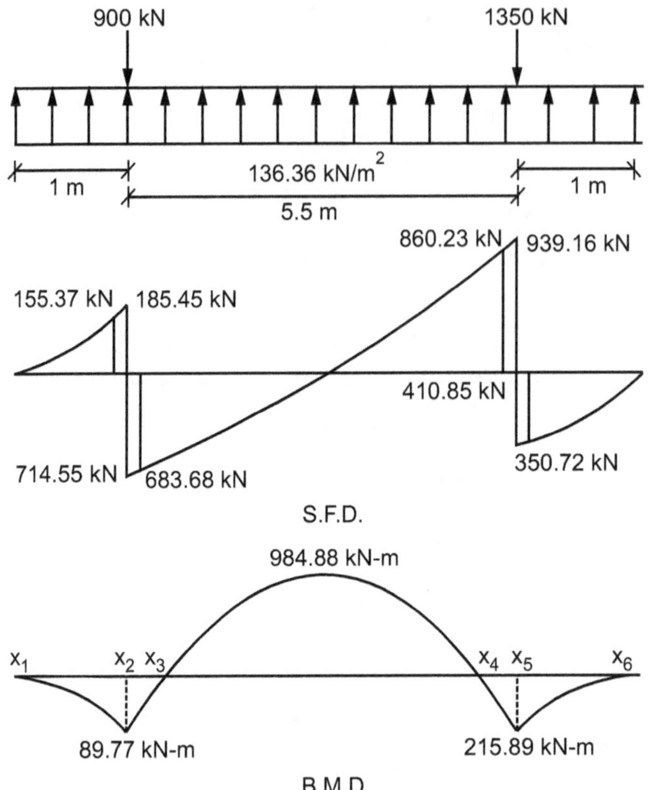

Fig. 14.12 : S.F.D. and B.M.D.

Step III : S.F. and B.M. :

$$B_x = B_1 + \left(\frac{B_2 - B_1}{L}\right) \cdot x$$

$$= 1.23 + \left(\frac{3.17 - 1.23}{7.5}\right) \cdot x = 1.23 + 0.26\,x$$

$$A_x = \frac{1}{2}(B_1 + B_x)\,x = \frac{1}{2}(1.23 + 1.23 + 0.26\,x)\ x$$

$$= (1.23 + 0.13\,x)\,x = 1.23\,x + 0.13\,x^2$$

$$\text{Distance of C.G.} = \left(\frac{2B_1 + B_x}{B_1 + B_x}\right) \cdot \frac{x}{3} = \left(\frac{2 \times 1.23 + 1.23 + 0.26\,x}{1.23 + 1.23 + 0.26\,x}\right) \cdot \frac{x}{3}$$

$$= \frac{x}{3}\left(\frac{3.69 + 0.26\,x}{2.46 + 0.26\,x}\right)$$

Hence total upward force to the left of x_1x_2

$$= P_0\,(1.23\,x + 0.13\,x^2)$$

$$= 136.36\ (1.23\ x + 0.13\ x^2)$$

S.F. at outer face of column A ($x = 0.85$ m)

$$= 136.36\ [1.23 \times 0.85 + 0.13 + (0.85)^2]$$
$$= 155.37\ \text{kN}$$

S.F. at just left of centre of column A ($x = 1$ m)

$$= 136.36\ (1.23 \times 1 + 0.13 \times 1^2)$$
$$= 185.45\ \text{kN}$$

S.F. at just right of centre of column A

$$= 900 - 185.45\ =\ 714.55\ \text{kN}$$

S.F. at inner face of column A ($x = 1.15$ m)

$$= 900 - 136.36\ [1.23 \times 1.15 + 0.13 \times (1.15)^2]$$
$$= 900 - 216.32\ =\ 683.68\ \text{kN}$$

S.F. at inner face of column B ($x = 6.5$ m)

$$= 136.36\ [1.23 \times 6.5 + 0.13 \times (6.5)^2] - 900$$
$$= 860.23\ \text{kN}$$

S.F. at just left of centre of column B ($x = 6.5$ m)

$$= 136.36\ (1.23 \times 6.5 + 0.13 \times (6.5)^2] - 900$$
$$= 939.16\ \text{kN}$$

S.F. at just right of centre of column B ($x = 6.5$ m)

$$= 900 + 1350 - 136.36\ [1.23 \times 6.5 + 0.13 \times (6.5)^2]$$
$$= 410.85\ \text{kN}$$

S.F. at outer face of column B ($x = 6.65$ m)

$$= 900 + 1350 - 136.36\ [1.23 \times 6.65 + 0.13 \times (6.65)^2]$$
$$= 350.72\ \text{kN}$$

Point of zero S.F. :

$$\text{S.F.}_x\ =\ 136.36\ (1.23 \times x + 0.13\ x^2) - 900$$
$$0\ =\ 167.72\ x + 17.73\ x^2 - 900$$
$$\therefore \qquad x\ =\ 3.82\ \text{m}$$

Bending moment :

B.M. at A ($x = 1$ m) $= p \times A_x \times \text{C.G.}$

$$= 136.36\ (1.23\ x + 0.13\ x^2) \times \left(\frac{3.69 + 0.26\ x}{2.46 + 0.26\ x}\right) \times \frac{x}{3}$$

$$= 136.36\ (1.23 \times 1 + 0.13 \times 1^2) \times \left(\frac{3.69 + 0.26 \times 1}{2.46 \times 0.26 \times 1}\right) \times \frac{1}{3}$$

$$= 89.77\ \text{kN-m}$$

B.M. at B $(x = 6.5 \text{ m})$ $= p \times A_x \times C.G.$

$$= 136.36 \,[1.23 \times 6.5 + 0.13 \times (6.5)^2]$$

$$\left(\frac{3.69 + 0.26 \times 6.5}{2.46 + 0.26 \times 6.5}\right) \times \frac{6.5}{3} - 900 \times 5.5$$

$$= 215.89$$

B.M. at zero S.F. (Max. B.M.) at $x = 3.82$ m

$$= 900 \times (3.82 - 1) - 136.36 \,[1.23 \times 3.82 + 0.13 \times (3.82)^2] \left(\frac{3.69 + 0.26 \times 3.82}{2.46 + 0.26 \times 3.82}\right) \times \frac{3.82}{3}$$

$$= 984.88 \text{ kN-m}$$

Step IV : Depth of footing : Depth of footing from B.M. consideration.

Width of footing at maximum B.M.

$$= B_1 + \left(\frac{B_2 - B_1}{2}\right) x$$

$$x = 3.82 \text{ m}$$

$\therefore$

$$b = 1.23 + \left(\frac{3.17 - 1.23}{7.5}\right) \times 3.82$$

$$= 2.218 \text{ m}$$

$$d = \sqrt{\frac{M_u}{R_u \cdot b}} = \sqrt{\frac{984.88 \times 10^6}{2.76 \times 2218}} = 400.92 \text{ mm}$$

$\therefore$

$$D = 400.92 + \text{Clear cover} + \frac{\phi}{2}$$

$$= 400.92 + 50 + \frac{20}{2} = 460.92$$

$\therefore$　　Provide overall depth $= 500$ mm

$\therefore$　　　　　　$d = 440$ mm

Step V : Area of reinforcement :

(a)　Area of reinforcement for hogging moment between A to B :

$$A_{st} = \frac{0.5\, f_{ck}}{f_y}\left[1 - \sqrt{1 - \frac{4.6\, M_u}{f_{ck}\, bd^2}}\right] bd$$

$$= \frac{0.5 \times 20}{415}\left[1 - \sqrt{1 - \frac{4.6 \times 984.88 \times 10^6}{20 \times 2218 \times (440)^2}}\right] \times 2218 \times 600$$

$$= 7351.92 \text{ mm}^2$$

Using 20 mm ϕ,

$\therefore$　　Number of bars $= \dfrac{7351.92}{490.87} = 14.97$

∴   Provide 15 bars of 25 mm diameter.

(b)   Area of reinforcement for sagging moment under column A :

Width under column A (x = 1 m)

$$= 1.23 + \left(\frac{3.17 - 1.23}{7.5}\right) \times 1 = 1.489 \text{ m}$$

$$A_{st} = \frac{0.5 \times 20}{415}\left[1 - \sqrt{1 - \frac{4.6 \times 89.77 \times 10^6}{20 \times 1489 \times (440)^2}}\right] \times 1489 \times 440$$

$$= 575.86 \text{ mm}^2$$

$$A_{st\,min} = \frac{0.12}{100} \times bD = \frac{0.12}{100} \times 1489 \times 440 = 786.19 > 575.86 \text{ mm}^2$$

∴ $A_{st} = 786.19 \text{ mm}^2$

Using 16 mm φ,

$$\text{Number of bars} = \frac{786.19}{201} = 3.91$$

Provide 4 bars of 16 mm diameter.

(c)   Area of reinforcement for sagging moment under column B :

Width under column B (x = 6.5 m)

$$= 1.23 + \left(\frac{3.17 - 1.23}{7.5}\right) \times 6.5 = 2.911 \text{ m}$$

$$A_{st} = \frac{0.5\,f_{ck}}{f_y}\left[1 - \sqrt{1 - \frac{4.6\,M_u}{f_{ck}\,bd^2}}\right] bd$$

$$= \frac{0.5 \times 20}{415}\left[1 - \sqrt{1 - \frac{4.6 \times 215.89 \times 10^6}{20 \times 2911 \times (440)^2}}\right] \times 2911 \times 440$$

$$= 1391 \text{ mm}^2$$

Using 16 mm φ,

$$\text{Number of bars} = \frac{1391}{201} = 6.92$$

Provide 7 bars of 16 mm diameter.

Step VI : Check depth for one way shear consideration :

(a)   Between X_2 - X_5 :

$$p_t = \frac{100\,A_{st}}{bd} = \frac{100 \times 15 \times 490.87}{2218 \times 440} = 0.75$$

∴ $\tau_c = 0.56$

$$V_{uc} = \tau_c \cdot bd = 0.56 \times 2218 \times 440 \times 10^{-3}$$

$$= 546.52 \text{ kN}$$

Shear force at critical section 'd' from face of column 'B' ($x = 6.06$ m)

$$= 136.36 \,(1.23\, x + 0.13\, x^2) - 900$$

$$= 136.36 \,[1.23 \times 6.06 + 0.13 \times (6.06)^2] - 900$$

$$= 767.39 \text{ kN}$$

$\therefore$ Shear reinforcement is provided for

$$V_s = V_{uD} - V_{uC} = 767.39 - 546.52 = 220.87 \text{ kN}$$

Provide 2-legged stirrups of 10 mm ϕ HYSD steel bars.

$\therefore$ $\text{Spacing} = \dfrac{A_{sv} \times 0.87\, f_y \cdot d}{V}$

$$= \dfrac{2 \times \dfrac{\pi}{4} \times 10^2 \times 0.87 \times 415 \times 600}{220.87 \times 10^3} = 154.96 \text{ mm}$$

Provide 2-legged stirrups of 10 mm ϕ HYSD steel bars of grade Fe 415 at 150 mm spacing.

(b) Between X_1 - X_2 :

$$p_t = \dfrac{100 \times 4 \times 201}{1489 \times 440}$$

$$= 0.12 < 0.15$$

$\therefore$ $\tau_c = 0.28$

$$V_{uC} = \tau_c\, bd$$

$$= 0.28 \times 1489 \times 440 \times 10^{-3}$$

$$= 183.44 \text{ kN}$$

Shear force is critical at a section 'd' from the face of column.

$\therefore$ $\text{S.F.} = (1.23\, x + 0.13\, x^2) \times 136.36$

$\therefore$ $x = (1 - 0.44) = 0.56$ m

$\therefore$ $\text{S.F.} = [1.23 \times 0.56 + 0.13 \times (0.56)^2] \times 136.36$

$$= 99.48 \text{ kN} < 183.44 \text{ kN}$$

(c) Between X_5 - X_6 :

$$p_t = \dfrac{100 \times 7 \times 201}{2911 \times 440} = 0.11 < 0.15$$

$\therefore$ $\tau_c = 0.28$

$\therefore \qquad V_{uc} = \tau_c\, bd$

$$= 0.28 \times 2911 \times 440 \times 10^{-3}$$

$$= 358.63 \text{ kN}$$

Shear force is critical at a section 'd' from face of column (x = 6.94 m)

$\therefore \qquad$ S.F. $= 900 + 1350 - 136.36\,[1.23 \times 6.94 + 0.13 \times (6.94)^2]$

$$= 232.22 \text{ kN} \ < \ 358.63 \text{ kN}$$

Step VII : Check depth for two way shear :

(i)   The critical section for two way shear shall be periphery at a distance d/2 from the face of column 'A'.

$\therefore \qquad b_o = 4\left(300 + \dfrac{440}{2} + \dfrac{440}{2}\right) = 2960 \text{ mm}$

Effective soil pressure acting upward $= 136.36 \text{ kN/m}^2$

$\qquad$ Shear force $=$ Column load – Upward pressure on the area within the periphery

$$= 900 - 136.36\,(0.74 \times 0.74)$$

$$= 825.33 \text{ kN}$$

$\qquad$ Nominal shear stress $= \dfrac{\text{Shear force}}{\text{Area}} = \dfrac{825.33 \times 10^3}{2960 \times 440} = 0.64 \text{ N/mm}^2$

$\qquad$ Permissible shear stress $= \tau_c = k_s \times 0.25\,\sqrt{f_{ck}}$

$$= 1 \times 0.25 \times \sqrt{20}$$

$$= 1.11 \text{ N/mm}^2 > 0.64 \text{ N/mm}^2$$

(ii)   The critical section for two way shear shall be periphery at a distance d/2 from the face of column 'B'.

$\therefore \qquad b_o = 4\left(400 + \dfrac{440}{2} + \dfrac{440}{2}\right) = 3360 \text{ mm}$

Effective soil pressure acting upward $= 136.36 \text{ kN/m}^2$

$\qquad$ Shear force $=$ Column load – Upward pressure on the area within the periphery

$$= 1350 - 136.36\,(0.84 \times 0.84)$$

$$= 1253.78 \text{ kN}$$

$\qquad$ Nominal shear stress $= \dfrac{\text{Shear force}}{\text{Area}} = \dfrac{1253.78 \times 10^3}{2960 \times 440} = 0.96 \text{ N/mm}^2$

$\therefore \qquad$ Permissible shear stress $= k \times 0.25\,\sqrt{f_{ck}}$

$$= 1 \times 0.25 \times \sqrt{20}$$

$$= 1.11 \text{ N/mm}^2 > 0.96 \text{ N/mm}^2$$

Step VIII : Reinforcement along width of footing :

(a)   Under column OA :

Width of footing at centre of column :

$$B_x = B_1 + \left(\dfrac{B_1 - B_2}{L}\right) x$$

$$= 1.23 + 0.26\, x$$

At $x = 1$ m, $B_x = 1.49$ m

The length of cantilever projection from the face of column

$$= \frac{1}{2}(1.49 - 0.3) = 0.595 \text{ m}$$

Width of footing along column

$$= (300 + 2 \times 440) = 1180 \text{ mm}$$

$$\text{Soil pressure on footing} = \frac{750}{1.49 \times 1.18} = 426.57 \text{ kN/m}^2$$

$\therefore$ Maximum bending moment $= \dfrac{426.57 \times (0.595)^2}{2} = 75.50$ kN-m

$\therefore$
$$A_{st} = \frac{0.5 \times 20}{415}\left[1 - \sqrt{1 - \frac{4.6\, M_u}{f_{ck}\, bd^2}}\right] bd$$

$$= \frac{0.5 \times 20}{415}\left[1 - \sqrt{1 - \frac{4.6 \times 75.50 \times 10^6}{20 \times 1000 \times (440)^2}}\right] \times 1000 \times 440$$

$$= 486.66 \text{ mm}^2$$

$$A_{st\,min} = \frac{0.12}{100} \times 1000 \times 500 = 600 \text{ mm}^2$$

Using 16 mm ϕ,

$$\text{Spacing} = \frac{1000 \times 201}{600} = 335 \text{ mm}$$

Provide 16 mm ϕ @ 330 mm c/c.

(b) Under column B :

Width of footing $= B_x$ (at $x = 6.5$ m)

$$B_x = 1.23 + 0.26\, x = 1.23 + 0.26 \times 6.5$$

$$= 2.92 \text{ m}$$

Length of cantilever projection $= \dfrac{1}{2}(2.9 - 0.4) = 1.25$ m

Width of footing along column $= (400 + 2 \times 440) = 1280$ mm

$\therefore$ Soil pressure on footing $= \dfrac{750}{2.92 \times 1.28}$

$$= 200.66 \text{ kN/m}^2$$

Maximum bending moment $= 200.66 \times \dfrac{(1.28)^2}{2}$

$$= 156.76 \text{ kN-m}$$

$$A_{st} = \frac{0.5 \times 20}{415}\left[1 - \sqrt{1 - \frac{4.6 \times 156.76 \times 10^6}{20 \times 1000 \times (440)^2}}\right] \times 1000 \times 440$$

$$= 1038 \text{ mm}^2 < 792 \text{ mm}^2$$

∴   Provide minimum reinforcement 16 mm ϕ @ 190 mm c/c.

Step IX : Check for development length :

$$\text{B.M.} = 136.36 \times \frac{1}{2}(2.46 + 0.26\,x)\;x \times \left(\frac{3.69 + 0.26\,x}{2.46 + 0.26\,x}\right)\cdot\frac{x}{3} - 900\,(x-1)$$

$$= 136.36\,(3.69 + 0.26\,x)\cdot\frac{x^2}{3} - 900\,x + 900$$

$$= \frac{136.36}{3}(3.69\,x^2 + 0.26\,x^3) - 900\,x + 900$$

Point of contraflexure :

$$\text{B.M.} = 0 = \frac{136.36}{3}(3.69\,x^2 + 0.26\,x^3) - 900\,x + 900$$

∴ $0 = 3.69\,x^2 + 0.26\,x^3 - 19.8\,x + 19.8$

∴ $x = 2.93$ m

S.F. at 2.93 m : S.F. $= 136.36\,(1.23\,x + 0.13\,x^2)$

$$= 900 - 136.36\,[1.23 \times 2.93 + 0.13 \times (2.93)^2]$$

$$= 256.39 \text{ kN}$$

∴ $\dfrac{1.3\,M_1}{V} + L_o > L_d$

M_1 = M.R. of steel available at zero B.M.

$$= 984 \text{ kN-m}$$

∴ $\dfrac{1.3 \times 984 \times 10^6}{256.39 \times 10^3} + 600 > \dfrac{0.87 \times 415 \times 25}{4 \times 1.6 \times 1.2}$

$$5589.27 > 1175.29$$

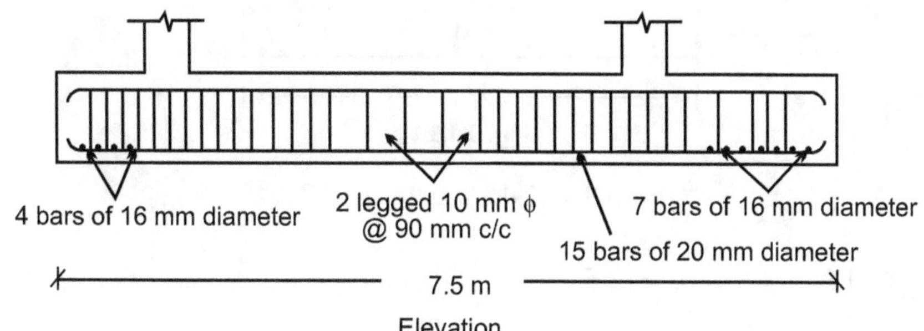

Fig. 14.13

Example 14.3 :

Design a combined footing for the following loads :

	Column A	Column B
Size	230×230	230×300
Working load	300 kN	400 kN

Centre to centre distance between columns is 2.4 m. Use M 20 and Fe 415.
S.B.C. = 150 kN/m².

Solution :

Step I : Design constants : M 20 and Fe 415

$$k_{u\ max} = 0.48$$

$$R_u = 0.36\ f_{ck}\ k_{u\ max}\ (1 - 0.42\ k_{u\ max})$$

$$= 0.36 \times 20 \times 0.48\ (1 - 0.42 \times 0.48)$$

$$= 2.76\ N/mm^2$$

Step II : Dimensions of footing :

Ultimate loads with F.S. = 1.5

$$W_{u_1} = 450\ kN$$

$$W_{u_2} = 600\ kN$$

Ultimate bearing capacity of soil = 225 kN/m²
Total column load = 450 + 600 = 1050 kN
Assume self weight of footing 10% of column load.

$\therefore \qquad S_w = 105\ kN$

$$\text{Area of footing required} = \frac{1200}{225} = 5.33\ m^2$$

$$1050\ x = 450 \times 2.4$$

$\therefore \qquad x = 1.03\ m\ \ \text{from column B}$

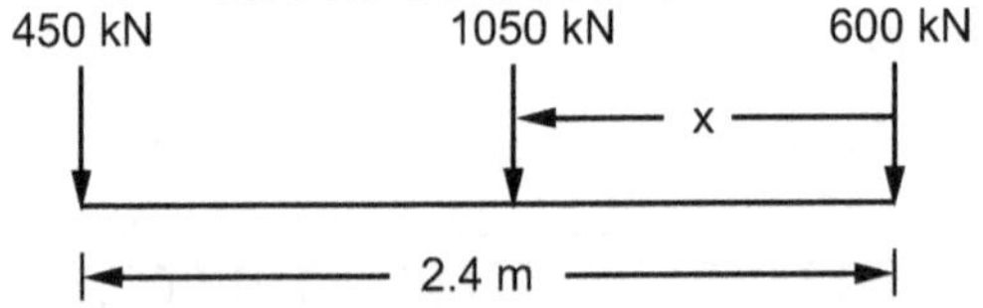

Fig. 14.14

$\therefore \qquad \dfrac{L}{2} = 0.5 + (2.4 - 1.03) = 1.87$

$\text{Adopt } \dfrac{L}{2} = 1.8\ m \qquad \therefore\ L = 3.6\ m$

$$B = \frac{5.33}{3.6} = 1.48\ \text{say } 1.5\ m$$

$$A_{f\ pro} = 3.6 \times 1.5 = 5.4 \text{ m}^2$$

$$\text{Net upward soil pressure} = \frac{1050}{5.4} = 194.44 \text{ kN/m}^2$$

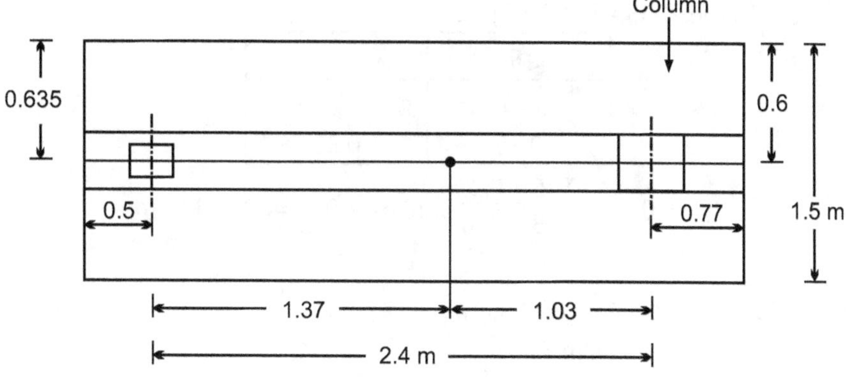

Fig. 14.15

Step III : Design of slab : Intensity of upward pressure $W_u = 194.44$ kN/m^2

Consider one meter width of slab (b = 1 m)

∴   Load per m run of slab $= 194.44 \times 1 = 194.44$ kN/m

$$\text{Maximum ultimate moment} = \frac{194.44 \times (0.635)^2}{2} = 39.19 \text{ kN-m}$$

For M 20 Fe 415 :

$$39.19 \times 10^6 = 0.138 \times 20 \times 1000 \times d_{req}^2$$

∴ $d_{req} = 119$ mm

Assume 16 mm bar and 50 mm clear cover.

∴ $D = 119 + \dfrac{16}{2} + 50 = 177$

Adopt D = 200 mm

$d_{pro} = 200 - 8 - 50 = 142$ mm

$$A_{st} = \frac{0.5 \times 20}{415}\left[1 - \sqrt{1 - \frac{4.6 \times 39.19 \times 10^6}{20 \times 1000 \times (142)^2}}\right] \times 1000 \times 142$$

$$= 877.22 \text{ mm}^2$$

For $\phi16$, $a_{st} = 201$ mm^2

$$\text{Spacing, S} = 1000 \times \frac{201}{877.22} = 229 \approx 220 \text{ mm c/c}$$

$$\text{Area pro} = 1000 \times \frac{201}{220} = 913.63 \text{ mm}^2$$

Step IV : Check the depth for one way shear consideration :

$$p_t = 100 \times \frac{913.63}{1000 \times 142} = 0.64\%$$

[From table 19 page 73 IS 453 : 2000]......

p_t	τ_c
0.5	0.3
0.75	0.35

$$\tau_c = 0.3 + \frac{(0.35 - 0.3)}{(0.75 - 0.5)} \times (0.64 - 0.5) = 0.328 \text{ N/mm}^2$$

[From table 20 page 73 IS 456 : 2000] ......

$$\tau_{c\ max} = 2.8 \text{ N/mm}^2$$

Value of k is 1.2 page no. 84.

$\therefore$　　Permissible shear stress $= 1.2 \times \tau_c$

$$= 1.2 \times 0.328$$

$$= \mathbf{0.454\ MPa}$$

$\therefore$　　Shear required by concrete $V_{uc} = 0.454 \times 1000 \times 142 \times 1000$

$$= \mathbf{95.47\ kN}$$

Design shear at distance d $= 142$ mm

From the face of column,

$$V_{uD} = 194.44 \times (0.635 - 0.142)$$

$$= 67.85 \text{ kN}$$

$\therefore$　　　　$V_{uC} > V_{uD}$

i.e.　　　　$95.47 > 67.85$

Step V : Check for development length :

$$L_d = \frac{0.87 \times 415}{4 \times 1.2} \times 16 = 868.4 \text{ mm}$$

Modified development length :

$$L_{dm} = L_d \times \frac{A_s}{A_{s\ pro}}$$

$$= 868.4 \times \frac{877.23}{913.63}$$

$$= 833.4 \text{ mm}$$

Available length of bar $= 635 - 50 + 89$

$$= 948 \text{ mm} > 833.4 \text{ mm} \quad \therefore \quad \text{Safe}$$

Step VI : Transverse reinforcement :

$$\text{Required } A_{st} = 0.15 \frac{bD}{100}$$

$$= \frac{0.15}{100} \times 1000 \times 200 = 300 \text{ mm}^2$$

Using ϕ 8 mm bars,

$$\text{Spacing} = 1000 \times \frac{50.26}{300}$$

$$= 167.5 \text{ mm}$$

Provide distribution steel of ϕ 8 @ 150 mm c/c.

Step VII : S.F.D. and B.M.D :

$$M_x = 0 = 291.6 \times \frac{x^2}{2} - 450\,(x - 0.43)$$

$$145.83\,x^2 - 450\,x + 193.5 = 0$$

$$\therefore \qquad x = 0.52 \text{ m and } x = 2.57 \text{ m}$$

Depth of beam from B.M. consideration :

$$86.47 \times 10^6 = 0.138 \times 20 \times 300 \times d_{req}^2$$

$$\therefore \qquad d_{req} = 323.15 \text{ mm}$$

$\therefore$ Provide total depth $= 400$ mm

$\therefore$ Effective depth provide $d_{pro} = 400 - 50 = 350$ mm

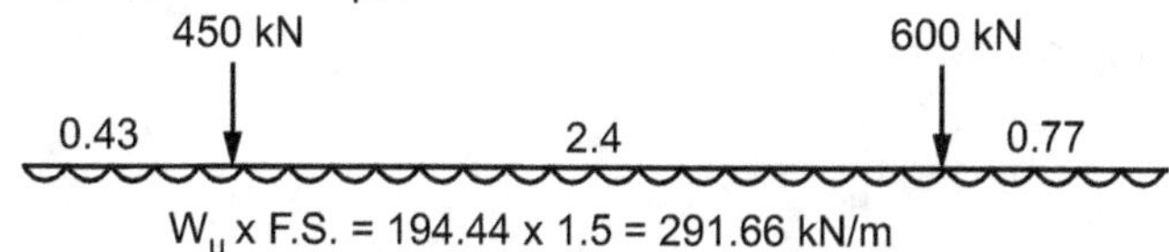

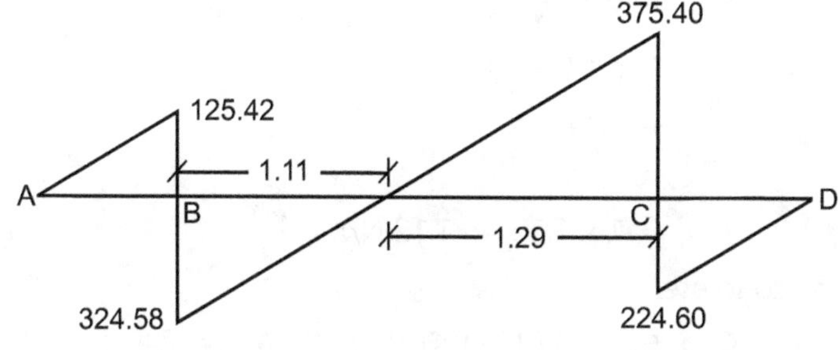

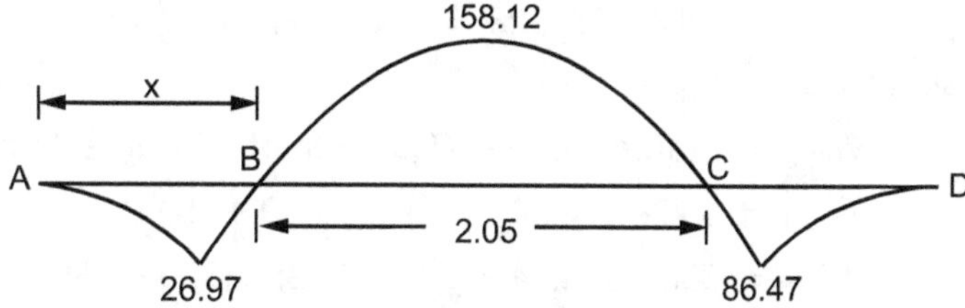

Fig. 14.16

Step VIII : Check for depth for two way shear :

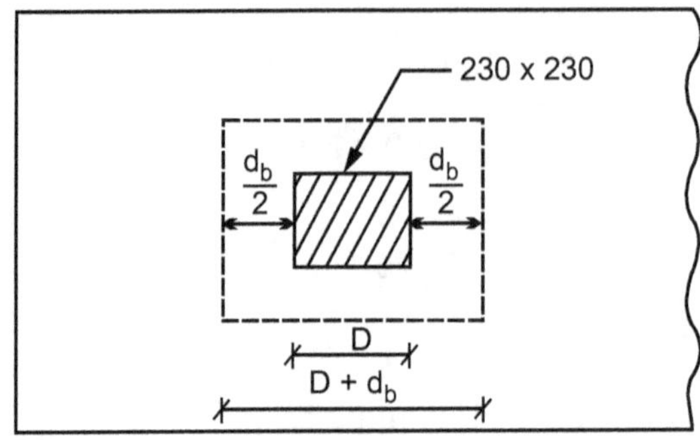

Fig. 14.17

$$b = 230 \text{ mm}$$
$$D = 300 \text{ mm}$$
$$d_b = 350 \text{ mm}$$
$$d_s = 142 \text{ mm}$$

$$\text{Area resisting two way shear} = 2\,(b \times d_b + d_s \times d_s) + 2\,(D + d_b)\,d_s$$
$$= 2\,(230 \times 350 + 142 \times 142) + 2\,(650) \times 142$$
$$= 385928 \text{ mm}^2$$

Shear stress resisted by concrete,

$$\tau_{uc} = \tau_{uc}' \times k_s$$

where

$$\tau_{uc}' = 0.25\,\sqrt{f_{ck}}$$
$$= 0.25 \times \sqrt{20}$$
$$= 1.12$$

$$k_s = 1$$

$$\therefore \quad \tau_{uc} = 1 \times 1.12 = 1.12 \text{ N/mm}^2$$

Shear resisted by concrete,

$$\tau_{uc\,2} = \tau_{uc} \times \text{Area resisting two way shear}$$
$$= 1.12 \times 385928 = 533.23 \text{ kN}$$

$$\text{Design shear} = V_{uD\,2}$$

$$\therefore \quad V_{uD\,2} = \text{Column load} - W_u \times \text{Area of critical section}$$
$$= 600 - 194.44 \times (b + d_s) \times (D + d_b)$$
$$= 600 - 194.44 \times (230 + 142) \times (300 + 350) \times 10^{-6}$$
$$= 453 \text{ kN} < V_{uc\,2}\,(553.23 \text{ kN}) \quad \therefore \text{ Safe}$$

Step IX : Area of reinforcement : Cantilever portion CD :

Length of cantilever from face of column

$$= \frac{291.66 \times (0.66)^2}{2} = 63.52 \text{ kN/m}$$

Assuming two rows,

$$d = 400 - 65 = 335 \text{ mm}$$

$$M_{u\,max} = 2.23 \times 300 \times (335)^2 \times 10^{-6}$$

$$= 75.08 \text{ kN-m} > 63.52 \text{ kN-m}$$

∴   Section is singly reinforced.

$$A_{st} = \frac{0.5 \times 20}{415}\left[1 - \sqrt{1 - \frac{4.6 \times 63.52 \times 10^6}{20 \times 300 \times (335)^2}}\right] \times 300 \times 335$$

$$= 600 \text{ mm}^2$$

Provide 3 ϕ 16 at bottom face area.

$$\text{Area provided} = 603 \text{ mm}^2$$

$$L_d = 54.4 \times 25 = 1359 \text{ mm}$$

Cantilever portion AB :

Length of cantilever from face of column

$$= 0.43 - \left(\frac{0.23}{2}\right)$$

∴   Ultimate moment $= \dfrac{291.66 \times (0.315)^2}{2} = 15 \text{ kN-m}$

$$A_{st} = \frac{0.5 \times 20}{415}\left[1 - \sqrt{1 - \frac{4.6 \times 15 \times 10^6}{20 \times 230 \times (335)^2}}\right] \times 230 \times 335$$

$$= 128.53 \text{ mm}^2$$

Provide 2 ϕ 12 at bottom face.

$$\text{Area provided} = 226 \text{ mm}^2$$

In the region BC between points of contraflexure the beam acts as T-beam.

$$b_f = \frac{l_o}{(l_o/b) + 4} + b_w$$

where

$$l_o = \text{Distance of point of contraflexure} = 2.05 \text{ m}$$

$$b = \text{Actual width of flange} = 1.5 \text{ m}$$

$$b_w = 230 \text{ mm}$$

∴

$$b_f = \frac{2050}{(2050/1500) + 4} + 230$$

$$= 612 \text{ mm}$$

$$\therefore \quad \text{Required } A_{st} = \frac{0.5 \times 20}{415}\left[1 - \sqrt{1 - \frac{4.6 \times 153.18 \times 10^6}{20 \times 612 \times (335)^2}}\right] \times 612 \times 335$$

$$= 1492.56 \text{ mm}^2$$

Provide 5 ϕ 20 mm.

$$\text{Area provided} = 1570 \text{ mm}^2$$

Step X : Design of shear reinforcement between portion B and C :

(i)   Maximum S.F. @ C = $V_{u\,max}$ = 375.40 kN

Shear at the point of contraflexure $= V_{uD}$

$$\therefore \qquad V_{uD} = 375.40 - 291.66 \times 0.26$$

$$= 300 \text{ kN}$$

$$p_t = \frac{100 \times 1570}{230 \times 335}$$

$$= 2.03\%$$

p_t	τ_c
2.0	0.79
2.25	0.81

$$\therefore \qquad \tau_{uc} = 0.79 + \frac{(0.81 - 0.79)}{(2.25 - 2.0)} \times (2.03 - 2.0)$$

$$= 0.792 \text{ N/mm}^2 \qquad \text{(Page 73 table 19 of IS 456 : 2000)}$$

Shear resisted by concrete : (V_{uc}) :

$$V_{uc} = \tau_{uc}\, bd$$

$$= 0.792 \times 230 \times \frac{335}{1000}$$

$$= 61 \text{ kN}$$

Shear resisted by minimum stirrups,

$$V_{usv\,min} = 0.4\, bd$$

$$= 0.4 \times 230 \times \frac{335}{1000}$$

$$= 30.82 \text{ kN}$$

$$V_{ur\,min} = 61 + 30.82 = 91.82 \text{ kN} \; < \; V_{uD} \text{ (300 kN)}$$

$\therefore$ Design for shear reinforcement is required.

Shear is to be resisted by stirrups.

$$V_{usv} = V_{uD} - V_{uc}$$

$$= 300 - 61$$
$$= 239 \text{ kN}$$

Using 10 mm diameter 4-legged stirrups,

$$\text{Spacing (S)} = \frac{0.87 \times 415 \times (4 \times 78.54) \times 325}{239 \times 1000}$$

$$= 154.24 \approx 150 \text{ mm}$$

Zone of shear reinforcement :

$$L_{s1} = \frac{(V_{u\,max} - V_{ur\,min})}{W_u} = \frac{(375.4 - 91.82)}{291.66}$$

$$= 0.97 \text{ m (from supports)}$$

Maximum shear at A $= V_{u\,max} = 324.58 \text{ kN}$

Shear at point of contraflexure $= V_{uD}$

$\therefore \qquad V_{uD} = 324.58 - 0.09 \times 291.66 = 298.33 \text{ kN}$

$V_{ur\,min} = 91.82 \text{ kN}$ as obtained above

$V_{us} = V_{uD} = V_{uc} = 298.33 - 61 = 237.33 \text{ kN}$

$$\text{Spacing (S)} = \frac{0.87 \times 415 \times 4 \times 78.54 \times 335}{237.33 \times 1000} = 154.24 \approx 150 \text{ mm c/c.}$$

Zone of shear reinforcement :

$$L_{s1} = \frac{(298.33 - 91.82)}{291.66} = 0.71 \text{ m}$$

For portion between two columns provide 10 mm diameter 4-legged stirrups at spacing 150 mm c/c from column C for distance of 0.97 m and from column B for distance of 0.71 m. For the remaining central portion of $(2.4 - 0.97 - 0.71) = 0.72$ m

Provide minimum shear reinforcement using 10 mm diameter 2-legged stirrups at spacing,

$$S = \frac{0.87 \times 415 \times 2 \times 78.54}{230 \times 300} = 92.14 \text{ mm}$$

$\therefore \qquad S = 90 \text{ mm (say)}$

Cantilever portion CD :

$$V_{u\,max} = 224.6 \text{ kN}$$

$$V_{uD} = 224.6 - 291.66 \left(\frac{300}{2} + 335\right) / 100$$

$$= 83.14 \text{ kN}$$

Since, $\qquad V_{usv\,min} = 30.82 \text{ kN}$

∴   Minimum shear reinforcement of 10 mm diameter 2-legged stirrups @ 190 mm c/c will be sufficiently in the cantilever portion of the beam.

Example 14.4 :

Two RC columns carry axial loads of 1200 kN and 900 kN respectively, placed 3.5 m c/c, safe bearing capacity of the underlying strata = 200 kN/m². Use M20, Fe500. The cantilever projection available from the centre line of the first column upto property line is 1.42 m. Design the combined slab type rectangular footing. Draw all details of reinforcement.

(Winter 2011, 25 Marks) [Dec. 11, 12, May 13]

Solution :

Step I : Design constants : M20 and Fe500.

$$R_u = 2.66$$

$$R_u = 0.36\, f_{ck}\, k_{u\,max}\, (1 - 0.42\, k_{u\,max})$$

∴ $$2.66 = 0.36 \times 20 \times k_{u\,max}\, (1 - 0.42\, k_{u\,max})$$

∴ $$k_{u\,max} - 0.42\, k_{u\,max}^2 = 0.369$$

∴ $$k_{u\,max}^2 - 2.38\, k_{u\,max} + 0.878 = 0$$

∴ $$k_{u\,max} = \frac{2.38 \pm \sqrt{(-2.38)^2 - 4 \times 0.878}}{2}$$

∴ $$k_{u\,max} = \frac{2.38 \pm 1.467}{2}$$

∴ $$k_{u\,max} = 0.46$$

Step II : Dimensions of footing : Load on footing

(i)   Ultimate load on column C_1 = 1.5 × 1200 = 1800 kN

(ii) Ultimate load on column C_2 = 1.5 × 900 = 1350 kN

(iii) Self weight of footing = 0.1 × 3150 = 315 kN

∴   Total load on footing = 3465 kN

∴   Required area of footing $= \dfrac{3465}{1.5 \times 200} = 11.55\ \text{m}^2$

$\sum M\ @\ C_2 = 0$

∴   3150 x = 1800 × 3.5

∴   x = 2 m from C_2

$\dfrac{1}{2}$ = 0.5 + (3.5 − 2) = 2 m

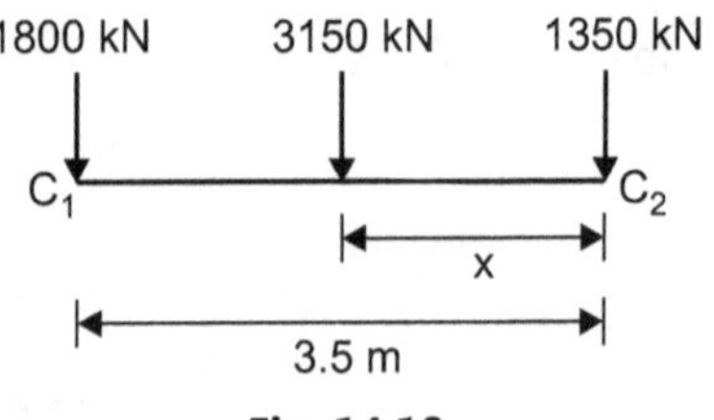

Fig. 14.18

∴   Adopt length of footing = 1.42 + 3.5 + 2 = 6.92 m ≈ 7 m

$$\text{Width} \;=\; \frac{A}{L} \;=\; \frac{11.55}{7} \;=\; 1.65 \text{ m}$$

Let $\bar{x}$ be the distance of C.G. of column loads $(C_1 + C_2)$ from centre line of column C_1.

$$\bar{x} \;=\; \frac{1350 \times 3.5}{3150} \;=\; 1.5 \text{ m}$$

$$l_1 + l_2 \;=\; 7 - 3.5 \;=\; 3.5 \text{ m}$$

$$\therefore \qquad 1.42 + l_2 \;=\; 3.5 \text{ m}$$

$$\therefore \qquad l_2 \;=\; 3.5 - 1.42 \;=\; 2.08 \text{ m}$$

$$\text{Net upward soil pressure} \;=\; \frac{3150}{7 \times 1.65} \;=\; 272.73 \text{ kN/m}^2 \;<\; 1.5 \times 200 \;=\; 300 \text{ kN/m}^2$$

Step III : SFD and BMD :

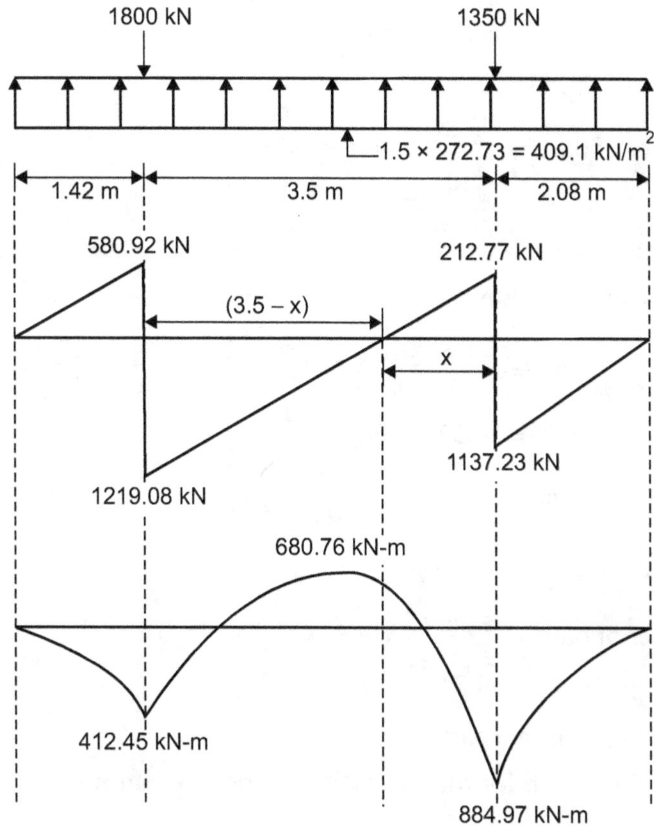

Fig. 14.19

$$\frac{x}{212.77} \;=\; \frac{(3.5 - x)}{1219.08}$$

$$1219.08\,x \;=\; 744.7 - 212.77\,x$$

$\therefore \qquad 1431.85 = 744.7$

$\therefore \qquad x = 0.52$ m

Step IV : Depth of footing :

$$d = \sqrt{\frac{M_u}{R_u b}} = \sqrt{\frac{680.76 \times 10^6}{2.66 \times 1650}} = 393.83 \text{ mm}$$

$$D = d + \text{clear cover} + \phi/2 = 393.82 + 50 + 16/2 = 451.82 \text{ mm}$$

Provide overall depth $= 500 \text{ mm} \Rightarrow d_{provided} = 500 - 50 - \dfrac{16}{2} = 442 \text{ mm}$

Step V : (a) Area of R/F for hogging B.M. between C_1 and C_2 :

$$A_{st} = \frac{0.5 \times 20}{500}\left[1 - \sqrt{1 - \frac{4.6 \times 680.76 \times 10^6}{20 \times 1650 \times 442^2}}\right] \times 1650 \times 442$$

$$= 4125.69 \text{ mm}^2$$

Using 25 mm ϕ.

$$\text{Number of bars} = \frac{4125.69}{\dfrac{\pi}{4} \times 25^2} = 8.40 \approx 9$$

Provide 9 bars of 25 mm ϕ.

(b) Area of R/F under column C_1 :

$$A_{st} = \frac{0.5 \times 20}{500}\left[1 - \sqrt{1 - \frac{4.6 \times 412.45 \times 10^6}{20 \times 1650 \times 442}}\right] \times 1650 \times 442$$

$$= 2332.77 \text{ mm}^2$$

$$\text{Minimum area of R/F} = 0.12\% \, bD = \frac{0.12}{100} \times 1650 \times 500 = 990 \text{ mm}^2$$

Using 25 mm ϕ bars,

$$\text{Number of bars} = \frac{2332.77}{\dfrac{\pi}{4} \times 25^2} = 4.75 \approx 5$$

$\therefore \qquad$ Provide 5, 25 mm ϕ bars.

Step VI : Check for depth for one way shear between columns :

(a) Between $X_2 - X_5$:

$$p_t = \frac{100 \, A_{st}}{bd} = \frac{100 \times 9 \times \dfrac{\pi}{4} \times 20^2}{1650 \times 442} = 0.6$$

p_t	p_c
0.5	0.49
0.6	?
0.75	0.57

$$\frac{0.25 - 0.08}{0.1 - x} \qquad \therefore x = \frac{0.1 \times 0.08}{0.25} = 0.032$$

$\therefore \qquad \tau_c = 0.49 + 0.032 = 0.522 \ \text{N/mm}^2$

$\therefore$ Shear resisted by concrete $= \tau_c \, bd/1000 = (0.522 \times 1650 \times 442)/1000 = 380.69 \ \text{kN}$

Shear force at critical section d from face of column on right side

$$= 212.72 - 409.1 \,(0.442 + 0.15)$$
$$= 212.72 - 409.1 \,(0.592)$$
$$= -29.4672$$

Design of shear R/F : $A_{sv} = 2 \times \dfrac{\pi}{4} \times 10^2 = 157.1 \ \text{mm}^2$

$\therefore \qquad$ Spacing of stirrups $= \dfrac{157.1 \times 0.87 \times 500 \times 442}{173.54 \times 10^3} = 174.05 \ \text{mm}$

Provide 2 legged stirrups of 10 mm ϕ steel bars of Fe500 at 160 mm c/c.

(b) Between $X_1 - X_2$:

$$p_t = \frac{100 \, A_{st}}{bd} = \frac{100 \times 5 \times \dfrac{\pi}{4} \times 25^2}{1650 \times 442} = 0.34$$

p_t	τ_c
0.25	0.36
0.34	?
0.50	0.49

$$\frac{0.25 - 0.13}{0.09 - x} \qquad \therefore x = \frac{0.09 \times 0.13}{0.25} = 0.0468$$

$\therefore \qquad \tau_c = 0.36 + 0.0468 = 0.4068 \ \text{N/mm}^2$

$\qquad \tau_{cbd} = 0.4068 \times 1650 \times 442/1000 = 296.68 \ \text{kN}$

$\quad 580.92 - 409.1 \times 0.407 = 414.41 \ \text{kN}$

Step VII : Check for depth for two-way shear :

(a) Under column C_1 : $b_o = 4 \left(230 + \dfrac{600}{2} + \dfrac{600}{2} \right) = 3320 \ \text{mm}$

$\qquad$ Soil pressure $= 195.65 \ \text{kN/m}^2$

$\qquad$ Shear force $= 600 - (195.65 \times 0.83 \times 0.83) = 465.22 \ \text{kN}$

$\qquad$ Nominal shear stress $= \tau_v = \dfrac{V}{bd} = \dfrac{465.22 \times 10^3}{3320 \times 600} = 0.23 \ \text{N/mm}^2$

$\qquad$ Permissible shear stress $= k_s \times 0.25 \sqrt{f_{ck}} = 1 \times 0.25 \sqrt{20} = 1.12 \ \text{N/mm}^2 > 0.23 \ \text{N/mm}^2$

(b) Under column C_2 : $\quad b_o = 4\left(300 + \dfrac{600}{2} + \dfrac{600}{2}\right) = 3600$ mm

$$\text{Shear force} = 750 - 195.65 \times 0.9 \times 0.9 = 591.62 \text{ kN}$$

$$\tau_v = \frac{V}{bd} = \frac{591.62 \times 10^3}{1000 \times 600} = 0.99 \text{ N/mm}^2$$

$$\text{Permissible shear stress} = k_s \times 0.25\sqrt{f_{ck}} = 1 \times 0.25\sqrt{20} = 1.11 \text{ N/mm}^2 > 0.99 \text{ N/mm}^2$$

Step VIII : R/F along width of footing :

(a) Under column C_1 :

$$\text{Projection} = \frac{1}{2}(1500 - 230) = 635 \text{ mm}$$

$$\text{Width} = 230 + 2 \times 292 = 814 \text{ mm}$$

$$\text{Soil pressure} = \frac{600 \times 10^3}{0.814 \times 1.5} = 491.4 \text{ kN/m}^2$$

$\therefore$ Maximum bending at face of column

$$= \frac{491.4 \times 0.635^2}{2} = 99.07 \text{ kN-m}$$

$\therefore$

$$d = \sqrt{\frac{M_u}{R_u b}} = \sqrt{\frac{99.07 \times 10^6}{2.66 \times 1000}} = 189.45 \text{ mm} < 442 \text{ mm}$$

$$A_{st} = \frac{0.5 \times 20}{500}\left[1 - \sqrt{1 - \frac{4.6 \times 99.07 \times 10^6}{20 \times 1000 \times 442^2}}\right] \times 1000 \times 442$$

$$= 1013.11 \text{ mm}^2 > A_{st\,min}$$

Using 16 mm ϕ bars,

$$\text{Spacing} = \frac{201 \times 1000}{1013.11} = 198.39 \text{ mm}$$

Provide 16 mm ϕ @ 190 mm c/c.

(b) Under column C_2 :

$$\text{Projection of footing} = \frac{1}{2}(1500 - 300) = 600 \text{ mm}$$

$$\text{Width of footing} = 300 + 2 \times 292 = 884 \text{ mm}$$

$$\text{Soil pressure} = \frac{750 \times 10^3}{0.884 \times 1.5} = 565.61 \text{ kN/m}^2$$

$$\text{Maximum bending force} = \frac{565.61 \times 0.6^2}{2} = 101.81 \text{ kN-m}$$

$$d = \sqrt{\frac{M_u}{R_u b}} = \sqrt{\frac{101.81 \times 10^6}{2.66 \times 1000}} = 192.01 \text{ mm} < 442 \text{ mm}$$

$$A_{st} = 1932.36 \text{ mm}^2$$

$$\text{Spacing} = \frac{201 \times 1000}{1932.36} = 104 \text{ mm}$$

Provide 16 mm ϕ @ 100 mm c/c.

Example 14.5 :

Design reinforced concrete combined rectangular footing for two columns A and B carrying working loads 600 kN and 850 kN respectively. Column A is 230 mm × 350 mm size and column B is 230 mm × 450 mm size. Centre to centre distance of columns is 3.4 m. Safe bearing capacity is 180 kN/m². Use M20 and TMT steel. Draw all details of reinforcements.

(Summer 2012, 25 Marks)

Solution :

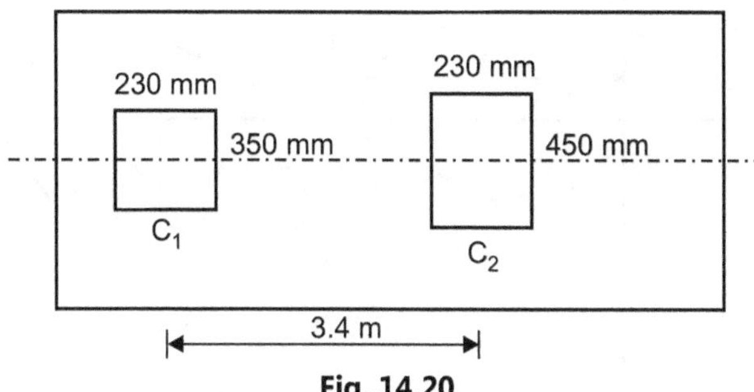

Fig. 14.20

Step I : Design constants :

$$k_{u\,max} = 0.48$$
$$R_u = 0.36\, f_{ck}\, k_{u\,max}\, (1 - 0.42\, k_{u\,max})$$
$$= 0.36 \times 20 \times 0.48\, (1 - 0.42 \times 0.48)$$
$$= 2.76 \text{ N/mm}^2$$

Step II : Dimensions of footing : Load on footing :

(i)   Ultimate load on column C_1 = 600 × 1.5 = 900 kN

(ii) Ultimate load on column C_2 = 850 × 1.5 = 1275 kN

(iii) Self weight of footing = 0.1 × 2175 = 217.5 kN

Total load = 2392.5 kN

$$\text{Required area of footing} = \frac{2392.5}{1.5 \times 180} = 8.86 \text{ m}^2$$

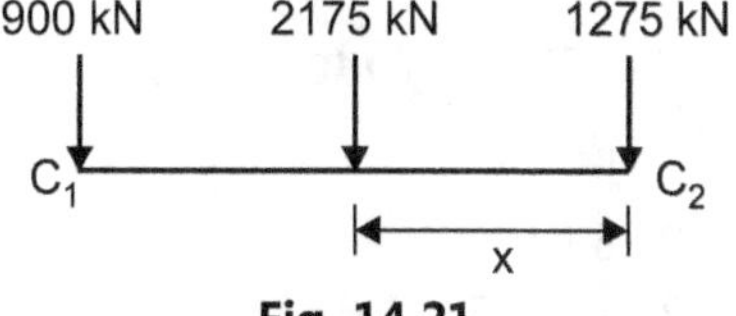

Fig. 14.21

$$900 \times 3.4 = 2175\, x$$

$\therefore$ $\quad x = 1.41$ m from C_2

$\therefore$ $\quad \dfrac{L}{2} = 0.5 + (3.4 - 1.41) = 2.49$ m

$\therefore$ Adopt length of footing $= 5.5$ m

$\therefore$ Width of footing $= \dfrac{8.86}{5.5} = 1.61$ m

$\therefore$ Provide dimensions of footing $= 1.65$ m $\times 5.5$ m

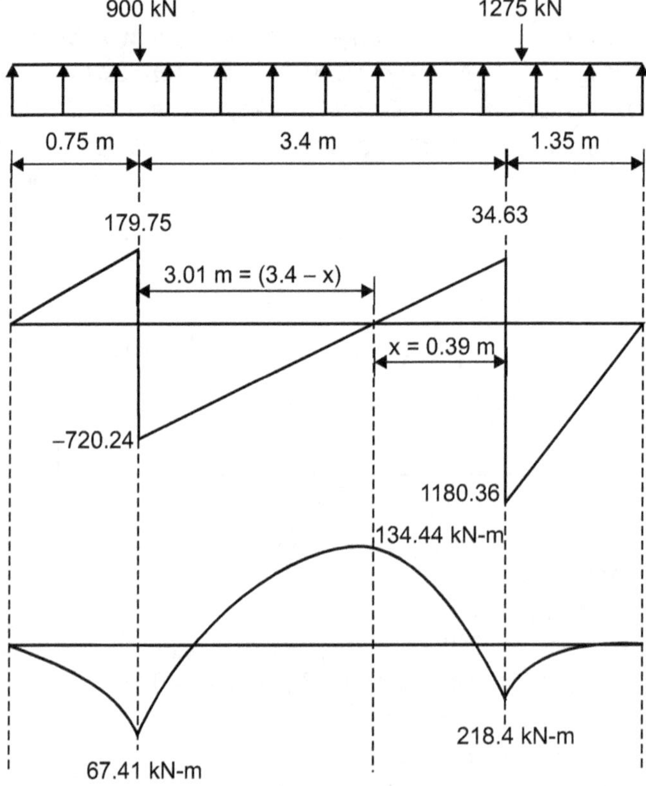

Fig. 14.22

Let $\bar{x}$ be the distance of C.G. of column loads $(C_1 + C_2)$ from centre line of column C_1.

$$\bar{x} = \dfrac{1275 \times 3.4}{2175} = 1.99 \text{ m} \approx 2 \text{ m}$$

$$l_1 + l_2 = 5.5 - 3.4 = 2.1 \text{ m}$$

$$l_1 + \bar{x} = \dfrac{L}{2} = \dfrac{5.5}{2} = 2.75 \text{ m}$$

$$l_1 + 2 = 2.75$$

$\therefore$ $\quad l_1 = 0.75$ m

$$l_2 = 2.1 - 0.75 = 1.35 \text{ m}$$

$\therefore$ Net upward soil pressure $= \dfrac{2175}{5.5 \times 1.65} = 239.67$ kN/m^2 $< 1.5 \times 180 = 270$ kN/m^2

Step III : SFD and BMD :

$$\frac{x}{94.63} = \frac{(3.4 - x)}{720.24}$$

$\therefore$ $720.24\,x = 321.74 - 94.63\,x$

$\therefore$ $814.87\,x = 321.74$

$\therefore$ $x = 0.39$ m

$$\frac{x}{94.69} = \frac{(3.4 - x)}{720.24}$$

$\therefore$ $720.24\,x = 321.74 - 94.63\,x$

$\therefore$ $814.87\,x = 321.74$

$\therefore$ $x = 0.39$ m

Step IV : Depth of footing :

$$d = \sqrt{\frac{M_u}{R_u b}} = \sqrt{\frac{218.4 \times 10^6}{2.76 \times 1650}} = 219 \text{ mm}$$

$$D = d + \text{clear cover} + \phi/2 = 219 + 50 + 16/2 = 277 \text{ mm}$$

Provide overall depth $= 350$ mm

$\therefore$ $d_{provided} = 350 - 50 - \dfrac{16}{2} = 292$ mm

Step V : (a) Area of R/F :

$$A_{st} = \frac{0.5\, f_{ck}}{f_y}\left[1 - \sqrt{1 - \frac{4.6\, M_u}{f_{ck}\, bd^2}}\right] bd$$

$$= \frac{0.5 \times 20}{415}\left[1 - \sqrt{1 - \frac{4.6 \times 218.4 \times 10^6}{20 \times 1650 \times 292^2}}\right] \times 1650 \times 292$$

$$= 2300.56 \text{ mm}^2$$

Number of bars $= \dfrac{2300.56}{201} = 11.44 \approx 12$

(b) A_{st} under column C_1 :

$$A_{st} = \frac{0.5\, f_{ck}}{f_y}\left[1 - \sqrt{1 - \frac{4.6\, M_u}{f_{ck}\, bd^2}}\right] bd$$

$$= \frac{0.5 \times 20}{415}\left[1 - \sqrt{1 - \frac{4.6 \times 67.41 \times 10^6}{20 \times 1650 \times 292^2}}\right] \times 1650 \times 292$$

$$= 658.39 \text{ mm}^2$$

$$A_{st\,min} = 0.12\% \, bD = \frac{0.12}{100} \times 1650 \times 350 = 693 \text{ mm}^2$$

$$\text{Number of bars} = \frac{693}{201} = 3.44 \approx 4$$

(c) A_{st} under column C_2 :

$$A_{st} = \frac{0.5 \times 20}{415}\left[1 - \sqrt{1 - \frac{4.6 \times 218.4 \times 10^6}{20 \times 1650 \times 292^2}}\right] \times 1650 \times 292$$

$$= 2300.56 \text{ mm}^2$$

$$\text{Number of bars} = \frac{2300.56}{201} = 11.44 \approx 12$$

Step VI : Check for depth for one-way shear between columns :

(a) Between $X_2 - X_5$:

$$p_t = \frac{100 \, A_{st}}{bd} = \frac{100 \times 13 \times \frac{\pi}{4} \times 16^2}{1650 \times 292} = 0.90$$

p_t	τ_c
0.75	0.56
1	0.62
0.9	0.6

$$\tau_c = 0.6 \text{ N/mm}^2$$

$\therefore$ Shear resisted by concrete $= \tau_c \, bd = 0.6 \times 1650 \times 292 \times 10^{-3} = 262.80$ kN

Shear force at critical section d from face of column on right side

$$= 465.32 - 293.48 \, (0.292 + 0.15)$$

$$= 335.60 \text{ kN} > 262.80 \text{ kN}$$

Design of shear R/F :

Design shear force = 335.6 kN

Shear strength of concrete (V_{UC}) = 181 kN

Shear R/F is provided for

$V_s = V_{UD} - V_{UC} = 335.6 - 162.06 = 173.54$ kN

Provide 2-legged stirrups at 10 mm ϕ HYSD steel bars.

$$\therefore \qquad A_{sv} = 2 \times \frac{\pi}{4} \times 10^2 = 157.1 \text{ mm}^2$$

$$\therefore \quad \text{Spacing of stirrups} = \frac{A_{sv} \times 0.87 \, f_y \, d}{V} = \frac{157.1 \times 0.87 \times 415 \times 292}{173.54 \times 10^3} = 95.43 \text{ mm}$$

Provide 2-legged stirrups of 10 mm ϕ HYSD steel bars of grade Fe415 at 90 mm spacing.

(b) Between $X_2 - X_2$:

$$p_t = \frac{100\,A_{st}}{bd} = \frac{100 \times 4 \times 201}{1650 \times 292} = 0.18$$

p_t	τ_c
0.15	0.28
0.25	0.36
0.18	0.304

Shear resisted by concrete = $\tau_c\,bd$ = $0.304 \times 1500 \times 292 \times 10^{-3}$ = 133.15 kN

Shear at critical section 'd' on left face of column A

$$= 184.91 - 293.48 \times 0.407 = 65.46 \text{ kN} < 133.15 \text{ kN}$$

(c) Between $X_5 - X_6$:

$$p_t = \frac{100\,A_{st}}{bd} = \frac{100 \times 7 \times 201}{1650 \times 292} = 0.32$$

p_t	τ_c
0.25	0.36
0.50	0.48
0.32	0.394

Shear resisted by concrete = $0.394 \times 1650 \times 292 \times 10^{-3}$ = 172.52 kN

Shear force at critical section 'd' on right side of column C_2

$$= 284.68 - 293.48 \left(\frac{0.3}{2} + 0.292 \right)$$

$$= 154.96 \text{ kN} < 172.57 \text{ kN}$$

Step VII : Check for depth for two-way shear :

(a)
$$b_o = 4 \left(230 + \frac{600}{2} + \frac{600}{2} \right) = 3320 \text{ mm}$$

Effective soil pressure acting upward = 195.65 kN/m^2

Shear force = Column load – Upward pressure on area within periphery

$$= 600 - (195.65 \times 0.83 \times 0.83)$$

$$= 465.22 \text{ kN}$$

Nominal shear stress = $\tau_v = \dfrac{V}{bd} = \dfrac{465.22 \times 10^3}{3320 \times 600} = 0.23$ N/mm^2

Permissible shear stress = $k_s \times 0.25 \sqrt{f_{ck}}$

$$= 1 \times 0.25 \sqrt{20} = 1.12 \text{ N/mm}^2 > 0.23 \text{ N/mm}^2$$

(b)
$$b_o = 4\left(300 + \frac{600}{2} + \frac{600}{2}\right) = 3600 \text{ mm}$$

$$\text{Shear force} = 750 - 195.65\,(0.9 \times 0.9) = 591.52 \text{ kN}$$

$$\text{Nominal shear stress} = \tau_v = \frac{V}{bd} = \frac{591.52 \times 10^3}{1000 \times 600} = 0.99 \text{ N/mm}^2$$

$$\text{Permissible shear stress} = k_s \times 0.25\sqrt{f_{ck}} = 1 \times 0.25\sqrt{20}$$

$$= 1.11 \text{ N/mm}^2 > 0.99 \text{ N/mm}^2$$

Step VIII : Reinforcement along width of footing :

(a) Under column C_1 :

Projection of footing along width

$$= \frac{1}{2}(1500 - 230) = 635 \text{ mm}$$

$$\text{Width of footing} = (230 + 2 \times 292)$$

$$= 814 \text{ mm}$$

$$\text{Soil pressure on the footing} = \frac{600 \times 10^3}{0.814 \times 1.5} = 491.4 \text{ kN/m}^2$$

Consider unit width of footing.

$\therefore$ Maximum bending at face of column

$$= \frac{491.40 \times 0.635^2}{2} = 99.07 \text{ kN-m}$$

$\therefore$
$$d = \sqrt{\frac{M_u}{R_u b}} = \sqrt{\frac{99.07 \times 10^6}{2.76 \times 1000}} = 189.45 \text{ mm} < 292 \text{ mm}$$

$\therefore$
$$A_{st} = \frac{0.5\,f_{ck}}{f_y}\left[1 - \sqrt{1 - \frac{4.6\,M_u}{f_{ac}\,bd^2}}\right]bd$$

$$= \frac{0.5 \times 20}{415}\left[1 - \sqrt{1 - \frac{4.6 \times 99.07 \times 10^6}{20 \times 1000 \times 292^2}}\right]1000 \times 292$$

$$= 1013.11 \text{ mm}^2 > A_{st\,min}$$

$$\text{Spacing} = \frac{\frac{\pi}{4} \times 16^2 \times 1000}{1013.11} = 198.39 \text{ mm}$$

Provide 16 mm ϕ @ 190 mm c/c.

(b) Under column C_2 :

$$\left[\begin{array}{c}\text{Projection of footing}\\\text{along width h}\end{array}\right] = \frac{1}{2}\,(1500 - 300) = 600 \text{ mm}$$

$$\text{Width of footing} = 300 + 2 \times 292 = 884 \text{ mm}$$

$$\text{Soil pressure on footing} = \frac{\text{Load}}{\text{Area}} = \frac{750 \times 10^3}{0.884 \times 1.5} = 565.61 \text{ kN/m}^2$$

$\therefore$ Maximum bending at face of column

$$= \frac{565.61 \times 0.6^2}{2} = 101.81 \text{ kN-m}$$

$$d = \sqrt{\frac{M_u}{R_u b}} = \sqrt{\frac{101.81 \times 10^6}{2.76 \times 1000}} = 192.01 \text{ mm} < 292 \text{ mm}$$

$$A_{st} = \frac{0.5 \times 20}{415}\left[1 - \sqrt{1 - \frac{4.6 \times 101.81 \times 10^6}{20 \times 1000 \times 292^2}}\right] \times 1000 \times 292$$

$$= 1932.36 \text{ mm}^2$$

$$\text{Spacing} = \frac{\frac{\pi}{4} \times 16^2 \times 1000}{1932.36} = 104 \text{ mm}$$

$\therefore$ Provide 16 mm ϕ @ 100 mm c/c.

Step IX : Distribution R/F : Provide 8 mm ϕ @ 100 mm c/c.

Step X : Check for development length :

$$\frac{1.3\,M_1}{V} + L_o > L_d$$

$$M_1 = \text{Moment of resistance of steel bars available at 0.3 m}$$

$$= 0.87\, f_y\, A_{st}\, (d - 0.42\, x_{u\,max})$$

$$= 0.87 \times 415 \times 2783.94\,(292 - 0.42 \times 0.48 \times 292)$$

$$= 234.32 \times 10^6 \text{ N-mm}$$

$$\text{S.F.} = 374.02 \times 10^3 \text{ N}$$

$$L_o = d \text{ or } 12\,\phi \text{ whichever is greater}$$

$$= 292 \text{ or } 12 \times 20$$

$$= 292 \text{ mm}$$

$$\therefore \quad L_d = \frac{0.87\, f_y\, \phi}{4\, \tau_b\, d}$$

$$= \frac{0.87 \times 415 \times 20}{4 \times 1.6 \times 1.2}$$

$$= 940.23 \text{ mm}$$

$$\therefore \quad \frac{1.3 \times 234.32 \times 10^6}{374.02 \times 10^3} + 292 = 1106.44 \text{ mm} > 940.23 \text{ mm}$$

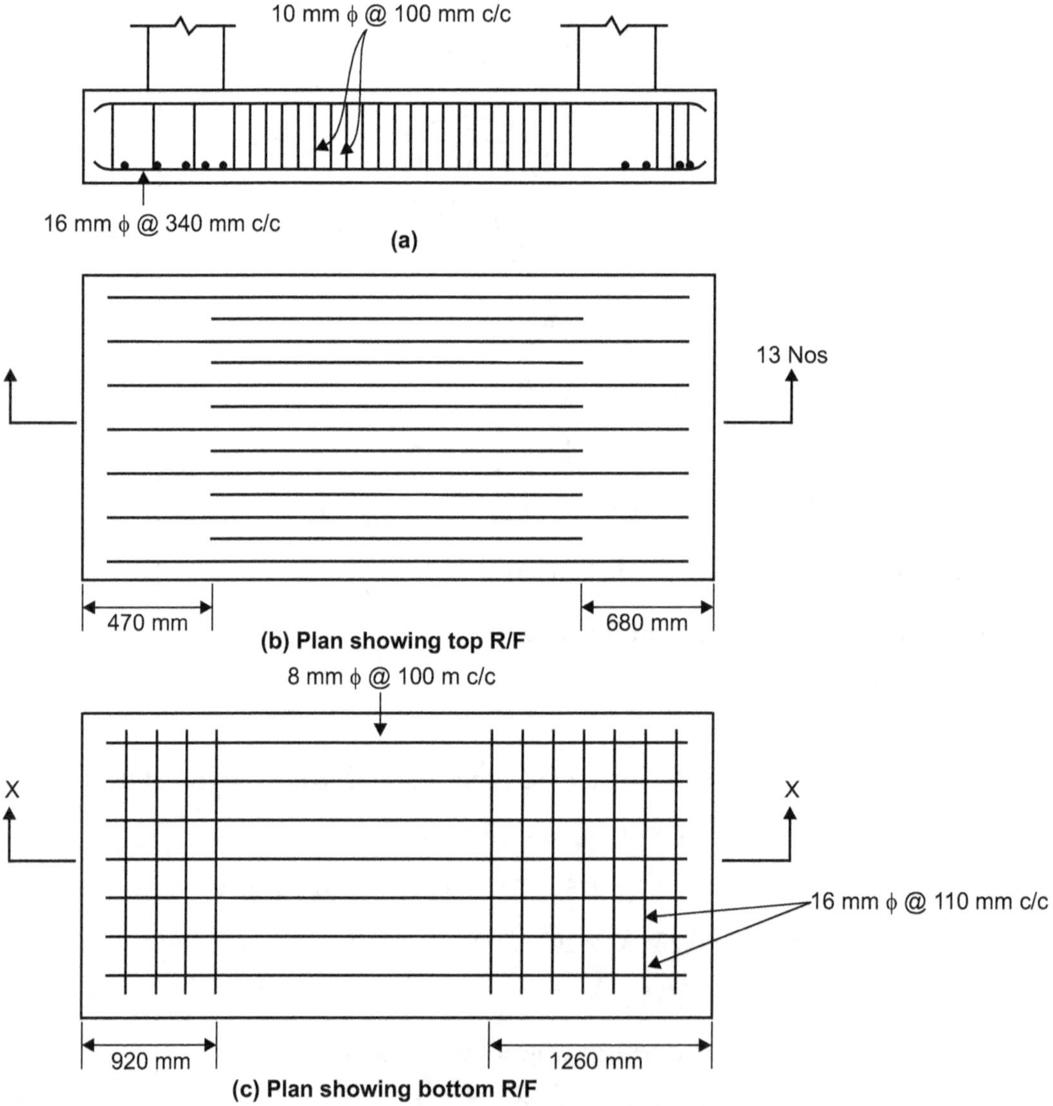

10 mm ϕ @ 100 mm c/c

16 mm ϕ @ 340 mm c/c

(a)

13 Nos

470 mm   680 mm

(b) Plan showing top R/F

8 mm ϕ @ 100 m c/c

X   X

16 mm ϕ @ 110 mm c/c

920 mm   1260 mm

(c) Plan showing bottom R/F

Fig. 14.23

IMPORTANT POINTS

- Types of combined footings.

- Steps for designing combined footings.

QUESTIONS

1. Design a reinforced concrete combined rectangular footing for two columns located apart. The overall sizes of columns are 350 mm × 350 mm and 600 mm × 600 mm and the loads on them are 900 kN and 1400 kN respectively. The safe bearing capacity of soil is 240 kN/m². Use M 25 and Fe 500.

2. Design a reinforced concrete combined rectangular footing for two columns located at 3.5 meter apart. The overall sizes of columns are 400 mm × 400 mm and 500 mm × 500 mm and the loads on them are 900 kN and 1350 kN respectively. The length of footing is restricted to 6.5 m. Use M 20 and Fe 415.

3. Two columns 5.1 m apart between centres carry loads of 1500 kN and 2500 kN respectively. The sizes of columns are 550 mm × 550 mm and 750 mm × 750 mm. Design a combined footing for the columns. The projections beyond the centres of columns parallel to the length of footing are limited to 0.8 m and 1.4 m respectively. Safe bearing capacity of soil is 300 kN/m². Use M 20 and Fe 415.

4. Design a strap footing to carry two column loads of 1100 kN and 2000 kN. The columns are 5.5 m apart. The sizes of columns are 400 mm × 400 mm and 550 mm × 550 mm respectively. The footing area under the columns are 1.25 m × 3.0 m and 2.75 m × 2.75 m and connected by a suitable strap beam. The safe bearing capacity of soil is 225 kN/m².

5. Two columns are 4.0 m apart, carry loads of 1500 kN and 2500 kN respectively. The sizes of columns are 500 mm × 600 mm and 700 mm × 800 mm respectively. The footing area under the columns are 2.2 m × 2.2 m and 3.2 m × 3.2 m and connecting by a suitable strap beam. The safe bearing capacity of soil is 400 kN/m². Use M 20 and Fe 500.

UNIVERSITY QUESTIONS

Dec. 2011

Q. 1   Two RC columns carry axial loads of 1200 kN and 900 kN respectively, placed 3.5 m c/c. Safe bearing capacity of the underlying strata = 200 kN/m². Use M20, Fe 500. The cantilever projection available from the centre line of the first column up to property line is 1.42 m. design the combined slab type rectangular footing. Draw all details of reinforcement. **(Example 14.4)**   **(25 Marks)**

May 2012

Q. 2 Design reinforced concrete combined rectangular footing for two columns A and B carrying working loads 600 kN and 850 kN respectively. Column A is 230 mm × 350 mm size and column B is 230 m × 450 mm size. Centre to centre distance of columns is 3.4 m, safe bearing capacity is 180 kN/m². Use M20 and TMT steel. Draw all details of reinforcements. **(Example 14.1)**   **(25 Marks)**

Dec. 2012

Q. 3 (a) Write a short note on combined footing wth strap beam.

(Section 14.2 and 14.4)   **(5 Marks)**

May 2013

Q. 4 Design a slab and beam type rectangular combined footing for two columns A and B carrying working load 650 kN and 80 kN respectively column A is 230 mm × 375 mm and column B is 230 mm × 40 mm. centre to centre distance between the columns is 3.0 and the property line is at 0.9 m from the faces of column A. Assume SBC of soil is 180 kN/m², use M 20 and Fe500. Draw detail of reinforcement in slab and central beam. **(Example 14.4)**   **(25 Marks)**

Dec. 2014

Q. 5 (a) At what situation, combined footing is recommended than isolated footing.

(Section 14.2)   **(5 Marks)**

May 2015

Q. 6 (a) State the necessity of combined footing and mentioned situations where it is to be provided.   **(Section 14.2) (5 Marks)**

Chapter 15
WATER TANKS

15.1 INTRODUCTION

Water tanks are very useful structures constructed for the storage of water for swimming, baths, sewage sanitation, etc. Water tanks are constructed of different materials such as

   (i)   Masonry.
   (ii) Plain concrete.
   (iii) Reinforced concrete.
   (iv) Prestressed concrete.
   (v)   Steel.

15.2 TYPES OF WATER TANKS

   (a)   Depending upon the shape, water tanks are classified as
      (i)   Circular water tanks.
      (ii) Rectangular water tanks.
   (b)   Depending upon the position with respect to ground, water tanks are classified as
      (i)   Tanks situated on the ground.
      (ii) Tanks situated under ground.
      (iii) Tanks situated above ground level also known as elevated water tanks.

15.3 PHILOSOPHY INVOLVED IN DESIGN OF WATER TANKS

I.S. codes on water tank basically specify provisions based on working stress method (W.S.M.). This is because cracking of concrete is not allowed in case of water tank surfaces which are in contact with water. So it restricts the allowable stresses. On the other face which is not in contact, one may go upto allowable stress in concrete and steel and may allow cracking of concrete.

15.4 MATERIALS OF CONCRETE AND STEEL

As per IS 3370.

   (a)   Concrete :
   (i)   Concrete mix shall not be less than M 20 (Clause 3.1 a, page no. 5 IS 3370 part I).
   (ii) Minimum cement in R.C.C. water tank shall be 330 kg/m^3.
   (iii) Concrete should be reasonably impervious.

Allowable stresses in concrete :

Table 15.1

Grade of concrete	Allowable stress in N/mm²		Allowable stress in shear in N/mm²
	In direct tension	In bending tension	
M 20	1.2	1.7	1.7
M 25	1.3	1.8	1.9
M 30	1.5	2.0	2.2
M 35	1.6	2.2	2.5
M 40	1.7	2.4	2.7

When thickness of wall ≤ 225 mm, check for tensile stress carried out on both surfaces. For non-retaining surface, recommendation in IS 456 shall be applied. For thickness greater than 225 mm, following stresses are taken into consideration.

Table 15.2

Grade of concrete	Allowable stress in N/mm²		Allowable stress in shear in N/mm²
	In direct tension	In bending tension	
M 20	5.0	7.0	0.8
M 25	6.0	8.5	0.9
M 30	8.0	10.0	1.0
M 35	9.0	11.5	1.1
M 40	10.0	13.0	1.2

According to clause no. 5.3 in IS 3370 part II following check is ensured for uncracked section.

$$\frac{t'}{t} + \frac{\sigma_{ct}'}{\sigma_{ct}} \leq 1$$

where, t' : Actual tensile stress in concrete under direct tension

           t : Allowable tensile stress in concrete under direct tension

       σ_{ct}' : Actual tensile stress in concrete in bending tension

       σ_{ct} : Allowable tensile stress in concrete in bending tension.

(b)   Allowable stresses in steel :

Refer Table 2 in IS 3370 part II :

Table 15.3

Nature of tensile stress	Permissible tensile stress in N/mm²	
	Fe 250	Fe 415
Tensile stress due to direct tension.	100	170
Tensile stress due to bending in steel near the liquid face or away from the liquid face when thickness is less than 225 mm.	100	170
Tensile stress in steel provided away from the liquid face in members of thickness greater than 225 mm.	125	200

15.5 MINIMUM REINFORCEMENT

The minimum reinforcement in tank walls and floors in each of two directions at right angles shall have an area of 0.3% of concrete section in that direction for sections upto 100 mm thick.

For sections between 100 mm to 450 mm, the minimum reinforcement in each direction shall be linearly reduced from 0.3% for 100 mm to 0.2% for 450 mm as shown in Fig. 15.1

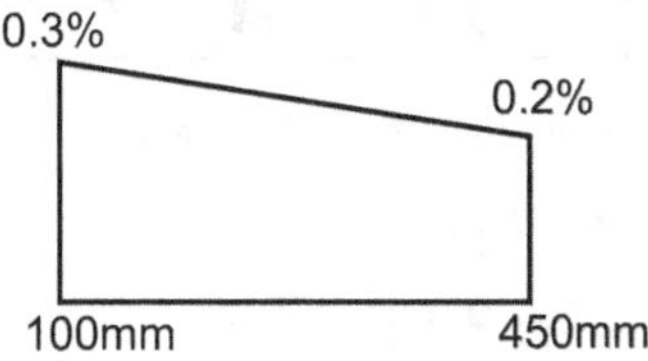

Fig. 15.1

For sections greater than 450 mm, minimum reinforcement shall be kept as 0.2%. In concrete sections of thickness 225 mm or greater, two layers of reinforcement shall be placed on near each face of the section.

15.6 DESIGN CONSTANTS FOR WORKING STRESS METHOD

(a) Modular ratio $= m = \dfrac{280}{3\sigma_{cbc}}$

(b) Neutral axis depth factor (k) :

$$k = \frac{m\,\sigma_{cbc}}{m\,\sigma_{cbc} + \sigma_{st}}$$

where σ_{cbc} : Stress in concrete in bending and compression.

σ_{st} : Stress in steel in tension.

(c)   Lever arm factor (j) :

$$j = \left(1 - \frac{k}{3}\right)$$

(d)   Moment resistance factor (Q) :

$$Q = \frac{1}{2}\,\sigma_{cbc} \times k \times j$$

For various combinations of concrete and steel, the value of various parameters will be tabulated as follows :

Table 15.4

Factor	Combination of concrete and steel			
	M 20 and Fe 250	**M 20 and Fe 415**	**M 25 and Fe 250**	**M 25 and Fe 415**
m	13.33	13.33	10.98	10.98
k	0.4	0.29	0.45	0.38
j	0.87	0.9	0.85	0.87
Q	1.21	0.91	1.63	2.63

15.7 TANKS SITUATED ON GROUND

We have to study circular and rectangular tanks situated on ground.

(A) Circular tanks situated on ground :

Circular tanks are preferred for large capacities.

Depending upon the connection of wall with base, circular tanks are classified into two parts :

(1)   Circular tanks with flexible joint between walls and base.

(2)   Circular tanks with rigid joint between walls and base.

(1) Circular tanks with flexible joint between walls and base :

In this type, the walls are designed as vertical cylinders subjected to water pressure. The intensity of water pressure at any depth h is wh; where w is unit weight of water.

Steps to be followed in design :

Step I : Design constants.

Step II : Fixation of dimensions.

(a)   Diameter of tank

$$\frac{\pi}{4}D^2 = \frac{\text{Volume of water tank}}{\text{Depth of water}}$$

(b)   Thickness of tank wall :

    (i)   150 mm.

    (ii)   30 mm per meter depth + 50 mm.

    (iii)   Thickness required to limit the tensile stress in concrete to 1.2 N/mm².

$$\text{Tensile stress } = \frac{T}{bt + (m-1)\,A_{st}}$$

Step III : Design of tank wall.

Step IV : Distribution steel.

Step V : Design of base slab.

15.8 DESIGN OF WATER TANK BY APPROXIMATE METHOD

The approximate method is based on the assumptions that cantilever action will take place for a height of $\frac{H}{3}$ or 1 m (whichever is more) above the base for the value of $\frac{H^2}{Dt}$ between 6 to 12 and for a height of $\frac{H}{4}$ or 1 m (whichever is more) for the value of $\frac{H^2}{Dt}$ between 12 to 30. For $\frac{H^2}{Dt}$ above 30, hoop action will be predominant and for $\frac{H^2}{Dt}$ below 6, usually cantilever action will be predominant.

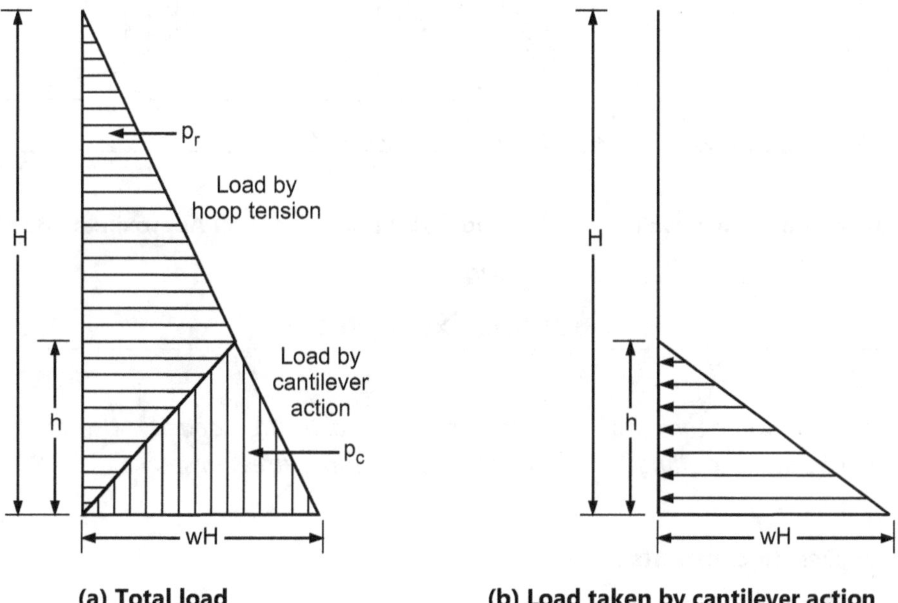

(a) Total load   **(b) Load taken by cantilever action**

Fig. 15.2 : Approximate method

Fig. 15.2 (a) shows the division of the hydrostatic pressure into loads taken by hoop action and loads taken by cantilever action. The load on the cantilever will be the area of the triangular load in Fig. 15.2 (b) and maximum. Cantilever B.M. occurs at the base of magnitude $\dfrac{1}{2}\,wH(h)\left(\dfrac{h}{3}\right) = \dfrac{wHh^2}{6}$.

The maximum hoop tension will occur at height h above base, the magnitude being given by $w\,(H-h)\,\dfrac{D}{2}$.

Steel for hoop tension is provided in the form of ring provided at both the faces. The spacings of the bars for hop tension will be kept equal upto height h. Above this height, the spacing of the rings can be increased.

15.9 EXAGGERATED BENT SHAPE OF WALL OF CIRCULAR WATER TANK FIXED AT BASE SLAB SHOWING ALL DETAILS

(SUMMER 2012, 5 MARKS)

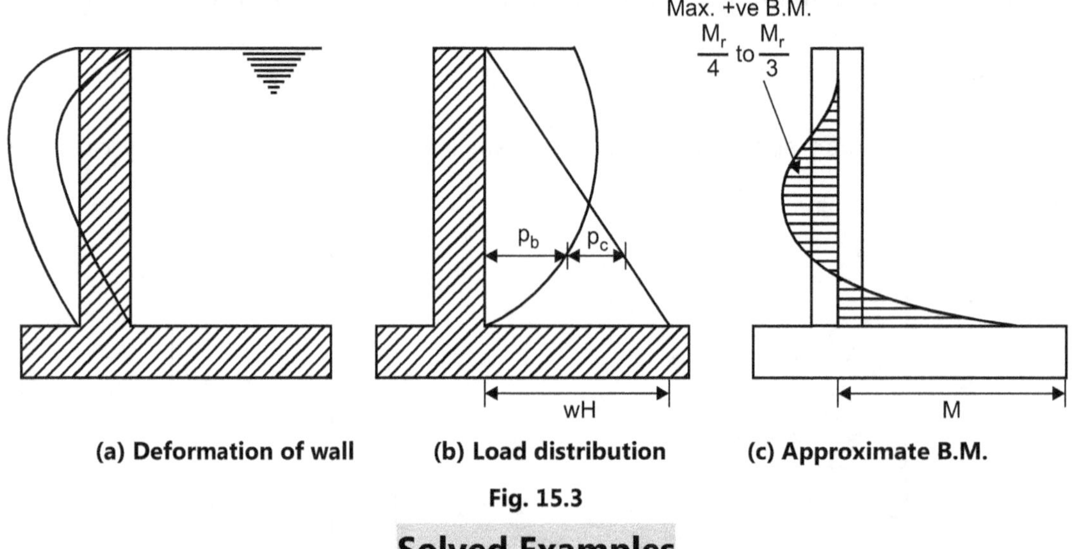

(a) Deformation of wall   **(b) Load distribution**   **(c) Approximate B.M.**

Fig. 15.3

Solved Examples

Example 15.1 :

Design a circular water tank with flexible base for 6 lakh litre capacity. Use M 25 Fe 415. Adopt depth of water excluding free board as 3.5 m. Assume stress in steel as 150 N/mm².

Solution :

Step I : Design constants :

Concrete grade M 25 and steel Fe 415.

According to IS : 456 – 2000,

$$\sigma_{cbc} = 8.5 \text{ MPa}$$

$$m = \frac{280}{3\sigma_{cbc}} = \frac{280}{3 \times 8.5} = 10.98$$

N.A. Depth factor :

$$k = \frac{m \cdot \sigma_{cbc}}{m \cdot \sigma_{cbc} + \sigma_{st}} = \frac{10.98 \times 8.5}{10.98 \times 8.5 + 150} = 0.383$$

Lever arm factor :

$$j = 1 - \frac{k}{3} = 1 - \frac{0.383}{3} = 0.872$$

$$Q = \frac{1}{2}\sigma_{cbc} \times k \times j$$

$$= \frac{1}{2} 8.5 \times 0.383 \times 0.872 = 1.169$$

Step II : Fixation of dimensions :

(i) **Diameter :** Shape is circular with internal diameter 'D'.

$$\text{Total height} = 3.5 \text{ m}$$
$$\text{Free board} = 0.2 \text{ m}$$
$$\text{Volume of tank} = 6 \text{ lakh litre} = 6 \times 10^5 \times 10^3 \text{ cm}^3$$
$$= 600 \text{ m}^3$$
$$= \text{Area} \times \text{Depth}$$

$\therefore \qquad\qquad \text{Area} = \dfrac{600}{3.5} = 171.42 \text{ m}^2$

$\therefore \qquad\qquad D = 14.77 \text{ m} \approx 15 \text{ m}$

$\therefore$ Internal diameter of tank $= 15 \text{ m}$

(ii) **Thickness of tank wall :** Thickness of tank wall will be from the following two :

I.   150 mm thickness of wall.

II. $\qquad\qquad t = 30 \times H + 50;$ whichever is more.

$$t = 30 \times 3.5 + 50$$
$$= 155 \text{ mm}$$

Let us adopt t = 200 mm. (Thickness is checked for limit tensile stress in concrete to 1.2 MPa).

Step III : Design of tank walls : Since, tank is with a flexible base, it will be designed as circular cylinders subjected to water pressures i.e. tank walls are designed only for hoop action.

(a) **Design for bottom part of wall :** Consider the bottom $\dfrac{3.5}{3} = 1.16 \text{ m}$

Maximum pressure intensity corresponding to the bottom of the 1 m height of wall.

$$P = wH = 9.81 \times 3.7$$

$$= 36.3 \text{ kN/m}^2$$

Maximum hoop tension, $\quad T = \dfrac{PD}{2}$

$$= \dfrac{36.29 \times 15}{2}$$

$$= 272.22 \text{ kN}$$

A_{st} calculations :

Permissible stress $= 150$ MPa

$\therefore \quad A_{st \text{ required}} = \dfrac{T}{\text{Permissible stress}} = \dfrac{272.22 \times 10^3}{150} = 1814.8 \text{ mm}^2$

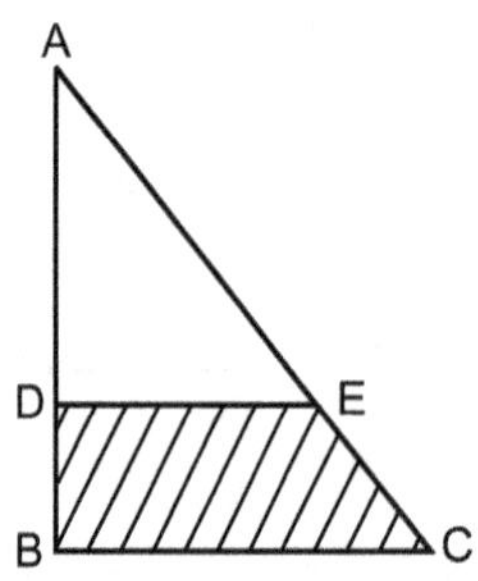

Fig. 15.4 (a)

Provided, $t = 200$ mm

$A_{st \text{ minimum}} = 0.3\,\%$

$$= \dfrac{0.3}{100} \times 1000 \times 200$$

$$= 600 \text{ mm}^2$$

$\therefore \quad A_{st \text{ required}} > A_{st \text{ minimum}}$

So provide $A_{st \text{ required}}$.

Provision of reinforcement :

Let us adopt $\phi 16$, $\quad a_{st} = 201 \text{ mm}^2$.

$$\text{Spacing, } S = 1000\,\dfrac{a_{st}}{A_{st}}$$

$$= 1000 \times \dfrac{201}{1814.8} = 110.78 \text{ mm}$$

So provide ϕ 16 @ 110 mm c/c along the wall upto 1 m.

Provide this reinforcement into two parts i.e. provide ϕ 16 @ 220 mm c/c. This reinforcement is applicable from B to D.

(b) Design for middle part of wall :

Consider 1.16 m in middle part of wall

   i.e.   F to D

Hoop tension at D can be found out.

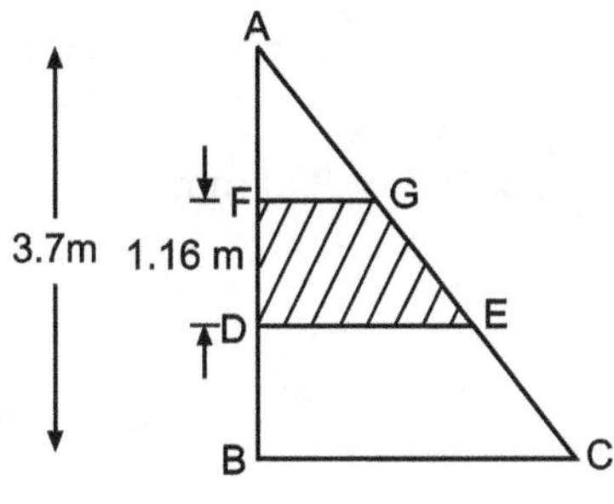

Fig. 15.4 (b)

Similarly, $P = 9.81 \times (3.7 - 1.16)$

$$= 24.91 \text{ kN/m}^2$$

$$\text{Hoop tension at D} = \frac{24.91 \times 15}{2} = 186.88 \text{ kN}$$

Consider same tension for 1.16 m above 'D' i.e. from D to F.

$$A_{st} = \frac{T_o}{\text{Permissible stress}} = \frac{186.88 \times 10^3}{150}$$

$$= 1245.86 \text{ mm}^2$$

$$A_{st\,min} = 600 \text{ mm}^2$$

Now, $A_{st\,reqd} > A_{st\,min}$

Hence, provide $A_{st\,reqd}$.

Provide ϕ 16 mm, $a_{st} = 201 \text{ mm}^2$.

$$\text{Spacing, } S = \frac{1000 \times 201}{1245.86} = 161.33 \text{ mm}$$

∴   Provide ϕ 16 mm @ 160 mm c/c divide this reinforcement in two parts i.e. provide ϕ 16 @ 320 mm near and away from water face for F to D, 1.16 m height of wall.

(c) Design of top 1.36 mm height of wall : For top 1.36 m height of wall maximum hoop tension will be at point 'F'.

$$\text{Hoop tension of 'F'} = 72.10 \text{ kN}$$

$$A_{st} = \frac{72.10 \times 10^3}{150} = 480.69 \text{ mm}^2$$

But $A_{st\ min}$ = 600 mm²

∴ $A_{st\ reqd}$ < $A_{st\ min}$

∴   Provide ϕ 10 mm.

$$\text{Spacing, S} = \frac{1000 \times 18.56}{480.69} = 163.43 \text{ mm}$$

∴   Provide 160 mm c/c.

Divide this reinforcement in two parts

$$S = 2 \times 160 = 320 \text{ mm}$$

∴   Provide ϕ 10 @ 320 mm c/c.

Step IV : Distribution steel :

Provide $A_{st\ min}$.

Provide ϕ 10 @ 320 mm c/c.

Step V : Design of base slab :

Provide base slab of minimum thickness = 150 mm.

$$A_{st} = A_{st\ min} = 0.3\ \% \ Ag$$

$$= \frac{0.3}{100} \times 1000 \times 200$$

$$= 600 \text{ m}^2$$

∴   Provide ϕ 10 mm, a_{st} = 78.54 mm² @ 120 mm c/c.

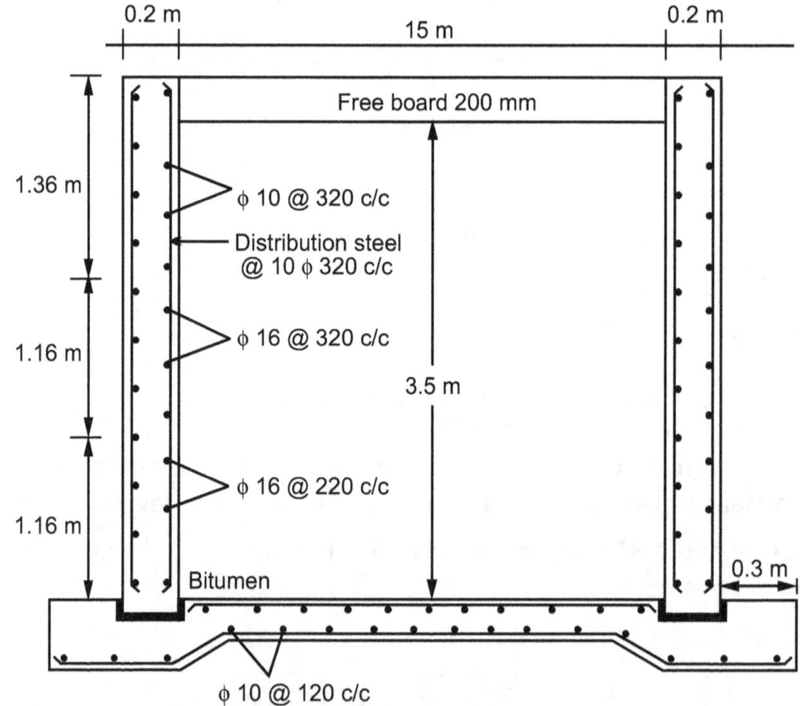

Fig. 15.5

Example 15.2 :

Design a circular water tank to the following particulars :

    (i)   Diameter of tank = 3.75 m.

    (ii)   Depth of water = 3 m.

    (iii)   Tank rests on ground.

    (iv)   Specific gravity of water = 9.81 kN/m³.

    Use M 20, Fe 415.

    Assume permissible stress in steel = 150 N/mm².

Step I : Design constants : Concrete grade M 20, steel Fe 415.

$$\sigma_{cbc} = 7 \text{ MPa}$$

$$\therefore \qquad m = \frac{280}{3\sigma_{cbc}} = \frac{280}{3 \times 7} = 13.333$$

Neutral axis depth factor :

$$k = \frac{m\,\sigma_{cbc}}{m\,\sigma_{cbc} + \sigma_{st}} = \frac{13.333 \times 7}{13.333 \times 7 + 150} = 0.39$$

Lever arm factor :

$$j = 1 - \frac{k}{3}$$

$$= 1 - \frac{0.39}{3} = 0.87$$

Moment of resistance factor :

$$Q = \frac{1}{2}\,\sigma_{cbc} \times k \times j$$

$$= \frac{1}{2} \times 7 \times 0.39 \times 0.87$$

$$= 1.187 \text{ N/mm}^2$$

Step II : Fixation of dimensions : Thickness of tank wall :

(a)   150 mm.

(b)   30 H + 50 = 30 × 3 + 50 = 140 mm.

Let us adopt,   t = 200 mm

Step III : Design of tank wall : Since tank is with a flexible base, it will be designed as circular cylinders subjected to water pressures i.e. tank walls are designed for hoop tension only.

(a)   Design for bottom part of wall : Consider the bottom $\frac{3}{3}$ = 1.0 m height of wall.

Maximum pressure intensity corresponding to the bottom of 1 m height of wall,

$$P = wH = 9.81 \times 3$$
$$= 29.43 \text{ kN/m}^2$$

Maximum hoop tension :

$$T = \frac{PD}{2} = \frac{29.43 \times 3.75}{2} = 55.18 \text{ kN}$$

Area of reinforcement :

Permissible stress = 150 MPa

$\therefore \qquad A_{st \text{ required}} = \dfrac{T}{\text{Permissible stress}} = \dfrac{55.18 \times 10^3}{150} = 367.87 \text{ mm}^2$

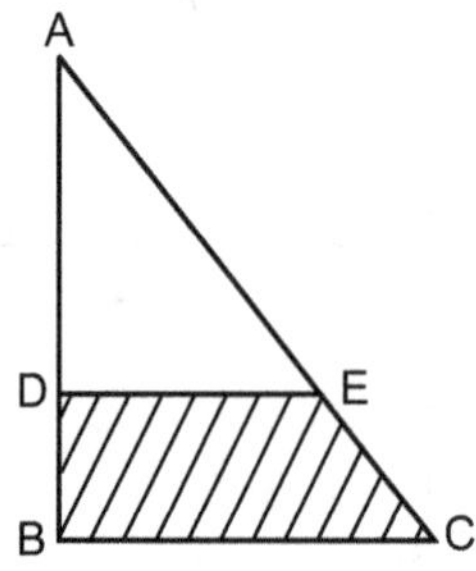

Fig. 15.6

$$A_{st \text{ min}} = 0.3\% \times \text{ Gross area}$$
$$= \frac{0.3}{100} \times 1000 \times 200$$
$$= 600 \text{ mm}^2$$
$$A_{st \text{ req.}} < A_{st \text{ min}}$$

So provide minimum steel.

Use 100 mm ϕ,   spacing $= \dfrac{1000 \times 78.54}{600}$

$$= 130.9 \text{ mm}$$

So provide 10 mm ϕ @ 130 mm c/c throughout the depth of water tank.

Step IV : Distribution steel : Provide minimum steel.

So provide 10 mm ϕ @ 130 mm c/c as vertical reinforcement.

Step V : Design of base slab : Provide base slab with minimum thickness = 150 mm. Provide minimum steel.

So provide 10 mm ϕ @ 130 mm c/c at top and bottom in the form of mesh.

(2) Circular tanks with a rigid joint between the walls and base :

In this type, the wall resists the water pressure partly by hoop action and partly by cantilever action. The tanks are designed by different methods as

    (a)   Dr. Reissner's method.

    (b)   Carpenter's simplification of Dr. Reissner's method.

    (c)   I.S. code method.

I.S. code method : The coefficients for bending moment, hoop tension and shear at the base of tank wall are determined by approximate method. These coefficients depend upon $\dfrac{H^2}{Dt}$ ratio.

Steps to be followed in design :

Step I : Design constants.

Step II : Fixation of dimensions.

$$\frac{\pi}{4} \times D^2 = \frac{\text{Volume of tank}}{\text{Height of water}}$$

Step III : Depth factor :

$\dfrac{H^2}{Dt}$ between 6 to 12 cantilever action predominant.

Coefficients are determined from table.

Step IV : Design of tank wall.

Step V : Distribution steel.

Step VI : Design of base slab.

Example 15.3 :

Design a circular water tank resting on firm ground with its wall fixed at its base. Assume height of the wall with F.B. as 4 m. Use M 20 Fe 415, capacity 8.2 lakh litre. Allowable stress = 150 N/mm².   **[Dec. 11,14]**

Solution :

Step I : Design constants : Material properties M 20, Fe 415.

$$\sigma_{cbc} = 7 \text{ MPa}$$

$$m = 13.33 \text{ MPa}$$

$$\sigma_{st} = 150 \text{ MPa}$$

$$k = \frac{m\,\sigma_{cbc}}{m\,\sigma_{cbc} + \sigma_{st}} = \frac{13.33 \times 7}{13.33 \times 7 + 150} = 0.383$$

$$j \; = \; 0.87$$

$$Q \; = \; \frac{1}{2}\, \sigma_{cbc}\, kj \; = \; 0.5 \times 7 \times 0.383 \times 0.87 \; = \; 1.169$$

Step II : Calculation of diameter and thickness of wall :

D – Internal diameter of tank

t – Thickness of wall of tank.

$$V \; = \; \frac{8.2 \times 10^5}{1000} \; = \; 820 \; m^3$$

Assume free board $= 0.2$ m

$$H \; = \; 4.2 \; m$$

$$Volume \; = \; Area \times Height$$

$$\therefore \quad 820 \; = \; \frac{\pi}{4} \times D^2 \times 4.2$$

$$\therefore \quad D \; = \; 16.15 \; m$$

Assume, $\quad D \; = \; 16.2 \; m$

$$t \; = \; 30\,H + 50$$

$$= \; 30 \times 4.2 + 50$$

$$= \; 176 \; mm$$

Step III : Depth factor :

$$\text{Depth factor} = \frac{H^2}{Dt} \; = \; \frac{(4.2)^2}{16.2 \times 176 \times 10^{-3}}$$

$$= \; 6.186$$

i.e. it is between 6 and 12.

So cantilever action will be predominant in wall for a height H/3 or 1 m from bottom, whichever is higher.

$$\therefore \quad h \; = \; \frac{H}{3} \; = \; \frac{4.2}{3} \; = \; 1.4 \; m \; \text{or 1 m whichever is more}$$

$$\therefore \quad h \; = \; 1.4 \; m$$

Step IV : Design of tank : Design of segment BD.

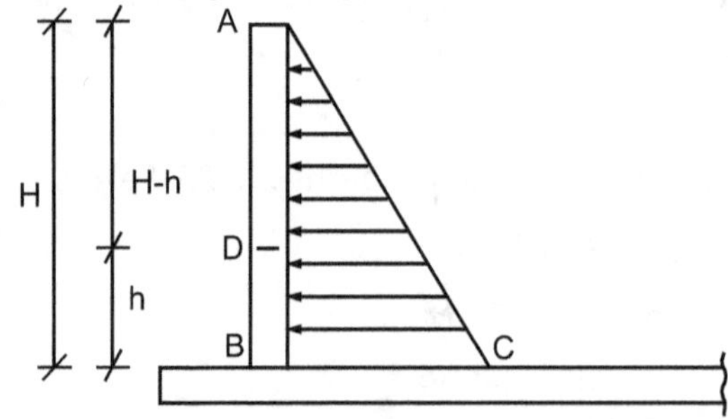

Fig. 15.7

$$Moment \; = \; Force \times Distance$$

$$\text{Force} \ = \ \frac{1}{2} \ wH \times 1.4$$

$$= \ 0.5 \times 9.81 \times 4.2 \times 1.4$$

$$= \ 28.84 \ kN$$

Check for depth :

$$\text{MR balanced} \ = \ Qbd^2$$

$$13.45 \times 10^6 \ = \ 1.169 \times 1000 \times d^2$$

$$d^2 \ = \ 11505.56$$

$$d_{reqd.} \ = \ 107.26 \ mm$$

As per IS 3370 part II clause no. 7.2.1,

$$d_{pro} \ = \ 176 - 25.6 \ = \ 145 \ mm$$

$$d_{reqd} \ < \ d_{pro}$$

Hence, the section is under reinforced.

Area of steel calculation :

$$A_{st} \ = \ \frac{BM_{max}}{\sigma_{st} \cdot j \cdot d}$$

$$= \ \frac{13.45 \times 10^6}{150 \times 0.872 \times 145} \ = \ 706.73 \ mm^2$$

Check for $A_{st \ min}$: As per IS code clause no. 7.11,

$$A_{st \ min} \ = \ 0.3 \ \% \ \text{of 100 m thickness}$$

$$= \ 0.2 \ \% \ \text{for 450 mm thickness}$$

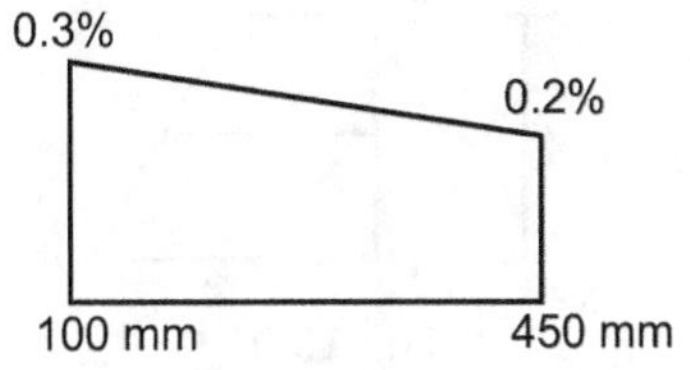

Fig. 15.8

So by interpolation of 176 mm thickness slab,

$$A_{st \ min} \ = \ 0.28\% \ \text{of Ag}$$

$$\therefore \qquad A_{st \ min} \ = \ \frac{0.28}{100} \times 1000 \times 176$$

$$= \ 492.8$$

$$\approx \ 490 \ mm^2$$

$\therefore \qquad$ Provide $A_{st\ calculated}$ = 706.73 mm^2

Spacing for 10 mm ϕ bar $= \dfrac{1000 \times 73.54}{706.73}$ = 111.13 mm $\approx$ 110 mm

Provide ϕ 10 @ 110 mm c/c on interface from bottom to $\dfrac{H}{3}$ = 1.4 m. No split. The vertical bar on inner side for part DA will be distribution reinforcement.

So curtail 50 % reinforcement to serve as distribution reinforcement on inner face or part DA.

Development length :

$$L_d = \frac{\phi\ \sigma_s}{4\ \tau_{bd}} = \frac{10 \times 150}{4 \times 0.8} = 468.75$$

Step V : Distribution reinforcement for part BD :

$$A_{std} = A_{st\ min} = 490 \text{ mm}^2$$

Using ϕ 8 mm bar,

$$\text{Spacing} = \frac{1000 \times 50.26}{490} = 102.57 \text{ mm} \approx 100 \text{ mm}$$

Provide ϕ 8 @ 200 c/c circular and vertical on outer + circular on inner face.

Design of DA : Design for hoop tension :

$$\text{Hoop tension} = \frac{PD}{2}$$

Pressure distribution diameter :

Let us consider two parts, each of 1.4 m.

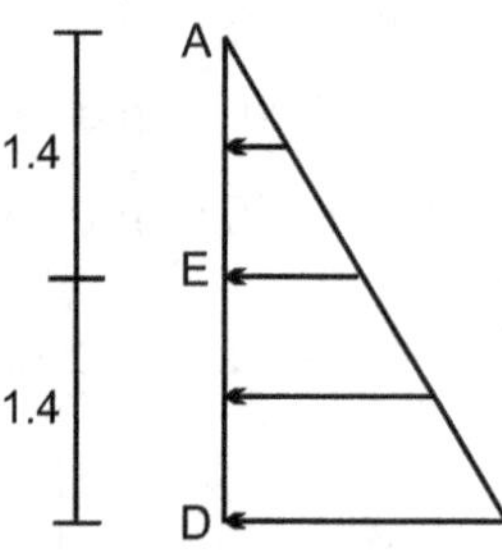

Fig. 15.9

Design for DE : Maximum hydrostatic pressure, P = 27.46 kN

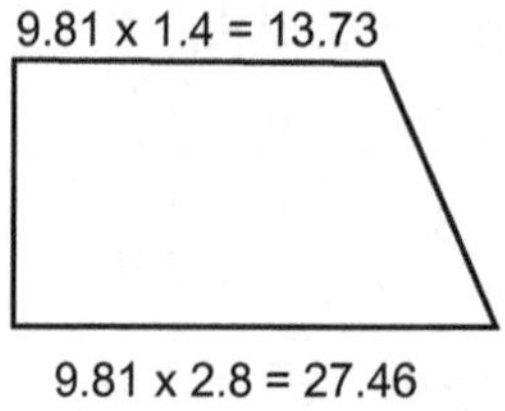

Fig. 15.10

$$\text{Hoop tension} = \frac{27.46 \times 16.2}{2} = 222.5$$

$$\begin{bmatrix} A_{st} \text{ in the form} \\ \text{of circular loops} \end{bmatrix} = \frac{t \times 10^3}{\sigma_{st}}$$

$$= \frac{222.5 \times 10^3}{150} = 1483.33 \text{ mm}^2$$

$$A_{st\ min} = 490 \text{ mm}^2$$

Spacing of ϕ 10 bars,

$$S = \frac{1000 \times 78.54}{1483.33} = 52.94 \text{ mm}$$

$$\approx 50 \text{ mm}$$

Split these loops on either face, so the spacing of loops on either face will be 100 mm for segment D.F. + should not be greater than 3D or 300 mm.

Segment EA :

$$\text{Hoop tension} = \frac{PD}{2} = \frac{13.73 \times 16.2}{2} = 111.21$$

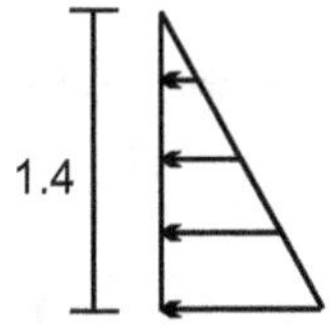

Fig. 15.11

$$\begin{bmatrix} A_{st} \text{ in the form} \\ \text{of circular loops} \end{bmatrix} = \frac{111.21 \times 10^3}{150} = 741.42 \text{ mm}^2$$

$$A_{st\ min} = 490 \text{ mm}$$

$$\text{Spacing for } \phi \text{ 8 mm bar} = \frac{1000 \times 50.26}{741.42} = 67.78 \text{ mm} \approx 65 \text{ mm}$$

Provide ϕ 8 @ 130 mm on either face in the form of loops and should not be greater than 3D or 300 mm.

Step VI : Design of base slab : Provide the base slab thickness of 150 mm since it is a fixed base.

$$\therefore \quad A_{st\ min} = 0.285 \% = \frac{0.285}{100} \times 1000 \times 150$$

$$= 428.57 \text{ mm}^2$$

$$\text{Spacing} = \frac{1000 \times 50.26}{428.57}$$

$$= 117.27 \text{ mm}$$

$$\approx 110 \text{ mm}$$

Provide ϕ 8 @ 110 mm c/c.

(B) Rectangular tanks resting on ground :

As material required for circular tank is minimum, but the form work for circular tanks is uneconomical, so for small capacities rectangular tanks are designed. In this type, walls are subjected to bending in two directions. Walls are considered as strips supported at corners as well as the walls act as cantilevers. Considering the length to width dimensions, walls are classified into two types.

(i) $\dfrac{L}{B} < 2$

(ii) $\dfrac{L}{B} \geq 2$

where,   L : Length of water tank.

                                B : Width of water tank.

(i) $\dfrac{L}{B} < 2$ **:** In this case, the walls are designed as continuous horizontal slab. The continuous strip of unit height can be analysed by moment distribution.

B.M. at ends of span $= \dfrac{Whl^2}{12}$.

producing tension on water side.

B.M. at centre of span $= \dfrac{Whl^2}{16}$.

producing tension away from water side.

(ii) $\dfrac{L}{B} \geq 2$ **:** In this type, long walls are designed as vertical cantilevers and short walls are designed as slabs spanning between the long walls with ends as fixed ends.

Though the short wall is considered as spanning between long wall, but it is possible that the short wall may have cantilever action for a certain height. So cantilever action for short wall is considered upto 1 m from bottom.

Pull in the walls :

(a) **Pull in the long wall :** Since the short wall span between the long walls at higher level, so the water pressure on short wall will be considered as tension for long wall.

Hence, tension per meter height of long wall $= \dfrac{W(H-1)}{2} \times B.$

(b)   Pull in the short wall :   Long wall is designed as cantilevers. So, generally no tension is acting upon the short wall. But generally the bottom 1 m height is considered spanning between short walls, which will produce tension on short wall.

Hence, tension on short wall = W(H – 1) × 1.

Analysis of tank wall section subjected to bending moment and pull :

Following approximate method is taken into consideration for analysis of wall subjected to moment and pull. Fig. 15.12 shows a section of wall subjected to moment and pull. Let two equal and opposite forces T be considered in the reinforcement. Steel is calculated for resulting moment.

$\therefore$ Resulting moment = M – Tx.

$\therefore$ Steel for resulting moment = A_{st_1} = $\dfrac{M - Tx}{\text{Safe stress in steel} \times \text{Lever arm}}$

Steel for pull = A_{st_2} = $\dfrac{\text{Pull}}{\text{Safe stress in steel}}$

Total steel = Steel for moment + Steel for pull

A_{st} = A_{st_1} + A_{st_2}

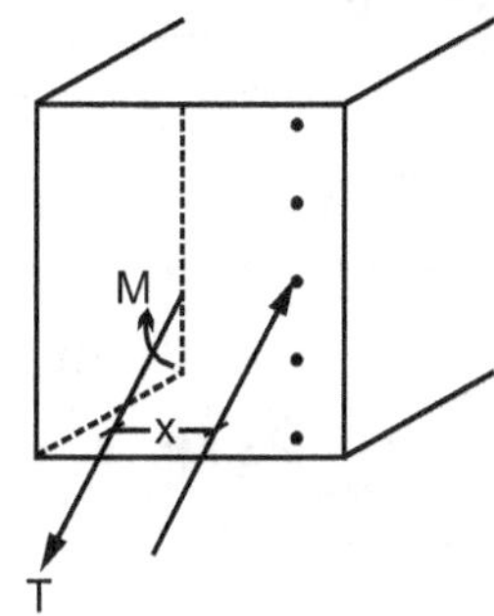

Fig. 15.12

Example 15.4 :

Design an open tank 4.5 m × 3.5 m × 3 m deep resting on firm ground. Use M 20 and Fe 415.

Solution :

Step I : Design constants :

Step II : Design of walls : L = 4.5 m, d = 3 m.

$$\therefore \qquad \frac{L}{d} = \frac{4.5}{3} = 1.5 < 2$$

Hence, tank walls will be designed as spanning horizontally.

Step III : Fixation of dimensions :

Thickness of wall shall not be less than

(a)   150 mm.

(b)   30 mm per meter depth + 50 $=$ $30 \times 3 + 50 =$ 140 mm.

(c)   60 mm per meter length of longer side $= 60 \times 4.5 =$ 270 mm.

$\therefore$ Provide a thickness of wall as 275 mm.

Effective span of short wall $= 3.5 + 0.275 = 3.775$ m

Effective span of long wall $= 4.5 + 0.275 = 4.775$ m

Step IV : Design of walls : Consider 1 m above the base slab.

$\therefore$ $\qquad\qquad\qquad\qquad$ $P = wh = 9810 \,(3.0 - 1.0) = 19620$ kN/m²

(i)   Design of long wall :

(a)   At the ends of the span :

$$\text{B.M.} = \frac{P \cdot l^2}{12} = 19620 \times \frac{(4.775)^2}{12} = 37279.02 \text{ N-m}$$

$$\text{Pull in the wall strip,} \quad T = \frac{PB}{2} = \frac{19620 \times 3.5}{2} = 34335 \text{ N}$$

Provide 16 mm ϕ bars at a clear cover of 25 mm.

$$\text{Effective cover} = 25 + 8 = 33 \text{ mm}$$
$$\text{Effective depth} = 275 - 33 = 242 \text{ mm}$$
$$\text{Effective cover} = 25 + 8 = 33 \text{ mm}$$

Resultant bending moment $= M - T \cdot x$

$$= 37279.02 - 34335 \times \left(d - \frac{t}{2} \right)$$

$$= 36117.15 - 34335 \times \left(0.242 - \frac{0.275}{2} \right)$$

$$= 33691.01 \text{ N-m}$$

$$\text{Steel for B.M.} = A_{st_1} = \frac{33691.01 \times 10^3}{170 \times 0.87 \times 242} = 941.31 \text{ mm}^2$$

$$\text{Steel for pull} = A_{st_2} = \frac{T}{\text{Allowable stress}} = \frac{34335}{170} = 201.97$$

$\therefore$ $\qquad$ Total steel required $= A_{st} = A_{st_1} + A_{st_2}$

$$= 941.31 + 201.97 = 1143.28 \text{ mm}^2$$

Use 16 mm ϕ.

$$\text{Spacing of 16 mm } \phi = \frac{1000 \times 201}{1143.28} = 175.81 \text{ mm}^2$$

Provide 16 mm ϕ @ 170 mm c/c.

(b) At the mid span :

$$\text{B.M. at mid span} = \frac{P\ell^2}{16} = \frac{19620 \times (4.775)^2}{16} = 27959.27 \text{ N-m}$$

$$\text{Resultant B.M.} = M - Tx$$

$$= 27959.2 - 34335 \left(0.242 - \frac{0.275}{2} \right)$$

$$= 24371.19 \text{ N-m}$$

$$\text{Steel for B.M.} = \frac{M}{\sigma_{st} \times \text{Lever arm}}$$

$$A_{st_1} = \frac{24371.19 \times 10^3}{200 \times 0.87 \times 242} = 578.78 \text{ mm}^2$$

$$\text{Steel for pull} = \frac{\text{Pull}}{\sigma_{st}} = \frac{34335}{200}$$

$$A_{st_2} = 171.68 \text{ mm}^2$$

$$\text{Total area of steel} = A_{st} = A_{st_1} + A_{st_2}$$

$$= 578.78 + 171.68 = 750.46 \text{ mm}^2$$

$$\text{Spacing of 16 mm } \phi = \frac{1000 \times 201}{750.46} = 267.83 \text{ mm}$$

Provide 16 mm ϕ @ 260 mm c/c.

(ii) Design of short wall :

(a) At the ends of the span :

$$P = wh = 9810 \times (3 - 1) = 19620 \text{ N/m}^2$$

$$\text{B.M. at ends of span} = \frac{Pb^2}{12} = \frac{19620 \times (3.775)^2}{12} = 23299.78 \text{ N-m}$$

$$\text{Pull in the short wall} = \frac{P\ell}{2} = \frac{19620 \times 4.5}{2} = 44145 \text{ N}$$

$$\text{Resultant bending moment} = M - Tx = 23299.78 - 44145 \left(0.242 - \frac{0.275}{2} \right)$$

$$= 18686.62 \text{ N-m}$$

$$\text{Steel for B.M.} = \frac{M}{\text{Stress} \times \text{Lever arm}}$$

$$= \frac{18686.62 \times 10^3}{170 \times 0.87 \times 242} = 522.09 \text{ mm}^2$$

$$\text{Steel for pull} = \frac{T}{\text{Stress}} = \frac{44145}{170} = 259.68 \text{ mm}^2$$

$$\therefore \quad \text{Total area of steel} = A_{st} = A_{st_1} + A_{st_2}$$

$$= 522.09 + 259.68 = 781.77 \text{ mm}^2$$

$$\text{Spacing of 16 mm } \phi = \frac{1000 \times 201}{781.77} = 257.11 \text{ mm}$$

Provide 16 mm ϕ @ 250 mm c/c.

(b) At the mid of the span :

$$\text{B.M. at mid of span} = \frac{Pb^2}{16} = \frac{19620 \times (3.775)^2}{16} = 17474.83 \text{ N-m}$$

Pull in the short wall $= 44145$ N

Resultant bending moment $= M - Tx$

$$= 17474.83 - 44145 \left(0.242 - \frac{0.275}{2} \right) = 12861.68 \text{ N-m}$$

$$\therefore \quad \text{Steel for B.M.} = \frac{M}{\text{Stress} \times \text{Lever arm}} = \frac{12861.68 \times 10^3}{200 \times 0.87 \times 242}$$

$$= 305.45 \text{ mm}^2$$

$$\text{Steel for pull} = \frac{T}{\text{Stress}} = \frac{44145}{200} = 220.73 \text{ mm}^2$$

$$\text{Total area of steel} = A_{st} = A_{st_1} + A_{st_2}$$

$$= 305.44 + 220.73 = 526.17 \text{ mm}^2$$

$$\text{Spacing of 16 mm } \phi = \frac{1000 \times 201}{526.17} = 382$$

Provide 16 mm ϕ @ 380 mm c/c.

Design at bottom 1 metre height of wall :

$$\left[\begin{array}{c} \text{Maximum intensity} \\ \text{at bottom} \end{array} \right] = pH$$

$$= 9810 \times 3 = 29430 \text{ N/m}^2$$

$$\therefore \quad \text{B.M. at bottom} = \frac{1}{2} \times pH \times 1 \times \left(\frac{1}{3} \times 1\right)$$

$$= \frac{1}{2} \times 29430 \times \frac{1}{3} = 4905 \text{ N-m}$$

Provide 10 mm vertical bars.

$$\therefore \quad \text{Effective cover} = \text{Clear cover} + \frac{\phi}{2}$$

$$= 25 + \frac{10}{2} = 30 \text{ mm}$$

$$\therefore \quad \text{Effective depth} = 275 - 30 = 245 \text{ mm}$$

$$\therefore \quad \text{Steel for B.M.} : A_{st} = \frac{M}{\text{Stress} \times \text{Lever arm}}$$

$$= \frac{4905 \times 10^3}{175 \times 0.87 \times 245}$$

$$= 133.13 \text{ mm}^2$$

Minimum reinforcement :

$$A_{st \, min} = \frac{0.3}{100} \times b \times t = \frac{0.3}{100} \times 1000 \times 275$$

$$= 825 \text{ mm}^2$$

$$\text{Spacing of 10 mm } \phi = \frac{1000 \times 78.53}{825} = 95.2 \text{ mm}$$

Provide 10 mm ϕ @ 90 mm c/c near each face.

Base slab : Base slab is provided 275 mm thick. Steel mesh of 10 mm ϕ @ 200 mm c/c is provided at top and bottom.

Example 15.5 :

Design a circular water tank of capacity 350000 litres, resting on ground and having rigid joints at base. Use M20 grade concrete with σ_{abc} = 7 N/mm^2, σ_{ct} = 1.20 N/mm^2, σ_{st} = 115 N/mm^2 and m = 13. Compare the value of the bending moments, shear force and hoop tension by

(i)   IS code method.

(ii) Approximate method.

Solution :

$$\text{Volume of tank} = \frac{350000}{1000} = 350 \text{ m}^3$$

Assuming H as 3 m, D = 12.20 m

Assume t = 30 (H) + 50 = 140 mm

(i) I.S. code method :

$$\frac{H^2}{Dt} = \frac{(3)^2}{12.20\,(0.14)} = 5.27$$

From Table 15.1,

Maximum tension is at 0.5 H i.e. 1.50 m from top

Magnitude of maximum number

$$= \left[0.477 + \frac{0.027}{1}(0.27)\right] wH \frac{D}{2}$$

$$= \frac{0.485}{2}(wHD)$$

$$= \frac{0.485}{2}(10000)(3)(12.20)$$

$$= 88755\ N$$

For exact location of maximum tension and its magnitude, the values of tension all along the height can be plotted by coefficients from Table 15.1. From the curve so plotted, maximum value can be obtained.

From Table 15.2,

The moment coefficient for base is found to be

$$= -\left[0.0222 - \frac{0.0035}{1}(0.27)\right]$$

$$= -0.0213$$

Minus sign indicates tension on the inner face.

$$\text{Maximum bending moment} = 0.0213\ wH^3$$

$$= 0.0213\,(10000)\,(3)^3$$

$$= 5751\ N/m$$

From Table 15.3,

$$\text{Coefficient for shear force} = \left[0.213 - \frac{0.016}{1}(0.27)\right]$$

$$= 0.209$$

$$\text{Magnitude of maximum S.F.} = 0.209\,(wH^2)$$

$$= 0.209\,(1000)\,(3^2)$$

$$= 18810\ N/m,\ \text{acting inward.}$$

(ii) By approximate method :

$$\frac{H^2}{Dt} = 5.27$$

As this is close to 6, height above base upto which cantilever action will be there is taken as $h = \dfrac{H}{3}$ or 1 m whichever is more.

In this case, both are same and h = 1 m, maximum hoop tension at this level

$$= w\,(H - h)\,\frac{D}{2}$$

$$= 10000\,(3 - 1)\,\frac{12.20}{2}$$

$$= 122000 \text{ N}$$

$$\text{Water pressure at bottom} = wH$$

$$= 30000 \text{ N/m}^2 \text{ per m.}$$

$$\text{Maximum B.M. (–ve)} = \frac{1}{2}\,(30000)\,(1)\left(\frac{1}{3}\right)$$

$$= 5000 \text{ Nm/m}$$

The above value shows that except in case of approximate method, values for design obtained from the other three methods are comparable.

Design by values obtained by IS code method :

For M20 grade of concrete with

$$\sigma_{cbc} = 7 \text{ N/mm}^2$$
$$\sigma_{ct} = 1.20 \text{ N/mm}^2$$
$$\sigma_{st} = 115 \text{ N/mm}^2 \text{ and}$$
$$m = 13$$

$$\text{N axis depth } n = k_d = \frac{7}{7 + \dfrac{115}{13}}\,d = 0.442\,d$$

$$jd = \left(1 - \frac{k}{3}\right)d = 0.853\,d$$

$$\text{Value of } Q = \frac{1}{2}\,(\sigma_{cbc})\,(k)\,(j)$$

$$= \frac{1}{2}\,(7)\,(0.442)\,(0.853)$$

$$= 1.3196 \text{ N/mm}^2$$

Effective depth required for B.M.

$$= \sqrt{\frac{5751\,(1000)}{(1000)\,(1.3196)}}$$

$$= 66 \text{ mm}$$

$$\text{Total thickness required} = 66 + 25 + 5$$

$$= 96 \text{ mm} \quad \text{say } 100 \text{ mm}$$

$$\text{With no crack basis, } d = \sqrt{\frac{6\,(5751)}{1.70}} \approx 142.47 \text{ mm}$$

From point of view of hoop tension,

$$A_{st} \text{ required} = \frac{88755}{115} = 771.80 \text{ mm}^2$$

Use 10 mm bars @ 100 mm c/c.

$$\text{Area of steel provided} = 785.40 \text{ mm}^2$$

$$\text{Thickness of concrete required} = \frac{1}{1.20\,(1000)}\,[88755 - 12\,(785.40)\,(1.20)]$$

$$= 64.53 \text{ mm}$$

If shrinkage effect be considered, thickness required

$$= \frac{1}{1000}\left[\frac{88755 + 2\,(10)^5\,(300)\,(10)^{-6}\,(785.40)}{1.20\left(\frac{4}{3}\right)} - 12\,(785.40)\right]$$

$$= 75.50 \text{ mm}$$

From point of view of maximum S.F. is 18810 N

$$\tau_c = \frac{18810}{(1000)\,(140 - 30)}$$

$$= 0.171 \text{ N/mm}^2 < \text{allowable}$$

$$t = 140 \text{ mm can be considered adequate}$$

$$\text{Effective depth, } d = 140 - (25 + 5)$$

$$= 110 \text{ mm}$$

$$A_{st \text{ required}} = \frac{5751\,(1000)}{115\,(0.853)\,(110)}$$

$$= 532.97 \text{ mm}^2$$

Use 10 mm @ 145 mm c/c.

$$A_{st\ provided} = 541.65\ mm^2$$

From Table 15.2,

$$\text{Maximum positive B.M.} = +\,0.005684\,(10000)\,(3)^3$$
$$= 1534.68\ Nm$$
$$\text{For these, } A_{st} = \frac{1534.68\,(1000)}{115\,(0.853)\,(110)}$$
$$= 142.23\ mm^2$$

Distribution reinforcement :

$$\text{Maximum reinforcement} = \frac{0.30}{100}\,(1000)\,(140)$$
$$= 420\ mm^2$$

Taking this as 0.30%.

Use 10 mm bars @ 175 mm c/c on the outer face also.

It is customary to provide a 100 mm haunch at the junction of wall and base. Reinforcement in the haunch may be provided in the form of 6 mm bars @ 150 mm c/c.

Design of base slab :

$$\text{Weight of side walls} = \pi\,(12.20 + 0.140)\,(0.140)\,(3.20)\,(24000)$$
$$= 416825.51\ N$$

Intensity of soil pressure below base slab,

i.e.
$$q = \frac{416825.51}{\dfrac{\pi}{4}\,(12.20 + 0.14)^2} = 3485.25\ N/m^2$$

Base slab B.M.s are obtained considering a circular slab.

Case I : If simply supported at ends :

$$M_r = M_\theta = \frac{3}{16}\,q \cdot R^2 \quad \text{at centre}$$

$$M_\theta = \frac{qR^2}{8} \quad \text{at edges}$$

Case II : If considered fixed at ends :

$$M_r = -\frac{qR^2}{8} \quad \text{at edges.}$$

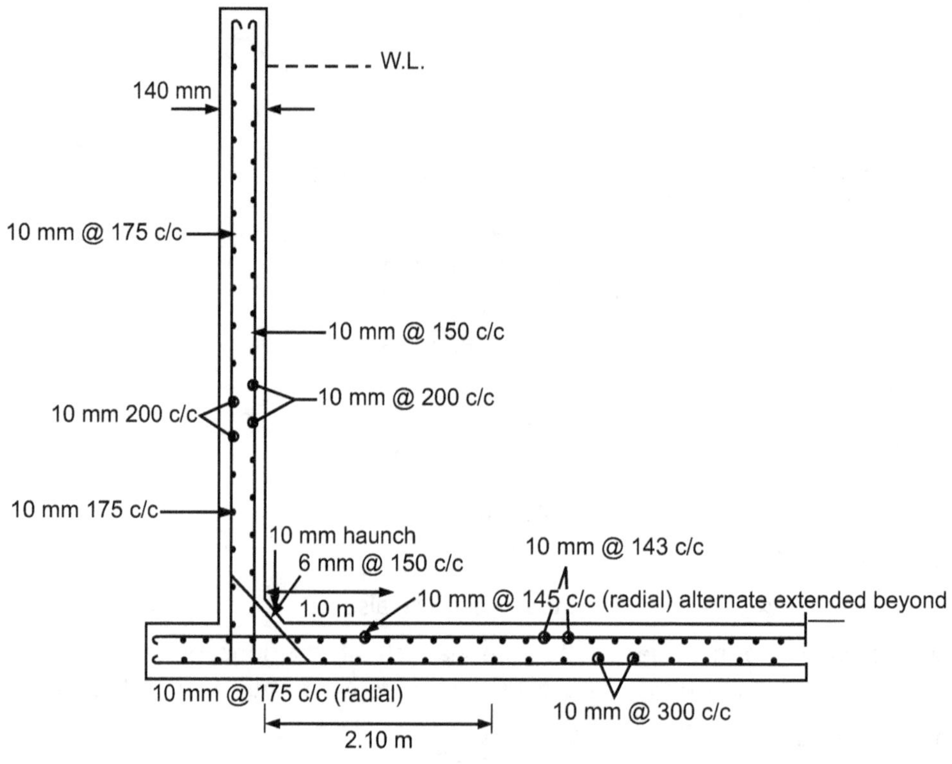

(a) Details of vertical wall and base slab

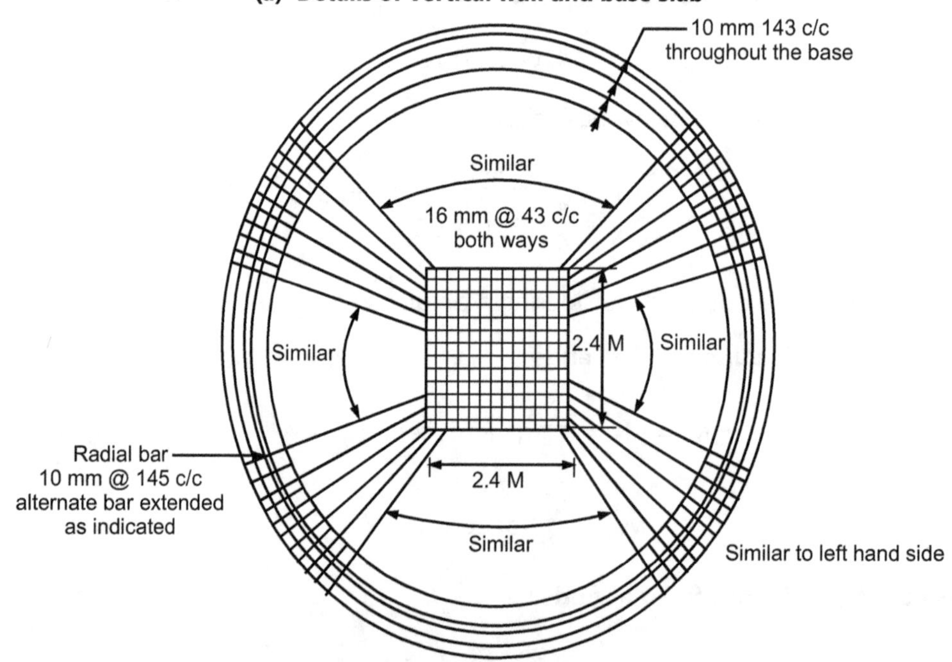

(b) Reinforcement on top of base slab

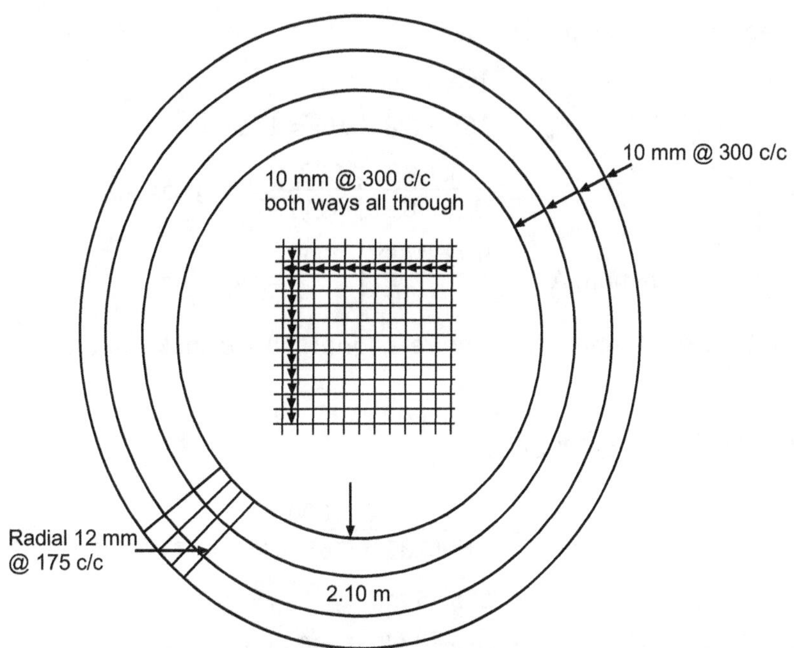

(c) Details of reinforcement

Fig. 15.13

$$M_\theta = \frac{qR^2}{16} \text{ at centre}$$

Considering partial flexity,

$$\text{Maximum positive, } M_r = M_\theta = \frac{8}{12}\left(\frac{3}{16}qR^2\right) = \frac{qR^2}{8}$$

$$\text{Maximum negative, } M_r = \frac{-qR^2}{16} \text{ at edges}$$

$$\text{At edges, } M_\theta = \frac{qR^2}{8} - \frac{qR^2}{16} = \frac{qR^2}{16}$$

$$\text{Maximum B.M.} = \frac{1}{8}(3485.25)\left[\frac{12.34}{2}\right]^2$$

$$= 16584.95 \text{ Nm}$$

$$d_{required} = \sqrt{\frac{16584.95\,(1000)}{1.32\,(1000)}}$$

$$= 112.09 \text{ mm}$$

$$\text{For no crack, } d = \sqrt{\frac{16584.95\,(6)}{1.70}} = 242 \text{ mm}$$

which can be reduced with reinforcement.

Make $\qquad$ $t = 165$ mm

with $\qquad$ $d_{av} = 165 - (28 + 16) = 121$ mm

$$A_{st} = \frac{16584.95\ (1000)}{(115)\ (0.853)\ (121)} = 1397.28\ \text{mm}^2$$

$$\text{Minimum } A_{st} = \frac{0.25\ (165)\ (1000)}{100} = 413\ \text{mm}^2$$

Use 16 mm bars @ 143 mm c/c at centre as grids. This will take care of both M_r and M_θ near centres.

For negative M_r of $\dfrac{qR^2}{16}$ i.e. 8292.48 Nm

$$A_{st\ required} = \frac{8292.48\ (1000)}{115\ (0.853)\ (165 - 36)}$$

$$= 655.55\ \text{mm}^2$$

Use 10 mm @ 120 mm c/c with increased 'd' of 130 mm.

Or 12 mm @ 175 mm c/c with d of 131 mm.

M_θ reinforcement to be placed on top all through.

Details of reinforcement are shown in Fig. 15.13.

Check bearing pressure on soil :

$$\text{Weight of side wall} = 416825.51\ \text{N}$$

$$\text{Weight of bottom slab} = \frac{\pi}{4}\ (12.20 + 0.28)^2\ (0.165)\ (24000)$$

$$= 484411.27\ \text{N}$$

Weight of water when tank is full

$$= \frac{\pi}{4}\ (12.20)^2\ (3)\ (10000)$$

$$= 3506959.90\ \text{N}$$

$$\text{Total} = 416825.51 + 484411.27 + 3506959.90$$

$$= 4408196.68\ \text{N}$$

$$\text{Maximum pressure on soil} = \frac{4408196.68}{\dfrac{\pi}{4} \times (12.48)^2}$$

$$= 36036.44\ \text{N/m}^2$$

Bearing pressure is low.

Example 15.6 :

Design circular reinforced concrete tank resting on ground to store 4 lakh litres of water. The tank wall is fixed at base and free at top. Take the safe bearing capacity of the supporting strata as 220 kN/m². Design the wall and bottom slab of the tank using IS code.

(Winter 2011, 20 Marks)

Solution :

Let the depth of tank be 3 m with free board as 300 mm. The diameter of tank D is

$$\frac{\pi}{4} \times D^2 (3 - 0.3) = \frac{400 \times 10^6}{10^6} \Rightarrow D = 13.73 \text{ m} \approx 13.75 \text{ m}$$

(i) Bottom 1 m height of wall :

Depth of water $= 2.7$ m

T_{max} at the base for 1 m height of wall $= \dfrac{whD}{2} = \dfrac{9810 \times 2.7 \times 13.75}{2} = 182098$ N

$$A_{st} = \frac{182098}{150} = 1214 \text{ mm}^2$$

Provide 12 bars of 12 mm ϕ.

Use mix M25, $\sigma_t = 13$ N/mm²

Let $t = $ Thickness of wall

$$\text{Tensile stress} = \frac{182098}{1000\, t + (11 - 1)\, 12 \times 113} = 13$$

$\therefore \qquad t = 126.51$ mm

Provide 140 mm thickness of wall uniformly throughout its height.

(ii) Middle 1 m height of wall :

Depth of water $= 1.7$ m

$$T = \frac{9810 \times 1.7 \times 13.75}{2} = 114654 \text{ N}$$

$$A_{st} = \frac{114654}{150} = 764.4 \text{ mm}^2$$

Provide 7 bars of 12 mm ϕ.

(iii) Top 1 m height of wall :

Depth of water $= 0.7$ m

$$T = \frac{9810 \times 0.7 \times 13.75}{2} = 47210 \text{ N}$$

$$A_{st} = \frac{47210}{150} = 314.7 \text{ mm}^2$$

Provide 4 bars of 10 mm ϕ in 0.7 m height and in rest 0.3 m free board height proportional steel may be provided i.e. 4 bars of 8 mm ϕ.

Hoop steel shall be provided equally on both faces.

$$A_{st} = 0.24 - (0.24 - 0.16) \times (140 - 100)/350 = 0.2309\% \text{ (Table 2 and 3)}$$

$$A_{st} = \frac{0.2309}{100} \times 140 \times 1000 = 323.2 \text{ mm}^2 \text{ on both faces}$$

$$= 161.6 \text{ mm}^2 \text{ on each face.}$$

Provide 8 mm ϕ @ 300 mm c/c on each face.

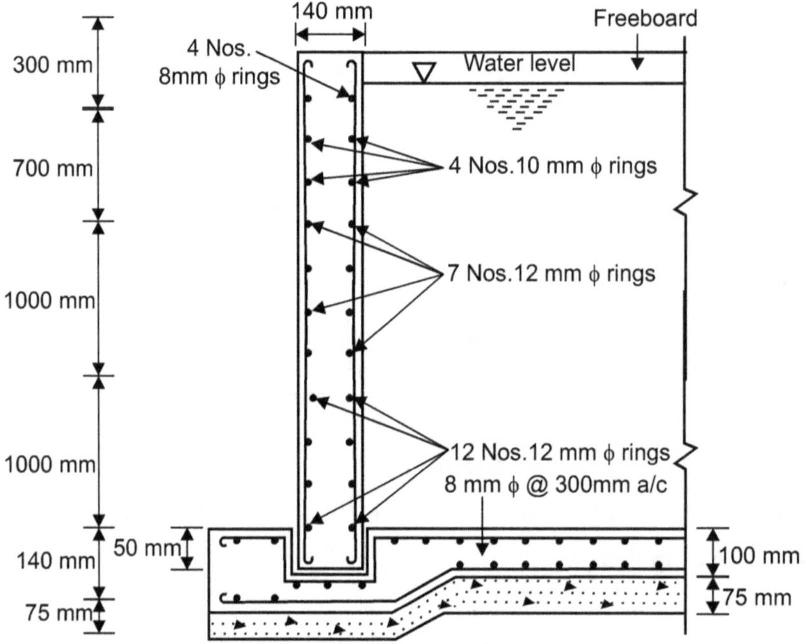

Fig. 15.14

Base slab : Provide 100 mm thick slab in M25.

$$A_{st\ min} = \frac{0.3}{100} \times 100 \times 1000 = 300 \text{ mm}^2 \text{ on both faces}$$

$$= 150 \text{ mm}^2 \text{ on each face}$$

Provide 8 mm ϕ @ 300 mm c/c both ways on top and bottom.

> **Example 15.7 :** *Design a rectangular water tank of capacity = 90000 lit. Height of tank = 3.3 m, including free board of 0.3 m. Use M20 Grade concrete and Fe415 steel. Sketch the reinforcement details. Assume suitable data if necessary.* **(Winter 2012, 20 Marks)**

Solution : 1. Data : Capacity of tank = 90,000 lit.

Size of tank = 6.5 m × 4.5 m (assume)

Free board = 0.3 m

M20 and Fe 415

σ_{cb} = 7 N/mm², σ_{st} = 115 N/mm² (on faces rear water face)

σ_{st} = 125 N/mm² (on faces away from water face)

m = 13, Q = 1.41, f = 0.84.

2. Dimensions of tank :

$$\text{Height of water} = \frac{90000 \times 10^3}{6500 \times 4500} = 3 \text{ m}$$

$$\text{Free board} = 0.3 \text{ m}$$

$\therefore$ Height of side walls = 3 + 0.3 = 3.3 m

$$L/B = 6.5/4.5 = 1.44 < 2$$

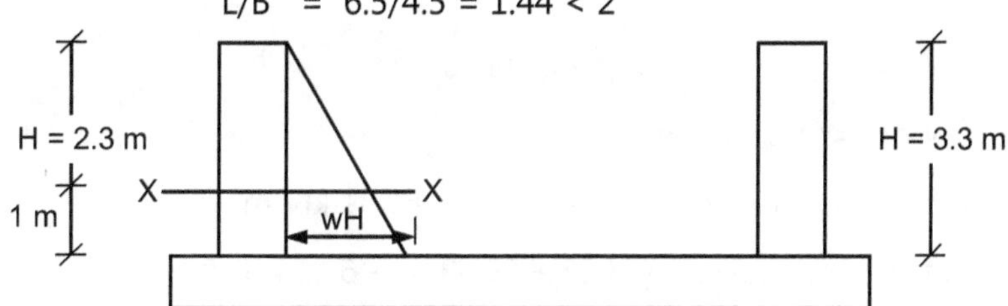

Fig. 15.15

It is assumed that the walls function as a continuous slab subjected to water pressure above (H/4) or 1 m from bottom and as a cantilever for the bottom 1 m.

Therefore, intensity of pressure

$$P = W (H - h) \text{ at X-X}$$
$$= 10 \times 2.5 = 25 \text{ kN/m}^2$$

Alternatively, design tables of IS : 3370 (Part IV) 1967 clause 2 can be used for computation of moments in tank walls.

3. Moments in side walls : L = 6.5 m, B = 4.5 m.

$$\frac{PL^2}{12} = \frac{25 \times 6.5^2}{12} = 88 \text{ kN-m}$$

$$\frac{PL^2}{8} = \frac{25 \times 6.5^2}{8} = 132 \text{ kN-m}$$

$$\frac{PB^2}{12} = \frac{25 \times 4.5^2}{12} = 42.18 \text{ kN-m}$$

$$\frac{PB^2}{8} = \frac{25 \times 4.5^2}{8} = 63.28 \text{ kN-m}$$

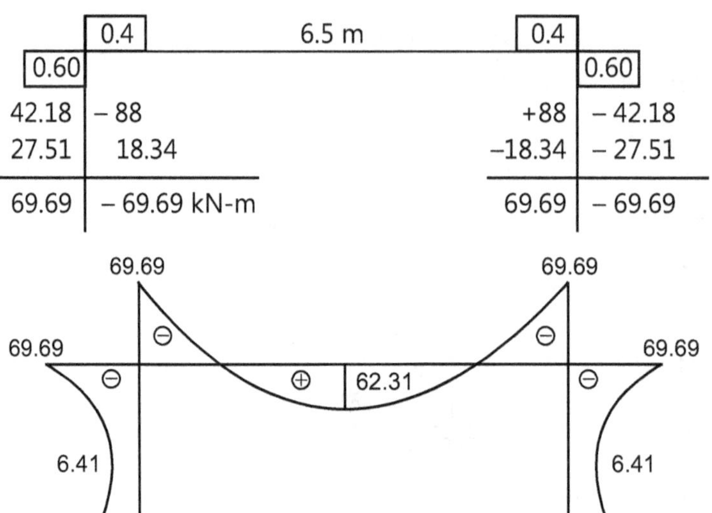

Fig. 15.16

Moment at support = 69.69 kN-m

Moment at centre (long walls) = (132 – 69.69) = 62.31 kN-m

Moment at centre (short walls) = (63.28 – 69.69) = – 6.41 kN-m

4. **Design of long and short walls :**

Maximum design moment = 69.69 kN-m

$$d = \sqrt{\frac{69.69 \times 10^6}{1.41 \times 1000}} = 222.3 \text{ mm}$$

Adopt effective depth = 235 mm

Overall depth = 270 mm

Direct tension in long wall, T = (0.5 × 25 × 4.5)

= 56.25 kN

Direct tension in short wall, T = (0.5 × 25 × 6.5) = 81.25 kN-m

$$A_{st \text{ (long wall corners)}} = \left(\frac{M - T_x}{\sigma_{st}\, y_d}\right) + \left(\frac{T}{\sigma_{st}}\right)$$

$$A_{st} = \left[\frac{69.69 \times 10^6 - (56.25 \times 10^3 \times 90)}{1000 \times 0.84 \times 235}\right] + \left[\frac{56.25 \times 10^3}{100}\right]$$

$$= 827.39 \text{ mm}^2$$

$$\text{Spacing of 16 mm } \phi \text{ bars } = \frac{1000 \times \frac{\pi}{4} \times 10^2}{827.39} = 94.90 \text{ mm} \approx 90 \text{ mm}$$

Adopt 10 mm ϕ bars @ 80 mm c/c (892.74 mm^2)

$$\text{R/F at centre of span (long walls) } = \frac{62.31 \times 10^6 - (63.28 \times 10^3 \times 90)}{12.5 \times 0.84 \times 235} + \frac{63.28 \times 10^3}{125}$$

$$= 2312.92 + 506.24 = 2819.16 \text{ mm}^2$$

Half of the bars from inner face at support are bent towards the outer face at centre providing an area of (0.5 × 892.74) = 446.37 mm^2. For the remaining area of (2819.16 − 446.37) = 2372.99 ≈ 2373 mm^2, provide 20 mm ϕ bars @ 130 mm c/c. For short-walls, bend 50% of the bars towards outer face at centre.

5. **Reinforcement for cantilever moment :** (For 1 m height from the bottom)

$$\text{Cantilever moment } = (3.3 \times 10 \times 1/2 \times 1/3) = 5.5 \text{ kN-m}$$

$$\therefore \quad A_{st} = \frac{5.5 \times 10^6}{100 \times 0.84 \times 235} = 278.62 \text{ mm}^2$$

$$A_{st\,min} = 0.3\% = \frac{0.3 \times 1000 \times 250}{100} = 750 \text{ mm}^2$$

$$\text{Reinforcement on each face } = 0.5 \times 750 = 375 \text{ mm}^2$$

$$\text{Spacing of 8 mm } \phi \text{ bars } = \frac{1000 \times 50}{375} = 130 \text{ mm c/c}$$

Adopt 8 mm ϕ bars @ 130 mm c/c on both faces.

6. **Base slab :**

The base slab rests on ground. Provide 200 mm base slab with 10 mm ϕ bars @ 300 mm c/c both ways on each face.

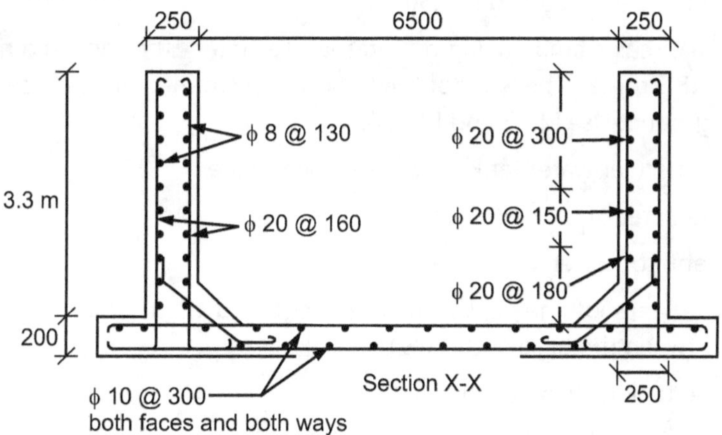

Fig. 15.17

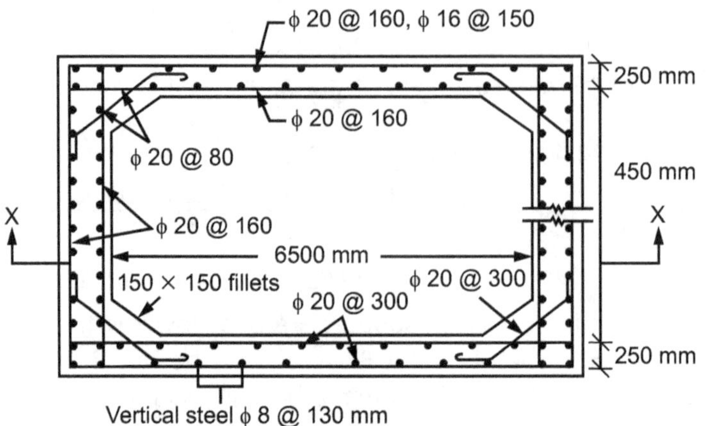

Fig. 15.18

IMPORTANT POINTS

- Types of water tanks.
- Design constants.
- Design steps for circular tanks situated on ground.
- Design steps for rectangular tanks resting on ground.

QUESTIONS

1. Design a circular tank for capacity of 500 litres. The maximum depth of water being 3.75 m. The walls of the tanks are restrained at the base. The tank rests on the ground. Use M 20 and Fe 250.

2. Design a circular tank having an internal diameter 10 m and the maximum depth of water 3.5 meter. The walls of the tanks are restrained at the base. The tanks rests on the ground. Use M 25 and Fe 415.

3. Design a circular water tank for the following data :

   (i)   Diameter of tank = 4.0 meter.

   (ii) Depth of water = 3.0 meter.

   (iii) The walls of the tanks are not restrained at the base (i.e. joint is flexible between the base and walls.)

   (iv) The tank rests on ground.

4. An open square tank 4.5 m × 4.5 m × 3.2 m deep rests on firm ground. Design the tank.

5. Design a rectangular tank 6 m × 2.9 m × 3 m with a maximum depth 2.75 m. The tank rests on ground 15 cm × 15 cm splays are provided at the junction of walls and base slab.

6. The circular water tank is proposed below the ground level, the details are as below :

Capacity = 10 lakh litres (open to sky)

Depth of water = 4.0 m

Free board = 0.50 m

Portion of water-tank above the ground level = 0.50 m

SBC of soil = 200 kN/sq.m.; ϕ = 25 degree;

Density of soil = 18 kN/cu.m.

IS : 3370 is recommended for analysis and design. Show the details of reinforcement.

Effect of water table can be neglected.

7. Design circular reinforced concrete tank resting on ground to store 4.5 lakh litres of water, the top of the tank is open. Take the safe bearing capacity of the supporting strata as 200 kN/m². Design the wall and bottom slab of the tank using IS code. Draw all details of reinforcements. Use M 20, Fe 415.

UNIVERSITY QUESTIONS

Dec. 2011

Q. 1 (a) Design circular reinforced concrete tank resting on ground to store 4 lakn liters of water. The tank wall is fixed at base and free at top. Take the safe bearing capacity of the supporting strata as 220 kN/m². Design the wall and bottom slab of the tank using IS code. **(Example 15.3)**   **(20 Marks)**

May 2012

Q. 2 (a) Draw exaggerated bent shape of wall of circular water tank fixed at base slab showing all details. **(Section 15.9)**   **(5 Marks)**

Dec. 2012

Q. 3 Design a Rectangular water tank of capacity = 9000 lit. Height of tank = 3.3 m, including free board of 0.3 m. Use M20 grade concrete and F415 steel. Sketch the reinforcement details. Assume suitable data if necessary.

(Example 15.7)   **(20 Marks)**

Dec. 2014

Q. 4   Design an open circular water tank with rigid joints rest on ground. The capacity of tank is 5.5×10^5 liters. The height of tank is restricted to 4.25 m. Use M20 and Fe415 materials. Also design the bottom slab of tank if S.B.C. of soil is 200 kN/m^2. Show pressure distribution diagram along the wall and reinforcement details.

(Example 15.3)   **(20 Marks)**

Dec. 2015

Q. 5   Design a rectangular water tank resting on ground of 3.0 lack liter capacity, open at top, the joint between wall and base slab is rigid, taking L/B ratio as 1.75 the safe bearing capacity of supporting strata is 200 kN/m^2. Design the wall and bottom slab of the tank. Draw details of reinforcement, use approximate method.

(Example 15.7)   **(20 Marks)**

◈ ◈ ◈

Marks: 30   **Time: 1.5 Hour**

---

1. (a) Explain in brief why high grade materials are used for prestressed concrete.   **(4 M)**

  (b) Explain the system of prestressing.   **(6 M)**

OR

2. (a) Explain in detail the loss of prestress due to friction.   **(5 M)**

  (b) Distinguish between RCC and PSC.   **(5 M)**

3. Design a post tensioned prestressed concrete I section beam for flexure to carry a live load of 10 kN/m over entire simply supported span of 15 m with M 40 grade of concrete and Freyssinet cable of 12/5 (f_y = 1750 Mpa) or 12/7 (fy = 1500 Mpa), including the design of end block. Draw sketches showing cable profiles and end block reinforcement details. Check fiber stresses in concrete and deflection.   **(10 M)**

OR

4. A post tensioned prestressed concrete two way slab, 6.5 × 9 m with discontinuous edges to support imposed load of 4 kN/m^2. Use S3 (three strands, each having cross sectional area 100 mm^2) having f_y = 1900 Mpa. Check the safety of the slab against collaps and deflection at services load take the grade of concrete = M40.   **(10 M)**

OR

5. Fig. 1 shows an intermediate frame of a multistoried building the frame are spaced 4 m centre to centre. Analyze a rigid jointed frame taking live load of and dead load 2.8 kN/m^2, 3 kN/m^2 for the panels with AB and BC respectively. The self weight of the beam may be taken as follows. Beams of 8 m span = 5.5 kN/m and beams of 4.5 m span = 3.5 kN/m. The relative stiffnesses of the members are marked on the Fig. 1. Use portal method for analyzing the frame for horizontal forces and proper substitute frame for vertical loads. Design the section for beam ABC for combined effect of vertical and horizontal loads. Adopt 15% redistribution of moments for vertical load moments. Use M20, Fe 415.   **(10 M)**

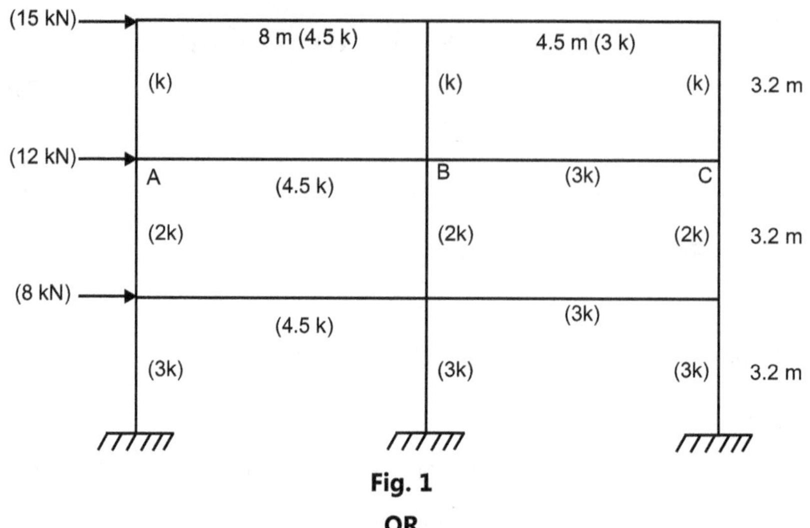

Fig. 1

OR

6. Analyze the rigid jointed frame as shown in Fig. 2 by cantilever method for lateral loads. Flexural rigidity for all members is same. Analyze beam GHI using proper substitute frame, if it is subjected to vertical ultimate live and dead load including its self weight of intensities 15 kN/m and 12 kN/m on span GH and 20 kN/m and 15 kN/m on HI respectively. The horizontal forces are shown in Fig. 2. Calculate maximum span moment for HI and support moment at H. Design section for combined effect of vertical and horizontal loads. Adopt 15% redistribution of moments for vertical load moment. Use M20 and Fe 500.   **(10 M)**

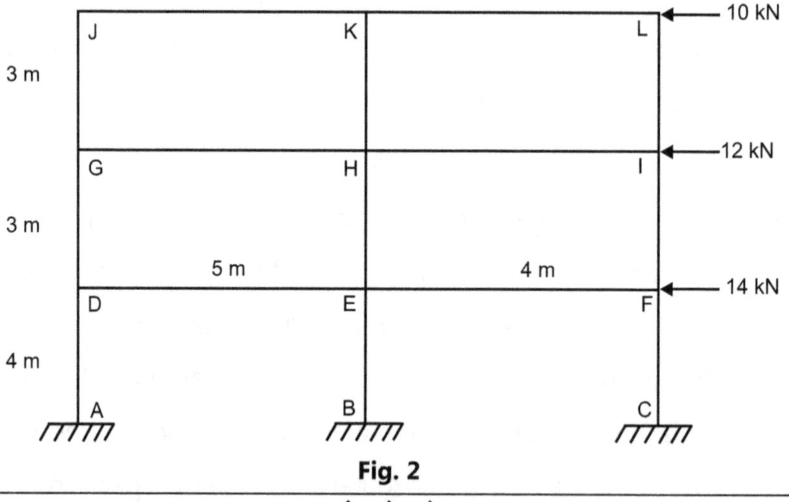

Fig. 2

◈ ◈ ◈

Sample Question Paper for
End-Semester Examination

Marks: 70   **Time: 3 Hour**

1. State the step by step procedure used in design of prestressed concrete flanged beam.

(10 M)

OR

2. Explain with sketch, why eccentric prestressing is preferable to concentric prestressing.

(10 M)

3. Explain Seismic coefficient method.   **(10 M)**

OR

4. Design a post tensioned prestressed concreted beam to carry a live load of 15 kN/m over simply supported span of 18 m only for flexure. The characteristic strength of concrete is 35 MPa. Use Freyssinet cables of 12/5 with f_y = 1750 MPa. Also design end block. Draw cable profiles at various sections. Check fiber stresses in concrete and deflection at mid-span.   **(10 M)**

5. Design a cantilever T-shaped retaining wall to retain soil, 4 m above the ground. The surcharge angle is 14° at the top of retaining wall. The unit weight of the soil is 17.5 kN/m^3, angle of repose is 35° and S.B.C of soil is 180 kN/m^2 at 1.2 m below ground level. Show the pressure distribution at base of wall and reinforcement details at toe slab, heel slab and vertical wall. Use M20 concrete and Fe415 steel.   **(16 M)**

OR

6. Design a T-shaped retaining wall for two layered leveled backfill for the following data.

Upper layer, height = 2.5 m, ϕ = 30°, density of material = 16 kN/m^3

Lower layer, Height = 2.5, ϕ = 32°, density of material = 18 kN/m^3

Safe bearing capacity of underlying strata is 195 kN/m^2 the coefficient of friction between base and underlying strata is 0.45. Draw lateral pressure diagram and details of reinforcement in stem and base slab including curtailment if any. Use M25 and Fe500.   **(16 M)**

7. At what situation, combined footing is recommended than isolated footing.   **(16 M)**

OR

8. Write a short note on combined footing with strap beam.   **(16 M)**

9. Draw exaggerated bent shape of wall of circular water tank fixed at base slab showing all details.   **(18 M)**

OR

10. Design circular reinforced concrete tank resting on ground to store 4 lakn liters of water. The tank wall is fixed at base and free at top. Take the safe bearing capacity of the supporting strata as 220 kN/m^2. Design the wall and bottom slab of the tank using IS code.   **(18 M)**